The Editor

JOHN PAUL RIQUELME is Professor of English at Boston University. He is the author of *Teller and Tale in Joyce's Fiction: Oscillating Perspectives* and *Harmony of Dissonances: T. S. Eliot, Romanticism, and Imagination*. His edited works include *Tess of the d'Urbervilles, Dracula, Joyce's Dislocutions: Essays on Reading as Translation,* and *Gothic and Modernism: Essaying Dark Literary Modernity.*

A NORTON CRITICAL EDITION

James Joyce

A PORTRAIT OF THE ARTIST AS A YOUNG MAN

AUTHORITATIVE TEXT
BACKGROUNDS AND CONTEXTS
CRITICISM

SECOND EDITION

Edited by

JOHN PAUL RIQUELME
BOSTON UNIVERSITY

Text Edited by

HANS WALTER GABLER
WITH WALTER HETTCHE

W. W. NORTON & COMPANY
Independent Publishers Since 1923

For Marie-Anne

". . . a Flower of the mountain yes. . . ."

W. W. Norton & Company has been independent since its founding in 1923, when William Warder Norton and Mary D. Herter Norton first published lectures delivered at the People's Institute, the adult education division of New York City's Cooper Union. The firm soon expanded its program beyond the Institute, publishing books by celebrated academics from America and abroad. By mid-century, the two major pillars of Norton's publishing program—trade books and college texts—were firmly established. In the 1950s, the Norton family transferred control of the company to its employees, and today—with a staff of five hundred and hundreds of trade, college, and professional titles published each year—W. W. Norton & Company stands as the largest and oldest publishing house owned wholly by its employees.

Copyright © 2022, 2007 by W. W. Norton & Company, Inc.

A revised excerpt from Hans Walter Gabler's introduction, the explanation of "symbols and sigla," and the text with line numbers and accompanying textual notes derive from A PORTRAIT OF THE ARTIST AS A YOUNG MAN by James Joyce, edited by Hans Walter Gabler with Walter Hettche. Copyright © 1993 by Hans Walter Gabler. This material reproduced here with the permission of Taylor & Francis Books, North America.

Manufacturing by Maple Press
Book design by Antonina Krass
Production manager: Stephen Sajdak

Library of Congress Cataloging-in-Publication Data

Names: Joyce, James, author. | Riquelme, John Paul, editor. | Gabler, Hans Walter, editor. | Hettche, Walter, editor.
Title: A portrait of the artist as a young man : authoritative text, backgrounds and contexts, criticism / James Joyce, John Paul Riquelme, Hans Walter Gabler, Walter Hettche.
Description: Second edition. | New York : W. W. Norton & Company, 2021. | Series: A Norton critical edition | Includes bibliographical references.
Identifiers: LCCN 2020043068 | ISBN 9780393643947 (paperback) | ISBN 9780393643961 (epub)
Classification: LCC PR6019.O9 P635 1999 | DDC 823/.912—dc23
LC record available at https://lccn.loc.gov/2020043068

W. W. Norton & Company, Inc., 500 Fifth Avenue, New York, N.Y. 10110
www.wwnorton.com
W. W. Norton & Company Ltd., 15 Carlisle Street, London W1D 3BS

1 2 3 4 5 6 7 8 9 0

Contents

Criticism

Preface

by John Paul Riquelme

During my first semester in college, decades ago, I was asked by an energetic Irish-American teacher, Gerald O'Grady, to read *A Portrait of the Artist as a Young Man* and some essays by the American theorist and critic Kenneth Burke. Like Stephen Dedalus in Joyce's narrative, I was facing a difficult initiation into adult life, yet I did not understand Joyce's challenging book when I tried to read it then, for the first time. Because I found it compelling, I reread the book several times during the following semester, trying to make better sense of it, without much success. It distracted me from other assignments; it left a permanent impression.

This edition of *A Portrait* is meant for all those students and other readers who recognize the book's achievement in its effect on them and who wish to understand the work more fully. The edition provides information and perspectives that may deepen readers' own conclusions about the book's implications, which are various and debatable. The annotations provided for the text are factual rather than interpretive.

The Text

The text of the narrative presented here is the authoritative version, established by Hans Walter Gabler with Walter Hettche, originally published with full editorial apparatus by Garland Publishing (1993). Included with that text is a selection of key notes from the Garland edition concerning textual variants. These notes, placed at page bottom, are meant to allow the interested reader easy access to options that were available during the editorial process. As Gabler explains in his "Introduction: Composition, Text, and Editing," Joyce's handwritten fair copy of the entire narrative, currently in the collection of the National Library of Ireland, provided the "copy-text," that is, the base text that was modified editorially. The text is, as Gabler puts it, "eclectic," a necessarily composite version, because textual changes were grafted onto the fair copy, changes warranted by later documents in the book's history. I am grateful to Gabler for allowing us to make more widely available the results of his careful editing work, including the selections from his textual notes for the Garland edition. "Why and How to Read the Textual Notes," which follows the editorial introduction, explains the enabling character of the notes for the reading process. In his introduction, Gabler discusses briefly the relevant composition and publication history of Joyce's book, including the particular prepublication documents that have survived. Readers interested in obtaining more details about that history will find ample, illuminating discussion in the longer introduction to the Garland edition and in Gabler's essay "The Genesis of *A Portrait of the Artist as a Young Man*."[1]

Backgrounds and Contexts

In the late 1940s and the 1950s, the period just after their author's death, Joyce's works received substantial positive critical attention. They were considered valuable largely on the basis of readings that involved attention to literary form and to so-called symbols, with little or no attention to historical and political contexts. At that time, modern literature had yet to be interpreted in light of empire-building and colonization. The literary canon was also narrower than it is now. For example, the writings of Oscar Wilde (1854–1900), one of Joyce's most important precursors, were still not widely discussed (a lingering effect of the scandal surrounding his conviction for acts of "gross indecency"). Over half a century later, critical approaches to literature attend more fully to issues of historical and social context, and the canon has changed. But reliable historical materials concerning many of our greatest modern writers have not been readily available to readers who are not specialists. The "Backgrounds and Contexts" section of this edition addresses that situation for Joyce's narrative by providing information about Irish history, especially political history, with an emphasis on significant events of the nineteenth century. This is the political history that Joyce would have grown up with and that his artist protagonist, Stephen Dedalus, knows from the inside. The documents concerning Irish history carry forward through 1916, the year of the Easter Rising, which marked a crucial turning point in Ireland's becoming a nation. The Easter Rising and *A Portrait of the Artist as a Young Man* are both products of Irish historical directions that emerged, on the streets of Dublin and in print, in 1916. Both signal something new and significant. The chronology that opens "Backgrounds and Contexts" provides a slightly longer historical perspective, reaching

---

1. *Critical Essays on James Joyce's "A Portrait of the Artist as a Young Man,"* ed. Philip Brady and James F. Carens (New York: G. K. Hall, 1998), 83–112.

back to the Insurrection of 1798 and forward to the 1937 Constitution of Ireland.

The nine illustrations within the section reflect graphically the history of violence—literal, political, and psychological—that informs
Stephen Dedalus's world. These visual texts include prejudicial
English political cartoons that represent the Irish, and in particular
their political leader, Charles Stewart Parnell (1846–1891), as
monstrous. The violence of internal Irish political disagreement is
reflected in the language and the cover of an anti-Parnell pamphlet,
The Discrowned King of Ireland. The extreme pressures on the
young are evident in the physical torments depicted in the woodcuts from *Hell Opened to Christians,* a pamphlet that could have
been distributed at retreats such as the one Stephen participates in
(Part III). The retreat's description of serpents devouring the souls
of sinners finds an aesthetic counterpart in the *Laocoön* sculpture
group, reproduced here, which plays a key role in Stephen's thinking about art.

Irish cultural revival provides an additional frame of reference
for reading *A Portrait.* The writings of Douglas Hyde (1860–1949)
and John Millington Synge (1871–1909) help illustrate the options
Joyce faced and presented to Stephen, because both Hyde and Synge
emphasize native Irish culture and because both took comparatively moderate stances on cultural politics. Though Joyce relocated
to the Continent, he paid continuing attention to Irish culture. Displaying a similar cosmopolitanism, Stephen Dedalus is not interested
in becoming fluent in Gaelic. He is headed toward Europe, not the
west of Ireland. His thinking about Ireland deserves comparison
with Synge's descriptions of traditional Irish living on the isolated
Aran Islands off the west coast. Indeed, Joyce would have known
Synge's book *The Aran Islands* (1907), aspects of which he evokes in
his presentation of Stephen.

Sharing Joyce's education by Jesuits, Stephen comes to know well
and to practice for a time the rigorous spiritual exercises recommended and formulated by St. Ignatius Loyola, the founder of the
Jesuit religious order. Excerpts from *The Spiritual Exercises,* including the meditation on hell, are provided as material that Stephen
would know by heart or nearly so. (*Hell Opened to Christians* would
have been a supplement to *The Spiritual Exercises.*)

Finally, the relevant contexts include aesthetic matters. As Joyce
reached maturity, he encountered the immensely influential Aesthetic
movement, whose most important English advocate was Walter Pater
(1839–1894). Every aspiring artist in the English-speaking world
during the 1890s read Pater's writings attentively. His response to
Leonardo's *Mona Lisa* (*La Gioconda*) and his suppressed and then
revised and reissued closing to *Studies in the History of the Renaissance*

(1873–93) were among the most widely read belle-lettristic passages of the late nineteenth century. Joyce imitates aspects of Pater's elaborate style late in Part IV, where it informs Stephen's thoughts. Oscar Wilde was influenced by Pater, but became an aesthete of a different kind. He was also the most successful Irish writer of the generation preceding Joyce's and Stephen's. When Joyce gave a title to his narrative about the artist, he may have had in mind Wilde's *The Picture of Dorian Gray* (1891), excerpts from which are provided.

Criticism

Joyce's works have attracted substantial attention from other writers, artists, theorists, and literary critics. Any selection from the wide, voluminous commentary on *A Portrait of the Artist as a Young Man* will necessarily be highly selective, even with regard to the kinds of commentary that have appeared. In this edition, the "Criticism" section presents work by four generations of commentators on both sides of the Atlantic. The critical commentaries are nearly all essays that have not been readily available through reprintings. Their arguments address matters of style, history, gender identity, the body, nation, empire, contrasting kinds of temporality, the narrative's place in literary history, and Joyce's relation to scientific thinking about development. Roughly half of the commentaries have appeared since I prepared the first edition. The "Selected Bibliography" presents suggestions for further research.

Acknowledgments

An edition of this kind results from collaborative efforts. I was fortunate to receive generous assistance from colleagues who exceed in number the limits of my memory, the space I have to thank them, and my ability to express my gratitude adequately. Primary among them is Hans Walter Gabler, whose careful, thoughtful, always well-informed attention to detail led to publication of the authoritative text of Joyce's narrative, which is here reprinted. He invariably responded patiently and supportively to the needs of the first edition, which he regularly anticipated. Equally important among the patient collaborators who made the work both possible and a pleasure is Carol Bemis at W. W. Norton & Company, who clearly believed in the importance of both editions and was willing to wait supportively for me to finish them. Her colleagues, Brian Baker for the first edition and then Rachel Goodman followed by Erika Nakagawa, provided timely, energetic assistance and imaginative ideas. Rachel and Erika kept the second edition moving forward with great alacrity. Erika managed permissions, routed proofs, incorporated editorial changes, and reminded me about many needed steps. The copyeditor was scrupulous. For both editions, Kurt Wildermuth enabled numerous improvements through his canny, meticulous attention to the volume's details. His commitment, goodwill, tact, and extensive knowledge made the final stages of the work especially rewarding. I and readers of this edition are in his debt because of his numerous suggestions for making it as accurate and accessible as possible.

I considered and revised the supplementary materials for this edition with the help of responses to a survey of faculty who had adopted the first edition. I am grateful to the thoughtful suggestions of the respondents, whose identities I do not know. When I began work on the first edition, I circulated a questionnaire concerning its possible contents to two dozen colleagues who teach and write about Joyce. I am grateful for the illuminating responses to that questionnaire, and to my other requests for information and advice, from Derek Attridge, Murray Beja, Christine van Boheemen, Rosa Maria Bollettieri Bosinelli, Richard Brown, Gregory Castle, Kevin Dettmar, Enda Duffy, Michael Patrick Gillespie, Michael Groden, Suzette Henke, Marjorie Howes, Nico Israel, Scott Klein, Patrick McGee, Jonathan Mulrooney, Vincent Pecora, Jean-Michel Rabaté, Bonnie Kime Scott, and Joseph Valente. Gregory Castle and Jonathan Mulrooney provided advice throughout the editing process, Castle primarily concerning critical commentaries and Mulrooney primarily concerning Joyce's relation to Catholicism. Howard Gray, S.J., shared his knowledge of St. Ignatius. William Brockman clarified some textual matters. The explanatory notes for the text are based on my independent research, but annotating a text as frequently commented on as Joyce's involves awareness of what other scholars have done. I consulted annotations by Chester Anderson, James Atherton, Seamus Deane, Don Gifford, and Jeri Johnson, whose efforts I acknowledge with thanks. For the new edition, Peter Nohrnberg was especially helpful as an interlocutor. Michael Patrick Gillespie and Daniel Fogel raised issues that resulted in new annotations. Peter Schwartz provided advice on a passage in German and Stephanie Nelson on a passage in nonstandard Greek.

I was able to complete much of the work on the first edition during a research leave in 2005 generously granted by the College of Arts and Sciences and the Humanities Foundation of Boston University. Special thanks go to Jeffrey Henderson, dean of CAS, and Katherine O'Connor, director of the Foundation, for their confidence and support. I also wish to thank my colleague Fred S. Kleiner, professor of art history and archaeology at Boston University, for explaining the strange history of the *Laocoön* sculpture group. Lindsey Gilbert, Mary Lawless, and Holly Schaaf, doctoral students in English in my department, provided dedicated assistance through their careful proofreading. My thanks go to Annie Diamond, who assisted me at the beginning of the revision process for the second edition, which I finished during a research leave from Boston University in 2019. I am most grateful for the university's generous support.

I am grateful to the journals, publishers, institutions, and individuals who gave permission for materials to appear. Rhoda Bilansky, the head of Interlibrary Loan at Mugar Memorial Library, Boston University, frequently obtained for extended use books and essays that were not locally available, including items that I never expected to see without travel to distant libraries. I received assistance as well from the staff of the British Library and the National Library of Ireland (Leabharlann Náisiúnta na hÉireann). At the National Library, Bernie McCann of Reprographics Services arranged for the copying of items in deteriorated, barely reproducible condition. Joanna Finegan, Curator of Prints and Drawings, and her colleague, Colette O'Flaherty, authorized reproduction of the library's copy of the 1916 Proclamation and expedited delivery of the image. Reproducing many of the illustrations for this volume would have been impossible without the resources and cooperation of the NLI.

My deepest debt is for support every day from my partner, Marie-Anne Verougstraete, who rendered all the illustrations for both editions, some of them from challenging originals. More importantly, she believed that the work was worth giving me the excessive amount of time that I needed to complete it.

Sources for the Annotations

Anderson, Chester G. "Explanatory Notes." *A Portrait of the Artist as a Young Man: Text, Criticism, and Notes.* Ed. Chester G. Anderson. New York: Viking, 1968.

Bradley, Bruce, S.J. *James Joyce's Schooldays.* New York: St. Martin's, 1982.

Catholic Encyclopedia. www.newadvent.org. [Cited as *Cath. Enc.*]

Connolly, S. J. *The Oxford Companion to Irish History.* Oxford, Eng.: Oxford UP, 1998.

Encyclopaedia Britannica, Eleventh Ed. London and New York: Encyclopaedia Britannica, 1910. [Cited as *Enc. Brit.*]

Gifford, Don. *Joyce Annotated: Notes for* Dubliners *and* A Portrait of the Artist as a Young Man. 2nd Ed. Berkeley: U of California P, 1982.

Holy Bible, the Douay Version of the Old Testament, the Confraternity Edition of the New Testament. New York: P. J. Kenedy & Sons, 1950. [This English version of the Bible was chosen as more appropriate than the King James Version for Joyce's text because the Douay-Confraternity translation is accepted by the Roman Catholic Church.]

Joyce, P. W. *English as We Speak It in Ireland*. 1910; rpt. Dublin: Wolfhound P, 1979.

Lalor, Brian, ed. *The Encyclopedia of Ireland*. New Haven and London: Yale UP, 2003.

Letters of James Joyce. Vol. I, corrected. Ed. Stuart Gilbert. New York: Viking, 1966. Vols. II–III. Ed. Richard Ellmann. New York: Viking, 1966.

Michael, Ian. *The Teaching of English, from the Sixteenth Century to 1870*. Cambridge, Eng.: Cambridge UP, 1987.

Mullin, Katherine. *James Joyce, Sexuality and Social Purity*. Cambridge, Eng.: Cambridge UP, 2003.

Nohrnberg, Peter C. L. "Building Up a Nation Once Again": Irish Masculinity, Violence, and the Cultural Politics of Sports in *A Portrait of the Artist as a Young Man* and *Ulysses*. *Joyce Studies Annual* (2010). Ed. Moshe Gold and Philip Sicker. New York: Fordham UP, 2011. 99–152.

Oxford English Dictionary. 2nd Ed. Ed. J. A. Simpson and E. S. C. Weiner. Oxford, Eng.: Clarendon, 1989. [Cited as *OED*.]

Shakespeare, William. *The Complete Works of Shakespeare*. 5th Ed. Ed. David Bevington. 2003; New York: Pearson Longman, 2007.

Sullivan, Kevin. *Joyce among the Jesuits*. New York: Columbia UP, 1957.

Introduction: Composition, Text, and Editing[†]

by Hans Walter Gabler

The seminal invention for *A Portrait of the Artist as a Young Man* was Joyce's narrative essay "A Portrait of the Artist."[1] The essay survives in Joyce's hand in a copybook belonging to his sister Mabel and bears the date 7/1/1904.[2] Submitted to the literary magazine *Dana* (as likely as not in the very copybook), it was rejected within less than a fortnight. According to Stanislaus Joyce in his *Dublin Diary*, the rejection spurred Joyce on to conceiving of an autobiographical novel, the opening chapters of which he supposedly wrote in the space of a couple of weeks.[3] Stanislaus also tells us that, as the brothers sat together in the kitchen on James Joyce's twenty-second birthday, February 2, 1904, James shared his plans for the novel with him, and he claims that he, Stanislaus, suggested the title *Stephen Hero*.

Joyce scholars have followed Richard Ellmann (*JJ*, 144–49) in taking Stanislaus's account altogether at face value. We have all persistently overlooked May Joyce's letter to James of September 1, 1916, in which she recalls James's reading the early chapters to their mother when they lived in St. Peter's Terrace, with the younger siblings put out of the room. May used to hide under the sofa to listen until, relenting, James allowed her to stay (*Letters* II, 382–83). This intimate memory puts the beginnings of Joyce's art in a different perspective. It suggests that he started his autobiographical

† Revised excerpt from "Introduction," *A Portrait of the Artist as a Young Man*, ed. Hans Walter Gabler with Walter Hettche (New York and London: Garland, 1993).

1. "A Portrait of the Artist" is most conveniently available in James Joyce, *Poems and Shorter Writings*, ed. Richard Ellmann, A. Walton Litz, and John Whittier-Ferguson. London: Faber and Faber, 1991, 211–18. The original is photographically reprinted in James Joyce, *A Portrait of the Artist as a Young Man. A Facsimile of Epiphanies, Notes, Manuscripts, and Typescripts*, prefaced and arranged by Hans Walter Gabler. New York and London: Garland Publishing, Inc., 1978 (vol. [7] of *The James Joyce Archive*, 63 vols., general editor Michael Groden), 70–85.

2. That is, January 7, 1904.

3. Stanislaus Joyce, *The Complete Dublin Diary*, ed. George H. Healey. Ithaca: Cornell UP, 1971, 11–13.

novel almost a year earlier than has hitherto been assumed, probably some months at least before August 1903, when his mother
died. The impulse thus seems to have sprung immediately from his
first experience of exile in Paris in 1902–03. "A Portrait of the Artist," of January 1904, can appear no longer as seminal for *Stephen
Hero*. Rather, defined as the conceptual outline for *A Portrait of the
Artist as a Young Man* that it has always been felt to be, it stands as
Joyce's first attempt to break away from his initial mode of autobiographical fiction. Against Stanislaus Joyce's idealizing of his brother's
triumphant heroism in defying *Dana,* we sense instead the stymy-
ing effect of that first public rejection. Digging his heels in and
continuing to write *Stephen Hero* was a retarding stage, even perhaps a retrogression, in Joyce's search for a sense of his art and a
narrative idiom all his own. *Stephen Hero* was to falter by mid-1905,
by which time Joyce was freeing himself from its fetters through
Dubliners.[4]

With eleven chapters of *Stephen Hero* written and its immediate
continuation conceived, Joyce left Dublin with Nora Barnacle, his
future wife, on October 8, 1904, for Trieste and Pola. Short narratives, too, were fermenting in his head. In the course of 1904, he
had published three stories in *The Irish Homestead:* "The Sisters,"
"Eveline," and "After the Race." They were the beginnings of *Dubliners,* to be enlarged into a book-length collection in Trieste. In
their exile, too, James and Nora soon found themselves to be expec-
tant parents. During Nora's pregnancy, Joyce carried *Stephen Hero*
forward through its "University episode," now the novel's only surviving fragment. Yet, closely coinciding with the birth of Giorgio
Joyce, he suspended work on it in June 1905.[5] From mid-1905, he
turned wholly to writing *Dubliners*. The protracted endeavor,
throughout 1906, to get the collection published ran persistently
foul even as, in 1906–07, he capped the sequence with "The Dead."

The Emerging Novel

The time devoted to writing *Dubliners* was the gestation period of a
fundamentally new conception for Joyce's autobiographical novel.

4. Hans Walter Gabler, *The Rocky Roads to* Ulysses. The National Library of Ireland
Joyce Studies 2004, no. 15. Dublin: National Library of Ireland, 2005.
5. The "University episode" fragment of eleven chapters—XV through XXV—was posthumously edited (erroneously as chapters XV through XXVI) by Theodore Spencer in
1944 and subsequently augmented by the text of a few stray additional manuscript
pages (James Joyce, *Stephen Hero,* ed. from the Manuscript in the Harvard College
Library by Theodore Spencer. A New Edition, Incorporating the Additional Manuscript Pages in the Yale University Library and the Cornell University Library, ed.
John J. Slocum and Herbert Cahoon. New York: New Directions, 1963). The *James
Joyce Archive,* vol. [8], collects and reprints photographically the "University episode"
and the stray manuscript pages.

Suspending it in 1905 had, as became apparent by 1907, been tan-
tamount to aborting the sixty-three-chapter project of *Stephen
Hero* in favor of beginning afresh a novel in five parts and naming it
A Portrait of the Artist as a Young Man. The first part was written
between September 8 and November 29, 1907. Reworked from
Stephen Hero, it omitted entirely the seven initial chapters of that
novel—those dealing with Stephen's childhood—and opened
immediately with Stephen's going to school (cf. *JJ,* 64). We may
assume[6] that this early version of Part I, of autumn 1907, included
neither the overture of the novel as eventually published ("Once
upon a time . . . *Apologise.*" [Part I, lines 1–41]) nor the Christmas-
dinner scene ([I, 716–1151]; this at first apparently belonged to Part
II of *A Portrait,* as drafted from materials reworked from *Stephen
Hero*). By April 7, 1908, the new novel had grown to three parts, but
was making no further progress. It was therefore sections of a work
he had grown despondent about that in early 1909 Joyce gave a fellow writer to read. The reader was Ettore Schmitz, or Italo Svevo,
at the time Joyce's language pupil. The supportive criticism he set
out in a letter of February 8, 1909 (*Letters* II, 226–27), suggests
that he had been given Parts I through III, plus a draft opening of
Part IV, in versions prior to those known from the published book.
Specifically—if inference may be trusted—the Christmas-dinner
scene was still a section of Part II, and the conclusion of Stephen's
confession in Part III was yet unwritten.

Schmitz's response encouraged Joyce to complete Part IV and
begin Part V. Yet this precipitated an apparently more serious crisis.
Sometime in 1911, Joyce threw the entire manuscript as it then
stood—313 manuscript leaves—in the fire.[7] Instantly rescued by a
family fire brigade, it apparently suffered no real harm and was
kept tied up in an old sheet for months before Joyce "sorted [it] out
and pieced [it] together as best [he] could" (*Letters* I, 136). This
reconstruction involved developing and rounding off Part V, thoroughly revising Parts I through III, and shaping the novel as a
whole into a stringent chiastic, or midcentered, design. It was an
effort of creation and re-creation occupying Joyce for over two, if
not three, years. On Easter Day 1913, he envisaged finishing the
book by the end of the year, but completing it spilled over into 1914.
The surviving fair copy bears the date line "Dublin 1904 | Trieste
1914" on its last page. Yet the date "1913" on the fair copy's title

---

6. For what follows, see my in-depth analysis in "The Genesis of *A Portrait of the Artist as
   a Young Man,*" *Critical Essays on James Joyce's "A Portrait of the Artist as a Young Man,*"
   ed. Philip Brady and James F. Carens. New York: G. K. Hall, 1998, 83–112.
7. It was not the *Stephen Hero* manuscript, therefore, as a persistent legend would have it,
   but an early *A Portrait* manuscript that was thus given over to the flames, a fact that a
   careful reading of Joyce's letter to Harriet Shaw Weaver of January 6, 1920, confirms
   (*Letters* I, 136).

page indicates that Joyce's Easter Day confidence was sufficiently
well founded. The design and much of the text were essentially
realized in 1913.

Joyce left the manuscript behind in Trieste when he moved to
Zurich in 1915. He retrieved it in 1919 and presented it to Harriet
Shaw Weaver (1876–1961) for Christmas (*Letters* I, 136), in gratitude for her support as his publisher and generous patron since
1914. Weaver saw to it that her Joyce manuscripts went into public
holdings. The entire work-in-progress lot of *Finnegans Wake* papers
in her trust should, she felt, go to Ireland. But Nora Joyce strongly
objected. Consequently, the British Museum in London received
them. In 1952, Weaver gave the fair copy of *A Portrait of the Artist
as a Young Man* to the National Library of Ireland.

The Serialization

On December 15, 1913, the American poet and critic Ezra Pound
(1885–1972) wrote to Joyce from London asking whether he had
anything publishable that Pound could place for him in any of the
British or American journals with which Pound had connections.[8]
He had heard about the young Irish writer exiled in faraway Trieste
through Joyce's fellow Irishman, then in London, the poet and playwright W. B. Yeats (1865–1939). During those vital years of his passion to discover the new writers and promote the new literature,
Pound was specifically associated with *The Egoist* (formerly titled
The Freewoman and *The New Freewoman*) under the editorship of
Dora Marsden. With the concurrent prospect of the British publisher Grant Richards's finally publishing *Dubliners*, Joyce wanted
Pound and *The Egoist* to consider his new novel. *The Egoist* began
to serialize *A Portrait of the Artist as a Young Man* in brief fortnightly installments on, as it happened, February 2, 1914, Joyce's
thirty-second birthday. Continuing through the spring and summer
of 1914 and for an entire year into World War I (despite recurring
difficulties then in delivering typescript copy from Austro-Hungarian
enemy territory to London), the serialization finished on September 1, 1915.

Owing to objections the British printers made for fear of prose-
cution for obscenity, *The Egoist* employed three printing houses in
succession, and even so the text underwent cuts from censorship
in production. The first paragraph of Part III, a couple of sentences in
the bird-girl conclusion to Part IV, a brief dialogue exchange about
farting, and the occurrence (twice) of the expletive "ballocks" in

---

8. *Pound/Joyce: The Letters of Ezra Pound to James Joyce, with Pound's Essays on Joyce*, ed.
Forrest Read. New York: New Directions, 1967, 17–18.

Part V were affected. Joyce did not read proof on the *Egoist* text. Nor, beyond Part II, did he receive the published text to read until sometimes many weeks or months after publication. (The wartime disturbances in communication were the obvious reason.) Nevertheless, he instantly spotted the censorship cuts in the published text. In Zurich, within neutral Switzerland, he was cut off from all the notes and manuscripts he had left behind in war-embroiled Trieste. Yet from a prodigious memory—a faculty that was essential to Joyce's writing throughout his life—he reprovided faultlessly words and sentences missing in the *Egoist* installments; with great determination, he insisted on an entirely uncensored text for the book publication.

Toward the First Edition

In the spring of 1915, several months before the end of the *Portrait* installments in *The Egoist,* Harriet Weaver, assisted by Ezra Pound, embarked upon a protracted search for a British publisher of the novel in book form. Grant Richards had the right of first refusal, contracted with the publishing of *Dubliners,* and declined. Martin Secker and, after long deliberation, Gerald Duckworth followed suit. Ezra Pound's attempts to interest John Lane—who in 1936 was to publish *Ulysses*—were unsuccessful. Duckworth's rejection of January 1916 was based on a reader's report from Edward Garnett, which documents how categorically *A Portrait*'s construction and style were beyond the expectations, and therefore the powers of perception, of even a most esteemed literary reader of the time.[9] Eventually, Harriet Weaver became a publisher and founded The Egoist Ltd. expressly to publish *A Portrait of the Artist as a Young Man* as a book. Yet, just as the established British publishers had refused to take on the novel, British printers now proved unwilling to touch it uncensored. (The then-recent legal proceedings against D. H. Lawrence's *The Rainbow* no doubt influenced their attitude.) Weaver's remaining hope was to arrange with an American partner to supply her with import sheets for a British edition. The promise of a satisfactory arrangement with John Marshall collapsed when Marshall absconded to Canada. It was with B. W. Huebsch of New York that a joint venture finally succeeded.

The Book Editions

B. W. Huebsch had become aware of Joyce through Grant Richards, who throughout 1916 negotiated with Huebsch to publish

9. Garnett's report is quoted in *JJ,* 403–04.

Dubliners in the United States with sheets imported from England. (The edition was brought out in December 1916, only a few weeks before that of *A Portrait*.) He was alerted to *A Portrait* through E. Byrne Hackett, an Irish-American bookseller and small-scale publisher to whom, on Ezra Pound's recommendation, Harriet Weaver had sent a set of uncorrected tearsheets, that is, the relevant columns cut from *The Egoist*. Hackett forwarded these to Huebsch, who on June 16, 1916,[1] offered "to print absolutely in accordance with the author's wishes, without deletion" (*Letters* I, 91). Providing him with copy to allow him to do so was now, in the middle of World War I, a transatlantic challenge involving efforts at communication between New York, London, and Zurich. John Marshall held a fully marked-up printer's copy, with corrections by Joyce in Parts I and II, author's corrections transferred into Parts III and IV by Harriet Weaver from lists Joyce had sent her, and Part V in the original typescript. But Marshall had disappeared, and all attempts to retrieve his set for Huebsch failed. (From this calamity, our greatest loss is that of the original Trieste typescript of Part V.) Weaver sent Huebsch a substitute copy with Parts III and IV marked up according to Joyce's lists, but Parts I, II, and V corrected merely through her recollection of Joyce's changes or, with respect to Part V, just her unaided impressions. Huebsch wisely refused to start printing from this copy, awaiting rather the receipt of Parts I, II, and V in exemplars Weaver had concurrently sent to Joyce to freshly mark up. These reached New York on October 6, and on October 17 Huebsch confirmed that the book was in the printer's hands. No proofreading other than Huebsch's house-proofing was feasible. Joyce was pressing for publication in 1916; this was even stipulated in the publishing contract. On December 29, a few copies were bound, to justify the date, "1916," on the first edition title page. In January 1917, the edition entered the American market, and 768 sets of sheets (for the 750 ordered) arrived in London to be bound and marketed by The Egoist Ltd.

Joyce found the first edition in need of extensive correction. By April 10, 1917, he had drawn up a handwritten list of "nearly 400" changes, which he sent to his literary agent, J. B. Pinker, to be typed with a carbon copy, so that, for safety's sake, two exemplars could be forwarded by separate mailings to New York. Yet by the time they arrived, Huebsch had already printed "a second edition

---

1. This was a year to the day after Joyce had written a postcard from Trieste to his brother Stanislaus, who, less protected by influential friends than James, had been interned as an enemy alien in a camp in Lower Austria. (James therefore wrote the card in rather shaky German [*Selected Letters*, 209].) He had written, so he informed his brother, the first chapter of his new novel, *Ulysses*—which was destined, as we now know, to be set on June 16, 1904.

from the first plates" unaltered. Weaver, who was also considering a second edition, refrained from extending her joint venture with Huebsch when she discovered that freshly imported sheets would not include Joyce's changes. She marked up instead an exemplar of the English first edition (American sheets) as printer's copy for the reset English second edition, published under the imprint of The Egoist Ltd. in 1918. (Weaver eventually gave this copy to the Bodleian Library in Oxford, where it is now shelved.) The "third English edition," published under the Egoist imprint in 1921, was, properly speaking, another issue of the first American edition, using more sheets imported from the United States.

In 1924, the publishing firm Jonathan Cape took over *A Portrait of the Artist as a Young Man* and published the "fourth English edition," which, in strict bibliographical terms, was the book's third edition. With the proofing and revising of *Ulysses* (1922) fresh in his memory, Joyce proofread the Jonathan Cape *Portrait* more thoroughly and consistently than any other of his books after their first publication. On July 11, he reported from Saint-Malo on work done before he left Paris, which involved resisting suggested censorial cuts[2] and insisting on the removal of the "perverted commas . . . by the sergeant-at-arms" (*Letters* III, 99–100). Cape complied on both counts—that is, he agreed to print without cuts and to remove the quotation marks and reset all dialogue with opening flush-left dialogue dashes. Joyce appears to have read three rounds of proof on the Cape edition. This marked the end of his attention to the text of *A Portrait of the Artist as a Young Man.*

This Edition

This Norton Critical Edition is a copy-text edition of *A Portrait of the Artist as a Young Man.*[3] The copy-text it is based on is provided by Joyce's fair-copy holograph, held by the National Library of Ireland and photographically reprinted in *The James Joyce Archive.* The surviving fragments of the typescript, the few *Egoist* galleys preserved, the *Egoist* serialization (1914–15), the first edition (B. W. Huebsch, 1916), the second edition (The Egoist Ltd., 1918), and the third edition (Jonathan Cape, 1924) have been collated against the fair copy; and the marked-up *Egoist* tearsheets, Joyce's lists of corrections,

2. Sylvia Beach, the American expatriate writer whose Parisian bookshop, Shakespeare and Company, published *Ulysses* in 1922, records her "amazement at the printer's queries in the margins." Sylvia Beach, *Shakespeare and Company.* London: Faber and Faber, 1960, 56.
3. That is, our edition has been constructed according to one of several alternative models of editing, other such models being, for instance, the diplomatic edition, the documentary edition, or the genetic or genetically oriented edition, as exemplified by James Joyce, *Ulysses. A Critical and Synoptic Edition.* 3 vols. Prepared by Hans Walter Gabler with Wolfhard Steppe and Claus Melchior. New York: Garland, 1984, 1986.

and Harriet Weaver's marked-up printer's copy for the 1918 British edition, as well as published and unpublished correspondence itemizing textual changes, have been checked. This comprehensive survey has been the basis for preparing the edited text.[4] Fundamentally, the edited text maintains the wording, spelling, and punctuation of its copy-text, although it emends obvious slips of the pen and authorial copying errors. Yet onto the copy-text it also grafts: first, Joyce's revisions on the typescript, in the serialization and in the book editions of 1916, 1918, and 1924; second, his restyling of capitalization and compound formation without hyphens (i.e., compounds in one word or two words) in the book editions; third, the styling of speech with dialogue dashes, as insisted on for the Jonathan Cape edition of 1924. Such editorial overwriting of the copy-text in terms of authorial revision and restyling later in time than the copy-text defines the edited text as a critically eclectic one.

The present edition adopts the edited text together with essentials of the apparatus from the Garland Critical Edition of 1993.[5] For a scholarly edition presents itself to its readers always as a network of discourses. Meshed with the edited text are commonly at least three further discursive strands, namely the so-called apparatus (that is, collation lists and notes answering to the editing); the explanatory material, or commentary; and the editorial introduction, essential particularly for arguing the rationale of the editing and for outlining the design of the edition. Each of these strands is represented in the present edition. Taking over the edited text wholly from the critical edition has also meant preserving the through line numbering for each part that, independent of book paginations, was devised identically for the Garland and Vintage editions of 1993. The present "Editorial Introduction," in its turn, is a revision and modification of the introduction in the Garland edition. The textual footnotes in this edition, furthermore, merge the three parts of the Garland edition's apparatus (i.e., its notes at the foot of the text pages, plus its appended "Emendation of Accidentals" and "Historical Collation" lists). Moreover, this Norton Critical Edition features prominently the fourth strand of a scholarly edition's constituent parts, the commentary. In fact, it does so doubly, both with bottom-of-the-page annotations and by means of the appended sections headed "Backgrounds and Contexts" and "Criticism."

---

4. Except for letters, all manuscript materials relevant to the constitution of the text have been photographically reprinted in *The James Joyce Archive*, vols. [7], [9], and [10].
5. James Joyce, *A Portrait of the Artist as a Young Man*, ed. Hans Walter Gabler with Walter Hettche. New York and London: Garland, 1993. There, the section "This Edition," on pages 10–18 within the introduction, discusses in detail the copy-text-editing rationale and procedures resulting in the edition's edited text.

Select Bibliography

Anderson, Chester G. "The Text of James Joyce's *A Portrait of the Artist as a Young Man.*" *Neuphilologische Mitteilungen* 65 (1964): 160–200.

Ellmann, Richard. *James Joyce.* Oxford, Eng.: Oxford UP, 1982 (*JJ*).

Gabler, Hans Walter. "Towards a Critical Text of James Joyce's *A Portrait of the Artist as a Young Man.*" *Studies in Bibliography* 27 (1974): 1–53.

Gabler, Hans Walter. "The Genesis of *A Portrait of the Artist as a Young Man.*" *Critical Essays on James Joyce's "A Portrait of the Artist as a Young Man."* Ed. Philip Brady and James F. Carens. New York: G. K. Hall, 1998, 83–112.

Gabler, Hans Walter. *The Rocky Roads to* Ulysses. The National Library of Ireland Joyce Studies 2004, no. 15. Dublin: National Library of Ireland, 2005.

Joyce, James. *A Portrait of the Artist as a Young Man.* Critical Ed. Ed. Hans Walter Gabler with Walter Hettche. New York and London: Garland, 1993.

Joyce, James. *A Portrait of the Artist as a Young Man.* Ed. Hans Walter Gabler with Walter Hettche. New York: Vintage, 1993.

Letters of James Joyce. Vol. I. Ed. Stuart Gilbert. New York: Viking, 1957, 1966. (*Letters* I)

Letters of James Joyce. Vols. II–III. Ed. Richard Ellmann. New York: Viking, 1966. (*Letters* II and III)

Selected Letters of James Joyce. Ed. Richard Ellmann. New York: Viking, 1975. (*Selected Letters*)

The James Joyce Archive. 63 vols. General editor Michael Groden. New York and London: Garland, 1977–79. Vol. [7]: *A Portrait of the Artist as a Young Man. A Facsimile of Epiphanies, Notes, Manuscripts, and Typescripts.* Prefaced and arranged by Hans Walter Gabler; vols. [9] and [10]: *A Portrait of the Artist as a Young Man. A Facsimile of the Final Holograph Manuscript.* Prefaced and arranged by Hans Walter Gabler.

Why and How to Read the Textual Notes

by Hans Walter Gabler and John Paul Riquelme

Readers of this edition should have little difficulty in drawing their gains from the annotations, contextual materials, and critical essays. But readers might benefit from some pointers on why and how to read and study the textual notes.

The copy-text for this edition is not a draft but a fair copy. Although it is not a document in which Joyce first wrote the text, the fair copy of *A Portrait of the Artist as a Young Man* shows distinct traces of continued writing in revisions that focus, or freshly generate, critically interpretable meaning. Such instances are recorded in the textual notes, and a decoding of the notes' formulaic foreshortenings opens the records up to interpretation. For instance, we find recorded, at Part I, lines 101–02 and lines 282–83, that Joyce originally used different numbers when, on the eve of Stephen Dedalus's sickness during his first term in Clongowes Wood College, Stephen changes from "seventyseven" to "seventysix" the number on a slip of paper inside his desk in the studyhall. Joyce erased something in the manuscript in both places. The total erasure at 101–02 is indicated by a ◇ in the footnote; but at 282–83, enough of the erased writing remains discernible to suggest that the word first written was "thirty." In itself, this information seems inert. But since we are reading not for information but to better understand and interpret a fictional text, we relate Joyce's minute revision of the numbers to the narrative. Because the next sentence at lines 283–84 talks about the Christmas vacation being far away, we may assume that the numbers count the days left until Christmas. Yet more significantly, this dating makes Stephen's sickness coincide with the death of the great Irish statesman Charles Stewart Parnell (1846–1891). Synchronizing historical time and fictional time, the parallel anchors Stephen's fantasy identifications with Parnell and Christ in the narrative's very structure.[1]

Throughout, the textual notes provide readers with the opportunity to understand aspects of the process by which the language for the narrative they are reading came into being through writing, revision, and editing. They also provide instances of verbal differences among the versions consulted during the establishing of the text printed in this edition. Some of the notes enable us to recognize Joyce's changes to the handwritten fair copy, as we have seen, or to a later typed or printed version, as part of his composing process. Some of those changes were corrections, such as the addition of a word that had been dropped during the transcribing of the fair copy from an earlier document or during the composing of new material for the fair copy. Other changes involved rewording that resulted in different meanings, through either substitution or addition of language. In effect, we have access to part of the writer's creative process. The notes also record differences between the fair copy and later versions of the text in typescript, in printed editions, or in changes that Joyce directed to be made. The changes may be corrections to errors committed by the typist or by printers, or they may reflect Joyce's decisions to modify the narrative's language. In either case, the differences can bring out contrasting meanings that affect our understanding of the passage's implications. We have access through the notes to processes of textual production between handwritten copy and printed versions, including this one. Those processes, which involve decisions made by the writer and his editors, extend a dimension already contained in the narrative, which in Part V presents Stephen Dedalus's process of composing his poem. Joyce has memorably evoked for us there the act of writing out by hand the text that Stephen is composing, but he has also given us the finished text as it is set up as a printed document.[2] The double vision of Stephen's poem as process and as result is one of the book's most vivid effects. The textual notes allow the reader to experience at points throughout the narrative, not just in the section concerning the poem, some of the oscillations between the

---

1. For a detailed analysis, see Hans Walter Gabler, "The Genesis of *A Portrait of the Artist as a Young Man*," *Critical Essays on James Joyce's "A Portrait of the Artist as a Young Man*," ed. Philip Brady and James F. Carens (New York: G. K. Hall, 1998), 106–08; or the essay "The Christmas Dinner Scene, Parnell's Death, and the Genesis of *A Portrait* . . . ," *James Joyce Quarterly* 13 (1976): 27–38.
2. The process of writing the "Villanelle" section itself into Part V has been analyzed from the fair copy in Gabler, "The Genesis of *A Portrait of the Artist as a Young Man*," 95–96. For an interpretive commentary concerning the relation of printed text to the acts of composing, writing out by hand, and reading, see John Paul Riquelme, "The Villanelle and the Source of Writing," *Teller and Tale in Joyce's Fiction* (Baltimore and London: Johns Hopkins UP, 1983), 73–83.

writer's handwritten text and the version that ultimately emerges as a published document.

The textual notes in this edition are an ample selection drawn from the footnotes pertaining to the establishing of the text editorially, as well as from the "Historical Collation" list in the 1993 Garland Critical Edition of *A Portrait of the Artist as a Young Man*. Some of the information from the "Historical Collation" not already also contained in the 1993 footnotes, concerning differences between versions of the text, has been shifted to the footnotes of this edition. The notes open with a line number and the reading in question from the line indicated. This so-called lemma is marked off by a square bracket. After the bracket follows a document indicator, marked off by a semicolon, for the source of the reading of this edition. Where the source is the copy-text—that is, Joyce's autograph fair-copy manuscript—the indicator (MS) is commonly absent, since implied, though it is given where especially warranted. For example, the first textual note for Part I begins:

12 *geen*] MS;

This means that in line 12, the word *"geen"* is written thus (with an *r* missing, as in a child's speech) in the fair copy; and a reason for emphasizing the MS spelling is that the conventional word ("green") appears in all published versions, prior to the text in this edition, established from that MS.

When the edition departs from its copy-text, the source of the adopted reading is always given. For example, the seventh textual note for Part I—

106 thrown--haha] aEg; jumped MS, Eg

—means that the language of line 106 from "thrown" through "haha" ("thrown his hat on the haha") has been accepted as a change away from the copy-text, that is, the MS, which contains only "jumped." As the "a" before the source indicator ("Eg") reports, Joyce changed the language on that later printing of the text, namely, in this case, the serial publication in *The Egoist*. In rare instances, the textual editors have decided uniquely for the critical edition not to retain the language of the MS, even though no document verifies Joyce's desire to have the change made. Such emendations of the MS are marked by "e"; if a document partially supports the change, it is mentioned after a colon. Any revision in the manuscript, such as a deletion, insertion, or cancellation, is indicated using the system presented in "Symbols and Sigla" (p. xxxii). For example, the note to IV, lines 385–86, places "the--keys" (followed by "MS") between superscript numerals and raised limit marks, as follows:

385–386 the--keys,] ^{71} the--keys $^{1\ulcorner}$ MS

This note indicates that all the language from "the" through "keys" ("the power of the keys") was added to the MS during the first level of revision. The addition is visible on the page of the manuscript here reproduced, written in above the sixth line of handwriting (p. xxxi). Such additions happen to be more frequent in Part IV than in the other parts. They are traces of the fact that the fair copy of Part IV is older than the fair copies of the other parts, and that therefore more instances of a later-stage revision are to be found on the MS for Part IV.[3] The note provides a reason and a basis for the reader to compare the passage before the addition was made to the passage.

Beyond documenting sources of readings, the notes frequently also report the language's textual history through typescript (TS) and *Egoist* serialization (Eg), as well as through the American first (16) and the British first and second editions (18 and 24). This record has been deemed especially pertinent where a departure in transmission from Joyce's MS has persisted into Chester G. Anderson's Viking edition (64), even though that first attempt at a critical edition was based on the rediscovery of the MS. For example, the first note for Part I, cited above, continues after "MS;" as follows:

green Eg–64

This note means (as indicated above) that the other published editions, from *The Egoist* through the 1964 edition, print "green," while the MS has "geen." Only exceptionally does the present edition give a textual history of its readings where the 1964 edition already reasserted Joyce's MS or a warranted change to it. The full textual record may be found in the 1993 Garland Critical Edition.[4]

In the printing of this edition, finally, as in the Garland and Vintage editions of 1993, end-of-line hyphenation occurs in two modes. The sign "=" marks a division for mere typographical reasons. Words so printed should always be cited as one undivided word. The regular hyphen indicates an authentic Joycean hyphen.

---

3. See Gabler, "The Genesis of *A Portrait of the Artist as a Young Man*," section I, especially pp. 85–86.

4. On only one occasion has an editorial decision of 1993 been reversed. At V. 2096 this edition does not follow the copy-text's "wenchers"; considering that form now an authorial slip of the pen, it emends according to all published texts and reads "wenches."

man. No King or emperor on this
earth has the power of the priest
of God. No angel or archangel
in heaven, no saint, not even
the Blessed Virgin herself, has
the power of a priest of God, the
power of the priest of God, the power, to loose, the power,
the power, the authority,
to make the great God of Heaven
come down upon the altar
and take the form of bread
and wine. What an awful
power, Stephen! —

A flame began to flutter
again on Stephen's cheek as he
heard in this proud address an
echo of his own proud musings.
How often had he seen himself
as a priest wielding calmly and
humbly the awful power of
which angels and saints stood
in reverence! His soul had
loved to muse in secret on
this desire. He had seen himself
a young and silent-mannered
priest, entering a confessional
swiftly, ascending the altar
steps, incensing, genuflecting,
accomplishing the vague acts
of the priesthood which pleased
him by reason of their
semblance of reality and of their
distance from it. In that dim
life which he had lived
through in his musings
he had assumed the voices

MS page for IV.382–402.

Symbols and Sigla

The symbols employed in the apparatus sections of this edition describe characteristic features of the writing and indicate sequences of correction and revision within the fair copy that provides the edition's copy-text.

⟨ ⟩	authorial deletion in the course of writing
⌐¹TEXT NEW¹⌐	text inserted/changed at first level of revision
⟨⌐¹⌐TEXT OLD⟩	text cancelled at first level of revision
⌐¹⟨TEXT OLD⟩ TEXT NEW¹⌐	text replaced at first level of revision
	The symbols ⌐ ⌐ delimit an area of change; a given number indicates the level, an additional letter identifies the agent ("A"=author; "s"=scribe)
∅	space reserved in the autograph
◇	erasure
☐	illegible character(s) or word(s)
|	line division in document

The document sigla employed in the apparatus sections are: MS, TS, Eg, 16, 18, 24, 64, as summarized above (p. xxx) and again identified in the opening textual footnote.

Following the lemma bracket in the emendations,

e   indicates a unique emendation in this edition;

e: indicates a unique emendation partially supported by the document identified after the colon;

a   prefixed to a document sigla (e.g., aEg, a16) indicates an authorial correction/revision in or to the document identified by the sigla.

The Text of
A PORTRAIT OF THE ARTIST
AS A YOUNG MAN

Edited, with Textual Notes, by

HANS WALTER GABLER
WITH WALTER HETTCHE

Explanatory Notes by

JOHN PAUL RIQUELME

Et ignotas animum dimittit in artes.[1]

Ovid, Metamorphoses. VIII.188.

1. "He turned his mind toward unknown arts" (Latin). The Roman poet Ovid (Publius Ovidius Naso, 43 BCE–17 CE) is presenting the decision of Daedalus, the legendary Athenian artist and inventor, to move beyond the limits of the known in his attempt to escape with his son, Icarus, from their island prison. After Daedalus had constructed a wooden device that made it possible for Queen Pasiphaë of Crete to have intercourse with a bull, her husband, King Minos, had Daedalus build a labyrinth to contain the Minotaur, the half-human, half-bull creature born of the union. Daedalus flew out of the labyrinth and escaped to Sicily with wings made in part of wax, but his son died after disregarding Daedalus's warning not to fly too close to the sun.

I

Once upon a time and a very good time it was there was a
moocow coming down along the road and this moocow that
was coming down along the road met a nicens little boy named
baby tuckoo . . . . .

His father told him that story: his father looked at him   5
through a glass:[1] he had a hairy face.

He was baby tuckoo. The moocow came down the road
where Betty Byrne lived: she sold lemon platt.[2]

> O, the wild rose blossoms
> On the little green place.   10

He sang that song. That was his song.

> O, the geen wothe botheth.

When you wet the bed first it is warm then it gets cold. His
mother put on the oilsheet. That had the queer smell.

His mother had a nicer smell than his father. She played on   15
the piano the sailor's hornpipe for him to dance. He danced:

> Tralala lala
> Tralala tralaladdy
> Tralala lala
> Tralala lala.   20

Uncle Charles and Dante clapped. They were older than his
father and mother but uncle Charles was older than Dante.

Dante had two brushes in her press.[3] The brush with the
maroon velvet back was for Michael Davitt and the brush with
the green velvet back was for Parnell.[4] Dante gave him a cachou[5]   25
every time he brought her a piece of tissue paper.

The Vances lived in number seven. They had a different
father and mother. They were Eileen's father and mother.
When they were grown up he was going to marry Eileen.

Copy-text: Holograph manuscript MS 920 and MS 921 at the National Library of Ireland
(MS); Collated texts: proofs and published text of the serialization in *The Egoist,* London
1914–15 (Eg); first edition, New York 1916 (16); second edition, London 1918 (18); third edition, London 1924 (24); 1964 Viking edition in the 1968 Viking Critical Library printing (64).

12 *geen*] MS; green Eg–64 [see pp. xxix–xxx]

1. Eyeglass or lens (*OED*); monocle.
2. Platted, or plaited (that is, intertwined), strands (*OED*) of lemon candy.
3. A cupboard for clothes and other personal belongings (*OED*).
4. The Irishmen Michael Davitt (1846–1906) and Charles Stewart Parnell (1846–1891)
   were the most influential nationalist political leaders in the 1880s, when the narrative opens,
   during campaigns for land-tenants' rights and Home Rule (limited autonomy) for Ireland.
5. A breath freshener and candy in the form of a pill made of cashew nut, licorice extract,
   and sugar (*OED*).

He hid under the table. His mother said: 30
—O, Stephen will apologise.
Dante said:
—O, if not, the eagles will come and pull out his eyes.

> Pull out his eyes,
> Apologise,   35
> Apologise,
> Pull out his eyes.
>
> Apologise,
> Pull out his eyes,
> Pull out his eyes,   40
> Apologise.

◆   ◆   ◆

The wide playgrounds were swarming with boys. All were
shouting and the prefects[6] urged them on with strong cries. The
evening air was pale and chilly and after every charge and thud
of the footballers[7] the greasy leather orb flew like a heavy bird   45
through the grey light. He kept on the fringe of his line, out of
sight of his prefect, out of the reach of the rude feet, feigning to
run now and then. He felt his body small and weak amid the
throng of players and his eyes were weak and watery. Rody
Kickham was not like that: he would be captain of the third   50
line[8] all the fellows said.

Rody Kickham was a decent fellow but Nasty Roche was a
stink. Rody Kickham had greaves in his number and a hamper
in the refectory.[9] Nasty Roche had big hands. He called the
Friday pudding dog-in-the-blanket. And one day he had asked: 55
—What is your name?
Stephen had answered:
—Stephen Dedalus.
Then Nasty Roche had said:
—What kind of a name is that?   60

---

30 He (NEW PARAGRAPH)] NO PARAGRAPH 16–64   59 Then] aEg; The MS, Eg

6. Senior students or teachers given the authority to supervise.
7. The unspecified game could be rugby, but "orb" could suggest a round ball appropriate for
   Gaelic football, revived in the 1880s, rather than the oval rugby ball. During Joyce's early
   years at school, however, both rugby and a rough, chaotic game "with English roots" (Nohrnberg, 104), "gravel football," were played. The latter involved a "not perfectly spherical"
   (Bradley, 49) ball. "Swarming" suggests the large number of boys who could engage in gravel
   football.
8. Youngest (for boys under thirteen) of three groups in the school, by contrast with the
   "lower" line (ages thirteen–fifteen) and the "higher" one (ages fifteen–eighteen).
9. Shin guards (OED) in a numbered cubby or small locker, and a food container in the
   dining area.

And when Stephen had not been able to answer Nasty
Roche had asked:
—What is your father?
Stephen had answered:
—A gentleman.   65
Then Nasty Roche had asked:
—Is he a magistrate?[1]
He crept about from point to point on the fringe of his line,
making little runs now and then. But his hands were bluish
with cold. He kept his hands in the sidepockets of his belted   70
grey suit. That was a belt round his jacket. And belt was also to
give a fellow a belt. One day a fellow had said to Cantwell:
—I'd give you such a belt in a second.
Cantwell had answered:
—Go and fight your match. Give Cecil Thunder a belt. I'd like   75
to see you. He'd give you a toe in the rump for yourself.
That was not a nice expression. His mother had told him
not to speak with the rough boys in the college. Nice mother!
The first day in the hall of the castle[2] when she had said good=
bye she had put up her veil double to her nose to kiss him: and   80
her nose and eyes were red. But he had pretended not to see
that she was going to cry. She was a nice mother but she was
not so nice when she cried. And his father had given him two
fiveshilling pieces for pocket money. And his father had told
him if he wanted anything to write home to him and, whatever   85
he did, never to peach on a fellow.[3] Then at the door of the
castle the rector had shaken hands with his father and mother,
his soutane[4] fluttering in the breeze, and the car had driven off
with his father and mother on it. They had cried to him from
the car, waving their hands: 90
—Goodbye, Stephen, goodbye!
—Goodbye, Stephen, goodbye!
He was caught in the whirl of a scrimmage[5] and, fearful of
the flashing eyes and muddy boots, bent down to look through
the legs. The fellows were struggling and groaning and their   95

---

71 jacket.] pocket. Eg–64

1. A member of the local judiciary; spread throughout Ireland outside Dublin, magistrates
   were frequently Protestants, but by the late decades of the nineteenth century, Catholics
   were sometimes appointed.
2. Central structure of Clongowes Wood College, founded 1814, the first and most prestigious boys' school established in Ireland by the Society of Jesus, a Roman Catholic religious
   order also known as the Jesuits.
3. Inform on an accomplice or associate (*OED*).
4. As a Roman Catholic priest, the head of the school, or rector, would have worn the traditional ecclesiastical outer garment, "a long buttoned gown or frock, with sleeves" (*OED*).
5. "A tussle for the ball among players (in various games)" (*OED*).

legs were rubbing and kicking and stamping. Then Jack
Lawton's yellow boots dodged out the ball and all the other
boots and legs ran after. He ran after them a little way and then
stopped. It was useless to run on. Soon they would be going
home for the holidays. After supper in the studyhall he would   100
change the number pasted up inside his desk from seventyseven
to seventysix.[6]

It would be better to be in the studyhall than out there in the
cold. The sky was pale and cold but there were lights in the
castle. He wondered from which window Hamilton Rowan   105
had thrown his hat on the haha[7] and had there been flowerbeds
at that time under the windows. One day when he had been
called to the castle the butler had shown him the marks of the
soldiers' slugs in the wood of the door and had given him a
piece of shortbread that the community[8] ate. It was nice and   110
warm to see the lights in the castle. It was like something in a
book. Perhaps Leicester Abbey was like that. And there were
nice sentences in Doctor Cornwell's Spelling Book.[9] They were
like poetry but they were only sentences to learn the spelling
from.   115

> *Wolsey died in Leicester Abbey*[1]
> *Where the abbots buried him.*
> *Canker is a disease of plants,*
> *Cancer one of animals.*

It would be nice to lie on the hearthrug before the fire,   120
leaning his head upon his hands, and think on those sentences.
He shivered as if he had cold slimy water next his skin. That
was mean of Wells to shoulder him into the square ditch[2] be=
cause he would not swop his little snuffbox for Wells's sea=
soned hacking chestnut,[3] the conqueror of forty. How cold and   125

---

101 seventyseven] aEg; ⁷¹⟨◇seven⟩ seventy-seven¹ʳ MS; seventy-seven Eg   102 seventysix.]
a Eg; ⁷¹ ⟨◇six.⟩ seventy-six.¹ʳ MS; seventy-six. Eg   106 thrown--haha] aEg; jumped MS, Eg
106 had(2)] Eg; were MS

6. Days remaining until Christmas. On Joyce's changes to the manuscript here, see
   pp. xxvii–xxviii.
7. Archibald Hamilton Rowan (1751–1834), an Irish nationalist imprisoned for sedition in
   1794, stopped at Clongowes Wood Castle (before it was a school) while escaping to
   France and reputedly threw his hat into the dry moat, or haha, around the Castle to mislead his pursuers.
8. Priests and other members of the order living and working together at the college.
9. In the middle of the nineteenth century, James Cornwell (1812–1902) published a number of books for instruction in grammar and composition, including *The Young Composer*
   (Michael).
1. Thomas Wolsey (c. 1474–1530), cardinal and lord chancellor of England, died at an
   abbey near Leicester in England on his way to trial for treason, having failed to secure
   from the pope a divorce for King Henry VIII from Catherine of Aragon.
2. The cesspool for the square, or urinal, behind the dormitory (Anderson).
3. Chestnut tied to a string to enable hacking, or striking against another chestnut until one
   breaks.

slimy the water had been! A fellow had once seen a big rat jump plop into the scum. He shivered and longed to cry. It would be so nice to be at home. Mother was sitting at the fire with Dante waiting for Brigid to bring in the tea. She had her feet on the fender and her jewelly slippers were so hot and they had such a lovely warm smell! Dante knew a lot of things. She had taught him where the Mozambique Channel was and what was the longest river in America and what was the name of the highest mountain in the moon. Father Arnall knew more than Dante because he was a priest but both his father and uncle Charles said that Dante was a clever woman and a wellread woman. And when Dante made that noise after dinner and then put up her hand to her mouth: that was heartburn.

A voice cried far out on the playground:

—All in!

Then other voices cried from the lower and third lines:

—All in! All in!

The players closed around, flushed and muddy, and he went among them, glad to go in. Rody Kickham held the ball by its greasy lace. A fellow asked him to give it one last: but he walked on without even answering the fellow. Simon Moonan told him not to because the prefect was looking. The fellow turned to Simon Moonan and said:

—We all know why you speak. You are McGlade's suck.[4]

Suck was a queer word. The fellow called Simon Moonan that name because Simon Moonan used to tie the prefect's false sleeves behind his back and the prefect used to let on to be angry. But the sound was ugly. Once he had washed his hands in the lavatory of the Wicklow Hotel and his father pulled the stopper up by the chain after and the dirty water went down through the hole in the basin. And when it had all gone down slowly the hole in the basin had made a sound like that: suck. Only louder.

To remember that and the white look of the lavatory made him feel cold and then hot. There were two cocks that you turned and water came out: cold and hot. He felt cold and then a little hot: and he could see the names printed on the cocks. That was a very queer thing.

And the air in the corridor chilled him too. It was queer and wettish. But soon the gas would be lit and in burning it made a light noise like a little song. Always the same: and when the fellows stopped talking in the playroom you could hear it.

127–128 He--home.] ABSENT Eg–64

4. Sycophant; someone who sucks up to another (schoolboy slang; OED).

It was the hour for sums. Father Arnall wrote a hard sum on
the board and then he said:

—Now then, who will win? Go ahead, York! Go ahead, Lan=   170
caster![5]

Stephen tried his best but the sum was too hard and he felt
confused. The little silk badge with the white rose on it that
was pinned on the breast of his jacket began to flutter. He was
no good at sums but he tried his best so that York might not   175
lose. Father Arnall's face looked very black but he was not in a
wax:[6] he was laughing. Then Jack Lawton cracked his fingers
and Father Arnall looked at his copybook and said:

—Right. Bravo Lancaster! The red rose wins. Come on now,
York! Forge ahead!   180

Jack Lawton looked over from his side. The little silk badge
with the red rose on it looked very rich because he had a blue
sailor top on. Stephen felt his own face red too, thinking of all
the bets about who would get first place in elements,[7] Jack
Lawton or he. Some weeks Jack Lawton got the card for first   185
and some weeks he got the card for first. His white silk badge
fluttered and fluttered as he worked at the next sum and heard
Father Arnall's voice. Then all his eagerness passed away and
he felt his face quite cool. He thought his face must be white
because it felt so cool. He could not get out the answer for the   190
sum but it did not matter. White roses and red roses: those
were beautiful colours to think of. And the cards for first place
and second place and third place were beautiful colours too:
pink and cream and lavender. Lavender and cream and pink
roses were beautiful to think of. Perhaps a wild rose might be   195
like those colours: and he remembered the song about the wild
rose blossoms on the little green place. But you could not have
a green rose. But perhaps somewhere in the world you could.

The bell rang and then the classes began to file out of the
rooms and along the corridors towards the refectory. He sat   200
looking at the two prints of butter on his plate but could not
eat the damp bread. The tablecloth was damp and limp. But he
drank off the hot weak tea which the clumsy scullion, girt with
a white apron, poured into his cup. He wondered whether the

169 he] ABSENT Eg–64

5. The House of York, whose emblem was the white rose, and the House of Lancaster,
   whose emblem was the red rose, opposed each other during the civil war in England later
   known as the War of the Roses. Ireland sided with York. Lancaster won.
6. Not angry (slang; *OED*).
7. As opposed to third *grammar*, the other division of the third line, the youngest students;
   the *elements* class studied spelling, grammar, writing, arithmetic, geography, history, and
   Latin (Gifford).

scullion's apron was damp too or whether all white things were 205
cold and damp. Nasty Roche and Saurin drank cocoa that their
people sent them in tins. They said they could not drink the tea;
that it was hogwash. Their fathers were magistrates, the fel=
lows said.

All the boys seemed to him very strange. They had all fa= 210
thers and mothers and different clothes and voices. He longed
to be at home and lay his head on his mother's lap. But he
could not: and so he longed for the play and study and prayers
to be over and to be in bed.

He drank another cup of hot tea and Fleming said: 215
—What's up? Have you a pain or what's up with you?
—I don't know, Stephen said.
—Sick in your breadbasket, Fleming said, because your face
looks white. It will go away.
—O yes, Stephen said. 220

But he was not sick there. He thought that he was sick in his
heart if you could be sick in that place. Fleming was very
decent to ask him. He wanted to cry. He leaned his elbows on
the table and shut and opened the flaps of his ears. Then he
heard the noise of the refectory every time he opened the flaps 225
of his ears. It made a roar like a train at night. And when he
closed the flaps the roar was shut off like a train going into a
tunnel. That night at Dalkey[8] the train had roared like that and
then, when it went into the tunnel, the roar stopped. He closed
his eyes and the train went on, roaring and then stopping; 230
roaring again, stopping. It was nice to hear it roar and stop and
then roar out of the tunnel again and then stop.

Then the higher line fellows began to come down along the
matting in the middle of the refectory, Paddy Rath and Jimmy
Magee and the Spaniard who was allowed to smoke cigars and 235
the little Portuguese who wore the woolly cap. And then the
lower line tables and the tables of the third line. And every
single fellow had a different way of walking.

He sat in a corner of the playroom pretending to watch a
game of dominos and once or twice he was able to hear for an 240
instant the little song of the gas. The prefect was at the door
with some boys and Simon Moonan was knotting his false
sleeves. He was telling them something about Tullabeg.[9]

Then he went away from the door and Wells came over to
Stephen and said: 245

8. Village on the coast south of Dublin.
9. Location of another Jesuit boys' school.

—Tell us, Dedalus, do you kiss your mother every night before
you go to bed?

Stephen answered:

—I do.

Wells turned to the other fellows and said: 250

—O, I say, here's a fellow says he kisses his mother every night
before he goes to bed.

The other fellows stopped their game and turned round,
laughing. Stephen blushed under their eyes and said:

—I do not.   255

Wells said:

—O, I say, here's a fellow says he doesn't kiss his mother
before he goes to bed.

They all laughed again. Stephen tried to laugh with them.
He felt his whole body hot and confused in a moment. What   260
was the right answer to the question? He had given two and
still Wells laughed. But Wells must know the right answer for
he was in third of grammar. He tried to think of Wells's mother
but he did not dare to raise his eyes to Wells's face. He did not
like Wells's face. It was Wells who had shouldered him into the   265
square ditch the day before because he would not swop his
little snuffbox for Wells's seasoned hacking chestnut, the con=
queror of forty. It was a mean thing to do; all the fellows said it
was. And how cold and slimy the water had been! And a fellow
had once seen a big rat jump plop into the scum.   270

The cold slime of the ditch covered his whole body; and,
when the bell rang for study and the lines filed out of the
playrooms, he felt the cold air of the corridor and staircase
inside his clothes. He still tried to think what was the right
answer. Was it right to kiss his mother or wrong to kiss his   275
mother? What did that mean, to kiss? You put your face up like
that to say goodnight and then his mother put her face down.
That was to kiss. His mother put her lips on his cheek; her lips
were soft and they wetted his cheek; and they made a tiny little
noise: kiss. Why did people do that with their two faces?   280

Sitting in the studyhall he opened the lid of his desk and
changed the number pasted up inside from seventyseven to
seventysix.[1] But the Christmas vacation was very far away: but
one time it would come because the earth moved round always.

There was a picture of the earth on the first page of his   285
geography: a big ball in the middle of clouds. Fleming had a

1. On Joyce's changes to the manuscript here, see pp. xxvii–xxviii.

box of crayons and one night during free study he had coloured
the earth green and the clouds maroon. That was like the two
brushes in Dante's press, the brush with the green velvet back
for Parnell and the brush with the maroon velvet back for   290
Michael Davitt. But he had not told Fleming to colour them
those colours. Fleming had done it himself.

He opened the geography to study the lesson; but he could
not learn the names of places in America. Still they were all
different places that had those different names. They were all in   295
different countries and the countries were in continents and the
continents were in the world and the world was in the universe.

He turned to the flyleaf of the geography and read what he
had written there: himself, his name and where he was.

Stephen Dedalus   300
Class of Elements
Clongowes Wood College
Sallins
County Kildare
Ireland   305
Europe
The World
The Universe

That was in his writing: and Fleming one night for a cod[2] had
written on the opposite page: 310

Stephen Dedalus is my name,
Ireland is my nation.
Clongowes is my dwellingplace
And heaven my expectation.

He read the verses backwards but then they were not poetry.   315
Then he read the flyleaf from the bottom to the top till he came
to his own name. That was he: and he read down the page
again. What was after the universe? Nothing. But was there
anything round the universe to show where it stopped before
the nothing place began? It could not be a wall but there could   320
be a thin thin line there all round everything. It was very big to
think about everything and everywhere. Only God could do
that. He tried to think what a big thought that must be but he
could think only of God. God was God's name just as his name
was Stephen. *Dieu* was the French for God and that was God's   325
name too; and when anyone prayed to God and said *Dieu* then
God knew at once that it was a French person that was pray=

2. As a prank.

ing. But though there were different names for God in all the
different languages in the world and God understood what all
the people who prayed said in their different languages still   330
God remained always the same God and God's real name was
God.

It made him very tired to think that way. It made him feel
his head very big. He turned over the flyleaf and looked wearily
at the green round earth in the middle of the maroon clouds.   335
He wondered which was right, to be for the green or for the
maroon, because Dante had ripped the green velvet back off
the brush that was for Parnell one day with her scissors and
had told him that Parnell was a bad man. He wondered if they
were arguing at home about that. That was called politics.   340
There were two sides in it: Dante was on one side and his
father and Mr Casey were on the other side but his mother and
uncle Charles were on no side. Every day there was something
in the paper about it.[3]

It pained him that he did not know well what politics meant   345
and that he did not know where the universe ended. He felt
small and weak. When would he be like the fellows in poetry
and rhetoric?[4] They had big voices and big boots and they
studied trigonometry. That was very far away. First came the
vacation and then the next term and then vacation again and   350
then again another term and then again the vacation. It was
like a train going in and out of tunnels and that was like the
noise of the boys eating in the refectory when you opened and
closed the flaps of the ears. Term, vacation; tunnel, out; noise,
stop. How far away it was! It was better to go to bed to sleep.   355
Only prayers in the chapel and then bed. He shivered and
yawned. It would be lovely in bed after the sheets got a bit hot.
First they were so cold to get into. He shivered to think how
cold they were first. But then they got hot and then he could
sleep. It was lovely to be tired. He yawned again. Night prayers 360
and then bed: he shivered and wanted to yawn. It would be
lovely in a few minutes. He felt a warm glow creeping up from
the cold shivering sheets, warmer and warmer till he felt warm
all over, ever so warm; ever so warm and yet he shivered a little
and still wanted to yawn.   365

The bell rang for night prayers and he filed out of the study=
hall after the others and down the staircase and along the

---

3. Newspaper coverage, often biased and sensational, began when Captain William O'Shea
   made public in 1889 the adulterous relationship between Parnell and O'Shea's wife,
   Katherine. The scandal divided the country and led to Parnell's being replaced in 1891 as
   leader of the Irish Parliamentary Party.
4. The two divisions of the higher line, the oldest group of boys.

corridors to the chapel. The corridors were darkly lit and the chapel was darkly lit. Soon all would be dark and sleeping. There was cold night air in the chapel and the marbles[5] were the colour the sea was at night. The sea was cold day and night: but it was colder at night. It was cold and dark under the seawall beside his father's house. But the kettle would be on the hob to make punch.

The prefect of the chapel prayed above his head and his memory knew the responses:

> O Lord, open our lips
> And our mouth shall announce Thy praise.
> Incline unto our aid, O God!
> O Lord, make haste to help us!

There was a cold night smell in the chapel. But it was a holy smell. It was not like the smell of the old peasants who knelt at the back of the chapel at Sunday mass. That was a smell of air and rain and turf and corduroy. But they were very holy peas= ants. They breathed behind him on his neck and sighed as they prayed. They lived in Clane,[6] a fellow said: there were little cottages there and he had seen a woman standing at the half= door of a cottage with a child in her arms as the cars had come past from Sallins. It would be lovely to sleep for one night in that cottage before the fire of smoking turf, in the dark lit by the fire, in the warm dark, breathing the smell of the peasants, air and rain and turf and corduroy. But, O, the road there between the trees was dark! You would be lost in the dark. It made him afraid to think of how it was.

He heard the voice of the prefect of the chapel saying the last prayer. He prayed it too against the dark outside under the trees.

> Visit, we beseech Thee, O Lord, this habitation and
> drive away from it all the snares of the enemy. May
> Thy holy angels dwell herein to preserve us in peace
> and may Thy blessing be always upon us through
> Christ, Our Lord. Amen.

His fingers trembled as he undressed himself in the dormi= tory. He told his fingers to hurry up. He had to undress and then kneel and say his own prayers and be in bed before the gas was lowered so that he might not go to hell when he died. He rolled his stockings off and put on his nightshirt quickly and

369 sleeping.] TS BEGINS

5. Pillars painted to look like marble (Anderson).
6. Village near Clongowes, whose chapel served as the parish church.

knelt trembling at his bedside and repeated his prayers quickly
quickly fearing that the gas would go down. He felt his shoul=
ders shaking as he murmured: 410

> God bless my father and my mother and spare them to
> me!
> God bless my little brothers and sisters and spare them
> to me!
> God bless Dante and uncle Charles and spare them to   415
> me!

He blessed himself and climbed quickly into bed and, tuck=
ing the end of the nightshirt under his feet, curled himself to=
gether under the cold white sheets, shaking and trembling. But
he would not go to hell when he died; and the shaking would   420
stop. A voice bade the boys in the dormitory goodnight. He
peered out for an instant over the coverlet and saw the yellow
curtains round and before his bed that shut him off on all sides.
The light was lowered quietly.

The prefect's shoes went away. Where? Down the staircase   425
and along the corridors or to his room at the end? He saw the
dark. Was it true about the black dog that walked there at night
with eyes as big as carriagelamps? They said it was the ghost of
a murderer. A long shiver of fear flowed over his body. He saw
the dark entrance hall of the castle. Old servants in old dress   430
were in the ironingroom above the staircase. It was long ago.
The old servants were quiet. There was a fire there but the hall
was still dark. A figure came up the staircase from the hall. He
wore the white cloak of a marshal; his face was pale and
strange; he held his hand pressed to his side. He looked out of   435
strange eyes at the old servants. They looked at him and saw
their master's face and cloak and knew that he had received his
deathwound. But only the dark was where they looked: only
dark silent air. Their master had received his deathwound on
the battlefield of Prague far away over the sea. He was standing   440
on the field; his hand was pressed to his side; his face was pale
and strange and he wore the white cloak of a marshal.

O how cold and strange it was to think of that! All the dark
was cold and strange. There were pale strange faces there, great
eyes like carriagelamps. They were the ghosts of murderers, the   445
figures of marshals who had received their deathwound on
battlefields far away over the sea. What did they wish to say
that their faces were so strange?

*Visit, we beseech Thee, O Lord, this habitation and drive
away from it all . . . .*   450

408–409 quickly quickly] quickly Eg; quickly, 16–24; quickly quickly, 64

Going home for the holidays! That would be lovely: the fellows had told him. Getting up on the cars[7] in the early wintry morning outside the door of the castle. The cars were rolling on the gravel. Cheers for the rector!

Hurray! Hurray! Hurray!   455

The cars drove past the chapel and all caps were raised. They drove merrily along the country roads. The drivers pointed with their whips to Bodenstown. The fellows cheered. They passed the farmhouse of the Jolly Farmer. Cheer after cheer after cheer. Through Clane they drove, cheering and   460 cheered. The peasant women stood at the halfdoors, the men stood here and there. The lovely smell there was in the wintry air: the smell of Clane: rain and wintry air and turf smoulder= ing and corduroy.

The train was full of fellows: a long long chocolate train   465 with cream facings. The guards went to and fro opening, closing, locking, unlocking the doors. They were men in dark blue and silver; they had silvery whistles and their keys made a quick music: click, click: click, click.

And the train raced on over the flat lands and past the Hill   470 of Allen. The telegraphpoles were passing, passing. The train went on and on. It knew. There were coloured lanterns in the hall of his father's house and ropes of green branches. There were holly and ivy round the pierglass and holly and ivy, green and red, twined round the chandeliers. There were red holly   475 and green ivy round the old portraits on the walls. Holly and ivy for him and for Christmas.

Lovely . . . . . .

All the people. Welcome home, Stephen! Noises of welcome. His mother kissed him. Was that right? His father was a mar=   480 shal now: higher than a magistrate. Welcome home, Stephen!

Noises . . . . .

There was a noise of curtainrings running back along the rods, of water being splashed in the basins. There was a noise of rising and dressing and washing in the dormitory: a noise of   485 clapping of hands as the prefect went up and down telling the fellows to look sharp. A pale sunlight showed the yellow cur= tains drawn back, the tossed beds. His bed was very hot and his face and body were very hot.

He got up and sat on the side of his bed. He was weak. He   490 tried to pull on his stocking. It had a horrid rough feel. The sunlight was queer and cold.

Fleming said:

7. Horse-drawn transportation.

—Are you not well?

He did not know; and Fleming said: 495

—Get back into bed. I'll tell McGlade you're not well.

—He's sick.

—Who is?

—Tell McGlade.

—Get back into bed.   500

—Is he sick?

A fellow held his arms while he loosened the stocking cling=
ing to his foot and climbed back into the hot bed.

He crouched down between the sheets, glad of their tepid
glow. He heard the fellows talk among themselves about him   505
as they dressed for mass. It was a mean thing to do, to shoulder
him into the square ditch, they were saying.

Then their voices ceased; they had gone. A voice at his bed
said:

—Dedalus, don't spy on us,[8] sure you won't?   510

Wells's face was there. He looked at it and saw that Wells
was afraid.

—I didn't mean to. Sure you won't?

His father had told him, whatever he did, never to peach on
a fellow. He shook his head and answered no and felt glad.   515
Wells said:

—I didn't mean to, honour bright. It was only for cod. I'm
sorry.

The face and the voice went away. Sorry because he was
afraid. Afraid that it was some disease. Canker was a disease of   520
plants and cancer one of animals: or another different. That
was a long time ago then out on the playgrounds in the evening
light, creeping from point to point on the fringe of his line, a
heavy bird flying low through the grey light. Leicester Abbey lit
up. Wolsey died there. The abbots buried him themselves.   525

It was not Wells's face, it was the prefect's. He was not
foxing.[9] No, no: he was sick really. He was not foxing. And he
felt the prefect's hand on his forehead; and he felt his forehead
warm and damp against the prefect's cold damp hand. That
was the way a rat felt, slimy and damp and cold. Every rat had   530
two eyes to look out of. Sleek slimy coats, little little feet
tucked up to jump, black shiny eyes to look out of. They could
understand how to jump. But the minds of rats could not
understand trigonometry. When they were dead they lay on

523 to] TS; of MS

8. Don't inform against me.
9. Pretending (slang; *OED*).

their sides. Their coats dried then. They were only dead things.   535

The prefect was there again and it was his voice that was saying that he was to get up, that Father Minister had said he was to get up and dress and go to the infirmary. And while he was dressing himself as quickly as he could the prefect said:

—We must pack off to Brother[1] Michael because we have the   540 collywobbles. Terrible thing to have the collywobbles! How we wobble when we have the collywobbles!

He was very decent to say that. That was all to make him laugh. But he could not laugh because his cheeks and lips were all shivery: and then the prefect had to laugh by himself.   545

The prefect cried:

—Quick march! Hayfoot! Strawfoot![2]

They went together down the staircase and along the corri= dor and past the bath. As he passed the door he remembered with a vague fear the warm turfcoloured bogwater, the warm   550 moist air, the noise of plunges, the smell of the towels, like medicine.

Brother Michael was standing at the door of the infirmary and from the door of the dark cabinet on his right came a smell like medicine. That came from the bottles on the shelves. The   555 prefect spoke to Brother Michael and Brother Michael answered and called the prefect sir. He had reddish hair mixed with grey and a queer look. It was queer that he would always be a brother. It was queer too that you could not call him sir because he was a brother and had a different kind of look. Was   560 he not holy enough or why could he not catch up on the others?

There were two beds in the room and in one bed there was a fellow: and when they went in he called out:

—Hello! It's young Dedalus! What's up?

—The sky is up, Brother Michael said.   565

He was a fellow out of third of grammar and, while Stephen was undressing, he asked Brother Michael to bring him a round of buttered toast.

—Ah, do! he said.

—Butter you up! said Brother Michael. You'll get your walking   570 papers in the morning when the doctor comes.

—Will I? the fellow said. I'm not well yet.

Brother Michael repeated:

541–542 Terrible--collywobbles! How--collywobbles!] MS; ABSENT TS–24   566 of(1)] of the Eg–64

1. Member of the Jesuit order who is part of the community but is not ordained.
2. Joking reference to using hay on the left foot and straw on the right to teach soldiers how to tell the difference between their feet when marching.

—You'll get your walking papers, I tell you.

He bent down to rake the fire. He had a long back like the long back of a tramhorse. He shook the poker gravely and nodded his head at the fellow out of third of grammar. 575

Then Brother Michael went away and after a while the fel=low out of third of grammar turned in towards the wall and fell asleep. 580

That was the infirmary. He was sick then. Had they written home to tell his mother and father? But it would be quicker for one of the priests to go himself to tell them. Or he would write a letter for the priest to bring.

> Dear Mother 585
>   I am sick. I want to go home. Please come and take
> me home. I am in the infirmary.
>   Your fond son,
>   Stephen

How far away they were! There was cold sunlight outside 590 the window. He wondered if he would die. You could die just the same on a sunny day. He might die before his mother came. Then he would have a dead mass in the chapel like the way the fellows had told him it was when Little had died. All the fel=lows would be at the mass, dressed in black, all with sad faces. 595 Wells too would be there but no fellow would look at him. The rector would be there in a cope of black and gold and there would be tall yellow candles on the altar and round the cata=falque.[3] And they would carry the coffin out of the chapel slowly and he would be buried in the little graveyard of the 600 community off the main avenue of limes. And Wells would be sorry then for what he had done. And the bell would toll slowly.

He could hear the tolling. He said over to himself the song that Brigid had taught him. 605

> *Dingdong! The castle bell!*
> *Farewell, my mother!*
> *Bury me in the old churchyard*
> *Beside my eldest brother.*
> *My coffin shall be black,* 610
> *Six angels at my back,*
> *Two to sing and two to pray*
> *And two to carry my soul away.*

601 limes.] Eg; chestnuts. MS–TS

3. Decorated structure that holds a coffin during funeral ceremonies (*OED*).

How beautiful and sad that was! How beautiful the words
were where they said *Bury me in the old churchyard!* A tremor   615
passed over his body. How sad and how beautiful! He wanted
to cry quietly but not for himself: for the words, so beautiful
and sad, like music. The bell! The bell! Farewell! O farewell!

The cold sunlight was weaker and Brother Michael was
standing at his bedside with a bowl of beeftea.[4] He was glad for   620
his mouth was hot and dry. He could hear them playing on the
playgrounds. It was after lunchtime. And the day was going on
in the college just as if he were there.

Then Brother Michael was going away and the fellow out of
third of grammar told him to be sure and come back and tell   625
him all the news in the paper. He told Stephen that his name
was Athy and that his father kept a lot of racehorses that were
spiffing jumpers and that his father would give a good tip to
Brother Michael any time he wanted it because Brother Mi=
chael was very decent and always told him the news out of the   630
paper they got every day up in the castle. There was every kind
of news in the paper: accidents, shipwrecks, sports and politics.

—Now it is all about politics in the paper, he said. Do your
people talk about that too?

—Yes, Stephen said.   635

—Mine too, he said.

Then he thought for a moment and said:

—You have a queer name, Dedalus, and I have a queer name
too, Athy. My name is the name of a town. Your name is like
Latin.   640

Then he asked:

—Are you good at riddles?

Stephen answered:

—Not very good.

Then he said: 645

—Can you answer me this one? Why is the county Kildare like
the leg of a fellow's breeches?

Stephen thought what could be the answer and then said:

—I give it up.

—Because there is a thigh in it, he said. Do you see the joke?   650
Athy is the town in the county Kildare and a thigh is the other
thigh.

—O, I see, Stephen said.

—That's an old riddle, he said.

---

622 It--lunchtime.] ABSENT TS–64

4. The juice of beef extracted by simmering (*OED*).

After a moment he said: 655
—I say!
—What? asked Stephen.
—You know, he said, you can ask that riddle another way?
—Can you? said Stephen.
—The same riddle, he said. Do you know the other way to ask   660
it?
—No, said Stephen.
—Can you not think of the other way? he said.

He looked at Stephen over the bedclothes as he spoke. Then
he lay back on the pillow and said: 665
—There is another way but I won't tell you what it is.

Why did he not tell it? His father, who kept the racehorses,
must be a magistrate too like Saurin's father and Nasty Roche's
father. He thought of his own father, of how he sang songs
while his mother played and of how he always gave him a   670
shilling when he asked for sixpence[5] and he felt sorry for him
that he was not a magistrate like the other boys' fathers. Then
why was he sent to that place with them? But his father had
told him that he would be no stranger there because his grand=
uncle had presented an address to the liberator[6] there fifty years   675
before. You could know the people of that time by their old
dress. It seemed to him a solemn time: and he wondered if that
was the time when the fellows in Clongowes wore blue coats
with brass buttons and yellow waistcoats and caps of rabbit=
skin and drank beer like grownup people and kept greyhounds   680
of their own to course the hares with.

He looked at the window and saw that the daylight had
grown weaker. There would be cloudy grey light over the play=
grounds. There was no noise on the playgrounds. The class
must be doing the themes or perhaps Father Arnall was reading   685
a legend[7] out of the book.

It was queer that they had not given him any medicine.
Perhaps Brother Michael would bring it back when he came.
They said you got stinking stuff to drink when you were in the
infirmary. But he felt better now than before. It would be nice   690
getting better slowly. You could get a book then. There was a

---

673 father] MS; uncle TS [BY INTERIM INSTRUCTION TO TYPIST? Eg REVERTS TO
father]   674 he] TS; we MS

5. In the British currency system, then in effect in Ireland, one shilling was worth twelve
   pence.
6. Daniel O'Connell (1775–1847), Irish political leader who worked for repeal of the Union
   with England and for Catholic emancipation (granted in 1829), the right of Catholics to
   hold high public offices, from which they had been excluded.
7. Story of a saint's life (OED).

book in the library about Holland. There were lovely foreign names in it and pictures of strangelooking cities and ships. It made you feel so happy.

How pale the light was at the window! But that was nice. The fire rose and fell on the wall. It was like waves. Someone had put coal on and he heard voices. They were talking. It was the noise of the waves. Or the waves were talking among them= selves as they rose and fell.

He saw the sea of waves, long dark waves rising and falling, dark under the moonless night. A tiny light twinkled at the pierhead where the ship was entering: and he saw a multitude of people gathered by the waters' edge to see the ship that was entering their harbour. A tall man stood on the deck, looking out towards the flat dark land: and by the light at the pierhead he saw his face, the sorrowful face of Brother Michael.

He saw him lift his hand towards the people and heard him say in a loud voice of sorrow over the waters:

—He is dead. We saw him lying upon the catafalque.

A wail of sorrow went up from the people.

—Parnell! Parnell! He is dead![8]

They fell upon their knees, moaning in sorrow.

And he saw Dante in a maroon velvet dress and with a green velvet mantle hanging from her shoulders walking proudly and silently past the people who knelt by the waters' edge.

◆   ◆   ◆

A great fire, banked high and red, flamed in the grate and under the ivytwined branches of the chandelier the Christmas table was spread. They had come home a little late and still dinner was not ready: but it would be ready in a jiffy, his mother had said. They were waiting for the door to open and for the servants to come in, holding the big dishes covered with their heavy metal covers.

All were waiting: uncle Charles, who sat far away in the shadow of the window, Dante and Mr Casey, who sat in the easychairs at either side of the hearth, Stephen, seated on a chair between them, his feet resting on the toasted boss.[9] Mr Dedalus looked at himself in the pierglass above the mantel= piece, waxed out his moustache ends and then, parting his coattails, stood with his back to the glowing fire: and still, from time to time, he withdrew a hand from his coattail to wax out one of his moustache ends. Mr Casey leaned his head to one

---

8. Parnell died October 6, 1891. On October 11, his body was brought by ship to Kingstown, now known as Dun Laoghaire.
9. A stuffed footstool without a wooden frame (*Letters* III, 129).

side and, smiling, tapped the gland of his neck with his fingers. And Stephen smiled too for he knew now that it was not true that Mr Casey had a purse of silver in his throat. He smiled to think how the silvery noise which Mr Casey used to make had deceived him. And when he had tried to open Mr Casey's hand to see if the purse of silver was hidden there he had seen that the fingers could not be straightened out: and Mr Casey had told him that he had got those three cramped fingers making a birthday present for Queen Victoria.[1]

Mr Casey tapped the gland of his neck and smiled at Ste= phen with sleepy eyes: and Mr Dedalus said to him:

—Yes. Well now, that's all right. O, we had a good walk, hadn't we, John? Yes . . . . . . I wonder if there's any likelihood of dinner this evening. Yes . . . . . O, well now, we got a good breath of ozone round the Head[2] today. Ay, bedad.

He turned to Dante and said:

—You didn't stir out at all, Mrs Riordan?

Dante frowned and said shortly:

—No.

Mr Dedalus dropped his coattails and went over to the side= board. He brought forth a great stone jar of whisky from the locker and filled the decanter slowly, bending now and then to see how much he had poured in. Then replacing the jar in the locker he poured out a little of the whisky into two glasses, added a little water and came with them back to the fireplace.

—A thimbleful, John, he said. Just to whet your appetite.

Mr Casey took the glass, drank, and placed it near him on the mantelpiece. Then he said:

—Well, I can't help thinking of our friend Christopher manu= facturing . . . .

He broke into a fit of laughter and coughing and added:

— . . . manufacturing that champagne for those fellows.

Mr Dedalus laughed loudly.

—Is it Christy? he said. There's more cunning in one of those warts on his bald head than in a pack of jack foxes.

He inclined his head, closed his eyes, and, licking his lips profusely, began to speak with the voice of the hotel keeper.

—And he has such a soft mouth when he's speaking to you, don't you know. He's very moist and watery about the dew= laps, God bless him.

755–756 glasses,--water] glasses ⌐¹, added a little water¹⌐ MS   756 with--back] back with the Eg–64

1. His hand has been crippled by forced labor during imprisonment for revolutionary activities.
2. Bray Head, a headland on the east coast, about twelve miles south of Dublin; near Bray, the village where Stephen's family resides.

Mr Casey was still struggling through his fit of coughing and laughter. Stephen, seeing and hearing the hotel keeper through his father's face and voice, laughed.

Mr Dedalus put up his eyeglass and, staring down at him, said quietly and kindly:

—What are you laughing at, you little puppy, you?

The servants entered and placed the dishes on the table. Mrs Dedalus followed and the places were arranged.

—Sit over, she said.

Mr Dedalus went to the end of the table and said:

—Now, Mrs Riordan, sit over. John, sit you down, my hearty.

He looked round to where uncle Charles sat and said:

—Now then, sir, there's a bird here waiting for you.

When all had taken their seats he laid his hand on the cover and then said quickly, withdrawing it:

—Now, Stephen.

Stephen stood up in his place to say the grace before meals:

    Bless us, O Lord, and these Thy gifts which through
Thy bounty we are about to receive through Christ
Our Lord. Amen.

All blessed themselves and Mr Dedalus with a sigh of pleas= ure lifted from the dish the heavy cover pearled around the edge with glistening drops.

Stephen looked at the plump turkey which had lain, trussed and skewered, on the kitchen table. He knew that his father had paid a guinea for it in Dunn's of D'Olier Street[3] and that the man had prodded it often at the breastbone to show how good it was: and he remembered the man's voice when he had said:

—Take that one, sir. That's the real Ally Daly.[4]

Why did Mr Barrett in Clongowes call his pandybat[5] a tur= key? It was not like a turkey. But Clongowes was far away: and the warm heavy smell of turkey and ham and celery rose from the plates and dishes and the great fire was banked high and red in the grate and the green ivy and red holly made you feel so happy and when dinner was ended the big plumpudding would be carried in, studded with peeled almonds and sprigs of holly, with bluish fire running around it and a little green flag flying from the top.

801 Mr] aTS; Father MS   802 It--turkey.] MS; ABSENT TS–64   808 a]ˇa ⟨□⟩ MS

3. Expensive shop for food in central Dublin. A guinea was a gold coin worth twenty-one shillings, that is, one pound and one shilling.
4. The real thing, the best (slang).
5. An instrument, often a reinforced leather strap, for punishing schoolboys with strokes on the open palm.

It was his first Christmas dinner and he thought of his little 810
brothers and sisters who were waiting in the nursery, as he had
often waited, till the pudding came. The deep low collar and
the Eton jacket made him feel queer and oldish: and that morn=
ing when his mother had brought him down to the parlour,
dressed for mass, his father had cried. That was because he was 815
thinking of his own father. And uncle Charles had said so too.

Mr Dedalus covered the dish and began to eat hungrily.
Then he said:

—Poor old Christy, he's nearly lopsided now with roguery.

—Simon, said Mrs Dedalus, you haven't given Mrs Riordan 820
any sauce.

Mr Dedalus seized the sauceboat.

—Haven't I? he cried. Mrs Riordan, pity the poor blind.

Dante covered her plate with her hands and said:

—No, thanks. 825

Mr Dedalus turned to uncle Charles.

—How are you off, sir?

—Right as the mail, Simon.

—You, John?

—I'm all right. Go on yourself. 830

—Mary? Here, Stephen, here's something to make your hair
curl.

He poured sauce freely over Stephen's plate and set the boat
again on the table. Then he asked uncle Charles was it tender.
Uncle Charles could not speak because his mouth was full but 835
he nodded that it was.

—That was a good answer our friend made to the canon.
What? said Mr Dedalus.

—I didn't think he had that much in him, said Mr Casey.

—*I'll pay you your dues, father, when you cease turning the* 840
house of God into a pollingbooth.

—A nice answer, said Dante, for any man calling himself a
catholic to give to his priest.

—They have only themselves to blame, said Mr Dedalus
suavely. If they took a fool's advice they would confine their 845
attention to religion.

—It is religion, Dante said. They are doing their duty in warn=
ing the people.

—We go to the house of God, Mr Casey said, in all humility to
pray to our Maker and not to hear election addresses. 850

—It is religion, Dante said again. They are right. They must
direct their flocks.

813 oldish:] old ⟨:⟩ ˥ˡish:ˡ˹ MS   840 *you*(1)] ˥ˡ*you*ˡ˹ MS; absent 16–24

—And preach politics from the altar, is it? asked Mr Dedalus.

—Certainly, said Dante. It is a question of public morality. A priest would not be a priest if he did not tell his flock what is right and what is wrong.   855

Mrs Dedalus laid down her knife and fork, saying:

—For pity' sake and for pity' sake let us have no political discussion on this day of all days in the year.

—Quite right, ma'am, said uncle Charles. Now, Simon, that's quite enough now. Not another word now.   860

—Yes, yes, said Mr Dedalus quickly.

He uncovered the dish boldly and said:

—Now then, who's for more turkey?

Nobody answered. Dante said: 865

—Nice language for any catholic to use!

—Mrs Riordan, I appeal to you, said Mrs Dedalus, to let the matter drop now.

Dante turned on her and said:

—And am I to sit here and listen to the pastors of my church   870
being flouted?

—Nobody is saying a word against them, said Mr Dedalus, so long as they don't meddle in politics.

—The bishops and priests of Ireland have spoken, said Dante, and they must be obeyed.   875

—Let them leave politics alone, said Mr Casey, or the people may leave their church alone.

—You hear? said Dante turning to Mrs Dedalus.

—Mr Casey! Simon! said Mrs Dedalus. Let it end now.

—Too bad! Too bad! said uncle Charles.   880

—What? cried Mr Dedalus. Were we to desert him at the bid= ding of the English people?[6]

—He was no longer worthy to lead, said Dante. He was a public sinner.

—We are all sinners and black sinners, said Mr Casey coldly.   885

—*Woe be to the man by whom the scandal cometh!* said Mrs Riordan. *It would be better for him that a millstone were tied about his neck and that he were cast into the depths of the sea rather than that he should scandalise one of these, my least little ones.* That is the language of the Holy Ghost.[7]   890

---

883 was] ⌐¹⟨is⟩ was¹⌐ [TWICE] MS

6. After the adultery scandal, the English prime minister, William Gladstone (1809–1898), leader of the Liberal Party, which had been allied with Parnell over Home Rule, pressed for Parnell's removal as head of the Irish Parliamentary Party.
7. In Christianity, the third person of the Holy Trinity (Father, Son, and Holy Ghost, or Holy Spirit) constituting a triune God (*OED*).

—And very bad language, if you ask me, said Mr Dedalus coolly.

—Simon! Simon! said uncle Charles. The boy.

—Yes, yes, said Mr Dedalus. I meant about the . . . . I was think= ing about the bad language of that railway porter. Well now, that's all right. Here, Stephen, show me your plate, old chap. Eat away now. Here.

He heaped up the food on Stephen's plate and served uncle Charles and Mr Casey to large pieces of turkey and splashes of sauce. Mrs Dedalus was eating little and Dante sat with her hands in her lap. She was red in the face. Mr Dedalus rooted with the carvers at the end of the dish and said:

—There's a tasty bit here we call the pope's nose.[8] If any lady or gentleman . . . . .

He held a piece of fowl up on the prong of the carvingfork. Nobody spoke. He put it on his own plate, saying:

—Well, you can't say but you were asked. I think I had better eat it myself because I'm not well in my health lately.

He winked at Stephen and, replacing the dishcover, began to eat again.

There was a silence while he ate. Then he said:

—Well now, the day kept up fine after all. There were plenty of strangers down too.

Nobody spoke. He said again:

—I think there were more strangers down than last Christmas.

He looked round at the others whose faces were bent to= wards their plates and, receiving no reply, waited for a moment and said bitterly:

—Well, my Christmas dinner has been spoiled anyhow.

—There could be neither luck nor grace, Dante said, in a house where there is no respect for the pastors of the church.

Mr Dedalus threw his knife and fork noisily on his plate.

—Respect! he said. Is it for Billy with the lip or for the tub of guts up in Armagh?[9] Respect!

—Princes of the church, said Mr Casey with slow scorn.

—Lord Leitrim's coachman,[1] yes, said Mr Dedalus.

---

898 plate] TS; table MS

8. The rump of the turkey.
9. William J. Walsh (1841–1921), archbishop of Dublin and primate of Ireland, and Michael Logue (1840–1924), archbishop of Armagh and primate of All Ireland, the top-ranking Irish prelates, denounced Parnell in a published statement (reprinted in this volume) signed by themselves and numerous bishops.
1. Any Irish person who collaborates with oppressors. In 1878, the earl of Leitrim, a land-lord with large holdings, hated for his treatment of tenants, was attacked and murdered; his Irish coachman attempted to protect him.

—They are the Lord's anointed, Dante said. They are an hon=
our to their country.

—Tub of guts, said Mr Dedalus coarsely. He has a handsome
face, mind you, in repose. You should see that fellow lapping   930
up his bacon and cabbage of a cold winter's day. O Johnny!

   He twisted his features into a grimace of heavy bestiality and
made a lapping noise with his lips.

—Really, Simon, said Mrs Dedalus, you should not speak that
way before Stephen. It's not right.   935

—O, he'll remember all this when he grows up, said Dante
hotly, the language he heard against God and religion and
priests in his own home.

—Let him remember too, cried Mr Casey to her from across
the table, the language with which the priests and the priests'   940
pawns broke Parnell's heart and hounded him into his grave.
Let him remember that too when he grows up.

—Sons of bitches! cried Mr Dedalus. When he was down they
turned on him to betray him and rend him like rats in a sewer.
Lowlived dogs! And they look it! By Christ, they look it!   945

—They behaved rightly, cried Dante. They obeyed their
bishops and their priests. Honour to them!

—Well, it is perfectly dreadful to say that not even for one day
of the year, said Mrs Dedalus, can we be free from these dread=
ful disputes!   950

   Uncle Charles raised his hands mildly and said:

—Come now, come now, come now! Can we not have our
opinions whatever they are without this bad temper and this
bad language? It is too bad surely.

   Mrs Dedalus spoke to Dante in a low voice but Dante said   955
loudly:

—I will not say nothing. I will defend my church and my
religion when it is insulted and spit on by renegade catholics.

   Mr Casey pushed his plate rudely into the middle of the
table and, resting his elbows before him, said in a harsh voice   960
to his host:

—Tell me, did I tell you that story about a very famous spit?

—You did not, John, said Mr Dedalus.

—Why then, said Mr Casey, it is a most instructive story. It
happened not long ago in the county Wicklow where we are   965
now.

   He broke off and, turning towards Dante, said with quiet
indignation:

---

949 of] in TS–64   960 harsh] hoarse TS–64   961 to--host:] ⌐¹⟨:⟩ to his host:¹⌐ MS

—And I may tell you, ma'am, that I, if you mean me, am no
renegade catholic. I am a catholic as my father was and his   970
father before him and his father before him again when we
gave up our lives rather than sell our faith.

—The more shame to you now, Dante said, to speak as you
do.

—The story, John, said Mr Dedalus smiling. Let us have the   975
story anyhow.

—Catholic indeed! repeated Dante ironically. The blackest[2]
protestant in the land would not speak the language I have
heard this evening.

Mr Dedalus began to sway his head to and fro, crooning like   980
a country singer.

—I am no protestant, I tell you again, said Mr Casey flushing.

Mr Dedalus, still crooning and swaying his head, began to
sing in a grunting nasal tone:

> O, come all you Roman catholics   985
> That never went to mass.

He took up his knife and fork again in good humour and set
to eating, saying to Mr Casey:

—Let us have the story, John. It will help us to digest.

Stephen looked with affection at Mr Casey's face which   990
stared across the table over his joined hands. He liked to sit
near him at the fire, looking up at his dark fierce face. But his
dark eyes were never fierce and his slow voice was good to
listen to. But why was he then against the priests? Because
Dante must be right then. But he had heard his father say that   995
she was a spoiled nun and that she had come out of the convent
in the Alleghanies when her brothers had got the money from
the savages for the trinkets and chainies.[3] Perhaps that made her
severe against Parnell. And she did not like him to play with
Eileen because Eileen was a protestant and when she was   1000
young she knew children that used to play with protestants and
the protestants used to make fun of the litany of the Blessed
Virgin. *Tower of Ivory*, they used to say, *House of Gold!*[4] How
could a woman be a tower of ivory or a house of gold? Who
was right then? And he remembered the evening in the infirm=   1005

977 Dante] ⁷⁾⟨◇⟩ Dante⁴ᵣ MS   992 fierce] ⁷¹fierce⁴ᵣ TS; ABSENT MS   997 brothers]
brother TS–64   998 and] and the TS–64

2. Most prejudiced against Catholics.
3. A spoiled nun would have renounced her vows or never completed her training. The
   Allegheny Mountains are in the eastern U.S. The brothers cheated African natives in
   their trading.
4. Phrases from the "Litany of Our Lady" (of Loreto) applied to the Virgin Mary.

ary in Clongowes, the dark waters, the light at the pierhead
and the moan of sorrow from the people when they had heard.

Eileen had long white hands. One evening when playing tig[5]
she had put her hands over his eyes: long and white and thin
and cold and soft. That was ivory: a cold white thing. That
was the meaning of *Tower of Ivory*.

—The story is very short and sweet, Mr Casey said. It was one
day down in Arklow, a cold bitter day, not long before the
chief[6] died. May God have mercy on him!

He closed his eyes wearily and paused. Mr Dedalus took a
bone from his plate and tore some meat from it with his teeth,
saying:

—Before he was killed, you mean.

Mr Casey opened his eyes, sighed and went on:

—It was down in Arklow one day. We were down there at a
meeting and after the meeting was over we had to make our
way to the railway station through the crowd. Such booing and
baaing, man, you never heard. They called us all the names in
the world. Well there was one old lady, and a drunken old
harridan she was surely, that paid all her attention to me. She
kept dancing along beside me in the mud bawling and scream=
ing into my face: *Priesthunter! The Paris Funds! Mr Fox! Kitty
O'Shea!*[7]

—And what did you do, John? asked Mr Dedalus.

—I let her bawl away, said Mr Casey. It was a cold day and to
keep up my heart I had (saving your presence, ma'am) a quid of
Tullamore[8] in my mouth and sure I couldn't say a word in any
case because my mouth was full of tobacco juice.

—Well, John?

—Well. I let her bawl away to her heart's content *Kitty O'Shea*
and the rest of it till at last she called that lady a name that I
won't sully this Christmas board nor your ears, ma'am, nor my
own lips by repeating.

He paused. Mr Dedalus, lifting his head from the bone,
asked:

—And what did you do, John?

—Do! said Mr Casey. She stuck her ugly old face up at me
when she said it and I had my mouth full of tobacco juice. I
bent down to her and *Phth!* says I to her like that.

5. Children's game also known as "tag" (*OED*).
6. Parnell.
7. Insults that refer to, respectively, the hunting down of priests during the time of the Penal
   Laws (first enacted 1695), the political funds that Parnell had private control of, a pseudonym he used during his affair with Mrs. O'Shea, and a nickname for Katherine O'Shea
   that has sexual connotations.
8. Chewing tobacco.

He turned aside and made the act of spitting.   1045
—*Phth!* says I to her like that, right into her eye.
He clapped a hand to his eye and gave a hoarse scream of
pain.
—*O Jesus, Mary and Joseph!* says she. *I'm blinded! I'm
blinded and drownded!*   1050
He stopped in a fit of coughing and laughter, repeating:
—*I'm blinded entirely!*
Mr Dedalus laughed loudly and lay back in his chair while
uncle Charles swayed his head to and fro.
Dante looked terribly angry and repeated while they   1055
laughed:
—Very nice! Ha! Very nice!
It was not nice about the spit in the woman's eye. But what
was the name the woman had called Kitty O'Shea that Mr
Casey would not repeat? He thought of Mr Casey walking   1060
through the crowds of people and making speeches from a
wagonette. That was what he had been in prison for and he
remembered that one night Sergeant O'Neill had come to the
house and had stood in the hall, talking in a low voice with his
father and chewing nervously at the chinstrap of his cap. And 1065
that night Mr Casey had not gone to Dublin by train but a car
had come to the door and he had heard his father say some=
thing about the Cabinteely road.[9]
He was for Ireland and Parnell and so was his father: and so
was Dante too for one night at the band on the esplanade she 1070
had hit a gentleman on the head with her umbrella because he
had taken off his hat when the band played *God save the
Queen* at the end.
Mr Dedalus gave a snort of contempt.
—Ah, John, he said. It is true for them. We are an unfortunate 1075
priestridden race and always were and always will be till the
end of the chapter.
Uncle Charles shook his head, saying:
—A bad business! A bad business!
Mr Dedalus repeated: 1080
—A priestridden Godforsaken race!
He pointed to the portrait of his grandfather on the wall to
his right.
—Do you see that old chap up there, John? he said. He was a
good Irishman when there was no money in the job. He was   1085

1066 not] ⁊¹not¹ᴦ MS

9. A road to Dublin that was sparsely used.

condemned to death as a whiteboy.[1] But he had a saying about
our clerical friends, that he would never let one of them put his
two feet under his mahogany.

Dante broke in angrily:

—If we are a priestridden race we ought to be proud of it! 1090
They are the apple of God's eye. *Touch them not*, says Christ,
for they are the apple of My eye.[2]

—And can we not love our country then? asked Mr Casey. Are
we not to follow the man that was born to lead us?

—A traitor to his country! replied Dante. A traitor, an adul= 1095
terer! The priests were right to abandon him. The priests were
always the true friends of Ireland.

—Were they, faith? said Mr Casey.

He threw his fist on the table and, frowning angrily, pro=
truded one finger after another. 1100

—Didn't the bishops of Ireland betray us in the time of the
union when bishop Lanigan presented an address of loyalty to
the marquess Cornwallis? Didn't the bishops and priests sell
the aspirations of this country in 1829 in return for catholic
emancipation? Didn't they denounce the fenian movement 1105
from the pulpit and in the confession box? And didn't they
dishonour the ashes of Terence Bellew MacManus?[3]

His face was glowing with anger and Stephen felt the glow
rise to his own cheek as the spoken words thrilled him. Mr
Dedalus uttered a guffaw of coarse scorn. 1110

—O, by God, he cried, I forgot little old Paul Cullen![4] Another
apple of God's eye!

Dante bent across the table and cried to Mr Casey:

—Right! Right! They were always right! God and morality and
religion come first. 1115

Mrs Dedalus, seeing her excitement, said to her:

—Mrs Riordan, don't excite yourself answering them.

1102 to] TS; of MS   1103 Didn't] Did⌐ⁿ't⌐ʳ MS   1104 this] MS; their TS–64

1. Name applied to violent protestors for tenants' rights who wore white shirts when they
   made their raids at night.
2. The phrase "apple of my eye" occurs in Zacharias 2:8, in the Old Testament; the words
   are not Christ's.
3. This paragraph refers to compromises made over a period of three decades after the Act
   of Union of 1800 on the way to achieving Catholic emancipation in 1829. James Lanigan
   was bishop of Ossory. Charles, Marquess Cornwallis, became viceroy and commander-in-
   chief of Ireland during the rebellion of 1798. The Fenian Brotherhood, also known as the
   Irish Republican Brotherhood, was a militant nationalist group active in Ireland and the
   U.S. beginning in the 1850s. When MacManus, a nationalist deported to Australia, was
   denied a state funeral in 1861, the Fenians organized their first significant public
   demonstration.
4. Archbishop of Dublin from 1852 to 1878; he condemned the Fenians and other forms of
   revolutionary nationalism.

—God and religion before everything! Dante cried. God and religion before the world!

Mr Casey raised his clenched fist and brought it down on the table with a crash.

—Very well, then, he shouted hoarsely, if it comes to that, no God for Ireland!

—John! John! cried Mr Dedalus, seizing his guest by the coat sleeve.

Dante stared across the table, her cheeks shaking. Mr Casey struggled up from his chair and bent across the table towards her, scraping the air from before his eyes with one hand as though he were tearing aside a cobweb.

—No God for Ireland! he cried. We have had too much God in Ireland. Away with God!

—Blasphemer! Devil! screamed Dante, starting to her feet and almost spitting in his face.

Uncle Charles and Mr Dedalus pulled Mr Casey back into his chair again, talking to him from both sides reasonably. He stared before him out of his dark flaming eyes, repeating:

—Away with God, I say!

Dante shoved her chair violently aside and left the table, upsetting her napkinring which rolled slowly along the carpet and came to rest against the foot of an easychair. Mrs Dedalus rose quickly and followed her towards the door. At the door Dante turned round violently and shouted down the room, her cheeks flushed and quivering with rage:

—Devil out of hell! We won! We crushed him to death! Fiend!

The door slammed behind her.

Mr Casey, freeing his arms from his holders, suddenly bowed his head on his hands with a sob of pain.

—Poor Parnell! he cried loudly. My dead king!

He sobbed loudly and bitterly.

Stephen, raising his terrorstricken face, saw that his father's eyes were full of tears.

❖   ❖   ❖

The fellows talked together in little groups.

One fellow said:

—They were caught near the Hill of Lyons.

—Who caught them?

—Mr Gleeson and the minister.[5] They were on a car.

The same fellow added:

—A fellow in the higher line told me.

5. Vice-rector.

Fleming asked:

—But why did they run away, tell us? 1160

—I know why, Cecil Thunder said. Because they had fecked[6] cash out of the rector's room.

—Who fecked it?

—Kickham's brother. And they all went shares in it.

But that was stealing. How could they have done that? 1165

—A fat lot you know about it, Thunder! Wells said. I know why they scut.[7]

—Tell us why.

—I was told not to, Wells said.

—O, go on, Wells, all said. You might tell us. We won't let it 1170 out.

Stephen bent forward his head to hear. Wells looked round to see if anyone was coming. Then he said secretly:

—You know the altar wine they keep in the press in the sac= risty? 1175

—Yes.

—Well, they drank that and it was found out who did it by the smell. And that's why they ran away, if you want to know.

And the fellow who had spoken first said:

—Yes, that's what I heard too from the fellow in the higher 1180 line.

The fellows were all silent. Stephen stood among them, afraid to speak, listening. A faint sickness of awe made him feel weak. How could they have done that? He thought of the dark silent sacristy. There were dark wooden presses there where the 1185 crimped surplices lay quietly folded.[8] It was not the chapel but still you had to speak under your breath. It was a holy place. He remembered the summer evening he had been there to be dressed as boatbearer,[9] the evening of the procession to the little altar in the wood. A strange and holy place. The boy that held 1190 the censer had swung it gently to and fro near the door with the silvery cap lifted by the middle chain to keep the coals lighting. That was called charcoal: and it had burned quietly as the fellow had swung it gently and had given off a weak sour smell.

1191, 1193, 1194(1), 1196, 1197 had] ⌐¹had¹⌐ MS   1194 had given] ⌐¹⟨gave⟩ had given¹⌐ MS

6. Stolen.
7. Ran away (from a word for the tail of a rabbit; *OED*).
8. The sacristy is the room of a church used for storing sacred vessels, valuable property, and vestments, the ritual robes worn by clergy and their assistants during rites and services. Surplices are loose-fitting, white gowns with wide sleeves (*OED*).
9. Person who carries the boat, the vessel containing the incense before it is put into the censer, or thurible, for burning during the mass (*OED*).

And then when all were vested he had stood holding out the   1195
boat to the rector and the rector had put a spoonful of incense
in and it had hissed on the red coals.

The fellows were talking together in little groups here and
there on the playground. The fellows seemed to him to have
grown smaller: that was because a sprinter[1] had knocked him   1200
down the day before, a fellow out of second of grammar. He
had been thrown by the fellow's machine lightly on the cinder=
path and his spectacles had been broken in three pieces and
some of the grit of the cinders had gone into his mouth.

That was why the fellows seemed to him smaller and farther   1205
away and the goalposts so thin and far and the soft grey sky so
high up. But there was no play on the football grounds for
cricket was coming: and some said that Barnes would be the
prof[2] and some said it would be Flowers. And all over the play=
grounds they were playing rounders and bowling twisters and   1210
lobs.[3] And from here and from there came the sounds of the
cricket bats through the soft grey air. They said: pick, pack,
pock, puck: like drops of water in a fountain slowly falling in
the brimming bowl.

Athy, who had been silent, said quietly: 1215
—You are all wrong.

All turned towards him eagerly.
—Why?
—Do you know?
—Who told you?   1220
—Tell us, Athy.

Athy pointed across the playground to where Simon
Moonan was walking by himself kicking a stone before him.
—Ask him, he said.

The fellows looked there and then said: 1225
—Why him?
—Is he in it?
—Tell us, Athy. Go on. You might if you know.

Athy lowered his voice and said:
—Do you know why those fellows scut? I will tell you but you   1230
must not let on you know.

He paused for a moment and then said mysteriously:

1197 in] in it 18—64

1. Bicyclist going full speed.
2. Probably the captain of the cricket team; cricket is a summer game.
3. Rounders is an English game resembling American baseball; twisters and lobs are ways of
   bowling, or delivering the ball, in cricket.

—They were caught with Simon Moonan and Tusker Boyle in
the square one night.

The fellows looked at him and asked: 1235
—Caught?
—What doing?
Athy said:
—Smugging.[4]
All the fellows were silent: and Athy said: 1240
—And that's why.

Stephen looked at the faces of the fellows but they were all
looking across the playground. He wanted to ask somebody
about it. What did that mean about the smugging in the
square? Why did the five fellows out of the higher line run   1245
away for that? It was a joke, he thought. Simon Moonan had
nice clothes and one night he had shown him a ball of creamy
sweets that the fellows of the football fifteen[5] had rolled down
to him along the carpet in the middle of the refectory when he
was at the door. It was the night of the match against the   1250
Bective Rangers and the ball was made just like a red and green
apple only it opened and it was full of the creamy sweets. And
one day Boyle had said that an elephant had two tuskers in=
stead of two tusks and that was why he was called Tusker
Boyle but some fellows called him Lady Boyle because he was   1255
always at his nails, paring them.

Eileen had long thin cool white hands too because she was a
girl. They were like ivory; only soft. That was the meaning of
Tower of Ivory but protestants could not understand it and
made fun of it. One day he had stood beside her looking into   1260
the hotel grounds. A waiter was running up a trail of bunting
on the flagstaff and a fox terrier was scampering to and fro on
the sunny lawn. She had put her hand into his pocket where his
hand was and he had felt how cool and thin and soft her hand
was. She had said that pockets were funny things to have: and   1265
then all of a sudden she had broken away and had run laughing
down the sloping curve of the path. Her fair hair had streamed
out behind her like gold in the sun. *Tower of Ivory. House of
Gold.* By thinking about things you could understand them.

But why in the square? You went there when you wanted to   1270
do something. It was all thick slabs of slate and water trickled
all day out of tiny pinholes and there was a queer smell of stale
water there. And behind the door of one of the closets there

1269 about] MS of TS–64

4. Probably homosexual contact but possibly masturbation (Mullin, 93).
5. Rugby, which eclipsed gravel football (see note 7, p. 6) during Joyce's time at Clongowes,
   is played with teams of fifteen.

was a drawing in red pencil of a bearded man in a Roman dress
with a brick in each hand and underneath was the name of the   1275
drawing:

 Balbus was building a wall.[6]

Some fellow had drawn it there for a cod. It had a funny
face but it was very like a man with a beard. And on the wall of
another closet there was written in backhand in beautiful writ=   1280
ing:

 Julius Caesar wrote The Calico Belly.[7]

Perhaps that was why they were there because it was a place
where some fellows wrote things for cod. But all the same it
was queer what Athy said and the way he said it. It was not a   1285
cod because they had run away. He looked with the others in
silence across the playground and began to feel afraid.

At last Fleming said:

—And we are all to be punished for what other fellows did?

—I won't come back, see if I do, Cecil Thunder said. Three   1290
days' silence in the refectory and sending us up for six and eight[8]
every minute.

—Yes, said Wells. And old Barrett has a new way of twisting
the note so that you can't open it and fold it again to see how
many ferulae[9] you are to get. I won't come back too.   1295

—Yes, said Cecil Thunder, and the prefect of studies[1] was in
second of grammar this morning.

—Let us get up a rebellion, Fleming said. Will we?

All the fellows were silent. The air was very silent and you
could hear the cricket bats but more slowly than before: pick,   1300
pock.

Wells asked:

—What is going to be done to them?

—Simon Moonan and Tusker are going to be flogged,[2] Athy
said, and the fellows in the higher line got their choice of   1305
flogging or being expelled.

—And which are they taking? asked the fellow who had
spoken first.

1278 fellow] fellows TS–18, 64 1283 there] aTS; in the square MS; there, Eg

6. A reference to the Latin classes. Balbus is mentioned in Cicero's *Letters to Atticus* 12.2
 (Anderson).
7. A takeoff on the title of Caesar's *Commentaries on the Gallic War* (*Commentarii de Bello
 Gallico*).
8. The number of strokes (with an implement), first three on each hand, then four on each
 hand.
9. Strokes with a cane or rod, from *ferula,* meaning rod (*OED*).
1. In charge of maintaining order in the conduct of classes.
2. Beaten with a rod (*OED*), in this case on the buttocks.

—All are taking expulsion except Corrigan, Athy answered.
He's going to be flogged by Mr Gleeson.   1310
—Is it Corrigan that big fellow? said Fleming. Why, he'd be
able for two of Gleeson!
—I know why, Cecil Thunder said. He is right and the other
fellows are wrong because a flogging wears off after a bit but a
fellow that has been expelled from college is known all his life   1315
on account of it. Besides Gleeson won't flog him hard.
—It's best of his play not to, Fleming said.
—I wouldn't like to be Simon Moonan and Tusker, Cecil
Thunder said. But I don't believe they will be flogged. Perhaps
they will be sent up for twice nine.[3]   1320
—No, no, said Athy. They'll both get it on the vital spot.
    Wells rubbed himself and said in a crying voice:
—Please, sir, let me off!
    Athy grinned and turned up the sleeves of his jacket, saying:

> It can't be helped;   1325
> It must be done.
> So down with your breeches
> And out with your bum.

The fellows laughed; but he felt that they were a little afraid.
In the silence of the soft grey air he heard the cricket bats from   1330
here and from there: pock. That was a sound to hear but if you
were hit then you would feel a pain. The pandybat made a
sound too but not like that. The fellows said it was made of
whalebone and leather with lead inside: and he wondered what
was the pain like. There were different kinds of pains for all the   1335
different kinds of sounds. A long thin cane would have a high
whistling sound and he wondered what was that pain like. It
made him shivery to think of it and cold: and what Athy said
too. But what was there to laugh at in it? It made him shivery:
but that was because you always felt like a shiver when you let   1340
down your trousers. It was the same in the bath when you
undressed yourself. He wondered who had to let them down,
the master or the boy himself. O how could they laugh about it
that way?
    He looked at Athy's rolledup sleeves and knuckly inky   1345
hands. He had rolled up his sleeves to show how Mr Gleeson
would roll up his sleeves. But Mr Gleeson had round shiny
cuffs and clean white wrists and fattish white hands and the

1332 would] ⌐¹would¹⌐ MS

3. Nine strokes per hand.

nails of them were long and pointed. Perhaps he pared them
too like Lady Boyle. But they were terribly long and pointed   1350
nails. So long and cruel they were though the white fattish
hands were not cruel but gentle. And though he trembled with
cold and fright to think of the cruel long nails and of the high
whistling sound of the cane and of the chill you felt at the end
of your shirt when you undressed yourself yet he felt a feeling   1355
of queer quiet pleasure inside him to think of the white fattish
hands, clean and strong and gentle. And he thought of what
Cecil Thunder had said: that Mr Gleeson would not flog Cor=
rigan hard. And Fleming had said he would not because it was
best of his play not to. But that was not why.   1360

A voice from far out on the playgrounds cried:
—All in!
And other voices cried:
—All in! All in!

During the writing lesson he sat with his arms folded, listen= 1365
ing to the slow scraping of the pens. Mr Harford went to and
fro making little signs in red pencil and sometimes sitting
beside the boy to show him how to hold the pen. He had tried
to spell out the headline for himself though he knew already
what it was for it was the last in the book. *Zeal without*   1370
prudence is like a ship adrift. But the lines of the letters were
like fine invisible threads and it was only by closing his right
eye tight tight and staring out of the left eye that he could make
out the full curves of the capital.

But Mr Harford was very decent and never got into a wax.   1375
All the other masters got into dreadful waxes. But why were
they to suffer for what fellows in the higher line did? Wells had
said that they had drunk some of the altar wine out of the press
in the sacristy and that it had been found out who had done it
by the smell. Perhaps they had stolen a monstrance[4] to run away 1380
with it and sell it somewhere. That must have been a terrible
sin, to go in quietly there at night, to open the dark press and
steal the flashing gold thing into which God was put on the
altar in the middle of flowers and candles at benediction[5] while
the incense went up in clouds at both sides as the fellow swung 1385
the censer and Dominic Kelly sang the first part by himself in

---

1361 playgrounds] playground Eg–64   1370 in] of TS–64   1375 But] MARKED FOR
PARAGRAPHING IN RUN-ON TEXT MS   1382 to(2)] ⁻¹to¹ᴿ MS

4. Open or transparent vessel made of gold or silver for showing the consecrated wafer of
   the Eucharist (*OED*).
5. In this case the "Benediction of the Blessed Sacrament," during which the consecrated
   host is exposed to the congregation (*Cath. Enc.*).

the choir. But God was not in it of course when they stole it.
But still it was a strange and a great sin even to touch it. He
thought of it with deep awe; a terrible and strange sin: it
thrilled him to think of it in the silence when the pens scraped   1390
lightly. But to drink the altar wine out of the press and be
found out by the smell was a sin too: but it was not terrible
and strange. It only made you feel a little sickish on account
of the smell of the wine. Because on the day when he had
made his first holy communion in the chapel he had shut his   1395
eyes and opened his mouth and put out his tongue a little: and
when the rector had stooped down to give him the holy com=
munion he had smelt a faint winy smell off the rector's breath
after the wine of the mass. The word was beautiful: wine. It
made you think of dark purple because the grapes were dark   1400
purple that grew in Greece outside houses like white temples.
But the faint smell off the rector's breath had made him feel
a sick feeling on the morning of his first communion. The day
of your first communion was the happiest day of your life.
And once a lot of generals had asked Napoleon what was the   1405
happiest day of his life. They thought he would say the day
he won some great battle or the day he was made an emperor.
But he said:
—Gentlemen, the happiest day of my life was the day on which
I made my first holy communion.   1410
    Father Arnall came in and the Latin lesson began and he
remained still, leaning on the desk with his arms folded. Father
Arnall gave out the themebooks and he said that they were
scandalous and that they were all to be written out again with
the corrections at once. But the worst of all was Fleming's   1415
theme because the pages were stuck together by a blot: and
Father Arnall held it up by a corner and said it was an insult to
any master to send him up such a theme. Then he asked Jack
Lawton to decline the noun *mare* and Jack Lawton stopped at
the ablative singular and could not go on with the plural.[6]   1420
—You should be ashamed of yourself, said Father Arnall
sternly. You, the leader of the class!
    Then he asked the next boy and the next and the next.
Nobody knew. Father Arnall became very quiet, more and
more quiet as each boy tried to answer and could not. But his   1425
face was blacklooking and his eyes were staring though his
voice was so quiet. Then he asked Fleming and Fleming said

1414 were] ONE PAGE MISSING IN TS

6. Lawton can decline (state the six grammatical cases for) the Latin noun *mare*, meaning sea,
   through the ablative, the last of the six, in the singular, but he does not know the plural.

that that word had no plural. Father Arnall suddenly shut the book and shouted at him:

—Kneel out there in the middle of the class. You are one of the idlest boys I ever met. Copy out your themes again the rest of you. 1430

Fleming moved heavily out of his place and knelt between the two last benches. The other boys bent over their theme= books and began to write. A silence filled the classroom and Stephen, glancing timidly at Father Arnall's dark face, saw that it was a little red from the wax he was in. 1435

Was that a sin for Father Arnall to be in a wax or was he allowed to get into a wax when the boys were idle because that made them study better or was he only letting on to be in a wax? It was because he was allowed because a priest would know what a sin was and would not do it. But if he did it one time by mistake what would he do to go to confession? Perhaps he would go to confession to the minister. And if the minister did it he would go to the rector: and the rector to the provin= cial: and the provincial to the general of the jesuits.[7] That was called the order: and he had heard his father say that they were all clever men. They could all have become highup people in the world if they had not become jesuits. And he wondered what Father Arnall and Paddy Barrett would have become and what Mr McGlade and Mr Gleeson would have become if they had not become jesuits. It was hard to think what because you would have to think of them in a different way with different coloured coats and trousers and with beards and moustaches and different kinds of hats. 1440 1445 1450 1455

The door opened quietly and closed. A quick whisper ran through the class: the prefect of studies. There was an instant of dead silence and then the loud crack of a pandybat on the last desk. Stephen's heart leapt up in fear.

—Any boys want flogging here, Father Arnall? cried the pre= fect of studies. Any lazy idle loafers that want flogging in this class? 1460

He came to the middle of the class and saw Fleming on his knees.

—Hoho! he cried. Who is this boy? Why is he on his knees? What is your name, boy? 1465

—Fleming, sir.

1434 other] others 64   1442 one] TS RESUMES

7. Stephen reproduces the hierarchy of positions within the Jesuits, but confession need not be addressed to a priest of higher rank. The general, or head, of the Jesuits has beneath him provincials, who are in charge of the Jesuits in provinces (such as Ireland), within which there are schools, such as Clongowes, run by a rector, in charge of the community.

—Hoho, Fleming! An idler of course. I can see it in your eye. Why is he on his knees, Father Arnall?

—He wrote a bad Latin theme, Father Arnall said, and he missed all the questions in grammar.

—Of course he did! cried the prefect of studies. Of course he did! A born idler! I can see it in the corner of his eye.

He banged his pandybat down on the desk and cried:

—Up, Fleming! Up, my boy!

Fleming stood up slowly.

—Hold out! cried the prefect of studies.

Fleming held out his hand. The pandybat came down on it with a loud smacking sound: one, two, three, four, five, six.

—Other hand!

The pandybat came down again in six loud quick smacks.

—Kneel down! cried the prefect of studies.

Fleming knelt down squeezing his hands under his armpits, his face contorted with pain, but Stephen knew how hard his hands were because Fleming was always rubbing rosin into them. But perhaps he was in great pain for the noise of the pandies was terrible. Stephen's heart was beating and flutter=ing.

—At your work, all of you! shouted the prefect of studies. We want no lazy idle loafers here, lazy idle little schemers. At your work, I tell you. Father Dolan will be in to see you every day. Father Dolan will be in tomorrow.

He poked one of the boys in the side with the pandybat, saying:

—You, boy! When will Father Dolan be in again?

—Tomorrow, sir, said Tom Furlong's voice.

—Tomorrow and tomorrow and tomorrow,[8] said the prefect of studies. Make up your minds for that. Every day Father Dolan. Write away. You, boy, who are you?

Stephen's heart jumped suddenly.

—Dedalus, sir.

—Why are you not writing like the others?

—I . . . . . my . . .

He could not speak with fright.

—Why is he not writing, Father Arnall?

—He broke his glasses, said Father Arnall, and I exempted him from work.

—Broke? What is this I hear? What is this your name is? said the prefect of studies.

—Dedalus, sir.

8. Part of Macbeth's response to the death of his wife (Shakespeare, *Macbeth* 5.5.19).

—Out here, Dedalus. Lazy little schemer. I see schemer in your
face. Where did you break your glasses?

Stephen stumbled into the middle of the class, blinded by
fear and haste.

—Where did you break your glasses? repeated the prefect of   1515
studies.

—The cinderpath, sir.

—Hoho! The cinderpath! cried the prefect of studies. I know
that trick.

Stephen lifted his eyes in wonder and saw for a moment   1520
Father Dolan's whitegrey not young face, his baldy whitegrey
head with fluff at the sides of it, the steel rims of his spectacles
and his nocoloured eyes looking through the glasses. Why did
he say that he knew that trick?

—Lazy idle little loafer! cried the prefect of studies. Broke my   1525
glasses! An old schoolboy trick! Out with your hand this mo=
ment!

Stephen closed his eyes and held out in the air his trembling
hand with the palm upwards. He felt the prefect of studies
touch it for a moment at the fingers to straighten it and then   1530
the swish of the sleeve of the soutane as the pandybat was lifted
to strike. A hot burning stinging tingling blow like the loud
crack of a broken stick made his trembling hand crumple to=
gether like a leaf in the fire: and at the sound and the pain
scalding tears were driven into his eyes. His whole body was   1535
shaking with fright, his arm was shaking and his crumpled
burning livid hand shook like a loose leaf in the air. A cry
sprang to his lips, a prayer to be let off. But though the tears
scalded his eyes and his limbs quivered with pain and fright he
held back the hot tears and the cry that scalded his throat.   1540

—Other hand! shouted the prefect of studies.

Stephen drew back his maimed and quivering right arm and
held out his left hand. The soutane sleeve swished again as the
pandybat was lifted and a loud crashing sound and a fierce
maddening tingling burning pain made his hand shrink to=   1545
gether with the palms and fingers in a livid quivering mass. The
scalding water burst forth from his eyes and, burning with
shame and agony and fear, he drew back his shaking arm in
terror and burst out into a whine of pain. His body shook with
a palsy of fright and in shame and rage he felt the scalding cry   1550
come from his throat and the scalding tears falling out of his
eyes and down his flaming cheeks.

—Kneel down! cried the prefect of studies.

1524 that(1)] absent TS–64

Stephen knelt down quickly pressing his beaten hands to his sides. To think of them beaten and swollen with pain all in a moment made him feel so sorry for them as if they were not his own but someone else's that he felt so sorry for. And as he knelt, calming the last sobs in his throat and feeling the burning tingling pain pressed in to his sides, he thought of the hands which he had held out in the air with the palms up and of the firm touch of the prefect of studies when he had steadied the shaking fingers and of the beaten swollen reddened mass of palm and fingers that shook helplessly in the air.

—Get at your work, all of you, cried the prefect of studies from the door. Father Dolan will be in every day to see if any boy, any lazy idle little loafer wants flogging. Every day. Every day.

The door closed behind him.

The hushed class continued to copy out the themes. Father Arnall rose from his seat and went among them, helping the boys with gentle words and telling them the mistakes they had made. His voice was very gentle and soft. Then he returned to his seat and said to Fleming and Stephen:

—You may return to your places, you two.

Fleming and Stephen rose and, walking to their seats, sat down. Stephen, scarlet with shame, opened a book quickly with one weak hand and bent down upon it, his face close to the page.

It was unfair and cruel: because the doctor had told him not to read without glasses and he had written home to his father that morning to send him a new pair. And Father Arnall had said that he need not study till the new glasses came. Then to be called a schemer before the class and to be pandied when he always got the card for first or second and was the leader of the Yorkists! How could the prefect of studies know that it was a trick? He felt the touch of the prefect's fingers as they had steadied his hand and at first he had thought that he was going to shake hands with him because the fingers were soft and firm: but then in an instant he had heard the swish of the soutane sleeve and the crash. It was cruel and unfair to make him kneel in the middle of the class then: and Father Arnall had told them both that they might return to their places without making any difference between them. He listened to Father Arnall's low and gentle voice as he corrected the themes. Perhaps he was sorry now and wanted to be decent. But it was unfair and cruel.

1555
1560
1565
1570
1575
1580
1585
1590
1595

1557 own] TS; hands MS   1557 so] ABSENT Eg–64   1575 and,--seats,] and⁷¹, walking--seats,¹ʳ MS   1587 had] ONE PAGE MISSING IN TS   1587 that] ABSENT Eg–64

The prefect of studies was a priest but that was cruel and unfair. And his whitegrey face and the nocoloured eyes behind the steelrimmed spectacles were cruel looking because he had steadied the hand first with his firm soft fingers and that was to hit it better and louder. 1600

—It's a stinking mean thing, that's what it is, said Fleming in the corridor as the classes were passing out in file to the refec= tory, to pandy a fellow for what is not his fault.

—You really broke your glasses by accident, didn't you? Nasty Roche asked. 1605

Stephen felt his heart filled by Fleming's words and did not answer.

—Of course he did! said Fleming. I wouldn't stand it. I'd go up and tell the rector on him.

—Yes, said Cecil Thunder eagerly, and I saw him lift the 1610 pandybat over his shoulder and he's not allowed to do that.

—Did they hurt much? Nasty Roche asked.

—Very much, Stephen said.

—I wouldn't stand it, Fleming repeated, from Baldyhead or any other Baldyhead. It's a stinking mean low trick, that's what 1615 it is. I'd go up straight up to the rector and tell him about it after dinner.

—Yes, do. Yes, do, said Cecil Thunder.

—Yes, do. Yes, go up and tell the rector on him, Dedalus, said Nasty Roche, because he said that he'd come in tomorrow 1620 again to pandy you.

—Yes, yes. Tell the rector, all said.

And there were some fellows out of second of grammar lis= tening and one of them said:

—The senate and the Roman people declared that Dedalus had 1625 been wrongly punished.[9]

It was wrong; it was unfair and cruel: and, as he sat in the refectory, he suffered time after time in memory the same hu= miliation until he began to wonder whether it might not really be that there was something in his face which made him look 1630 like a schemer and he wished he had a little mirror to see. But there could not be; and it was unjust and cruel and unfair.

He could not eat the blackish fish fritters they got on Wednesdays in lent[1] and one of his potatoes had the mark of the spade in it. Yes, he would do what the fellows had told him. He 1635

1614 or] TS RESUMES   1616 up(1)] ABSENT Eg–64

9. A statement modeled on decrees by the Roman Senate.
1. The period of forty days of penitence before Easter, during which dietary restrictions apply involving abstinence and fasting; in this case, fish has been substituted for meat.

would go up and tell the rector that he had been wrongly punished. A thing like that had been done before by somebody in history, by some great person whose head was in the books of history. And the rector would declare that he had been wrongly punished because the senate and the Roman people 1640 always declared that the man who did that had been wrongly punished. Those were the great men whose names were in Richmal Magnall's Questions.[2] History was all about those men and what they did and that was what Peter Parley's Tales about Greece and Rome were all about.[3] Peter Parley himself was on 1645 the first page in a picture. There was a road over a heath with grass at the side and little bushes: and Peter Parley had a broad hat like a protestant minister and a big stick and he was walk= ing fast along the road to Greece and Rome.

It was easy what he had to do. All he had to do was when 1650 the dinner was over and he came out in his turn to go on walking but not out to the corridor but up the staircase on the right that led to the castle. He had nothing to do but that: to turn to the right and walk fast up the staircase and in half a minute he would be in the low dark narrow corridor that led 1655 through the castle to the rector's room. And every fellow had said that it was unfair, even the fellow out of second of gram= mar who had said that about the senate and the Roman people.

What would happen? He heard the fellows of the higher line stand up at the top of the refectory and heard their steps as 1660 they came down the matting: Paddy Rath and Jimmy Magee and the Spaniard and the Portuguese and the fifth was big Corrigan who was going to be flogged by Mr Gleeson. That was why the prefect of studies had called him a schemer and pandied him for nothing: and, straining his weak eyes, tired 1665 with the tears, he watched big Corrigan's broad shoulders and big hanging black head passing in the file. But he had done something and besides Mr Gleeson would not flog him hard: and he remembered how big Corrigan looked in the bath. He had skin the same colour as the turfcoloured bogwater in the 1670 shallow end of the bath and when he walked along the side his feet slapped loudly on the wet tiles and at every step his thighs shook a little because he was fat.

1641 man] men TS—64   1656 had] ⌐¹had¹⌐ MS

2. *Historical and Miscellaneous Questions for the Use of Young People* (1800), a textbook, widely reprinted throughout the nineteenth century, concerning mythology, astronomy, architecture, and other topics, by Richmal Mangnall (1769–1820), whose name is misspelled (*Enc. Brit.* 17.572).
3. "Peter Parley" was the pseudonym of Samuel Goodrich (1793–1860), author of *Peter Parley's Tales about Ancient Rome* (1833) and many other books for the young with similar titles (*Enc. Brit.* 12.238).

The refectory was half empty and the fellows were still passing out in file. He could go up the staircase because there 1675 was never a priest or a prefect outside the refectory door. But he could not go. The rector would side with the prefect of studies and think it was a schoolboy trick and then the prefect of studies would come in every day the same only it would be worse because he would be dreadfully waxy at any fellow 1680 going up to the rector about him. The fellows had told him to go but they would not go themselves. They had forgotten all about it. No, it was best to forget all about it: and perhaps the prefect of studies had only said he would come in. No, it was best to hide out of the way because when you were small and 1685 young you could often escape that way.

The fellows at his table stood up. He stood up and passed out among them in the file. He had to decide. He was coming near the door. If he went on with the fellows he could never go up to the rector because he could not leave the playground for 1690 that. And if he went and was pandied all the same all the fellows would make fun and talk about young Dedalus going up to the rector to tell on the prefect of studies.

He was walking down along the matting and he saw the door before him. It was impossible: he could not. He thought 1695 of the baldy head of the prefect of studies with the cruel no= coloured eyes looking at him and he heard the voice of the prefect of studies asking him twice what his name was. Why could he not remember the name when he was told the first time? Was he not listening the first time or was it to make fun 1700 out of the name? The great men in the history had names like that and nobody made fun of them. It was his own name that he should have made fun of if he wanted to make fun. Dolan: it was like the name of a woman that washed clothes.

He had reached the door and, turning quickly to the right, 1705 walked up the stairs: and, before he could make up his mind to come back, he had entered the low dark narrow corridor that led to the castle. And as he crossed the threshold of the door of the corridor he saw, without turning his head to look, that all the fellows were looking after him as they went filing by. 1710

He passed along the narrow dark corridor, passing little doors that were the doors of the rooms of the community. He peered in front of him and right and left through the gloom and thought that those must be portraits. It was dark and silent and his eyes were weak and tired with tears so that he could not 1715 see. But he thought they were the portraits of the saints and

great men of the order who were looking down on him silently
as he passed: saint Ignatius Loyola holding an open book and
pointing to the words *Ad Majorem Dei Gloriam* in it, saint
Francis Xavier pointing to his chest, Lorenzo Ricci with his   1720
berretta on his head like one of the prefects of the lines, the
three patrons of holy youth, saint Stanislaus Kostka, saint
Aloysius Gonzaga and blessed John Berchmans, all with young
faces because they died when they were young, and Father
Peter Kenny sitting in a chair wrapped in a big cloak.[4]   1725

He came out on the landing above the entrance hall and
looked about him. That was where Hamilton Rowan had
passed and the marks of the soldiers' slugs were there. And it
was there that the old servants had seen the ghost in the white
cloak of a marshal.   1730

An old servant was sweeping at the end of the landing. He
asked him where was the rector's room and the old servant
pointed to the door at the far end and looked after him as he
went on to it and knocked.

There was no answer. He knocked again more loudly and   1735
his heart jumped when he heard a muffled voice say:
—Come in!

He turned the handle and opened the door and fumbled for
the handle of the green baize door inside. He found it and
pushed it open and went in.   1740

He saw the rector sitting at a desk writing. There was a skull
on the desk and a strange solemn smell in the room like the old
leather of chairs.

His heart was beating fast on account of the solemn place he
was in and the silence of the room: and he looked at the skull   1745
and at the rector's kindlooking face.
—Well, my little man, said the rector. What is it?

Stephen swallowed down the thing in his throat and said:
—I broke my glasses, sir.

The rector opened his mouth and said: 1750
—O!

Then he smiled and said:
—Well, if we broke our glasses we must write home for a new
pair.
—I wrote home, sir, said Stephen, and Father Arnall said I am   1755
not to study till they come.

---

4. Saint Ignatius of Loyola (1491–1556), a Spanish priest, founded the Society of Jesus, recognized by the Roman Catholic Church in 1540. The Latin motto of the Jesuits means "To the
greater glory of God." Francis Xavier (1506–1552) was Loyola's most important disciple.
Lorenzo Ricci (1703–1775) was a general of the Jesuits. The three patrons were all youthful
Jesuit saints of the sixteenth and seventeenth centuries. Peter Kenney, S.J. (1779–1841),
whose name is here spelled Kenny, founded Clongowes Wood College, dedicated to Gonzaga.

—Quite right! said the rector.

Stephen swallowed down the thing again and tried to keep his legs and his voice from shaking.

—But, sir . . . .

—Yes?

—Father Dolan came in today and pandied me because I was not writing my theme.

The rector looked at him in silence and he could feel the blood rising to his face and the tears about to rise to his eyes.

The rector said:

—Your name is Dedalus, isn't it?

—Yes, sir.

—And where did you break your glasses?

—On the cinderpath, sir. A fellow was coming out of the bicycle house and I fell and they got broken. I don't know the fellow's name.

The rector looked at him again in silence. Then he smiled and said:

—O, well, it was a mistake. I am sure Father Dolan did not know.

—But I told him I broke them, sir, and he pandied me.

—Did you tell him that you had written home for a new pair? the rector asked.

—No, sir.

—O, well then, said the rector, Father Dolan did not under= stand. You can say that I excuse you from your lessons for a few days.

Stephen said quickly for fear his trembling would prevent him:

—Yes, sir, but Father Dolan said he will come in tomorrow to pandy me again for it.

—Very well, the rector said. It is a mistake and I shall speak to Father Dolan myself. Will that do now?

Stephen felt the tears wetting his eyes and murmured:

—O yes, sir, thanks.

The rector held his hand across the side of the desk where the skull was and Stephen, placing his hand in it for a moment, felt a cool moist palm.

—Good day now, said the rector, withdrawing his hand and bowing.

—Good day, sir, said Stephen.

He bowed and walked quietly out of the room, closing the doors carefully and slowly.

But when he had passed the old servant on the landing and was again in the low narrow dark corridor he began to walk faster and faster. Faster and faster he hurried on through the gloom, excitedly. He bumped his elbow against the door at the end and, hurrying down the staircase, walked quickly through the two corridors and out into the air. 1805

He could hear the cries of the fellows on the playgrounds. He broke into a run and, running quicker and quicker, ran across the cinderpath and reached the third line playground, panting.

The fellows had seen him running. They closed round him in 1810 a ring, pushing one against another to hear.

—Tell us! Tell us!

—What did he say?

—Did you go in?

—What did he say? 1815

—Tell us! Tell us!

He told them what he had said and what the rector had said and, when he had told them, all the fellows flung their caps spinning up into the air and cried:

—Hurroo! 1820

They caught their caps and sent them up again spinning skyhigh and cried again:

—Hurroo! Hurroo!

They made a cradle of their locked hands and hoisted him up among them and carried him along till he struggled to get 1825 free. And when he had escaped from them they broke away in all directions, flinging their caps again into the air and whis= tling as they went spinning up and crying:

—Hurroo!

And they gave three groans for Baldyhead Dolan and three 1830 cheers for Conmee and they said he was the decentest rector that was ever in Clongowes.

The cheers died away in the soft grey air. He was alone. He was happy and free: but he would not be anyway proud with Father Dolan. He would be very quiet and obedient: and he 1835 wished that he could do something kind for him to show him that he was not proud.

The air was soft and grey and mild and evening was coming. There was the smell of evening in the air, the smell of the fields in the country where they digged up turnips to peel them and 1840 eat them when they went out for a walk to Major Barton's, the smell there was in the little wood beyond the pavilion where the gallnuts[5] were.

5. A gallnut is a growth on a tree caused by insects (*OED*).

The fellows were practising long shies and bowling lobs and
slow twisters.[6] In the soft grey silence he could hear the bump of   1845
the balls: and from here and from there through the quiet air
the sound of the cricket bats: pick, pack, pock, puck: like drops
of water in a fountain falling softly in the brimming bowl.

II

Uncle Charles smoked such black twist[1] that at last his out=   1
spoken nephew suggested to him to enjoy his morning smoke
in a little outhouse[2] at the end of the garden.
—Very good, Simon. All serene, Simon, said the old man tran=
quilly. Anywhere you like. The outhouse will do me nicely: it   5
will be more salubrious.
—Damn me, said Mr Dedalus frankly, if I know how you can
smoke such villainous awful tobacco. It's like gunpowder, by
God.
—It's very nice, Simon, replied the old man. Very cool and   10
mollifying.
Every morning, therefore, uncle Charles repaired to his out=
house but not before he had creased and brushed scrupulously
his back hair and brushed and put on his tall hat. While he
smoked the brim of his tall hat and the bowl of his pipe were   15
just visible beyond the jambs of the outhouse door. His arbour,
as he called the reeking outhouse which he shared with the cat
and the garden tools, served him also as a soundingbox: and
every morning he hummed contentedly one of his favourite
songs: O, twine me a bower or Blue eyes and golden hair or   20
The Groves of Blarney while the grey and blue coils of smoke
rose slowly from his pipe and vanished in the pure air.
During the first part of the summer in Blackrock[3] uncle
Charles was Stephen's constant companion. Uncle Charles was
a hale old man with a well tanned skin, rugged features and   25
white side whiskers. On week days he did messages between
the house in Carysfort Avenue and those shops in the main
street of the town with which the family dealt. Stephen was

1–2 outspoken] MS; ABSENT TS–64 MS   8 such] ⁻¹such¹ᒋ TS

6. In cricket, a shy is a throw (OED), while lobs and twisters are ways of bowling, that is,
delivering the ball to the batsman (Enc. Brit. 7.439–40).
1. Dark, that is, strong tobacco.
2. A shed, such as a toolhouse (OED), not in this case a privy (as American usage could
suggest).
3. Located five miles south of Dublin on Dublin Bay.

glad to go with him on these errands for uncle Charles helped
him very liberally to handfuls of whatever was exposed in open 30
boxes and barrels outside the counter. He would seize a hand=
ful of grapes and sawdust or three or four American apples and
thrust them generously into his grandnephew's hand while the
shopman smiled uneasily; and on Stephen's feigning reluctance
to take them, he would frown and say: 35
—Take them, sir. Do you hear me, sir? They're good for your
bowels.

When the order list had been booked the two would go on
to the park where an old friend of Stephen's father, Mike
Flynn, would be found seated on a bench, waiting for them. 40
Then would begin Stephen's run round the park. Mike Flynn
would stand at the gate near the railway station, watch in
hand, while Stephen ran round the track in the style Mike
Flynn favoured, his head high lifted, his knees well lifted and
his hands held straight down by his sides. When the morning 45
practice was over the trainer would make his comments and
sometimes illustrate them by shuffling along for a yard or so
comically in an old pair of blue canvas shoes. A small ring of
wonderstruck children and nursemaids would gather to watch
him and linger even when he and uncle Charles had sat down 50
again and were talking athletics and politics. Though he had
heard his father say that Mike Flynn had put some of the best
runners of modern times through his hands Stephen often
glanced with mistrust at his trainer's flabby stubblecovered
face, as it bent over the long stained fingers through which he 55
rolled his cigarette, and with pity at the mild lustreless blue
eyes which would look up suddenly from the task and gaze
vaguely into the bluer distance while the long swollen fingers
ceased their rolling and grains and fibres of tobacco fell back
into the pouch. 60

On the way home uncle Charles would often pay a visit to
the chapel and, as the font was above Stephen's reach, the old
man would dip his hand and then sprinkle the water briskly
about Stephen's clothes and on the floor of the porch. While he
prayed he knelt on his red handkerchief and read above his 65
breath from a thumbblackened prayerbook wherein catch=
words were printed at the foot of every page. Stephen knelt at
his side respecting, though he did not share, his piety. He often
wondered what his granduncle prayed for so seriously. Perhaps
he prayed for the souls in purgatory or for the grace of a happy 70

48 an] TS; ABSENT MS   58 bluer] blue TS–64

death: or perhaps he prayed that God might send him back a
part of the big fortune he had squandered in Cork.[4]

On Sundays Stephen with his father and his granduncle took
their constitutional. The old man was a nimble walker in spite
of his corns and often ten or twelve miles of the road were   75
covered. The little village of Stillorgan was the parting of the
ways. Either they went to the left towards the Dublin moun=
tains or along the Goatstown road and thence into Dundrum,
coming home by Sandyford. Trudging along the road or
standing in some grimy wayside publichouse his elders spoke   80
constantly of the subjects nearest their hearts, of Irish politics,
of Munster and of the legends of their own family, to all of
which Stephen lent an avid ear. Words which he did not under=
stand he said over and over to himself till he had learned them
by heart: and through them he had glimpses of the real world   85
about him. The hour when he too would take his part in the
life of that world seemed drawing near and in secret he began
to make ready for the great part which he felt awaited him the
nature of which he only dimly apprehended.

His evenings were his own; and he pored over a ragged   90
translation of *The Count of Monte Cristo*.[5] The figure of that
dark avenger stood forth in his mind for whatever he had heard
or divined in childhood of the strange and terrible. At night he
built up on the parlour table an image of the wonderful island
cave out of transfers and paper flowers and coloured tissue   95
paper and strips of the silver and golden paper in which choc=
olate is wrapped. When he had broken up this scenery, weary
of its tinsel, there would come to his mind the bright picture of
Marseilles, of sunny trellisses and of Mercedes. Outside Black=
rock, on the road that led to the mountains, stood a small   100
whitewashed house in the garden of which grew many rose=
bushes: and in this house, he told himself, another Mercedes
lived. Both on the outward and on the homeward journey he
measured distance by this landmark: and in his imagination he
lived through a long train of adventures, marvellous as those in 105
the book itself, towards the close of which there appeared an
image of himself, grown older and sadder, standing in a
moonlit garden with Mercedes who had so many years before

81 nearest] nearer TS–64   86 his] ABSENT Eg–64

4. The main city of County Cork, which is located in Munster, the southern province, one
of the four traditional geographical areas of Ireland.
5. A French novel of betrayal, escape, and revenge, by Alexandre Dumas *père* (1802–1870),
in which the hero, Edmond Dantès, escapes from prison and returns to Marseilles, a
French port on the Mediterranean, to avenge the deception that led his betrothed, Mercedes, to marry another man in the belief that Dantès was dead.

slighted his love, and with a sadly proud gesture of refusal, saying:

—Madam, I never eat muscatel grapes.

He became the ally of a boy named Aubrey Mills and founded with him a gang of adventurers in the avenue. Aubrey carried a whistle dangling from his buttonhole and a bicycle lamp attached to his belt while the others had short sticks thrust daggerwise through theirs. Stephen, who had read of Napoleon's plain style of dress, chose to remain unadorned and thereby heightened for himself the pleasure of taking counsel with his lieutenant before giving orders. The gang made forays into the gardens of old maids or went down to the castle[6] and fought a battle on the shaggy weedgrown rocks, coming home after it weary stragglers with the stale odours of the foreshore in their nostrils and the rank oils of the seawrack upon their hands and in their hair.

Aubrey and Stephen had a common milkman and often they drove out in the milkcar to Carrickmines[7] where the cows were at grass. While the men were milking the boys would take turns in riding the tractable mare round the field. But when autumn came the cows were driven home from the grass: and the first sight of the filthy cowyard at Stradbrook[8] with its foul green puddles and clots of liquid dung and steaming brantroughs sickened Stephen's heart. The cattle which had seemed so beau= tiful in the country on sunny days revolted him and he could not even look at the milk they yielded.

The coming of September did not trouble him this year for he knew he was not to be sent back to Clongowes. The practice in the park came to an end when Mike Flynn went into hospi= tal. Aubrey was at school and had only an hour or two free in the evening. The gang fell asunder and there were no more nightly forays or battles on the rocks. Stephen sometimes went round with the car which delivered the evening milk: and these chilly drives blew away his memory of the filth of the cowyard and he felt no repugnance at seeing the cowhairs and hayseeds on the milkman's coat. Whenever the car drew up before a house he waited to catch a glimpse of a well scrubbed kitchen or of a softly lighted hall and to see how the servant would hold the jug and how she would close the door. He thought it

128 mare] aEg; horse MS—Eg   136 he knew] MS; ABSENT Eg—64 MS

6. A Martello tower, one of the defensive fortifications built on Ireland's east coast during the Napoleonic Wars (1803–06) in case of invasion.
7. A village located inland three miles south of Blackrock.
8. A locale one mile southeast of Blackrock.

should be a pleasant life enough, driving along the roads every
evening to deliver milk, if he had warm gloves and a fat bag of
gingernuts in his pocket to eat from. But the same foreknowl=   150
edge which had sickened his heart and made his limbs sag
suddenly as he raced round the park, the same intuition which
had made him glance with mistrust at his trainer's flabby
stubblecovered face as it bent heavily over his long stained
fingers, dissipated any vision of the future. In a vague way he   155
understood that his father was in trouble and that this was the
reason why he himself had not been sent back to Clongowes.
For some time he had felt the slight changes in his house; and
these changes in what he had deemed unchangeable were so
many slight shocks to his boyish conception of the world. The   160
ambition which he felt astir at times in the darkness of his soul
sought no outlet. A dusk like that of the outer world obscured
his mind as he heard the mare's hoofs clattering along the
tramtrack on the Rock Road and the great can swaying and
rattling behind him.   165

   He returned to Mercedes and, as he brooded upon her im=
age, a strange unrest crept into his blood. Sometimes a fever
gathered within him and led him to rove alone in the evening
along the quiet avenues. The peace of the gardens and the
kindly lights in the windows poured a tender influence into his   170
restless heart. The noise of children at play annoyed him and
their silly voices made him feel, even more keenly than he had
felt at Clongowes, that he was different from others. He did
not want to play. He wanted to meet in the real world the
unsubstantial image which his soul so constantly beheld. He   175
did not know where to seek it or how: but a premonition which
led him on told him that this image would, without any overt
act of his, encounter him. They would meet quietly as if they
had known each other and had made their tryst, perhaps at one
of the gates or in some more secret place. They would be alone,   180
surrounded by darkness and silence: and in that moment of
supreme tenderness he would be transfigured. He would fade
into something impalpable under her eyes and then, in a mo=
ment, he would be transfigured.[9] Weakness and timidity and
inexperience would fall from him in that magic moment.   185

◆   ◆   ◆

151 limbs] legs Eg–64   169 avenues.] avenue. TS–64

9. Transformed, but "transfigured" would carry a religious overtone for Stephen. The Transfiguration is the high point of Jesus's public life, the moment in which his divinity is
ravishingly revealed to some of his disciples. The manifestation of the divine glory is
celebrated by Catholics annually as the Feast of the Transfiguration.

Two great yellow caravans[1] had halted one morning before
the door and men had come tramping into the house to dis=
mantle it. The furniture had been hustled out through the front
garden which was strewn with wisps of straw and rope ends
and into the huge vans at the gate. When all had been safely   190
stowed the vans had set off noisily down the avenue: and from
the window of the railway carriage, in which he had sat with
his redeyed mother, Stephen had seen them lumbering heavily
along the Merrion Road.

The parlour fire would not draw that evening and Mr Deda=   195
lus rested the poker against the bars of the grate to attract the
flame. Uncle Charles dozed in a corner of the half furnished
uncarpeted room and near him the family portraits leaned
against the wall. The lamp on the table shed a weak light over
the boarded floor, muddied by the feet of the vanmen. Stephen   200
sat on a footstool beside his father listening to a long and
incoherent monologue. He understood little or nothing of it at
first but he became slowly aware that his father had enemies
and that some fight was going to take place. He felt, too, that
he was being enlisted for the fight, that some duty was being   205
laid upon his shoulders. The sudden flight from the comfort
and revery of Blackrock, the passage through the gloomy foggy
city, the thought of the bare cheerless house in which they were
now to live made his heart heavy: and again an intuition or
foreknowledge of the future came to him. He understood also   210
why the servants had often whispered together in the hall and
why his father had often stood on the hearthrug, with his back
to the fire, talking loudly to uncle Charles who urged him to sit
down and eat his dinner.

—There's a crack of the whip left in me yet, Stephen, old chap,   215
said Mr Dedalus, poking at the dull fire with fierce energy.
We're not dead yet, sonny. No, by the Lord Jesus (God forgive
me) nor half dead.

Dublin was a new and complex sensation. Uncle Charles
had grown so witless that he could no longer be sent out on   220
errands and the disorder in settling in the new house left Ste=
phen freer than he had been in Blackrock. In the beginning he
contented himself with circling timidly round the neighbouring
square or, at most, going half way down one of the side streets:
but when he had made a skeleton map of the city in his mind he   225
followed boldly one of its central lines until he reached the

1. Covered carts, or vans (*OED*), in this case for moving household goods.

customhouse.[2] He passed unchallenged among the docks and along the quays wondering at the multitude of corks that lay bobbing on the surface of the water in a thick yellow scum, at the crowds of quay porters and the rumbling carts and the   230 illdressed bearded policeman. The vastness and strangeness of the life suggested to him by the bales of merchandise stacked along the walls or swung aloft out of the holds of steamers wakened again in him the unrest which had sent him wan= dering in the evening from garden to garden in search of   235 Mercedes. And amid this new bustling life he might have fancied himself in another Marseilles but that he missed the bright sky and the sunwarmed trellisses of the wineshops. A vague dissatisfaction grew up within him as he looked on the quays and on the river and on the lowering skies and yet he   240 continued to wander up and down day after day as if he really sought someone that eluded him.

He went once or twice with his mother to visit their rela= tives: and, though they passed a jovial array of shops lit up and adorned for Christmas, his mood of embittered silence did not   245 leave him. The causes of his embitterment were many, remote and near. He was angry with himself for being young and the prey of restless foolish impulses, angry also with the change of fortune which was reshaping the world about him into a vision of squalor and insincerity. Yet his anger lent nothing to the   250 vision. He chronicled with patience what he saw, detaching himself from it and tasting its mortifying flavour in secret.

He was sitting on the backless chair in his aunt's kitchen. A lamp with a reflector hung on the japanned wall[3] of the fire= place and by its light his aunt was reading the evening paper   255 that lay on her knees. She looked a long time at a smiling picture that was set in it and said musingly:

—The beautiful Mabel Hunter![4]

A ringletted girl stood on tiptoe to peer at the picture and said softly: 260

—What is she in, mud?

—In the pantomime, love.

---

228 wondering] ⌐A⌐wondering⌐A⌐ aTS; ABSENT MS   232 stacked] stocked TS–64   252 tasting] testing 16–18, 64   252 secret.] FIVE TO SIX LINES, PLUS TWO PAGES MISSING IN TS

2. The central line would be Gardiner Street, which runs along one side of Mountjoy Square, in the neighborhood where the family now lives, about 1.5 miles north of the River Liffey in Dublin. Gardiner Street leads to the Custom House (1791), a large governmental building on the river.
3. A wall finished with a black, glossy varnish (OED).
4. Probably a stage performer in pantomimes, dramatic performances of tales loosely linking singing, dancing, and jokes (OED).

The child leaned her ringletted head against her mother's sleeve, gazing on the picture and murmured, as if fascinated:

—The beautiful Mabel Hunter! 265

As if fascinated, her eyes rested long upon those demurely taunting eyes and she murmured again devotedly:

—Isn't she an exquisite creature?

And the boy who came in from the street, stamping crook= edly under his stone[5] of coal, heard her words. He dropped his 270 load promptly on the floor and hurried to her side to see. But she did not raise her easeful head to let him see. He mauled the edges of the paper with his reddened and blackened hands, shouldering her aside and complaining that he could not see.

He was sitting in the narrow breakfast room high up in the 275 old darkwindowed house. The firelight flickered on the wall and beyond the window a spectral dusk was gathering upon the river. Before the fire an old woman was busy making tea and, as she bustled at her task, she told in a low voice of what the priest and the doctor had said. She told too of certain changes 280 that she had seen in her of late and of her odd ways and sayings. He sat listening to the words and following the ways of adventure that lay open in the coals, arches and vaults and winding galleries and jagged caverns.

Suddenly he became aware of something in the doorway. A 285 skull appeared suspended in the gloom of the doorway. A feeble creature like a monkey was there, drawn thither by the sound of voices at the fire. A whining voice came from the door, asking:

—Is that Josephine? 290

The old bustling woman answered cheerily from the fire= place:

—No, Ellen. It's Stephen.

—O . . . . O, good evening, Stephen.

He answered the greeting and saw a silly smile break out 295 over the face in the doorway.

—Do you want anything, Ellen? asked the old woman at the fire.

But she did not answer the question and said:

—I thought it was Josephine. I thought you were Josephine, 300 Stephen.

And, repeating this several times, she fell to laughing feebly.

---

281 that—seen] that she seen Eg; they had seen 16–24; she had seen 64   295 out] ABSENT Eg–64

5. A unit of measure weighing fourteen pounds (*OED*).

He was sitting in the midst of a children's party at Harold's Cross.[6] His silent watchful manner had grown upon him and he took little part in the games. The children, wearing the spoils of their crackers, danced and romped noisily and, though he tried to share their merriment, he felt himself a gloomy figure amid the gay cocked hats and sunbonnets.

But when he had sung his song and withdrawn into a snug corner of the room he began to taste the joy of his loneliness. The mirth, which in the beginning of the evening had seemed to him false and trivial, was like a soothing air to him, passing gaily by his senses, hiding from other eyes the feverish agitation of his blood while through the circling of the dancers and amid the music and laughter her glances travelled to his corner, flattering, taunting, searching, exciting his heart.

In the hall the children who had stayed latest were putting on their things: the party was over. She had thrown a shawl about her and, as they went together towards the tram, sprays of her fresh warm breath flew gaily above her cowled head and her shoes tapped blithely on the glassy road.

It was the last tram. The lank brown horses knew it and shook their bells to the clear night in admonition. The conduc= tor talked with the driver, both nodding often in the green light of the lamp. On the empty seats of the tram were scattered a few coloured tickets. No sound of footsteps came up or down the road. No sound broke the peace of the night save when the lank brown horses rubbed their noses together and shook their bells.

They seemed to listen, he on the upper step and she on the lower. She came up to his step many times and went down to hers again between their phrases and once or twice stood close beside him for some moments on the upper step, forgetting to go down, and then went down. His heart danced upon her movements like a cork upon a tide. He heard what her eyes said to him from beneath their cowl and knew that in some dim past, whether in life or in revery, he had heard their tale before. He saw her urge her vanities, her fine dress and sash and long black stockings, and knew that he had yielded to them a thou= sand times. Yet a voice within him spoke above the noise of his dancing heart, asking him would he take her gift to which he had only to stretch out his hand. And he remembered the day when he and Eileen had stood looking into the hotel grounds,

---

315 glances] glance Eg–64   340 above] Eg; ABSENT MS

6. A suburb of Dublin, just beyond the Grand Canal to the southwest.

watching the waiters running up a trail of bunting on the
flagstaff and the foxterrier scampering to and fro on the sunny   345
lawn, and how, all of a sudden, she had broken out into a peal
of laughter and had run down the sloping curve of the path.
Now, as then, he stood listlessly in his place, seemingly a
tranquil watcher of the scene before him.

—She too wants me to catch hold of her, he thought. That's   350
why she came with me to the tram. I could easily catch hold of
her when she comes up to my step: nobody is looking. I could
hold her and kiss her.

But he did neither: and, when he was sitting alone in the
deserted tram, he tore his ticket into shreds and stared gloomily   355
at the corrugated footboard.

The next day he sat at his table in the bare upper room for
many hours. Before him lay a new pen, a new bottle of ink and
a new emerald exercise.[7] From force of habit he had written at
the top of the first page the initial letters of the jesuit motto: 360
A. M. D. G.[8] On the first line of the page appeared the title of
the verses he was trying to write: To E— C—. He knew it was
right to begin so for he had seen similar titles in the collected
poems of Lord Byron.[9] When he had written this title and
drawn an ornamental line underneath he fell into a daydream   365
and began to draw diagrams on the cover of the book. He saw
himself sitting at his table in Bray the morning after the dis=
cussion at the Christmas dinnertable, trying to write a poem
about Parnell on the back of one of his father's second moiety
notices.[1] But his brain had then refused to grapple with the   370
theme and, desisting, he had covered the page with the names
and addresses of certain of his classmates:

>   Roderick Kickham
>   John Lawton
>   Anthony MacSwiney   375
>   Simon Moonan

Now it seemed as if he would fail again but, by dint of
brooding on the incident, he thought himself into confidence.
During this process all those elements which he deemed com=
mon and insignificant fell out of the scene. There remained no   380

---

379 those] these 64

7. A composition book for school assignments, in this case with an emerald-green cover.
8. Abbreviation of the Jesuit motto, *Ad Majorem Dei Gloriam* (Latin; "To the greater glory of
   God"), which students were required to write at the top of assignments.
9. George Gordon, Lord Byron (1788–1824), English Romantic poet.
1. Legal notices for payments due on the second half (moiety, *OED*) of a bill.

trace of the tram itself nor of the trammen nor of the horses: nor did he and she appear vividly. The verses told only of the night and the balmy breeze and the maiden lustre of the moon. Some undefined sorrow was hidden in the hearts of the protag= onists as they stood in silence beneath the leafless trees and when the moment of farewell had come the kiss, which had been withheld by one, was given by both. After this the letters L. D. S.[2] were written at the foot of the page and, having hidden the book, he went into his mother's bedroom and gazed at his face for a long time in the mirror of her dressingtable.

But his long spell of leisure and liberty was drawing to its end. One evening his father came home full of news which kept his tongue busy all through dinner. Stephen had been awaiting his father's return for there had been mutton hash that day and he knew that his father would make him dip his bread in the gravy. But he did not relish the hash for the mention of Clon= gowes had coated his palate with a scum of disgust.

—I walked bang into him, said Mr Dedalus for the fourth time, just at the corner of the square.

—Then I suppose, said Mrs Dedalus, he will be able to arrange it. I mean, about Belvedere.[3]

—Of course he will, said Mr Dedalus. Don't I tell you he's provincial of the order[4] now?

—I never liked the idea of sending him to the christian brothers[5] myself, said Mrs Dedalus.

—Christian brothers be damned! said Mr Dedalus. Is it with Paddy Stink and Mickey Mud? No, let him stick to the jesuits in God's name since he began with them. They'll be of service to him in after years. Those are the fellows that can get you a position.

—And they're a very rich order, aren't they, Simon?

—Rather. They live well, I tell you. You saw their table at Clongowes. Fed up, by God, like gamecocks.

Mr Dedalus pushed his plate over to Stephen and bade him finish what was on it.

—Now then, Stephen, he said. You must put your shoulder to the wheel, old chap. You've had a fine long holiday.

—O, I'm sure he'll work very hard now, said Mrs Dedalus. Especially when he has Maurice with him.

—O, Holy Paul, I forgot about Maurice, said Mr Dedalus.

2. *Laus Deo Semper* (Latin; "Praise to God Always"), a Jesuit motto, often written at the end of assignments.
3. Belvedere College, a day school run by the Jesuits, close to Mountjoy Square.
4. High-ranking member of the Jesuit order, in charge of the province, Ireland.
5. The Irish Christian Brothers, a lay order of the Catholic Church, ran schools for students unable to pay the fees charged by the Jesuits.

Here, Maurice! Come here, you thickheaded ruffian! Do you
know I'm going to send you to a college where they'll teach you
to spell c.a.t: cat. And I'll buy you a nice little penny handker=
chief to keep your nose dry. Won't that be grand fun?

Maurice grinned at his father and then at his brother. Mr   425
Dedalus screwed his glass into his eye and stared hard at both
his sons. Stephen mumbled his bread[6] without answering his
father's gaze.

—By the bye, said Mr Dedalus at length, the rector, or provin=
cial, rather, was telling me that story about you and Father   430
Dolan. You're an impudent thief, he said.

—O, he didn't, Simon!

—Not he! said Mr Dedalus. But he gave me a great account of
the whole affair. We were chatting, you know, and one word
borrowed another. And, by the way, who do you think he told   435
me will get that job in the corporation?[7] But I'll tell you that
after. Well, as I was saying, we were chatting away quite
friendly and he asked me did our friend here wear glasses still
and then he told me the whole story.

—And was he annoyed, Simon?   440

—Annoyed! Not he! *Manly little chap!* he said.

Mr Dedalus imitated the mincing nasal tone of the provin=
cial.

—Father Dolan and I, when I told them all at dinner about it,
Father Dolan and I had a great laugh over it. *You better mind*   445
yourself, Father Dolan, said I, *or young Dedalus will send you*
up for twice nine. We had a famous laugh together over it. Ha!
Ha! Ha!

Mr Dedalus turned to his wife and interjected in his natural
voice: 450

—Shows you the spirit in which they take the boys there. O, a
jesuit for your life, for diplomacy!

He reassumed the provincial's voice and repeated:

—*I told them all at dinner about it and Father Dolan and I and*
all of us we all had a hearty laugh together over it. Ha! Ha! Ha!   455

◆   ◆   ◆

The night of the Whitsuntide[8] play had come and Stephen
from the window of the dressingroom looked out on the small

426 both] a16; both of MS, Eg–16   455 *all* (2)] all MS, Eg–18; ABSENT 64   456 The]
TS RESUMES

6. Tore his bread into small pieces (*OED*).
7. Dublin Corporation, the government bureaucracy in Dublin.
8. The week that includes the seventh Sunday following Easter, Whitsunday (or Pentecost),
   which marks the Holy Spirit's descent on the apostles. On the Holy Spirit, see note 7, p. 27.

grassplot across which lines of Chinese lanterns were stretched.
He watched the visitors come down the steps from the house
and pass into the theatre. Stewards in evening dress, old Belve=   460
dereans, loitered in groups about the entrance to the theatre
and ushered in the visitors with ceremony. Under the sudden
glow of a lantern he could recognize the smiling face of a priest.

The Blessed Sacrament had been removed from the taber=
nacle[9] and the first benches had been driven back so as to leave   465
the dais of the altar and the space before it free. Against the
walls stood companies of barbells and Indian clubs; the dumb=
bells were piled in one corner: and in the midst of countless
hillocks of gymnasium shoes and sweaters and singlets in
untidy brown parcels there stood the stout leatherjacketed   470
vaulting horse waiting its turn to be carried up on to the stage.
A large bronze shield, tipped with silver, leaned against the
panel of the altar also waiting its turn to be carried up on to the
stage and set in the middle of the winning team at the end of
the gymnastic display.   475

Stephen, though in deference to his reputation for essay=
writing he had been elected secretary to the gymnasium, had no
part in the first section of the programme: but in the play
which formed the second section he had the chief part, that of a
farcical pedagogue. He had been cast for it on account of his   480
stature and grave manners for he was now at the end of his
second year at Belvedere and in number two.[1]

A score of the younger boys in white knickers and singlets
came pattering down from the stage, through the vestry[2] and
into the chapel. The vestry and chapel were peopled with eager   485
masters and boys. The plump bald sergeantmajor was testing
with his foot the springboard of the vaulting horse. The lean
young man in a long overcoat, who was to give a special
display of intricate club swinging, stood near watching with
interest, his silvercoated clubs peeping out of his deep side=   490
pockets. The hollow rattle of the wooden dumbbells was heard

465 back] ABSENT 64   471 on to] on TS–64   473 on to] on 64   477 had(2)] had
had TS–64   488 to] TS; ABSENT MS

9. The consecrated bread, or Host, has been removed from its container, the tabernacle, to
prevent any accidents to it during the play.
1. This statement contradicts the one at II.653–54, which places Stephen in number six at
the end of his first term at Belvedere. Stephen would have had to enroll at Belvedere in
number three in order to be in number two during his second year. If he did enter in
number three, the later statement is inaccurate. If he entered in number six, he is in his
fifth year when he is in number two, not his second. The inconsistency, or "vague" chronology (Bradley, 6), is Joyce's, going back to the book's holograph MS. Joyce's own age
when he entered Belvedere College throws no clarifying light on the matter, because he
did not rigorously align the sequence of his experiences there with Stephen's.
2. Room adjoining the chapel, in which ritual robes are kept (OED).

as another team made ready to go up on the stage: and in
another moment the excited prefect was hustling the boys
through the vestry like a flock of geese, flapping the wings of
his soutane nervously and crying to the laggards to make haste.   495
A little troop of Neapolitan peasants were practising their steps
at the end of the chapel, some arching their arms above their
heads, some swaying their baskets of paper violets and curtsey=
ing. In a dark corner of the chapel at the gospel side of the altar[3]
a stout old lady knelt amid her copious black skirts. When she   500
stood up a pinkdressed figure, wearing a curly golden wig and
an oldfashioned straw sunbonnet, with black pencilled eye=
brows and cheeks delicately rouged and powdered, was dis=
covered. A low murmur of curiosity ran round the chapel at the
discovery of this girlish figure. One of the prefects, smiling and   505
nodding his head, approached the dark corner and, having
bowed to the stout old lady, said pleasantly:
—Is this a beautiful young lady or a doll that you have here,
Mrs Tallon?
Then, bending down to peer at the smiling painted face un-   510
der the leaf of the bonnet, he exclaimed:
—No! Upon my word I believe it's little Bertie Tallon after all!
Stephen at his post by the window heard the old lady and
the priest laugh together and heard the boys' murmur of ad=
miration behind him as they pressed forward to see the little   515
boy who had to dance the sunbonnet dance by himself. A
movement of impatience escaped him. He let the edge of the
blind fall and, stepping down from the bench on which he had
been standing, walked out of the chapel.
He passed out of the schoolhouse and halted under the shed   520
that flanked the garden. From the theatre opposite came the
muffled noise of the audience and sudden brazen clashes of the
soldiers' band. The light spread upwards from the glass roof
making the theatre seem a festive ark, anchored amid the hulks
of houses, her frail cables of lanterns looping her to her moor=   525
ings. A sidedoor of the theatre opened suddenly and a shaft of
light flew across the grassplots. A sudden burst of music issued
from the ark, the prelude of a waltz: and when the sidedoor
closed again the listener could hear the faint rhythm of the
music. The sentiment of the opening bars, their languor and   530

497 arching] MS; circling TS [MISREADING]–64   515 pressed] MS; passed TS–64
524 amid] MS; among TS–64 MS

3. To the left of the altar, as the congregation sees it, where the priest reads the Gospels (the
   first four books of the New Testament), but not the Epistles (the letters from apostles
   included as books of the New Testament), which are read from the right side of the altar.

supple movement, evoked the incommunicable emotion which
had been the cause of all his day's unrest and of his impatient
movement of a moment before. His unrest issued from him like
a wave of sound: and on the tide of flowing music the ark was
journeying, trailing her cables of lanterns in her wake. Then a   535
noise like dwarf artillery broke the movement. It was the
clapping that greeted the entry of the dumbbell team on the
stage.

At the far end of the shed near the street a speck of pink
light showed in the darkness and as he walked towards it he   540
became aware of a faint aromatic odour. Two boys were
standing in the shelter of the doorway, smoking, and before he
reached them he had recognised Heron by his voice.

—Here comes the noble Dedalus! cried a high throaty voice.
Welcome to our trusty friend!   545

This welcome ended in a soft peal of mirthless laughter as
Heron salaamed and then began to poke the ground with his
cane.

—Here I am, said Stephen, halting and glancing from Heron
to his friend.   550

The latter was a stranger to him but in the darkness, by the
aid of the glowing cigarette tips, he could make out a pale
dandyish face, over which a smile was travelling slowly, a tall
overcoated figure and a hard hat. Heron did not trouble him=
self about an introduction but said instead: 555

—I was just telling my friend Wallis what a lark it would be
tonight if you took off the rector in the part of the school=
master. It would be a ripping good joke.

Heron made a poor attempt to imitate for his friend Wallis
the rector's pedantic bass and then, laughing at his failure,   560
asked Stephen to do it.

—Go on, Dedalus, he urged. You can take him off rippingly.
*He that will not hear the churcha let him be to theea as the
heathena and the publicana.*[4]

The imitation was prevented by a mild expression of anger   565
from Wallis in whose mouthpiece the cigarette had become too
tightly wedged.

—Damn this blankety blank holder, he said, taking it from his
mouth and smiling and frowning upon it tolerantly. It's always
getting stuck like that. Do you use a holder?   570

542 the(2)] a TS–64

4. A send-up of the rector repeating Jesus's words from Matthew 18:17: "And if he refuse to
hear them, appeal to the Church, but if he refuse to hear even the Church, let him be to
thee as the heathen and the publican."

—I don't smoke, answered Stephen.

—No, said Heron, Dedalus is a model youth. He doesn't smoke and he doesn't go to bazaars and he doesn't flirt and he doesn't damn anything or damn all.

Stephen shook his head and smiled in his rival's flushed and mobile face, beaked like a bird's. He had often thought it strange that Vincent Heron had a bird's face as well as a bird's name. A shock of pale hair lay on the forehead like a ruffled crest: the forehead was narrow and bony and a thin hooked nose stood out between the closeset prominent eyes which were light and inexpressive. The rivals were school friends. They sat together in class, knelt together in the chapel, talked together after beads[5] over their lunches. As the fellows in number one[6] were undistinguished dullards Stephen and Heron had been during the year the virtual heads of the school. It was they who went up to the rector together to ask for a free day or to get a fellow off.

—O, by the way, said Heron suddenly, I saw your governor going in.

The smile waned on Stephen's face. Any allusion made to his father by a fellow or by a master put his calm to rout in a moment. He waited in timorous silence to hear what Heron might say next. Heron, however, nudged him expressively with his elbow and said:

—You're a sly dog, Dedalus!

—Why so? said Stephen.

—You'd think butter wouldn't melt in your mouth, said Heron. But I'm afraid you're a sly dog.

—Might I ask you what you are talking about? said Stephen urbanely.

—Indeed you might, answered Heron. We saw her, Wallis, didn't we? And deucedly pretty she is too. And so inquisitive! *And what part does Stephen take, Mr Dedalus? And will Stephen not sing, Mr Dedalus?* Your governor was staring at her through that eyeglass of his for all he was worth so that I think the old man has found you out too. I wouldn't care a bit, by Jove. She's ripping, isn't she, Wallis?

—Not half bad, answered Wallis quietly as he placed his holder once more in a corner of his mouth.

A shaft of momentary anger flew through Stephen's mind at these indelicate allusions in the hearing of a stranger. For him

575

580

585

590

595

600

605

610

608—Not] TS;—Hot MS   609 a] the 64

5. After saying prayers using rosary beads.
6. The final year of study.

there was nothing amusing in a girl's interest and regard. All day he had thought of nothing but their leavetaking on the steps of the tram at Harold's Cross, the stream of moody emotions it had made to course through him and the poem he had written about it. All day he had imagined a new meeting with her for he knew that she was to come to the play. The old restless moodiness had again filled his heart as it had done on the night of the party but had not found an outlet in verse. The growth and knowledge of two years of boyhood stood between then and now, forbidding such an outlet: and all day the stream of gloomy tenderness within him had started forth and re= turned upon itself in dark courses and eddies, wearying him in the end until the pleasantry of the prefect and the painted little boy had drawn from him a movement of impatience.

—So you may as well admit, Heron went on, that we've fairly found you out this time. You can't play the saint on me any more, that's one sure five.[7]

A soft peal of mirthless laughter escaped from his lips and, bending down as before, he struck Stephen lightly across the calf of the leg with his cane, as if in jesting reproof.

Stephen's moment of anger had already passed. He was nei= ther flattered nor confused but simply wished the banter to end. He scarcely resented what had seemed to him at first a silly indelicateness for he knew that the adventure in his mind stood in no danger from their words: and his face mirrored his rival's false smile.

—Admit! repeated Heron, striking him again with his cane across the calf of the leg.

The stroke was playful but not so lightly given as the first one had been. Stephen felt the skin tingle and glow slightly and almost painlessly; and bowing submissively, as if to meet his companion's jesting mood, began to recite the *Confiteor*.[8] The episode ended well for both Heron and Wallis laughed indul= gently at the irreverence.

The confession came only from Stephen's lips and, while they spoke the words, a sudden memory had carried him to another scene called up, as if by magic, at the moment when he had noted the faint cruel dimples at the corners of Heron's smiling lips and had felt the familiar stroke of the cane against his calf and had heard the familiar word of admonition:

615

620

625

630

635

640

645

650

---

618 heart] breast TS [misreading]–64   632 moment] 24 [cf 610, not 625]; movement MS–18

7. That's something guaranteed.
8. The prayer said at the beginning of confession, which opens with this Latin word meaning "I confess."

—Admit!

It was towards the close of his first term in the college when he was in number six.[9] His sensitive nature was still smarting under the lashes of an undivined and squalid way of life. His soul was still disquieted and cast down by the dull phenome= non of Dublin. He had emerged from a two years' spell of revery to find himself in the midst of a new scene, every event and figure of which affected him intimately, disheartened him or allured him and, whether alluring or disheartening, filled him always with unrest and bitter thoughts. All the leisure that his school life left him was passed in the company of subversive writers whose gibes and violence of speech set up a ferment in his brain before they passed out of it into his crude writings.

The essay was for him the chief labour of his week and every Tuesday, as he marched from home to the school, he read his fate in the incidents of the way, pitting himself against some figure ahead of him and quickening his pace to outstrip it be= fore a certain goal was reached or planting his steps scrupu= lously in the spaces of the patchwork of the footpath and telling himself that he would be first and not first in the weekly essay.

On a certain Tuesday the course of his triumphs was rudely broken. Mr Tate, the English master, pointed his finger at him and said bluntly:

—This fellow has heresy in his essay.

A hush fell on the class. Mr Tate did not break it but dug with his hand between his crossed thighs while his heavily starched linen creaked about his neck and wrists. Stephen did not look up. It was a raw spring morning and his eyes were still smarting and weak. He was conscious of failure and of detec= tion, of the squalor of his own mind and home, and felt against his neck the raw edge of his turned and jagged collar.

A short loud laugh from Mr Tate set the class more at ease.

—Perhaps you didn't know that, he said.

—Where? asked Stephen.

Mr Tate withdrew his delving hand and spread out the es= say.

—Here. It's about the Creator and the soul. Rrm . . . rrm . . . . . rrm . . . Ah! *without a possibility of ever approaching nearer.* That's heresy.

655

660

665

670

675

680

685

690

660 him] ABSENT Eg—64   661 that] which TS—64

9. The group of students six years from finishing. See the gloss for II.481–82, regarding the discrepancy about his initial year of study. If he entered in number six, the play occurs in his fifth academic year at the college, but if the statement at II.481–82 is correct, he entered in number three, and the play occurs in his second year at Belvedere.

Stephen murmured:

—I meant *without a possibility of ever reaching.*

It was a submission and Mr Tate, appeased, folded up the
essay and passed it across to him, saying: 695

—O . . . Ah! *ever reaching.* That's another story.

But the class was not so soon appeased. Though nobody
spoke to him of the affair after class he could feel about him a
vague general malignant joy.

A few nights after this public chiding he was walking with a   700
letter along the Drumcondra Road when he heard a voice cry:

—Halt!

He turned and saw three boys of his own class coming to=
wards him in the dusk. It was Heron who had called out and,
as he marched forward between his two attendants, he cleft the   705
air before him with a thin cane, in time to their steps. Boland,
his friend, marched beside him, a large grin on his face, while
Nash came on a few steps behind, blowing from the pace and
wagging his great red head.

As soon as the boys had turned into Clonliffe Road together   710
they began to speak about books and writers, saying what
books they were reading and how many books there were in
their fathers' bookcases at home. Stephen listened to them in
some wonderment for Boland was the dunce and Nash the idler
of the class. In fact after some talk about their favourite writers 715
Nash declared for Captain Marryat[1] who, he said, was the
greatest writer.

—Fudge! said Heron. Ask Dedalus. Who is the greatest writer,
Dedalus?

Stephen noted the mockery in the question and said: 720

—Of prose, do you mean?

—Yes.

—Newman,[2] I think.

—Is it Cardinal Newman? asked Boland.

—Yes, answered Stephen.   725

The grin broadened on Nash's freckled face as he turned to
Stephen and said:

—And do you like Cardinal Newman, Dedalus?

—O, many people say that Newman has the best prose style,
Heron said to the other two in explanation. Of course, he's not   730
a poet.

729 people] MS; ABSENT TS–64

1. Captain Frederick Marryat (1792–1848), English naval officer, who wrote adventure
   stories.
2. John Henry, Cardinal Newman (1801–1890), a prominent English Protestant clergyman,
   who converted to Catholicism, became a cardinal, and defended his faith in writings that
   were widely admired.

—And who is the best poet, Heron? asked Boland.

—Lord Tennyson,[3] of course, answered Heron.

—O, yes, Lord Tennyson, said Nash. We have all his poetry at
home in a book.   735

At this Stephen forgot the silent vows he had been making
and burst out:

—Tennyson a poet! Why, he's only a rhymester!

—O, get out! said Heron. Everyone knows that Tennyson is the
greatest poet.   740

—And who do you think is the greatest poet? asked Boland,
nudging his neighbour.

—Byron, of course, answered Stephen.

Heron gave the lead and all three joined in a scornful laugh.

—What are you laughing at? asked Stephen.   745

—You, said Heron. Byron the greatest poet! He's only a poet for
uneducated people.

—He must be a fine poet! said Boland.

—You may keep your mouth shut, said Stephen, turning on
him boldly. All you know about poetry is what you wrote up   750
on the slates in the yard and were going to be sent to the loft
for.

Boland, in fact, was said to have written on the slates in the
yard a couplet about a classmate of his who often rode home
from the college on a pony: 755

> As Tyson was riding into Jerusalem
> He fell and hurt his Alec Kafoozelum.

This thrust put the two lieutenants to silence but Heron
went on:

—In any case Byron was a heretic and immoral too.   760

—I don't care what he was, cried Stephen hotly.

—You don't care whether he was a heretic or not? said Nash.

—What do you know about it? shouted Stephen. You never
read a line of anything in your life except a trans[4] or Boland
either.   765

—I know that Byron was a bad man, said Boland.

—Here. Catch hold of this heretic, Heron called out.

In a moment Stephen was a prisoner.

—Tate made you buck up the other day, Heron went on, about
the heresy in your essay.   770

—I'll tell him tomorrow, said Boland.

---

761 hotly.] TS; ⁷¹Hotly.ˡ˥ MS   762 don't] aEg; ABSENT MS–Eg

3. Alfred, Lord Tennyson (1809–1892), poet laureate of England.
4. A translation, used as a shortcut by students instead of the text in the original language.

—Will you? said Stephen. You'd be afraid to open your lips.
—Afraid?
—Ay. Afraid of your life.
—Behave yourself! cried Heron, cutting at Stephen's legs with   775
his cane.

It was the signal for their onset. Nash pinioned his arms
behind while Boland seized a long cabbage stump which was
lying in the gutter. Struggling and kicking under the cuts of the
cane and the blows of the knotty stump Stephen was borne   780
back against a barbed wire fence.
—Admit that Byron was no good.
—No.
—Admit.
—No.   785
—Admit.
—No. No.

At last after a fury of plunges he wrenched himself free. His
tormentors set off towards Jones's Road, laughing and jeering
at him, while he, half blinded with tears, stumbled on, clench=   790
ing his fists madly and sobbing.

While he was still repeating the *Confiteor* amid the indul=
gent laughter of his hearers and while the scenes of that
malignant episode were still passing sharply and swiftly before
his mind he wondered why he bore no malice now to those   795
who had tormented him. He had not forgotten a whit of their
cowardice and cruelty but the memory of it called forth no
anger from him. All the descriptions of fierce love and hatred
which he had met in books had seemed to him therefore unreal.
Even that night as he stumbled homewards along Jones's Road   800
he had felt that some power was divesting him of that sudden=
woven anger as easily as a fruit is divested of her soft ripe peel.

He remained standing with his two companions at the end
of the shed, listening idly to their talk or to the bursts of ap=
plause in the theatre. She was sitting there among the others,   805
perhaps waiting for him to appear. He tried to recall her
appearance but could not. He could remember only that she had
worn a shawl about her head like a cowl and that her dark eyes
had invited and unnerved him. He wondered had he been in her
thoughts as she had been in his. Then in the dark and unseen   810
by the other two he rested the tips of the fingers of one hand
upon the palm of the other hand, scarcely touching it and yet
pressing upon it lightly. But the pressure of her fingers had

790 half--on,] aEg; torn and flushed and panting, stumbled after them, half blinded with
tears, MS; half blinded with tears, TS–Eg; torn and flushed and panting, stumbled after
them half blinded with tears, 64   791 sobbing.] TS ENDS   802 her] its Eg–64

been lighter and steadier: and suddenly the memory of their
touch traversed his brain and body like an invisible warm   815
wave.

A boy came towards them, running along under the shed.
He was excited and breathless.

—O, Dedalus, he cried, Doyle is in a great bake[5] about you.
You're to go in at once and get dressed for the play. Hurry up,   820
you better.

—He's coming now, said Heron to the messenger with a
haughty drawl, when he wants to.

The boy turned to Heron and repeated:

—But Doyle is in an awful bake.   825

—Will you tell Doyle with my best compliments that I damned
his eyes? answered Heron.

—Well, I must go now, said Stephen who cared little for such
points of honour.

—I wouldn't, said Heron, damn me if I would. That's no way   830
to send for one of the senior boys. In a bake, indeed! I think it's
quite enough that you're taking a part in his bally old play.

This spirit of quarrelsome comradeship which he had ob=
served lately in his rival had not seduced Stephen from his
habits of quiet obedience. He mistrusted the turbulence and   835
doubted the sincerity of such comradeship which seemed to
him a sorry anticipation of manhood. The question of honour
here raised was, like all such questions, trivial to him. While his
mind had been pursuing its intangible phantoms and turning in
irresolution from such pursuit he had heard about him the   840
constant voices of his father and of his masters, urging him to
be a gentleman above all things and urging him to be a good
catholic above all things. These voices had now come to be
hollowsounding in his ears. When the gymnasium had been
opened he had heard another voice urging him to be strong and   845
manly and healthy and when the movement towards national
revival had begun to be felt in the college yet another voice had
bidden him be true to his country and help to raise up her
fallen language and tradition.[6] In the profane world, as he
foresaw, a wordly voice would bid him raise up his father's   850
fallen state by his labours and, meanwhile, the voice of his
schoolcomrades urged him to be a decent fellow, to shield
others from blame or to beg them off and to do his best to get

839–840 turning--irresolution] Eg–64; turning back in irresoluteness MS

5. In an angry state of mind.
6. The opening of the gymnasium suggests the work of the Gaelic Athletic Association,
   while "national revival" refers to the Gaelic League (founded 1893), which advocated use
   of the Irish language instead of English.

free days for the school. And it was the din of all these hollow=
sounding voices that made him halt irresolutely in the pursuit   855
of phantoms. He gave them ear only for a time but he was
happy only when he was far from them, beyond their call,
alone or in the company of phantasmal comrades.

In the vestry a plump freshfaced jesuit and an elderly man, in
shabby blue clothes, were dabbling in a case of paints and   860
chalks. The boys who had been painted walked about or stood
still awkwardly, touching their faces in a gingerly fashion with
their furtive fingertips. In the middle of the vestry a young
jesuit, who was then on a visit to the college, stood rocking
himself rhythmically from the tips of his toes to his heels and   865
back again, his hands thrust well forward into his sidepockets.
His small head set off with glossy red curls and his newly
shaven face agreed well with the spotless decency of his soutane
and with his spotless shoes.

As he watched this swaying form and tried to read for him=   870
self the legend of the priest's mocking smile there came into
Stephen's memory a saying which he had heard from his father
before he had been sent to Clongowes, that you could always
tell a jesuit by the style of his clothes. At the same moment he
thought he saw a likeness between his father's mind and that of   875
this smiling welldressed priest: and he was aware of some des=
ecration of the priest's office or of the vestry itself, whose si=
lence was now routed by loud talk and joking and its air
pungent with the smells of the gasjets and the grease.

While his forehead was being wrinkled and his jaws painted   880
black and blue by the elderly man he listened distractedly to the
voice of the plump young jesuit which bade him speak up and
make his points clearly. He could hear the band playing *The
Lily of Killarney*[7] and knew that in a few moments the curtain
would go up. He felt no stage fright but the thought of the part   885
he had to play humiliated him. A remembrance of some of his
lines made a sudden flush rise to his painted cheeks. He saw her
serious alluring eyes watching him from among the audience
and their image at once swept away his scruples, leaving his
will compact. Another nature seemed to have been lent him: 890
the infection of the excitement and youth about him entered
into and transformed his moody mistrustfulness. For one rare
moment he seemed to be clothed in the real apparel of boy=
hood: and, as he stood in the wings among the other players, he
shared the common mirth amid which the drop scene was   895

7. The overture to the opera of that name (first performed in 1862); composed by Julius
Benedict (1804–1885), German-born composer who worked primarily in England.

hauled upwards by two ablebodied priests with violent jerks and all awry.

A few moments after he found himself on the stage amid the garish gas and the dim scenery, acting before the innumerable faces of the void. It surprised him to see that the play which he had known at rehearsals for a disjointed lifeless thing had suddenly assumed a life of its own. It seemed now to play itself, he and his fellow actors aiding it with their parts. When the curtain fell on the last scene he heard the void filled with applause and, through a rift in the side scene, saw the simple body before which he had acted magically deformed, the void of faces breaking at all points and falling asunder into busy groups.

He left the stage quickly and rid himself of his mummery[8] and passed out through the chapel into the college garden. Now that the play was over his nerves cried for some further adventure. He hurried onwards as if to overtake it. The doors of the theatre were all open and the audience had emptied out. On the lines which he had fancied the moorings of an ark a few lanterns swung in the night breeze, flickering cheerlessly. He mounted the steps from the garden in haste, eager that some prey should not elude him, and forced his way through the crowd in the hall and past the two jesuits who stood watching the exodus and bowing and shaking hands with the visitors. He pushed onward nervously, feigning a still greater haste and faintly conscious of the smiles and stares and nudges which his powdered head left in its wake.

When he came out on the steps he saw his family waiting for him at the first lamp. In a glance he noted that every figure of the group was familiar and ran down the steps angrily.

—I have to leave a message down in George's Street,[9] he said to his father quickly. I'll be home after you.

Without waiting for his father's questions he ran across the road and began to walk at breakneck speed down the hill. He hardly knew where he was walking. Pride and hope and desire like crushed herbs in his heart sent up vapours of maddening incense before the eyes of his mind. He strode down the hill amid the tumult of suddenrisen vapours of wounded pride and fallen hope and baffled desire. They streamed upwards before his anguished eyes in dense and maddening fumes and passed away above him till at last the air was clear and cold again.

A film still veiled his eyes but they burned no longer. A

8. Literally his costume, but also the mood of the performance.
9. Name of a lane near the Liffey, 1.5 miles from the College.

power, akin to that which had often made anger or resentment
fall from him, brought his steps to rest. He stood still and
gazed up at the sombre porch of the morgue and from that to   940
the dark cobbled laneway at its side. He saw the word *Lotts* on
the wall of the lane and breathed slowly the rank heavy air.
—That is horse piss and rotted straw, he thought. It is a good
odour to breathe. It will calm my heart. My heart is quite calm
now. I will go back.   945

◆   ◆   ◆

Stephen was once again seated beside his father in the corner
of a railway carriage at Kingsbridge.[1] He was travelling with his
father by the night mail to Cork. As the train steamed out of
the station he recalled his childish wonder of years before and
every event of his first day in Clongowes. But he felt no wonder   950
now. He saw the darkening lands slipping past him, the silent
telegraphpoles passing his window swiftly every four seconds,
the little glimmering stations, manned by a few silent sentries,
flung by the mail behind her and twinkling for a moment in the
darkness like fiery grains flung backwards by a runner.   955
He listened without sympathy to his father's evocation of
Cork and of scenes of his youth, a tale broken by sighs or
draughts from his pocket flask whenever the image of some
dead friend appeared in it or whenever the evoker remembered
suddenly the purpose of his actual visit. Stephen heard but   960
could feel no pity. The images of the dead were all strange to
him save that of uncle Charles, an image which had lately been
fading out of memory. He knew, however, that his father's
property was going to be sold by auction and in the manner of
his own dispossession he felt the world give the lie rudely to his 965
phantasy.
At Maryborough he fell asleep. When he awoke the train
had passed out of Mallow and his father was stretched asleep
on the other seat. The cold light of the dawn lay over the
country, over the unpeopled fields and the closed cottages. The   970
terror of sleep fascinated his mind as he watched the silent
country or heard from time to time his father's deep breath or
sudden sleepy movement. The neighbourhood of unseen
sleepers filled him with strange dread as though they could
harm him; and he prayed that the day might come quickly. His   975
prayer, addressed neither to God nor saint, began with a shiver,
as the chilly morning breeze crept through the chink of the

950 in] at Eg–64   959 evoker] Eg; evoked MS

1. Dublin railway station (now Heuston Station) for trains going west and south.

carriage door to his feet, and ended in a trail of foolish words
which he made to fit the insistent rhythm of the train: and
silently, at intervals of four seconds, the telegraphpoles held the   980
galloping notes of the music between punctual bars. This furi=
ous music allayed his dread and, leaning against the window=
ledge, he let his eyelids close again.

They drove in a jingle[2] across Cork while it was still early
morning and Stephen finished his sleep in a bedroom of the   985
Victoria Hotel.[3] The bright warm sunlight was streaming
through the window and he could hear the din of traffic. His
father was standing before the dressingtable, examining his
hair and face and moustache with great care, craning his neck
across the waterjug and drawing it back sideways to see the   990
better. While he did so he sang softly to himself with quaint
accent and phrasing:

> 'Tis youth and folly
> Makes young men marry,
> So here, my love, I'll   995
> No longer stay.
> What can't be cured, sure,
> Must be injured, sure,
> So I'll go to
> Amerikay.   1000
>
> My love she's handsome,
> My love she's boney:
> She's like good whisky
> When it is new;
> But when 'tis old   1005
> And growing cold
> It fades and dies like
> The mountain dew.

The consciousness of the warm sunny city outside his win=
dow and the tender tremors with which his father's voice   1010
festooned the strange sad happy air drove off all the mists of
the night's ill humour from Stephen's brain. He got up quickly
to dress and, when the song had ended, said:
—That's much prettier than any of your other *come-all-yous*.[4]
—Do you think so? asked Mr Dedalus.   1015

984 drove--across] ˥¹⟨reached⟩ drove--across¹˥ MS   1002 *boney:*] e:64; boney: MS, Eg;
bony: aEg–24; *bonny:* 64

2. A covered two-wheeled, horse-drawn car (*OED*).
3. The most expensive hotel in Cork at the time.
4. Irish ballads, many of which begin "Come all you."

—I like it, said Stephen.

—It's a pretty old air, said Mr Dedalus, twirling the points of his moustache. Ah, but you should have heard Mick Lacy sing it! Poor Mick Lacy! He had little turns for it, grace notes he used to put in that I haven't got. That was the boy could sing a *come-all-you*, if you like.   1020

Mr Dedalus had ordered drisheens[5] for breakfast and during the meal he crossexamined the waiter for local news. For the most part they spoke at cross purposes when a name was mentioned, the waiter having in mind its present holder and Mr Dedalus his father or perhaps his grandfather.   1025

—Well, I hope they haven't moved the Queen's College[6] any= how, said Mr Dedalus, for I want to show it to this youngster of mine.

Along the Mardyke[7] the trees were in bloom. They entered   1030 the grounds of the college and were led by the garrulous porter across the quadrangle. But their progress across the gravel was brought to a halt after every dozen or so paces by some reply of the porter's.

—Ah, do you tell me so? And is poor Pottlebelly dead?   1035
—Yes, sir. Dead, sir.

During these halts Stephen stood awkwardly behind the two men, weary of the subject and waiting restlessly for the slow march to begin again. By the time they had crossed the quad= rangle his restlessness had risen to fever. He wondered how his   1040 father, whom he knew for a shrewd suspicious man, could be duped by the servile manners of the porter: and the lively southern speech which had entertained him all the morning now irritated his ears.

They passed into the anatomy theatre where Mr Dedalus,   1045 the porter aiding him, searched the desks for his initials. Ste= phen remained in the background, depressed more than ever by the darkness and silence of the theatre and by the air it wore of jaded and formal study. On the desk before him he read the word *Foetus* cut several times in the dark stained wood. The   1050 sudden legend startled his blood: he seemed to feel the absent students of the college about him and to shrink from their company. A vision of their life, which his father's words had been powerless to evoke, sprang up before him out of the word cut in the desk. A broadshouldered student with a moustache   1055

1020 boy] boy who Eg–64   1025 its] the Eg–64

5. Blood sausages (P. W. Joyce, 251).
6. One of the three nonsectarian institutions of that name, located in Cork, Belfast, and Galway, at which Catholics could pursue higher education.
7. A promenade in the western part of Cork city.

was cutting in the letters with a jackknife, seriously. Other students stood or sat near him laughing at his handiwork. One jogged his elbow. The big student turned on him, frowning. He was dressed in loose grey clothes and had tan boots.

Stephen's name was called. He hurried down the steps of the theatre so as to be as far away from the vision as he could be and, peering closely at his father's initials, hid his flushed face.

But the word and the vision capered before his eyes as he walked back across the quadrangle and towards the college gate. It shocked him to find in the outer world a trace of what he had deemed till then a brutish and individual malady of his own mind. His recent monstrous reveries came thronging into his memory. They too had sprung up before him, suddenly and furiously, out of mere words. He had soon given in to them and allowed them to sweep across and abase his intellect, wonder= ing always where they came from, from what den of monstrous images, and always weak and humble towards others, restless and sickened of himself when they had swept over him.

—Ay, bedad! And there's the Groceries[8] sure enough! cried Mr Dedalus. You often heard me speak of the Groceries, didn't you, Stephen. Many's the time we went down there when our names had been marked, a crowd of us, Harry Peard and little Jack Mountain and Bob Dyas and Maurice Moriarty, the Frenchman, and Tom O'Grady and Mick Lacy that I told you of this morning and Joey Corbet and poor little goodhearted Johnny Keevers of the Tantiles.

The leaves of the trees along the Mardyke were astir and whispering in the sunlight. A team of cricketers passed, agile young men in flannels and blazers, one of them carrying the long green wicketbag. In a quiet bystreet a German band of five players in faded uniforms and with battered brass instruments was playing to an audience of street arabs[9] and leisurely mess= enger boys. A maid in a white cap and apron was watering a box of plants on a sill which shone like a slab of limestone in the warm glare. From another window open to the air came the sound of a piano, scale after scale rising into the treble.

Stephen walked on at his father's side, listening to stories he had heard before, hearing again the names of the scattered and dead revellers who had been the companions of his father's youth. And a faint sickness sighed in his heart. He recalled his own equivocal position in Belvedere, a free boy,[1] a leader afraid of his own authority, proud and sensitive and suspicious, bat=

8. A pub that also sold household items and nonperishable food.
9. Street urchins, children from the slums.
1. Student on scholarship, who pays no fees.

tling against the squalor of his life and against the riot of his
mind. The letters cut in the stained wood of the desk stared
upon him, mocking his bodily weakness and futile enthusiasms   1100
and making him loathe himself for his own mad and filthy
orgies. The spittle in his throat grew bitter and foul to swallow
and the faint sickness climbed to his brain so that for a moment
he closed his eyes and walked on in darkness.

He could still hear his father's voice.   1105
—When you kick out for yourself, Stephen, (as I daresay you
will one of those days) remember, whatever you do, to mix
with gentlemen. When I was a young fellow I tell you I enjoyed
myself. I mixed with fine decent fellows. Everyone of us could
do something. One fellow had a good voice, another fellow   1110
was a good actor, another could sing a good comic song, an=
other was a good oarsman or a good racketplayer, another
could tell a good story and so on. We kept the ball rolling
anyhow and enjoyed ourselves and saw a bit of life and we
were none the worse of it either. But we were all gentlemen,   1115
Stephen, (at least I hope we were) and bloody good honest
Irishmen too. That's the kind of fellows I want you to associate
with, fellows of the right kidney. I'm talking to you as a friend,
Stephen. I don't believe in playing the stern father. I don't
believe a son should be afraid of his father. No, I treat you as   1120
your grandfather treated me when I was a young chap. We
were more like brothers than father and son. I'll never forget
the first day he caught me smoking. I was standing at the end
of the South Terrace one day with some maneens[2] like myself
and sure we thought we were grand fellows because we had   1125
pipes stuck in the corners of our mouths. Suddenly the gov=
ernor passed. He didn't say a word or stop even. But the next
day, Sunday, we were out for a walk together and when we
were coming home he took out his cigar case and said: *By the
bye, Simon, I didn't know you smoked*: or something like that.   1130
—Of course I tried to carry it off as best I could. *If you want a
good smoke*, he said, *try one of these cigars. An American
captain made me a present of them last night in Queenstown.*[3]

Stephen heard his father's voice break into a laugh which
was almost a sob.   1135
—He was the handsomest man in Cork at that time, by God he
was! The women used to stand to look after him in the street.

He heard the sob passing loudly down his father's throat
and opened his eyes with a nervous impulse. The sunlight

2. "Little man," used derisively (Irish dialect).
3. A port (now known as Cobh) on the southern coast of County Cork from which many
   Irish emigrated for America and elsewhere.

breaking suddenly on his sight turned the sky and clouds into a 1140
fantastic world of sombre masses with lakelike spaces of dark
rosy light. His very brain was sick and powerless. He could
scarcely interpret the letters of the signboards of the shops. By
his monstrous way of life he seemed to have put himself be=
yond the limits of reality. Nothing moved him or spoke to him 1145
from the real world unless he heard in it an echo of the
infuriated cries within him. He could respond to no earthly or
human appeal, dumb and insensible to the call of summer and
gladness and companionship, wearied and dejected by his fa=
ther's voice. He could scarcely recognise as his his own 1150
thoughts, and repeated slowly to himself:
—I am Stephen Dedalus. I am walking beside my father whose
name is Simon Dedalus. We are in Cork, in Ireland. Cork is a
city. Our room is in the Victoria Hotel. Victoria and Stephen
and Simon. Simon and Stephen and Victoria. Names. 1155
    The memory of his childhood suddenly grew dim. He tried
to call forth some of its vivid moments but could not. He
recalled only names: Dante, Parnell, Clane, Clongowes. A little
boy had been taught geography by an old woman who kept
two brushes in her wardrobe. Then he had been sent away 1160
from home to a college. In the college he had made his first
communion and eaten slim jim[4] out of his cricket cap and
watched the firelight leaping and dancing on the wall of a little
bedroom in the infirmary and dreamed of being dead, of mass
being said for him by the rector in a black and gold cope, of 1165
being buried then in the little graveyard of the community off
the main avenue of limes. But he had not died then. Parnell had
died. There had been no mass for the dead in the chapel and no
procession. He had not died but he had faded out like a film in
the sun. He had been lost or had wandered out of existence for 1170
he no longer existed. How strange to think of him passing out
of existence in such a way, not by death but by fading out in
the sun or by being lost and forgotten somewhere in the uni=
verse! It was strange to see his small body appear again for a
moment: a little boy in a grey belted suit. His hands were in his 1175
sidepockets and his trousers were tucked in at the knees by
elastic bands.
    On the evening of the day on which the property was sold
Stephen followed his father meekly about the city from bar to
bar. To the sellers in the market, to the barmen and barmaids, 1180

1167 limes.] Eg; chestnuts. MS

4. A sugar-coated sweet that was sold in long strips (*Letters* III, 129).

to the beggars who importuned him for a lob[5] Mr Dedalus told
the same tale, that he was an old Corkonian, that he had been
trying for thirty years to get rid of his Cork accent up in Dublin
and that Peter Pickackafox beside him was his eldest son but
that he was only a Dublin jackeen.[6]   1185

They had set out early in the morning from Newcombe's
coffeehouse where Mr Dedalus' cup had rattled noisily against
its saucer and Stephen had tried to cover that shameful sign of
his father's drinkingbout of the night before by moving his
chair and coughing. One humiliation had succeeded another: 1190
the false smiles of the market sellers, the curvettings and
oglings of the barmaids with whom his father flirted, the com=
pliments and encouraging words of his father's friends. They
had told him that he had a great look of his grandfather and
Mr Dedalus had agreed that he was an ugly likeness. They had   1195
unearthed traces of a Cork accent in his speech and made him
admit that the Lee was a much finer river than the Liffey. One
of them in order to put his Latin to the proof had made him
translate short passages from Dilectus[7] and asked him whether
it was correct to say: *Tempora mutantur nos et mutamur in illis*   1200
or *Tempora mutantur et nos mutamur in illis.*[8] Another, a brisk
old man, whom Mr Dedalus called Johnny Cashman, had
covered him with confusion by asking him to say which were
prettier, the Dublin girls or the Cork girls.

—He's not that way built, said Mr Dedalus. Leave him alone.   1205
He's a levelheaded thinking boy who doesn't bother his head
about that kind of nonsense.

—Then he's not his father's son, said the little old man.

—I don't know, I'm sure, said Mr Dedalus, smiling com=
placently.   1210

—Your father, said the little old man to Stephen, was the
boldest flirt in the city of Cork in his day. Do you know that?

Stephen looked down and studied the tiled floor of the bar
into which they had drifted.

—Now don't be putting ideas into his head, said Mr Dedalus.   1215
Leave him to his Maker.

1184 Pickackafox] MS; Pickackafax Eg–64   1200 *Tempora--illis*] e:Eg, 18; Tempora
mutantur et nos cum illis mutamur MS   1201 *Tempora--illis*.] Eg; Tempora mutantur et
nos mutamur cum illis. MS   1201 *in*] Eg; cum MS

5. Money (Irish dialect).
6. A conceited lower-class person (Irish dialect).
7. A misspelling for *Delectus*, from the title, *Delectus Bententiarum*, of an early nineteenth-
   century anthology of Latin sentences by Richard Valpy (1754–1836), to accompany his
   grammar, both widely used for teaching Latin in schools.
8. Two metrically different ways of expressing the sentiment that times change and that we
   change with them, or because of them (Latin).

—Yerra, sure I wouldn't put any ideas into his head. I'm old
enough to be his grandfather. And I am a grandfather, said the
little old man to Stephen. Do you know that?
—Are you? asked Stephen.   1220
—Bedad I am, said the little old man. I have two bouncing
grandchildren out at Sunday's Well.[9] Now then! What age do
you think I am? And I remember seeing your grandfather in his
red coat riding out to hounds. That was before you were born.
—Ay, or thought of, said Mr Dedalus.   1225
—Bedad I did! repeated the little old man. And, more than
that, I can remember even your greatgrandfather, old John Ste=
phen Dedalus, and a fierce old fireeater he was. Now then!
There's a memory for you!
—That's three generations—four generations, said another of   1230
the company. Why, Johnny Cashman, you must be nearing the
century.
—Well, I'll tell you the truth, said the little old man. I'm just
twentyseven years of age.
—We're as old as we feel, Johnny, said Mr Dedalus. And just   1235
finish what you have there and we'll have another. Here, Tim
or Tom or whatever your name is, give us the same again here.
By God, I don't feel more than eighteen myself. There's that
son of mine there not half my age and I'm a better man than he
is any day of the week.   1240
—Draw it mild now, Dedalus. I think it's about time for you to
take a back seat, said the gentleman who had spoken before.
—No, by God! asserted Mr Dedalus. I'll sing a tenor song
against him or I'll vault a fivebarred gate against him or I'll run
with him after the hounds across the country as I did thirty   1245
years ago along with the Kerry Boy and the best man for it.
—But he'll beat you here, said the little old man, tapping his
forehead and raising his glass to drain it.
—Well, I hope he'll be as good a man as his father. That's all I
can say, said Mr Dedalus.   1250
—If he is, he'll do, said the little old man.
—And thanks be to God, Johnny, said Mr Dedalus, that we
lived so long and did so little harm.
—But did so much good, Simon, said the little old man
gravely. Thanks be to God we lived so long and did so much   1255
good.
    Stephen watched the three glasses being raised from the
counter as his father and his two cronies drank to the memory

1241 about] ABSENT Eg—64

9. A suburb of Cork city, just over a mile from the center.

of their past. An abyss of fortune or of temperament sundered
him from them. His mind seemed older than theirs: it shone   1260
coldly on their strifes and happiness and regrets like a moon
upon a younger earth. No life or youth stirred in him as it had
stirred in them. He had known neither the pleasure of compan=
ionship with others nor the vigour of rude male health nor filial
piety. Nothing stirred within his soul but a cold and cruel and   1265
loveless lust. His childhood was dead or lost and with it his
soul capable of simple joys: and he was drifting amid life like
the barren shell of the moon.

> Art thou pale for weariness
> Of climbing heaven and gazing on the earth   1270
> Wandering companionless . . . . ?[1]

He repeated to himself the lines of Shelley's fragment. Its
alternation of sad human ineffectiveness with vast inhuman
cycles of activity chilled him: and he forgot his own human
and ineffectual grieving.   1275

◆ ◆ ◆

Stephen's mother and his brother and one of his cousins
waited at the corner of quiet Foster Place while he and his
father went up the steps and along the colonnade where the
highland sentry was parading. When they had passed into the
great hall and stood at the counter Stephen drew forth his   1280
orders on the governor of the bank of Ireland for thirty and
three pounds; and these sums, the moneys of his exhibition[2] and
essay prize, were paid over to him rapidly by the teller in notes
and in coin respectively. He bestowed them in his pockets with
feigned composure and suffered the friendly teller, to whom his   1285
father chatted, to take his hand across the broad counter and
wish him a brilliant career in after life. He was impatient of
their voices and could not keep his feet at rest. But the teller
still deferred the serving of others to say that he was living in
changed times and that there was nothing like giving a boy the   1290
best education that money could buy. Mr Dedalus lingered in
the hall gazing about him and up at the roof and telling Ste=
phen, who urged him to come out, that they were standing in
the house of commons of the old Irish parliament.

1273 ineffectiveness] a16 [CF UNPUBLISHED LETTER TO HARRIET SHAW WEAVER, c. 20 NOV.
1917, BRITISH LIBRARY]; ineffectualness MS–16   1289 that] ABSENT Eg–64

1. Opening of "To the Moon," by the English Romantic poet Percy Bysshe Shelley
   (1792–1822).
2. Award made because of his performance on the annual competitive, national school
   examinations.

—God help us! he said piously. To think of the men of those ¹²⁹⁵
times, Stephen, Hely Hutchinson and Flood and Henry Grattan
and Charles Kendal Bushe,³ and the noblemen we have now,
leaders of the Irish people at home and abroad. Why, by God,
they wouldn't be seen dead in a ten acre field with them. No,
Stephen, old chap, I'm sorry to say that they are only as I roved ¹³⁰⁰
out one fine May morning in the merry month of sweet July.⁴

A keen October wind was blowing round the bank. The
three figures standing at the edge of the muddy path had
pinched cheeks and watery eyes. Stephen looked at his thinly
clad mother and remembered that a few days before he had ¹³⁰⁵
seen a mantle priced at twenty guineas in the window of Bar=
nardo's.

—Well, that's done, said Mr Dedalus.

—We had better go to dinner, said Stephen. Where?

—Dinner? said Mr Dedalus. Well, I suppose we had better, ¹³¹⁰
what?

—Some place that's not too dear, said Mrs Dedalus.

—Underdone's?⁵

—Yes. Some quiet place.

—Come along, said Stephen quickly. It doesn't matter about ¹³¹⁵
the dearness.

He walked on before them with short nervous steps, smiling.
They tried to keep up with him, smiling also at his eagerness.

—Take it easy like a good young fellow, said his father. We're
not out for the half mile, are we? ¹³²⁰

For a swift season of merrymaking the money of his prizes
ran through Stephen's fingers. Great parcels of groceries and
delicacies and dried fruits arrived from the city. Every day he
drew up a bill of fare for the family and every night led a party
of three or four to the theatre to see *Ingomar* or *The Lady of* ¹³²⁵
*Lyons.*⁶ In his coat pockets he carried squares of Vienna choc=
olate for his guests while his trousers' pockets bulged with
masses of silver and copper coins. He bought presents for
everyone, overhauled his room, wrote out resolutions, marshal=
led his books up and down their shelves, pored upon all kinds ¹³³⁰

1306 window] windows Eg–64

3. Irish statesmen and orators of the late eighteenth and early nineteenth centuries: John
   Hely-Hutchinson (1724–1794), Henry Flood (1732–1791), Henry Grattan (1746–
   1820), and Charles Kendal Bushe (1767–1843).
4. Mr. Dedalus's joking transformation of the opening line of the ballad "The Bonny
   Labouring Boy" expresses his skepticism about the leaders of the day.
5. The family's joking nickname for some expensive restaurant.
6. Two plays with happy endings for the young male heroes, Ingomar in *Ingomar the Barbar-
   ian* (1851), by the English actress and dramatist Maria Lovell (1803–1877), and Claude
   Melnotte in *The Lady of Lyons* (1838), by the English novelist and playwright Edward
   Bulwer-Lytton (1803–1873).

of price lists, drew up a form of commonwealth for the household by which every member of it held some office, opened a loan bank for his family and pressed loans on willing borrowers so that he might have the pleasure of making out receipts and reckoning the interests on the sums lent. When he could do no more he drove up and down the city in trams. Then the season of pleasure came to an end. The pot of pink enamel paint gave out and the wainscot of his bedroom re= mained with its unfinished and illplastered coat.

His household returned to its usual way of life. His mother had no further occasion to upbraid him for squandering his money. He too returned to his old life at school and all his novel enterprises fell to pieces. The commonwealth fell, the loan bank closed its coffers and its books on a sensible loss,[7] the rules of life which he had drawn about himself fell into desue= tude.

How foolish his aim had been! He had tried to build a breakwater of order and elegance against the sordid tide of life without him and to dam up, by rules of conduct and active interests and new filial relations, the powerful recurrence of the tides within him. Useless. From without as from within the waters had flowed over his barriers: their tides began once more to jostle fiercely above the crumbled mole.[8]

He saw clearly too his own futile isolation. He had not gone one step nearer the lives he had sought to approach nor bridged the restless shame and rancour that divided him from father and mother and brother and sister. He felt that he was hardly of the one blood with them but stood to them rather in the mystical kinship of fosterage, fosterchild and fosterbrother.

He burned to appease the fierce longings of his heart before which everything else was idle and alien. He cared little that he was in mortal sin,[9] that his life had grown to be a tissue of subterfuges and falsehood. Beside the savage desire within him to realise the enormities which he brooded on nothing was sacred. He bore cynically with the shameful details of his secret riots in which he exulted to defile with patience whatever im= age had attracted his eyes. By day and by night he moved among distorted images of the outer world. A figure that had seemed to him by day demure and innocent came towards him

1335

1340

1345

1350

1355

1360

1365

1344 loan] Eg [CF 1333]; loans MS   1352 waters] water Eg–18, 64

7. Perceptible, that is, substantial, loss.
8. "A massive structure, esp. of stone, serving as a pier or breakwater" (OED).
9. Sin that causes spiritual death; by contrast with venial sin, which is pardonable because not grave (OED).

by night through the winding darkness of sleep, her face trans= 1370
figured by a lecherous cunning, her eyes bright with brutish
joy. Only the morning pained him with its dim memory of dark
orgiastic riot, its keen and humiliating sense of transgression.

He returned to his wanderings. The veiled autumnal even=
ings led him from street to street as they had led him years 1375
before along the quiet avenues of Blackrock. But no vision of
trim front gardens or of kindly lights in the windows poured a
tender influence upon him now. Only at times, in the pauses of
his desire, when the luxury that was wasting him gave room to
a softer languor, the image of Mercedes traversed the back= 1380
ground of his memory. He saw again the small white house and
the garden of rosebushes on the road that led to the mountains
and he remembered the sadly proud gesture of refusal which he
was to make there, standing with her in the moonlit garden
after years of estrangement and adventure. At those moments 1385
the soft speeches of Claude Melnotte rose to his lips and eased
his unrest. A tender premonition touched him of the tryst he
had then looked forward to and, in spite of the horrible reality
which lay between his hope of then and now, of the holy
encounter he had then imagined at which weakness and timid= 1390
ity and inexperience were to fall from him.

Such moments passed and the wasting fires of lust sprang up
again. The verses passed from his lips and the inarticulate cries
and the unspoken brutal words rushed forth from his brain to
force a passage. His blood was in revolt. He wandered up and 1395
down the dark slimy streets peering into the gloom of lanes and
doorways, listening eagerly for any sound. He moaned to him=
self like some baffled prowling beast. He wanted to sin with
another of his kind, to force another being to sin with him and
to exult with her in sin. He felt some dark presence moving 1400
irresistibly upon him from the darkness, a presence subtle and
murmurous as a flood filling him wholly with itself. Its mur=
mur besieged his ears like the murmur of some multitude in
sleep; its subtle streams penetrated his being. His hands
clenched convulsively and his teeth set together as he suffered 1405
the agony of its penetration. He stretched out his arms in the
street to hold fast the frail swooning form that eluded him and
incited him: and the cry that he had strangled for so long in his
throat issued from his lips. It broke from him like a wail of
despair from a hell of sufferers and died in a wail of furious 1410
entreaty, a cry for an iniquitous abandonment, a cry which was

1379 him] Eg; ABSENT MS

but the echo of an obscene scrawl which he had read on the oozing wall of a urinal.

He had wandered into a maze of narrow and dirty streets. From the foul laneways he heard bursts of hoarse riot and wrangling and the drawling of drunken singers. He walked onward, undismayed, wondering whether he had strayed into the quarter of the jews. Women and girls dressed in long vivid gowns traversed the street from house to house. They were leisurely and perfumed. A trembling seized him and his eyes grew dim. The yellow gasflames arose before his troubled vi= sion against the vapoury sky, burning as if before an altar. Before the doors and in the lighted halls groups were gathered, arrayed as for some rite. He was in another world: he had awakened from a slumber of centuries.

He stood still in the middle of the roadway, his heart clam= ouring against his bosom in a tumult. A young woman dressed in a long pink gown laid her hand on his arm to detain him and gazed into his face. She said gaily:

—Good night, Willie dear!

Her room was warm and lightsome. A huge doll sat with her legs apart in the copious easychair beside the bed. He tried to bid his tongue speak that he might seem at ease, watching her as she undid her gown, noting the proud conscious movements of her perfumed head.

As he stood silent in the middle of the room she came over to him and embraced him gaily and gravely. Her round arms held him firmly to her and he, seeing her face lifted to him in serious calm and feeling the warm calm rise and fall of her breast, all but burst into hysterical weeping. Tears of joy and relief shone in his delighted eyes and his lips parted though they would not speak.

She passed her tinkling hand through his hair, calling him a little rascal.

—Give me a kiss, she said.

His lips would not bend to kiss her. He wanted to be held firmly in her arms, to be caressed slowly, slowly, slowly. In her arms he felt that he had suddenly become strong and fearless and sure of himself. But his lips would not bend to kiss her.

With a sudden movement she bowed his head and joined her lips to his and he read the meaning of her movements in her frank uplifted eyes. It was too much for him. He closed his eyes, surrendering himself to her, body and mind, conscious of

nothing in the world but the dark pressure of her softly parting
lips. They pressed upon his brain as upon his lips as though   1455
they were the vehicle of a vague speech; and between them he
felt an unknown and timid pressure, darker than the swoon of
sin, softer than sound or odour.

III

The swift December dusk had come tumbling clownishly after
its dull day and as he stared through the dull square of the
window of the schoolroom he felt his belly crave for its food.
He hoped there would be stew for dinner, turnips and carrots
and bruised potatoes and fat mutton pieces to be ladled out in   5
thick peppered flourfattened sauce. Stuff it into you, his belly
counselled him.

It would be a gloomy secret night. After early nightfall the
yellow lamps would light up here and there the squalid quarter
of the brothels. He would follow a devious course up and down   10
the streets, circling always nearer and nearer in a tremor of fear
and joy, until his feet led him suddenly round a dark corner.
The whores would be just coming out of their houses making
ready for the night, yawning lazily after their sleep and settling
the hairpins in their clusters of hair. He would pass by them   15
calmly waiting for a sudden movement of his own will or a
sudden call to his sinloving soul from their soft perfumed flesh.
Yet as he prowled in quest of that call his senses, stultified only
by his desire, would note keenly all that wounded and shamed
them, his eyes a ring of porter froth on a clothless table or a   20
photograph of two soldiers standing to attention or a gaudy
playbill, his ears the drawling jargon of greeting:
—Hello, Bertie, any good in your mind?
—Is that you, pigeon?
—Number ten. Fresh Nelly is waiting on you.   25
—Good night, husband! Coming in to have a short time?

The equation on the page of his scribbler began to spread
out a widening tail, eyed and starred like a peacock's: and
when the eyes and stars of its indices had been eliminated be=
gan slowly to fold itself together again. The indices appearing   30
and disappearing were eyes opening and closing; the eyes
opening and closing were stars being born and being quenched.
The vast cycle of starry life bore his weary mind outward to its

verge and inward to its centre, a distant music accompanying
him outward and inward. What music? The music came nearer   35
and he recalled the words, the words of Shelley's fragment
upon the moon wandering companionless, pale for weariness.[1]
The stars began to crumble and a cloud of fine stardust fell
through space.

The dull light fell more faintly upon the page whereon an=   40
other equation began to unfold itself slowly and to spread
abroad its widening tail. It was his own soul going forth to
experience, unfolding itself sin by sin, spreading abroad the
balefire[2] of its burning stars and folding back upon itself, fading
slowly, quenching its own lights and fires. They were   45
quenched: and the cold darkness filled chaos.

A cold lucid indifference reigned in his soul. At his first
violent sin he had felt a wave of vitality pass out of him and had
feared to find his body or his soul maimed by the excess.
Instead the vital wave had carried him on its bosom out of   50
himself and back again when it receded: and no part of body or
soul had been maimed but a dark peace had been established
between them. The chaos in which his ardour extinguished
itself was a cold indifferent knowledge of himself. He had
sinned mortally not once but many times and he knew that,   55
while he stood in danger of eternal damnation for the first sin
alone, by every succeeding sin he multiplied his guilt and his
punishment. His days and works and thoughts could make no
atonement for him, the fountains of sanctifying grace having
ceased to refresh his soul. At most by an alms given to a   60
beggar, whose blessing he fled from, he might hope wearily to
win for himself some measure of actual grace.[3] Devotion had
gone by the board. What did it avail to pray when he knew that
his soul lusted after its own destruction? A certain pride, a
certain awe, withheld him from offering to God even one   65
prayer at night though he knew it was in God's power to take
away his life while he slept and hurl his soul hellward ere he
could beg for mercy. His pride in his own sin, his loveless awe
of God told him that his offence was too grievous to be atoned
for in whole or in part by a false homage to the Allseeing and   70
Allknowing.

—Well now, Ennis, I declare you have a head and so has my

1. See II.1269–71 and note 1, p. 84.
2. Bonfire (OED).
3. According to Catholic doctrine, God's grace can manifest itself in the individual as a
   permanent state of habitual grace, or sanctifying grace, which can be lost because of
   mortal sin, that is, sin that deadens the soul. Impulsive moral acts constitute a second
   contrasting form, actual grace, which lasts only during the act (Cath. Enc.).

stick! Do you mean to say that you are not able to tell me what a surd[4] is?

The blundering answer stirred the embers of his contempt of his fellows. Towards others he felt neither shame nor fear. On Sunday mornings as he passed the churchdoor he glanced coldly at the worshippers who stood bareheaded, four deep, outside the church, morally present at the mass which they could neither see nor hear. Their dull piety and the sickly smell of the cheap hairoil with which they had anointed their heads repelled him from the altar they prayed at. He stooped to the evil of hypocrisy with others, sceptical of their innocence which he could cajole so easily.

On the wall of his bedroom hung an illuminated scroll, the certificate of his prefecture in the college of the sodality of the Blessed Virgin Mary.[5] On Saturday mornings when the sodality met in the chapel to recite the little office[6] his place was a cushioned kneelingdesk at the right of the altar from which he led his wing of boys through the responses. The falsehood of his position did not pain him. If at moments he felt an impulse to rise from his post of honour and, confessing before them all his unworthiness, to leave the chapel, a glance at their faces restrained him. The imagery of the psalms of prophecy soothed his barren pride. The glories of Mary held his soul captive: spikenard and myrrh and frankincense, symbolising the preciousness of God's gifts to her soul, rich garments, symbol= ising her royal lineage, her emblems, the lateflowering plant and lateblossoming tree, symbolising the agelong gradual growth of her cultus among men. When it fell to him to read the lesson towards the close of the office he read it in a veiled voice, lulling his conscience to its music:

> Quasi cedrus exaltata sum in Libanon et quasi cu= pressus in monte Sion. Quasi palma exaltata sum in Gades et quasi plantatio rosae in Jericho. Quasi uliva speciosa in campis et quasi platanus exaltata sum juxta aquam in plateis. Sicut cinnamomum et balsamum aro= matizans odorem dedi et quasi myrrha electa dedi suavitatem odoris.[7]

84 easily.] Eg; lightly. MS

4. An irrational number.
5. His leadership of the devotional group dedicated to the Virgin Mary.
6. Readings drawn from the Bible to honor the Virgin Mary.
7. Latin version of a passage from Ecclesiasticus (not Ecclesiastes), a book in the Old Testament canon, not accepted by Protestants. In English: "I was exalted like a cedar in Libanus, and as a cypress tree on mount Sion. I was exalted like a palm tree in Cades, and as a rose plant in Jericho: As a fair olive tree in the plains, and as a plane tree by the water in the streets, was I exalted. I gave a sweet smell like cinnamon, and aromatical balm: I yielded a sweet odour like the best myrrh" (24:17–20).

His sin, which had covered him from the sight of God, had   110
led him nearer to the refuge of sinners. Her eyes seemed to
regard him with mild pity; her holiness, a strange light glowing
faintly upon her frail flesh, did not humiliate the sinner who
approached her. If ever he was impelled to cast sin from him
and to repent the impulse that moved him was the wish to be   115
her knight. If ever his soul, reentering her dwelling shyly after
the frenzy of his body's lust had spent itself, was turned to=
wards her whose emblem is the morning star, *bright and
musical, telling of heaven and infusing peace,*[8] it was when her
names were murmured softly by lips whereon there still lin=   120
gered foul and shameful words, the savour itself of a lewd kiss.

That was strange. He tried to think how it could be but the
dusk, deepening in the schoolroom, covered over his thought.
The bell rang. The master marked the sums and cuts[9] to be done
for the next lesson and went out. Heron, beside Stephen, began   125
to hum tunelessly:

> *My excellent friend Bombados.*[1]

Ennis, who had gone to the yard, came back, saying:
—The boy from the house is coming up for the rector.

A tall boy behind Stephen rubbed his hands and said: 130
—That's game ball.[2] We can scut the whole hour. He won't be
in till after half two. Then you can ask him questions on the
catechism,[3] Dedalus.

Stephen, leaning back and drawing idly on his scribbler,
listened to the talk about him which Heron checked from time   135
to time by saying:
—Shut up, will you. Don't make such a bally racket!

It was strange too that he found an arid pleasure in follow=
ing up to the end the rigid lines of the doctrines of the church
and penetrating into obscure silences only to hear and feel the   140
more deeply his own condemnation. The sentence of saint
James which says that he who offends against one command=

---

123 thought.] MS; thoughts. Eg–64   127 *Bombados.*] e:Eg, aEg; *Pompados| My dearest
and best Patake* MS; *Pompados.* Eg

8. The Virgin Mary is associated with the morning star in the "Litany of Our Lady" (of
   Loreto), alluded to in Part I (p. 30); the italicized language is quoted from John Henry
   Cardinal Newman's "The Glories of Mary for the Sake of Her Son," in his *Discourses to
   Mixed Congregations* (1849).
9. Mathematics schoolwork to be done from material in a text of Euclid's *Geometry* (*Letters*
   III, 129).
1. A line probably from a music-hall pantomime.
2. The final ball, the deciding factor.
3. An instructional treatise concerning a religion's principles in the form of questions and
   answers (*OED*).

ment becomes guilty of all[4] had seemed to him first a swollen phrase until he had begun to grope in the darkness of his own state. From the evil seed of lust all other deadly sins[5] had sprung   145
forth: pride in himself and contempt of others, covetousness in using money for the purchase of unlawful pleasure, envy of those whose vices he could not reach to and calumnious murmuring against the pious, gluttonous enjoyment of food, the dull glowering anger amid which he brooded upon his   150
longing, the swamp of spiritual and bodily sloth in which his whole being had sunk.

As he sat in his bench gazing calmly at the rector's shrewd harsh face his mind wound itself in and out of the curious questions proposed to it. If a man had stolen a pound in his   155
youth and had used that pound to amass a huge fortune how much was he obliged to give back, the pound he had stolen only or the pound together with the compound interest accru= ing upon it or all his huge fortune? If a layman in giving baptism pour the water before saying the words is the child   160
baptised? Is baptism with a mineral water valid? How comes it that while the first beatitude[6] promises the kingdom of heaven to the poor of heart the second beatitude promises also to the meek that they shall possess the land? Why was the sacrament of the eucharist[7] instituted under the two species of bread and   165
wine if Jesus Christ be present body and blood, soul and divin= ity, in the bread alone and in the wine alone? Does a tiny particle of the consecrated bread contain all the body and blood of Jesus Christ or a part only of the body and blood? If the wine change into vinegar and the host crumble into cor=   170
ruption after they have been consecrated is Jesus Christ still present under their species as God and as man?
—Here he is! Here he is!

A boy from his post at the window had seen the rector come from the house. All the catechisms were opened and all heads   175
bent upon them silently. The rector entered and took his seat on the dais. A gentle kick from the tall boy in the bench behind urged Stephen to ask a difficult question.

---

168 bread] Eg; ABSENT MS

4. In the New Testament, James 2:10: "For whoever keeps the whole law, but offends in one point, has become guilty in all."
5. All seven sins deadly to the soul are mentioned: lust, pride, covetousness, envy, gluttony, anger, and sloth.
6. A declaration of blessedness. Stephen is thinking about Jesus's statements in Matthew 3–11 concerning the blessed.
7. The Christian sacrament, or religious rite, in which consecrated bread and wine are consumed.

The rector did not ask for a catechism to hear the lesson from. He clasped his hands on the desk and said: 180
—The retreat will begin on Wednesday afternoon in honour of saint Francis Xavier whose feast day is Saturday. The retreat will go on from Wednesday to Friday. On Friday confessions will be heard all the afternoon after beads. If any boys have special confessors perhaps it will be better for them not to   185
change. Mass will be on Saturday morning at nine o'clock and general communion for the whole college. Saturday will be a free day. Sunday of course. But Saturday and Sunday being free days some boys might be inclined to think that Monday is a free day also. Beware of making that mistake. I think you,   190
Lawless, are likely to make that mistake.
—I, sir? Why, sir?
A little wave of quiet mirth broke forth over the class of boys from the rector's grim smile. Stephen's heart began slowly to fold and fade with fear like a withering flower.   195
The rector went on gravely:
—You are all familiar with the story of the life of saint Francis Xavier, I suppose, the patron of your college. He came of an old and illustrious Spanish family and you remember that he was one of the first followers of saint Ignatius. They met in   200
Paris where Francis Xavier was professor of philosophy at the university. This young and brilliant nobleman and man of let=
ters entered heart and soul into the ideas of our glorious founder and you know that he, at his own desire, was sent by saint Ignatius to preach to the Indians. He is called, as you   205
know, the apostle of the Indies. He went from country to country in the east, from Africa to India, from India to Japan, baptising the people. He is said to have baptised as many as ten thousand idolaters in one month. It is said that his right arm had grown powerless from having been raised so often over the   210
heads of those whom he baptised. He wished then to go to China to win still more souls for God but he died of fever on the island of Sancian.[8] A great saint, saint Francis Xavier! A great soldier of God!
The rector paused and then, shaking his clasped hands be=   215
fore him, went on:
—He had the faith in him that moves mountains. Ten thou=
sand souls won for God in a single month! That is a true conqueror, true to the motto of our order *ad majorem Dei*

183 Friday] Eg; Fridays MS   183 confessions] MS; confession Eg–64

8. Off the Chinese coast.

gloriam! A saint who has great power in heaven, remember: 220
power to intercede for us in our grief, power to obtain what=
ever we pray for if it be for the good of our souls, power above
all to obtain for us the grace to repent if we be in sin. A great
saint, saint Francis Xavier! A great fisher of souls![9]

He ceased to shake his clasped hands and, resting them   225
against his forehead, looked right and left of them keenly at his
listeners out of his dark stern eyes.

In the silence their dark fire kindled the dusk into a tawny
glow. Stephen's heart had withered up like a flower of the
desert that feels the simoom[1] coming from afar.   230

◆   ◆   ◆

—*Remember only thy last things and thou shalt not sin for
ever*—words taken, my dear little brothers in Christ, from the
book of Ecclesiastes, seventh chapter, fortieth verse.[2] In the
name of the Father and of the Son and of the Holy Ghost.
Amen.   235

Stephen sat in the front bench of the chapel. Father Arnall
sat at a table to the left of the altar. He wore about his shoul=
ders a heavy cloak; his pale face was drawn and his voice
broken with rheum. The figure of his old master, so strangely
rearisen, brought back to Stephen's mind his life at Clongowes: 240
the wide playgrounds, swarming with boys, the square ditch,
the little cemetery off the main avenue of limes where he had
dreamed of being buried, the firelight on the wall of the infirm=
ary where he lay sick, the sorrowful face of Brother Michael.
His soul, as these memories came back to him, became again a   245
child's soul.

—We are assembled here today, my dear little brothers in
Christ, for one brief moment far away from the busy bustle of
the outer world to celebrate and to honour one of the greatest
of saints, the apostle of the Indies, the patron saint also of your   250
college, saint Francis Xavier. Year after year for much longer
than any of you, my dear little boys, can remember or than I
can remember the boys of this college have met in this very
chapel to make their annual retreat before the feast day of their
patron saint. Time has gone on and brought with it its changes.   255
Even in the last few years what changes can most of you not

242 limes] Eg; chestnuts MS

9. The implied comparison is to Jesus's disciples Peter and Andrew, to whom Jesus said,
"Come, follow me, and I will make you fishers of men" (Matthew 4:19).
1. A hot, dry wind carrying dust (*OED*).
2. From Ecclesiasticus (see note 7, p. 91): "In all thy works remember thy last end, and thou
shalt never sin" (7:40).

remember? Many of the boys who sat in those front benches a few short years ago are perhaps now in distant lands, in the burning tropics or immersed in professional duties or in sem= inaries or voyaging over the vast expanse of the deep or, it may 260 be, already called by the great God to another life and to the rendering up of their stewardship. And still as the years roll by, bringing with them changes for good and bad, the memory of the great saint is honoured by the boys of his college who make every year their annual retreat on the days preceding the feast 265 day set apart by our holy mother the church to transmit to all the ages the name and fame of one of the greatest sons of catholic Spain.

Now what is the meaning of this word *retreat* and why is it allowed on all hands to be a most salutary practice for all who 270 desire to lead before God and in the eyes of men a truly chris= tian life? A retreat, my dear boys, signifies a withdrawal for a while from the cares of our life, the cares of this workaday world, in order to examine the state of our conscience, to reflect on the mysteries of holy religion and to understand 275 better why we are here in this world. During these few days I intend to put before you some thoughts concerning the four last things. They are, as you know from your catechism, death, judgment, hell and heaven. We shall try to understand them fully during these few days so that we may derive from the 280 understanding of them a lasting benefit to our souls. And re= member, my dear boys, that we have been sent into this world for one thing and for one thing alone: to do God's holy will and to save our immortal souls. All else is worthless. One thing alone is needful, the salvation of one's soul. What doth it profit 285 a man to gain the whole world if he suffer the loss of his immortal soul?[3] Ah, my dear boys, believe me there is nothing in this wretched world that can make up for such a loss.

I will ask you therefore, my dear boys, to put away from your minds during these few days all worldly thoughts, 290 whether of study or pleasure or ambition, and to give all your attention to the state of your souls. I need hardly remind you that during the days of the retreat all boys are expected to preserve a quiet and pious demeanour and to shun all loud unseemly pleasure. The elder boys, of course, will see that this 295 custom is not infringed and I look especially to the prefects and

258 short] MS; ABSENT Eg–64   269 Now] PARAGRAPH INDENT MS; DIALOGUE DASH 16–64: HERE AND THROUGHOUT SERMONS

3. Based on Matthew 16:26: "For what doth it profit a man, if he gain the whole world, and suffer the loss of his own soul?"

officers of the sodality of Our Blessed Lady and of the sodality of the holy angels to set a good example to their fellowstu= dents.

Let us try therefore to make this retreat in honour of saint Francis with our whole heart and our whole mind. God's bless= ing will then be upon all your year's studies. But, above and beyond all, let this retreat be one to which you can look back in after years when maybe you are far from this college and among very different surroundings, to which you can look back with joy and thankfulness and give thanks to God for having granted you this occasion of laying the first foundation of a pious honourable zealous christian life. And if, as may so happen, there be at this moment in these benches any poor soul which has had the unutterable misfortune to lose God's holy grace and to fall into grievous sin I fervently trust and pray that this retreat may be the turningpoint in the life of that soul. I pray to God through the merits of His zealous servant Francis Xavier that such a soul may be led to sincere repentance and that the holy communion on saint Francis' day of this year may be a lasting covenant between God and that soul. For just and unjust, for saint and sinner alike, may this retreat be a mem= orable one.

Help me, my dear little brothers in Christ. Help me by your pious attention, by your own devotion, by your outward de= meanour. Banish from your minds all worldly thoughts and think only of the last things, death, judgment, hell and heaven. He who remembers these things, says Ecclesiastes, shall not sin for ever. He who remembers the last things will act and think with them always before his eyes. He will live a good life and die a good death, believing and knowing that, if he has sacri= ficed much in this earthly life, it will be given to him a hundredfold and a thousandfold more in the life to come, in the kingdom without end—a blessing, my dear boys, which I wish you from my heart; one and all, in the name of the Father and of the Son and of the Holy Ghost. Amen.

As he walked home with silent companions a thick fog seemed to compass his mind. He waited in stupor of mind till it should lift and reveal what it had hidden. He ate his dinner with surly appetite and, when the meal was over and the greasestrewn plates lay abandoned on the table, he rose and went to the window, clearing the thick scum from his mouth with his tongue and licking it from his lips. So he had sunk to the state of a beast that licks his chaps after meat. This was the

end: and a faint glimmer of fear began to pierce the fog of his   340
mind. He pressed his face against the pane of the window and
gazed out into the darkening street. Forms passed this way and
that way through the dull light. And that was life. The letters
of the name of Dublin lay heavily upon his mind, pushing one
another surlily hither and thither with slow boorish insistence.   345
His soul was fattening and congealing into a gross grease,
plunging ever deeper in its dull fear into a sombre threatening
dusk, while the body that was his stood, listless and dishon=
oured, gazing out of darkened eyes, helpless, perturbed and
human for a bovine god to stare upon.   350

The next day brought death and judgment, stirring his soul
slowly from its listless despair. The faint glimmer of fear be=
came a terror of spirit as the hoarse voice of the preacher blew
death into his soul. He suffered its agony. He felt the deathchill
touch the extremities and creep onward towards the heart, the   355
film of death veiling the eyes, the bright centres of the brain
extinguished one by one like lamps, the last sweat oozing upon
the skin, the powerlessness of the dying limbs, the speech
thickening and wandering and failing, the heart throbbing
faintly and more faintly, all but vanquished, the breath, the   360
poor timid breath, the poor helpless human spirit, sobbing and
sighing, gurgling and rattling in the throat. No help! No help!
He, he himself, his body to which he had yielded was dying.
Into the grave with it! Nail it down into a wooden box, the
corpse. Carry it out of the house on the shoulders of hirelings.   365
Thrust it out of men's sight into a long hole in the ground, into
the grave, to rot, to feed the mass of its creeping worms and to
be devoured by scuttling plumpbellied rats.

And while the friends were still standing in tears by the
bedside the soul of the sinner was judged. At the last moment   370
of consciousness the whole earthly life passed before the vision
of the soul and, ere it had time to reflect, the body had died and
the soul stood terrified before the judgmentseat. God, who had
long been merciful, would then be just. He had long been
patient, pleading with the sinful soul, giving it time to repent,   375
sparing it yet awhile. But that time had gone. Time was to sin
and to enjoy, time was to scoff at God and at the warnings of
His holy church, time was to defy His majesty, to disobey His
commands, to hoodwink one's fellow men, to commit sin after
sin and sin after sin and to hide one's corruption from the sight   380
of men. But that time was over. Now it was God's turn: and He
was not to be hoodwinked or deceived. Every sin would then

come forth from its lurkingplace, the most rebellious against
the divine will and the most degrading to our poor corrupt
nature, the tiniest imperfection and the most heinous atrocity.   385
What did it avail then to have been a great emperor, a great
general, a marvellous inventor, the most learned of the learned?
All were as one before the judgmentseat of God. He would
reward the good and punish the wicked. One single instant was
enough for the trial of a man's soul. One single instant after the   390
body's death, the soul had been weighed in the balance. The
particular judgment was over and the soul had passed to the
abode of bliss or to the prison of purgatory or had been hurled
howling into hell.

   Nor was that all. God's justice had still to be vindicated   395
before men: after the particular there still remained the general
judgment. The last day had come. The doomsday was at hand.
The stars of heaven were falling upon the earth like the figs
cast by the figtree which the wind has shaken. The sun, the
great luminary of the universe, had become as sackcloth of   400
hair. The moon was bloodred. The firmament was as a scroll
rolled away. The archangel Michael, the prince of the heavenly
host, appeared glorious and terrible against the sky. With one
foot on the sea and one foot on the land he blew from the
archangelical trumpet the brazen death of time. The three   405
blasts of the angel filled all the universe. Time is, time was but
time shall be no more. At the last blast the souls of universal
humanity throng towards the valley of Jehoshaphat, rich and
poor, gentle and simple, wise and foolish, good and wicked.
The soul of every human being that has ever existed, the souls   410
of all those who shall yet be born, all the sons and daughters of
Adam, all are assembled on that supreme day. And lo the
supreme judge is coming! No longer the lowly Lamb of God,
no longer the meek Jesus of Nazareth, no longer the Man of
Sorrows, no longer the Good Shepherd, He is seen now coming   415
upon the clouds, in great power and majesty, attended by nine
choirs of angels, angels and archangels, principalities, powers
and virtues, thrones and dominations, cherubim and seraphim,
God Omnipotent, God Everlasting. He speaks: and His voice is
heard even at the farthest limits of space, even in the bottom=   420
less abyss. Supreme Judge, from His sentence there will be and
can be no appeal. He calls the just to His side bidding them
enter into the kingdom, the eternity of bliss prepared for them.
The unjust He casts from Him, crying in His offended majesty:
Depart from me, ye cursed, into everlasting fire which was   425

prepared for the devil and his angels.[4] O what agony then for the miserable sinners! Friend is torn apart from friend, children from their parents, husbands from their wives. The poor sinner holds out his arms to those who were dear and near to him in this earthly world, to those whose simple piety perhaps he made a mock of, to those who counselled him and tried to lead him on the right path, to a kind brother, to a loving sister, to the mother and father who loved him so dearly. But it is too late: the just turn away from the wretched damned souls which now appear before the eyes of all in their hideous and evil character. O you hypocrites, O you whited sepulchres, O you who present a smooth smiling face to the world while your soul within is a foul swamp of sin, how will it fare with you in that terrible day?

And this day will come, shall come, must come: the day of death and the day of judgment. It is appointed unto man to die and after death the judgment. Death is certain. The time and manner are uncertain, whether from long disease or from some unexpected accident: the Son of God cometh at an hour when you little expect Him. Be therefore ready every moment, seeing that you may die at any moment. Death is the end of us all. Death and judgment, brought into the world by the sin of our first parents, are the dark portals that close our earthly exist= ence, the portals that open into the unknown and the unseen, portals through which every soul must pass, alone, unaided save by its good works, without friend or brother or parents or master to help it, alone and trembling. Let that thought be ever before our minds and then we cannot sin. Death, a cause of terror to the sinner, is a blessed moment for him who has walked in the right path, fulfilling the duties of his station in life, attending to his morning and evening prayers, approaching the holy sacrament frequently and performing good and mer= ciful works. For the pious and believing catholic, for the just man, death is no cause of terror. Was it not Addison, the great English writer, who, when on his deathbed, sent for the wicked young earl of Warwick to let him see how a christian can meet his end? He it is and he alone, the pious and believing christian, who can say in his heart:

427 children] MS; children are torn Eg–64 MS   429 and near] MS; ABSENT Eg–64 MS
451 parents] MS; parent Eg–64

4. According to Jesus, this will be said to the damned, or goats, when they are separated from the sheep at the Last Judgment (Matthew 24:41).

O grave, where is thy victory?
O death, where is thy sting?[5]   465

Every word of it was for him. Against his sin, foul and
secret, the whole wrath of God was aimed. The preacher's
knife had probed deeply into his diseased conscience and he felt
now that his soul was festering in sin. Yes, the preacher was
right. God's turn had come. Like a beast in its lair his soul had   470
lain down in its own filth but the blasts of the angel's trumpet
had driven him forth from the darkness of sin into the light.
The words of doom cried by the angel shattered in an instant
his presumptuous peace. The wind of the last day blew through
his mind; his sins, the jeweleyed harlots of his imagination, fled   475
before the hurricane, squeaking like mice in their terror and
huddled under a mane of hair.

As he crossed the square, walking homeward, the light
laughter of a girl reached his burning ears. The frail gay sound
smote his heart more strongly than a trumpetblast, and, not   480
daring to lift his eyes, he turned aside and gazed, as he walked,
into the shadow of the tangled shrubs. Shame rose from his
smitten heart and flooded his whole being. The image of Emma
appeared before him and, under her eyes, the flood of shame
rushed forth anew from his heart. If she knew to what his mind   485
had subjected her or how his brutelike lust had torn and
trampled upon her innocence! Was that boyish love? Was that
chivalry? Was that poetry? The sordid details of his orgies stank
under his very nostrils: the sootcoated packet of pictures which
he had hidden in the flue of the fireplace and in the presence of   490
whose shameless or bashful wantonness he lay for hours sin=
ning in thought and deed: his monstrous dreams, peopled by
apelike creatures and by harlots with gleaming jewel eyes: the
foul long letters he had written in the joy of guilty confession
and carried secretly for days and days only to throw them   495
under cover of night among the grass in the corner of a field or
beneath some hingeless door or in some niche in the hedges
where a girl might come upon them as she walked by and read
them secretly. Mad! Mad! Was it possible he had done these

---

474 peace.] Eg; piece. MS   479 ears.] ear. Eg–64   482 shadow] Eg; shadows MS

5. "The Dying Christian to His soul," lines 17–18, by the English poet Alexander Pope
(1688–1744). Joseph Addison (1672–1719) collaborated with the Irish writer Sir Richard
Steele (1672–1729) and served as chief secretary for Ireland (1708–10, 1714–15), the
number two position in the English administration of the island. Although Pope is quoted
in this passage as if in harmony with Addison, the estrangement between the writers was
clear during their lives and in Pope's derision of Addison as "Atticus" in "An Epistle to
Dr. Arbuthnot" (1735).

things? A cold sweat broke out upon his forehead as the foul   500
memories condensed within his brain.

When the agony of shame had passed from him he tried to
raise his soul from its abject powerlessness. God and the
Blessed Virgin were too far from him: God was too great and
stern and the Blessed Virgin too pure and holy. But he imagined   505
that he stood near Emma in a wide land and, humbly and in
tears, bent and kissed the elbow of her sleeve.

In a wide land under a tender lucid evening sky, a cloud
drifting westward amid a pale green sea of heaven, they stood
together, children that had erred. Their error had offended   510
deeply God's majesty, though it was the error of two children,
but it had not offended her whose beauty *is not like earthly
beauty, dangerous to look upon, but like the morning star
which is its emblem, bright and musical.*[6] The eyes were not
offended which she turned upon them nor reproachful. She   515
placed their hands together, hand in hand, and said, speaking
to their hearts:
—Take hands, Stephen and Emma. It is a beautiful evening
now in heaven. You have erred but you are always my children.
It is one heart that loves another heart. Take hands together,   520
my dear children, and you will be happy together and your
hearts will love each other.

The chapel was flooded by the dull scarlet light that filtered
through the lowered blinds: and through the fissure between
the last blind and the sash a shaft of wan light entered like a   525
spear and touched the embossed brasses of the candlesticks
upon the altar that gleamed like the battleworn mail armour of
angels.

Rain was falling on the chapel, on the garden, on the college.
It would rain for ever, noiselessly. The water would rise inch   530
by inch, covering the grass and shrubs, covering the trees and
houses, covering the monuments and the mountain tops. All
life would be choked off, noiselessly: birds, men, elephants,
pigs, children: noiselessly floating corpses amid the litter of the
wreckage of the world. Forty days and forty nights the rain   535
would fall till the waters covered the face of the earth.

It might be. Why not?
—*Hell has enlarged its soul and opened its mouth without any
limits*—words taken, my dear little brothers in Christ Jesus,
from the book of Isaias, fifth chapter, fourteenth verse. In the   540

---

508 a(1)] the Eg—64   536 covered] Eg; had covered MS

6. From Newman's "The Glories of Mary for the Sake of Her Son" in *Discourses to Mixed Congregations,* quoted on p. 92.

name of the Father and of the Son and of the Holy Ghost. Amen.

The preacher took a chainless watch from a pocket within his soutane and, having considered its dial for a moment in silence, placed it silently before him on the table.   545

He began to speak in a quiet tone.

—Adam and Eve, my dear boys, were, as you know, our first parents and you will remember that they were created by God in order that the seats in heaven left vacant by the fall of Lucifer and his rebellious angels might be filled again. Lucifer,   550 we are told, was a son of the morning, a radiant and mighty angel; yet he fell: he fell and there fell with him a third part of the host of heaven: he fell and was hurled with his rebellious angels into hell. What his sin was we cannot say. Theologians consider that it was the sin of pride, the sinful thought con=   555 ceived in an instant: *non serviam: I will not serve.*[7] That instant was his ruin. He offended the majesty of God by the sinful thought of one instant and God cast him out of heaven into hell for ever.

Adam and Eve were then created by God and placed in   560 Eden, that lovely garden in the plain of Damascus resplendent with sunlight and colour, teeming with luxuriant vegetation. The fruitful earth gave them her bounty: beasts and birds were their willing servants: they knew not the ills our flesh is heir to, disease and poverty and death: all that a great and generous   565 God could do for them was done. But there was one condition imposed on them by God: obedience to His word. They were not to eat of the fruit of the forbidden tree.

Alas, my dear little boys, they too fell. The devil, once a shining angel, a son of the morning, now a foul fiend came to   570 them in the shape of a serpent, the subtlest of all the beasts of the field. He envied them. He, the fallen great one, could not bear to think that man, a being of clay, should possess the inheritance which he by his sin had forfeited for ever. He came to the woman, the weaker vessel, and poured the poison of his   575 eloquence into her ear, promising her (O, the blasphemy of that promise!) that if she and Adam ate of the forbidden fruit they would become as gods, nay as God Himself. Eve yielded to the wiles of the archtempter. She ate the apple and gave it also to

---

561 that--Damascus] that lovely garden ⌐¹in the plain of Damascus¹⌐ MS; in the plain of Damascus, that lovely garden Eg–64   563 and] Eg; are MS   570–571 to them] MS; ABSENT Eg–64

7. Based on Jeremias 2:20. See also note 3, p. 211.

Adam who had not the moral courage to resist her. The poison   580
tongue of Satan had done its work. They fell.

And then the voice of God was heard in that garden, calling
His creature man to account: and Michael, prince of the heav=
enly host, with a sword of flame in his hand appeared before
the guilty pair and drove them forth from Eden into the world,   585
the world of sickness and striving, of cruelty and disappoint=
ment, of labour and hardship, to earn their bread in the sweat
of their brow. But even then how merciful was God! He took
pity on our poor degraded first parents and promised that in
the fulness of time He would send down from heaven One who   590
would redeem them, make them once more children of God
and heirs to the kingdom of heaven: and that One, that
Redeemer of fallen man, was to be God's onlybegotten Son, the
Second Person of the Most Blessed Trinity, the Eternal Word.

He came. He was born of a virgin pure, Mary the virgin   595
mother. He was born in a poor cowhouse in Judea and lived as
a humble carpenter for thirty years until the hour of His
mission had come. And then, filled with love for men, He went
forth and called to men to hear the new gospel.

Did they listen? Yes, they listened but would not hear. He   600
was seized and bound like a common criminal, mocked at as a
fool, set aside to give place to a public robber, scourged with
five thousand lashes, crowned with a crown of thorns, hustled
through the streets by the jewish rabble and the Roman sol=
diery, stripped of His garments and hanged upon a gibbet and   605
His side was pierced with a lance and from the wounded body
of Our Lord water and blood issued continually.

Yet even then, in that hour of supreme agony, Our Merciful
Redeemer had pity for mankind. Yet even there, on the hill of
Calvary, He founded the holy catholic church against which, it   610
is promised, the gates of hell shall not prevail. He founded it
upon the rock of ages[8] and endowed it with His grace, with
sacraments and sacrifice, and promised that if men would obey
the word of His church they would still enter into eternal life
but if, after all that had been done for them, they still persisted   615
in their wickedness there remained for them an eternity of
torment: hell.

The preacher's voice sank. He paused, joined his palms for
an instant, parted them. Then he resumed:

—Now let us try for a moment to realise, as far as we can, the   620 ·
nature of that abode of the damned which the justice of an

589 pity] Eg; absent MS   589 first] MS; absent Eg–64 MS   612 it] Eg; absent MS

8. That is, Peter, referred to as "this rock" in Matthew 16:18.

offended God has called into existence for the eternal punish=
ment of sinners. Hell is a strait and dark and foulsmelling
prison, an abode of demons and lost souls, filled with fire and
smoke. The straitness of this prison house is expressly designed   625
by God to punish those who refused to be bound by His laws.
In earthly prisons the poor captive has at least some liberty of
movement, were it only within the four walls of his cell or in
the gloomy yard of his prison. Not so in hell. There, by reason
of the great number of the damned, the prisoners are heaped   630
together in their awful prison the walls of which are said to be
four thousand miles thick: and the damned are so utterly
bound and helpless that, as a blessed saint, saint Anselm, writes
in his book on similitudes,[9] they are not even able to remove
from the eye a worm that gnaws it.   635

They lie in exterior darkness. For, remember, the fire of hell
gives forth no light. As, at the command of God, the fire of the
Babylonian furnace lost its heat but not its light so, at the
command of God, the fire of hell, while retaining the intensity
of its heat, burns eternally in darkness. It is a neverending   640
storm of darkness, dark flames and dark smoke of burning
brimstone, amid which the bodies are heaped one upon another
without even a glimpse of air. Of all the plagues with which the
land of the Pharaohs was smitten one plague alone, that of
darkness, was called horrible. What name, then, shall we give   645
to the darkness of hell which is to last not for three days alone
but for all eternity?

The horror of this strait and dark prison is increased by its
awful stench. All the filth of the world, all the offal and scum
of the world, we are told, shall run there as to a vast reeking   650
sewer when the terrible conflagration of the last day has purged
the world. The brimstone too which burns there in such pro=
digious quantity fills all hell with its intolerable stench: and the
bodies of the damned themselves exhale such a pestilential
odour that, as saint Bonaventure says, one of them alone would   655
suffice to infect the whole world. The very air of this world,
that pure element, becomes foul and unbreathable when it has
been long enclosed. Consider then what must be the foulness of
the air of hell. Imagine some foul and putrid corpse that has
lain rotting and decomposing in the grave, a jellylike mass of   660
liquid corruption. Imagine such a corpse a prey to flames,
devoured by the fire of burning brimstone and giving off dense

623 a] aEg; ABSENT MS–Eg

9. Saint Anselm of Canterbury (1033–1109), a Benedictine theologian, wrote important
   treatises but not one on similitudes.

choking fumes of nauseous loathsome decomposition. And
then imagine this sickening stench, multiplied a millionfold and
a millionfold again from the millions upon millions of fetid   665
carcases massed together in the reeking darkness, a huge and
rotting human fungus. Imagine all this and you will have some
idea of the horror of the stench of hell.

But this stench is not, horrible though it is, the greatest
physical torment to which the damned are subjected. The   670
torment of fire is the greatest torment to which the tyrant has
ever subjected his fellowcreatures. Place your finger for a mo=
ment in the flame of a candle and you will feel the pain of fire.
But our earthly fire was created by God for the benefit of man,
to maintain in him the spark of life and to help him in the   675
useful arts whereas the fire of hell is of another quality and was
created by God to torture and punish the unrepentant sinner.
Our earthly fire also consumes more or less rapidly according
as the object which it attacks is more or less combustible so
that human ingenuity has even succeeded in inventing chemical   680
preparations to check or frustrate its action. But the sulphu=
reous brimstone which burns in hell is a substance which is
specially designed to burn for ever and for ever with unspeak=
able fury. Moreover our earthly fire destroys at the same time
as it burns so that the more intense it is the shorter is its dur=   685
ation: but the fire of hell has this property that it preserves that
which it burns and though it rages with incredible intensity it
rages for ever.

Our earthly fire again, no matter how fierce or widespread it
may be, is always of a limited extent: but the lake of fire in hell   690
is boundless, shoreless and bottomless. It is on record that the
devil himself, when asked the question by a certain soldier, was
obliged to confess that if a whole mountain were thrown into
the burning ocean of hell it would be burned up in an instant
like a piece of wax. And this terrible fire will not afflict the   695
bodies of the damned only from without but each lost soul will
be a hell unto itself, the boundless fire raging in its very vitals.
O, how terrible is the lot of those wretched beings! The blood
seethes and boils in the veins, the brains are boiling in the skull,
the heart in the breast glowing and bursting, the bowels a   700
redhot mass of burning pulp, the tender eyes flaming like mol=
ten balls.

And yet what I have said as to the strength and quality and
boundlessness of this fire is as nothing when compared to its
intensity, an intensity which it has as being the instrument   705
chosen by divine design for the punishment of soul and body
alike. It is a fire which proceeds directly from the ire of God,

working not of its own activity but as an instrument of divine
vengeance. As the waters of baptism cleanse the soul with the
body so do the fires of punishment torture the spirit with the   710
flesh. Every sense of the flesh is tortured and every faculty of
the soul therewith: the eyes with impenetrable utter darkness,
the nose with noisome odours, the ears with yells and howls
and execrations, the taste with foul matter, leprous corruption,
nameless suffocating filth, the touch with redhot goads and   715
spikes, with cruel tongues of flame. And through the several
torments of the senses the immortal soul is tortured eternally in
its very essence amid the leagues upon leagues of glowing fires
kindled in the abyss by the offended majesty of the Omnipotent
God and fanned into everlasting and ever increasing fury by the   720
breath of the anger of the Godhead.

Consider finally that the torment of this infernal prison is
increased by the company of the damned themselves. Evil com=
pany on earth is so noxious that even the plants, as if by
instinct, withdraw from the company of whatsoever is deadly   725
or hurtful to them. In hell all laws are overturned: there is no
thought of family or country, of ties or relationship. The
damned howl and scream at one another, their torture and rage
intensified by the presence of beings tortured and raging like
themselves. All sense of humanity is forgotten. The yells of the 730
suffering sinners fill the remotest corners of the vast abyss. The
mouths of the damned are full of blasphemies against God and
of hatred for their fellow sufferers and of curses against those
souls which were their accomplices in sin. In olden times it was
the custom to punish the parricide, the man who had raised his   735
murderous hand against his father, by casting him into the
depths of the sea in a sack in which were placed a cock, a
monkey and a serpent. The intention of those lawgivers who
framed such a law, which seems cruel in our times, was to
punish the criminal by the company of hateful and hurtful   740
beasts. But what is the fury of those dumb beasts compared
with the fury of execration which bursts from the parched lips
and aching throats of the damned in hell when they behold in
their companions in misery those who aided and abetted them
in sin, those whose words sowed the first seeds of evil thinking 745
and evil living in their minds, those whose immodest sugges=
tions led them on to sin, those whose eyes tempted and allured
them from the path of virtue. They turn upon those accom=

718 leagues(2)] Eg; ABSENT MS   727 or relationship.] of relationship. Eg; of relationships. 16–64

plices and upbraid them and curse them. But they are helpless
and hopeless: it is too late now for repentance.   750

Last of all consider the frightful torment to those damned
souls, tempters and tempted alike, of the company of the devils.
These devils will afflict the damned in two ways, by their pres=
ence and by their reproaches. We can have no idea of how
horrible these devils are. Saint Catherine of Siena once saw a   755
devil and she has written that, rather than look again for one
single instant on such a frightful monster, she would prefer to
walk until the end of her life along a track of red coals. These
devils, who were once beautiful angels, have become as hideous
and ugly as they once were beautiful. They mock and jeer at   760
the lost souls whom they dragged down to ruin. It is they, the
foul demons, who are made in hell the voices of conscience.
Why did you sin? Why did you lend an ear to the temptings of
fiends? Why did you turn aside from your pious practices and
good works? Why did you not shun the occasions of sin? Why   765
did you not leave that evil companion? Why did you not give
up that lewd habit, that impure habit? Why did you not listen
to the counsels of your confessor? Why did you not, even after
you had fallen the first or the second or the third or the fourth
or the hundredth time, repent of your evil ways and turn to   770
God who only waited for your repentance to absolve you of
your sins? Now the time for repentance has gone by. Time is,
time was but time shall be no more! Time was to sin in secrecy,
to indulge in that sloth and pride, to covet the unlawful, to
yield to the promptings of your lower nature, to live like the   775
beasts of the field, nay worse than the beasts of the field for
they, at least, are but brutes and have not reason to guide them:
time was but time shall be no more. God spoke to you by so
many voices but you would not hear. You would not crush out
that pride and anger in your heart, you would not restore those   780
illgotten goods, you would not obey the precepts of your holy
church nor attend to your religious duties, you would not
abandon those wicked companions, you would not avoid those
dangerous temptations. Such is the language of those fiendish
tormentors, words of taunting and of reproach, of hatred and   785
of disgust. Of disgust, yes! For even they, the very devils, when
they sinned sinned by such a sin as alone was compatible with
such angelical natures, a rebellion of the intellect: and they,
even they, the foul devils must turn away, revolted and dis=
gusted, from the contemplation of those unspeakable sins by   790
which degraded man outrages and defiles the temple of the
Holy Ghost, defiles and pollutes himself.[1]

1. The body is referred to as the temple of the Holy Spirit in 1 Corinthians 6:18–19.

O, my dear little brothers in Christ, may it never be our lot
to hear that language! May it never be our lot, I say! In the last
day of terrible reckoning I pray fervently to God that not a   795
single soul of those who are in this chapel today may be found
among those miserable beings whom the Great Judge shall
command to depart for ever from His sight, that not one of us
may ever hear ringing in his ears the awful sentence of rejec=
tion: *Depart from me, ye cursed, into everlasting fire which*   800
was prepared for the devil and his angels![2]

He came down the aisle of the chapel, his legs shaking and
the scalp of his head trembling as though it had been touched
by ghostly fingers. He passed up the staircase and into the
corridor along the walls of which the overcoats and water=   805
proofs hung like gibbeted malefactors, headless and dripping
and shapeless. And at every step he feared that he had already
died, that his soul had been wrenched forth of the sheath of his
body, that he was plunging headlong through space.

He could not grip the floor with his feet and sat heavily at   810
his desk, opening one of his books at random and poring over
it. Every word for him! It was true. God was almighty. God
could call him now, call him as he sat at his desk, before he had
time to be conscious of the summons. God had called him. Yes?
What? Yes? His flesh shrank together as it felt the approach of   815
the ravenous tongues of flames, dried up as it felt about it the
swirl of stifling air. He had died. Yes. He was judged. A wave
of fire swept through his body: the first. Again a wave. His
brain began to glow. Another. His brain was simmering and
bubbling within the cracking tenement of the skull. Flames   820
burst forth from his skull like a corolla,[3] shrieking like voices:
—Hell! Hell! Hell! Hell! Hell!

Voices spoke near him:
—On hell.
—I suppose he rubbed it into you well.   825
—You bet he did. He put us all into a blue funk.[4]
—That's what you fellows want: and plenty of it to make you
work.

He leaned back weakly in his desk. He had not died. God
had spared him still. He was still in the familiar world of the 830
school. Mr Tate and Vincent Heron stood at the window,

---

2. The separation of the damned from the saved at the Last Judgment (Matthew 24:41);
   quoted on pp. 99–100.
3. Crown (*OED*).
4. Ill humor (*OED*).

talking, jesting, gazing out at the bleak rain, moving their
heads.

—I wish it would clear up. I had arranged to go for a spin on
the bike with some fellows out by Malahide.[5] But the roads   835
must be kneedeep.

—It might clear up, sir.

The voices that he knew so well, the common words, the
quiet of the classroom when the voices paused and the silence
was filled by the sound of softly browsing cattle as the other   840
boys munched their lunches tranquilly, lulled his aching soul.

There was still time. O Mary, refuge of sinners, intercede for
him! O Virgin Undefiled, save him from the gulf of death!

The English lesson began with the hearing of the history.
Royal persons, favourites, intriguers, bishops passed like mute   845
phantoms behind their veil of names. All had died: all had been
judged. What did it profit a man to gain the whole world if he
lost his soul? At last he had understood: and human life lay
around him, a plain of peace whereon antlike men laboured in
brotherhood, their dead sleeping under quiet mounds. The el=   850
bow of his companion touched him and his heart was touched:
and when he spoke to answer a question of his master he heard
his own voice full of the quietude of humility and contrition.

His soul sank back deeper into depths of contrite peace, no
longer able to suffer the pain of dread and sending forth, as she   855
sank, a faint prayer. Ah yes, he would still be spared; he would
repent in his heart and be forgiven: and then those above,
those in heaven, would see what he would do to make up for the
past: a whole life, every hour of life. Only wait.

—All, God! All, all!   860

A messenger came to the door to say that confessions were
being heard in the chapel. Four boys left the room; and he
heard others passing down the corridor. A tremulous chill blew
round his heart, no stronger than a little wind, and yet, listen=
ing and suffering silently, he seemed to have laid an ear against   865
the muscle of his own heart, feeling it close and quail, listening
to the flutter of its ventricles.

No escape. He had to confess, to speak out in words what he
had done and thought, sin after sin. How? How?

—Father, I . . .   870

The thought slid like a cold shining rapier into his tender
flesh: confession. But not there in the chapel of the college. He
would confess all, every sin of deed and thought, sincerely: but
not there among his school companions. Far away from there

5. Fishing village north of Dublin.

in some dark place he would murmur out his own shame: and   875
he besought God humbly not to be offended with him if he did
not dare to confess in the college chapel: and in utter abjection
of spirit he craved forgiveness mutely of the boyish hearts
about him.

Time passed.   880

He sat again in the front bench of the chapel. The daylight
without was already failing and, as it fell slowly through the
dull red blinds, it seemed that the sun of the last day was going
down and that all souls were being gathered for the judgment.

—*I am cast away from the sight of Thine eyes:* words taken,   885
my dear little brothers in Christ, from the Book of Psalms,
thirtieth chapter, twentythird verse. In the name of the Father
and of the Son and of the Holy Ghost. Amen.

The preacher began to speak in a quiet friendly tone. His
face was kind and he joined gently the fingers of each hand,   890
forming a frail cage by the union of their tips.

—This morning we endeavoured, in our reflection upon hell,
to make what our holy founder calls in his book of spiritual
exercises, the composition of place.[6] We endeavoured, that is, to
imagine with the senses of the mind, in our imagination, the   895
material character of that awful place and of the physical tor=
ments which all who are in hell endure. This evening we shall
consider for a few moments the nature of the spiritual torments
of hell.

Sin, remember, is a twofold enormity. It is a base consent to   900
the promptings of our corrupt nature, to the lower instincts, to
that which is gross and beastlike; and it is also a turning away
from the counsel of our higher nature, from all that is pure and
holy, from the Holy God Himself. For this reason mortal sin is
punished in hell by two different forms of punishment, physical   905
and spiritual.

Now of all these spiritual pains by far the greatest is the pain
of loss, so great, in fact, that in itself it is a torment greater
than all the others. Saint Thomas,[7] the greatest doctor of the
church, the angelic doctor, as he is called, says that the worst   910
damnation consists in this that the understanding of man is
totally deprived of divine light and his affection obstinately
turned away from the goodness of God. God, remember, is a
being infinitely good and therefore the loss of such a being

6. Saint Ignatius of Loyola's *Spiritual Exercises* stresses the efficacy in meditation of visual-
   izing the actual place being contemplated.
7. Saint Thomas Aquinas (1224 or 1225–1274), Dominican theologian, whose *Summa
   Theologica* eventually became central in Catholic thought.

must be a loss infinitely painful. In this life we have not a very 915
clear idea of what such a loss must be but the damned in hell,
for their greater torment, have a full understanding of that
which they have lost and understand that they have lost it
through their own sins and have lost it for ever. At the very
instant of death the bonds of the flesh are broken asunder and 920
the soul at once flies towards God. The soul tends towards
God as towards the center of her existence. Remember, my
dear little boys, our souls long to be with God. We come from
God, we live by God, we belong to God: we are His, inalien=
ably His. God loves with a divine love every human soul and 925
every human soul lives in that love. How could it be otherwise?
Every breath that we draw, every thought of our brain, every
instant of life proceed from God's inexhaustible goodness. And
if it be pain for a mother to be parted from her child, for a man
to be exiled from hearth and home, for friend to be sundered 930
from friend, O think what pain, what anguish it must be for
the poor soul to be spurned from the presence of the supremely
good and loving Creator Who has called that soul into exist=
ence from nothingness and sustained it in life and loved it with
an immeasurable love. This, then, to be separated for ever from 935
its greatest good, from God, and to feel the anguish of that
separation, knowing full well that it is unchangeable, this is the
greatest torment which the created soul is capable of bearing,
poena damni, the pain of loss.

The second pain which will afflict the souls of the damned in 940
hell is the pain of conscience. Just as in dead bodies worms are
engendered by putrefaction so in the souls of the lost there
arises a perpetual remorse from the putrefaction of sin, the
sting of conscience, the worm, as Pope Innocent the Third calls
it, of the triple sting. The first sting inflicted by this cruel worm 945
will be the memory of past pleasures. O what a dreadful mem=
ory will that be! In the lake of alldevouring flame the proud
king will remember the pomps of his court, the wise but wicked
man his libraries and instruments of research, the lover of ar=
tistic pleasures his marbles and pictures and other art treasures, 950
he who delighted in the pleasures of the table his gorgeous
feasts, his dishes prepared with such delicacy, his choice wines;
the miser will remember his hoard of gold, the robber his
illgotten wealth, the angry and revengeful and merciless mur=
derers their deeds of blood and violence in which they revelled, 955
the impure and adulterous the unspeakable and filthy pleasures
in which they delighted. They will remember all this and loathe
themselves and their sins. For how miserable will all those
pleasures seem to the soul condemned to suffer in hellfire for

ages and ages. How they will rage and fume to think that they   960
have lost the bliss of heaven for the dross of earth, for a few
pieces of metal, for vain honours, for bodily comforts, for a
tingling of the nerves. They will repent indeed: and this is the
second sting of the worm of conscience, a late and fruitless
sorrow for sins committed. Divine justice insists that the under=   965
standing of those miserable wretches be fixed continually on
the sins of which they were guilty and, moreover, as saint
Augustine[8] points out, God will impart to them His own
knowledge of sin so that sin will appear to them in all its
hideous malice as it appears to the eyes of God Himself. They   970
will behold their sins in all their foulness and repent but it will
be too late and then they will bewail the good occasions which
they neglected. This is the last and deepest and most cruel sting
of the worm of conscience. The conscience will say: You had
time and opportunity to repent and would not. You were   975
brought up religiously by your parents. You had the sacraments
and graces and indulgences[9] of the church to aid you. You had
the minister of God to preach to you, to call you back when
you had strayed, to forgive you your sins, no matter how many,
how abominable, if only you had confessed and repented. No.   980
You would not. You flouted the ministers of holy religion, you
turned your back on the confessional, you wallowed deeper
and deeper in the mire of sin. God appealed to you, threatened
you, entreated you to return to Him. O what shame, what
misery! The ruler of the universe entreated you, a creature   985
of clay, to love Him Who made you and to keep His law.
No. You would not. And now, though you were to flood all
hell with your tears if you could still weep, all that sea of
repentance would not gain for you what a single tear of true
repentance shed during your mortal life would have gained for   990
you. You implore now a moment of earthly life wherein to
repent: in vain. That time is gone: gone for ever.

Such is the threefold sting of conscience, the viper which
gnaws the very heart's core of the wretches in hell so that filled
with hellish fury they curse themselves for their folly and curse   995
the evil companions who have brought them to such ruin and
curse the devils who tempted them in life and now mock them
and torture them in eternity and even revile and curse the
Supreme Being Whose goodness and patience they scorned and
slighted but Whose justice and power they cannot evade.   1000

8. Early Church father (354–430), who wrote the *Confessions* and the *City of God*.
9. The seven Catholic sacraments are baptism, confirmation, the Eucharist, penance, matri-
    mony, ordination, and extreme unction. An indulgence is the remission of punishment
    for a sin (*OED*).

The next spiritual pain to which the damned are subjected is
the pain of extension. Man, in this earthly life, though he be
capable of many evils, is not capable of them all at once inas=
much as one evil corrects and counteracts another just as one
poison frequently corrects another. In hell on the contrary one   1005
torment, instead of counteracting another, lends it still greater
force: and moreover as the internal faculties are more perfect
than the external senses so are they more capable of suffering.
Just as every sense is afflicted with a fitting torment so is every
spiritual faculty; the fancy with horrible images, the sensitive   1010
faculty with alternate longing and rage, the mind and under=
standing with an interior darkness more terrible even than the
exterior darkness which reigns in that dreadful prison. The
malice, impotent though it be, which possesses these demon
souls is an evil of boundless extension, of limitless duration, a   1015
frightful state of wickedness which we can scarcely realise
unless we bear in mind the enormity of sin and the hatred God
bears to it.

Opposed to this pain of extension and yet coexistent with it
we have the pain of intensity. Hell is the center of all evils and,   1020
as you know, things are more intense at their centers than at
their remotest points. There are no contraries or admixtures of
any kind to temper or soften in the least the pains of hell. Nay,
things which are good in themselves become evil in hell. Com=
pany, elsewhere a source of comfort to the afflicted, will be   1025
there a continual torment: knowledge, so much longed for as
the chief good of the intellect, will there be hated worse than
ignorance: light, so much coveted by all creatures from the lord
of creation down to the humblest plant in the forest, will be
loathed intensely. In this life our sorrows are either not very   1030
long or not very great because nature either overcomes them by
habits or puts an end to them by sinking under their weight.
But in hell the torments cannot be overcome by habit for while
they are of terrible intensity they are at the same time of con=
tinual variety, each pain, so to speak, taking fire from another   1035
and reendowing that which has enkindled it with a still fiercer
flame. Nor can nature escape from these intense and various
tortures by succumbing to them for the soul in hell is sustained
and maintained in evil so that its suffering may be the greater.
Boundless extension of torment, incredible intensity of suffer=   1040
ing, unceasing variety of torture—this is what the divine
majesty, so outraged by sinners, demands, this is what the
holiness of heaven, slighted and set aside for the lustful and low

1020 all] MS; ABSENT Eg–64   1038 in hell] ABSENT Eg–64

pleasures of the corrupt flesh, requires, this is what the blood
of the innocent Lamb of God, shed for the redemption of   1045
sinners, trampled upon by the vilest of the vile, insists upon.

Last and crowning torture of all the tortures of that awful
place is the eternity of hell. Eternity! O dread and dire word.
Eternity! What mind of man can understand it? And, remem=
ber, it is an eternity of pain. Even though the pains of hell were   1050
not so terrible as they are yet they would become infinite as
they are destined to last for ever. But while they are everlasting
they are at the same time, as you know, intolerably intense,
unbearably extensive. To bear even the sting of an insect for all
eternity would be a dreadful torment. What must it be then to   1055
bear the manifold tortures of hell for ever. For ever! For all
eternity! Not for a year or for an age but for ever. Try to
imagine the awful meaning of this. You have often seen the
sand on the seashore. How fine are its tiny grains! And how
many of those tiny little grains go to make up the small handful   1060
which a child grasps in its play. Now imagine a mountain of
that sand, a million miles high, reaching from the earth to the
farthest heavens, and a million miles broad, extending to re=
motest space, and a million miles in thickness: and imagine
such an enormous mass of countless particles of sand multi=   1065
plied as often as there are leaves in the forest, drops of water in
the mighty ocean, feathers on birds, scales on fish, hairs on
animals, atoms in the vast expanse of the air: and imagine that
at the end of every million years a little bird came to that
mountain and carried away in its beak a tiny grain of that sand.   1070
How many millions upon millions of centuries would pass be=
fore that bird had carried away even a square foot of that
mountain, how many eons upon eons of ages before it had
carried away all. Yet at the end of that immense stretch of time
not even one instant of eternity could be said to have ended. At   1075
the end of all those billions and trillions of years eternity would
have scarcely begun. And if that mountain rose again after it
had been all carried away and if the bird came again and
carried it all away again grain by grain: and if it so rose and
sank as many times as there are stars in the sky, atoms in the   1080
air, drops of water in the sea, leaves on the trees, feathers upon
birds, scales upon fish, hairs upon animals, at the end of all
those innumerable risings and sinkings of that immeasurably
vast mountain not one single instant of eternity could be said to
have ended: even then, at the end of such a period, after that   1085
eon of time the mere thought of which makes our very brain
reel dizzily, eternity would have scarcely begun.

A holy saint (one of our own fathers I believe it was) was

once vouchsafed a vision of hell. It seemed to him that he stood in the midst of a great hall, dark and silent save for the ticking of a great clock. The ticking went on unceasingly; and it seemed to this saint that the sound of the ticking was the ceaseless repetition of the words: ever, never; ever, never. Ever to be in hell, never to be in heaven; ever to be shut off from the presence of God, never to enjoy the beatific vision;[1] ever to be eaten with flames, gnawed by vermin, goaded with burning spikes, never to be free from those pains; ever to have the conscience upbraid one, the memory enrage, the mind filled with darkness and despair, never to escape; ever to curse and revile the foul demons who gloat fiendishly over the misery of their dupes, never to behold the shining raiment of the blessed spirits; ever to cry out of the abyss of fire to God for an instant, a single instant, of respite from such awful agony, never to receive, even for an instant, God's pardon; ever to suffer, never to enjoy; ever to be damned, never to be saved; ever, never; ever, never. O what a dreadful punishment! An eternity of endless agony, of endless bodily and spiritual torment, without one ray of hope, without one moment of cessation, of agony limitless in extent, limitless in intensity, of torment infinitely lasting, infinitely varied, of torture that sustains eternally that which it eternally devours, of anguish that everlastingly preys upon the spirit while it racks the flesh, an eternity, every instant of which is itself an eternity, and that eternity an eternity of woe. Such is the terrible punishment decreed for those who die in mortal sin by an almighty and a just God.

Yes, a just God! Men, reasoning always as men, are aston=ished that God should mete out an everlasting and infinite pun=ishment in the fires of hell for a single grievous sin. They reason thus because, blinded by the gross illusion of the flesh and the darkness of human understanding, they are unable to comprehend the hideous malice of mortal sin. They reason thus because they are unable to comprehend that even venial sin[2] is of such a foul and hideous nature that even if the omnipotent Creator could end all the evil and misery in the world, the wars, the diseases, the robberies, the crimes, the deaths, the murders, on condition that He allowed a single venial sin to pass unpunished, a single venial sin, a lie, an angry look, a moment of wilful sloth, He, the great omnipotent God could not do so because sin, be it in thought or deed, is a trans=

---

1. Direct apprehension of God, reserved for the blessed in heaven.
2. A thought, word, or deed at odds with God's law but that is, by contrast with a mortal sin, pardonable (*Cath. Enc.*).

gression of His law and God would not be God if He did not 1130
punish the transgressor.

A sin, an instant of rebellious pride of the intellect, made
Lucifer and a third part of the cohorts of angels fall from their
glory. A sin, an instant of folly and weakness, drove Adam and
Eve out of Eden and brought death and suffering into the 1135
world. To retrieve the consequences of that sin the onlybegot=
ten Son of God came down to earth, lived and suffered and
died a most painful death, hanging for three hours on the cross.

O, my dear little brethren in Christ Jesus, will we then
offend that good Redeemer and provoke His anger? Will we 1140
trample again upon that torn and mangled corpse? Will we spit
upon that face so full of sorrow and love? Will we too, like the
cruel jews and the brutal soldiers, mock that gentle and com=
passionate Saviour Who trod alone for our sakes the awful
winepress of sorrow? Every word of sin is a wound in His 1145
tender side. Every sinful act is a thorn piercing His head. Every
impure thought, deliberately yielded to, is a keen lance trans=
fixing that sacred and loving heart. No, no. It is impossible for
any human being to do that which offends so deeply the divine
majesty, that which is punished by an eternity of agony, that 1150
which crucifies again the Son of God and makes a mockery of
Him.

I pray to God that my poor words may have availed today to
confirm in holiness those who are in a state of grace, to
strengthen the wavering, to lead back to the state of grace the 1155
poor soul that has strayed if any such be among you. I pray to
God, and do you pray with me, that we may repent of our sins.
I will ask you now, all of you, to repeat after me the act of
contrition, kneeling here in this humble chapel in the presence
of God. He is there in the tabernacle burning with love for 1160
mankind, ready to comfort the afflicted. Be not afraid. No
matter how many or how foul the sins if only you repent of
them they will be forgiven you. Let no worldly shame hold you
back. God is still the merciful Lord Who wishes not the eternal
death of the sinner but rather that he be converted and live. 1165

He calls you to Him. You are His. He made you out of
nothing. He loved you as only a God can love. His arms are
open to receive you even though you have sinned against Him.
Come to Him, poor sinner, poor vain and erring sinner. Now is
the acceptable time. Now is the hour. 1170

The priest rose and turning towards the altar knelt upon the
step before the tabernacle in the fallen gloom. He waited till all

1144 Who] ⟨w⟩ Who MS   1144 sakes] sake Eg–64

in the chapel had knelt and every least noise was still. Then
raising his head he repeated the act of contrition,[3] phrase by
phrase, with fervour. The boys answered him phrase by phrase. 1175
Stephen, his tongue cleaving to his palate, bowed his head,
praying with his heart.

> —*O my God!*—
> —*O my God!*—
> —*I am heartily sorry*—   1180
> —*I am heartily sorry*—
> —*for having offended Thee*—
> —*for having offended Thee*—
> —*and I detest my sins*—
> —*and I detest my sins*—   1185
> —*above every other evil*—
> —*above every other evil*—
> —*because they displease Thee, my God*—
> —*because they displease Thee, my God*—
> —*Who art so deserving*—   1190
> —*Who art so deserving*—
> —*of all my love*—
> —*of all my love*—
> —*and I firmly purpose*—
> —*and I firmly purpose*—   1195
> —*by Thy holy grace*—
> —*by Thy holy grace*—
> —*never more to offend Thee*—
> —*never more to offend Thee*—
> —*and to amend my life*—   1200
> —*and to amend my life*—

◆   ◆   ◆

He went up to his room after dinner in order to be alone
with his soul: and at every step his soul seemed to sigh: at every
step his soul mounted with his feet, sighing in the ascent,
through a region of viscid[4] gloom.   1205

He halted on the landing before the door and then, grasping
the porcelain knob, opened the door quickly. He waited in fear,
his soul pining within him, praying silently that death might
not touch his brow as he passed over the threshold, that the
fiends that inhabit darkness might not be given power over   1210
him. He waited still at the threshold as at the entrance to some
dark cave. Faces were there; eyes: they waited and watched.

3. Formal prayer expressing sorrow for having sinned; the specific prayer spoken in this
   instance follows.
4. Thick and adhesive, sticky.

—We knew perfectly well of course that though it was bound
to come to the light he would find considerable difficulty in
endeavouring to try to induce himself to try to endeavour to   1215
ascertain the spiritual plenipotentiary[5] and so we knew of
course perfectly well—

Murmuring faces waited and watched; murmurous voices
filled the dark shell of the cave. He feared intensely in spirit
and in flesh but, raising his head bravely, he strode into the   1220
room firmly. A doorway, a room, the same room, same win=
dow. He told himself calmly that those words had absolutely
no sense which had seemed to rise murmurously from the dark.
He told himself that it was simply his room with the door
open.   1225

He closed the door and, walking swiftly to the bed, knelt
beside it and covered his face with his hands. His hands were
cold and damp and his limbs ached with chill. Bodily unrest
and chill and weariness beset him, routing his thoughts. Why
was he kneeling there like a child saying his evening prayers?   1230
To be alone with his soul, to examine his conscience, to meet
his sins face to face, to recall their times and manners and
circumstances, to weep over them. He could not weep. He
could not summon them to his memory. He felt only an ache of
soul and body, his whole being, memory, will, understanding,   1235
flesh, benumbed and weary.

That was the work of devils, to scatter his thoughts and
overcloud his conscience, assailing him at the gates of the cow=
ardly and sincorrupted flesh: and, praying God timidly to
forgive him his weakness, he crawled up on to the bed and,   1240
wrapping the blankets closely about him, covered his face again
with his hands. He had sinned. He had sinned so deeply against
heaven and before God that he was not worthy to be called
God's child.

Could it be that he, Stephen Dedalus, had done those things?   1245
His conscience sighed in answer. Yes, he had done them, se=
cretly, filthily, time after time, and, hardened in sinful impeni=
tence, he had dared to wear the mask of holiness before the
tabernacle itself while his soul within was a living mass of
corruption. How came it that God had not struck him dead?   1250
The leprous company of his sins closed about him, breathing
upon him, bending over him from all sides. He strove to forget

1213 though] a16; although MS–16, 64   1247 time,] MS, a16; time aEg

5. An inflated way to refer to a priest or some other individual empowered to deal with
   spiritual difficulties, including sin; a spiritual ambassador, with full powers.

them in an act of prayer, huddling his limbs closer together and binding down his eyelids: but the senses of the soul would not be bound and, though his eyes were shut fast, he saw the places 1255 where he had sinned and, though his ears were tightly covered, he heard. He desired with all his will not to hear or see. He desired till his frame shook under the strain of his desire and until the senses of his soul closed. They closed for an instant and then opened. He saw. 1260

A field of stiff weeds and thistles and tufted nettlebunches. Thick among the tufts of rank stiff growth lay battered canis= ters and clots and coils of solid excrement. A faint marshlight struggled upwards from all the ordure through the bristling greygreen weeds. An evil smell, faint and foul as the light, 1265 curled upwards sluggishly out of the canisters and from the stale crusted dung.

Creatures were in the field; one, three, six: creatures were moving in the field, hither and thither. Goatish creatures with human faces, hornybrowed, lightly bearded and grey as india= 1270 rubber. The malice of evil glittered in their hard eyes, as they moved hither and thither, trailing their long tails behind them. A rictus of cruel malignity lit up greyly their old bony faces. One was clasping about his ribs a torn flannel waistcoat, an= other complained monotonously as his beard stuck in the 1275 tufted weeds. Soft language issued from their spittleless lips as they swished in slow circles round and round the field, winding hither and thither through the weeds, dragging their long tails amid the rattling canisters. They moved in slow circles, circling closer and closer, to enclose, to enclose, soft language issuing 1280 from their lips, their long swishing tails besmeared with stale shite, thrusting upwards their terrific faces . . . . .

Help!

He flung the blankets from him madly to free his face and neck. That was his hell. God had allowed him to see the hell 1285 reserved for his sins: stinking, bestial, malignant, a hell of lech= erous goatish fiends. For him! For him!

He sprang from the bed, the reeking odour pouring down his throat, clogging and revolting his entrails. Air! The air of heaven! He stumbled towards the window, groaning and al= 1290 most fainting with sickness. At the washstand a convulsion seized him within: and, clasping his cold forehead wildly, he vomited profusely in agony.

When the fit had spent itself he walked weakly to the win=

1254 the(2)] MS; his Eg–64   1256 ears] Eg; eyes MS   1257 or] a16; nor MS–16
1264 struggled] struggling Eg–24

dow and, lifting the sash, sat in a corner of the embrasure and 1295
leaned his elbow upon the sill. The rain had drawn off; and
amid the moving vapours from point to point of light the city
was spinning about herself a soft cocoon of yellowish haze.
Heaven was still and faintly luminous and the air sweet to
breathe, as in a thicket drenched with showers: and amid peace 1300
and shimmering lights and quiet fragrances he made a covenant
with his heart.

He prayed:

—*He once had meant to come on earth in heavenly glory but
we sinned: and then He could not safely visit us but with a* 1305
shrouded majesty and a bedimmed radiance for He was God.
So He came Himself in weakness not in power and He sent
thee, a creature in His stead, with a creature's comeliness and
lustre suited to our state. And now thy very face and form, dear
mother, speak to us of the Eternal; not like earthly beauty, 1310
dangerous to look upon, but like the morning star which is thy
emblem, bright and musical, breathing purity, telling of heaven
and infusing peace. O harbinger of day! O light of the pilgrim!
Lead us still as thou hast led. In the dark night, across the bleak
wilderness guide us on to our Lord Jesus, guide us home.[6] 1315

His eyes were dimmed with tears and, looking humbly up to
heaven, he wept for the innocence he had lost.

When evening had fallen he left the house and the first touch
of the damp dark air and the noise of the door as it closed
behind him made ache again his conscience, lulled by prayer 1320
and tears. Confess! Confess! It was not enough to lull the con=
science with a tear and a prayer. He had to kneel before the
minister of the Holy Ghost and tell over his hidden sins truly
and repentantly. Before he heard again the footboard of the
housedoor trail over the threshold as it opened to let him in, 1325
before he saw again the table in the kitchen set for supper he
would have knelt and confessed. It was quite simple.

The ache of conscience ceased and he walked onward swiftly
through the dark streets. There were so many flagstones on the
footpath of that street and so many streets in that city and so 1330
many cities in the world. Yet eternity had no end. He was in
mortal sin. Even once was a mortal sin. It could happen in an
instant. But how so quickly? By seeing or by thinking of seeing.
The eyes see the thing, without having wished first to see. Then
in an instant it happens. But does that part of the body under= 1335

1301 fragrances] fragrance Eg–64

6. The passage is nearly identical to one in Newman's "The Glories of Mary," quoted on
pp. 92 and 102.

stand or what? The serpent, the most subtle beast of the field. It must understand when it desires in one instant and then prolongs its own desire instant after instant, sinfully. It feels and understands and desires. What a horrible thing! Who made it to be like that, a bestial part of the body able to understand bestially and desire bestially? Was that then he or an inhuman thing moved by a lower soul than his soul? His soul sickened at the thought of a torpid snaky life feeding itself out of the tender marrow of his life and fattening upon the slime of lust. O why was that so? O why?

He cowered in the shadow of the thought, abasing himself in the awe of God Who had made all things and all men. Mad= ness. Who could think such a thought? And, cowering in darkness and abject, he prayed mutely to his angel guardian to drive away with his sword the demon that was whispering to his brain.

The whisper ceased and he knew then clearly that his own soul had sinned in thought and word and deed wilfully through his own body. Confess! He had to confess every sin. How could he utter in words to the priest what he had done? Must, must. Or how could he explain without dying of shame? Or how could he have done such things without shame? A madman, a loathsome madman! Confess! O he would indeed to be free and sinless again! Perhaps the priest would know. O dear God!

He walked on and on through illlit streets, fearing to stand still for a moment lest it might seem that he held back from what awaited him, fearing to arrive at that towards which he still turned with longing. How beautiful must be a soul in the state of grace when God looked upon it with love!

Frowsy girls sat along the curbstones before their baskets. Their dank hair hung trailed over their brows. They were not beautiful to see as they crouched in the mire. But their souls were seen by God; and if their souls were in a state of grace they were radiant to see: and God loved them, seeing them.

A wasting breath of humiliation blew bleakly over his soul to think of how he had fallen, to feel that those souls were dearer to God than his. The wind blew over him and passed on to the myriads and myriads of other souls on whom God's favour shone now more and now less, stars now brighter and now dimmer, sustained and failing. And the glimmering souls passed away, sustained and failing, merged in a moving breath. One soul was lost; a tiny soul: his. It flickered once and went out, forgotten, lost. The end: black cold void waste.

1365 baskets.] aEg; baskets of herrings. MS–Eg

Consciousness of place came ebbing back to him slowly over
a vast tract of time unlit, unfelt, unlived. The squalid scene   1380
composed itself around him; the common accents, the burning
gasjets in the shops, odours of fish and spirits and wet sawdust,
moving men and women. An old woman was about to cross
the street, an oilcan in her hand. He bent down and asked her
was there a chapel near.   1385

—A chapel, sir? Yes, sir. Church Street chapel.

—Church?

She shifted the can to her other hand and directed him: and,
as she held out her reeking withered right hand under its fringe
of shawl, he bent lower towards her, saddened and soothed by   1390
her voice.

—Thank you.

—You are quite welcome, sir.

The candles on the high altar had been extinguished but the
fragrance of incense still floated down the dim nave. Bearded   1395
workmen with pious faces were guiding a canopy out through
a sidedoor, the sacristan aiding them with quiet gestures and
words. A few of the faithful still lingered, praying before one of
the sidealtars or kneeling in the benches near the confessionals.
He approached timidly and knelt at the last bench in the body,   1400
thankful for the peace and silence and fragrant shadow of the
church. The board on which he knelt was narrow and worn
and those who knelt near him were humble followers of Jesus.
Jesus too had been born in poverty and had worked in the shop
of a carpenter, cutting boards and planing them, and had first   1405
spoken of the kingdom of God to poor fishermen, teaching all
men to be meek and humble of heart.

He bowed his head upon his hands, bidding his heart be
meek and humble that he might be like those who knelt beside
him and his prayer as acceptable as theirs. He prayed beside   1410
them but it was hard. His soul was foul with sin and he dared
not ask forgiveness with the simple trust of those whom Jesus,
in the mysterious ways of God, had called first to His side, the
carpenters, the fishermen, poor and simple people following a
lowly trade, handling and shaping the wood of trees, mending   1415
their nets with patience.

A tall figure came down the aisle and the penitents stirred:
and, at the last moment glancing up swiftly, he saw a long grey
beard and the brown habit of a capuchin.[7] The priest entered
the box and was hidden. Two penitents rose and entered the   1420

---

7. The Capuchin monks, a division of the Franciscans, are named for the cowl (Italian,
   cappuccio) that is part of their brown, white-belted habits (*OED*).

confessional at either side. The wooden slide was drawn back and the faint murmur of a voice troubled the silence.

His blood began to murmur in his veins, murmuring like a sinful city summoned from its sleep to hear its doom. Little flakes of fire fell and powdery ashes fell softly, alighting on the houses of men. They stirred, waking from sleep, troubled by the heated air.

The slide was shot back. The penitent emerged from the side of the box. The farther slide was drawn. A woman entered quietly and deftly where the first penitent had knelt. The faint murmur began again.

He could still leave the chapel. He could stand up, put one foot before the other and walk out softly and then run, run, run swiftly through the dark streets. He could still escape from the shame. O what shame! His face was burning with shame. Had it been any terrible crime but that one sin! Had it been murder! Little fiery flakes fell and touched him at all points, shameful thoughts, shameful words, shameful acts. Shame covered him wholly like fine glowing ashes falling continually. To say it in words! His soul, stifling and helpless, would cease to be.

The slide was shot back. A penitent emerged from the far= ther side of the box. The near slide was drawn. A penitent entered where the other penitent had come out. A soft whisper= ing noise floated in vaporous cloudlets out of the box. It was the woman: soft whispering cloudlets, soft whispering vapour, whispering and vanishing.

He beat his breast with his fist humbly, secretly under cover of the wooden armrest. He would be at one with others and with God. He would love his neighbour. He would love God Who had made and loved him. He would kneel and pray with others and be happy. God would look down on him and on them and would love them all.

It was easy to be good. God's yoke was sweet and light. It was better never to have sinned, to have remained always a child, for God loved little children and suffered them to come to Him. It was a terrible and a sad thing to sin. But God was merciful to poor sinners who were truly sorry. How true that was! That was indeed goodness.

The slide was shot to suddenly. The penitent came out. He was next. He stood up in terror and walked blindly into the box.

1425

1430

1435

1440

1445

1450

1455

1460

1435 O--shame.] ABSENT Eg—64

At last it had come. He knelt in the silent gloom and raised
his eyes to the white crucifix suspended above him. God could
see that he was sorry. He would tell all his sins. His confession
would be long, long. Everybody in the chapel would know then   1465
what a sinner he had been. Let them know. It was true. But
God had promised to forgive him if he was sorry. He was
sorry. He clasped his hands and raised them towards the white
form, praying with his darkened eyes, praying with all his
trembling body, swaying his head to and fro like a lost crea=   1470
ture, praying with whimpering lips.
—Sorry! Sorry! O sorry!
The slide clicked back and his heart bounded in his breast.
The face of an old priest was at the grating, averted from him,
leaning upon a hand. He made the sign of the cross and prayed   1475
of the priest to bless him for he had sinned. Then, bowing his
head, he repeated the *Confiteor*[8] in fright. At the words *my
most grievous fault* he ceased, breathless.
—How long is it since your last confession, my child?
—A long time, father.   1480
—A month, my child?
—Longer, father.
—Three months, my child?
—Longer, father.
—Six months?   1485
—Eight months, father.
    He had begun. The priest asked:
—And what do you remember since that time?
    He began to confess his sins: masses missed, prayers not
said, lies.   1490
—Anything else, my child?
    Sins of anger, envy of others, gluttony, vanity, disobedience.
—Anything else, my child?
    Sloth.
—Anything else, my child?   1495
    There was no help. He murmured:
—I . . . . committed sins of impurity, father.
    The priest did not turn his head.
—With yourself, my child?
—And . . . with others.   1500
—With women, my child?
—Yes, father.
—Were they married women, my child?

---

8. The prayer said at the beginning of confession.

He did not know. His sins trickled from his lips, one by one, trickled in shameful drops from his soul festering and oozing like a sore, a squalid stream of vice. The last sins oozed forth, sluggish, filthy. There was no more to tell. He bowed his head, overcome. 1505

The priest was silent. Then he asked:

—How old are you, my child? 1510

—Sixteen, father.

The priest passed his hand several times over his face. Then, resting his forehead against his hand, he leaned towards the grating and, with eyes still averted, spoke slowly. His voice was weary and old. 1515

—You are very young, my child, he said, and let me implore of you to give up that sin. It is a terrible sin. It kills the body and it kills the soul. It is the cause of many crimes and misfortunes. Give it up, my child, for God' sake. It is dishonourable and unmanly. You cannot know where that wretched habit will lead you or where it will come against you. As long as you commit that sin, my poor child, you will never be worth one farthing to God. Pray to our mother Mary to help you. She will help you, my child. Pray to Our Blessed Lady when that sin comes into your mind. I am sure you will do that, will you not? You repent of all those sins. I am sure you do. And you will promise God now that by His holy grace you will never offend Him any more by that wicked sin. You will make that solemn promise to God, will you not? 1520 1525

—Yes, father. 1530

The old and weary voice fell like sweet rain upon his quak= ing parching heart. How sweet and sad!

—Do so, my poor child. The devil has led you astray. Drive him back to hell when he tempts you to dishonour your body in that way—the foul spirit who hates Our Lord. Promise God now that you will give up that sin, that wretched wretched sin. 1535

Blinded by his tears and by the light of God's mercifulness he bent his head and heard the grave words of absolution spoken and saw the priest's hand raised above him in token of forgiveness.[9] 1540

—God bless you, my child. Pray for me.

He knelt to say his penance, praying in a corner of the dark nave: and his prayers ascended to heaven from his purified heart like perfume streaming upwards from a heart of white rose. 1545

9. That is, making the sign of the cross.

The muddy streets were gay. He strode homeward, con=
scious of an invisible grace pervading and making light his
limbs. In spite of all he had done it. He had confessed and God
had pardoned him. His soul was made fair and holy once more,
holy and happy.   1550

It would be beautiful to die if God so willed. It was beautiful
to live if God so willed, to live in grace a life of peace and
virtue and forbearance with others.

He sat by the fire in the kitchen, not daring to speak for
happiness. Till that moment he had not known how beautiful 1555
and peaceful life could be. The green square of paper pinned
round the lamp cast down a tender shade. On the dresser was a
plate of sausages and white pudding and on the shelf there were
eggs. They would be for the breakfast in the morning after the
communion in the college chapel. White pudding and eggs and 1560
sausages and cups of tea. How simple and beautiful was life
after all! And life lay all before him.

In a dream he fell asleep. In a dream he rose and saw that it
was morning. In a waking dream he went through the quiet
morning towards the college.   1565

The boys were all there, kneeling in their places. He knelt
among them, happy and shy. The altar was heaped with fra=
grant masses of white flowers: and in the morning light the pale
flames of the candles among the white flowers were clear and
silent as his own soul.   1570

He knelt before the altar with his classmates, holding the
altar cloth with them over a living rail of hands. His hands
were trembling: and his soul trembled as he heard the priest
pass with the ciborium[1] from communicant to communicant.
—*Corpus Domini nostri.*   1575

Could it be? He knelt there sinless and timid: and he would
hold upon his tongue the host and God would enter his purified
body.
—*In vitam eternam. Amen.*

Another life! A life of grace and virtue and happiness! It was 1580
true. It was not a dream from which he would wake. The past
was past.
—*Corpus Domini nostri.*[2]

The ciborium had come to him.

---

1. Covered receptacle for the consecrated wafers of the Eucharist.
2. Latin phrases, meaning "Unto life eternal," "Amen," and "The body of our Lord," spoken
   by priests during administration of the Eucharist.

IV

Sunday was dedicated to the mystery of the Holy Trinity,[1]
Monday to the Holy Ghost, Tuesday to the Guardian Angels,
Wednesday to saint Joseph, Thursday to the Most Blessed Sac=
rament of the Altar, Friday to the Suffering Jesus, Saturday to
the Blessed Virgin Mary.   5

Every morning he hallowed himself anew in the presence of
some holy image or mystery. His day began with an heroic
offering of its every moment of thought or action for the inten=
tions of the sovereign pontiff[2] and with an early mass. The raw
morning air whetted his resolute piety; and often as he knelt   10
among the few worshippers at the sidealtar, following with his
interleaved prayerbook[3] the murmur of the priest, he glanced up
for an instant towards the vested figure standing in the gloom
between the two candles which were the old and the new
testaments and imagined that he was kneeling at mass in the   15
catacombs.[4]

His daily life was laid out in devotional areas. By means of
ejaculations[5] and prayers he stored up ungrudgingly for the
souls in purgatory centuries of days and quarantines[6] and years;
yet the spiritual triumph which he felt in achieving with ease so   20
many fabulous ages of canonical penances did not wholly re=
ward his zeal of prayer since he could never know how much
temporal punishment he had remitted by way of suffrage for
the agonising souls: and, fearful lest in the midst of the purga=
torial fire, which differed from the infernal only in that it was   25
not everlasting, his penance might avail no more than a drop of
moisture, he drove his soul daily through an increasing circle of
works of supererogation.[7]

Every part of his day, divided by what he regarded now as
the duties of his station in life, circled about its own centre of   30
spiritual energy. His life seemed to have drawn near to eternity;
every thought, word and deed, every instance of consciousness

---

23 by--suffrage] ⁻¹by--suffrageˡ⁻ MS   32 instance] 16; instant MS–Eg

1. In Catholic doctrine, a mystery is something incomprehensible to human intelligence,
   such as the infinite, eternal nature of God (*Cath. Enc.*). On the Holy Trinity, see note 7,
   p. 27.
2. A heroic offering is a vow to donate all of one's good deeds to the spiritual well-being of
   another person, in this case the pope (*Cath. Enc.*).
3. Prayerbook supplemented with devotional material placed between the pages out of piety
   by the person using the book.
4. Subterranean tombs used by early Christians to hide their worship services from the
   Romans.
5. Short prayers emotionally performed.
6. Periods of forty days of strict ecclesiastical penance (*Cath. Enc.*).
7. Works that go beyond duty in an attempt to reach perfection (*Cath. Enc.*).

could be made to revibrate radiantly in heaven: and at times his
sense of such immediate repercussion was so lively that he
seemed to feel his soul in devotion pressing like fingers the   35
keyboard of a great cash register and to see the amount of his
purchase start forth immediately in heaven not as a number but
as a frail column of incense or as a slender flower.

The rosaries too which he said constantly (for he carried his
beads loose in his trousers' pockets that he might tell them as   40
he walked the streets) transformed themselves into coronals of
flowers of such vague unearthly texture that they seemed to
him as hueless and odourless as they were nameless. He offered
up each of his three daily chaplets[8] that his soul might grow
strong in each of the three theological virtues, in faith in the 45
Father Who had created him, in hope in the Son Who had
redeemed him and in love of the Holy Ghost Who had sanc=
tified him: and this thrice triple prayer he offered to the Three
Persons through Mary in the name of her joyful and sorrowful
and glorious mysteries.   50

On each of the seven days of the week he further prayed that
one of the seven gifts of the Holy Ghost[9] might descend upon
his soul and drive out of it day by day the seven deadly sins
which had defiled it in the past: and he prayed for each gift on
its appointed day, confident that it would descend upon him,   55
though it seemed to him strange at times that wisdom and
understanding and knowledge were so distinct in their nature
that each should be prayed for apart from the others. Yet he
believed that at some future stage of his spiritual progress this
difficulty would be removed when his sinful soul had been   60
raised up from its weakness and enlightened by the Third Per=
son of the Most Blessed Trinity. He believed this all the more
and with trepidation because of the divine gloom and silence
wherein dwelt the unseen Paraclete,[1] Whose symbols were a
dove and a mighty wind, to sin against Whom was a sin be=   65
yond forgiveness, the eternal, mysterious, secret Being to
Whom, as God, the priests offered up mass once a year, robed
in the scarlet of the tongues of fire.[2]

43 as(1)] ⌐¹as⌐ MS   45–48 the(2)--offered] Eg, aEg; the Father, in hope in the Son, in
charity in the Holy Ghost, and as daily offerings of thanksgiving MS   56 seemed]
⌐ˢseemedˢ⌐ MS   56 to--strange] strange to him Eg–64   68 the(1)] ⌐¹the⌐ MS   68 of--
fire.] ⌐¹of the tongues of fire⌐. MS

8. Three groups of fifty-five beads, each representing a prayer, that make up the rosary (OED).
9. Wisdom, understanding, counsel, fortitude, knowledge, piety, and fear of the Lord (Isaias
   11:2–3).
1. The Holy Spirit or Holy Ghost, the third person of the Trinity.
2. At Pentecost, the seventh Sunday after Easter (Whitsunday), the priests' red robes represent the descent of the Holy Spirit on the apostles as tongues of fire (Acts 2:3).

The imagery through which the nature and kinship of the
Three Persons of the Trinity were darkly shadowed forth in the   70
books of devotion which he read (the Father contemplating
from all eternity as in a mirror His Divine Perfections and
thereby begetting eternally the Eternal Son and the Holy Spirit
proceeding out of Father and Son from all eternity) were easier
of acceptance by his mind by reason of their august incompre=   75
hensibility than was the simple fact that God had loved his soul
from all eternity, for ages before he had been born into the
world, for ages before the world itself had existed. He had
heard the names of the passions of love and hate pronounced
solemnly on the stage and in the pulpit, had found them set   80
forth solemnly in books, and had wondered why his soul was
unable to harbour them for any time or to force his lips to utter
their names with conviction. A brief anger had often invested
him but he had never been able to make it an abiding passion
and had always felt himself passing out of it as if his very body   85
were being divested with ease of some outer skin or peel. He
had felt a subtle, dark and murmurous presence penetrate his
being and fire him with a brief iniquitous lust: it too had
slipped beyond his grasp leaving his mind lucid and indifferent.
This, it seemed, was the only love and that the only hate his   90
soul would harbour.

But he could no longer disbelieve in the reality of love since
God Himself had loved his individual soul with divine love
from all eternity. Gradually, as his soul was enriched with
spiritual knowledge, he saw the whole world forming one vast   95
symmetrical expression of God's power and love. Life became a
divine gift for every moment and sensation of which, were it
even the sight of a single leaf hanging on the twig of a tree, his
soul should praise and thank the Giver. The world for all its
solid substance and complexity no longer existed for his soul   100
save as a theorem of divine power and love and universality. So
entire and unquestionable was this sense of the divine meaning
in all nature granted to his soul that he could scarcely under=
stand why it was in any way necessary that he should continue
to live. Yet that also was part of the divine purpose and he   105
dared not question its use, he above all others who had sinned
so deeply and so foully against the divine purpose. Meek and
abased by this consciousness of the one eternal omnipresent
perfect reality his soul took up again her burden of pieties,
masses and prayers and sacraments and mortifications: and   110

78 He no paragraph] NEW PARAGRAPH Eg–64   105 also] MS; ABSENT Eg–64

only then for the first time since he had brooded on the great mystery of love did he feel within him a warm movement like that of some newly born life or virtue of the soul itself. The attitude of rapture in sacred art, the raised and parted hands, the parted lips and eyes as of one about to swoon, became for   115 him an image of the soul in prayer, humiliated and faint before her Creator.

But he had been forewarned of the dangers of spiritual exal= tation and did not allow himself to desist from even the least or lowliest devotion, striving also by constant mortification to   120 undo the sinful past rather than to achieve a saintliness fraught with peril. Each of his senses was brought under a rigorous discipline. In order to mortify the sense of sight he made it his rule to walk in the street with downcast eyes, glancing neither to right nor left and never behind him. His eyes shunned every   125 encounter with the eyes of women. From time to time also he balked them by a sudden effort of the will, as by lifting them suddenly in the middle of an unfinished sentence and closing the book. To mortify his hearing he exerted no control over his voice which was then breaking, neither sang nor whistled and   130 made no attempt to flee from noises which caused him painful nervous irritation such as the sharpening of knives on the knifeboard, the gathering of cinders on the fireshovel and the twigging[3] of the carpet. To mortify his smell was more difficult as he found in himself no instinctive repugnance to bad odours,   135 whether they were the odours of the outdoor world such as those of dung and tar or the odours of his own person among which he had made many curious comparisons and experi= ments. He found in the end that the only odour against which his sense of smell revolted was a certain stale fishy stink like   140 that of longstanding urine: and whenever it was possible he subjected himself to this unpleasant odour. To mortify the taste he practised strict habits at table, observed to the letter all the fasts of the church and sought by distraction to divert his mind from the savours of different foods. But it was to the mortifi=   145 cation of touch that he brought the most assiduous ingenuity of inventiveness. He never consciously changed his position in bed, sat in the most uncomfortable positions, suffered patiently every itch and pain, kept away from the fire, remained on his knees all through the mass except at the gospels,[4] left parts of   150

---

3. Beating (OED) or, possibly, brushing vigorously with a broom.
4. Rather than sitting part of the time, he remained on his knees except when everyone was expected to stand.

his neck and face undried so that the air might sting them and, whenever he was not saying his beads, carried his arms stiffly at his sides like a runner and never in his pockets or clasped behind him.

He had no temptations to sin mortally. It surprised him however to find that at the end of his course of intricate piety and selfrestraint he was so easily at the mercy of childish and unworthy imperfections. His prayers and fasts availed him little for the suppression of anger at hearing his mother sneeze or at being disturbed in his devotions. It needed an immense effort of his will to master the impulse which urged him to give outlet to such irritation. Images of the outbursts of trivial anger which he had often noted among his masters, their twitching mouths, closeshut lips and flushed cheeks, recurred to his memory, dis= couraging him, for all his practice of humility, by the compari= son. To merge his life in the common tide of other lives was harder for him than any fasting or prayer and it was his constant failure to do this to his own satisfaction which caused in his soul at last a sensation of spiritual dryness together with a growth of doubts and scruples. His soul traversed a period of desolation in which the sacraments themselves seemed to have turned into dried up sources. His confession became a channel for the escape of scrupulous and unrepented imperfections. His actual reception of the eucharist did not bring him the same dissolving moments of virginal selfsurrender as did those spiri= tual communions made by him sometimes at the close of some visit to the Blessed Sacrament.[5] The book which he used for these visits was an old neglected book written by saint Alphon= sus Liguori with fading characters and sere foxpapered leaves.[6] A faded world of fervent love and virginal responses seemed to be evoked for his soul by the reading of its pages in which the imagery of the canticles[7] was interwoven with the communi= cant's prayers. An inaudible voice seemed to caress the soul, telling her names and glories, bidding her arise as for espousal and come away, bidding her look forth, a spouse, from Amana and from the mountains of the leopards; and the soul seemed to answer with the same inaudible voice, surrendering herself:

155

160

165

170

175

180

185

151 the] ABSENT Eg–64   151–152 and, whenever--beads,] and ⁊¹, whenever--beads,ⁱʳ MS

5. Visits alone to the church, between masses, to pray.
6. Saint Alphonsus Liguori (1696–1787) wrote various books, including *The Visits to the Most Holy Sacrament,* the one probably meant here, whose pages have become foxed, or discolored by decay (*OED*).
7. The Old Testament book known as the Canticle of Canticles in the Catholic tradition and as the Song of Solomon (or Song of Songs) in the Protestant tradition. The Canticle pres-ents an allegory of the soul as the bride and lover of God.

Inter ubera mea commorabitur.[8]

This idea of surrender had a perilous attraction for his mind
now that he felt his soul beset once again by the insistent voices   190
of the flesh which began to murmur to him again during his
prayers and meditations. It gave him an intense sense of power
to know that he could, by a single act of consent, in a moment
of thought, undo all that he had done. He seemed to feel a
flood slowly advancing towards his naked feet and to be wait=   195
ing for the first faint timid noiseless wavelet to touch his
fevered skin. Then, almost at the instant of that touch, almost
at the verge of sinful consent, he found himself standing far
away from the flood upon a dry shore, saved by a sudden act of
the will or a sudden ejaculation: and, seeing the silver line of   200
the flood far away and beginning again its slow advance to=
wards his feet, a new thrill of power and satisfaction shook his
soul to know that he had not yielded nor undone all.

When he had eluded the flood of temptation many times in
this way he grew troubled and wondered whether the grace   205
which he had refused to lose was not being filched from him
little by little. The clear certitude of his own immunity grew
dim and to it succeeded a vague fear that his soul had really
fallen unawares. It was with difficulty that he won back his old
consciousness of his state of grace by telling himself that he had   210
prayed to God at every temptation and that the grace which he
had prayed for must have been given to him inasmuch as God
was obliged to give it. The very frequency and violence of
temptations showed him at last the truth of what he had heard
about the trials of the saints. Frequent and violent temptations   215
were a proof that the citadel of the soul had not fallen and that
the devil raged to make it fall.

Often when he had confessed his doubts and scruples, some
momentary inattention at prayer, a movement of trivial anger
in his soul or a subtle wilfulness in speech or act, he was bidden   220
by his confessor to name some sin of his past life before absol=
ution was given him. He named it with humility and shame and
repented of it once more. It humiliated and shamed him to
think that he would never be freed from it wholly, however
holily he might live or whatever virtues or perfections he might   225
attain. A restless feeling of guilt would always be present with
him: he would confess and repent and be absolved, confess and
repent again and be absolved again, fruitlessly. Perhaps that

214 heard] Eg; ABSENT MS   227 would] ⌐¹would¹⌐ MS

8. "He shall abide between my breasts" (Latin; Canticle 1:12).

first hasty confession wrung from him by the fear of hell had
not been good? Perhaps, concerned only for his imminent   230
doom, he had not had sincere sorrow for his sin? But the surest
sign that his confession had been good and that he had had
sincere sorrow for his sin was, he knew, the amendment of his
life.
—I have amended my life, have I not? he asked himself.   235

◆ ◆ ◆

The director stood in the embrasure of the window, his back
to the light, leaning an elbow on the brown crossblind and, as
he spoke and smiled, slowly dangling and looping the cord of
the other blind. Stephen stood before him, following for a mo=
ment with his eyes the waning of the long summer daylight   240
above the roofs or the slow deft movements of the priestly
fingers. The priest's face was in total shadow but the waning
daylight from behind him touched the deeply grooved temples
and the curves of the skull. Stephen followed also with his ears
the accents and intervals of the priest's voice as he spoke   245
gravely and cordially of indifferent themes, the vacation which
had just ended, the colleges of the order abroad, the transfer=
ence of masters. The grave and cordial voice went on easily
with its tale and in the pauses Stephen felt bound to set it on
again with respectful questions. He knew that the tale was a   250
prelude and his mind waited for the sequel. Ever since the
message of summons had come for him from the director his
mind had struggled to find the meaning of the message: and
during the long restless time he had sat in the college parlour
waiting for the director to come in his eyes had wandered from   255
one sober picture to another around the walls and his mind had
wandered from one guess to another until the meaning of the
summons had almost become clear. Then just as he was wish=
ing that some unforeseen cause might prevent the director from
coming he had heard the handle of the door turning and the   260
swish of a soutane.

The director had begun to speak of the dominican and fran=
ciscan orders and of the friendship between saint Thomas and
saint Bonaventure.[9] The capuchin dress, he thought, was rather
too   265

Stephen's face gave back the priest's indulgent smile and, not

256 had] ABSENT Eg–64

9. Saint Thomas Aquinas (see note 7, p. 111), and Saint Bonaventure (1221–1274), a Franciscan, would have known each other at the University of Paris.

being anxious to give an opinion, he made a slight dubitative
movement with his lips.

—I believe, continued the director, that there is some talk now
among the capuchins themselves of doing away with it and   270
following the example of the other franciscans.

—I suppose they would retain it in the cloister, said Stephen.

—O certainly, said the director. For the cloister it is all right
but for the street I really think it would be better to do away
with it, don't you?   275

—It must be troublesome, I imagine.

—Of course it is: of course. Just imagine, when I was in Bel=
gium I used to see them out cycling in all kinds of weather with
this thing up about their knees! It was really ridiculous. *Les
jupes*,[1] they call them in Belgium.   280

The vowel was so modified as to be indistinct.

—What do they call them?

—*Les jupes*.

—O.

Stephen smiled again in answer to the smile which he could   285
not see on the priest's shadowed face, its image or spectre only
passing rapidly across his mind as the low discreet accent fell
upon his ear. He gazed calmly before him at the waning sky,
glad of the cool of the evening and of the faint yellow glow
which hid the tiny flame kindling upon his cheek.   290

The names of articles of dress worn by women or of certain
soft and delicate stuffs used in their making brought always to
his mind a delicate and sinful perfume. As a boy he had imag=
ined the reins by which horses are driven as slender silken
bands and it had shocked him to feel at Stradbrooke the greasy 295
leather of harness. It had shocked him too when he had felt for
the first time beneath his tremulous fingers the brittle texture of
a woman's stocking for, retaining nothing of all he read save
that which seemed to him an echo or a prophecy of his own
state, it was only amid softworded phrases or within rosesoft   300
stuffs that he dared to conceive of the soul or body of a woman
moving with tender life.

But the phrase on the priest's lips was disingenuous for he
knew that a priest should not speak lightly on that theme. The
phrase had been spoken lightly with design and he felt that his 305
face was being searched by the eyes in the shadow. Whatever
he had heard or read of the craft of jesuits he had put aside

275 with it,] with, Eg–16, 64   281 was] ⌐was⌐ MS   289 of(3)] a16; ABSENT MS–16,
64   295 had] ABSENT Eg–64

1. "The skirts" (French).

frankly as not borne out by his own experience. His masters, even when they had not attracted him, had seemed to him always intelligent and serious priests, athletic and highspirited prefects. He thought of them as men who washed their bodies briskly with cold water and wore clean cold linen. During all the years he had lived among them in Clongowes and in Bel= vedere he had received only two pandies and, though these had been dealt him in the wrong, he knew that he had often escaped punishment. During all those years he had never heard from any of his masters a flippant word: it was they who had taught him christian doctrine and urged him to live a good life and, when he had fallen into grievous sin, it was they who had led him back to grace. Their presence had made him diffident of himself when he was a muff[2] in Clongowes and it had made him diffident of himself also while he had held his equivocal position in Belvedere. A constant sense of this had remained with him up to the last year of his school life. He had never once disobeyed or allowed turbulent companions to seduce him from his habit of quiet obedience: and, even when he doubted some statement of a master, he had never presumed to doubt openly. Lately some of their judgments had sounded a little childish in his ears and had made him feel a regret and pity as though he were slowly passing out of an accustomed world and were hearing its language for the last time. One day when some boys had gathered round a priest under the shed near the chapel he had heard the priest say:

—I believe that Lord Macaulay[3] was a man who probably never committed a mortal sin in his life, that is to say, a deliberate mortal sin.[4]

Some of the boys had then asked the priest if Victor Hugo were not the greatest French writer. The priest had answered that Victor Hugo had never written half so well when he had turned against the church as he had written when he was a catholic.

—But there are many eminent French critics, said the priest, who consider that even Victor Hugo, great as he certainly was, had not so pure a French style as Louis Veuillot.[5]

---

340 had written] aEg; wrote MS–Eg

2. Someone without skill, a beginner (colloquial; *OED*).
3. Thomas Babington Macaulay, 1st Baron Macaulay (1800–1859), English essayist and historian.
4. A mortal sin is by definition deliberate, that is, intended.
5. The contrast drawn between these two Frenchmen, Victor Hugo (1802–1885), a famous writer, and Louis Veuillot (1813–1883), a journalist who openly supported the Catholic Church, is unwarranted.

The tiny flame which the priest's allusion had kindled upon   345
Stephen's cheek had sunk down again and his eyes were still
fixed calmly on the colourless sky. But an unresting doubt flew
hither and thither before his mind. Masked memories passed
quickly before him: he recognized scenes and persons yet he
was conscious that he had failed to perceive some vital circum=   350
stance in them. He saw himself walking about the grounds
watching the sports in Clongowes and eating slim jim out of his
cricketcap. Some jesuits were walking round the cycletrack in
the company of ladies. The echoes of certain expressions used
in Clongowes sounded in remote caves of his mind.   355

His ears were listening to these distant echoes amid the si=
lence of the parlour when he became aware that the priest was
addressing him in a different voice.

—I sent for you today, Stephen, because I wished to speak to
you on a very important subject.   360
—Yes, sir.
—Have you ever felt that you had a vocation?

Stephen parted his lips to answer yes and then withheld the
word suddenly. The priest waited for the answer and added:
—I mean have you ever felt within yourself, in your soul, a   365
desire to join the order. Think.
—I have sometimes thought of it, said Stephen.

The priest let the blindcord fall to one side and, uniting his
hands, leaned his chin gravely upon them, communing with
himself.   370
—In a college like this, he said at length, there is one boy or
perhaps two or three boys whom God calls to the religious life.
Such a boy is marked off from his companions by his piety, by
the good example he shows to others. He is looked up to by
them; he is chosen perhaps as prefect by his fellow sodalists.   375
And you, Stephen, have been such a boy in this college, prefect
of Our Blessed Lady's sodality. Perhaps you are the boy in this
college whom God designs to call to Himself.

A strong note of pride reinforcing the gravity of the priest's
voice made Stephen's heart quicken in response.   380
—To receive that call, Stephen, said the priest, is the greatest
honour that the Almighty God can bestow upon a man. No
king or emperor on this earth has the power of the priest
of God. No angel or archangel in heaven, no saint, not even

the Blessed Virgin herself has the power of a priest of God: the   385
power of the keys, the power to bind and to loose from sin,[6] the
power of exorcism, the power to cast out from the creatures of
God the evil spirits that have power over them, the power, the
authority, to make the great God of Heaven come down upon
the altar and take the form of bread and wine. What an awful   390
power, Stephen!

A flame began to flutter again on Stephen's cheek as he
heard in this proud address an echo of his own proud musings.
How often had he seen himself as a priest wielding calmly and
humbly the awful power of which angels and saints stood in   395
reverence! His soul had loved to muse in secret on this desire.
He had seen himself, a young and silentmannered priest, en=
tering a confessional swiftly, ascending the altarsteps, in=
censing, genuflecting, accomplishing the vague acts of the
priesthood which pleased him by reason of their semblance of   400
reality and of their distance from it. In that dim life which he
had lived through in his musings he had assumed the voices and
gestures which he had noted with various priests. He had bent
his knee sideways like such a one, he had shaken the thurible[7]
only slightly like such a one, his chasuble[8] had swung open like   405
that of such another as he had turned to the altar again after
having blessed the people. And above all it had pleased him to
fill the second place in those dim scenes of his imagining. He
shrank from the dignity of celebrant because it displeased him
to imagine that all the vague pomp should end in his own   410
person or that the ritual should assign to him so clear and final
an office. He longed for the minor sacred offices, to be vested
with the tunicle of subdeacon[9] at high mass, to stand aloof from
the altar, forgotten by the people, his shoulders covered with a
humeral veil, holding the paten within its folds,[1] or when the   415
sacrifice had been accomplished, to stand as deacon in a dal=
matic of cloth of gold[2] on the step below the celebrant, his

385–386 the--keys,] ⌐¹the--keys¹ʳ MS   386–388 the (3)--them,] ⌐¹the--them,¹ʳ MS   406
had] ⌐¹had¹ʳ MS   407 him] ⌐¹him¹ʳ MS   412 minor sacred] ⌐¹minor sacrded¹ʳ MS
412–413 offices, to--tunicle] offices⌐¹, to--tunicle¹ʳ MS   413 subdeacon] aEg; ⌐¹sub-|¹ʳ
deacon MS; sub-deacon Eg   415 holding--folds,] ⌐¹holding--folds,¹ʳ MS   415 or] ⌐¹⟨and
then⟩ or¹ʳ MS   416 accomplished,] accomplish⟨ing⟩ed, MS   416 as deacon] ⌐¹⟨once
again⟩ as deacon¹ʳ MS

6. The power of entry to heaven by acting as confessor and giving absolution (Matthew
   16:19).
7. The container for burning incense during the mass.
8. Sleeveless outer vestment worn by a priest during the mass.
9. The short tunic worn by the assistant to the deacon; the deacon assists the priest.
1. The veil is a cloth that the subdeacon wears on his shoulder during mass to wrap sacred
   vessels when he touches them; these vessels include the paten, the plate for the consecrated Host.
2. The wide-sleeved vestment, open at the sides, that deacons wear during mass, of a fabric
   woven wholly or partially from gold.

hands joined and his face towards the people, and sing the
chant *Ite, missa est.*[3] If ever he had seen himself celebrant it was
as in the pictures of the mass in his child's massbook, in a   420
church without worshippers, save for the angel of the sacrifice,
at a bare altar and served by an acolyte scarcely more boyish
than himself. In vague sacrificial or sacramental acts alone his
will seemed drawn to go forth to encounter reality: and it was
partly the absence of an appointed rite which had always con=   425
strained him to inaction whether he had allowed silence to
cover his anger or pride or had suffered only an embrace he
longed to give.

He listened in reverent silence now to the priest's appeal and
through the words he heard even more distinctly a voice bid=   430
ding him approach, offering him secret knowledge and secret
power. He would know then what was the sin of Simon Magus[4]
and what the sin against the Holy Ghost[5] for which there was
no forgiveness. He would know obscure things, hidden from
others, from those who were conceived and born children of   435
wrath. He would know the sins, the sinful longings and sinful
thoughts and sinful acts, of others, hearing them murmured
into his ear in the confessional under the shame of a darkened
chapel by the lips of women and of girls: but rendered immune
mysteriously at his ordination by the imposition of hands his   440
soul would pass again uncontaminated to the white peace of
the altar. No touch of sin would linger upon the hands with
which he would elevate and break the host; no touch of sin
would linger on his lips in prayer to make him eat and drink
damnation to himself, not discerning the body of the Lord.[6] He   445
would hold his secret knowledge and secret power, being as
sinless as the innocent: and he would be a priest for ever
according to the order of Melchisedech.[7]

—I will offer up my mass tomorrow morning, said the direc=
tor, that Almighty God may reveal to you His holy will. And   450
let you, Stephen, make a novena to your patron saint, the first

---

421 worshippers, save--sacrifice,] worshippers ⌐|, save--sacrifice,|⌐ MS   425 an appointed]
⌐|⟨a⟩ an appointed|⌐ MS   438 ear] MS; ears Eg–64   451 patron] MS; holy patron Eg
[SETTING ERROR]–64

3. Latin words, meaning "Go, the mass is finished," spoken to release the congregation at
   the end of the mass.
4. The sin of simony, from Simon, known as "Magus" because he was considered a "sor-
   cerer" or "magician" (Latin), who tried to buy their spiritual powers from the apostles.
5. To sin against the Holy Ghost is to confound him with evil, to deny maliciously the divine
   character of divine works (*Cath. Enc.*); but the theological debates about the precise
   character of this sin may make it particularly mysterious for Stephen.
6. Without recognizing Christ's divine presence in the Host.
7. A priest mentioned in the Old Testament (Genesis 14:18), who is treated in the New Testament (Hebrews 5:6) as a precursor of Jesus; by implication a forerunner of Catholic priests.

martyr,[8] who is very powerful with God, that God may en=
lighten your mind. But you must be quite sure, Stephen, that
you have a vocation because it would be terrible if you found
afterwards that you had none. Once a priest always a priest,   455
remember. Your catechism tells you that the sacrament of Holy
Orders is one of those which can be received only once because
it imprints on the soul an indelible spiritual mark which can
never be effaced. It is before you must weigh well, not after. It
is a solemn question, Stephen, because on it may depend the   460
salvation of your eternal soul. But we will pray to God to=
gether.

He held open the heavy halldoor and gave his hand as if
already to a companion in the spiritual life. Stephen passed out
on to the wide platform above the steps and was conscious of   465
the caress of mild evening air. Towards Findlater's church a
quartet of young men were striding along with linked arms,
swaying their heads and stepping to the agile melody of their
leader's concertina. The music passed in an instant, as the first
bars of sudden music always did, over the fantastic fabrics of   470
his mind, dissolving them painlessly and noiselessly as a sudden
wave dissolves the sandbuilt turrets of children. Smiling at the
trivial air he raised his eyes to the priest's face and, seeing in it
a mirthless reflection of the sunken day, detached his hand
slowly which had acquiesced faintly in that companionship.   475

As he descended the steps the impression which effaced his
troubled selfcommunion was that of a mirthless mask reflecting
a sunken day from the threshold of the college. The shadow,
then, of the life of the college passed gravely over his conscious=
ness. It was a grave and ordered and passionless life that   480
awaited him, a life without material cares. He wondered how
he would pass the first night in the novitiate[9] and with what
dismay he would wake the first morning in the dormitory. The
troubling odour of the long corridors of Clongowes came back
to him and he heard the discreet murmur of the burning   485
gasflames. At once from every part of his being unrest began to
irradiate. A feverish quickening of his pulses followed and a din
of meaningless words drove his reasoned thoughts hither and
thither confusedly. His lungs dilated and sank as if he were
inhaling a warm moist unsustaining air and he smelt again the   490

---

458 an indelible] ⌐¹⟨a⟩ indelible¹⌐ MS   473 in] ⌐¹in¹⌐ MS

8. That is, make a devotion lasting nine days, dedicated to Saint Stephen, the first Christian
   martyr, who was stoned for blasphemy.
9. The probationary period before an aspiring priest can formally enter a religious order;
   also the residence for aspirants during that period.

warm moist air which hung in the bath in Clongowes above the sluggish turfcoloured water.

Some instinct, waking at these memories, stronger than edu= cation or piety, quickened within him at every near approach to that life, an instinct subtle and hostile, and armed him against acquiescence. The chill and order of the life repelled him. He saw himself rising in the cold of the morning and filing down with the others to early mass and trying vainly to struggle with his prayers against the fainting sickness of his stomach. He saw himself sitting at dinner with the community of a college. What then had come of that deeprooted shyness of his which had made him loth to eat or drink under a strange roof? What had come of the pride of his spirit which had always made him conceive himself as a being apart in every order?

The Reverend Stephen Dedalus, S. J.[1]

His name in that new life leaped into characters before his eyes and to it there followed a mental sensation of an unde= fined face or colour of a face. The colour faded and became strong like a changing glow of pallid brick red. Was it the raw reddish glow he had so often seen on wintry mornings on the shaven gills of the priests? The face was eyeless and sourfa= voured and devout, shot with pink tinges of suffocated anger. Was it not a mental spectre of the face of one of the jesuits whom some of the boys called Lantern Jaws and others Foxy Campbell?

He was passing at that moment before the jesuit house in Gardiner Street and wondered vaguely which window would be his if he ever joined the order. Then he wondered at the vagueness of his wonder, at the remoteness of his own soul from what he had hitherto imagined her sanctuary, at the frail hold which so many years of order and obedience had of him when once a definite and irrevocable act of his threatened to end for ever, in time and in eternity, his freedom. The voice of the director urging upon him the proud claims of the church and the mystery and power of the priestly office repeated itself idly in his memory. His soul was not there to hear and greet it and he knew now that the exhortation he had listened to had already fallen into an idle formal tale. He would never swing the thurible before the tabernacle as priest. His destiny was to be elusive of social or religious orders. The wisdom of the

501 come] MS; become Eg–64   513 pink] ⌐¹pink¹⌐ MS   520 own] ABSENT 16, 64

1. Society of Jesus, that is, a member of the Jesuits.

priest's appeal did not touch him to the quick. He was destined to learn his own wisdom apart from others or to learn the wisdom of others himself wandering among the snares of the world.   535

The snares of the world were its ways of sin. He would fall. He had not yet fallen but he would fall silently, in an instant. Not to fall was too hard, too hard: and he felt the silent lapse of his soul, as it would be at some instant to come, falling, falling but not yet fallen, still unfallen but about to fall.   540

He crossed the bridge over the stream of the Tolka[2] and turned his eyes coldly for an instant towards the faded blue shrine of the Blessed Virgin which stood fowlwise on a pole in the middle of a hamshaped encampment of poor cottages. Then, bending to the left, he followed the lane which led up to   545 his house. The faint sour stink of rotted cabbages came to= wards him from the kitchen gardens on the rising ground above the river. He smiled to think that it was this disorder, the misrule and confusion of his father's house and the stagnation of vegetable life, which was to win the day in his soul. Then a   550 short laugh broke from his lips as he thought of that solitary farmhand in the kitchen gardens behind their house whom they had nicknamed the man with the hat. A second laugh, taking rise from the first after a pause, broke from him involuntarily as he thought of how the man with the hat worked, considering   555 in turn the four points of the sky and then regretfully plunging his spade in the earth.

He pushed open the latchless door of the porch and passed through the naked hallway into the kitchen. A group of his brothers and sisters was sitting round the table. Tea was nearly   560 over and only the last of the second watered tea[3] remained in the bottoms of the small glassjars and jampots which did ser= vice for teacups. Discarded crusts and lumps of sugared bread, turned brown by the tea which had been poured over them, lay scattered on the table. Little wells of tea lay here and there on   565 the board and a knife with a broken ivory handle was stuck through the pith of a ravaged turnover.

The sad quiet greyblue glow of the dying day came through the window and the open door, covering over and allaying quietly a sudden instinct of remorse in Stephen's heart. All that   570 had been denied them had been freely given to him, the eldest:

2. Ballybough Bridge, over the Tolka River in north Dublin.
3. Weak tea, either watered to make it go further or brewed by using the tea leaves a second time, here because of financial difficulties.

but the quiet glow of evening showed him in their faces no sign
of rancour.

He sat near them at the table and asked where his father and
mother were. One answered:
—Goneboro toboro lookboro atboro aboro houseboro.

Still another removal! A boy named Fallon in Belvedere had
often asked him with a silly laugh why they moved so often. A
frown of scorn darkened quickly his forehead as he heard again
the silly laugh of the questioner.

He asked:
—Why are we on the move again, if it's a fair question?

The same sister answered:
—Becauseboro theboro landboro lordboro willboro putboro
usboro outboro.

The voice of his youngest brother from the farther side of
the fireplace began to sing the air *Oft in the Stilly Night.*[4] One
by one the others took up the air until a full choir of voices was
singing. They would sing so for hours, melody after melody,
glee after glee, till the last pale light died down on the horizon,
till the first dark nightclouds came forth and night fell.

He waited for some moments, listening, before he too took
up the air with them. He was listening with pain of spirit to the
overtone of weariness behind their frail fresh innocent voices.
Even before they set out on life's journey they seemed weary
already of the way.

He heard the choir of voices in the kitchen echoed and mul=
tiplied through an endless reverberation of the choirs of endless
generations of children: and heard in all the echoes an echo also
of the recurring note of weariness and pain. All seemed weary
of life even before entering upon it. And he remembered that
Newman had heard this note also in the broken lines of Virgil
*giving utterance, like the voice of Nature herself, to that pain
and weariness yet hope of better things which has been the
experience of her children in every time.*[5]

◆   ◆   ◆

He could wait no longer.

From the door of Byron's publichouse to the gate of Clon=
tarf[6] chapel, from the gate of Clontarf chapel to the door of
Byron's publichouse and then back again to the chapel and
then back again to the publichouse he had paced slowly at first

578 silly] ⌐¹silly⌐ᴵ MS

4. First, and identifying, line of a popular song from *National Airs*, by the Irish poet Thomas Moore (1779–1852).
5. From Cardinal Newman's *An Essay in Aid of a Grammar of Assent* (1870).
6. Clontarf is east of Dublin on Dublin Bay.

planting his steps scrupulously in the spaces of the patchwork
of the footpath, then timing their fall to the fall of verses. A full
hour had passed since his father had gone in with Dan Crosby,
the tutor, to find out from him something about the university.[7]
For a full hour he had paced up and down, waiting: but he   615
could wait no longer.

He set off abruptly for the Bull,[8] walking rapidly lest his
father's shrill whistle might call him back; and in a few mo=
ments he had rounded the curve at the police barrack and was
safe.   620

Yes, his mother was hostile to the idea as he had read from
her listless silence. Yet her mistrust pricked him more keenly
than his father's pride and he thought coldly how he had
watched the faith which was fading down in his soul aging and
strengthening in her eyes. A dim antagonism gathered force   625
within him and darkened his mind as a cloud against her dis=
loyalty: and when it passed cloudlike leaving his mind serene
and dutiful towards her again he was made aware dimly and
without regret of a first noiseless sundering of their lives.

The university! So he had passed beyond the challenge of the   630
sentries who had stood as guardians of his boyhood and had
sought to keep him among them, that he might be subject to
them and serve their ends. Pride after satisfaction uplifted him
like long slow waves. The end he had been born to serve yet
did not see had led him to escape by an unseen path: and now it 635
beckoned to him once more and a new adventure was about to
be opened to him. It seemed to him that he heard notes of fitful
music leaping upwards a tone and downwards a diminished
fourth, upwards a tone and downwards a major third, like
triplebranching flames leaping fitfully, flame after flame, out of 640
a midnight wood. It was an elfin prelude, endless and formless:
and, as it grew wilder and faster, the flames leaping out of
time, he seemed to hear from under the boughs and grasses
wild creatures racing, their feet pattering like rain upon the
leaves. Their feet passed in pattering tumult over his mind, the 645
feet of hares and rabbits, the feet of harts and hinds and ante=
lopes, until he heard them no more and remembered only a
proud cadence from Newman: *Whose feet are as the feet of
harts and underneath the everlasting arms.*[9]

7. This teacher could give advice and information about University College, Dublin, a
   Catholic institution founded in 1854 with Newman as rector and affiliated with the
   Jesuits from 1883 to 1908.
8. The seawall from Clontarf into Dublin Bay.
9. From Newman's *The Idea of the University Defined and Illustrated* (1852).

The pride of that dim image brought back to his mind the   650
dignity of the office he had refused. All through his boyhood he
had mused upon that which he had so often thought to be his
destiny and when the moment had come for him to obey the
call he had turned aside, obeying a wayward instinct. Now
time lay between: the oils of ordination would never anoint his   655
body. He had refused. Why?

He turned seaward from the road at Dollymount[1] and as he
passed on to the thin wooden bridge he felt the planks shaking
with the tramp of heavily shod feet. A squad of christian
brothers was on its way back from the Bull and had begun to   660
pass, two by two, across the bridge. Soon the whole bridge was
trembling and resounding. The uncouth faces passed him two
by two, stained yellow or red or livid by the sea and, as he
strove to look at them with ease and indifference, a faint stain
of personal shame and commiseration rose to his own face.   665
Angry with himself he tried to hide his face from their eyes by
gazing down sideways into the shallow swirling water under
the bridge but he still saw a reflection therein of their topheavy
silk hats and humble tapelike collars and loosely hanging cleri=
cal clothes.   670
—Brother Hickey.

Brother Quaid.

Brother MacArdle.

Brother Keogh.

Their piety would be like their names, like their faces, like   675
their clothes: and it was idle for him to tell himself that their
humble and contrite hearts, it might be, paid a far richer tribute
of devotion than his had ever been, a gift tenfold more accept=
able than his elaborate adoration. It was idle for him to move
himself to be generous towards them, to tell himself that if he   680
ever came to their gates, stripped of his pride, beaten and in
beggar's weeds, that they would be generous towards him,
loving him as themselves. Idle and embittering, finally, to ar=
gue, against his own dispassionate certitude, that the com=
mandment of love bade us not to love our neighbour as   685
ourselves with the same amount and intensity of love but to
love him as ourselves with the same kind of love.

He drew forth a phrase from his treasure and spoke it softly
to himself:

678 of] ⌐of⌐ MS   684 dispassionate] ⌐dis⌐passionate MS

1. Adjacent and to the north of Clontarf.

—A day of dappled seaborne clouds.[2]   690

The phrase and the day and the scene harmonised in a
chord. Words. Was it their colours?[3] He allowed them to glow
and fade, hue after hue: sunrise gold, the russet and green of
apple orchards, azure of waves, the greyfringed fleece of
clouds. No, it was not their colours: it was the poise and   695
balance of the period itself. Did he then love the rhythmic rise
and fall of words better than their associations of legend and
colour? Or was it that, being as weak of sight as he was shy of
mind, he drew less pleasure from the reflection of the glowing
sensible world through the prism of a language manycoloured   700
and richly storied than from the contemplation of an inner
world of individual emotions mirrored perfectly in a lucid
supple periodic prose?[4]

He passed from the trembling bridge on to firm land again.
At that instant, as it seemed to him, the air was chilled; and   705
looking askance towards the water he saw a flying squall dark=
ening and crisping suddenly the tide. A faint click at his heart, a
faint throb in his throat told him once more of how his flesh
dreaded the cold infrahuman odour of the sea: yet he did not
strike across the downs on his left but held straight on along   710
the spine of rocks that pointed against the river's mouth.

A veiled sunlight lit up faintly the grey sheet of water where
the river was embayed.[5] In the distance along the course of the
slowflowing Liffey slender masts flecked the sky and, more
distant still, the dim fabric of the city lay prone in haze. Like a 715
scene on some vague arras,[6] old as man's weariness, the image
of the seventh city of christendom was visible to him across the
timeless air, no older nor more weary nor less patient of subjec=
tion than in the days of the thingmote.[7]

Disheartened, he raised his eyes towards the slowdrifting   720
clouds, dappled and seaborne. They were voyaging across the
deserts of the sky, a host of nomads on the march, voyaging
high over Ireland, westward bound. The Europe they had come
from lay out there beyond the Irish Sea, Europe of strange
tongues and valleyed and woodbegirt and citadelled and of   725
entrenched and marshalled races. He heard a confused music

2. Remembered from Hugh Miller's *The Testimony of the Rocks* (1857), a theological tract,
   where Miller has "breeze-borne," rather than seaborne.
3. "Rhetorical modes or figures; ornaments of style or diction, embellishments" (*OED*).
4. Prose characterized by periodic sentences, in which the main clause or its verb is postponed until the end.
5. Formed into a bay.
6. Tapestry.
7. A mound, removed in the seventeenth century, where public councils were held during
   the Scandinavian occupation of Dublin from the ninth to the eleventh centuries.

within him as of memories and names which he was almost
conscious of but could not capture even for an instant; then the
music seemed to recede, to recede, to recede: and from each
receding trail of nebulous music there fell always one long=   730
drawn calling note, piercing like a star the dusk of silence.
Again! Again! Again! Again! A voice from beyond the world
was calling.

—Hello, Stephanos![8]
—Here comes The Dedalus!   735
—Ao! . . . Eh, give it over, Dwyer, I'm telling you or I'll give you
a stuff in the kisser[9] for yourself . . . . Ao!
—Good man, Towser! Duck him!
—Come along, Dedalus! Bous Stephanoumenos! Bous Steph=
aneforos![1]   740
—Duck him! Guzzle him now, Towser!
—Help! Help! . . . Ao!

   He recognised their speech collectively before he distin=
guished their faces. The mere sight of that medley of wet
nakedness chilled him to the bone. Their bodies, corpsewhite   745
or suffused with a pallid golden light or rawly tanned by the
sun, gleamed with the wet of the sea. Their divingstone, poised
on its rude supports and rocking under their plunges, and the
roughhewn stones of the sloping breakwater over which they
scrambled in their horseplay gleamed with cold wet lustre. The   750
towels with which they smacked their bodies were heavy with
cold seawater: and drenched with cold brine was their matted
hair.

   He stood still in deference to their calls and parried their
banter with easy words. How characterless they looked: Shuley   755
without his deep unbuttoned collar, Ennis without his scarlet
belt with the snaky clasp and Connolly without his Norfolk
coat with the flapless sidepockets! It was a pain to see them and
a swordlike pain to see the signs of adolescence that made
repellent their pitiable nakedness. Perhaps they had taken ref= 760
uge in number and noise from the secret dread in their souls.
But he, apart from them and in silence, remembered in what
dread he stood of the mystery of his own body.

—Stephanos Dedalos! Bous Stephanoumenos! Bous Stephane=
foros!   765

---

732 Again!(4)] MS; ABSENT Eg–64   747 sun,] 18; suns, MS–16, 64

8. "Wreath," "crown" (Greek).
9. A hit in the mouth (colloquial).
1. "Ox as wreath-bearer for the sacrifice," with a play on Stephen's name that suggests "ox
   as Stephen's soul" (Greek).

Their banter was not new to him and now, as always, it
flattered his mild proud sovereignty. Now, as never before, his
strange name seemed to him a prophecy. So timeless seemed
the grey warm air, so fluid and impersonal his own mood, that
all ages were as one to him. A moment before the ghost of   770
the ancient kingdom of the Danes had looked forth through the
vesture of the hazewrapped city. Now, at the name of the
fabulous artificer,[2] he seemed to hear the noise of dim waves
and to see a winged form flying above the waves and slowly
climbing the air. What did it mean? Was it a quaint device   775
opening a page of some medieval book of prophecies and sym=
bols, a hawklike man flying sunward above the sea, a prophecy
of the end he had been born to serve and had been following
through the mists of childhood and boyhood, a symbol of the
artist forging anew in his workshop out of the sluggish matter   780
of the earth a new soaring impalpable imperishable being?

His heart trembled; his breath came faster and a wild spirit
passed over his limbs as though he were soaring sunward. His
heart trembled in an ecstasy of fear and his soul was in flight.
His soul was soaring in an air beyond the world and the body   785
he knew was purified in a breath and delivered of incertitude
and made radiant and commingled with the element of the
spirit. An ecstasy of flight made radiant his eyes and wild his
breath and tremulous and wild and radiant his windswept
limbs.   790

—One! Two! . . . Look out!
—O, Cripes, I'm drownded!
—One! Two! Three and away!
—Me next! Me next!
—One! . . . Uk!   795
—Stephaneforos!

His throat ached with a desire to cry aloud, the cry of a
hawk or eagle on high, to cry piercingly of his deliverance to
the winds. This was the call of life to his soul not the dull gross
voice of the world of duties and despair, not the inhuman voice   800
that had called him to the pale service of the altar. An instant
of wild flight had delivered him and the cry of triumph which
his lips withheld cleft his brain.
—Stephaneforos!

766 now,--always,] now Eg--64   792 Cripes,] cripes, 64

2. Daedalus, the inventor (see note 1, p. 3).

What were they now but cerements[3] shaken from the body of   805
death—the fear he had walked in night and day, the incertitude
that had ringed him round, the shame that had abased him
within and without—cerements, the linens of the grave?

His soul had arisen from the grave of boyhood, spurning her
graveclothes. Yes! Yes! Yes! He would create proudly out of the   810
freedom and power of his soul, as the great artificer whose
name he bore, a living thing, new and soaring and beautiful,
impalpable, imperishable.

He started up nervously from the stoneblock for he could no
longer quench the flame in his blood. He felt his cheeks aflame   815
and his throat throbbing with song. There was a lust of wan=
dering in his feet that burned to set out for the ends of the
earth. On! On! his heart seemed to cry. Evening would deepen
above the sea, night fall upon the plains, dawn glimmer before
the wanderer and show him strange fields and hills and faces.   820
Where?

He looked northward towards Howth.[4] The sea had fallen
below the line of seawrack on the shallow side of the break=
water and already the tide was running out fast along the
foreshore. Already one long oval bank of sand lay warm and   825
dry amid the wavelets. Here and there warm isles of sand
gleamed above the shallow tide: and about the isles and around
the long bank and amid the shallow currents of the beach were
lightclad gayclad figures wading and delving.

In a few moments he was barefoot, his stockings folded in   830
his pockets and his canvas shoes dangling by their knotted laces
over his shoulders: and, picking a pointed salteaten stick out of
the jetsam among the rocks, he clambered down the slope of
the breakwater.

There was a long rivulet in the strand: and, as he waded   835
slowly up its course, he wondered at the endless drift of sea=
weed. Emerald and black and russet and olive, it moved
beneath the current, swaying and turning. The water of the
rivulet was dark with endless drift and mirrored the highdrift=
ing clouds. The clouds were drifting above him silently and   840
silently the seatangle was drifting below him; and the grey
warm air was still: and a new wild life was singing in his veins.

Where was his boyhood now? Where was the soul that had
hung back from her destiny, to brood alone upon the shame of
her wounds and in her house of squalor and subterfuge to   845

805 cerements] a16; the cerements MS—16

3. Graveclothes.
4. Headland on Dublin Bay's northeast coast.

queen it in faded cerements and in wreaths that withered at the touch? Or where was he?

He was alone. He was unheeded, happy and near to the wild heart of life. He was alone and young and wilful and wild= hearted, alone amid a waste of wild air and brackish waters and the seaharvest of shells and tangle and veiled grey sunlight and gayclad lightclad figures of children and girls and voices childish and girlish in the air.   850

A girl stood before him in midstream: alone and still, gazing out to sea. She seemed like one whom magic had changed into the likeness of a strange and beautiful seabird. Her long slender bare legs were delicate as a crane's and pure save where an emerald trail of seaweed had fashioned itself as a sign upon the flesh. Her thighs, fuller and softhued as ivory, were bared al= most to the hips where the white fringes of her drawers were like featherings of soft white down. Her slateblue skirts were kilted boldly about her waist and dovetailed behind her. Her bosom was as a bird's, soft and slight; slight and soft as the breast of some darkplumaged dove. But her long fair hair was girlish; and girlish, and touched with the wonder of mortal beauty, her face.   855   860   865

She was alone and still, gazing out to sea; and when she felt his presence and the worship of his eyes her eyes turned to him in quiet sufferance of his gaze, without shame or wantonness. Long, long she suffered his gaze and then quietly withdrew her eyes from his and bent them towards the stream, gently stirring the water with her foot hither and thither. The first faint noise of gently moving water broke the silence, low and faint and whispering, faint as the bells of sleep; hither and thither, hither and thither: and a faint flame trembled on her cheek.   870   875

—Heavenly God! cried Stephen's soul in an outburst of pro= fane joy.

He turned away from her suddenly and set off across the strand. His cheeks were aflame; his body was aglow; his limbs were trembling. On and on and on and on he strode, far out over the sands, singing wildly to the sea, crying to greet the advent of the life that had cried to him.   880

Her image had passed into his soul for ever and no word had broken the holy silence of his ecstasy. Her eyes had called him and his soul had leaped at the call. To live, to err, to fall, to triumph, to recreate life out of life! A wild angel had appeared to him, the angel of mortal youth and beauty, an envoy from the fair courts of life, to throw open before him in an instant of ecstasy the gates of all the ways of error and glory. On and on and on and on!   885   890

He halted suddenly and heard his heart in the silence. How far had he walked? What hour was it?

There was no human figure near him nor any sound borne to him over the air. But the tide was near the turn and already the day was on the wane. He turned landward and ran towards   895
the shore and, running up the sloping beach, reckless of the sharp shingle, found a sandy nook amid a ring of tufted sand= knolls and lay down there that the peace and silence of the evening might still the riot of his blood.

He felt above him the vast indifferent dome and the calm   900
processes of the heavenly bodies: and the earth beneath him, the earth that had borne him, had taken him to her breast.

He closed his eyes in the languor of sleep. His eyelids trembled as if they felt the vast cyclic movement of the earth and her watchers, trembled as if they felt the strange light of   905
some new world. His soul was swooning into some new world, fantastic, dim, uncertain as under sea, traversed by cloudy shapes and beings. A world, a glimmer or a flower? Glimmer= ing and trembling, trembling and unfolding, a breaking light, an opening flower, it spread in endless succession to itself,   910
breaking in full crimson and unfolding and fading to palest rose, leaf by leaf and wave of light by wave of light, flooding all the heavens with its soft flushes, every flush deeper than other.

Evening had fallen when he woke and the sand and arid grasses of his bed glowed no longer. He rose slowly and, re=   915
calling the rapture of his sleep, sighed at its joy.

He climbed to the crest of the sandhill and gazed about him. Evening had fallen. A rim of the young moon cleft the pale waste of sky like the rim of a silver hoop embedded in grey sand: and the tide was flowing in fast to the land with a low   920
whisper of her waves, islanding a few last figures in distant pools.

V

He drained his third cup of watery tea to the dregs and set to chewing the crusts of fried bread that were scattered near him, staring into the dark pool of the jar. The yellow dripping had been scooped out like a boghole and the pool under it brought back to his memory the dark turfcoloured water of the bath in   5
Clongowes. The box of pawntickets at his elbow had just been

rifled and he took up idly one after another in his greasy fingers the blue and white dockets, scrawled and sanded and creased and bearing the name of the pledger as Daly or MacEvoy.[1]

—1 Pair Buskins

 1 D. Coat

 3 Articles and White

 1 Man's Pants

Then he put them aside and gazed thoughtfully at the lid of the box, speckled with lousemarks, and asked vaguely:

—How much is the clock fast now?

His mother straightened the battered alarmclock that was lying on its side in the middle of the kitchen mantelpiece until its dial showed a quarter to twelve and then laid it once more on its side.

—An hour and twentyfive minutes, she said. The right time now is twenty past ten. The dear knows[2] you might try to be in time for your lectures.

—Fill out the place for me to wash, said Stephen.

—Katey, fill out the place for Stephen to wash.

—Boody, fill out the place for Stephen to wash.

—I can't. I'm going for blue. Fill it out, you, Maggie.

When the enamelled basin had been fitted into the well of the sink and the old washingglove flung on the side of it he allowed his mother to scrub his neck and root into the folds of his ears and into the interstices at the wings of his nose.

—Well, it's a poor case, she said, when a university student is so dirty that his mother has to wash him.

—But it gives you pleasure, said Stephen calmly.

An earsplitting whistle was heard from upstairs and his mother thrust a damp overall into his hands, saying:

—Dry yourself and hurry out for the love of goodness.

A second shrill whistle, prolonged angrily, brought one of the girls to the foot of the staircase.

—Yes, father?

—Is your lazy bitch of a brother gone out yet?

—Yes, father.

—Sure?

—Yes, father.

—Hm!

10—1] NO DIALOGUE DASH TO INDICATE THE LIST AS AUDIBLY SPOKEN Eg–64

1. Aliases used when items were pawned.
2. "God knows" (polite anglicized form of a Gaelic expression; P. W. Joyce, 69; Gifford, 223).

The girl came back making signs to him to be quick and go out quietly by the back. Stephen laughed and said:

—He has a curious idea of genders if he thinks a bitch is masculine.

—Ah, it's a scandalous shame for you, Stephen, said his 50 mother, and you'll live to rue the day you set your foot in that place. I know how it has changed you.

—Good morning, everybody, said Stephen smiling and kissing the tips of his fingers in adieu.

The lane behind the terrace was waterlogged and as he went 55 down it slowly, choosing his steps amid heaps of wet rubbish, he heard a mad nun screeching in the nuns' madhouse beyond the wall:[3]

—Jesus! O Jesus! Jesus!

He shook the sound out of his ears by an angry toss of his 60 head and hurried on, stumbling through the mouldering offal, his heart already bitten by an ache of loathing and bitterness. His father's whistle, his mother's mutterings, the screech of an unseen maniac were to him now so many voices offending and threatening to humble the pride of his youth. He drove their 65 echoes even out of his heart with an execration: but as he walked down the avenue and felt the grey morning light falling about him through the dripping trees and smelt the strange wild smell of the wet leaves and bark his soul was loosed of her miseries. 70

The rainladen trees of the avenue evoked in him, as always, memories of the girls and women in the plays of Gerhart Hauptmann:[4] and the memory of their pale sorrows and the fragrance falling from the wet branches mingled in a mood of quiet joy. His morning walk across the city had begun: and he 75 foreknew that as he passed the sloblands of Fairview[5] he would think of the cloistral silverveined prose of Newman, that as he walked along the North Strand Road, glancing idly at the win= dows of the provision shops, he would recall the dark humour of Guido Cavalcanti[6] and smile, that as he went by Baird's 80 stonecutting works in Talbot Place the spirit of Ibsen[7] would blow through him like a keen wind, a spirit of wayward boyish beauty, and that passing a grimy marine dealer's shop beyond

3. St. Vincent's Lunatic Asylum, run by the Sisters of Charity and located in Fairview, just across the Tolka River in northeast Dublin, where the Dedalus family lives, on Royal Ter-race (now Inverness Road).
4. Gerhardt Hauptmann (1862–1946), German writer.
5. Tidal flatlands where the Tolka enters Dublin Bay.
6. Italian poet (c. 1255–1300).
7. Henrik Ibsen (1828–1906), Norwegian dramatist.

the Liffey he would repeat the song by Ben Jonson which
begins: 85

I was not wearier where I lay.[8]

   His mind when wearied of its search for the essence of
beauty amid the spectral words of Aristotle or Aquinas turned
often for its pleasure to the dainty songs of the Elizabethans.
His mind, in the vesture of a doubting monk, stood often in   90
shadow under the windows of that age, to hear the grave and
mocking music of the lutenists or the frank laughter of waist=
coateers[9] until a laugh too low, a phrase, tarnished by time, of
chambering[1] and false honour stung his monkish pride and
drove him on from his lurkingplace.   95

   The lore which he was believed to pass his days brooding
upon so that it had rapt him from the companionships of youth
was only a garner of slender sentences from Aristotle's poetics
and psychology and a *Synopsis Philosophiae Scholasticae ad
mentem divi Thomae.*[2] His thinking was a dusk of doubt and   100
selfmistrust lit up at moments by the lightnings of intuition, but
lightnings of so clear a splendour that in those moments the
world perished about his feet as if it had been fireconsumed:
and thereafter his tongue grew heavy and he met the eyes of
others with unanswering eyes for he felt that the spirit of   105
beauty had folded him round like a mantle and that in revery at
least he had been acquainted with nobility. But when this brief
pride of silence upheld him no longer he was glad to find him=
self still in the midst of common lives, passing on his way amid
the squalor and noise and sloth of the city fearlessly and with a 110
light heart.

   Near the hoardings[3] on the canal he met the consumptive
man with the doll's face and the brimless hat coming towards
him down the slope of the bridge with little steps, tightly but=
toned into his chocolate overcoat and holding his furled um=   115
brella a span or two from him like a diviningrod. It must be
eleven, he thought, and peered into a dairy to see the time. The
clock in the dairy told him that it was five minutes to five but,
as he turned away, he heard a clock somewhere near him but
unseen beating eleven strokes in swift precision. He laughed as 120

---

8. From *The Vision of Delight* (1617), by the English poet and dramatist Ben Jonson
   (1572–1637).
9. Low-class prostitutes (*OED*).
1. Sexual indulgences, lewdness (*OED*).
2. Selections from Aristotle's writings pertaining to literature, the *Poetics,* and to the mind,
   De Sensu (Of the Senses) and *De Anima (Of the Soul),* and a book whose Latin title in English
   would be *A Synopsis of Scholastic Philosophy for the Understanding of Saint Thomas.*
3. Fence made of boards, where bills are posted (*OED*).

he heard it for it made him think of MacCann; and he saw him
a squat figure in a shooting jacket and breeches and with a fair
goatee standing in the wind at Hopkins' corner and heard him
say:
—Dedalus, you're an antisocial being, wrapped up in yourself. 125
I'm not. I'm a democrat: and I'll work and act for social liberty
and equality among all classes and sexes in the United States of
the Europe of the future.
    Eleven! Then he was late for that lecture too. What day of
the week was it? He stopped at a newsagent's to read the 130
headline of a placard. Thursday. Ten to eleven; English: eleven
to twelve; French: twelve to one; physics. He fancied to himself
the English lecture and felt, even at that distance, restless and
helpless. He saw the heads of his classmates meekly bent as
they wrote in their notebooks the points they were bidden to 135
note, nominal definitions, essential definitions[4] and examples or
dates of birth and death, chief works, a favourable and an
unfavourable criticism side by side. His own head was unbent
for his thoughts wandered abroad and whether he looked
around the little class of students or out of the window across 140
the desolate gardens of the green an odour assailed him of
cheerless cellardamp and decay. Another head than his, right
before him in the first benches, was poised squarely above its
bending fellows like the head of a priest appealing without
humility to the tabernacle for the humble worshippers about 145
him. Why was it that when he thought of Cranly he could
never raise before his mind the entire image of his body but
only the image of the head and face? Even now against the grey
curtain of the morning he saw it before him like the phantom
of a dream, the face of a severed head or deathmask, crowned 150
on the brows by its stiff black upright hair as by an iron crown.
It was a priestlike face, priestlike in its pallor, in the wide=
winged nose, in the shadowings below the eyes and along the
jaws, priestlike in the lips that were long and bloodless and
faintly smiling: and Stephen, remembering swiftly how he had 155
told Cranly of all the tumults and unrest and longings in his
soul, day after day and night by night only to be answered by
his friend's listening silence, would have told himself that it
was the face of a guilty priest who heard confessions of those
whom he had not power to absolve but that he felt again in 160
memory the gaze of its dark womanish eyes.

137 and(1)] or Eg—64   159–160 of--whom] Eg; ABSENT MS

4. For Aristotle in the *Posterior Analytics*, definitions that focus on effects produced are
nominal, while those that focus on cause, or "essence," are essential.

Through this image he had a glimpse of a strange dark
cavern of speculation but at once turned away from it feeling
that it was not yet the hour to enter it. But the nightshade of his
friend's listlessness seemed to be diffusing in the air around him   165
a tenuous and deadly exhalation: and he found himself
glancing from one casual word to another on his right or left in
stolid wonder that they had been so silently emptied of instan=
taneous sense until every mean shop legend bound his mind
like the words of a spell and his soul shrivelled up sighing with   170
age as he walked on in a lane among heaps of dead language.
His own consciousness of language was ebbing from his brain
and trickling into the very words themselves which set to band
and disband themselves in wayward rhythms:

> The ivy whines upon the wall   175
> And whines and twines upon the wall
> The ivy whines upon the wall
> The yellow ivy on the wall
> Ivy, ivy up the wall.

Did any one ever hear such drivel? Lord Almighty! Who ever   180
heard of ivy whining on a wall? Yellow ivy: that was all right.
Yellow ivory also. And what about ivory ivy?
The word now shone in his brain, clearer and brighter than
any ivory sawn from the mottled tusks of elephants. *Ivory,
ivoire, avorio, ebur.*[5] One of the first examples that he had   185
learnt in Latin had run: *India mittit ebur*:[6] and he recalled the
shrewd northern face of the rector who had taught him to
construe the Metamorphoses of Ovid[7] in a courtly English,
made whimsical by the mention of porkers and potsherds and
chines of bacon. He had learnt what little he knew of the laws   190
of Latin verse from a ragged book written by a Portuguese
priest:

Contrahit orator, variant in carmine vates.[8]

The crises and victories and secessions in Roman history
were handed on to him in the trite words *in tanto discrimine*[9]   195
and he had tried to peer into the social life of the city of cities
through the words *implere ollam denariorum* which the rector

<hr>

5. Words for ivory in English, French, Italian, and Latin.
6. "India sends ivory."
7. These mythological narratives about transformations among humans, animals, and plants,
   by the Roman poet Ovid (Publius Ovidius Naso, 43 BCE–17 CE), provide the book's epigraph (p. 3).
8. Literally, "the orator summarizes; the poet amplifies in song" (Latin), but in the *Prosodia,*
   by the Portuguese Jesuit Emmanuel Alvarez (1562–1582), the subject is prose rhythm.
9. "In such a great crisis" (Latin).

V   157

had rendered sonorously as the filling of a pot with denaries.[1]
The pages of his timeworn Horace[2] never felt cold to the touch
even when his own fingers were cold: they were human pages: 200
and fifty years before they had been turned by the human
fingers of John Duncan Inverarity and by his brother William
Malcolm Inverarity. Yes, those were noble names on the dusky
flyleaf and, even for so poor a Latinist as he, the dusky verses
were as fragrant as though they had lain all those years in   205
myrtle and lavender and vervain: but yet it wounded him to
think that he would never be but a shy guest at the feast of the
world's culture and that the monkish learning, in terms of
which he was striving to forge out an esthetic philosophy, was
held no higher by the age he lived in than the subtle and   210
curious jargons of heraldry and falconry.

The grey block of Trinity[3] on his left, set heavily in the city's
ignorance like a great dull stone set in a cumbrous ring, pulled
his mind downward: and while he was striving this way and
that to free his feet from the fetters of the reformed conscience[4]   215
he came upon the droll statue of the national poet of Ireland.[5]

He looked at it without anger: for, though sloth of the body
and of the soul crept over it like unseen vermin, over the
shuffling feet and up the folds of the cloak and around the
servile head, it seemed humbly conscious of its indignity. It   220
was a Firbolg in the borrowed cloak of a Milesian;[6] and he
thought of his friend Davin, the peasant student. It was a
jesting name between them but the young peasant bore with it
lightly, saying:

—Go on, Stevie. I have a hard head, you tell me. Call me what   225
you will.

The homely version of his christian name on the lips of his
friend had touched Stephen pleasantly when first heard for he
was as formal in speech with others as they were with him.
Often, as he sat in Davin's rooms in Grantham Street, wonder=   230
ing at his friend's wellmade boots that flanked the wall pair by
pair and repeating for his friend's simple ear the verses and
cadences of others which were the veils of his own longing and

228 had] ⌐had⌐ MS

1. The phrase translates the Latin of the preceding line; "denaries" were Roman coins.
2. Quintus Horatius Flaccus (65–8 BCE), Roman poet.
3. Trinity College, a Protestant, Anglo-Irish institution that Catholics did not attend, first because they were barred from admission and later because the Catholic establishment forbade enrollment.
4. The post-Reformation, that is, Protestant, English attitudes represented by Trinity College.
5. The statue of Thomas Moore outside the gates of Trinity College is "droll," or amusing, because it presents him in a toga. Not officially Ireland's national poet, Moore was popular for his sentimentally Irish writing.
6. An early inhabitant of Ireland, a Firbolg, trying to dress up like one of the more civilized invaders, the Milesians.

dejection, the rude Firbolg mind of his listener had drawn his
mind towards it and flung it back again, drawing it by a quiet   235
inbred courtesy of attention or by a quaint turn of old English
speech or by the force of its delight in rude bodily skill (for
Davin had sat at the feet of Michael Cusack, the Gael),[7]
repelling swiftly and suddenly by a grossness of intelligence or
by a bluntness of feeling or by a dull stare of terror in the eyes   240
the terror of soul of a starving Irish village in which the curfew[8]
was still a nightly fear.

Side by side with his memory of the deeds of prowess of his
uncle Mat Davin, the athlete,[9] the young peasant worshipped
the sorrowful legend of Ireland. The gossip of his fellowstu=   245
dents which strove to render the flat life of the college signifi=
cant at any cost loved to think of him as a young fenian.[1] His
nurse had taught him Irish and shaped the rude imagination by
the broken lights of Irish myth. He stood towards this myth
upon which no individual mind had ever drawn out a line of   250
beauty and to its unwieldy tales that divided against themselves
as they moved down the cycles[2] in the same attitude as towards
the Roman catholic religion, the attitude of a dullwitted loyal
serf. Whatsoever of thought or of feeling came to him from
England or by way of English culture his mind stood armed   255
against in obedience to a password: and of the world that lay
beyond England he knew only the foreign legion of France in
which he spoke of serving.

Coupling this ambition with the young man's diffident hu=
mour Stephen had often called him one of the tame geese:[3] and   260
there was even a point of irritation in the name pointed against
that very reluctance of speech and deed in his friend which
seemed so often to stand between Stephen's mind, eager of
speculation, and the hidden ways of Irish life.

One night the young peasant, his spirit stung by the violent   265
or luxurious language in which Stephen escaped from the cold
silence of intellectual revolt, had called up before Stephen's
mind a strange vision. The two were walking slowly towards

248 the] MS; his Eg–64   251 against] ABSENT Eg–18, 64   259 diffident] MS; ABSENT
Eg–64

7. Cusack (1847–1906) was involved in founding the Gaelic Athletic Association (1884).
8. Curfew, including the extinguishing of lights, was imposed by the English early in the
   eighteenth century and again as part of the Coercion Acts from 1800 to 1921.
9. Maurice Davin (1864–1927), a founder of the Gaelic Athletic Association, held international athletic records.
1. Militant Irish nationalist.
2. Ancient Irish heroic legends, grouped into "cycles," such as the Fenian Cycle, which
   focused on Finn Mac Cumhaill.
3. A play on the "wild geese," Irish Catholic soldiers who, after William III reconquered
   Ireland, fled to the Continent in 1691 and served in foreign armies.

Davin's rooms through the dark narrow streets of the poorer
jews.   270
—A thing happened to myself, Stevie, last autumn coming on
winter and I never told it to a living soul and you are the first
person now I ever told it to. I disremember if it was October or
November. It was October because it was before I came up
here to join the matriculation class.   275

Stephen had turned his smiling eyes towards his friend's
face, flattered by his confidence and won over to sympathy by
the speaker's simple accent.
—I was away all that day from my own place, over in Butte=
vant (I don't know if you know where that is) at a hurling   280
match[4] between the Croke's Own Boys and the Fearless Thurles
and by God, Stevie, that was the hard fight. My first cousin
Fonsy Davin was stripped to his buff that day minding cool[5] for
the Limericks but he was up with the forwards half the time
and shouting like mad. I never will forget that day. One of the   285
Crokes made a woful wipe at him one time with his camaun
and I declare to God he was within an aim's ace of getting it at
the side of the temple. O, honest to God, if the crook of it
caught him that time he was done for.
—I am glad he escaped, Stephen had said with a laugh, but   290
surely that's not the strange thing that happened you?
—Well, I suppose that doesn't interest you but leastways there
was such noise after the match that I missed the train home and
I couldn't get any kind of a yoke[6] to give me a lift for, as luck
would have it, there was a mass meeting that same day over in   295
Castletownroche[7] and all the cars in the country were there. So
there was nothing for it only to stay the night or to foot it out.
Well, I started to walk and on I went and it was coming on
night when I got into the Ballyhoura hills, that's better than ten
miles from Kilmallock and there's a long lonely road after that.   300
You wouldn't see the sign of a christian house along the road or
hear a sound. It was pitch dark almost. Once or twice I stopped
by the way under a bush to redden my pipe and only for the
dew was thick I'd have stretched out there and slept. At last
after a bend of the road I spied a little cottage with a light in   305
the window. I went up and knocked at the door. A voice asked

---

269 rooms] room 64

4. The match to be played in a town in County Cork involves hurling, a traditional game
   resembling both lacrosse and hockey played with a bladed stick known as a *camaun* or
   camann.
5. Played shirtless minding the goal. "Cool" is anglicized from the Irish *cúl*, meaning goal.
6. Conveyance, transportation.
7. A political meeting in a town five miles from Buttevant.

who was there and I answered I was over at the match in
Buttevant and was walking back and that I'd be thankful for a
glass of water. After a while a young woman opened the door
and brought me out a big mug of milk. She was half undressed   310
as if she was going to bed when I knocked and she had her hair
hanging: and I thought by her figure and by something in the
look of her eyes that she must be carrying a child. She kept me
in talk a long while at the door and I thought it strange because
her breast and her shoulders were bare. She asked me was I   315
tired and would I like to stop the night there. She said she was
all alone in the house and that her husband had gone that
morning to Queenstown with his sister to see her off. And all
the time she was talking, Stevie, she had her eyes fixed on my
face and she stood so close to me I could hear her breathing.   320
When I handed her back the mug at last she took my hand to
draw me in over the threshold and said: *Come in and stay the
night here. You've no call to be frightened. There's no-one in it
but ourselves* . . . . I didn't go in, Stevie. I thanked her and
went on my way again, all in a fever. At the first bend of the   325
road I looked back and she was standing in the door.

The last words of Davin's story sang in his memory and the
figure of the woman in the story stood forth reflected in other
figures of the peasant women whom he had seen standing in
the doorways at Clane[8] as the college cars drove by, as a type of   330
her race and his own, a batlike soul waking to the conscious=
ness of itself in darkness and secrecy and loneliness and,
through the eyes and voice and gesture of a woman without
guile, calling the stranger to her bed.

A hand was laid on his arm and a young voice cried: 335
—Ah, gentleman, your own girl, sir! The first handsel[9] today,
gentleman. Buy that lovely bunch. Will you, gentleman?

The blue flowers which she lifted towards him and her
young blue eyes seemed to him at that instant images of guile=
lessness: and he halted till the image had vanished and he saw   340
only her ragged dress and damp coarse hair and hoydenish
face.
—Do, gentleman! Don't forget your own girl, sir!
—I have no money, said Stephen.
—Buy them lovely ones, will you, sir? Only a penny.   345
—Did you hear what I said? asked Stephen, bending towards
her. I told you I had no money. I tell you again now.

326 in] MS; at Eg–64

8. A village near Clongowes.
9. "First money taken by a trader in the morning" (*OED*).

—Well, sure, you will some day, sir, please God, the girl
answered after an instant.

—Possibly, said Stephen, but I don't think it likely.   350

He left her quickly, fearing that her intimacy might turn to
gibing and wishing to be out of the way before she offered her
ware to another, a tourist from England or a student of Trinity.
Grafton Street along which he walked prolonged that moment
of discouraged poverty. In the roadway at the head of the street   355
a slab was set to the memory of Wolfe Tone[1] and he remem=
bered having been present with his father at its laying. He re=
membered with bitterness that scene of tawdry tribute. There
were four French delegates in a brake and one, a plump smiling
young man, held, wedged on a stick, a card on which were   360
printed the words: *Vive l'Irlande!*[2]

But the trees in Stephen's Green were fragrant of rain and
the rainsodden earth gave forth its moral odour, a faint in=
cense rising upward through the mould from many hearts. The
soul of the gallant venal city which his elders had told him of   365
had shrunk with time to a faint mortal odour rising from the   .
earth and he knew that in a moment when he entered the
sombre college he would be conscious of a corruption other
than that of Buck Egan and Burnchapel Whaley.[3]

It was too late to go upstairs to the French class. He crossed   370
the hall and took the corridor to the left which led to the
physics theatre. The corridor was dark and silent but not un=
watchful. Why did he feel that it was not unwatchful? Was it
because he had heard that in Buck Whaley's time there was a
secret staircase there? Or was the jesuit house extraterritorial[4]   375
and was he walking among aliens? The Ireland of Tone and of
Parnell[5] seemed to have receded in space.

He opened the door of the theatre and halted in the chilly
grey light that struggled through the dusty windows. A figure
was crouching before the large grate and by its leanness and   380
greyness he knew that it was the dean of studies lighting the

1. A memorial placed at one corner of Stephen's Green in 1898, the centenary of the Insurrection of 1798 against the English, to honor (Theobald) Wolfe Tone (1763–1798), who,
after accompanying French forces into Ireland to fight for independence, was captured
and died by his own hand during his imprisonment.
2. This sign, held by French representatives in a carriage, reads "Long live Ireland!" (French).
3. Confused reference, probably not to John "Bully" Egan (c. 1750–1810) but to Thomas
"Buck" Whaley (1766–1800), son of Richard "Burnchapel" Whaley (c. 1700–1769). All
had reputations for extreme behavior, but the Whaleys were noted for corruption, including involvement with the Hellfire Club, a licentious group of rakes reputed to practice
Satanism. Stephen associates the Whaleys with the college because Whaley's house, 86
Stephen's Green, became part of University College.
4. Not a part of Ireland, presumably because of the tie to the Vatican, an independent state,
and because of the attitudes Stephen associates with the Jesuit house.
5. Heroic figures associated with sacrifice and Irish independence.

fire. Stephen closed the door quietly and approached the fire=
place.

—Good morning, sir! Can I help you?

The priest looked up quickly and said: 385

—One moment now, Mr Dedalus, and you will see. There is
an art in lighting a fire. We have the liberal arts and we have
the useful arts. This is one of the useful arts.

—I will try to learn it, said Stephen.

—Not too much coal, said the dean, working briskly at his 390
task, that is one of the secrets.

He produced four candle butts from the sidepockets of his
soutane and placed them deftly among the coals and twisted
papers. Stephen watched him in silence. Kneeling thus on the
flagstone to kindle the fire and busied with the disposition of 395
his wisps of paper and candle butts he seemed more than ever a
humble server making ready the place of sacrifice in an empty
temple, a levite of the Lord. Like a levite's robe of plain linen
the faded worn soutane draped the kneeling figure of one
whom the canonicals or the bellbordered ephod[6] would irk and 400
trouble. His very body had waxed old in lowly service of the
Lord—in tending the fire upon the altar, in bearing tidings se=
cretly, in waiting upon worldlings, in striking swiftly when
bidden—and yet had remained ungraced by aught of saintly or
of prelatic beauty. Nay, his very soul had waxed old in that 405
service without growing towards light and beauty or spreading
abroad a sweet odour of her sanctity—a mortified will no more
responsive to the thrill of its obedience than was to the thrill of
love or combat his aging body, spare and sinewy, greyed with a
silverpointed down. 410

The dean rested back on his hunkers[7] and watched the sticks
catch. Stephen, to fill the silence, said:

—I am sure I could not light a fire.

—You are an artist, are you not, Mr Dedalus? said the dean,
glancing up and blinking his pale eyes. The object of the artist 415
is the creation of the beautiful. What the beautiful is is another
question.

He rubbed his hands slowly and drily over the difficulty.

—Can you solve that question now? he asked.

—Aquinas, answered Stephen, says *Pulcra sunt quae visa* 420
placent.[8]

---

6. The robe of an assistant, or levite, by contrast with the more splendid garments.
7. On his heels (P. W. Joyce, 275, 269); squatting with hams close to heels (*OED*).
8. "Those things are beautiful that please the eye" (Latin), an adaptation of Aquinas's statement in *Summa Theologica* (I.5.4), "*Pulchra enim dicuntur quae visa placent*" ("Those
   things are called beautiful that please the eye").

—This fire before us, said the dean, will be pleasing to the eye. Will it therefore be beautiful?

—In so far as it is apprehended by the sight, which I suppose means here esthetic intellection, it will be beautiful. But Aqui= nas also says *Bonum est in quod tendit appetitus.*[9] In so far as it satisfies the animal craving for warmth fire is a good. In hell however it is an evil.

—Quite so, said the dean, you have certainly hit the nail on the head.

He rose nimbly and went towards the door, set it ajar and said:

—A draught is said to be a help in these matters.

As he came back to the hearth, limping slightly but with a brisk step, Stephen saw the silent soul of a jesuit look out at him from the pale loveless eyes. Like Ignatius he was lame but in his eyes burned no spark of Ignatius' enthusiasm. Even the legendary craft of the company,[1] a craft subtler and more secret than its fabled books of secret subtle wisdom, had not fired his soul with the energy of apostleship. It seemed as if he used the shifts and lore and cunning of the world, as bidden to do, for the greater glory of God, without joy in their handling or hatred of that in them which was evil but turning them, with a firm gesture of obedience, back upon themselves: and for all this silent service it seemed as if he loved not at all the master and little, if at all, the ends he served. *Similiter atque senis baculus,*[2] he was, as the founder would have had him, like a staff in an old man's hand, to be left in a corner, to be leaned on in the road at nightfall or in stress of weather, to lie with a lady's nosegay on a garden seat, to be raised in menace.

The dean returned to the hearth and began to stroke his chin.

—When may we expect to have something from you on the esthetic question? he asked.

—From me! said Stephen in astonishment. I stumble on an idea once a fortnight if I am lucky.

—These questions are very profound, Mr Dedalus, said the dean. It is like looking down from the cliffs of Moher[3] into the depths. Many go down into the depths and never come up. Only the trained diver can go down into those depths and explore them and come to the surface again.

9. "The good inheres in what is desired" (Latin), another adaptation of Aquinas from the same passage.
1. The Jesuits.
2. Stephen translates this comparison, quoted in Latin, from Ignatius Loyola's constitution of the Society of Jesus.
3. Steep coastal cliffs in County Clare, on Ireland's west coast.

—If you mean speculation, sir, said Stephen, I also am sure
that there is no such thing as free thinking inasmuch as all
thinking must be bound by its own laws.

—Ha!   465

—For my purpose I can work on at present by the light of one
or two ideas of Aristotle and Aquinas.

—I see. I quite see your point.

—I need them only for my own use and guidance until I have
done something for myself by their light. If the lamp smokes or   470
smells I shall try to trim it. If it does not give light enough I
shall sell it and buy or borrow another.

—Epictetus[4] also had a lamp, said the dean, which was sold for
a fancy price after his death. It was the lamp he wrote his
philosophical dissertations by. You know Epictetus?   475

—An old gentleman, said Stephen coarsely, who said that the
soul is very like a bucketful of water.

—He tells us in his homely way, the dean went on, that he put
an iron lamp before a statue of one of the gods and that a thief
stole the lamp. What did the philosopher do? He reflected that   480
it was in the character of a thief to steal and determined to buy
an earthen lamp next day instead of the iron lamp.

A smell of molten tallow came up from the dean's candle
butts and fused itself in Stephen's consciousness with the jin=
gle of the words, bucket and lamp and lamp and bucket. The   485
priest's voice too had a hard jingling tone. Stephen's mind
halted by instinct, checked by the strange tone and the imagery
and by the priest's face which seemed like an unlit lamp or a
reflector hung in a false focus. What lay behind it or within it?
A dull torpor of the soul or the dullness of the thundercloud,   490
charged with intellection and capable of the gloom of God?

—I meant a different kind of lamp, sir, said Stephen.

—Undoubtedly, said the dean.

—One difficulty, said Stephen, in esthetic discussion is to
know whether words are being used according to the literary   495
tradition or according to the tradition of the marketplace. I
remember a sentence of Newman's in which he says of the
Blessed Virgin that she was detained in the full company of the
saints. The use of the word in the marketplace is quite differ=
ent. *I hope I am not detaining you.*   500

—Not in the least, said the dean politely.

---

472 or borrow] absent Eg–64   479 one of] Eg; absent MS   481 in] Eg; absent MS

4. Greek Stoic philosopher (c. 55–c. 135), whose *Discourses* include the comparison of the
soul to a container of water and the story of the lamps mentioned below.

—No, no, said Stephen smiling, I mean . . . .

—Yes, yes: I see, said the dean quickly, I quite catch the point: *detain*.

He thrust forward his under jaw and uttered a dry short   505 cough.

—To return to the lamp, he said, the feeding of it is also a nice problem. You must choose the pure oil and you must be careful when you pour it in not to overflow it, not to pour in more than the funnel can hold.   510

—What funnel? asked Stephen.

—The funnel through which you pour the oil into your lamp.

—That? said Stephen. Is that called a funnel? Is it not a tun= dish?[5]

—What is a tundish?   515

—That. The . . . the funnel.

—Is that called a tundish in Ireland? asked the dean. I never heard the word in my life.

—It is called a tundish in Lower Drumcondra,[6] said Stephen laughing, where they speak the best English.   520

—A tundish! said the dean reflectively. That is a most interest= ing word. I must look that word up. Upon my word I must.

His courtesy of manner rang a little false and Stephen looked at the English convert with the same eyes as the elder brother in the parable may have turned on the prodigal.[7] A humble fol=   525 lower in the wake of clamorous conversions, a poor English= man in Ireland, he seemed to have entered on the stage of jesuit history when that strange play of intrigue and suffering and envy and struggle and indignity had been all but given through —a latecomer, a tardy spirit.[8] From what had he set out? Per=   530 haps he had been born and bred among serious dissenters,[9] seeing salvation in Jesus only and abhorring the vain pomps of the establishment. Had he felt the need of an implicit faith amid the welter of sectarianism and the jargon of its turbulent schisms, six principle men, peculiar people, seed and snake   535 baptists, supralapsarian dogmatists?[1] Had he found the true church all of a sudden in winding up to the end like a reel of cotton some finespun line of reasoning upon insufflation or the

519 Lower] Eg; ABSENT MS

5. An English word, found in Shakespeare, now little used, but not Irish in origin.
6. Northern suburb of Dublin.
7. The story of the obedient son and his prodigal younger brother is told in Luke 15:11–32.
8. Late convert, long after the highly publicized conversions, including Newman's, which occurred in 1845.
9. Protestants who were not members of the Anglican Church, the established Church in England.
1. Dissenting sects, all Baptist, with distinctive beliefs.

imposition of hands or the procession of the Holy Ghost?[2] Or
had Lord Christ touched him and bidden him follow, like that   540
disciple who had sat at the receipt of custom,[3] as he sat by the
door of some zincroofed chapel,[4] yawning and telling over his
church pence?

The dean repeated the word yet again.

—Tundish! Well now, that is interesting!   545

—The question you asked me a moment ago seems to me more
interesting. What is that beauty which the artist struggles to
express from lumps of earth, said Stephen coldly.

The little word seemed to have turned a rapier point of his
sensitiveness against this courteous and vigilant foe. He felt   550
with a smart of dejection that the man to whom he was speak=
ing was a countryman of Ben Jonson. He thought:

—The language in which we are speaking is his before it is
mine. How different are the words *home, Christ, ale, master* on
his lips and on mine! I cannot speak or write these words with=   555
out unrest of spirit. His language, so familiar and so foreign,
will always be for me an acquired speech. I have not made or
accepted its words. My voice holds them at bay. My soul frets
in the shadow of his language.

—And to distinguish between the beautiful and the sublime,   560
the dean added. To distinguish between moral beauty and ma=
terial beauty. And to inquire what kind of beauty is proper to
each of the various arts. These are some interesting points we
might take up.

Stephen, disheartened suddenly by the dean's firm dry tone,   565
was silent. The dean also was silent: and through the silence a
distant noise of many boots and confused voices came up the
staircase.

—In pursuing these speculations, said the dean conclusively,
there is however the danger of perishing of inanition. First you   570
must take your degree. Set that before you as your first aim.
Then, little by little, you will see your way. I mean in every
sense, your way in life and in thinking. It may be uphill pedal=
ling at first. Take Mr Moonan. He was a long time before he
got to the top. But he got there.   575

—I may not have his talent, said Stephen quietly.

---

2. Aspects of Catholic beliefs that are implicitly being compared to the idiosyncratic views
   of the dissenting sects. Insufflation involves breathing on someone to represent the coming of the Holy Ghost. The imposition, or laying on, of hands can pass on authority or
   expel evil. The doctrine of the Trinity (see note 7, p. 27) involves the Holy Ghost's proceeding from the Father and the Son together.
3. Matthew, who was collecting taxes when Jesus called him (Matthew 9:9).
4. In England, a freestanding place of worship for a dissenting sect is called a chapel rather
   than a church.

—You never know, said the dean brightly. We never can say what is in us. I most certainly should not be despondent. *Per aspera ad astra.*[5]

He left the hearth quickly and went towards the landing to   580
oversee the arrival of the first arts' class.

Leaning against the fireplace Stephen heard him greet briskly and impartially every student of the class and could almost see the frank smiles of the coarser students. A desolating pity be= gan to fall like a dew upon his easily embittered heart for this   585
faithful servingman of the knightly Loyola, for this halfbrother of the clergy, more venal than they in speech, more steadfast of soul than they, one whom he would never call his ghostly fa= ther: and he thought how this man and his companions had earned the name of worldlings at the hands not of the un=   590
worldly only but of the worldly also for having pleaded, during all their history, at the bar of God's justice for the souls of the lax and the lukewarm and the prudent.

The entry of the professor was signalled by a few rounds of Kentish fire[6] from the heavy boots of those students who sat on   595
the highest tier of the gloomy theatre under the grey cob= webbed windows. The calling of the roll began and the re= sponses to the names were given out in all tones until the name of Peter Byrne was reached.

—Here!   600

A deep bass note in response came from the upper tier, followed by coughs of protest along the other benches.

The professor paused in his reading and called the next name:

—Cranly!   605

No answer.

—Mr Cranly!

A smile flew across Stephen's face as he thought of his friend's studies.

—Try Leopardstown![7] said a voice from the bench behind.   610

Stephen glanced up quickly but Moynihan's snoutish face outlined on the grey light was impassive. A formula was given out. Amid the rustling of the notebooks Stephen turned back again and said:

—Give me some paper for God' sake.   615

5. "Through difficulties to the stars" (Latin).
6. Extended hand clapping or, in this case, foot stamping; the expression is "said to have originated in reference to meetings held in Kent in 1828–1829" in opposition to proposed Catholic Emancipation (*OED*).
7. A track for horseracing, six miles south of central Dublin.

—Are you as bad as that? asked Moynihan with a broad grin.

He tore a sheet from his scribbler and passed it down, whis=
pering:

—In case of necessity any layman or woman can do it.

The formula which he wrote obediently on the sheet of   620
paper, the coiling and uncoiling calculations of the professor,
the spectrelike symbols of force and velocity fascinated and
jaded Stephen's mind. He had heard some say that the old
professor was an atheist freemason.[8] O the grey dull day! It
seemed a limbo of painless patient consciousness through   625
which souls of mathematicians might wander, projecting long
slender fabrics from plane to plane of ever rarer and paler
twilight, radiating swift eddies to the last verges of a universe
ever vaster, farther and more impalpable.

—So we must distinguish between elliptical and ellipsoidal.   630
Perhaps some of you gentlemen may be familiar with the works
of Mr W. S. Gilbert. In one of his songs he speaks of the
billiard sharp who is condemned to play:

>   On a cloth untrue
>   With a twisted cue
>   And elliptical billiard balls.[9]   635

He means a ball having the form of the ellipsoid of the princi=
pal axes of which I spoke a moment ago.

Moynihan leaned down towards Stephen's ear and mur=
mured:

—What price ellipsoidal balls! Chase me, ladies, I'm in the   640
cavalry!

His fellowstudent's rude humour ran like a gust through the
cloister of Stephen's mind, shaking into gay life limp priestly
vestments that hung upon the walls, setting them to sway and   645
caper in a sabbath of misrule. The forms of the community
emerged from the gustblown vestments, the dean of studies,
the portly florid bursar with his cap of grey hair, the president,
the little priest with feathery hair who wrote devout verses, the
squat peasant form of the professor of economics, the tall form   650
of the young professor of mental science discussing on the
landing a case of conscience with his class like a giraffe crop=
ping high leafage among a herd of antelopes, the grave troubled
prefect of the sodality, the plump roundheaded professor of

---

634 *untrue*] ⁷¹⟨*that's new*⟩ *untrue*¹ʳ MS

8. A contradiction in terms, because Freemasonry requires belief in God.
9. From the last act of the light opera *The Mikado* (1885), by W. S. Gilbert (1836–1911)
   and Arthur Sullivan (1842–1900).

Italian with his rogue's eyes. They came ambling and stum= 655
bling, tumbling and capering, kilting their gowns for leap frog,
holding one another back, shaken with deep false laughter,
smacking one another behind and laughing at their rude mal=
ice, calling to one another by familiar nicknames, protesting
with sudden dignity at some rough usage, whispering two and 660
two behind their hands.

   The professor had gone to the glass cases on the sidewall
from a shelf of which he took down a set of coils, blew away
the dust from many points and, bearing it carefully to the table,
held a finger on it while he proceeded with his lecture. He 665
explained that the wires in modern coils were of a compound
called platinoid lately discovered by F. W. Martino.[1]

   He spoke clearly the initials and surname of the discoverer.
Moynihan whispered from behind:

—Good old Fresh Water Martin!   670

—Ask him, Stephen whispered back with weary humour, if he
wants a subject for electrocution. He can have me.

   Moynihan, seeing the professor bend over the coils, rose in
his bench and, clacking noiselessly the fingers of his right hand,
began to call with the voice of a slobbering urchin: 675

—Please, teacher! Please, teacher! This boy is after saying a
bad word, teacher.

—Platinoid, the professor said solemnly, is preferred to Ger=
man silver because it has a lower coefficient of resistance
variation by changes of temperature. The platinoid wire is in= 680
sulated and the covering of silk that insulates it is wound
double on the ebonite bobbins just where my finger is. If it
were wound single an extra current would be induced in the
coils. The bobbins are saturated in hot paraffinwax . . .

   A sharp Ulster[2] voice said from the bench below Stephen: 685

—Are we likely to be asked questions on applied science?

   The professor began to juggle gravely with the terms pure
science and applied science. A heavybuilt student wearing gold
spectacles stared with some wonder at the questioner. Moyni=
han murmured from behind in his natural voice: 690

—Isn't MacAlister a devil for his pound of flesh?

   Stephen looked down coldly on the oblong skull beneath

---

657 false] fast 64   682 double] MS; ABSENT Eg–64

1. Fernando Wood Martin (1863–1933), American chemist, may be meant. *Encyclopedia
   Britannica* mentions "Martino" as having introduced platinoid but gives no identifying
   information (*Enc. Brit.* 6:857n.2).
2. One of the four traditional provinces of Ireland, located in the northeast portion of the
   island, where Protestants are in the majority.

him overgrown with tangled twinecoloured hair. The voice, the accent, the mind of the questioner offended him and he allowed the offence to carry him towards wilful unkindness, bidding his 695 mind think that the student's father would have done better had he sent his son to Belfast[3] to study and have saved some= thing on the trainfare by so doing.

The oblong skull beneath did not turn to meet this shaft of thought and yet the shaft came back to its bowstring: for he 700 saw in a moment the student's wheypale face.

—That thought is not mine, he said to himself quickly. It came from the comic Irishman in the bench behind. Patience. Can you say with certitude by whom the soul of your race was bartered and its elect betrayed—by the questioner or by the 705 mocker? Patience. Remember Epictetus. It is probably in his character to ask such a question at such a moment in such a tone and to pronounce the word *science* as a monosyllable.

The droning voice of the professor continued to wind itself slowly round and round the coils it spoke of, doubling, 710 trebling, quadrupling its somnolent energy as the coil multi= plied its ohms of resistance.

Moynihan's voice called from behind in echo to a distant bell:

—Closing time, gents! 715

The entrance hall was crowded and loud with talk. On a table near the door were two photographs in frames and be= tween them a long roll of paper bearing an irregular tail of signatures. MacCann went briskly to and fro among the stu= dents, talking rapidly, answering rebuffs and leading one after 720 another to the table. In the inner hall the dean of studies stood talking to a young professor, stroking his chin gravely and nod= ding his head.

Stephen, checked by the crowd at the door, halted irresol= utely. From under the wide falling leaf of a soft hat Cranly's 725 dark eyes were watching him.

—Have you signed? Stephen asked.

Cranly closed his long thinlipped mouth, communed with himself an instant and answered:

—*Ego habeo.*[4] 730

—What is it for?

—*Quod?*[5]

—What is it for?

---

3. Largest city in Ulster and the location of Queen's University.
4. "I have." The first in a series of joking statements in simplified Latin.
5. "What?"

Cranly turned his pale face to Stephen and said blandly and bitterly:

—*Per pax universalis.*[6]

Stephen pointed to the Czar's photograph[7] and said:

—He has the face of a besotted Christ.

The scorn and anger in his voice brought Cranly's eyes back from a calm survey of the walls of the hall.

—Are you annoyed? he asked.

—No, answered Stephen.

—Are you in bad humour?

—No.

—*Credo ut vos sanguinarius mendax estis,* said Cranly, *quia facies vostra monstrat ut vos in damno malo humore estis.*[8]

Moynihan, on his way to the table, said in Stephen's ear:

—MacCann is in tiptop form. Ready to shed the last drop. Brandnew world. No stimulants and votes for the bitches.

Stephen smiled at the manner of this confidence and, when Moynihan had passed, turned again to meet Cranly's eyes.

—Perhaps you can tell me, he said, why he pours his soul so freely into my ear. Can you?

A dull scowl appeared on Cranly's forehead. He stared at the table where Moynihan had bent to write his name on the roll, and then said flatly:

—A sugar![9]

—*Quis est in malo humore,* said Stephen, *ego aut vos?*[1]

Cranly did not take up the taunt. He brooded sourly on his judgment and repeated with the same flat force:

—A flaming bloody sugar, that's what he is!

It was his epitaph for all dead friendships and Stephen won=dered whether it would ever be spoken in the same tone over his memory. The heavy lumpish phrase sank slowly out of hearing like a stone through a quagmire. Stephen saw it sink as he had seen many an other, feeling its heaviness depress his heart. Cranly's speech, unlike that of Davin, had neither rare phrases of Elizabethan English nor quaintly turned versions of Irish idioms. Its drawl was an echo of the quays of Dublin given back by a bleak decaying seaport, its energy an echo of

---

766 an other,] MS; another, Eg–64

6. "For universal peace."
7. Photograph of Czar Nicholas II (1868–1918) of Russia, on display with one of his wife, Czarina Alexandra Feodorovna (1872–1918).
8. "I believe that you are a bloody liar and from the expression on your face that you are in a damned bad mood."
9. A euphemistic play on the word *shit*, with which *sugar* shares an initial sound (*Letters* III, 129–30).
1. "Who is in a bad mood, me or you?"

the sacred eloquence of Dublin given back flatly by a Wicklow pulpit.[2]

The heavy scowl faded from Cranly's face as MacCann marched briskly towards them from the other side of the hall.

—Here you are! said MacCann cheerily.   775

—Here I am! said Stephen.

—Late as usual. Can you not combine the progressive tendency[3] with a respect for punctuality?

—That question is out of order, said Stephen. Next business.

His smiling eyes were fixed on a silverwrapped tablet of milk   780
chocolate which peeped out of the propagandist's breastpocket. A little ring of listeners closed round to hear the war of wits. A lean student with olive skin and lank black hair thrust his face between the two, glancing from one to the other at each phrase and seeming to try to catch each flying phrase in his open moist   785
mouth. Cranly took a small grey handball from his pocket and began to examine it closely, turning it over and over.

—Next business? said MacCann. Hom!

He gave a loud cough of laughter, smiled broadly and tugged twice at the strawcoloured goatee which hung from his   790
blunt chin.

—The next business is to sign the testimonial.

—Will you pay me anything if I sign? asked Stephen.

—I thought you were an idealist, said MacCann.

The gipsylike student looked about him and addressed the   795
onlookers in an indistinct bleating voice.

—By hell, that's a queer notion. I consider that notion to be a mercenary notion.

His voice faded into silence. No heed was paid to his words. He turned his olive face, equine in expression, towards Ste=   800
phen, inviting him to speak again.

MacCann began to speak with fluent energy of the Czar's rescript,[4] of Stead,[5] of general disarmament, arbitration in cases of international disputes, of the signs of the times, of the new humanity and the new gospel of life which would make it the   805
business of the community to secure as cheaply as possible the greatest possible happiness of the greatest possible number.

2. Davin, who grew up on the land, retains in his speaking the influence of Elizabethan English combined with Irish turns of phrase. By contrast, Cranly's speech is a degenerated version of eighteenth-century Irish orators' eloquence.

3. Progressive political beliefs, that is, socialistic attitudes.

4. Nicholas II's "Peace Rescript" (1898), which led to a peace conference in The Hague in 1899 and to discussions involving the people, issues, and attitudes mentioned in the paragraph.

5. William Thomas Stead (1849–1912), English journalist, who actively opposed war and published The United States of Europe (1899).

The gipsy student responded to the close of the period by crying:

—Three cheers for universal brotherhood!

—Go on, Temple, said a stout ruddy student near him. I'll stand you a pint after.

—I'm a believer in universal brotherhood, said Temple, glancing about him out of his dark oval eyes. Marx is only a bloody cod.[6]

Cranly gripped his arm tightly to check his tongue, smiling uneasily, and repeated:

—Easy, easy, easy!

Temple struggled to free his arm but continued, his mouth flecked by a thin foam:

—Socialism was founded by an Irishman and the first man in Europe who preached the freedom of thought was Collins.[7] Two hundred years ago. He denounced priestcraft. The philosopher of Middlesex. Three cheers for John Anthony Collins!

A thin voice from the verge of the ring replied:

—Pip! pip!

Moynihan murmured beside Stephen's ear:

—And what about John Anthony's poor little sister:

Lottie Collins lost her drawers;
Won't you kindly lend her yours?[8]

Stephen laughed and Moynihan, pleased with the result, murmured again:

—We'll have five bob each way on John Anthony Collins.[9]

—I am waiting for your answer, said MacCann briefly.

—The affair doesn't interest me in the least, said Stephen wearily. You knew that well. Why do you make a scene about it?

—Good! said MacCann, smacking his lips. You are a reaction= ary then?

—Do you think you impress me, Stephen asked, when you flourish your wooden sword?

—Metaphors! said MacCann bluntly. Come to facts.

Stephen blushed and turned aside. MacCann stood his ground and said with hostile humour:

---

823 priestcraft. The] priestcraft, the Eg–64   836 knew] know Eg–64

6. Fool.
7. Anthony Collins (1676–1729), English theologian, author of *A Discourse of Free-thinking* (1713), that is, thinking free of institutionalized religion and its dogma.
8. The joking rhyme refers to an English music-hall performer of the 1890s.
9. Five shillings to place and five to show, as though Collins were a race horse (*Letters* III, 130).

—Minor poets, I suppose, are above such trivial questions as   845
the question of universal peace.

Cranly raised his head and held the handball between the
two students by way of a peaceoffering, saying:

—*Pax super totum sanguinarium globum.*[1]

Stephen, moving away the bystanders, jerked his shoulder   850
angrily in the direction of the Czar's image, saying:

—Keep your icon. If we must have a Jesus let us have a legit=
imate Jesus.

—By hell, that's a good one! said the gipsy student to those
about him. That's a fine expression. I like that expression   855
immensely.

He gulped down the spittle in his throat as if he were gulp=
ing down the phrase and, fumbling at the peak of his tweed
cap, turned to Stephen, saying:

—Excuse me, sir, what do you mean by that expression you   860
uttered just now?

Feeling himself jostled by the students near him, he said to
them:

—I am curious to know now what he meant by that ex=
pression.   865

He turned again to Stephen and said in a whisper:

—Do you believe in Jesus? I believe in man. Of course, I don't
know if you believe in man. I admire you, sir. I admire the
mind of man independent of all religions. Is that your opinion
about the mind of Jesus?   870

—Go on, Temple, said the stout ruddy student returning, as
was his wont, to his first idea, that pint is waiting for you.

—He thinks I'm an imbecile, Temple explained to Stephen,
because I'm a believer in the power of mind.

Cranly linked his arms into those of Stephen and his admirer   875
and said:

—*Nos ad manum ballum jocabimus.*[2]

Stephen, in the act of being led away, caught sight of
MacCann's flushed bluntfeatured face.

—My signature is of no account, he said politely. You are right   880
to go your way. Leave me to go mine.

—Dedalus, said MacCann crisply, I believe you're a good fel=
low but you have yet to learn the dignity of altruism and the
responsibility of the human individual.

A voice said: 885

---

881 your] Eg; your own MS

1. More joking Latin: "Peace over the entire bloody globe."
2. Modified Latin: "Let's go play handball."

—Intellectual crankery is better out of this movement than in
it.

Stephen, recognising the harsh tone of MacAlister's voice,
did not turn in the direction of the voice. Cranly pushed sol=
emnly through the throng of students, linking Stephen and   890
Temple like a celebrant attended by his ministers on his way to
the altar.

Temple bent eagerly across Cranly's breast and said:
—Did you hear MacAlister what he said? That youth is jealous
of you. Did you see that? I bet Cranly didn't see that. By hell, I   895
saw that at once.

As they crossed the inner hall the dean of studies was in the
act of escaping from the student with whom he had been con=
versing. He stood at the foot of the staircase, a foot on the
lowest step, his threadbare soutane gathered about him for   900
the ascent with womanish care, nodding his head often and
repeating:
—Not a doubt of it, Mr Hackett! Very true! Not a doubt of it!

In the middle of the hall the prefect of the college sodality
was speaking earnestly, in a soft querulous voice, with a   905
boarder. As he spoke he wrinkled a little his freckled brow and
bit, between his phrases, at a tiny bone pencil.
—I hope the matric men will all come. The first arts men are
pretty sure. Second arts too. We must make sure of the new=
comers.[3]   910

Temple bent again across Cranly, as they were passing
through the doorway, and said in a swift whisper:
—Do you know that he is a married man? He was a married
man before they converted him. He has a wife and children
somewhere. By hell, I think that's the queerest notion I ever   915
heard! Eh?

His whisper trailed off into sly cackling laughter. The mo=
ment they were through the doorway Cranly seized him rudely by
the neck and shook him, saying:
—You flaming floundering fool! I'll take my dying bible there   920
isn't a bigger bloody ape, do you know, than you in the whole
flaming bloody world!

Temple wriggled in his grip, laughing still with sly content,
while Cranly repeated flatly at every rude shake:
—A flaming flaring bloody idiot!   925

903 true!] fine! Eg–64

3. First-, second-, and third-year students, called by the names of the examinations they
were required to take at the end of each year; "matric": short for matriculation.

They crossed the weedy garden together. The president, wrapped in a heavy loose cloak, was coming towards them along one of the walks, reading his office. At the end of the walk he halted before turning and raised his eyes. The students saluted, Temple fumbling as before at the peak of his cap. They walked forward in silence. As they neared the alley Stephen could hear the thuds of the players' hands and the wet smacks of the ball and Davin's voice crying out excitedly at each stroke.

The three students halted round the box on which Davin sat to follow the game. Temple, after a few moments, sidled across to Stephen and said:

—Excuse me, I wanted to ask you do you believe that Jean Jacques Rousseau[4] was a sincere man?

Stephen laughed outright. Cranly, picking up the broken stave of a cask from the grass at his foot, turned swiftly and said sternly:

—Temple, I declare to the living God if you say another word, do you know, to anybody on any subject I'll kill you *super spottum*.[5]

—He was like you, I fancy, said Stephen, an emotional man.

—Blast him, curse him! said Cranly broadly. Don't talk to him at all. Sure you might as well be talking, do you know, to a flaming chamberpot as talking to Temple. Go home, Temple. For God' sake go home.

—I don't care a damn about you, Cranly, answered Temple, moving out of reach of the uplifted stave and pointing at Ste= phen. He's the only man I see in this institution that has an individual mind.

—Institution! Individual! cried Cranly. Go home, blast you, for you're a hopeless bloody man.

—I'm an emotional man, said Temple. That's quite rightly expressed. And I'm proud that I'm an emotionalist.

He sidled out of the alley, smiling slily. Cranly watched him with a blank expressionless face.

—Look at him! he said. Did you ever see such a go-by-the-wall?

His phrase was greeted by a strange laugh from a student who lounged against the wall, his peaked cap down on his eyes. The laugh, pitched in a high key and coming from a so muscu=

930

935

940

945

950

955

960

965

950 God'] God's Eg—64

4. Swiss thinker (1712–1778), whose writings about the contractual responsibilities of governments to the people anticipated the French Revolution.
5. "On the spot" (simplified Latin).

lar frame, seemed like the whinny of an elephant. The student's body shook all over and, to ease his mirth, he rubbed both his hands delightedly over his groins.

—Lynch is awake, said Cranly.

Lynch, for answer, straightened himself and thrust forward 970 his chest.

—Lynch puts out his chest, said Stephen, as a criticism of life.

Lynch smote himself sonorously on the chest and said:

—Who has anything to say about my girth?

Cranly took him at the word and the two began to tussle. 975 When their faces had flushed with the struggle they drew apart, panting. Stephen bent down towards Davin who, intent on the game, had paid no heed to the talk of the others.

—And how is my little tame goose? he asked. Did he sign too?

Davin nodded and said: 980

—And you, Stevie?

Stephen shook his head.

—You're a terrible man, Stevie, said Davin, taking the short pipe from his mouth. Always alone.

—Now that you have signed the petition for universal peace, 985 said Stephen, I suppose you will burn that little copybook I saw in your room.

As Davin did not answer Stephen began to quote:

—Long pace, fianna! Right incline, fianna! Fianna, by num= bers, salute, one, two![6]   990

—That's a different question, said Davin. I'm an Irish nation= alist, first and foremost. But that's you all out. You're a born sneerer, Stevie.

—When you make the next rebellion with hurleysticks,[7] said Stephen, and want the indispensable informer, tell me. I can 995 find you a few in this college.

—I can't understand you, said Davin. One time I hear you talk against English literature. Now you talk against the Irish in= formers. What with your name and your ideas. . . . Are you Irish at all?   1000

—Come with me now to the office of arms[8] and I will show you the tree of my family, said Stephen.

—Then be one of us, said Davin. Why don't you learn Irish? Why did you drop out of the league class[9] after the first lesson?

967 body] aEg; trunk MS–Eg

6. Military drill instructions from Davin's Fenian handbook. "Fianna" means warriors (Gaelic).
7. The bladed sticks used in the traditional Irish game of hurling.
8. Coats of arms, that is, genealogies.
9. Gaelic League class to learn Irish.

—You know one reason why, answered Stephen.   1005
   Davin tossed his head and laughed.
—O, come now, he said. Is it on account of that certain young
lady and Father Moran? But that's all in your own mind,
Stevie. They were only talking and laughing.
   Stephen paused and laid a friendly hand upon Davin's   1010
shoulder.
—Do you remember, he said, when we knew each other first.
The first morning we met you asked me to show you the
way to the matriculation class, putting a very strong stress on
the first syllable. You remember? Then you used to address the   1015
jesuits as father,[1] you remember? I ask myself about you: *Is
he as innocent as his speech?*
—I'm a simple person, said Davin. You know that. When you
told me that night in Harcourt Street those things about your
private life, honest to God, Stevie, I was not able to eat my   1020
dinner. I was quite bad. I was awake a long time that night.
Why did you tell me those things?
—Thanks, said Stephen. You mean I am a monster.
—No, said Davin, but I wish you had not told me.
   A tide began to surge beneath the calm surface of Stephen's   1025
friendliness.
—This race and this country and this life produced me, he
said. I shall express myself as I am.
—Try to be one of us, repeated Davin. In your heart you are an
Irishman but your pride is too powerful.   1030
—My ancestors threw off their language and took on another,
Stephen said. They allowed a handful of foreigners to subject
them. Do you fancy I am going to pay in my own life and
person debts they made? What for?
—For our freedom, said Davin.   1035
—No honourable and sincere man, said Stephen, has given up
to you his life and his youth and his affections from the days of
Tone to those of Parnell but you sold him to the enemy or
failed him in need or reviled him and left him for another. And
you invite me to be one of you. I'd see you damned first.   1040
—They died for their ideals, Stevie, said Davin. Our day will
come yet,[2] believe me.
   Stephen, following his own thought, was silent for an in=
stant.

1031 on] MS; ABSENT Eg–64

1. A form of address that Davin brings from the country. More worldly city dwellers address
   Jesuits as "sir."
2. Fenian slogan.

—The soul is born, he said vaguely, first in those moments I 1045
told you of. It has a slow and dark birth, more mysterious than
the birth of the body. When the soul of a man is born in this
country there are nets flung at it to hold it back from flight.
You talk to me of nationality, language, religion. I shall try to
fly by those nets.   1050
    Davin knocked the ashes from his pipe.
—Too deep for me, Stevie, he said. But a man's country comes
first. Ireland first, Stevie. You can be a poet or a mystic after.
—Do you know what Ireland is? asked Stephen with cold
violence. Ireland is the old sow that eats her farrow.   1055
    Davin rose from his box and went towards the players,
shaking his head sadly. But in a moment his sadness left him
and he was hotly disputing with Cranly and the two players
who had finished their game. A match of four was arranged,
Cranly insisting, however, that his ball should be used. He let it 1060
rebound twice or thrice to his hand and then struck it strongly
and swiftly towards the base of the alley, exclaiming in answer
to its thud:
—Your soul!
    Stephen stood with Lynch till the score began to rise. Then 1065
he plucked him by the sleeve to come away. Lynch obeyed,
saying:
—Let us eke[3] go, as Cranly has it.
    Stephen smiled at this sidethrust. They passed back through
the garden and out through the hall where the doddering porter 1070
was pinning up a notice in the frame. At the foot of the steps
they halted and Stephen took a packet of cigarettes from his
pocket and offered it to his companion.
—I know you are poor, he said.
—Damn your yellow insolence, answered Lynch.   1075
    This second proof of Lynch's culture made Stephen smile
again.
—It was a great day for European culture, he said, when you
made up your mind to swear in yellow.[4]
    They lit their cigarettes and turned to the right. After a 1080
pause Stephen began:
—Aristotle has not defined pity and terror.[5] I have. I say . . .

1053 a(2)] a16; ABSENT MS–16, 64   1061 then] ABSENT Eg–64

3. Lynch echoes Cranly's habitual speech, in which he misuses the archaic word "eke,"
   meaning also (*Letters* III, 130).
4. Lynch jokingly transforms the conventional use of *bloody* as a swear by his substitution
   (*Letters* III, 130).
5. Terms that Aristotle uses in his *Poetics* to describe the achievement of catharsis in tragedy.

Lynch halted and said bluntly:

—Stop! I won't listen! I am sick. I was out last night on a yellow drunk with Horan and Goggins.   1085

Stephen went on:

—Pity is the feeling which arrests the mind in the presence of whatsoever is grave and constant in human sufferings and unites it with the human sufferer. Terror is the feeling which arrests the mind in the presence of whatsoever is grave and 1090 constant in human sufferings and unites it with the secret cause.

—Repeat, said Lynch.

Stephen repeated the definitions slowly.

—A girl got into a hansom a few days ago, he went on, in 1095 London. She was on her way to meet her mother whom she had not seen for many years. At the corner of a street the shaft of a lorry shivered the window of the hansom in the shape of a star. A long fine needle of the shivered glass pierced her heart. She died on the instant. The reporter called it a tragic death. It 1100 is not. It is remote from terror and pity according to the terms of my definitions.

The tragic emotion, in fact, is a face looking two ways, towards terror and towards pity, both of which are phases of it. You see I use the word *arrest*. I mean that the tragic emotion 1105 is static. Or rather the dramatic emotion is. The feelings ex= cited by improper art are kinetic, desire or loathing. Desire urges us to possess, to go to something, loathing urges us to abandon, to go from something. These are kinetic emotions. The arts which excite them, pornographical or didactic, are 1110 therefore improper arts. The esthetic emotion (I use the general term) is therefore static. The mind is arrested and raised above desire and loathing.

—You say that art must not excite desire, said Lynch. I told you that one day I wrote my name in pencil on the backside of 1115 the Venus of Praxiteles in the Museum.[6] Was that not desire?

—I speak of normal natures, said Stephen. You also told me that when you were a boy in that charming carmelite school[7] you ate pieces of dried cowdung.

Lynch broke again into a whinny of laughter and again 1120 rubbed both his hands over his groins but without taking them from his pockets.

—O, I did! I did! he cried.

---

6. Plaster cast of a nude Venus by the Greek sculptor Praxiteles (4th century BCE), which stood in the National Museum.
7. Run by the Carmelites, the order of Our Lady of Mount Carmel.

Stephen turned towards his companion and looked at him for a moment boldly in the eyes. Lynch, recovering from his laughter, answered his look from his humbled eyes. The long slender flattened skull beneath the long pointed cap brought before Stephen's mind the image of a hooded reptile. The eyes, too, were reptilelike in glint and gaze. Yet at that instant, humbled and alert in their look, they were lit by one tiny human point, the window of a shrivelled soul, poignant and selfembittered. 1125

1130

—As for that, Stephen said in polite parenthesis, we are all animals. I also am an animal.

—You are, said Lynch. 1135

—But we are just now in a mental world, Stephen continued. The desire and loathing excited by improper esthetic means are really not esthetic emotions not only because they are kinetic in character but also because they are not more than physical. Our flesh shrinks from what it dreads and responds to the stimulus of what it desires by a purely reflex action of the nerv= ous system. Our eyelid closes before we are aware that the fly is about to enter our eye. 1140

—Not always, said Lynch critically.

—In the same way, said Stephen, your flesh responded to the stimulus of a naked statue but it was, I say, simply a reflex action of the nerves. Beauty expressed by the artist cannot awaken in us an emotion which is kinetic or a sensation which is purely physical. It awakens, or ought to awaken, or induces, or ought to induce, an esthetic stasis, an ideal pity or an ideal terror, a stasis called forth, prolonged and at last dissolved by what I call the rhythm of beauty. 1145

1150

—What is that exactly? asked Lynch.

—Rhythm, said Stephen, is the first formal esthetic relation of part to part in any esthetic whole or of an esthetic whole to its part or parts or of any part to the esthetic whole of which it is a part. 1155

—If that is rhythm, said Lynch, let me hear what you call beauty: and, please remember, though I did eat a cake of cow= dung once, that I admire only beauty. 1160

Stephen raised his cap as if in greeting. Then, blushing slightly, he laid his hand on Lynch's thick tweed sleeve.

—We are right, he said, and the others are wrong. To speak of these things and to try to understand their nature and, having understood it, to try slowly and humbly and constantly to 1165

1138 not esthetic] Eg, aEg; unesthetic MS; not æsthetic Eg; unesthetic 64   1151 dis-
solved] Eg; ABSENT MS

express, to press out again, from the gross earth or what it
brings forth, from sound and shape and colour which are the
prison gates of our soul, an image of the beauty we have come
to understand—that is art.

They had reached the canal bridge[8] and, turning from their   1170
course, went on by the trees. A crude grey light, mirrored in the
sluggish water, and a smell of wet branches over their heads
seemed to war against the course of Stephen's thought.

—But you have not answered my question, said Lynch. What
is art? What is the beauty it expresses?   .   1175

—That was the first definition I gave you, you sleepyheaded
wretch, said Stephen, when I began to try to think out the
matter for myself. Do you remember the night? Cranly lost his
temper and began to talk about Wicklow bacon.

—I remember, said Lynch. He told us about them flaming fat   1180
devils of pigs.

—Art, said Stephen, is the human disposition of sensible or
intelligible matter for an esthetic end. You remember the pigs
and forget that. You are a distressing pair, you and Cranly.

Lynch made a grimace at the raw grey sky and said: 1185

—If I am to listen to your esthetic philosophy give me at least
another cigarette. I don't care about it. I don't even care about
women. Damn you and damn everything. I want a job of five
hundred a year. You can't get me one.

Stephen handed him the packet of cigarettes. Lynch took the   1190
last one that remained, saying simply:

—Proceed!

—Aquinas, said Stephen, says that is beautiful the apprehen=
sion of which pleases.

Lynch nodded.   1195

—I remember that, he said. *Pulcra sunt quae visa placent.*

—He uses the word *visa*, said Stephen, to cover esthetic appre=
hension of all kinds, whether through sight or hearing or
through any other avenue of apprehension. This word, though
it is vague, is clear enough to keep away good and evil which   1200
excite desire and loathing. It means certainly a stasis and not a
kinesis. How about the true? It produces also a stasis of the
mind. You would not write your name in pencil across the
hypothenuse of a rightangled triangle.

—No, said Lynch. Give me the hypothenuse of the Venus of   1205
Praxiteles.

1197–98 apprehension] MS; apprehensions Eg–64

8. Over the Grand Canal in south Dublin.

—Static therefore, said Stephen. Plato, I believe, said that beauty is the splendour of truth.[9] I don't think that it has a meaning but the true and the beautiful are akin. Truth is beheld by the intellect which is appeased by the most satisfying relations of the intelligible: beauty is beheld by the imagination which is appeased by the most satisfying relations of the sen= sible. The first step in the direction of truth is to understand the frame and scope of the intellect itself, to comprehend the act itself of intellection. Aristotle's entire system of philosophy rests upon his book of psychology and that, I think, rests on his statement that the same attribute cannot at the same time and in the same connection belong to and not belong to the same subject.[1] The first step in the direction of beauty is to under= stand the frame and scope of the imagination, to comprehend the act itself of esthetic apprehension. Is that clear?

—But what is beauty? asked Lynch impatiently. Out with an= other definition. Something we see and like! Is that the best you and Aquinas can do?

—Let us take woman, said Stephen.

—Let us take her! said Lynch fervently.

—The Greek, the Turk, the Chinese, the Copt, the Hottentot, said Stephen, all admire a different type of female beauty. That seems to be a maze out of which we cannot escape. I see however two ways out. One is this hypothesis: that every physi= cal quality admired by men in women is in direct connection with the manifold functions of women for the propagation of the species. It may be so. The world, it seems, is drearier than even you, Lynch, imagined. For my part I dislike that way out. It leads to eugenics rather than to esthetic. It leads you out of the maze into a new gaudy lectureroom where MacCann, with one hand on *The Origin of Species*[2] and the other hand on the new testament, tells you that you admired the great flanks of Venus because you felt that she would bear you burly offspring and admired her great breasts because you felt that she would give good milk to her children and yours.

—Then MacCann is a sulphuryellow liar, said Lynch energeti= cally.

—There remains another way out, said Stephen laughing.

—To wit? said Lynch.

9. Plato comments on truth and beauty in his dialogues that concern art, the *Symposium* and the *Phaedrus*.

1. Aristotle wrote about the mind, but he never produced a book narrowly about psychology. Stephen correctly claims that Aristotle's prohibition against contradiction is central to his thinking about identity.

2. Published in 1859 by the English naturalist Charles Darwin (1809–1882), whose claims about evolution posed challenges to Christian beliefs.

—This hypothesis, Stephen began.

A long dray laden with old iron came round the corner of sir Patrick Dun's hospital covering the end of Stephen's speech with the harsh roar of jangled and rattling metal. Lynch closed his ears and gave out oath after oath till the dray had passed. 1250 Then he turned on his heel rudely. Stephen turned also and waited for a few moments till his companion's illhumour had had its vent.

—This hypothesis, Stephen repeated, is the other way out: that, though the same object may not seem beautiful to all 1255 people, all people who admire a beautiful object find in it certain relations which satisfy and coincide with the stages themselves of all esthetic apprehension. These relations of the sensible, visible to you through one form and to me through another, must be therefore the necessary qualities of beauty. 1260 Now, we can return to our old friend saint Thomas for another pennyworth of wisdom.

Lynch laughed.

—It amuses me vastly, he said, to hear you quoting him time after time like a jolly round friar. Are you laughing in your 1265 sleeve?

—MacAlister, answered Stephen, would call my esthetic the= ory applied Aquinas. So far as this side of esthetic philosophy extends Aquinas will carry me all along the line. When we come to the phenomenon of artistic conception, artistic gesta= 1270 tion and artistic reproduction I require a new terminology and a new personal experience.

—Of course, said Lynch. After all Aquinas, in spite of his intellect, was exactly a good round friar. But you will tell me about the new personal experience and new terminology some 1275 other day. Hurry up and finish the first part.

—Who knows? said Stephen smiling. Perhaps Aquinas would understand me better than you. He was a poet himself. He wrote a hymn for Maundy Thursday. It begins with the words *Pange lingua gloriosi*.[3] They say it is the highest glory of the 1280 hymnal. It is an intricate and soothing hymn. I like it: but there is no hymn that can be put beside that mournful and majestic processional song, the *Vexilla Regis* of Venantius Fortunatus.[4]

1270 phenomenon] MS; phenomena Eg–64

3. Partial Latin title of a hymn, sung on Maundy Thursday, the day before Good Friday, *Pange Lingua Gloriosi Corporis Mysterium* ("Tell, My Tongue, of the Mystery of Christ's Glorious Body"). The hymn is by Fortunatus (6th century), not Aquinas (*Cath. Enc.*).

4. Partial Latin title of another hymn sung on Maundy Thursday, *Vexilla Regis Prodeunt* ("The Banners of the King Advance").

Lynch began to sing softly and solemnly in a deep bass
voice: 1285

> Impleta sunt quae concinit
> David fideli carmine
> Dicendo nationibus
> Regnavit a ligno Deus.[5]

—That's great! he said, well pleased. Great music!   1290
They turned into Lower Mount Street. A few steps from the
corner a fat young man, wearing a silk neckcloth, saluted them
and stopped.
—Did you hear the results of the exams? he asked. Griffin was
plucked. Halpin and O'Flynn are through the home civil.   1295
Moonan got fifth place in the Indian. O'Shaughenessy got four=
teenth.[6] The Irish fellows in Clarke's gave them a feed last night.
They all ate curry.
His pallid bloated face expressed benevolent malice and, as
he had advanced through his tidings of success, his small   1300
fatencircled eyes vanished out of sight and his weak wheezing
voice out of hearing.
In reply to a question of Stephen's his eyes and his voice
came forth again from their lurkingplaces.
—Yes. MacCullagh and I, he said. He's taking pure mathemat= 1305
ics and I'm taking constitutional history. There are twenty
subjects. I'm taking botany too. You know I'm a member of the
field club.
He drew back from the other two in a stately fashion and
placed a plump woollengloved hand on his breast from which   1310
muttered wheezing laughter at once broke forth.
—Bring us a few turnips and onions the next time you go out
said Stephen drily, to make a stew.
The fat student laughed indulgently and said:
—We are all highly respectable people in the field club. Last 1315
Saturday we went out to Glenmalure,[7] seven of us.
—With women, Donovan? said Lynch.
Donovan again laid his hand on his chest and said:
—Our end is the acquisition of knowledge.
Then he said quickly: 1320

1289 Regnavit] Eg; Regnavi MS   1299 malice] Eg, 16; mirth MS; malice, Eg

5. The second stanza of *Pange Lingua*, these lines concern David's having foretold in his
   songs that God would rule the nations from a tree, that is, a cross.
6. The exam results pertain to gaining a place in the British civil service, the government
   administration at home and abroad. "Plucked" means failed. "Through" means success, in
   this case for posts in the United Kingdom. Doing well on the "Indian" exams enables serving in the British Empire's administration of India.
7. Valley in County Wicklow.

—I hear you are writing some essay about esthetics.

Stephen made a vague gesture of denial.

—Goethe and Lessing,[8] said Donovan, have written a lot on that subject, the classical school and the romantic school and all that. The *Laocoon*[9] interested me very much when I read it. Of course it is idealistic, German, ultraprofound. 1325

Neither of the others spoke. Donovan took leave of them urbanely.

—I must go, he said softly and benevolently. I have a strong suspicion, amounting almost to a conviction, that my sister 1330 intended to make pancakes today for the dinner of the Don= ovan family.

—Goodbye, Stephen said in his wake. Don't forget the turnips for me and my mate.

Lynch gazed after him, his lip curling in slow scorn till his 1335 face resembled a devil's mask:

—To think that that yellow pancakeeating excrement can get a good job, he said at length, and I have to smoke cheap ciga= rettes!

They turned their faces towards Merrion Square and went 1340 on for a little in silence.

—To finish what I was saying about beauty, said Stephen, the most satisfying relations of the sensible must therefore corre= spond to the necessary phases of artistic apprehension. Find these and you find the qualities of universal beauty. Aquinas 1345 says: *ad pulcritudinem tria requiruntur, integritas, consonantia, claritas*. I translate it so: *Three things are needed for beauty, wholeness, harmony and radiance*. Do these correspond to the phases of apprehension? Are you following?

—Of course, I am, said Lynch. If you think I have an excre= 1350 mentitious intelligence run after Donovan and ask him to listen to you.

Stephen pointed to a basket which a butcher's boy had slung inverted on his head.

—Look at that basket, he said. 1355

—I see it, said Lynch.

—In order to see that basket, said Stephen, your mind first of all separates the basket from the rest of the visible universe which is not the basket. The first phase of apprehension is a bounding line drawn about the object to be apprehended. An 1360

8. Johann Wolfgang von Goethe (1749–1832) and Gotthold Ephraim Lessing (1729–1781), German writers.
9. Lessing's book of that title (1766), on the differences in character and value between literature as a temporal art and sculpture as a spatial art, involves centrally the large Greek sculpture of Laocoön and his two sons struggling with serpents (see p. 323).

esthetic image is presented to us either in space or in time.
What is audible is presented in time, what is visible is presented
in space. But temporal or spatial the esthetic image is first
luminously apprehended as selfbounded and selfcontained
upon the immeasurable background of space or time which is   1365
not it. You apprehend it as *one* thing. You see it as one whole.
You apprehend its wholeness. That is *integritas*.
—Bull's eye! said Lynch laughing. Go on.
—Then, said Stephen, you pass from point to point, led by its
formal lines; you apprehend it as balanced part against part   1370
within its limits; you feel the rhythm of its structure. In other
words the synthesis of immediate perception is followed by the
analysis of apprehension. Having first felt that it is *one* thing
you feel now that it is a *thing*. You apprehend it as complex,
multiple, divisible, separable, made up of its parts, the result of   1375
its parts and their sum, harmonious. That is *consonantia*.
—Bull's eye again! said Lynch wittily. Tell me now what is
claritas and you win the cigar.
—The connotation of the word, Stephen said, is rather vague.
Aquinas uses a term which seems to be inexact. It baffled me   1380
for a long time. It would lead you to believe that he had in
mind symbolism or idealism, the supreme quality of beauty
being a light from some other world, the idea of which the
matter is but the shadow, the reality of which it is but the
symbol. I thought he might mean that *claritas* is the artistic   1385
discovery and representation of the divine purpose in anything
or a force of generalisation which would make the esthetic
image a universal one, make it outshine its proper conditions.
But that is literary talk. I understand it so. When you have
apprehended that basket as one thing and have then analysed it   1390
according to its form and apprehended it as a thing you make
the only synthesis which is logically and esthetically permiss=
ible. You see that it is that thing which it is and no other thing.
The radiance of which he speaks is the scholastic *quidditas*, the
whatness of a thing. This supreme quality is felt by the artist   1395
when the esthetic image is first conceived in his imagination.
The mind in that mysterious instant Shelley likened beautifully
to a fading coal.[1] The instant wherein that supreme quality of
beauty, the clear radiance of the esthetic image, is apprehended
luminously by the mind which has been arrested by its whole=   1400
ness and fascinated by its harmony is the luminous silent stasis

1384–85 is] a16; was MS–16 [THREE TIMES]

1. The comparison, in "A Defence of Poetry" (1821), suggests that some invisible power,
like a wind, from within causes a fleeting glow.

of esthetic pleasure, a spiritual state very like to that cardiac condition which the Italian physiologist Luigi Galvani, using a phrase almost as beautiful as Shelley's, called the enchantment of the heart.[2]   1405

Stephen paused and, though his companion did not speak, felt that his words had called up around them a thoughten= chanted silence.

—What I have said, he began again, refers to beauty in the wider sense of the word, in the sense which the word has in the   1410 literary tradition. In the marketplace it has another sense. When we speak of beauty in the second sense of the term our judgment is influenced in the first place by the art itself and by the form of that art. The image, it is clear, must be set between the mind or senses of the artist himself and the mind or senses   1415 of others. If you bear this in memory you will see that art necessarily divides itself into three forms progressing from one to the next. These forms are: the lyrical form, the form wherein the artist presents his image in immediate relation to himself; the epical form, the form wherein he presents his image in   1420 mediate relation to himself and to others; the dramatic form, the form wherein he presents his image in immediate relation to others.

—That you told me a few nights ago, said Lynch, and we began the famous discussion.   1425

—I have a book at home, said Stephen, in which I have written down questions which are more amusing than yours were. In finding the answers to them I found the theory of esthetic which I am trying to explain. Here are some questions I set myself: *Is a chair finely made tragic or comic? Is the portrait of*   1430 *Mona Lisa good if I desire to see it? Is the bust of sir Philip Crampton*[3] *lyrical, epical or dramatic? Can excrement or a child or a louse be a work of art? If not, why not?*

—Why not, indeed? said Lynch laughing.

—*If a man hacking in fury at a block of wood*, Stephen con=   1435 tinued, *make there an image of a cow is that image a work of art? If not, why not?*

—That's a lovely one, said Lynch laughing again. That has the true scholastic stink.

—Lessing, said Stephen, should not have taken a group of   1440 statues to write of. The art, being inferior, does not present the

2. Galvani (1737–1798), an Italian scientist, described the pause in a frog's heartbeat when the frog's heart was pierced with a needle.
3. A grotesque bust of Crampton (1777–1858), a famous surgeon, once stood near Trinity College on a drinking fountain.

forms I spoke of distinguished clearly one from another. Even
in literature, the highest and most spiritual art, the forms are
often confused. The lyrical form is in fact the simplest verbal
vesture of an instant of emotion, a rhythmical cry such as ages   1445
ago cheered on the man who pulled at the oar or dragged
stones up a slope. He who utters it is more conscious of the
instant of emotion than of himself as feeling emotion. The
simplest epical form is seen emerging out of lyrical literature
when the artist prolongs and broods upon himself as the centre 1450
of an epical event and this form progresses till the centre of
emotional gravity is equidistant from the artist himself and
from others. The narrative is no longer purely personal. The
personality of the artist passes into the narration itself, flowing
round and round the persons and the action like a vital sea.   1455
This progress you will see easily in that old English ballad
Turpin Hero which begins in the first person and ends in the
third person.[4] The dramatic form is reached when the vitality
which has flowed and eddied round each person fills every
person with such vital force that he or she assumes a proper   1460
and intangible esthetic life. The personality of the artist at first
a cry or a cadence or a mood and then a fluid and lambent
narrative finally refines itself out of existence, impersonalises
itself, so to speak. The esthetic image in the dramatic form is
life purified in and reprojected from the human imagination.   1465
The mystery of esthetic like that of material creation is accom=
plished. The artist, like the God of the creation, remains within
or behind or beyond or above his handiwork, invisible, refined
out of existence, indifferent, paring his fingernails.[5]
—Trying to refine them also out of existence, said Lynch.   1470
   A fine rain began to fall from the high veiled sky and they
turned into the duke's lawn to reach the national library[6] before
the shower came.
—What do you mean, Lynch asked surlily, by prating about
beauty and the imagination in this miserable Godforsaken is=   1475
land? No wonder the artist retired within or behind his handi=
work after having perpetrated this country.
   The rain fell faster. When they passed through the passage

---

4. Some versions of this ballad about the eighteenth-century highwayman Dick Turpin
   include the shift in person.
5. This statement resembles one made by the French novelist Gustave Flaubert
   (1821–1880) in a famous letter of 1857, where he asserts that the artist in the work must
   be like God in the created world, invisible, all powerful, felt everywhere but not seen.
6. The Duke of Leinster's residence, called Leinster House (originally Kildare House), and
   its small lawn are in the same complex of buildings as the National Library.

beside Kildare house they found many students sheltering un=
der the arcade of the library. Cranly leaning against a pillar 1480
was picking his teeth with a sharpened match, listening to some
companions. Some girls stood near the entrance door. Lynch
whispered to Stephen:

—Your beloved is here.

Stephen took his place silently on the step below the group 1485
of students, heedless of the rain which fell fast, turning his eyes
towards her from time to time. She too stood silently among
her companions. She has no priest to flirt with, he thought with
conscious bitterness, remembering how he had seen her
last. Lynch was right. His mind, emptied of theory and courage, 1490
lapsed back into a listless peace.

He heard the students talking among themselves. They
spoke of two friends who had passed the final medical exam=
ination, of the chances of getting places on ocean liners, of
poor and rich practices.   1495

—That's all a bubble. An Irish country practice is better.

—Hynes was two years in Liverpool and he says the same. A
frightful hole he said it was. Nothing but midwifery cases. Half
a crown cases.[7]

—Do you mean to say it is better to have a job here in the 1500
country than in a rich city like that? I know a fellow . . . .

—Hynes has no brains. He got through by stewing, pure
stewing.[8]

—Don't mind him. There's plenty of money to be made in a
big commercial city.   1505

—Depends on the practice.

—*Ego credo ut vita pauperum est simpliciter atrox, simpliciter
sanguinarius atrox, in Liverpoolio.*[9]

Their voices reached his ears as if from a distance in inter=
rupted pulsation. She was preparing to go away with her 1510
companions.

The quick light shower had drawn off, tarrying in clusters of
diamonds among the shrubs of the quadrangle where an exha=
lation was breathed forth by the blackened earth. Their trim
boots prattled as they stood on the steps of the colonnade 1515
talking quietly and gaily, glancing at the clouds, holding their

1479 Kildare house] a16 [cf unpublished letter to harriet shaw weaver, c. 20 Nov.
1917, british library]; the Royal Irish Academy MS–16, 64

7. Poor Irish inhabitants of this large English city across the Irish Channel could not afford
   medical care.
8. Hard study rather than natural ability.
9. Joke Latin: "I believe that the life of the poor is simply frightful, simply bloody frightful,
   in Liverpool."

umbrellas at cunning angles against the few last raindrops, closing them again, holding their skirts demurely.

And if he had judged her harshly? If her life were a simple rosary of hours, her life simple and strange as a bird's life, gay   1520
in the morning, restless all day, tired at sundown? Her heart simple and wilful as a bird's heart?

◆   ◆   ◆

Towards dawn he awoke. O what sweet music! His soul was all dewy wet. Over his limbs in sleep pale cool waves of light had passed. He lay still, as if his soul lay amid cool waters,   1525
conscious of faint sweet music. His mind was waking slowly to a tremulous morning knowledge, a morning inspiration. A spirit filled him, pure as the purest water, sweet as dew, moving as music. But how faintly it was inbreathed, how passionlessly as if the seraphim themselves were breathing upon him! His   1530
soul was waking slowly, fearing to awake wholly. It was that windless hour of dawn when madness wakes and strange plants open to the light and the moth flies forth silently.

An enchantment of the heart! The night had been enchanted. In dream or vision he had known the ecstasy of seraphic life.[1]   1535
Was it an instant of enchantment only or long hours and days and years and ages?

The instant of inspiration seemed now to be reflected from all sides at once from a multitude of cloudy circumstance of what had happened or of what might have happened. The in=   1540
stant flashed forth like a point of light and now from cloud on cloud of vague circumstance confused form was veiling softly its afterglow. O! In the virgin womb of the imagination the word was made flesh. Gabriel the seraph had come to the virgin's chamber.[2] An afterglow deepened within his spirit,   1545
whence the white flame had passed, deepening to a rose and ardent light. That rose and ardent light was her strange wilful heart, strange that no man had known or would know, wilful from before the beginning of the world: and lured by that ardent roselike glow the choirs of the seraphim were falling   1550
from heaven.

> Are you not weary of ardent ways,
> Lure of the fallen seraphim?
> Tell no more of enchanted days.

1. The life of the seraphs, the highest ranking angels.
2. The passage echoes New Testament passages concerning the future birth of Jesus. At the moment "the Word was made flesh" (John 1:14), Gabriel, an archangel, not a seraph, announces to Mary the character of her pregnancy (Luke 1:26–38).

The verses passed from his mind to his lips and, murmuring 1555
them over, he felt the rhythmic movement of a villanelle[3] pass
through them. The roselike glow sent forth its rays of rhyme;
ways, days, blaze, praise, raise. Its rays burned up the world,
consumed the hearts of men and angels: the rays from the rose
that was her wilful heart. 1560

> Your eyes have set man's heart ablaze
> And you have had your will of him.
> Are you not weary of ardent ways?

And then? The rhythm died away, ceased, began again to
move and beat. And then? Smoke, incense ascending from the 1565
altar of the world.

> Above the flame the smoke of praise
> Goes up from ocean rim to rim.
> Tell no more of enchanted days.

Smoke went up from the whole earth, from the vapoury 1570
oceans, smoke of her praise. The earth was like a swinging
swaying smoking censer, a ball of incense, an ellipsoidal ball.
The rhythm died out at once; the cry of his heart was broken.
His lips began to murmur the first verses over and over; then
went on stumbling through half verses, stammering and 1575
baffled; then stopped. The heart's cry was broken.

The veiled windless hour had passed and behind the panes
of the naked window the morning light was gathering. A bell
beat faintly very far away. A bird twittered; two birds, three.
The bell and the birds ceased: and the dull white light spread 1580
itself east and west, covering the world, covering the roselight
in his heart.

Fearing to lose all he raised himself suddenly on his elbow to
look for paper and pencil. There was neither on the table; only
the soup plate he had eaten the rice from for supper and the 1585
candlestick with its tendrils of tallow and its paper socket,
singed by the last flame. He stretched his arm wearily towards
the foot of the bed, groping with his hand in the pockets of the
coat that hung there. His fingers found a pencil and then a
cigarette packet. He lay back and, tearing open the packet, 1590
placed the last cigarette on the window ledge and began to
write out the stanzas of the villanelle in small neat letters on the
rough cardboard surface.

1572 swaying smoking] swaying Eg–24; smoking swaying 64   1580 birds] bird Eg–64

3. Complex French poetic form using only two rhymes and requiring specific repetitions of
   rhymes and lines. For the exact pattern see p. 321.

Having written them out he lay back on the lumpy pillow, murmuring them again. The lumps of knotted flock under his 1595 head reminded him of the lumps of knotted horsehair in the sofa of her parlour on which he used to sit, smiling or serious, asking himself why he had come, displeased with her and with himself, confounded by the print of the Sacred Heart[4] above the untenanted sideboard. He saw her approach him in a lull of the 1600 talk and beg him to sing one of his curious songs. Then he saw himself sitting at the old piano, striking chords softly from its speckled keys and singing, amid the talk which had risen again in the room, to her who leaned beside the mantelpiece a dainty song of the Elizabethans, a sad and sweet loth to depart, the 1605 victory chant of Agincourt,[5] the happy air of Greensleeves.[6] While he sang and she listened, or feigned to listen, his heart was at rest but when the quaint old songs had ended and he heard again the voices in the room he remembered his own sarcasm: the house where young men are called by their chris= 1610 tian names a little too soon.

At certain instants her eyes seemed about to trust him but he had waited in vain. She passed now dancing lightly across his memory as she had been that night at the carnival ball. Her white dress a little lifted, a white spray nodding in her hair. She 1615 danced lightly in the round. She was dancing towards him and, as she came, her eyes were a little averted and a faint glow was on her cheek. At the pause in the chain of hands her hand had lain in his an instant, a soft merchandise.

—You are a great stranger now.   1620
—Yes. I was born to be a monk.
—I am afraid you are a heretic.
—Are you much afraid?

For answer she had danced away from him along the chain of hands, dancing lightly and discreetly, giving herself to none. 1625 The white spray nodded to her dancing and when she was in shadow the glow was deeper on her cheek.

A monk! His own image started forth a profaner of the cloister, a heretic franciscan, willing and willing not to serve, spinning like Gherardino da Borgo San Donnino[7] a lithe web of 1630 sophistry and whispering in her ear.

1624 him] aEg; ABSENT MS–Eg

4. A representation of Jesus, frequently hung on the walls of Irish Catholic homes, with his heart showing to indicate his love.
5. Where the English defeated the French (1415).
6. A sixteenth-century English ballad in which the singer complains to the lady Greensleeves about her disdaining him.
7. Thirteenth-century Franciscan who was condemned for heresy because of his efforts to return the order to stricter practices.

No, it was not his image. It was the image of the young priest in whose company he had seen her last, looking at him out of dove's eyes, toying with the pages of her Irish phrase= book.

1635

—Yes, yes, the ladies are coming round to us. I can see it every day. The ladies are with us. The best helpers the language has.

—And the church, Father Moran?

—The church too. Coming round too. The work is going ahead there too. Don't fret about the church.

1640

Bah! he had done well to leave the room in disdain. He had done well not to salute her on the steps of the library. He had done well to leave her to flirt with her priest, to toy with a church which was the scullerymaid of christendom.

Rude brutal anger routed the last lingering instant of ecstasy from his soul. It broke up violently her fair image and flung the fragments on all sides. On all sides distorted reflections of her image started from his memory: the flowergirl in the ragged dress with damp coarse hair and a hoyden's face who had called herself his own girl and begged his handsel, the kitchen= girl in the next house who sang over the clatter of her plates with the drawl of a country singer the first bars of *By Killarney's Lakes and Fells*,[8] a girl who had laughed gaily to see him stumble when the iron grating in the footpath near Cork Hill had caught the broken sole of his shoe, a girl he had glanced at, attracted by her small ripe mouth as she passed out of Jacob's biscuit factory, who had cried to him over her shoul= der:

1645

1650

1655

—Do you like what you seen of me, straight hair and curly eyebrows?

1660

And yet he felt that, however he might revile and mock her image, his anger was also a form of homage. He had left the classroom in disdain that was not wholly sincere, feeling that perhaps the secret of her race lay behind those dark eyes upon which her long lashes flung a quick shadow. He had told him= self bitterly as he walked through the streets that she was a figure of the womanhood of her country, a batlike soul waking to the consciousness of itself in darkness and secrecy and lone= liness, tarrying a while, loveless and sinless, with her mild lover and leaving him to whisper of innocent transgressions in the latticed ear of a priest.[9] His anger against her found vent in

1665

1670

1632 was(2)] was like Eg–64   1643 well] Eg; ABSENT MS   1659 seen] aEg; saw MS–Eg   1669 a while,] awhile, Eg–64

8. Ballad from the opera *Inisfallen*, by the Irish composer Michael Balfe (1808–1870).
9. "Latticed" from being pressed up against the separating grid in the confessional.

coarse railing at her paramour, whose name and voice and features offended his baffled pride: a priested peasant, with a brother a policeman in Dublin and a brother a potboy in Moycullen.[1] To him she would unveil her soul's shy nakedness, 1675 to one who was but schooled in the discharging of a formal rite rather than to him, a priest of the eternal imagination, trans= muting the daily bread of experience into the radiant body of everliving life.[2]

The radiant image of the eucharist united again in an instant 1680 his bitter and despairing thoughts, their cries arising unbroken in a hymn of thanksgiving.

> Our broken cries and mournful lays
> Rise in one eucharistic hymn.
> Are you not weary of ardent ways?   1685
>
> While sacrificing hands upraise
> The chalice flowing to the brim.
> Tell no more of enchanted days.

He spoke the verses aloud from the first lines till the music and rhythm suffused his mind, turning it to quiet indulgence; 1690 then copied them painfully to feel them the better by seeing them; then lay back on his bolster.

The full morning light had come. No sound was to be heard: but he knew that all around him life was about to awaken in common noises, hoarse voices, sleepy prayers. Shrinking from 1695 that life he turned towards the wall, making a cowl of the blanket and staring at the great overblown scarlet flowers of the tattered wallpaper. He tried to warm his perishing joy in their scarlet glow, imagining a roseway from where he lay upwards to heaven all strewn with scarlet flowers. Weary! 1700 Weary! He too was weary of ardent ways.

A gradual warmth, a languorous weariness passed over him descending along his spine from his closely cowled head. He felt it descend and, seeing himself as he lay, smiled. Soon he would sleep.   1705

He had written verses for her again after ten years. Ten years before she had worn her shawl cowlwise about her head, send= ing sprays of her warm breath into the night air, tapping her foot upon the glassy road. It was the last tram; the lank brown horses knew it and shook their bells to the clear night in 1710

1675 Moycullen.] aEg; Athenry. MS–Eg   1676 in] Eg; to MS   1677 the] MS; ABSENT 64

1. Someone serving pots of drinks in a pub in Moycullen, a village in County Galway.
2. Stephen understands his role as artist as essentially similar to that of a Catholic priest, who transforms bread into the consecrated Host.

admonition. The conductor talked with the driver, both nod=
ding often in the green light of the lamp. They stood on the
steps of the tram, he on the upper, she on the lower. She came
up to his step many times between their phrases and went
down again and once or twice remained beside him forgetting   1715
to go down and then went down. Let be! Let be!

Ten years from that wisdom of children to his folly. If he
sent her the verses? They would be read out at breakfast amid
the tapping of eggshells. Folly indeed! The brothers would
laugh and try to wrest the page from each other with their   1720
strong hard fingers. The suave priest, her uncle, seated in his
armchair, would hold the page at arm's length, read it smiling
and approve of the literary form.

No, no: that was folly. Even if he sent her the verses she
would not show them to others. No, no: she could not.   1725

He began to feel that he had wronged her. A sense of her
innocence moved him almost to pity her, an innocence he had
never understood till he had come to the knowledge of it
through sin, an innocence which she too had not understood
while she was innocent or before the strange humiliation of her   1730
nature[3] had first come upon her. Then first her soul had begun
to live as his soul had when he had first sinned: and a tender
compassion filled his heart as he remembered her frail pallor
and her eyes, humbled and saddened by the dark shame of
womanhood.   1735

While his soul had passed from ecstasy to languor where had
she been? Might it be, in the mysterious ways of spiritual life,
that her soul at those same moments had been conscious of his
homage? It might be.

A glow of desire kindled again his soul and fired and ful=   1740
filled all his body. Conscious of his desire she was waking from
odorous sleep, the temptress of his villanelle. Her eyes, dark
and with a look of languor, were opening to his eyes. Her
nakedness yielded to him, radiant, warm, odorous and lavish=
limbed, enfolded him like a shining cloud, enfolded him like   1745
water with a liquid life: and like a cloud of vapour or like
waters circumfluent in space the liquid letters of speech, sym=
bols of the element of mystery, flowed forth over his brain.

>   Are you not weary of ardent ways?
>   Lure of the fallen seraphim.   1750
>   Tell no more of enchanted days.

1749 ways?] e:MS; ways, Eg–64

3. Her menstrual period.

Your eyes have set man's heart ablaze
And you have had your will of him.
Are you not weary of ardent ways?

Above the flame the smoke of praise   1755
Goes up from ocean rim to rim.
Tell no more of enchanted days.

Our broken cries and mournful lays
Rise in one eucharistic hymn.
Are you not weary of ardent ways?   1760

While sacrificing hands upraise
The chalice flowing to the brim.
Tell no more of enchanted days.

And still you hold our longing gaze
With languorous look and lavish limb.   1765
Are you not weary of ardent ways?
Tell no more of enchanted days.

◆   ◆   ◆

What birds were they?

He stood on the steps of the library to look at them, leaning
wearily on his ashplant.[4] They flew round and round the jutting   1770
shoulder of a house in Molesworth Street.[5] The air of the late
March evening made clear their flight, their dark darting
quivering bodies flying clearly against the sky as against a
limphung cloth of smoky tenuous blue.

He watched their flight: bird after bird: a dark flash, a   1775
swerve, a flash again, a dart aside, a curve, a flutter of wings.
He tried to count them before all their darting quivering bodies
passed: six, ten, eleven: and wondered were they odd or even in
number. Twelve, thirteen: for two came wheeling down from
the upper sky. They were flying high and low but ever round   1780
and round in straight and curving lines and ever flying from left
to right, circling about a temple of air.

He listened to their cries: like the squeak of mice behind the
wainscot: a shrill twofold note. But the notes were long and
shrill and whirring, unlike the cry of vermin, falling a third or a   1785
fourth and trilled as the flying beaks clove the air. Their cry
was shrill and clear and fine and falling like threads of silken
light unwound from whirring spools.

1765 *limb.*] e:MS, Eg; limb. MS; *limb!* Eg–64   1769 He NEW PARAGRAPH] NO PARAGRAPH
Eg–64   1783 their] the Eg–64

4. Sapling of the ash tree used as a walking stick (*OED*).
5. Off Kildare Street at the National Library and the National Museum.

The inhuman clamour soothed his ears in which his
mother's sobs and reproaches murmured insistently and the   1790
dark frail quivering bodies wheeling and fluttering and swerv=
ing round an airy temple of the tenuous sky soothed his eyes
which still saw the image of his mother's face.

Why was he gazing upwards from the steps of the porch,
hearing their shrill twofold cry, watching their flight? For an   1795
augury of good or evil? A phrase of Cornelius Agrippa[6] flew
through his mind and then there flew hither and thither shape=
less thoughts from Swedenborg[7] on the correspondence of birds
to things of the intellect and of how the creatures of the air
have their knowledge and know their times and seasons be=   1800
cause they, unlike man, are in the order of their life and have
not perverted that order by reason.

And for ages men had gazed upward as he was gazing at
birds in flight. The colonnade above him made him think
vaguely of an ancient temple and the ashplant on which he   1805
leaned wearily of the curved stick of an augur. A sense of fear
of the unknown moved in the heart of his weariness, a fear of
symbols and portents, of the hawklike man whose name he
bore soaring out of his captivity on osierwoven wings, of
Thoth, the god of writers, writing with a reed upon a tablet   1810
and bearing on his narrow ibis head the cusped moon.[8]

He smiled as he thought of the god's image for it made him
think of a bottlenosed judge in a wig, putting commas into a
document which he held at arm's length and he knew that he
would not have remembered the god's name but that it was like   1815
an Irish oath.[9] It was folly. But was it for this folly that he was
about to leave for ever the house of prayer and prudence into
which he had been born and the order of life out of which he
had come?

They came back with shrill cries over the jutting shoulder of   1820
the house, flying darkly against the fading air. What birds were
they? He thought that they must be swallows who had come
back from the south. Then he was to go away? for they were
birds ever going and coming, building ever an unlasting home

1823 away?] away 18–64

6. Heinrich Cornelius Agrippa von Nettesheim (1486–1535), German occult philosopher,
who discusses augury (divination by means of birds) in his *De Occulta Philosophia* (1531).
7. Emmanuel Swedenborg (1688–1772), Swedish mystical philosopher and scientist.
8. Thoth, the ancient Egyptian god of wisdom and writing, was frequently depicted in
human form with an ibis head crowned by the moon's horns.
9. *Thauss ag Dhee* (phonetically spelled), meaning "God knows," and its modified version,
thauss ag fee, meaning "the dear knows," an expression Stephen's mother uses (see
p. 152) (Gifford, 268; P. W. Joyce, 69).

under the eaves of men's houses and ever leaving the homes   1825
they had built to wander.

> *Bend down your faces, Oona and Aleel.*
> *I gaze upon them as the swallow gazes*
> *Upon the nest under the eave before*
> *He wander the loud waters.*[1]   1830

A soft liquid joy like the noise of many waters flowed over
his memory and he felt in his heart the soft peace of silent
spaces of fading tenuous sky above the waters, of oceanic si=
lence, of swallows flying through the seadusk over the flowing
waters.   1835

A soft liquid joy flowed through the words where the soft
long vowels hurtled noiselessly and fell away, lapping and
flowing back and ever shaking the white bells of their waves in
mute chime and mute peal and soft low swooning cry: and he
felt that the augury he had sought in the wheeling darting birds   1840
and in the pale space of sky above him had come forth from his
heart like a bird from a turret quietly and swiftly.

Symbol of departure or of loneliness? The verses crooned in
the ear of his memory composed slowly before his remember=
ing eyes the scene of the hall on the night of the opening of the   1845
national theatre.[2] He was alone at the side of the balcony,
looking out of jaded eyes at the culture of Dublin in the stalls
and at the tawdry scenecloths and human dolls framed by the
garish lamps of the stage. A burly policeman sweated behind
him and seemed at every moment about to act. The catcalls   1850
and hisses and mocking cries ran in rude gusts round the hall
from his scattered fellowstudents.

—A libel on Ireland!

—Made in Germany![3]

—Blasphemy!   1855

—We never sold our faith!

—No Irish woman ever did it!

—We want no amateur atheists.

1837 noiselessly] noiselessly⟨,⟩ MS   1839 mute] ⁻¹ mute¹⌐ MS [TWICE]   1841–42 from--
heart] ⁻¹from--heart¹⌐ MS   1844 the--of] ⁻¹the--of¹⌐ MS   1845 the opening of] ⁻¹the
opening of¹⌐ MS

1. Opening of Cathleen's dying farewell in the play *The Countess Cathleen* (1892), by the
   Irish poet and dramatist W. B. Yeats (1865–1939; see pp. 299–300).
2. May 8, 1899, when *The Countess Cathleen,* the first production of the Irish Literary
   Theatre, drew protests because Cathleen gives up her soul to feed her people.
3. At the time, Germany would have been thought of as largely Protestant and Jewish, by
   contrast with Catholic Ireland.

—We want no budding buddhists.[4]

A sudden soft hiss fell from the windows above him and he 1860
knew that the electric lamps had been switched on in the
readers' room. He turned into the pillared hall, now calmly lit,
went up the staircase and passed in through the clicking
turnstile.

Cranly was sitting over near the dictionaries. A thick book, 1865
opened at the frontispiece, lay before him on the wooden rest.
He leaned back in his chair, inclining his ear like that of a
confessor to the face of the medical student who was reading to
him a problem from the chess page of a journal. Stephen sat
down at his right and the priest at the other side of the table 1870
closed his copy of *The Tablet*[5] with an angry snap and stood up.

Cranly gazed after him blandly and vaguely. The medical
student went on in a softer voice:

—Pawn to king's fourth.[6]

—We had better go, Dixon, said Stephen in warning. He has 1875
gone to complain.

Dixon folded the journal and rose with dignity, saying:

—Our men retired in good order.

—With guns and cattle, added Stephen, pointing to the title-
page of Cranly's book on which was printed *Diseases of the* 1880
Ox.

As they passed through a lane of the tables Stephen said:

—Cranly, I want to speak to you.

Cranly did not answer or turn. He laid his book on the
counter and passed out, his wellshod feet sounding flatly on the 1885
floor. On the staircase he paused and gazing absently at Dixon
repeated:

—Pawn to king's bloody fourth.

—Put it that way if you like, Dixon said.

He had a quiet toneless voice and urbane manners and on a 1890
finger of his plump clean hand he displayed at moments a
signet ring.

As they crossed the hall a man of dwarfish stature came
towards them. Under the dome of his tiny hat his unshaven
face began to smile with pleasure and he was heard to murmur. 1895
The eyes were melancholy as those of a monkey.

1860 soft] e; brief MS; swift Eg–64 [REVISION MISREAD? CF 2071, 2076]   1860 fell--him]
⁻¹⟨was heard⟩ fell--him¹ʳ MS   1862 readers'] reader's 16–64   1863 went] ⁻¹⟨and going⟩
went¹ʳ MS   1880 printed] a16; written MS–16   1890 toneless] Eg; ringless MS

4. Yeats and others involved in the nationalist literary revival held occult beliefs, partici-
   pated in séances, and explored Eastern religions and thought. See pp. 299–304 for some
   of Yeats's early writings that made a significant impression on Joyce.
5. A conservative Catholic weekly.
6. A typical opening move in chess.

—Good evening, captain, said Cranly, halting.

—Good evening, gentlemen, said the stubblegrown monkeyish face.

—Warm weather for March, said Cranly. They have the win= 1900
dows open upstairs.

Dixon smiled and turned his ring. The blackish monkey=
puckered face pursed its human mouth with gentle pleasure
and its voice purred:

—Delightful weather for March. Simply delightful. 1905

—There are two nice young ladies upstairs, captain, tired of
waiting, Dixon said.

Cranly smiled and said kindly:

—The captain has only one love: sir Walter Scott. Isn't that so,
captain? 1910

—What are you reading now, captain? Dixon asked. *The Bride
of Lammermoor?*[7]

—I love old Scott, the flexible lips said. I think he writes some=
thing lovely. There is no writer can touch sir Walter Scott.

He moved a thin shrunken brown hand gently in the air in 1915
time to his praise and his thin quick eyelids beat often over his
sad eyes.

Sadder to Stephen's ear was his speech: a genteel accent, low
and moist, marred by errors:[8] and listening to it he wondered
was the story true and was the thin blood that flowed in his 1920
shrunken frame noble and come of an incestuous love?

The park trees were heavy with rain and rain fell still and
ever in the lake, lying grey like a shield. A game of swans[9] flew
there and the water and the shore beneath were fouled with
their greenwhite slime. They embraced softly impelled by the 1925
grey rainy light, the wet silent trees, the shieldlike witnessing
lake, the swans. They embraced without joy or passion, his
arm about his sister's neck. A grey woollen cloak was wrapped
athwart from her shoulder to her waist: and her fair head was
bent in willing shame. He had loose redbrown hair and tender 1930
shapely strong freckled hands. Face? There was no face seen.
The brother's face was bent upon her fair rainfragrant hair.
The hand freckled and strong and shapely and caressing was
Davin's hand.

He frowned angrily upon his thought and on the shrivelled 1935

1902 blackish] black⌐¹ish¹⌐ MS   1906 of] Eg; ABSENT MS   1921 noble and] ⌐¹noble
and¹⌐ MS   1921 of an] ⌐¹of an¹⌐ MS   1923 A--of] Eg; Old MS   1929 athwart] MS;
athwart her Eg–64

7. Novel (1819) by the Scottish writer Sir Walter Scott (1771–1832).
8. A combination of upper-class pronunciation and grammatical mistakes.
9. A flock kept for pleasure (*OED*).

mannikin who had called it forth. His father's gibes at the Bantry gang[1] leaped out of his memory. He held them at a distance and brooded uneasily on his own thought again. Why were they not Cranly's hands? Had Davin's simplicity and in= nocence stung him more secretly?   1940

He walked on across the hall with Dixon, leaving Cranly to take leave elaborately of the dwarf.

Under the colonnade Temple was standing in the midst of a little group of students. One of them cried:

—Dixon, come over till you hear. Temple is in grand form.   1945

Temple turned on him his dark gipsy eyes.

—You're a hypocrite, O'Keeffe, he said. And Dixon's a smiler. By hell, I think that's a good literary expression.

He laughed slily, looking in Stephen's face, repeating:

—By hell, I'm delighted with that name. A smiler.   1950

A stout student who stood below them on the steps said:

—Come back to the mistress, Temple. We want to hear about that.

—He had, faith, Temple said. And he was a married man too. And all the priests used to be dining there. By hell, I think they   1955 all had a touch.[2]

—We shall call it riding a hack to spare the hunter,[3] said Dixon.

—Tell us, Temple, O'Keeffe said. How many quarts of porter have you in you?

—All your intellectual soul is in that phrase, O'Keeffe, said   1960 Temple with open scorn.

He moved with a shambling gait round the group and spoke to Stephen.

—Did you know that the Forsters are the kings of Belgium?[4] he asked.   1965

Cranly came out through the door of the entrance hall, his hat thrust back on the nape of his neck and picking his teeth with care.

—And here's the wiseacre, said Temple. Do you know that about the Forsters?   1970

He paused for an answer. Cranly dislodged a figseed from his teeth on the point of his rude toothpick and gazed at it intently.

1958 How] how Eg–64   1972 rude] Eg; ABSENT MS

1. A group of politicians from the town of Bantry, in County Cork, who were considered Parnell's betrayers, including Timothy Healy (1855–1931), who led the opposition to Parnell within the Irish Parliamentary Party after the adultery scandal.
2. Sexual contact.
3. Riding a workhorse instead of a more valuable, better-looking one.
4. A drunken claim, perhaps made jokingly as a play on the tendency to see Irish origins in unlikely places.

—The Forster family, Temple said, is descended from Baldwin the First, king of Flanders. He was called the Forester. Forester and Forster are the same name. A descendant of Baldwin the First, captain Francis Forster, settled in Ireland and married the daughter of the last chieftain of Clanbrassil. Then there are the Blake Forsters. That's a different branch.[5] ₁₉₇₅

—From Baldhead, king of Flanders, Cranly repeated, rooting again deliberately at his gleaming uncovered teeth. ₁₉₈₀

—Where did you pick up all that history? O'Keeffe asked.

—I know all the history of your family too, Temple said, turning to Stephen. Do you know what Giraldus Cambrensis[6] says about your family? ₁₉₈₅

—Is he descended from Baldwin too? asked a tall consumptive student with dark eyes.

—Baldhead, Cranly repeated, sucking at a crevice in his teeth.

—*Pernobilis et pervetusta familia*,[7] Temple said to Stephen.

The stout student who stood below them on the steps farted briefly. Dixon turned towards him saying in a soft voice: ₁₉₉₀

—Did an angel speak?

Cranly turned also and said vehemently but without anger:

—Goggins, you're the flamingest dirty devil I ever met, do you know. ₁₉₉₅

—I had it on my mind to say that, Goggins answered firmly. It did no-one any harm, did it?

—We hope, Dixon said suavely, that it was not of the kind known to science as a *paulo post futurum*.[8]

—Didn't I tell you he was a smiler? said Temple, turning right and left. Didn't I give him that name? ₂₀₀₀

—You did. We're not deaf, said the tall consumptive.

Cranly still frowned at the stout student below him. Then, with a snort of disgust, he shoved him violently down the steps.

—Go away from here, he said rudely. Go away, you stinkpot. And you are a stinkpot. ₂₀₀₅

Goggins skipped down on to the gravel and at once returned to his place with good humour. Temple turned back to Stephen and asked:

—Do you believe in the law of heredity? ₂₀₁₀

—Are you drunk or what are you or what are you trying to say? asked Cranly, facing round on him with an expression of wonder.

---

5. More drunken claims parodying the enthusiasm for Irish genealogies.
6. Twelfth-century Welsh historian who wrote about Ireland.
7. "From a noble and venerable family" (Latin).
8. Latin name of a Greek verb tense for an event that will happen soon, jokingly used to express the hope that Goggins's fart has no future aspect.

—The most profound sentence ever written, Temple said with
enthusiasm, is the sentence at the end of the zoology. Repro=   2015
duction is the beginning of death.

He touched Stephen timidly at the elbow and said eagerly:
—Do you feel how profound that is because you are a poet?

Cranly pointed his long forefinger.
—Look at him! he said with scorn to the others. Look at   2020
Ireland's hope!

They laughed at his words and gesture. Temple turned on
him bravely, saying:
—Cranly, you're always sneering at me. I can see that. But I
am as good as you are any day. Do you know what I think   2025
about you now as compared with myself?
—My dear man, said Cranly urbanely, you are incapable, do
you know, absolutely incapable of thinking.
—But do you know, Temple went on, what I think of you and
of myself compared together?   2030
—Out with it, Temple! the stout student cried from the steps.
Get it out in bits!

Temple turned right and left, making sudden feeble gestures
as he spoke.
—I'm a ballocks,[9] he said, shaking his head in despair. I am.   2035
And I know I am. And I admit it that I am.

Dixon patted him lightly on the shoulder and said mildly:
—And it does you every credit, Temple.
—But he, Temple said, pointing to Cranly. He is a ballocks too
like me. Only he doesn't know it. And that's the only difference   2040
I see.

A burst of laughter covered his words. But he turned again
to Stephen and said with a sudden eagerness:
—That word is a most interesting word. That's the only Eng=
lish dual number.[1] Did you know?   2045
—Is it? Stephen said vaguely.

He was watching Cranly's firmfeatured suffering face, lit up
now by a smile of false patience. The gross name had passed
over it like foul water poured over an old stone image, patient
of injuries: and, as he watched him, he saw him raise his hat in   2050
salute and uncover the black hair that stood up stiffly from his
forehead like an iron crown.

She passed out from the porch of the library and bowed
across Stephen in reply to Cranly's greeting. He also? Was there

2025 are] MS; ABSENT Eg–64   2051 up] ABSENT 18–24

9. Literally, a testicle; figuratively, a clumsy person.
1. Grammatical form that expresses a pair but is treated as singular.

not a slight flush on Cranly's cheek? Or had it come forth at   2055
Temple's words? The light had waned. He could not see.

Did that explain his friend's listless silence, his harsh com=
ments, the sudden intrusions of rude speech with which he had
shattered so often Stephen's ardent wayward confessions? Ste=
phen had forgiven freely for he had found this rudeness also in   2060
himself towards himself. And he remembered an evening when
he had dismounted from a borrowed creaking bicycle to pray
to God in a wood near Malahide.[2] He had lifted up his arms
and spoken in ecstasy to the sombre nave of the trees, knowing
that he stood on holy ground and in a holy hour. And when   2065
two constabularymen had come into sight round a bend in the
gloomy road he had broken off his prayer to whistle loudly an
air from the last pantomime.

He began to beat the frayed end of his ashplant against the
base of a pillar. Had Cranly not heard him? Yet he could wait.   2070
The talk about him ceased for a moment: and a soft hiss fell
again from a window above. But no other sound was in the air
and the swallows whose flight he had followed with idle eyes
were sleeping.

She had passed through the dusk. And therefore the air was   2075
silent save for one soft hiss that fell. And therefore the tongues
about him had ceased their babble. Darkness was falling.

Darkness falls from the air.[3]

A trembling joy, lambent as a faint light, played like a fairy
host around him. But why? Her passage through the darkening   2080
air or the verse with its black vowels and its opening sound,
rich and lutelike?

He walked away slowly towards the deeper shadows at the
end of the colonnade, beating the stone softly with his stick to
hide his revery from the students whom he had left: and   2085
allowed his mind to summon back to itself the age of Dowland
and Byrd and Nash.[4]

Eyes, opening from the darkness of desire, eyes that dimmed
the breaking east. What was their languid grace but the soft=
ness of chambering? And what was their shimmer but the   2090
shimmer of the scum that mantled the cesspool of the court of a

2076 soft] Eg; brief MS   2089 grace] Eg; ABSENT MS

2. Coastal village north of Dublin.
3. Misrecollection of the line, which concerns brightness falling, from "A Litany in Time of
   Plague" (1592), by the English poet and dramatist Thomas Nashe (1567–1601).
4. The Elizabethan and Jacobean era in England. Elizabeth I reigned 1558–1603. James I
   reigned 1603–25. John Dowland (c. 1563–1626) and William Byrd (1543–1623) were
   composers. "Nash" is a variation of "Nashe" (see previous note).

slobbering Stuart.[5] And he tasted in the language of memory
ambered wines,[6] dying fallings of sweet airs, the proud pavan:[7]
and saw with the eyes of memory kind gentlewomen in Covent
Garden[8] wooing from their balconies with sucking mouths and   2095
the poxfouled wenches of the taverns and young wives that,
gaily yielding to their ravishers, clipped[9] and clipped again.

The images he had summoned gave him no pleasure. They
were secret and enflaming but her image was not entangled by
them. That was not the way to think of her. It was not even the   2100
way in which he thought of her. Could his mind then not trust
itself? Old phrases, sweet only with a disinterred sweetness like
the figseeds Cranly rooted out of his gleaming teeth.

It was not thought nor vision though he knew vaguely that
her figure was passing homeward through the city. Vaguely   2105
first and then more sharply he smelt her body. A conscious
unrest seethed in his blood. Yes, it was her body that he smelt:
a wild and languid smell: the tepid limbs over which his music
had flowed desirously and the secret soft linen upon which her
flesh distilled odour and a dew.   2110

A louse crawled over the nape of his neck and, putting his
thumb and forefinger deftly beneath his loose collar, he caught
it. He rolled its body, tender yet brittle as a grain of rice, be=
tween thumb and finger for an instant before he let it fall from
him and wondered would it live or die. There came to his mind   2115
a curious phrase from Cornelius a Lapide[1] which said that the
lice born of human sweat were not created by God with the
other animals on the sixth day. But the tickling of the skin of
his neck made his mind raw and red. The life of his body,
illclad, illfed, louseeaten, made him close his eyelids in a sud=   2120
den spasm of despair: and in the darkness he saw the brittle
bright bodies of lice falling from the air and turning often as
they fell. Yes: and it was not darkness that fell from the air. It
was brightness.

2096 wenches] Eg–64; wenchers MS, 93   2107 that] ABSENT Eg–64   2119 red. The]
red⟨,⟩. ⟨t⟩ The MS

5. James I of England, who has often been compared unfavorably with his predecessor,
   Elizabeth I.
6. Perfumed with ambergris (OED).
7. An Elizabethan dance.
8. An area in the eastern part of central London that developed in the 1630s under the guidance of the English architect and stage designer Inigo Jones (1573–1652), who incorporated what had been primarily a market for flowers, fruits, and vegetables into a piazza.
   When Charles II (1630–1685) let theaters reopen in 1660 after eighteen years of Puritan
   repression and allowed women to act in public for the first time, the first theater was in
   Covent Garden. Stephen's imagined memories have moved forward half a century from
   Dowland, Byrd, and Nash.
9. Embraced.
1. Flemish Jesuit (1567–1637), who made the following claim.

Brightness falls from the air.   2125

He had not even remembered rightly Nash's line. All the images it had awakened were false. His mind bred vermin. His thoughts were lice born of the sweat of sloth.

He came back quickly along the colonnade towards the group of students. Well then let her go and be damned to her. 2130 She could love some clean athlete who washed himself every morning to the waist and had black hair on his chest. Let her.

Cranly had taken another dried fig from the supply in his pocket and was eating it slowly and noisily. Temple sat on the pediment of a pillar, leaning back, his cap pulled down on his 2135 sleepy eyes. A squat young man came out of the porch, a leather portfolio tucked under his armpit. He marched towards the group, striking the flags[2] with the heels of his boots and with the ferrule[3] of his heavy umbrella. Then, raising the um= brella in salute, he said to all: 2140
—Good evening, sirs.

He struck the flags again and tittered while his head trembled with a slight nervous movement. The tall consump= tive student and Dixon and O'Keeffe were speaking in Irish and did not answer him. Then, turning to Cranly, he said: 2145
—Good evening, particularly to you.

He moved the umbrella in indication and tittered again. Cranly, who was still chewing the fig, answered with loud movements of his jaws.
—Good? Yes. It is a good evening.   2150

The squat student looked at him seriously and shook his umbrella gently and reprovingly.
—I can see, he said, that you are about to make obvious remarks.
—Um, Cranly answered, holding out what remained of the 2155 halfchewed fig and jerking it towards the squat student's mouth in sign that he should eat.

The squat student did not eat it but, indulging his special humour, said gravely, still tittering and prodding his phrase with his umbrella: 2160
—Do you intend that . . .

He broke off, pointed bluntly to the munched pulp of the fig and said loudly:
—I allude to that.
—Um, Cranly said as before.   2165

2133 dried] ⌐¹dried¹⌐ MS

2. Flagstones (*OED*).
3. Metal ring or cap to protect the end of a stick.

—Do you intend that now, the squat student said, as *ipso facto*[4]
or, let us say, as so to speak?

Dixon turned aside from his group, saying:

—Goggins was waiting for you, Glynn. He has gone round to
the Adelphi[5] to look for you and Moynihan. What have you   2170
there? he asked, tapping the portfolio under Glynn's arm.

—Examination papers, Glynn answered. I give them monthly
examinations to see that they are profiting by my tuition.

He also tapped the portfolio and coughed gently and smiled.

—Tuition! said Cranly rudely. I suppose you mean the bare=   2175
footed children that are taught by a bloody ape like you. God
help them!

He bit off the rest of the fig and flung away the butt.

—I suffer little children to come unto me,[6] Glynn said amiably.

—A bloody ape, Cranly repeated with emphasis, and a blas=   2180
phemous bloody ape!

Temple stood up and, pushing past Cranly, addressed
Glynn:

—That phrase you said now, he said, is from the new testa=
ment about suffer the children to come to me.   2185

—Go to sleep again, Temple, said O'Keeffe.

—Very well, then, Temple continued, still addressing Glynn,
and if Jesus suffered the children to come why does the church
send them all to hell if they die unbaptised? Why is that?

—Were you baptised yourself, Temple? the consumptive stu=   2190
dent asked.

—But why are they sent to hell if Jesus said they were all to
come? Temple said, his eyes searching in Glynn's eyes.

Glynn coughed and said gently, holding back with difficulty
the nervous titter in his voice and moving his umbrella at every   2195
word:

—And, as you remark, if it is thus I ask emphatically whence
comes this thusness.

—Because the church is cruel like all old sinners, Temple said.

—Are you quite orthodox on that point, Temple? Dixon said   2200
suavely.

—Saint Augustine says that about unbaptised children going to
hell, Temple answered, because he was a cruel old sinner too.

—I bow to you, Dixon said, but I had the impression that
limbo existed for such cases.   2205

2193 in] ⁻¹in ˥ˊ MS

4. "By that very fact" (Latin); part of the meaningless babble of the conversation (*Letters* III, 130).
5. Adelphi Hotel, near the National Library.
6. Alludes to Mark 10:14.

—Don't argue with him, Dixon, Cranly said brutally. Don't talk to him or look at him. Lead him home with a sugan[7] the way you'd lead a bleating goat.

—Limbo! Temple cried. That's a fine invention too. Like hell.

—But with the unpleasantness left out, Dixon said.   2210

He turned smiling to the others and said:

—I think I am voicing the opinions of all present in saying so much.

—You are, Glynn said in a firm tone. On that point Ireland is united.   2215

He struck the ferrule of his umbrella on the stone floor of the colonnade.

—Hell, Temple said. I can respect that invention of the grey spouse of Satan.[8] Hell is Roman, like the walls of the Romans, strong and ugly. But what is limbo?   2220

—Put him back into the perambulator, Cranly, O'Keeffe called out.

Cranly made a swift step towards Temple, halted, stamping his foot and crying as if to a fowl:

—Hoosh!   2225

Temple moved away nimbly.

—Do you know what limbo is? he cried. Do you know what we call a notion like that in Roscommon?[9]

—Hoosh! Blast you! Cranly cried, clapping his hands.

—Neither my arse nor my elbow! Temple cried out scornfully.   2230
And that's what I call limbo.

—Give us that stick here, Cranly said.

He snatched the ashplant roughly from Stephen's hand and sprang down the steps: but Temple, hearing him move in pur= suit, fled through the dusk like a wild creature, nimble and 2235 fleetfooted. Cranly's heavy boots were heard loudly charging across the quadrangle and then returning heavily, foiled and spurning the gravel at each step.

His step was angry and with an angry abrupt gesture he thrust the stick back into Stephen's hand. Stephen felt that his 2240 anger had another cause but, feigning patience, touched his arm slightly and said quietly:

—Cranly, I told you I wanted to speak to you. Come away.

Cranly looked at him for a few moments and asked:

—Now?   2245

2224 and] MS; ABSENT Eg–64   2236 heard] heard ⟨in⟩ MS

7. A straw or hay rope (Gaelic; P. W. Joyce, 338).
8. Sin, in *Paradise Lost* (book two), by the English poet John Milton (1608–1674).
9. In the west of Ireland, both a town and a county.

—Yes, now, Stephen said. We can't speak here. Come away.

They crossed the quadrangle together without speaking. The birdcall from *Siegfried*[1] whistled softly followed them from the steps of the porch. Cranly turned: and Dixon, who had whistled, called out: 2250

—Where are you fellows off to? What about that game, Cranly?

They parleyed in shouts across the still air about a game of billiards to be played in the Adelphi hotel. Stephen walked on alone and out into the quiet of Kildare Street. Opposite   2255 Maple's hotel he stood to wait, patient again. The name of the hotel, a colourless polished wood, and its colourless quiet front stung him like a glance of polite disdain. He stared angrily back at the softly lit drawingroom of the hotel in which he imagined the sleek lives of the patricians of Ireland housed in calm. They   2260 thought of army commissions and land agents: peasants greeted them along the roads in the country: they knew the names of certain French dishes and gave orders to jarvies[2] in highpitched provincial voices which pierced through their skintight accents.

How could he hit their conscience or how cast his shadow   2265 over the imagination of their daughters, before their squires begat upon them, that they might breed a race less ignoble than their own? And under the deepened dusk he felt the thoughts and desires of the race to which he belonged flitting like bats across the dark country lanes, under trees by the edges of   2270 streams and near the poolmottled bogs. A woman had waited in the doorway as Davin had passed by at night and, offering him a cup of milk, had all but wooed him to her bed: for Davin had the mild eyes of one that could be secret. But him no woman's eyes had wooed.   2275

His arm was taken in a strong grip and Cranly's voice said:

—Let us eke go.

They walked southward in silence. Then Cranly said:

—That blithering idiot Temple! I swear to Moses, do you know, that I'll be the death of that fellow one time.   2280

But his voice was no longer angry and Stephen wondered was he thinking of her greeting to him under the porch.

They turned to the left and walked on as before. When they had gone on so for some time Stephen said:

—Cranly, I had an unpleasant quarrel this evening.   2285

2266 imagination] imaginations 16–64   2274 that] who Eg–64   2278 southward] Eg; northward MS

1. Musical passage from the opera *Siegfried* (1876), by the German composer Richard Wagner (1813–1883).
2. Hackney coachmen (*OED*).

—With your people? Cranly asked.

—With my mother.

—About religion?

—Yes, Stephen answered.

    After a pause Cranly asked: 2290

—What age is your mother?

—Not old, Stephen said. She wishes me to make my easter duty.

—And will you?

—I will not, Stephen said.

—Why not? Cranly said.   2295

—I will not serve, answered Stephen.

—That remark was made before,[3] Cranly said calmly.

—It is made behind now, said Stephen hotly.

    Cranly pressed Stephen's arm, saying: 2300

—Go easy, my dear man. You're an excitable bloody man, do you know.

    He laughed nervously as he spoke and, looking up into Ste= phen's face with moved and friendly eyes, said:

—Do you know that you are an excitable man?   2305

—I daresay I am, said Stephen, laughing also.

    Their minds, lately estranged, seemed suddenly to have been drawn closer, one to the other.

—Do you believe in the eucharist?[4] Cranly asked.

—I do not, Stephen said.   2310

—Do you disbelieve then?

—I neither believe in it nor disbelieve in it, Stephen answered.

—Many persons have doubts, even religious persons, yet they overcome them or put them aside, Cranly said. Are your doubts on that point too strong?   2315

—I do not wish to overcome them, Stephen answered.

    Cranly, embarrassed for a moment, took another fig from his pocket and was about to eat it when Stephen said:

—Don't, please. You cannot discuss this question with your mouth full of chewed fig.   2320

    Cranly examined the fig by the light of a lamp under which he halted. Then he smelt it with both nostrils, bit a tiny piece, spat it out and threw the fig rudely into the gutter. Addressing it as it lay, he said:

---

3. Made before by Satan, who according to tradition said *"non serviam"* when he fell. This Latin phrase occurs and is translated into English in one of the sermons of Part III (line 556), where it is attributed to Lucifer, another name for Satan. Joyce could have encoun= tered the Latin in the Vulgate Bible, the early fifth-century translation from Greek and Hebrew attributed primarily to St. Jerome (347–420 CE). In Jeremias 2:20, it applies to Israel's rejection of God, not Satan's.

4. Believe that the consecrated bread and wine are the body and blood of Christ.

—Depart from me, ye cursed, into everlasting fire![5]   2325
  Taking Stephen's arm he went on again and said:
—Do you not fear that those words may be spoken to you on
the day of judgment?
—What is offered me on the other hand? Stephen asked. An
eternity of bliss in the company of the dean of studies?   2330
—Remember, Cranly said, that he would be glorified.
—Ay, Stephen said somewhat bitterly. Bright, agile, impassible
and, above all, subtle.
—It is a curious thing, do you know, Cranly said dispassion=
ately, how your mind is supersaturated with the religion in   2335
which you say you disbelieve. Did you believe in it when you
were at school? I bet you did.
—I did, Stephen answered.
—And were you happier then? Cranly asked softly. Happier
than you are now, for instance?   2340
—Often happy, Stephen said, and often unhappy. I was some=
one else then.
—How someone else? What do you mean by that statement?
—I mean, said Stephen, that I was not myself as I am now, as I
had to become.   2345
—Not as you are now, not as you had to become, Cranly
repeated. Let me ask you a question. Do you love your mother?
  Stephen shook his head slowly.
—I don't know what your words mean, he said simply.
—Have you never loved anyone? Cranly asked.   2350
—Do you mean women?
—I am not speaking of that, Cranly said in a colder tone. I ask
you if you ever felt love towards anyone or anything.
  Stephen walked on beside his friend, staring gloomily at the
footpath.   2355
—I tried to love God, he said at length. It seems now I failed. It
is very difficult. I tried to unite my will with the will of God
instant by instant. In that I did not always fail. I could perhaps
do that still . . . . .
  Cranly cut him short by asking: 2360
—Has your mother had a happy life?
—How do I know? Stephen said.
—How many children had she?
—Nine or ten, Stephen answered. Some died.
—Was your father . . . . Cranly interrupted himself for an in=   2365
stant: and then said: I don't want to pry into your family

---

5. Gospel of St. Matthew 25:41, with mention in the full passage that the fire was prepared
specifically for Satan and his angels.

affairs. But was your father what is called well-to-do? I mean when you were growing up?

—Yes, Stephen said.

—What was he? Cranly asked after a pause.   2370

Stephen began to enumerate glibly his father's attributes.

—A medical student, an oarsman, a tenor, an amateur actor, a shouting politician, a small landlord, a small investor, a drinker, a good fellow, a storyteller, somebody's secretary, something in a distillery, a taxgatherer, a bankrupt and at   2375 present a praiser of his own past.

Cranly laughed, tightening his grip on Stephen's arm, and said:

—The distillery is damn good.

—Is there anything else you want to know? Stephen asked.   2380

—Are you in good circumstances at present?

—Do I look it? Stephen asked bluntly.

—So then, Cranly went on musingly, you were born in the lap of luxury.

He used the phrase broadly and loudly as he often used   2385 technical expressions as if he wished his hearer to understand that they were used by him without conviction.

—Your mother must have gone through a good deal of suffer= ing, he said then. Would you not try to save her from suffering more even if . . . . or would you?   2390

—If I could, Stephen said. That would cost me very little.

—Then do so, Cranly said. Do as she wishes you to do. What is it for you? You disbelieve in it. It is a form: nothing else. And you will set her mind at rest.

He ceased and, as Stephen did not reply, remained silent.   2395 Then, as if giving utterance to the process of his own thought, he said:

—Whatever else is unsure in this stinking dunghill of a world a mother's love is not. Your mother brings you into the world, carries you first in her body. What do we know about what she   2400 feels? But whatever she feels, it, at least, must be real. It must be. What are our ideas or ambitions? Play. Ideas! Why, that bloody bleating goat Temple has ideas. MacCann has ideas too. Every jackass going the roads thinks he has ideas.

Stephen, who had been listening to the unspoken speech   2405 behind the words, said with assumed carelessness:

—Pascal, if I remember rightly, would not suffer his mother to kiss him as he feared the contact of her sex.[6]

---

6. An unconfirmed story but in line with the extreme, conservative Catholicism of the French philosopher Blaise Pascal (1623–1662).

—Pascal was a pig, said Cranly.

—Aloysius Gonzaga,[7] I think, was of the same mind, Stephen 2410
said.

—And he was another pig then, said Cranly.

—The church calls him a saint, Stephen objected.

—I don't care a flaming damn what anyone calls him, Cranly
said rudely and flatly. I call him a pig. 2415

Stephen, preparing the words neatly in his mind, continued:

—Jesus too seems to have treated his mother with scant cour=
tesy in public but Suarez,[8] a jesuit theologian and Spanish
gentleman, has apologised for him.

—Did the idea ever occur to you, Cranly asked, that Jesus was 2420
not what he pretended to be?

—The first person to whom that idea occurred, Stephen
answered, was Jesus himself.

—I mean, Cranly said, hardening in his speech, did the idea
ever occur to you that he was himself a conscious hypocrite, 2425
what he called the jews of his time, a whited sepulchre?[9] Or, to
put it more plainly, that he was a blackguard?

—That idea never occurred to me, Stephen answered. But I am
curious to know are you trying to make a convert of me or a
pervert[1] of yourself? 2430

He turned towards his friend's face and saw there a raw
smile which some force of will strove to make finely significant.

Cranly asked suddenly in a plain sensible tone:

—Tell me the truth. Were you at all shocked by what I said?

—Somewhat, Stephen said. 2435

—And why were you shocked, Cranly pressed on in the same
tone, if you feel sure that our religion is false and that Jesus
was not the son of God?

—I am not at all sure of it, Stephen said. He is more like a son
of God than a son of Mary. 2440

—And is that why you will not communicate,[2] Cranly asked,
because you are not sure of that too, because you feel that the
host too may be the body and blood of the son of God and not
a wafer of bread? And because you fear that it may be?

—Yes, Stephen said quietly. I feel that and I also fear it. 2445

---

7. A young saint (1568–1591), patron of youth and of Clongowes Wood College, who is
reputed to have held attitudes about the body similar to Pascal's.
8. Francisco Suarez (1548–1617).
9. Jesus denounced the hypocrisy of the scribes and Pharisees, a self-righteous ancient Jewish sect, by comparing them to "whited sepulchres, which outwardly appear to men beautiful, but within are full of dead men's bones, and of all uncleanness" (Matthew 23:27).
1. In a religious context, someone who turns away from a faith, the opposite of a convert,
who turns toward it (OED).
2. Receive Holy Communion (OED).

—I see, Cranly said.

Stephen, struck by his tone of closure, reopened the dis=
cussion at once by saying:

—I fear many things: dogs, horses, firearms, the sea, thunder=
storms, machinery, the country roads at night.   2450

—But why do you fear a bit of bread?

—I imagine, Stephen said, that there is a malevolent reality
behind those things I say I fear.

—Do you fear then, Cranly asked, that the God of the Roman
catholics would strike you dead and damn you if you made a   2455
sacrilegious communion?

—The God of the Roman catholics could do that now, Stephen
said. I fear more than that the chemical action which would be
set up in my soul by a false homage to a symbol behind which
are massed twenty centuries of authority and veneration.   2460

—Would you, Cranly asked, in extreme danger commit that
particular sacrilege? For instance, if you lived in the penal days?[3]

—I cannot answer for the past, Stephen replied. Possibly not.

—Then, said Cranly, you do not intend to become a protes=
tant?   2465

—I said that I had lost the faith, Stephen answered, but not
that I had lost selfrespect. What kind of liberation would that
be to forsake an absurdity which is logical and coherent and to
embrace one which is illogical and incoherent?

They had walked on towards the township of Pembroke[4] and   2470
now, as they went on slowly along the avenues, the trees and
the scattered lights in the villas soothed their minds. The air of
wealth and repose diffused about them seemed to comfort their
neediness. Behind a hedge of laurel a light glimmered in the
window of a kitchen and the voice of a servant was heard   2475
singing as she sharpened knives. She sang in short broken bars
Rosie O'Grady.[5]

Cranly stopped to listen, saying:

—*Mulier cantat.*[6]

The soft beauty of the Latin word touched with an enchant=   2480
ing touch the dark of the evening, with a touch fainter and
more persuading than the touch of music or of a woman's
hand. The strife of their minds was quelled. The figure of

3. The period from 1697 until Catholic Emancipation in 1829, when laws prohibited Catholics in Ireland from practicing their religion and denied them civil rights.
4. Township (1863–1930) comprised of Donnybrook, Ballsbridge, Sandymount, and Ring-
send, east and south of central Dublin.
5. "Sweet Rosie O'Grady" was a popular song credited to the music-hall singer Maude
Nugent (1877–1958), also known as Maude Jerome. Cranly remembers the well-known
refrain.
6. "A woman is singing" (Latin).

woman as she appears in the liturgy of the church passed si=
lently through the darkness: a whiterobed figure, small and   2485
slender as a boy and with a falling girdle. Her voice, frail and
high as a boy's, was heard intoning from a distant choir the
first words of a woman which pierce the gloom and clamour of
the first chanting of the passion:

—*Et tu cum Jesu Galilaeo eras.*[7]   2490

And all hearts were touched and turned to her voice, shining
like a young star, shining clearer as the voice intoned the pro=
paroxyton[8] and more faintly as the cadence died.

The singing ceased. They went on together, Cranly repeating
in strongly stressed rhythm the end of the refrain: 2495

> *And when we are married*
> *O, how happy we'll be*
> *For I love sweet Rosie O'Grady*
> *And Rosie O'Grady loves me.*

—There's real poetry for you, he said. There's real love.   2500

He glanced sideways at Stephen with a strange smile and
said:

—Do you consider that poetry? Or do you know what the
words mean?

—I want to see Rosie first, said Stephen.   2505

—She's easy to find, Cranly said.

His hat had come down on his forehead. He shoved it back:
and in the shadow of the trees Stephen saw his pale face,
framed by the dark, and his large dark eyes. Yes. His face was
handsome: and his body was strong and hard. He had spoken   2510
of a mother's love. He felt then the sufferings of women, the
weaknesses of their bodies and souls: and would shield them
with a strong and resolute arm and bow his mind to them.

Away then: it is time to go. A voice spoke softly to Stephen's
lonely heart, bidding him go and telling him that his friendship   2515
was coming to an end. Yes: he would go. He could not strive
against another. He knew his part.

—Probably I shall go away, he said.

—Where? Cranly asked.

—Where I can, Stephen said.   2520

—Yes, Cranly said. It might be difficult for you to live here
now. But is it that that makes you go?

2484 liturgy--the] ⁷¹liturgy--theⁱʳ MS

7. "Thou also wast with Jesus the Galilean" (Matthew 26:69), spoken to Peter just before he
   denies knowing Jesus. In Latin here as part of the mass sung on Palm Sunday, the Sunday
   before Easter.
8. A word accented on the third to last syllable, as in the word itself.

—I have to go, Stephen answered.

—Because, Cranly continued, you need not look upon yourself as driven away if you do not wish to go or as a heretic or an outlaw. There are many good believers who think as you do. Would that surprise you? The church is not the stone building nor even the clergy and their dogmas. It is the whole mass of those born into it. I don't know what you wish to do in life. Is it what you told me the night we were standing outside Har= court Street station?[9]

—Yes, Stephen said, smiling in spite of himself at Cranly's way of remembering thoughts in connection with places. The night you spent half an hour wrangling with Doherty about the shortest way from Sallygap to Larras.[1]

—Pothead! Cranly said with calm contempt. What does he know about the way from Sallygap to Larras? Or what does he know about anything for that matter? And the big slobbering washingpot head of him!

He broke out into a loud long laugh.

—Well? Stephen said. Do you remember the rest?

—What you said, is it? Cranly asked. Yes, I remember it. To discover the mode of life or of art whereby your spirit could express itself in unfettered freedom.

Stephen raised his hat in acknowledgment.

—Freedom! Cranly repeated. But you are not free enough yet to commit a sacrilege. Tell me, would you rob?

—I would beg first, Stephen said.

—And if you got nothing would you rob?

—You wish me to say, Stephen answered, that the rights of property are provisional and that in certain circumstances it is not unlawful to rob. Everyone would act in that belief. So I will not make you that answer. Apply to the jesuit theologian Juan Mariana de Talavera[2] who will also explain to you in what circumstances you may lawfully kill your king and whether you had better hand him his poison in a goblet or smear it for him upon his robe or his saddlebow. Ask me rather would I suffer others to rob me or, if they did, would I call down upon them what I believe is called the chastisement of the secular arm.

—And would you?

—I think, Stephen said, it would pain me as much to do so as to be robbed.

2544 itself] aEg; it MS–Eg

9. Rail station (functioning until 1959) south of the west side of Stephen's Green.
1. In the Wicklow Mountains, south of Dublin; where Cranly's family lives.
2. Spanish Jesuit (1536–1623).

—I see, Cranly said.

He produced his match and began to clean the crevice be= tween two teeth. Then he said carelessly: 2565

—Tell me, for example, would you deflower a virgin?

—Excuse me, Stephen said politely. Is that not the ambition of most young gentlemen?

—What then is your point of view? Cranly asked.

His last phrase, soursmelling as the smoke of charcoal and 2570 disheartening, excited Stephen's brain over which its fumes seemed to brood.

—Look here, Cranly, he said. You have asked me what I would do and what I would not do. I will tell you what I will do and what I will not do. I will not serve that in which I no longer 2575 believe whether it call itself my home, my fatherland or my church: and I will try to express myself in some mode of life or art as freely as I can and as wholly as I can, using for my defence the only arms I allow myself to use, silence, exile and cunning.   2580

Cranly seized his arm and steered him round so as to lead him back towards Leeson Park.[3] He laughed almost slily and pressed Stephen's arm with an elder's affection.

—Cunning indeed! he said. Is it you? You poor poet, you!

—And you made me confess to you, Stephen said, thrilled by 2585 his touch, as I have confessed to you so many other things, have I not?

—Yes, my child,[4] Cranly said, still gaily.

—You made me confess the fears that I have. But I will tell you also what I do not fear. I do not fear to be alone or to be 2590 spurned for another or to leave whatever I have to leave. And I am not afraid to make a mistake, even a great mistake, a lifelong mistake and perhaps as long as eternity too.

Cranly, now grave again, slowed his pace and said:

—Alone, quite alone. You have no fear of that. And you know 2595 what that word means? Not only to be separate from all others but to have not even one friend.

—I will take the risk, said Stephen.

—And not to have any one person, Cranly said, who would be more than a friend, more even than the noblest and truest 2600 friend a man ever had.

2564 his match] ⁷¹his match¹ʳ MS   2581–82 lead him] a16; head MS; lead Eg–16; head 64   2596 word] Eg; words MS

3. Leading to the Leeson Street Bridge over the Grand Canal and back toward Stephen's Green.
4. Words a priest would speak in the confessional to someone confessing.

His words seemed to have struck some deep chord in his own nature. Had he spoken of himself, of himself as he was or wished to be? Stephen watched his face for some moments in silence. A cold sadness was there. He had spoken of himself, of 2605 his own loneliness which he feared.

—Of whom are you speaking? Stephen asked at length.

Cranly did not answer.

◆　◆　◆

20 March: Long talk with Cranly on the subject of my re= volt. He had his grand manner on. I supple and suave. Attacked 2610 me on the score of love for one's mother. Tried to imagine his mother: cannot. Told me once, in a moment of thoughtlessness, his father was sixtyone when he was born. Can see him. Strong farmer type. Pepper and salt suit. Square feet. Unkempt grizzled beard. Probably attends coursing matches.[5] Pays his 2615 dues regularly but not plentifully to Father Dwyer of Larras. Sometimes talks to girls after nightfall. But his mother? Very young or very old? Hardly the first. If so, Cranly would not have spoken as he did. Old then. Probably: and neglected. Hence Cranly's despair of soul: the child of exhausted loins. 2620

21 March, morning: Thought this in bed last night but was too lazy and free to add it. Free, yes. The exhausted loins are those of Elizabeth and Zachary. Then is he the precursor. Item: he eats chiefly belly bacon and dried figs. Read locusts and wild honey. Also, when thinking of him, saw always a stern severed 2625 head or deathmask as if outlined on a grey curtain or veronica. Decollation they call it in the fold. Puzzled for the moment by saint John at the Latin gate. What do I see? A decollated precursor trying to pick the lock.[6]

21 March, night: Free. Soulfree and fancyfree. Let the dead 2630 bury the dead. Ay. And let the dead marry the dead.[7]

22 March: In company with Lynch followed a sizable hos=

2623 Elizabeth] ⁻¹⟨Anna⟩ Elizabeth¹ʳ MS   2623 Zachary.] ⁻¹⟨Joachim⟩ Zachary¹ʳ. MS   2623 is he] he is Eg–64

5. Matches in which greyhounds pursue hares (*OED*).
6. The details of the entry link Cranly to John the Baptist, whose parents, Elizabeth and Zachary, were old. When he was a hermit, John lived on locusts and wild honey. He suffered decollation, or beheading, when Salomé tricked her stepfather, Herod, into granting her wish. Stephen compares the severed head to a deathmask and to a veronica, a cloth bearing the image of Jesus's face, after the cloth used by Saint Veronica to wipe his face on his way to the cross. John the Baptist was the precursor of Jesus, but Saint John "at the Latin gate" is John the Apostle. They are linked by their names but also by the fact that the Lateran Church (at the Latin gate in Rome), where John the Apostle miraculously escaped from the Romans, is consecrated to John the Baptist. John the Baptist figuratively opened the door for Jesus and figuratively picked the lock of the Latin gate for John the Apostle.
7. Stephen cites and then transforms Luke 9:60, "Let the dead bury their dead."

pital nurse. Lynch's idea. Dislike it. Two lean hungry grey=
hounds walking after a heifer.

23 *March*: Have not seen her since that night. Unwell? Sits at   2635
the fire perhaps with mamma's shawl on her shoulders. But not
peevish. A nice bowl of gruel? Won't you now?

24 *March*: Began with a discussion with my mother. Subject:
B. V. M.[8] Handicapped by my sex and youth. To escape held up
relations between Jesus and Papa against those between Mary   2640
and her son. Said religion is not a lying-in hospital.[9] Mother
indulgent. Said I have a queer mind and have read too much.
Not true. Have read little and understood less. Then she said I
would come back to faith because I had a restless mind. This
means to leave church by backdoor of sin and reenter through   2645
the skylight of repentance. Cannot repent. Told her so and
asked for sixpence. Got threepence.

Then went to college. Other wrangle with little roundhead
rogue's eye Ghezzi.[1] This time about Bruno the Nolan.[2] Began in
Italian and ended in pidgin English. He said Bruno was a ter=   2650
rible heretic. I said he was terribly burned. He agreed to this
with some sorrow. Then gave me recipe for what he calls
risotto alla bergamasca.[3] When he pronounces a soft *o* he pro=
trudes his full carnal lips as if he kissed the vowel. Has he? And
could he repent? Yes, he could: and cry two round rogue's   2655
tears, one from each eye.

Crossing Stephen's, that is, my green, remembered that his
countrymen and not mine had invented what Cranly the other
night called our religion. A quartet of them, soldiers of the
ninetyseventh infantry regiment, sat at the foot of the cross and   2660
tossed up dice for the overcoat of the crucified.

Went to library. Tried to read three reviews. Useless. She is
not out yet. Am I alarmed? About what? That she will never be
out again. Blake wrote:

> *I wonder if William Bond will die.*   2665
> *For assuredly he is very ill.*

Alas, poor William!

8. The Blessed Virgin Mary.
9. Maternity hospital.
1. Italian teacher at University College.
2. Giordano Bruno (1548–1600), Italian Dominican and philosopher, was born in Nola; he
   was burned at the stake as a heretic.
3. "Risotto as prepared in Bergamo" (Italian), ostensibly a rice dish typical of northern Italy,
   but a dish known by that name has never been identified.

I was once at a diorama in Rotunda.[4] At the end were pic=
tures of big nobs. Among them William Ewart Gladstone, just
then dead. Orchestra played *O Willie, we have missed you.*[5]   2670
A race of clodhoppers.

25 March, morning: A troubled night of dreams. Want to get
them off my chest.

A long curving gallery. From the floor ascend pillars of dark
vapours. It is peopled by the images of fabulous kings, set in   2675
stone. Their hands are folded upon their knees in token of
weariness and their eyes are darkened for the errors of men go
up before them for ever as dark vapours.

Strange figures advance from a cave. They are not as tall as
men. One does not seem to stand quite apart from another.   2680
Their faces are phosphorescent, with darker streaks. They peer
at me and their eyes seem to ask me something. They do not
speak.

30 March: This evening Cranly was in the porch of the
library, proposing a problem to Dixon and her brother. A   2685
mother let her child fall into the Nile. Still harping on the
mother. A crocodile seized the child. Mother asked it back.
Crocodile said all right if she told him what he was going to do
with the child, eat it or not eat it.

This mentality, Lepidus would say, is indeed bred out of   2690
your mud by the operation of your sun.[6]

And mine? Is it not too? Then into Nilemud with it!

1 April: Disapprove of this last phrase.

2 April: Saw her drinking tea and eating cakes in Johnston,
Mooney and O'Brien's. Rather, lynxeyed Lynch saw her as we   2695
passed. He tells me Cranly was invited there by brother. Did he
bring his crocodile? Is he the shining light now? Well, I dis=
covered him. I protest I did. Shining quietly behind a bushel of
Wicklow bran.

3 April: Met Davin at the cigar shop opposite Findlater's   2700
church.[7] He was in a black sweater and had a hurleystick.
Asked me was it true I was going away and why. Told him the

2668 Rotunda.] ⌐⟨Leinster Hall⟩ Rotunda¹ᴵ. MS   2679 from] as from Eg–24

4. A group of buildings used for various public purposes, at the end of Sackville (now
   O'Connell) Street at Rutland (now Parnell) Square. "Diorama": a forerunner of the
   cinema.
5. The passage evokes various Williams, starting with the English Romantic poet William
   Blake (1757–1827), whose poem "William Bond" is cited, and ending with the line from
   the song "Willie, We Have Missed You" (1854), by the American songwriter Stephen Collins Foster (1826–1864). On Gladstone, see note 6, p. 27.
6. In Shakespeare's *Antony and Cleopatra,* Lepidus says drunkenly, "Your serpent of Egypt is
   bred now of your mud by the operation of your sun; so is your crocodile" (2.7.26–27).
7. Presbyterian church in Rutland (now Parnell) Square.

shortest way to Tara was via Holyhead.[8] Just then my father
came up. Introduction. Father polite and observant. Asked
Davin if he might offer him some refreshment. Davin could   2705
not, was going to a meeting. When we came away father told
me he had a good honest eye. Asked me why I did not join a
rowing club. I pretended to think it over. Told me then how he
broke Pennyfeather's heart.[9] Wants me to read law. Says I was
cut out for that. More mud, more crocodiles.   2710

5 *April:* Wild spring. Scudding clouds. O life! Dark stream of
swirling bogwater on which appletrees have cast down their
delicate flowers. Eyes of girls among the leaves. Girls demure
and romping. All fair or auburn: no dark ones. They blush
better. Houp-la!   2715

6 *April:* Certainly she remembers the past. Lynch says all
women do. Then she remembers the time of her childhood—
and mine if I was ever a child. The past is consumed in the
present and the present is living only because it brings forth the
future. Statues of women, if Lynch be right, should always be   2720
fully draped, one hand of the woman feeling regretfully her
own hinder parts.

6 *April: later:* Michael Robartes remembers forgotten beauty
and, when his arms wrap her round, he presses in his arms the
loveliness which has long faded from the world. Not this. Not   2725
at all. I desire to press in my arms the loveliness which has not
yet come into the world.[1]

10 *April:* Faintly, under the heavy night, through the silence
of the city which has turned from dreams to dreamless sleep as
a weary lover whom no caresses move, the sound of hoofs   2730
upon the road. Not so faintly now as they come near the
bridge; and in a moment as they pass the darkened windows
the silence is cloven by alarm as by an arrow. They are heard
now far away, hoofs that shine amid the heavy night as gems,
hurrying beyond the sleeping fields to what journey's end—   2735
what heart?—bearing what tidings?

11 *April:* Read what I wrote last night. Vague words for a
vague emotion. Would she like it? I think so. Then I should
have to like it also.

13 *April:* That tundish has been on my mind for a long time.   2740
I looked it up and find it is English and good old blunt English

2741 is] MS; ABSENT Eg–64

8. Taking the ferry to Holyhead, the Welsh port across the Irish Channel, is the most direct
   route to Tara, the seat of the ancient kings of Ireland.
9. A stock phrase suggesting with a touch of irony disappointed love (*Letters* III, 130).
1. Stephen rejects the sentiment expressed in Yeats's poem "Michael Robartes Remembers
   Forgotten Beauty" (1896) (see p. 300).

too. Damn the dean of studies and his funnel! What did he
come here for to teach us his own language or to learn it from
us. Damn him one way or the other!

14 April: John Alphonsus Mulrennan has just returned from
the west of Ireland (European and Asiatic papers please copy).
He told us he met an old man there in a mountain cabin. Old
man had red eyes and short pipe. Old man spoke Irish.
Mulrennan spoke Irish. Then old man and Mulrennan spoke
English. Mulrennan spoke to him about universe and stars. Old
man sat, listened, smoked, spat. Then said:
—Ah, there must be terrible queer creatures at the latter end of
the world.

I fear him. I fear his redrimmed horny eyes. It is with him I
must struggle all through this night till day come, till he or I lie
dead, gripping him by the sinewy throat till . . . . Till what? Till
he yield to me? No. I mean him no harm.

15 April: Met her today pointblank in Grafton Street. The
crowd brought us together. We both stopped. She asked me
why I never came, said she had heard all sorts of stories about
me. This was only to gain time. Asked me was I writing poems.
About whom? I asked her. This confused her more and I felt
sorry and mean. Turned off that valve at once and opened the
spiritual-heroic refrigerating apparatus, invented and patented
in all countries by Dante Alighieri.[2] Talked rapidly of myself
and my plans. In the midst of it unluckily I made a sudden
gesture of a revolutionary nature. I must have looked like a
fellow throwing a handful of peas up into the air. People began
to look at us. She shook hands a moment after and, in going
away, said she hoped I would do what I said.

Now I call that friendly, don't you?

Yes. I liked her today. A little or much? Don't know. I liked
her—and it seems a new feeling to me. Then, in that case, all
the rest, all that I thought I thought and all that I felt I felt, all
the rest before now, in fact . . . . . . O, give it up, old chap! Sleep it
off!

16 April: Away! Away!

The spell of arms and voices: the white arms of roads, their
promise of close embraces and the black arms of tall ships that
stand against the moon, their tale of distant nations. They are
held out to say: We are alone. Come. And the voices say with

2745

2750

2755

2760

2765

2770

2775

2780

2768 up] ABSENT 18–64

2. In *La Vita Nuova* (*The New Life*), Dante (1265–1321) presents his idealized adoration,
   free of physical desire, for Beatrice Portinari, whom he first met as a child. Beatrice
   appears later as a guide to spiritual salvation in Dante's *Divine Comedy.*

them: We are your kinsmen. And the air is thick with their company as they call to me, their kinsman, making ready to go, shaking the wings of their exultant and terrible youth.

26 April: Mother is putting my new secondhand clothes in order. She prays now, she says, that I may learn in my own life and away from home and friends what the heart is and what it feels. Amen. So be it. Welcome, O life! I go to encounter for the millionth time the reality of experience and to forge in the smithy of my soul the uncreated conscience of my race.[3]

27 April: Old father, old artificer, stand me now and ever in good stead.

Dublin 1904
Trieste 1914

2792 stead.] stead. RECTANGLE BLOT BELOW MS   2793 Dublin] ⟨Cabra⟩, Dublin MS   2794 Trieste] Trieste, ⟨Austria⟩ MS

3. Can be understood as biologically based, but can also mean, more broadly, "tribe, nation, or people" (*OED*), and was often used with that meaning in Joyce's youth. "Uncreated": can mean "not brought into being," but also means "self-existent or eternal" as an attribute of something divine (*OED*).

Related Writings by Joyce

JAMES JOYCE

Chamber Music†

Chamber Music (1907) consists of thirty-four love poems in language of a refined kind that the volume's title suggests, plus two more poems, one about hearing the noise of flowing waters (XXXV) and one with violent, visionary details (XXXVI, provided below). The Irish poet W. B. Yeats (1865–1939) expressed admiration for XXXVI. In the highly musical episode 11 of Joyce's *Ulysses* (1922), the character Leopold Bloom contemplates a pun on "chamber music" because of the tinkling sound of urine hitting a chamber pot. However, such an ironic implication did not play a role in the choice of this book's title, suggested by Joyce's brother Stanislaus. Indeed, not long before publication Joyce expressed an ambivalence regarding the "too complacent" title: "I should prefer a title which to a certain extent repudiated the book without altogether disparaging it" (Letter to Stanislaus, 18 October 1906, in Richard Ellmann, ed., *Selected Letters of James Joyce*, 121). The statement captures Joyce's mixed attitude toward his early work and toward his younger self projected by it.

XII

What counsel has the hooded moon
   Put in thy heart, my shyly sweet,
Of Love in ancient plenilune,[1]
   Glory and stars beneath his feet—
A sage that is but kith and kin
With the comedian Capuchin?[2]

---

† From *Chamber Music* (London: Elkin Mathews, 1907), unnumbered pages.
1. A full moon. Joyce could have encountered this word in the prose and poetry of Algernon Charles Swinburne (1837–1909), an English decadent poet mentioned in *Ulysses*, episode 1, or in the poetry of Andrew Lang, whose villanelle "To the Nightingale in September" (p. 321 below) includes it.
2. The Capuchin monks, a division of the Franciscans, are named for the cowl (Italian, *cappuccio*) that is part of their brown, white-belted habits (*OED*). "Comedian" suggests disparagingly that the priest is clownlike.

Believe me rather that am wise
   In disregard of the divine,
A glory kindles in those eyes
   Trembles to starlight. Mine, O Mine!
No more be tears in moon or mist
For thee, sweet sentimentalist.

XXXIII

Now, O now, in this brown land
   Where Love did so sweet music make
We two shall wander, hand in hand,
   Forbearing for old friendship' sake,
Nor grieve because our love was gay
Which now is ended in this way.

A rogue in red and yellow dress
   Is knocking, knocking at the tree;
And all around our loneliness
   The wind is whistling merrily.
The leaves—they do not sigh at all
When the year takes them in the fall.

Now, O now, we hear no more
   The villanelle[1] and roundelay!
Yet will we kiss, sweetheart, before
   We take sad leave at close of day.
Grieve not, sweetheart, for anything—
The year, the year is gathering.

XXXVI

I hear an army charging upon the land,
   And the thunder of horses plunging, foam about their knees:
Arrogant, in black armour, behind them stand,
   Disdaining the reins, with fluttering whips, the charioteers.

They cry unto the night their battle-name:
   I moan in sleep when I hear afar their whirling laughter.
They cleave the gloom of dreams, a blinding flame,
   Clanging, clanging upon the heart as upon an anvil.

---

1. We have corrected Joyce's habitual misspelling of "villanelle" as "vilanelle," which occurs
   in the first edition of *Chamber Music*.

They come shaking in triumph their long, green hair:
 They come out of the sea and run shouting by the shore.
My heart, have you no wisdom thus to despair?
 My love, my love, my love, why have you left me alone?

DIEGO ANGELI

[A Novel of the Jesuits (1918)]†

Joyce published this translation of a laudatory review of *A Portrait* by Diego Angeli (1869–1937) in *The Egoist*, where the narrative appeared in installments during 1914–15. Angeli's review was originally published in *Il Marzocco* 22:3 (12 August 1917): 2–3 as "Un Romanzo di Gesuiti" ("A Novel of the Jesuits").

Extract from "Il Marzocco"

FLORENCE, AUGUST 12, 1917

Mr. James Joyce is a young Irish novelist whose last book, *A Portrait of the Artist as a Young Man,* has raised a great tumult of discussion among English-speaking critics. It is easy to see why. An Irishman, he has found in himself the strength to proclaim himself a citizen of a wider world; a catholic, he has had the courage to cast his religion from him and to proclaim himself an atheist; and a writer, inheriting the most traditionalist of all European literatures, he has found a way to break free from the tradition of the old English novel and to adopt a new style consonant with a new conception. In a word such an effort was bound to tilt against all the feelings and cherished beliefs of his fellowcountrymen but, carried out, as it is here, with a fine and youthful boldness, it has won the day. His book is not alone an admirable work of art and thought; it is also a cry of revolt: it is the desire of a new artist to look upon the world with other eyes, to bring to the front his individual theories and to compel a listless public to reflect that there are another literature and another esthetic apprehension beyond those foisted upon us, with a bountifulness at times nauseating, by the general purveying of pseudo-romantic prose and by fashionable publishers, with their seriocomic booklists, and by the weekly and monthly magazines. And let us admit that such a cry of revolt has been uttered at the right moment and that it is in itself the promise of a fortunate renascence.

† From *The Egoist* 5:2 (February 1918): 30.

For, to tell the truth, English fiction seemed lately to have gone astray amid the sentimental niceties of Miss Beatrice Harraden, the police-aided plottiness of Sir Conan Doyle, the stupidities of Miss Corelli or, at best, the philosophical and sociological disquisitions of Mrs. Humphrey Ward.[1] The intention seemed to be to satisfy the largest circle of readers and all that remain within the pale of tradition by trying to put again on the market old dusty ideas and by avoiding sedulously all conflict with the esthetic, moral and political susceptibilities of the majority. For this reason in the midst of the great revolution of the European novel English writers continued to remain in their "splendid isolation" and could not or would not open their eyes to what was going on around them. Literature, however, like all the other arts underwent a gradual transformation and Mr. Joyce's book marks its definite date in the chronology of English literature. I think it well to put so much on record here not only for that which it signifies actually but also for that which in time it may bring forth.

The phenomenon is all the more important in that Mr. Joyce's *Portrait* contains two separate elements, each of which is significant and worthy of analysis: its ethical content and the form wherewith this content is clothed. When one has read the book to the end one understands why most English and American critics have raised an outcry against both form and content, understanding, for the most part, neither one nor the other. Accustomed as they are to the usual novels, enclosed in a set framework, they found themselves in this case out of their depth and hence their talk of immorality, impiety, naturalism and exaggeration. They have not grasped the subtlety of the psychological analysis nor the synthetic value of certain details and certain sudden arrests of movement. Possibly their own protestant upbringing renders the moral development of the central character incomprehensible to them. For Mr. Joyce is a catholic and, more than that, a catholic brought up in a jesuit college. One must have passed many years of one's own life in a seminary of the society of Jesus, one must have passed through the same experiences and undergone the same crises to understand the profound analysis, the keenness of observation shown in the character of Stephen Dedalus. No writer, so far as I know, has penetrated deeper in the examination of the influence, sensual rather than spiritual, of the society's exercises.

＊　＊　＊

1. British best-selling novelist (1851–1920) and a leading opponent of women's suffrage. Beatrice Harraden (1864–1936), English suffragette and best-selling novelist. Sir Arthur Conan Doyle (1859–1930), British writer best known for his widely read Sherlock Holmes stories. Miss Corelli: popular English novelist Mary Mackay (1855–1924), who wrote under the name Marie Corelli.

For this analysis so purely modern, so cruelly and boldly true, the writer needed a style which would break down the tradition of the six shilling novel:[2] and this style Mr. Joyce has fashioned for himself. The brushwork of the novel reminds one of certain modern paintings in which the planes interpenetrate and the external vision seems to partake of the sensations of the onlooker. It is not so much the narrative of a life as its reminiscence but it is a reminiscence whole, complete and absolute, with all those incidents and details which tend to fix indelibly each feature of the whole. He does not lose time explaining the wherefore of these sensations of his nor even tell us their reason or origin: they leap up in his pages as do the memories of a life we ourselves have lived without apparent cause, without logical sequence. But it is exactly such a succession of past visions and memories which makes up the sum of every life. In this evocation of reality Mr. Joyce is truly a master. The majority of English critics remark, with easy superficiality, that he thinks himself a naturalist simply because he does not shrink from painting certain brutal episodes in words more brutal still. This is not so: his naturalism goes much deeper. Certainly there is a difference, formal no less than substantial, between his book and, let us say, *La Terre* of Emile Zola.[3] Zola's naturalism is romantic whereas the naturalism of Mr. Joyce is impressionist, the profound synthetic naturalism of some pictures of Cézanne or Maquet,[4] the naturalism of the late impressionists who single out the characteristic elements of a landscape or a scene or a human face. And all this he expresses in a rapid and concise style, free from every picturesque effect, every rhetorical redundancy, every needless image or epithet. Mr. Joyce tells us what he must tell in the least number of words; his palette is limited to a few colours. But he knows what to choose for his end and therefore half a page of his dry precise angular prose expresses much more (and with much more telling effect)

---

2. The six shilling novel emerged after works of fiction began to be serialized in twenty parts in England in the middle of the nineteenth century. Once the final part was published, the novel would be reprinted as a single volume priced at six shillings, considerably less than the price of novels before the turn to serialization. The price reduction drew a wider audience for what were often narratives of domestic realism. Angeli contrasts Joyce's narrative with this earlier form because it was not a work of domestic realism meant for a wide audience.
3. Novel (1887) by this grittily realistic French writer (1840–1902), controversial for the violence and sexuality in its depiction of rural life.
4. Paul Cézanne (1839–1906), French painter. Maquet is an error for the surname of Albert Marquet (1875–1947), French painter. By synthetic naturalism, Angeli seems to mean Cézanne's tendency to paint scenes, people, and objects in a representational, that is, recognizable, way but with an emphasis on their geometrical shapes. Cézanne is often treated as a bridge between nineteenth-century painting and more abstract painting that emerged in the twentieth century. It is not clear why he would link the two painters by means of synthetic naturalism, since Marquat was known for using strong colors rather than emphasizing geometry. He was, however, like Cézanne, committed to leaving behind nineteenth-century conventions of painting.

than all that wearisome research of images and colour of which we have lately heard and read so much.

And that is why Mr. Joyce's book has raised such a great clamour of discussion. He is a new writer in the glorious company of English literature, a new writer with a new form of his own and new aims, and he comes at a moment when the world is making a new constitution and a new social ordinance.[5] We must welcome him with joy. He is one of those rude craftsmen who open up paths whereon many will yet follow. It is the first streak of the dawn of a new art visible on the horizon. Let us hail it therefore as the herald of a new day.

JAMES JOYCE

Stephen Dedalus after *A Portrait*

Starting in 1918, the American avant-garde journal *The Little Review* published versions of the first thirteen episodes of *Ulysses* (1922) and part of the fourteenth episode, of the eighteen total in the book. This serial publication ceased at the end of 1920 because of objections by the postal authorities concerning obscenity, and *Ulysses* was banned in the United States for over a dozen years. Although Joyce made many revisions to these early versions, some small and some large, before book publication, the extensive presentation of Stephen Dedalus in the serialized episodes carried over largely intact to the book. The serialized episodes are the first published presentation after the appearance of *A Portrait* of Stephen's life following his sojourn in Paris, a destination that is not specified at the end of *A Portrait*.

Although Stephen plays a large role in *Ulysses*, the later book is only in part a sequel to *A Portrait*, because the narrative concerns centrally as well Leopold Bloom and his wife, Molly. More space is devoted to the Blooms, and Leopold overshadows Stephen as the narrative's main character. Stephen, however, remains a key figure. In Joyce's early draft of an autobiographical narrative, *Stephen Hero*, which he abandoned and which was published only posthumously, Stephen's surname was Daedalus (a pseudonym Joyce had used in publishing some early stories). For the more streamlined narrative of *A Portrait*, he changed the spelling to Dedalus. Although a few critics have treated the Stephens of the two narratives prior to *Ulysses* as the same character, conflating them is dubious, given the change in name, the scant overlap in narrative detail, and the shifts in style and structure. By contrast, the continuity between the Stephen of *A Portrait* and the Stephen of *Ulysses* has been widely accepted. *Ulysses* moves us forward in

5. Although the phrasing is optimistic and future-oriented, Angeli published his review in the midst of World War I, the worst period of destruction in European history up until that time. He sees Joyce as part of a new order that would replace the old discredited social order responsible for immense destruction.

Stephen's life to the events of a single day, Thursday 16 June 1904, following his return from Paris, his destination when he leaves Dublin after the end of *A Portrait*. He returns following the death of his mother, for whom he is in mourning. In other words, there is a gap in time and in significant action between the last journal entry in *A Portrait* and the opening of *Ulysses*. Details concerning Paris and his mother's death emerge as memories in the later book, some of them vivid and recurring. One recollection of Paris in episode 3 suggests that Stephen was there in February 1904. We know neither the date of Stephen's departure for Paris nor the date of his mother's death.

In the first of three opening episodes, all featuring Stephen, he starts the day in dialogue with Buck Mulligan, his medical student friend with whom he shares lodgings on the outskirts of Dublin. Buck's Oxford acquaintance, the Englishman Haines, is staying with them. In episode 2, Stephen is at work, teaching a history class to young students at a school and in conversation with the headmaster, Mr. Deasy, an opinionated Protestant from the north of Ireland, who pays him his salary and asks for Stephen's help in placing a letter about hoof-and-mouth disease in a local newspaper. In episode 3, Stephen walks along the beach in the direction of Dublin. His thoughts are presented at length in these initial episodes but most extensively in episode 3, during which he speaks to no one. We see him making notes for a poem on a scrap of paper that he tears from the corner of Deasy's letter, and he urinates.

After three morning episodes focusing on Leopold Bloom, in episode 7, which starts at noon, Stephen plays a significant role (as does Bloom, though they do not interact). In part V of *A Portrait*, we hear Stephen in oral performance, presenting his thinking about art to his friend Vincent Lynch, and we see him produce a villanelle. In episode 7, he narrates a brief realistic story of his own production for the most part to a character referred to as "professor" MacHugh while they and others are on their way from the newspaper office to a pub, where Stephen has offered to buy drinks. MacHugh is well educated but does not appear to be employed as a professor. Stephen's narration follows three stylistically elevated spoken performances by other characters in the newspaper office, none of them original. Two of the recitations mention the biblical figure Moses, whom Stephen alludes to in the title that he gives his contrasting story. In episode 9, Stephen engages in a polylogue with a group of literary people in the National Library of Ireland, starting at 2 p.m. He presents his imaginative, carefully detailed, but less than historically accurate speculations about the possible autobiographical significance of several works by Shakespeare. Episode 10, which begins at 3 p.m., is divided into nineteen brief unnumbered and untitled narrative segments, each focusing primarily on a short sequence of action but also including snippets of narration pertaining to the action in one or more of the other segments. The thirteenth segment, presented here, concentrates on Stephen, including his encounter with one of his siblings, Dilly. After episode 10, Stephen plays significant roles in episodes 14–17, in which Leopold Bloom takes an interest in Stephen, who is drinking too much, keeps him from being arrested, helps Stephen sober up, and then has a conversation with him over hot cocoa at the Blooms' home, before Stephen leaves. Only part of episode 14 appeared in *The Little Review*, and the styles of that episode and of all the episodes involving Stephen following episode 10 are so far removed from realism that the narrative details are often obscure or open to speculation, compared to the more realistically presented details in earlier episodes and in *A Portrait*. As a consequence, the selections below stop with the encounter with his sister in episode 10.

Critics and other readers of *Ulysses* usually refer to the unnumbered, untitled episodes by the Homeric names that Joyce assigned to them but did not include in the book. The excerpts below are presented by episode numbers, with the Homeric titles in brackets as a reminder that they do not actually appear in *The Little Review* or the book. Most readers of the episodes who encountered them in *The Little Review* and in the book would not have been aware of the Homeric titles that critics of the narrative use.

The Little Review was a small operation focused on publishing issues with high-quality contents. Sometimes the proofreading was uneven, and mistakes were made in designating correctly the volume and issue numbers. As a consequence, the volume and issue numbers provided below, which have been adopted by scholars to identify the sequence of issues bibliographically, may not correspond to the numbers on the physical issues. In the excerpts, obvious or distracting printer's errors and inconsistencies have been silently corrected, but differences from later printed versions have been allowed to stand, except where noted.

All of the issues of *The Little Review* containing episodes of *Ulysses* are available online at the Modernist Journals Project.

From *Episode I* [*Telemachus*]†

STATELY, plump Buck Mulligan came from the stairhead, bearing a bowl of lather on which a mirror and a razor lay crossed. A yellow dressing gown, ungirdled, was sustained gently behind him on the mild morning air. He held the bowl aloft and intoned:

—*Introibo ad altare Dei.*[1]

Halted, he peered down the dark winding stairs and called up coarsely:

—Come up, Kinch.[2] Come up, you fearful jesuit.

Solemnly he came forward and mounted the round gunrest. He faced about and blessed gravely thrice the tower,[3] the surrounding

---

† From *The Little Review* 4:11 (March 1918): 4–7, 9–10.
1. "I will go to God's altar." The words spoken by the priest at the opening of the Roman Catholic Latin Mass as the ritual was practiced in Joyce's time.
2. Mulligan's nickname for Stephen, for reasons that are not clear.
3. The Martello tower where they live, in Sandycove, on Dublin Bay southeast of Dublin's center. Martello towers were used for coastal defense in the nineteenth century.

country and the awaking mountains. Then, catching sight of Stephen Dedalus, he bent towards him and made rapid crosses in the air, gurgling in his throat and shaking his head. Stephen Dedalus, displeased and sleepy, leaned his arms on the top of the staircase and looked coldly at the shaking gurgling face that blessed him, equine in its length, and at the light untonsured hair, grained and hued like pale oak.

Buck Mulligan peeped an instant under the mirror and then covered the bowl smartly.

—Back to barracks, he said sternly.

He added in a preacher's tone:

—For this, O dearly beloved, is the genuine christine: body and soul and blood and ouns. Slow music, please. Shut your eyes, gents. One moment. A little trouble about those white corpuscles. Silence, all.

He peered sideways up and gave a long low whistle of call, then paused awhile in rapt attention, his even white teeth glistening here and there with gold points. Chrysostomos.[4]

—Thanks, old chap, he cried briskly. That will do nicely. Switch off the current, will you?

He skipped off the gunrest and looked gravely at his watcher, gathering about his legs the loose folds of his gown. The plump shadowed face and sullen oval jowl recalled a prelate, patron of arts in the middle ages. A pleasant smile broke quietly over his lips.

—The mockery of it! he said gaily. Your absurd name, an ancient Greek!

He pointed his finger in friendly jest and went over to the parapet, laughing to himself. Stephen Dedalus stepped up, followed him wearily halfway and sat down on the edge of the gunrest, watching him still as he propped his mirror on the parapet, dipped the brush in the bowl and lathered cheeks and neck.

Buck Mulligan's gay voice went on:

—My name is absurd too. Malachi, Mulligan, two dactyls. But it has a Hellenic ring, hasn't it? Tripping and sunny like the buck himself. We must go to Athens. Will you come if I can get the aunt to fork out twenty quid?

He laid the brush aside and, laughing with delight, cried:

—Will he come? The jejune jesuit.

Ceasing, he began to shave with care.

—Tell me, Mulligan, Stephen said quietly.

—Yes, my love?

—How long is Haines going to stay in this tower?

4. "Golden-mouthed" (Greek), the epithet applied to St. John Chrysostom, an Early Church father renowned for his oratory. It applies literally to Mulligan's dental work.

Buck Mulligan showed a shaven cheek over his right shoulder.

—God, isn't he dreadful? he said frankly. A ponderous Saxon. He thinks you're not a gentleman. God, these bloody English! Bursting with money and indigestion. Because he comes from Oxford. You know, Dedalus, you have the real Oxford manner. He can't make you out. O, my name for you is the best: Kinch, the knifeblade.

He shaved warily over his chin.

—He was raving all night about a black panther, Stephen said. Where is his guncase?

—A woeful lunatic, Mulligan said. Were you in a funk?

—I was, Stephen said with energy and growing fear. Out here in the dark with a man I don't know raving and moaning to himself about shooting a black panther. You saved men from drowning. I'm not a hero, however. If he stays on here I am off.

Buck Mulligan frowned at the lather on his razorblade. He hopped down from his perch and began to search his trouser pockets hastily.

—Scutter, he cried thickly.

He came over to the gunrest and, thrusting a hand into Stephen's upper pocket, said:

—Give us a loan of your noserag to wipe my razor.

Stephen suffered him to pull out and hold up on show by its corner a dirty crumpled handkerchief. Buck Mulligan wiped the razorblade neatly. Then, gazing over the handkerchief, he said:

—The bard's noserag. A new art colour for our Irish poets: snotgreen. You can almost taste it, can't you?

He mounted to the parapet again and gazed out over Dublin bay, his fair oakpale hair stirring slightly.

—God! he said quietly. Isn't the sea what Algy calls it: a great sweet mother.[5] The snotgreen sea. The scrotumtightening sea. *Epi oinopa ponton.*[6] Ah, Dedalus, the Greeks! She is our great sweet mother. Come and look.

Stephen stood up and went over to the parapet. Leaning on it, he looked down on the water.

—Our mighty mother! Buck Mulligan said.

He turned abruptly his quick searching eyes from the sea to Stephen's face.

—The aunt thinks you killed your mother, he said. That's why she won't let me have anything to do with you.

—Someone killed her, Stephen said gloomily.

—You could have knelt down, damn it, Kinch, when your dying

5. The English poet Algernon Charles Swinburne (1837–1909) refers to the sea as "the great sweet mother" in "The Triumph of Time" (1866).
6. "Over the winedark sea," a reference to Homer's presentation of the sea in *The Odyssey*.

mother asked you, Buck Mulligan said. I'm hyperborean[7] as much as you. But to think of your mother begging you with her last breath to kneel down and pray for her. And you refused. There is something sinister in you . . . .

He broke off and lathered again lightly his farther cheek. A tolerant smile curled his lips.

—But a lovely mummer![8] he murmured to himself. Kinch, the loveliest mummer of them all!

He shaved evenly and with care, in silence, seriously.

Stephen, an elbow rested on the jagged granite, leaned his palm against his brow and gazed at the fraying edge of his shiny black coatsleeve. Pain, that was not yet the pain of love, fretted his heart. Silently, in a dream she had come to him after her death, her wasted body within its loose brown graveclothes giving off an odour of wax and rosewood, her breath, that had bent upon him, mute, reproachful, a faint odour of wetted ashes. Across the threadbare cuffedge he saw the sea, hailed as a great sweet mother by the wellfed voice beside him. The ring of bay and skyline held a dull green mass of liquid. A bowl of white china had stood beside her deathbed, holding the green sluggish bile which she had torn up from her rotting liver by fits of loud groaning vomiting.

Buck Mulligan wiped again his razorblade.

—Ah, poor dogsbody![9] he said in a kind voice. I must give you a shirt and a few noserags. How are the secondhand breeks?

—They fit well enough, Stephen answered.

Buck Mulligan attacked the hollow beneath his underlip.

—The mockery of it, he said contentedly. Secondleg they should be. God knows what poxy bowsy left them off. I have a lovely pair with a hair stripe, grey. You'll look spiffing in them. I'm not joking, Kinch. You look damn well when you're dressed.

—Thanks, Stephen said. I can't wear them if they are grey.

—He can't wear them, Buck Mulligan told his face in the mirror. Etiquette is etiquette. He kills his mother but he can't wear grey trousers.

He folded his razor neatly and with stroking palps of fingers felt the smooth skin.

Stephen turned his gaze from the sea and to the plump face with its smokeblue mobile eyes.

—That fellow I was with in the Ship last night, said Buck

7. Aloof, living at a distance from ordinary people. In the word's background is the race in Greek mythology that lived in a region of sun and abundance beyond (*huber*) the north wind (*boreas*).
8. Actor, often with a derogatory implication; sometimes, more specifically, a masked or disguised actor in a visiting troupe that performed traditional holiday plays.
9. An underling; someone who does menial work.

Mulligan, says you have g. p. i. He's up in Dottyville with Conolly
Norman. General paralysis of the insane!

He swept the mirror a half circle in the air to flash the tidings
abroad in sunlight now radiant on the sea. His curling shaven lips
laughed and the edges of his white glittering teeth. Laughter seized
all his strong wellknit trunk.

—Look at yourself, he said, you dreadful bard!

Stephen bent forward and peered at the mirror held out to him,
cleft by a crooked crack. Hair on end. As he and others see me.
Who chose this face for me? It asks me too. I pinched it out of the
skivvy's room, Buck Mulligan said. It does her all right. The aunt
always keeps plain looking servants for Malachi. Lead him not into
temptation. And her name is Ursula.

Laughing again, he brought the mirror away from Stephen's
peering eyes.

—The rage of Caliban at not seeing his face in a mirror, he said.
If Wilde were only alive to see you![1]

Drawing back and pointing, Stephen said with bitterness:

—It is a symbol of Irish art. The cracked lookingglass of a
servant.[2]

Buck Mulligan suddenly linked his arm in Stephen's and walked
with him round the tower, his razor and mirror clacking in the
pocket where he had thrust them.

—It's not fair to tease you like that, Kinch, is it? he said kindly.
God knows you have more spirit than any of them.

Parried again. He fears the lancet of my art as I fear that of
his.

—The cracked lookingglass of a servant! Tell that to the oxy chap
downstairs and touch him for a guinea. He's stinking with money
and thinks you're not a gentleman. His old fellow made his tin by
selling jalap to Zulus or some bloody swindle or other. God, Kinch,
if you and I could only work together we might do something for the
island. Hellenise it.

Cranly's arm.[3] His arm.

*   *   *

1. Caliban is a character in Shakespeare's *The Tempest*, specifically a native servant of Prospero, duke of Milan, on the island on which Prospero and his daughter live after being
exiled by his usurping brother. In the nineteenth century, the English sometimes associated the Irish with the brutish Caliban. Oscar Wilde mentions Caliban prominently in
the epigrams that constitute the "preface" to *The Picture of Dorian Gray* (see p. 335
below).
2. Wilde is the source of this image, though in his dialogue "The Decay of Lying" (1889) the
phrase refers not to a servant but to the role of the artist in a conception of art as realistic
that treats it as a mirror.
3. Stephen's close friend Cranly presses his arm with "affection" late in Part V of *A Portrait*
(p. 218).

—Look at the sea. What does it care about offences? Chuck Loyola,[4] Kinch, and come on down. The Sassenach[5] wants his morning rashers.

His head halted again for a moment at the top of the staircase, level with the roof:

—Don't mope over it all day, he said. I'm inconsequent. Give up the moody brooding.

His head vanished but the drone of his descending voice boomed out of the stairhead.

> —*And no more turn aside and brood*
> *Upon love's bitter mystery*
> *For Fergus rules the brazen cars.*[6]

Woodshadows floated silently by through the morning peace from the stairhead seaward where he gazed. Inshore and farther out the mirror of water whitened, spurned by light-shod hurrying feet. White breast of the dim sea. The twining stresses, two by two. A hand plucking the harpstrings, merging their twining chords. Wavewhite wedded words shimmering on the dim tide.

A cloud began to cover the sun slowly, wholly, shadowing the bay in deeper green. It lay beneath him, a bowl of bitter waters. Fergus' song. I sang it alone in the house, holding down the long dark chords. Her door was open: she wanted to hear my music. Silent with awe and pity I went to her bedside. She was crying in her wretched bed. For those words, Stephen: love's bitter mystery.

Where now?

Her secrets: old feather fans, tassled dancecards, powdered with musk, a gaud of amber beads in her locked drawer. A birdcage hung in the sunny window of her house when she was a girl. She heard old Royce sing in the pantomime of Turko the Terrible[7] and laughed with others when he sang:

> *I am the boy*
> *That can enjoy*
> *Invisibility.*

Phantasmal mirth, folded away: musk perfumed.

And no more turn aside and brood.

Folded away in the memory of nature with her toys. Memories beset his brooding brain. Her glass of water from the kitchen tap when she had approached the sacrament. A cored apple, filled with

---

4. Saint Ignatius of Loyola (1491–1556), Spanish priest and founder of the Society of Jesus (Jesuits).
5. An often derogatory term for the English (Gaelic).
6. From "Who Goes with Fergus?" by W. B. Yeats (see p. 300).
7. A popular pantomime, that is, theatrical entertainment primarily for children, by Edwin Hamilton (1849–1919), filled with magical transformations.

brown sugar, roasting for her at the hob on a dark autumn evening. Her shapely fingernails reddened by the blood of squashed lice from the children's shirts.

In a dream, silently, she had come to him, her wasted body within its loose graveclothes giving off an odour of wax and rosewood, her breath bent over him with mute secret words, a faint odour of wetted ashes.

Her glazing eyes, staring out of death, to shake and bend my soul. On me alone. The ghostcandle to light her agony. Ghostly light on the tortured face. Her hoarse loud breath rattling in horror, while all prayed on their knees. Her eyes on me to strike me down. *Liliata rutilantium te confessorum turma circumdet: iubilantium te virginum chorus excipiat.*[8]

Ghoul! Chewer of corpses!

No, mother! Let me be and let me live.

*   *   *

From *Episode II* [*Nestor*][†]

*   *   *

A stick struck the door and a voice in the corridor called:

—Hockey.

They broke asunder, sidling out of their benches, leaping them. Quickly they were gone and from the lumber room came the rattle of sticks and clamour of their boots and tongues.

Sargent who alone had lingered came forward slowly, showing an open copybook. His thick hair and scraggy neck gave witness of unreadiness and through his misty glasses weak eyes looked up pleading. On his cheek, dull and bloodless, a soft stain of ink lay, dateshaped, recent and damp as a snail's bed.

He held out his copybook. The word *Sums* was written on the headline. Beneath were sloping figures and at the foot a crooked signature with blind loops and a blot. Cyril Sargent: his name and seal.

—Mr. Deasy told me to write them out all again, he said, and show them to you, sir.

Stephen touched the edges of the book. Futility.

—Do you understand how to do them now? he asked.

—Numbers eleven to fifteen, Sargent answered. Mr. Deasy said I was to copy them off the board, sir.

—Can you do them yourself? Stephen asked.

---

8. A prayer spoken at the bedside of the dying that asks in Latin for "the throng of confessors, bright like lilies, to gather around you and for the choir of joyous virgins to receive you."

† From *The Little Review* 4:12 (April 1918): 27–28, 32–34.

—No, sir.

Ugly and futile: lean neck and thick hair and a stain of ink, a snail's bed. Yet someone had loved him, borne him in her arms and in her heart. But for her the race of the world would have trampled him under foot, a squashed boneless snail. She had loved his weak watery blood drained from her own. Was that then real? The only true thing in life? She was no more: the trembling skeleton of a twig burnt in the fire, an odour of rosewood and wetted ashes. She had saved him from being trampled under foot and had gone, scarcely having been. A poor soul gone to heaven: and on a heath beneath winking stars a fox, red reek of rapine in his fur, with merciless bright eyes scraped in the earth, listened, scraped up the earth, listened, scraped and scraped.

Sitting at his side Stephen solved out the problem. He proves by algebra that Shakespeare's ghost is Hamlet's grandfather.[1] Sargent peered askance, through his slanted glasses. Hockeysticks rattled in the lumberroom: the hollow knock of a ball and calls from the field.

Across the page the symbols moved in grave morrice,[2] in the mummery of their letters, wearing quaint caps of squares and cubes. Give hands, traverse, bow to partner: so: imps of fancy of the Moors. Gone too from the world, Averroes and Moses Maimonides,[3] dark men in mien and movement, flashing in their mocking mirrors the obscure soul of the world, a darkness shining in brightness which brightness could not comprehend.

—Do you understand now? Can you work the second for yourself?

—Yes, sir.

In long shaky strokes Sargent copied the data. Waiting always for a word of help his hand moved faithfully the unsteady symbols, a faint hue of shame flickering behind his dull skin. *Amor matris*: subjective and objective genitive.[4] With her weak blood and wheysour milk she fed him and hid from sight of others his swaddlingbands.

Like him was I, these sloping shoulders, this gracelessness. My

---

1. Stephen is recalling Mulligan's joking characterization in episode 1 (a comment not reprinted here) of Stephen's speculations about Shakespeare, which Stephen presents in episode 9.
2. A traditional English dance distantly associated with the Moors.
3. Averroës (1126–1198), Spanish-Arabian philosopher, and Moses Maimonides (1135–1204), Spanish rabbi and philosopher; both argued for the relevance of the Greek philosopher Aristotle (384–322 BCE) to the philosophical thinking associated with their respective religious-philosophical traditions, Muslim and Jewish.
4. The Latin phrase can be translated as "love of the mother," that is, either the mother's love of the child or the child's love of the mother. The ambiguity of the genitive (possessive) construction gives it both subjective and objective meanings, grammatically speaking.

childhood bends beside me. Too far for me to lay a hand of comfort there, once or lightly. Mine is far and his secret as our eyes. Secrets, silent, stony, sit in the dark palaces of both our hearts; secrets weary of their tyranny: tyrants willing to be dethroned.

The sum was done.

—It is very simple, Stephen said as he stood up.

—Yes, sir. Thanks, Sargent answered.

He dried the page with a sheet of thin blotting paper and carried his copybook back to his desk.

—You had better get your stick and go out to the others, Stephen said as he followed towards the door the boy's graceless form.

—Yes, sir.

*   *   *

—Mark my words, Mr. Dedalus, he said. England is in the hands of the jews. In all the highest places: her finance, her press. And they are the signs of a nation's decay. Wherever they gather they eat up the nation's vital strength. I have seen it coming these years. As sure as we are standing here the jew merchants are already at their work of destruction. Old England is dying.

He stepped swiftly off, his eyes coming to blue life as they passed a broadsunbeam. He faced about and back again.

—Dying, he said, if not dead by now.

> *The harlot's cry from street to street*
> *Shall weave old England's windingsheet.* [5]

His eyes open wide in vision stared sternly across the sunbeam in which he halted.

—A merchant, Stephen said, is one who buys cheap and sells dear, jew or gentile, is he not?

—They sinned against the light, Mr. Deasy said gravely. And you can see the darkness in their eyes. And that is why they are wanderers on the earth to this day.

On the steps of the Paris stock exchange the goldskinned men quoting prices on their gemmed fingers. Gabble of geese. They swarmed loud, uncouth, about the temple, their heads thick plotting under maladroit silk hats. Not theirs: these clothes, this speech, these gestures. Their full slow eyes belied the words, the gestures eager and unoffending, but knew the rancours massed about them and knew their zeal was vain. Vain patience to heap and hoard. Time surely would scatter all. A hoard heaped by the

---

5. From "Auguries of Innocence" (c. 1803) by the English Romantic poet William Blake (1757–1827).

roadside: plundered and passing on. Their eyes knew their years of wandering and, patient, knew the dishonours of their flesh.

—Who has not? Stephen said.

—What do you mean? Mr. Deasy asked.

He came forward a pace and stood by the table. His underjaw fell sideways open uncertainly. Is this old wisdom? He waits to hear from me.

—History, Stephen said, is a nightmare from which I am trying to awake.

From the playfield the boys raised a shout. A whirring whistle: goal.

—The ways of the Creator are not our ways, Mr. Deasy said. All history moves towards one great goal, the manifestation of God.

Stephen jerked his thumb towards the window, saying:

—That is God.

Hooray! Ay! Whrrwhee!

—What? Mr. Deasy asked.

—A shout in the street, Stephen answered, shrugging his shoulders.

* * *

From *Episode III* [*Proteus*][†]

INELUCTABLE modality[1] of the visible: at least that if no more, thought through my eyes. Signatures of all things I am here to read, seaspawn and seawrack, the nearing tide, that rusty boot. Snotgreen, bluesilver, rust: coloured signs. Limits of the diaphane.[2] But he adds: in bodies. Then he was aware of them, bodies, before of them coloured. How? By knocking his sconce against them, sure. Go easy. Bald he was and a millionaire, *maestro di color che sanno.*[3] Limit of the diaphane in. Why in? Diaphane, adiaphane. If you can put your five fingers through it it is a gate, if not a door. Shut your eyes and see.

Stephen closed his eyes to hear his boots crush crackling wrack and shells. You are walking through it howsomeever. I am, a stride at a time. A very short space of time through very short times of space. Five, six: the *Nacheinander.*[4] Exactly: and that is the ineluctable modality of the audible. Open your eyes. No. Jesus! If I fell

† From *The Little Review* 5:1 (May 1918): 37, 39–41, 46–48.
1. Something ineluctable is inescapable, that is, necessary. In psychology, a modality is "a category of sense perception" (*OED*).
2. Transparent ("adiaphane," below, is its opposite).
3. Aristotle was reputed to be bald. In Italian, Dante (1265–1321) calls him "master of them that know" (*Inferno* 4.131).
4. "After each other" (in time). As a German adverb, this word is not capitalized, nor is *nebeneinander* (below): "next to each other" (in space).

over a cliff that beetles o'er his base, fell through the *Nebeneinander* ineluctably. I am getting on nicely in the dark. My ash sword
hangs at my side. Tap with it: they do. My two feet in his boots are
at the end of my two legs, *nebeneinander*. Sounds solid: made by
the mallet of Los demiurgos.[5] Am I walking into eternity along Sandymount strand? Crush, crack, crick, crick. Wild sea money. * * *

* * *

   Houses of decay, mine, his and all. You told the Clongowes gen-
try you had an uncle a judge and an uncle a general in the army.
Come out of them, Stephen. Beauty is not there. Nor in the stag-
nant bay of Marsh's library where you read the fading prophecies of
Joachim Abbas.[6] For whom? The hundredheaded rabble of the
cathedral close. A hater of his kind ran from them to the wood of
madness, his mane foaming in the moon, his eyeballs stars.
Houyhnhnm, horsenostrilled. The oval equine faces, Temple, Buck
Mulligan, Foxy Campbell, Lanternjaws. Abbas father, furious dean
what offence laid fire to their brains? Paff! *Descende, calve, ut ne
amplius decalveris.*[7] A garland of grey hair on his comminated[8] head
see him now clambering down to the footpace, (*descende*), clutching a monstrance, basiliskeyed. Get down, baldpoll! A choir gives
back menace and echo, assisting about the altar's horns, the snorted
Latin of jackpriests moving burly in their albs,[9] tonsured and oiled
and gelded, fat with the fat of the kidneys of wheat. And at the
same instant perhaps a priest round the corner is elevating it.
Dringdring! And two streets off another locking it into a pyx.[1]
Dringadring! And in a ladychapel another taking housel all to his
own cheek. Dringdring! Down, up, forward, back. Occam[2] thought
of that, invincible doctor. A misty English morning the imp tickled
his brain. Bringing his host down and kneeling he heard twine with
his second bell the first bell in the transept (he is lifting his) and,

---

5. Los is the name that William Blake gave in several of his poetic works to a figure who
   creates central elements of the human world. Demiurgos is the transliteration of the
   Greek word that the philosopher Plato (c. 427–c. 347 BCE) assigned in his dialogue
   Timaeus to the fashioner of the material universe.
6. Joachim of Flora (c. 1135–1202), abbot of the abbey of Santa Maria di Corazzo in Cal-
   abria, some of whose prophetic writings interpreting the Old Testament Book of Revelation were condemned by the Church after his death, though he was never declared a
   heretic. See the excerpt from Yeats's "The Tables of the Law" (p. 301).
7. "Descend, bald one, lest you lose more hair" (Latin).
8. Threatened.
9. An alb is a long white garment worn by clergy, often with a rope belt.
1. Priests in different locations are elevating the consecrated bread eaten during the Christian sacrament, or religious rite, called the Eucharist, or they are putting the bread into a
   pyx, the container in which it is kept.
2. William of Occam, or Ockham (c. 1285–1349), English theologian who argued that the
   true body of Christ was not to be confused with the many manifestations of Christ during
   simultaneous celebrations of the Eucharist.

rising, heard (now I am lifting) their two bells (he is kneeling) twang in diphthong.

Cousin Stephen, you will never be a saint. Isle of saints. You were awfully holy, weren't you? You prayed to the Blessed Virgin that you might not have a red nose. You prayed to the devil in Serpentine avenue that the buxom widow in front might lift her clothes still more from the wet street. *O si, certo!*[3] Sell your soul for that, do, dyed rags pinned round a squaw. More tell me, more still! On the top of the Howth tram alone crying to the rain: *naked women! naked women!* What about that, eh?

What about what? what else were they invented for?

Reading two pages apiece of seven books every night eh? I was young. You bowed to yourself in the mirror, stepping forward to applause earnestly, striking face. Hurray for the Goddamned idiot! Hray! No-one saw: tell no-one. Books you were going to write with letters for titles. Have you read his F? O yes, but I prefer Q. Yes, but W is wonderful. O yes, W. Remember your epiphanies on green oval leaves, deeply deep, copies to be sent if you died to all the great libraries of the world, including Alexandria?[4] Someone was to read them there after a few thousand years, a mahamanvantara.[5] Pico della Mirandola like.[6] Ay, very like a whale.[7] When one reads these strange pages of one long gone one feels that one is at one with one who once . . . . [8]

*   *   *

My Latin quarter hat. God, we simply must dress the character. I want puce gloves. You were a student, weren't you? Of what in the other devil's name? Paysayenn. P.C.N., you know: *physiques, chimiques et naturelles.*[9] Aha. Eating your groatsworth of *mou en civet,*[1] fleshpots of Egypt, elbowed by belching cabmen. Just say in the most natural tone: when I was in Paris I used to. Yes, used to carry punched tickets to prove an alibi if they arrested you for murder somewhere. Justice. On the night of the seventeenth of February 1904

3. "Oh yes, certainly" (Italian).
4. The ancient world's most celebrated library, in Alexandria, Egypt, purportedly damaged by a fire inadvertently caused by Julius Caesar in 48 CE and then in decline under Roman rule, along with the city. The details of its ultimate dissolution are uncertain.
5. In Hinduism, an exceedingly long period of time, many thousands of years.
6. Giovanni Pico della Mirandola (1463–1494), Italian philosopher whose esoteric writings were banned by the Church. See the excerpt from Walter Pater's essay on Pico della Mirandola (p. 325).
7. Words spoken by Polonius in *Hamlet* (3.2.382), when he is agreeing with Hamlet's comment about a cloud resembling a whale.
8. Stephen is imitating Walter Pater's style in an exaggerated way.
9. Physics, chemistry, and biology, the subjects that Stephen traveled to Paris to pursue as premedical studies. "Paysayenn" is Stephen's recalling the French pronunciation of the abbreviation.
1. An inexpensive stew made from an animal's lung.

the prisoner was seen by two witnesses. Other fellow did it: other me. Hat, tie, overcoat, nose. *Lui, c'est moi.*[2] You seem to have enjoyed yourself.

Proudly walking. Whom were you trying to walk like? Forget: a dispossessed. With mother's money order, eight shillings, the barrier of the post office shut in your face by the usher. Hunger toothache. *Encore deux minutes.*[3] Look clock. Must get. *Fermé.*[4] Hired dog! Shoot him to bloody bits with a bang shotgun, bits man spattered walls all brass buttons. Bits all khrrrklak in place clack back. Not hurt? O, that's all right. Shake hands. See what I meant, see? O, that's all right. Shake a shake. O, that's all only all right.—

You were going to do wonders, what? Missionary to Europe after fiery Columbanus.[5] Pretending to speak broken English as you dragged your valise, porter threepence, across the slimy pier at Newhaven. *Comment?*[6] Rich booty you brought back; five tattered numbers of *Pantalon Blanc et Culotte Rouge;*[7] a blue French telegram, curiosity to show:

—Mother dying come home father.

The aunt thinks you killed your mother. That's why she won't.

* * *

* * * If I were suddenly naked here as I sit? I am not. Across the sands of all the world, followed by the sun's flaming sword, to the west, to evening lands. She trudges, schlepps, trains, drags, trascines her load. A tide westering, moondrawn, in her wake. Tides, myriad-islanded, within her, blood not mine, *oinopa ponton,* a winedark sea. Behold the handmaid of the moon. In sleep the wet sign calls her hour, bids her rise. Bridebed, childbed, bed of death, ghost-candled. *Omnis caro ad te veniet.*[8] He comes, pale vampire, through storm his eyes, his bat sails bloodying the sea, mouth to her mouth's kiss.

Here. Put a pin in that chap, will you? My tablet. Mouth to her kiss. No. Must be two of em. Glue em well. Mouth to her mouth's kiss.

His lips lipped and mouthed fleshless lips of air: mouth to her moomb. Oomb, allwombing tomb. His mouth moulded issuing breath, unspeeched: ooeeehah: roar of cataractic planets, globed,

2. "I am he" (French). A play on the French king Louis XIV's assertion *"L'état, c'est moi"* ("I am the state").
3. "Another two minutes" (French).
4. "Closed" (French).
5. Irish saint (540–615 CE), who left Ireland to be a missionary in Europe.
6. "What?" (French). Stephen was pretending not to understand English.
7. Apparently the name of a French magazine, though one of exactly that name (white trousers and red knee breeches) has not been identified.
8. "All flesh shall come to thee" (Latin; Psalms 64:3; also from the Introit of the Requiem Mass).

blazing, roaring wayawayawayawayawayawayaway. Paper. The banknotes, blast them. Old Deasy's letter. Here. Thanking you for the hospitality tear the blank end off. Turning his back to the sun he bent over far to a table of rock and scribbled words. That's twice I forgot to take slips from the library counter.

His shadow lay over the rocks as he bent, ending. Why not endless till the farthest star? Darkly they are there behind this light, darkness shining in the brightness, delta of Cassiopeia, worlds. Me sits there with his augur's rod of ash, in borrowed sandals, by day beside a livid sea, unbeheld, in violet night walking beneath a reign of uncouth stars. I throw this ended shadow from me, call it back. Endless, would it be mine, form of my form? Who watches me here? Who ever anywhere will read these written words? Signs on a white field. Somewhere to someone in your flutiest voice. The good bishop of Cloyne[9] took the veil of the temple out of his shovel hat: veil of space with coloured emblems hatched on its field. Hold hard. Coloured on a flat: yes, that's right. Flat I see, then think distance, near, far, flat I see, east, back. Ah, see now! Falls back suddenly frozen in stereoscope. Click does the trick. You find my words dark. Darkness is in our souls do you not think? Flutier. Our souls, shamewounded by our sins, cling to us yet more, a woman to her lover clinging, the more the more.

She trusts me, her hand gentle, the longlashed eyes. Now where the blue hell am I bringing her beyond the veil? Into the ineluctable modality of the ineluctable visuality. She, she, she. What she? The virgin at Hodges Figgis' window on Monday looking in for one of the alphabet books you were going to write. Keen glance you gave her. Wrist through the braided jesse of her sunshade. She lives in Leeson park, a lady of letters. Talk that to someone else, Stevie: a pickmeup. Bet she wears those curse of God stays suspenders and yellow stockings, darned with lumpy wool. Talk about apple dumpling, *piuttosto*.[1] Where are your wits?

Touch me. Soft eyes. Soft soft soft hand. I am lonely here. O, touch me soon, now. What is that word known to all men? I am quiet here alone. Sad too. Touch, touch me.

He lay back at full stretch over the sharp rocks, cramming the scribbled note and pencil into a pocket, his hat tilted down on his eyes. That is Kevin Egan's[2] movement I made, nodding for his nap. *Hlo! Bonjour.* Under its leaf he watched through peacocktwittering lashes the southing sun. I am caught in this burning scene. Pan's

9. George Berkeley (1685–1753), bishop in the Church of Ireland and idealist philosopher.
1. "Rather" (Italian).
2. Name for a fictitious Irish political exile living in Paris.

hour, the faunal noon. Among gumheavy serpentplants, milkoozing fruits, where on the tawny waters leaves lie wide. Pain is far.

And no more turn aside and brood.

His gaze brooded on his broadtoed boots, a buck's castoffs, *nebeneinander.* He counted the creases of rucked leather wherein another's foot had nested warm. The foot that beat the ground in tripudium,[3] foot I dislove. But you were delighted when Esther Osvalt's shoe went on you: girl I knew in Paris. *Tiens, quel petit pied!*[4] Staunch friend, a brother soul: Wilde's love that dare not speak its name.[5] He now will leave me. And the blame? As I am. All or not at all.

In long lassos from the Cock lake the water flowed full, covering greengoldenly lagoons of sand, rising, flowing. My ashplant[6] will float away. I shall wait. No, they will pass on, passing chafing against the low rocks, swirling, passing. Better get this job over quick. Listen: a fourworded wavespeech: seesoo, hrss, rsseeiss ooos. Vehement breath of waters amid seasnakes, rearing horses, rocks. In cups of rocks it slops: flop, slop, slap: bounded in barrels. And, spent, its speech ceases. It flows purling, widely flowing, floating foampool, flower unfurling.

*   *   *

From *Episode VII* [*Aeolus*][†]

I have money.

—Gentlemen, Stephen said. May I suggest that the house do now adjourn?

—It is not a French compliment? Mr. O'Madden Burke asked.[1]

—All who are in favour say ay, Lenehan announced. The contrary no. I declare it carried. To which particular boosingshed . . ? Mooney's?

He led the way.

Mr. O'Madden Burke, following close, said with an ally's lunge of his umbrella:

—*Lay on, Macduff!*[2]

---

3. "A beating the ground with the feet, a leaping or dancing, a religious dance" (*OED*, in the Latin etymology of *tripudiate*).
4. "Look, what a small foot!" (French).
5. The phrase comes from a poem by Lord Alfred Douglas (1870–1945), who was Oscar Wilde's lover. Wilde asserted when put on trial for indecent acts that it referred to an ideal affection that an older man felt toward a younger man.
6. Walking stick made from an ash sapling.
† From *The Little Review* 5:6 (October 1918): 120–23.
1. The meaning of the question and the intention behind it are obscure.
2. *Macbeth* 5.8.32. In the last scene of the play, just before he is killed, Macbeth invites Macduff to fight.

—Chip of the old block! the editor cried, slapping Stephen on the shoulder. Let us go. Where are those bloody keys?

He fumbled in his pocket, pulling out the crushed typesheets.

—Foot and mouth. I know. That'll be all right. That'll go in.[3] Where are they?

He thrust the sheets back and went into the inner office.

J.J. O'Molloy, about to follow him in, said quietly to Stephen:

—I hope you will live to see it published. Myles, one moment.

He went into the inner office, closing the door behind him.

—Come along, Stephen, the professor said. That is fine, isn't it? It has the prophetic vision.

The first newsboy came pattering down the stairs at their heels and rushed out into the street, yelling:

—Racing special!

Dublin.

They turned to the left along Abbey street.

—I have a vision too, Stephen said.

—Yes? the professor said, skipping to get into step. Crawford will follow. Another newsboy shot past them, yelling as he ran:

—Racing special!

Dubliners.

—Two Dublin vestals, Stephen said, elderly and pious, have lived fifty and fiftythree years in Fumbally's lane.

—Where is that? the professor asked.

—Off Blackpitts, Stephen said.

Damp night reeking of hungry dough. Against the wall. Face glistening tallow under her fustian shawl. Frantic hearts. Akasic records.[4] Quicker, darlint!

On now. Let there be life.

—They want to see the views of Dublin from the top of Nelson's pillar.[5] They save up three and tenpence in a red tin letterbox moneybox. They shake out threepenny bits and a sixpence and coax out the pennies with the blade of a knife. Two and three in silver and one and seven in coppers. They put on their bonnets and best clothes and take their umbrellas for fear it may come on to rain.

—Wise virgins, professor MacHugh said.

---

3. The editor of the newspaper is indicating that he will print the letter that Stephen has delivered from Mr. Deasy, the head of the school where Stephen teaches, concerning the foot and mouth disease affecting cattle.
4. A collection of all human experience, past, present, and future, according to the occult religion of theosophy, which draws on the work of Helena Petrovna Blavatsky (1831–1891).
5. An imposing granite column, popular with tourists, in the center of Dublin, built in 1809 to commemorate the English victory at the Battle of Trafalgar (1805). Because it was topped with a statue of the English naval hero Admiral Horatio Nelson (1758–1805), Irish nationalists objected to it. An explosion destroyed it in 1966.

—They buy oneandfourpenceworth of brawn[6] and four slices of panloaf at the north city diningrooms in Marlborough street from Miss Kate Collins, proprietress . . They purchase four and twenty ripe plums from a girl at the foot of Nelson's pillar to take off the thirst of the brawn. They give two threepenny bits to the gentleman at the turnstile and begin to waddle slowly up the winding staircase, grunting, encouraging each other, afraid of the dark, panting, one asking the other have you the brawn, praising God and the Blessed Virgin, threatening to come down, peeping at the airslits. Glory be to God. They had no idea it was that high.

Their names are Anne Kearns and Florence MacCabe. Anne Kearns has the lumbago for which she rubs on Lourdes[7] water given her by a lady who got a bottleful from a passionist father. Florence MacCabe takes a crubeen and a bottle of double X[8] for supper every Saturday.

—Antithesis, the professor said, nodding twice. I can see them. What's keeping our friend?

He turned.

A bevy of scampering newsboys rushed down the steps, scampering in all directions, yelling, their white papers fluttering. Hard after them Myles Crawford appeared on the steps, his hat aureoling his scarlet face, talking with J. J. O'Molloy.

—Come along, the professor cried waving his arm.

He set off again to walk by Stephen's side.

—Yes, he said, I see them.

*   *   *

—When they have eaten the brawn and the bread and wiped their twenty fingers in the paper the bread was wrapped in they go nearer the railings.

—Something for you, the professor explained to Myles Crawford. Two old Dublin women on the top of Nelson's pillar.

—That's new, Myles Crawford said. Out for the waxies' Dargle.[9] Two old trickies, what?

—But they are afraid the pillar will fall, Stephen went on. They see the roofs and argue about where the different churches are: Rathmines' blue dome, Adam and Eve's, saint Laurence O'Toole's. But it makes them giddy to look so they pull up their skirts . . . .

—Easy all, Myles Crawford said. We're in the archdiocese here.

6. Boar's meat.
7. Water from a spring at Lourdes, in southern France, where the Virgin Mary is said to have appeared to a girl.
8. A pig's foot, or a dish made from pig's feet, and a bottle of Guinness stout.
9. A holiday outing by working-class people. Waxies are shoemakers. The River Dargle was a holiday destination for well-off Dubliners.

—And settle down on their striped petticoats, peering up at the statue of the onehandled adulterer.[1]

—Onehandled adulterer! the professor cried. I like that. I see the idea. I see what you mean.

—It gives them a crick in their necks, Stephen said, and they are too tired to look up or down or to speak. They put the bag of plums between them and eat the plums out of it, one after another wiping off with their handkerchiefs the plumjuice that dribbles out of their mouths and spitting the plumstones slowly out between the railways.

He gave a sudden loud young laugh as a close. Lenehan and Mr. O'Madden Burke, hearing, turned, beckoned and led on across towards Mooney's.

—Finished? Myles Crawford said. So long as they do no worse.

—You remind me of Antisthenes, the professor said, a disciple of Gorgias the sophist. It is said of him that none could tell if he were bitterer against others or against himself. He was the son of a noble and a bondwoman. And he wrote a book in which he took away the palm of beauty from Argive Helen and handed it to poor Penelope.[2]

Poor Penelope. Penelope Rich.[3]

They made ready to cross O'Connell street.

—But what do you call it? Myles Crawford asked. Where did they get the plums?

—Call it, wait, the professor said, opening his long lips wide to reflect. Call it, let me see. Call it: *deus nobis haec otia fecit.*[4]

—No, Stephen said, I call it *A Pisgah Sight of Palestine.*[5]

—I see, the professor said.

He laughed richly.

—I see, he said again with new pleasure. Moses and the promised land. We gave him that idea, he added to J. J. O'Molloy.

J. J. O'Molloy sent a weary sidelong glance towards the statue and held his peace.

—I see, the professor said.

---

1. Admiral Nelson lost part of his right arm at the Battle of Santa Cruz de Tenerife (1797) and had a famous affair with the married Emma, Lady Hamilton (1765–1815).
2. Antisthenes (c. 446–c. 366 BCE) was a Greek philosopher who studied with Gorgias (483–375 BCE). His book, now lost, argued that the virtue of Penelope, wife of Odysseus, made her more beautiful than Helen, wife of Menelaus, whose renowned beauty contributed to the war between Greece and Troy. Calling Helen Argive does not mean she was literally from the city of Argos. Argive was used to refer generally to the ancient Greeks who fought against Troy.
3. English noblewoman (1563–1607), notorious for court intrigue and adultery, by contrast with Penelope in Homer's *Odyssey*.
4. "It is a god who gave us this peace" (Latin; Virgil, *Eclogues* 1.6).
5. In the Old Testament, God let Moses see the promised land from Mount Pisgah but did not allow him to enter it (Deuteronomy 34:1–5).

He halted on Sir John Gray's pavement island[6] and peered aloft at Nelson through the meshes of his wry smile.

—Onehandled adulterer, he said grimly. That tickles me I must say.

—Tickled the old ones too, Myles Crawford said, if the truth was known.

*   *   *

From *Episode IX* [*Scylla and Charybdis*][†]

*   *   *

—Our young Irish bards, John Eglinton censured, have yet to create a figure which the world will set beside Saxon Shakespeare's Hamlet though I admire him, as old Ben did, on this side idolatry.[1]

—All these questions are purely academic,[2] Russell oracled out of his shadow. I mean, whether Hamlet is Shakespeare or James I or Essex. Clergyman's discussions of the historicity of Jesus. Art has to reveal to us ideas, formless spiritual essences. The supreme question about a work of art is out of how deep a life does it spring. The painting of Gustave Moreau is the painting of ideas. The deepest poetry of Shelley, the words of Hamlet bring our mind into contact with the eternal wisdom, Plato's world of ideas. All the rest is the speculation of schoolboys for schoolboys.

A. E. has been telling some interviewer. Wall, tarnation strike me!

—The schoolmen[3] were schoolboys first, Stephen said superpolitely. Aristotle was once Plato's schoolboy.

—And has remained so, one should hope, John Eglinton sedately said. One can see him, a model schoolboy with his diploma under his arm.

He laughed again at the now smiling bearded face.

Formless spiritual. Father, Son and Holy Breath.[4] This verily is that. I am the fire upon the altar. I am the sacrificial butter.

---

6. The memorial statue, close to Nelson's column, of John Gray (1815–1875), nationalist politician and newspaper owner, who supported Home Rule (limited autonomy) for Ireland.

† From *The Little Review* 5:12 (April 1919) and 6:1 (May 1919): 154–58, 179–81.

1. Refers to a comment by Ben Jonson (1572–1637), poet and playwright, in his *Timber, or Discoveries Made upon Men and Matter* (1641).

2. "Of no consequence, irrelevant" (*OED*). I.e., more abstruse than the pronouncements of George Russell (1867–1935), who used the pseudonym A.E., Irish writer and editor who was part of a Dublin theosophical group.

3. Plato treated the material world as secondary to a world of abstract forms. Aristotle studied with him. "Schoolmen" refers to medieval philosophers whose work originated in monastic schools.

4. In Christianity, the three persons of the Holy Trinity. The third person is usually called the Holy Spirit or Holy Ghost.

Dunlop, Judge, the noblest Roman of them all, A. E., Arval in heaven hight, K. H., their master. Adepts of the great white lodge always watching to see if they can help. The Christ with the bride-sister, moisture of light, born of a virgin, repentant sophia, departed to the plane of buddhi. Mrs. Cooper Oakley once glimpsed our very illustrious sister H. P. B.'s elemental.[5]

O, fie! Out on't![6] *Pfuiteufel!* You naughtn't to look, missus, so you naugh't when a lady's ashowing of her elemental.

Mr. Best entered, tall, young, mild, light. He bore in his hand with grace a notebook, new, large, clean, bright.

—That model schoolboy, Stephen said, would find Hamlet's musings about the afterlife of his princely soul, the improbable, insignificant and undramatic monologue, as shallow as Plato's.

John Eglinton, frowning, said, waxing wroth:

—Upon my word it makes my blood boil to hear anyone compare Aristotle with Plato.

—Which of the two, Stephen asked, would have banished me from his commonwealth?[7]

Unsheathe your dagger definitions. Streams of tendency and eons they worship. God: noise in the street: very peripatetic. Space: what you damn well have to see. Through spaces smaller than red globules of man's blood they creepycrawl after Blake's buttocks into eternity of which this vegetable world is but a shadow.[8] Hold to the now, the here, through which all future plunges to the past.

* * *

—He will have it that "Hamlet" is a ghost story, John Eglinton said for Mr. Best's behoof. Like the fat boy in Pickwick[9] he wants to make our flesh creep.

> *List! List! O list!*
> *My flesh hears him creeping, hears.*
> *If thou didst ever. . . . .*[1]

5. For H. P. Blavatsky, see note 4, p. 247. In theosophy, an elemental seems to be a center of force, but its precise character is unclear. This paragraph touches on various aspects of occult thinking and practice and people involved in the spiritualist movement, including A.E.
6. Stephen is drawing on Hamlet's language (*Hamlet*, especially 1.2.135 but also 2.2.588).
7. Plato banished poets from his utopia in his dialogue *The Republic* because they made things up.
8. Stephen is mixing aspects of William Blake's *Milton* (Book I, Plate 29, ll. 19–22) concerning the vegetable world with the scene at the end of Dante's *Inferno* (Canto 34) when Dante the pilgrim and Virgil crawl over Satan's buttocks as they leave Hell for Purgatory.
9. Joe in *The Pickwick Papers* (1837), the first novel by Charles Dickens (1812–1870).
1. Based on what the Ghost says to Hamlet (*Hamlet* 1.5.23–24). This excerpt from episode 9 includes several other references to that famous scene, among others. With his frequent citations and echoes of Shakespeare's works and references to Shakespeare's life, Stephen demonstrates his mastery of a large canon. As he challenges his listeners and the episode's readers to match his knowledge and to keep up, Stephen argues speculatively for

—What is a ghost? Stephen said with tingling energy. One who has faded into impalpability through death, through absence, through change of manners. Elizabethan London lay as far from Stratford as corrupt Paris lies from virgin Dublin. Who is the ghost, returning to the world that has forgotten him? Who is king Hamlet?

John Eglinton shifted his spare body, leaning back to judge.

Lifted.

—It is this hour of a June day, Stephen said, begging with a swift glance their hearing. The flag is up on the playhouse by the bankside. The bear Sackerson growls in the pit near it, Paris garden. Canvasclimbers who sailed with Drake[2] chew their sausages among the groundlings.

Local colour. Work in all you know. Make them accomplices.

—Shakespeare has left the huguenot's house[3] in Silver street and walks by the swanmews along the riverbank. But he does not stay to feed the pen chivying her game of cygnets[4] towards the rushes. The swan of Avon has other thoughts.

Composition of place. Ignatius Loyola, make haste to help me!

—The play begins. A player comes on under the shadow, clad in the castoff mail of a court buck, a wellset man with a bass voice. He is the ghost king Hamlet, and the player Shakespeare. He speaks the words to Burbage,[5] the young player who stands before him, calling him by a name:

Hamlet, I am thy father's spirit

bidding him list. To a son he speaks, the son of his soul, the prince, young Hamlet and to the son of his body, Hamnet Shakespeare who has died in Stratford that his namesake may live for ever.

Is it possible that that player Shakespeare, a ghost by absence, and in the vesture of buried Denmark, a ghost by death, speaking his own words to his own son's name (had Hamnet Shakespeare lived he would have been prince Hamlet's twin) is it possible, I want to know, or probable that he did not draw or foresee the logical conclusion of those premises: you are this dispossessed son. I am the murdered father: your mother is the guilty queen, Ann Shakespeare, born Hathaway?

---

an estrangement in Shakespeare's marriage, based on the ostensible adultery of his wife, Anne, with details of the playwright's family life reflected variously in the plays.

2. Sir Francis Drake (c. 1540–1596), English navigator and naval hero. The Paris Garden, on the banks of the River Thames in London near Shakespeare's Globe Theatre, was famous for its bear pit and its bear Sackerson.

3. Shakespeare is believed to have lived for a time on Silver Street in London in the house of a Huguenot, that is, a French Protestant.

4. A pen is a female swan, game is the collective noun for swans, and cygnets are young swans. To chivy is to chase.

5. Richard Burbage (1567–1619), famous actor in Shakespeare's company.

—But this prying into the family life of a great man, Russell began impatiently.

Art thou there, truepenny?[6]

—Interesting only to the parish clerk. I mean, we have the plays. I mean when we read the poetry of "King Lear" what is it to us how the poet lived? As for living our servants can do that for us, Villiers de l'Isle said.[7] Peeping and prying into greenroom gossip of the day, the poet's drinking, the poet's debts. We have "King Lear": and it is immortal.

Mr. Best's face appealed to, agreed.

Flow over them with your waves and with your waters, Mananaan, Mananaan MacLir. . . . .[8]

By the way, that pound he lent you when you were hungry?

I wanted it.

Take thou this noble.

You spent most of it in . . . .

Do you intend to pay it back?

O, yes.

When? Now?

Well . . . no.

When, then?

I paid my way. I paid my way.

Steady on. He's from north of Boyne water.[9] You owe it.

Wait. Five months. Molecules all change. I am other I now. Other I got pound.

Buzz. Buzz.[1]

But I, entelechy, form of forms, am I by memory under ever changing forms.

I that sinned and prayed and fasted.

A child Conmee saved from pandies.

I, I and I. I.

A.E.I.O.U.

—Do you mean to fly in the face of the tradition of three centuries? John Eglinton's carping voice asked. Her ghost at least has been laid for ever. She died, for literature at least, before she was born.

—She died, Stephen retorted, sixtyseven years after she was born. She saw him into and out of the world. She took his first

---

6. Hamlet addresses the Ghost as "truepenny," or honest old fellow (*Hamlet* 1.5.159).
7. In the play *Axël* (1891), by Auguste Villiers del l'Isle Adam (1838–1889). W. B. Yeats used the statement as an epigraph in *The Secret Rose* (1897) (see pp. 299–300).
8. From the play *Deirdre* (1901), by George Russell. MacLir is king of the Celtic Otherworld, realm of deities and the dead.
9. Ulster, that is, northern Ireland, the majority Protestant part of the island, is north of the Boyne River. Russell was born in County Armagh, Ulster.
1. Hamlet says this to Polonius (*Hamlet* 2.2.393).

embraces. She bore his children and she laid pennies on his eyes to keep his eyelids closed when he lay on his deathbed.

Mother's deathbed. Candle. The sheeted mirror. Who brought me into this world lies there, bronzelidded, under few cheap flowers. *Liliata rutilantium.*

I wept alone.

John Eglinton looked in the tangled glowworm of his lamp.

—The world believes that Shakespeare made a mistake,[2] he said, and got out of it as quickly and as best he could.

—Bosh! Stephen said rudely. A man of genius makes no mistakes. His errors are volitional and are the portals of discovery.

* * *

—I was prepared for paradoxes from what Malachi Mulligan told us but I may as well warn you that if you want to shake my belief that Shakespeare is Hamlet you have a stern task before you.

Bear with me.

Stephen withstood the bane of miscreant eyes, glinting stern under wrinkling brows. A basilisk. *E quando vede l'uomo l'attosca.* Messer Brunetto, I thank thee for the word.[3]

—As we, or mother Dana, weave and unweave our bodies,[4] Stephen said, from day to day, their molecules shuttled to and fro, so does the artist weave and unweave his image. And as the mole on my right breast is where it was when I was born, though all my body has been woven of new stuff time after time so through the ghost of the unquiet father the image of the unliving son looks forth.[5] In the intense instant of imagination, when the mind, Shelley says, is a fading coal,[6] that which I was is that which I am and that which in possibility I may come to be. So in the future, the sister of the past, I may see myself as I sit here now but by reflection from that which then I shall be.

2. The supposed mistake would have been his marriage to Anne Hathaway, which is central to Stephen's speculations concerning the biographical implications of some of Shakespeare's plays.
3. The Florentine writer Brunetto Latini (c. 1220–1294) wrote about the basilisk, a mythical reptile that could kill with a look. The Italian means "and when it gazes at a man, it poisons him."
4. In *The Odyssey*, Penelope weaves a tapestry by day but unweaves it at night as a strategy for delaying marriage to one of her many suitors. "Dana": Ancient Celtic goddess, whose name Stephen's interlocutor here, John Eglinton (pen name of William Magee, 1868–1961), used as the title for the magazine he published from May 1904 through April 1905.
5. In his speculations about Shakespeare's life and works, Stephen aligns the Ghost of Hamlet's father with the playwright and Hamlet with Shakespeare's dead son, Hamnet.
6. The Romantic poet Percy Bysshe Shelley (1792–1822) makes the comparison in "A Defence of Poetry" (1821), suggesting that an invisible power, like a wind, from within causes a fleeting glow. Stephen meditates on the comparison quite differently in part V of *A Portrait* (V.1398), where he does not present the moment's temporal complexity.

Drummond of Hawthornden helped you at that stile.[7]

* * *

He laughed to free his mind from his mind's bondage.

Judge Eglinton summed up.

—The truth is midway, he affirmed. He is the ghost and the prince. He is all in all.

—He is, Stephen said. The boy of act one is the mature man of act five. All in all. In "Cymbeline", in "Othello" he is bawd and cuckold. He acts and is acted on. His unremitting intellect is the Iago ceaselessly[8] that the moor in him shall suffer.

—Cuckoo! Cuckoo! Buck Mulligan clucked lewdly. O word of fear!

Dark dome received, reverbed.

—And what a character is Iago! undaunted John Eglinton exclaimed. When all is said Dumas *fils* (or is it Dumas *père*) is right. After God Shakespeare has created most.

—Man delights him not nor woman neither, Stephen said. He returns after a life of absence—to that spot of earth where he was born, where he has always been a silent witness and there, his journey of life ended, he plants his mulberrytree in the earth. Then dies, Gravediggers bury Hamlet *père* and Hamlet *fils*. If you like the last scene look long on it: prosperous Prospero, the good man rewarded, Lizzie, grandpa's lump of love, and nuncle Richie, the bad man taken off by poetic justice to the place where the bad niggers go.[9] He found in the world without as actual what was in his world within as possible. Maeterlinck says: If Socrates leave his house today he will find the sage seated on his doorstep, if Judas go forth tonight it is to Judas his steps will tend.[1] Every life is many

7. Turnstile, here meaning Stephen's rhetorical turn. "Stile" refers literally to steps, often in a ladderlike arrangement, that allow people to negotiate a wall or fence. Stephen's figurative meaning involves help in overcoming a difficulty. In "A Cypress Grove" (1623), a prose meditation on mortality, the Scottish poet William Drummond of Hawthornden (1585–1649) contrasts being alive in the present with the future after death and the past before birth.

8. The word "willing," which appears after "ceaselessly" in the book version, is missing here. In Shakespeare's *Othello*, Iago hates Othello, who is a Moor.

9. Apparently a play on Old Ned's having "gone where the good Niggas go" in "Old Uncle Ned," an 1848 minstrel song by Stephen Foster (1826–1864). In this paragraph, Stephen implies that Shakespeare late in life can be identified with Prospero, the central figure of his final play, *The Tempest*. Lizzie is Shakespeare's granddaughter, Elizabeth Hall, and Richie is one of Shakespeare's brothers, Richard, but the episode is so freewheeling in its associations and speculations around names that Lizzie and Richie also suggest, however distantly, the names of English monarchs.

1. Maurice Maeterlinck (1862–1949), Belgian writer, in *La Sagesse et la destinée* (*Wisdom and Destiny*) (1898). Socrates (c. 470–399 BCE), Greek philosopher with whom Plato studied. Judas Iscariot (died c. 30–33 CE), a disciple of Jesus whose betrayal of him led to Jesus's arrest and crucifixion.

days, day after day. We walk through ourselves, meeting robbers,
ghosts, giants, old men, young men, wives, but always meeting ourselves. The playwright who wrote this world and wrote it badly (He
gave us light first and the sun two days later), the lord of things as
they are whom the most Roman of catholics call *dio boia*, hangman
god, is doubtless all in all in all of us, ostler and butcher, and would
be bawd and cuckold too but that in the economy of heaven, foretold by Hamlet, there are no more marriages, glorified man being a
wife unto himself.

*   *   *

—You are a delusion, said roundly John Eglinton to Stephen. You
have brought us all this way to show us a French triangle.[2] Do you
believe your own theory?

—No, Stephen said promptly.

—Are you going to write it? Mr. Best asked. You ought to make it
a dialogue, don't you know, like the Platonic dialogues Wilde wrote.[3]

John Eglinton smiled doubly.

—Well, in that case, he said, I don't see why you should expect
payment for it since you don't believe it yourself. Dowden believes[4]
there is some mystery in "Hamlet" but will say no more. Herr
Bleibtreu,[5] the man Piper met in Berlin who is working up that Rutland theory, believes that the secret is hidden in the Stratford monument.[6] He is going to visit the present duke, Piper says, and prove
to him that his ancestor wrote the plays. It will come as a surprise
to his grace. But he believes his theory.

I believe, O Lord, help my unbelief. That is, help me to believe or
help me to unbelieve? Who helps to believe? *Egomen.*[7] Who to
unbelieve? Other chap.

—You are the only contributor to *Dana* who asks for pieces of
silver. Then I don't know about the next number. Fred Ryan wants
a space for an article on economics.

2. A *ménage à trois*, that is, an adulterous relationship between a married couple and a third
   person.
3. Plato wrote dialogues, as did Wilde (see note 2, p. 236).
4. Edward Dowden (1843–1913), Irish critic and poet, in *Shakspere* [sic]: *A Critical Study
   of His Mind and Art* (1875).
5. Karl August Bleibtreu (1859–1928), German writer, who wrote *Der Wahre Shakespeare*
   [*The True Shakespeare*] (1907).
6. The Church of the Holy Trinity at Stratford-upon-Avon, about 90 miles northwest of
   London, contains both a funerary monument to Shakespeare and his gravesite, with a
   stone slab on which is carved his epitaph. The town is Shakespeare's birthplace and burial
   site. It is commonly referred to as Stratford and at times in this episode as Avon. Little is
   known of Shakespeare's private life, but it appears that his wife, Anne, remained in Stratford when he went to London to pursue his career in the theater. He returned to Stratford to live with his wife when his engagement with the London theater eventually
   decreased.
7. The usage here is not standard Greek, but it suggests "I myself" or "I on the one hand,"
   by contrast with "Other chap."

Fraidrine. Two pieces of silver he lent me. Tide you over. Economics.

—For a guinea, Stephen said, you can publish this interview.

* * *

From *Episode X* [*Wandering Rocks*]†

Stephen Dedalus watched through the webbed window the lapidary's fingers prove a timedulled chain. Dust webbed the window. Dust darkened the toiling fingers with their vulture nails. Dust slept on dull coils of bronze and silver, lozenges of cinnabar, on rubies, leprous and winedark stones.

Born all in the dark wormy earth, cold specks of fire, evil lights shining in the darkness. Muddy swinesnouts, hands, root and root, gripe and wrest them.

She dances in a foul gloom where gum burns with garlic. A sailorman, rustbearded, sips from a beaker rum and eyes her. A long and seafed silent rut. She dances, capers, wagging her sowish haunches and her hips, on her gross belly flapping a ruby egg.

Old Russell with a smeared shammy rag, burnished again his gem, turned it and held it at the point of his Moses' beard. Grandfather ape gloating on a stolen hoard.

And you who wrest old images from the burial earth! The brainsick words of sophists: Antisthenes. A lore of drugs. Orient and immortal wheat standing from everlasting to everlasting.

Two old women from their whiff of the briny drudged through Irishtown along London bridge road, one with a sanded unbrella, one with a midwife's bag in which eleven cockles rolled.[1]

The whirr of flapping leathern bands and hum of dynamos from the powerhouse urged Stephen to be on. Beingless beings. Stop! Throb always without you and the throb always within. Your heart you sing of. I between them. Where? Between two roaring worlds where they swirl, I. Shatter them, one and both. But stun myself too in the blow. Shatter me you who can. Bawd and butcher, were the words. I say! Not yet awhile. A look around.

Yes, quite true. Very large and wonderful and keeps famous time. You say right, Sir, a Monday morning. Twas so, indeed.[2]

Stephen went down Bedford row. In Clohisey's window a faded print of Heenan boxing Sayers held his eye. Staring backers with square hats stood round the ropering. The heavyweights in light

---

1. This interpolation refers to something Stephen sees on the beach in episode 3.
2. Hamlet says this to Polonius (*Hamlet* 2.2.387–88).

loincloths proposed gently each to other his bulbous fists. And they are throbbing: heroes' hearts.

He turned and halted by the slanted bookcart.

—Twopence each, the huckster said. Four for sixpence.

Tattered pages. *The Irish Beekeeper. Life and Miracles of the Curé of Ars. Pocket Guide to Killarney.*

I might find here one of my pawned schoolprizes. *Stephano Dedalo, alumno optimo, palmam ferenti.*[3]

Father Conmee, having read his little hours, walked through the hamlet of Donnycarney, murmuring vespers.[4]

Binding too good probably. What is this? Eighth and ninth book of Moses. Secret of all secrets. Seal of King David. Thumbed pages: read and read. Who has passed here before me? How to soften chapped hands. Recipe for white wine vinegar. How to win a woman's love. For me this. Say the following talisman three times with hands folded:

—*Se el yilo nebrakada femininum! Amor me solo! Sanktus! Amen.*[5]

Who wrote this? Charms and invocations of the most blessed abbot Peter Salanka to all true believers divulged. As good as any other abbot's charms, as mumbling Joachim's. Down, baldynoddle, or we'll wool your wool.

—What are you doing here, Stephen?

Dilly's high shoulders and shabby dress.

Shut the book quick. Don't let see.

—What are you doing? Stephen said.

A Stuart face of nonesuch Charles,[6] lank locks falling at its sides. It glowed as she crouched feeding the fire with broken boots. I told her of Paris. Late lieabed under a quilt of old overcoats fingering a pinchbeck bracelet, Dan Kelly's token. *Nebrakada femininum.*

—What have you there? Stephen asked.

—I bought it from the other cart for a penny, Dilly said, laughing nervously. Is it any good?

My eyes they say she has. Do others see me so? Quick, far and daring. Shadow of my mind.

He took the coverless book from her hand. Bué's French primer.

—What did you buy that for? He asked. To learn French?

She nodded, reddening and closing tight her lips.

Show no surprise. Quite natural.

---

3. "To Stephen Dedalus, best student, winner of the palm (prize)" (Latin).
4. Interpolation of a moment involving Father Conmee, who appears at the beginning of the episode.
5. This line is a statement of uncertain meaning in mixed languages; the second half suggests something like "love me only" and then "Holy" before the closing amen.
6. Charles I (1600–1649), a member of the House of Stuart who ruled 1625–49.

—Here, Stephen said. It's all right. Mind Maggie doesn't pawn it on you. I suppose all my books are gone.

—Some, Dilly said. We had to.

She is drowning. Save her. All against us. She will drown me with her, eyes and hair. Lank coils of seaweed hair around me, my heart, my soul. Salt green death.

We.

Misery! Misery!

BACKGROUNDS
AND CONTEXTS

Political Nationalism:
Irish History, 1798–1916

KEY DATES, EVENTS, AND FIGURES

1798 **Insurrection of 1798,** led by the radical **Society of United Irishmen;** the unsuccessful rebellion, inspired in part by the French and American revolutions, resulted in possibly thirty thousand deaths. United Irish leaders included (**Theobald**) **Wolfe Tone** (1763–1798), founder of the modern Irish republican movement, who committed suicide before he could be executed.

1801 **United Kingdom of Great Britain and Ireland** established as a response to the Insurrection by an **Act of Union** (1800) passed under English pressure by both Irish and English parliaments. Irish Parliament dissolved, with Irish representatives then elected to the House of Commons in Westminster. Under the Union, the English government intervened frequently in Irish public affairs (education, public health) and exercised centralized control.

1803 **Rebellion of 1803,** an unsuccessful uprising in Dublin by remnants of the United Irishmen led by **Robert Emmet** (1778–1803), who was captured, hanged, and beheaded.

1828 Election of **Daniel O'Connell** (1775–1847), "The Liberator," to Parliament, despite prohibition against Catholic representatives; election led to Catholic Emancipation in 1829. O'Connell then worked for repeal of the Union.

1842–48 **Young Ireland Movement,** made up of nationalists dissatisfied with O'Connell's moderate political directions and willing to use force; leaders included Charles Gavin Duffy, Thomas Davis, and John Blake Dillon.

1845–49 **The Great Famine,** involving repeated failures of the potato crop due to a fungus, resulted in a **population loss** from death and emigration of 20–25 percent (possibly two million of eight million). **Insufficiency of English aid** resulted in bitterness that fueled future separatist activities in Ireland and among Irish who had emigrated. **John Mitchel** (1815–1875), a Young Irelander, memorably captured the post-famine Irish view when he wrote, "The Almighty, indeed, sent the potato blight, but the English created the famine."

1848   **Rebellion of 1848,** led by Young Ireland in the same year as violent revolutionary activity in France and other European countries; the unsuccessful action put an end to the Young Ireland Movement.

1858   **Fenian Brotherhood,** also known as the **Irish Republican Brotherhood,** a militant nationalist group, established in Dublin by James Stephens (1824–1901) soon after a parallel organization sprang up in America.

1867   **Rising of 1867,** led by the Fenians at scattered locations around Ireland, quickly put down by the forces of the Crown. Attempt to break a Fenian prisoner out of Clerkenwell Prison, London, later in the year involved an explosion that killed several people.

1870   **Disestablishment of the Church of Ireland** (Anglican), which had been the state Church, under the English monarch, since 1537.

1879   Irish National **Land League** founded in Dublin by **Michael Davitt** (1846–1906) to advocate peasant ownership of the land. **Charles Stewart Parnell** (1846–1891) named president.

1881   **Land League** leaders, including Parnell, **imprisoned in Kilmainham Jail** near Dublin; **League outlawed** for advocating nonpayment of rent.

1882   **Kilmainham "treaty,"** an agreement between Parnell and the English government, that made some land reforms possible and resulted in the release of Land League leaders from jail. The agreement was a step toward negotiations for Home Rule (limited autonomy). Lord Frederick Cavendish, the new Irish chief secretary (English official in charge of administering Ireland), and the undersecretary, T. H. Burke, assassinated in the **Phoenix Park murders,** by the **Invincibles,** an extremist nationalist group. The horrific murders, involving surgical knives, undermined the immediate chances for Home Rule. Already existing **Coercion Acts,** meant to keep Irish unrest under tight control, were renewed and strengthened.

Parnell established the **National League** to replace the suppressed Land League and to focus on establishing Home Rule constitutionally rather than on land reform.

1884   **Gaelic Athletic Association** founded—an openly nationalist, at times actively political organization that fostered traditional Irish sports, such as hurling and Gaelic football, and discouraged foreign sports. In 1890–91, the GAA supported Parnell's attempt to retain his leadership.

1886   **Home Rule Bill defeated.** Introduced by the English prime minister, William Gladstone (1809–1898), leader of the Liberals, in cooperation with Parnell, the bill would have given partial autonomy to Ireland.

1891   **Parnell removed** as leader of the Irish Parliamentary Party after he is denounced by Michael Davitt and the Catholic clergy following his involvement in a divorce trial and adultery scandal.

1893   Second **Home Rule Bill defeated.**
Gaelic League founded, with **Douglas Hyde** (1860–1949) as president, to revive the Irish language, both spoken and literary.

1914   Third **Home Rule Bill passed,** but never implemented because of the outbreak of **World War I** that year and Irish demands for separation from England after the Rising of 1916.

1916   **Easter Rising** and **Proclamation of the Irish Republic** by elements of the Irish Republican Brotherhood and the smaller Irish Citizens Army in Dublin, with scattered supporting events elsewhere. Harsh British response, including the quick execution of the leaders and the imposition of martial law, led to widespread support for the separatist movement and eventually to a contested treaty with England (1922) that partitioned the island into Northern Ireland (six counties) and the Irish Free State (twenty-six counties). The Anglo-Irish Treaty triggered the Irish Civil War (1922–23). The partition persists between Northern Ireland, under English dominion, and the country often called "The Republic of Ireland," whose official name is Éire/Ireland, as established in the 1937 Constitution of Ireland.

JOHN MITCHEL

[On the Great Famine, 1845–49: English Intentions][†]

John Mitchel (1815–1875), Irish political writer, responded to the Great Famine (1845–49) by advocating revolution to create an independent Ireland. Mitchel's castigation of the English for not doing enough to help the Irish strongly influenced later nationalist thinking. He was reacting to the pervasive suffering in Ireland because of the famine, reflected in a 20–25 percent decline in the population, including excess mortality that has been reasonably estimated at over one million (Connolly 361, 228–29).

Letter I

* * *

TO THE HON A. STEPHENS (OF GEORGIA)

Sir—

To be the historiographer of defeat and humiliation is not a task to be coveted, especially by one of the defeated. Neither can the world bring itself to take much interest in that side of human affairs. It sympathizes with success; it lends an ear to the successful; and inclines to believe what they affirm. Nevertheless, I have undertaken to narrate, for especial behoof of American readers, the last Conquest of Ireland; meaning by the word "last," not the final conquest, but the last up to this date: for it is probable that the island will need to be conquered again.

I have chosen the form of letters, and have asked permission to address them to you; for two reasons—first, that I may never forget I am writing for the information of Americans, and must explain many things which to Irish readers would need no explanation—and next, that having my correspondent always present to my mind, and personifying in him the rather select American audience whom one would especially desire to address, I may be more completely withheld from all declamation, exaggeration and vituperation—may eschew adjectives, cleave unto substantives, and in short come to the point.

* * *

---

† From *The Last Conquest of Ireland (Perhaps)* (Dublin: The Irishman Office, 1861), pp. 1–4, 165–66, 310–11, 321–25. One of Mitchel's footnotes has been omitted.

* * * [T]here are some circumstances which perplex an inquirer who derives his information from the English periodical press. That an island which is said to be an integral part of the richest empire on the globe—and the most fertile portion of that empire— with British Constitution, *Habeas Corpus*, Members of Parliament, and Trial by Jury—should in five years lose two and a half millions of its people (more than one-fourth) by hunger and fever, the consequence of hunger, and flight beyond sea to escape from hunger— while that empire of which it is said to be a part, was all the while advancing in wealth, prosperity and comfort, at a faster pace than ever before—is a matter that seems to ask elucidation. In the year 1841, Ireland, a country precisely half the size of your State of Georgia, had a population of 8,175,124. The natural increase of population in Ireland, through all her former troubles, would have given upwards of nine millions in 1851; but in 1851 the Census Commissioners find in Ireland but 6,515,794 living souls. (*Thom's Official Directory.*)[1]

Another thing, which to a spectator must appear anomalous, is that during each of those five years of "famine," from '46 to '51— that famine-struck land produced more than double the needful sustenance for all her own people; and of the best and choicest kind. Governor Wise, of Virginia, was in Brazil while the ends of the earth were resounding with the cry of Irish starvation; and was surprised to see unloaded at Rio abundance of the best quality of packed beef from Ireland. He surmised that the superiority of this Irish beef in all markets, depended on the greater care in its packing, and recommended attention to that matter in his own country. That the people who were dying of hunger did, in each year of their agony, produce upon Irish ground, of wheat and other grain, and of cattle and poultry, more than double the amount that they could all by any gluttony devour, is a fact that must be not only asserted, but in another letter proved beyond doubt.

* * *

Letter XIII

* * *

This is the estate of a certain Marquis of Conyngham: and for him those desolate people, while health lasts, and they may still keep body and soul together, outside the Poorhouse, are for ever

---

1. *Thom's Irish Almanac and Official Directory,* published in Dublin by Alexander Thom beginning in 1844.

employed in making up a *subsidy*, called rent; which that district
sends half-yearly to be consumed in England, or wherever else it
may please their noble proprietor to devour their hearts' blood and
the marrow of their bones.

So it is; and so it was, even before Famine, with almost the whole
of that coast region. The landlords were all absentees. All the grain
and cattle the people could raise were never enough to make up the
rent: it all went away, of course; it was all consumed in England;
but Ireland received in exchange stamped rent receipts. Of course
there were no improvements,—because *they* would have only raised
the rent; and in ordinary years many thousands of those poor
people lived mainly on sea-weed some months of every year. But
this was trespass and robbery; for the sea-weed belonged to the lord
of the manor, who frequently made examples of the depredators.[2]

Can you picture in your mind a race of white men reduced to
this condition? White men! Yes of the highest and purest blood
and breed of men. The very region I have described to you was
once—before British civilization overtook us—the abode of the
strongest and richest clans in Ireland; the Scotic MacCauras; the
Norman Clan-Gerralt, (or Geraldin or Fitzgerald)—the Norman MacWilliams (or De Burgo, or Burke)—the princely and
munificent O'Briens and O'Donnells, founders of many monaster-
ies, chiefs of glittering hosts, generous patrons of Ollamh, Bard,
and Brehon; sea-roving Macnamaras and O'Malleys, whose ships
brought from Spain wine and horses,—from England fair-haired,
white-armed Saxon slaves, "tall, handsome women," as the chroniclers call them, fit to weave wool or embroider mantles in the house
of a king.

After a struggle of six or seven centuries, after many bloody wars
and sweeping confiscations, English "civilization" prevailed,—
and had brought the clans to the condition I have related. The
ultimate idea of English civilization being that "the sole *nexus*
between man and man is cash payment,"—and the "Union" having
finally determined the course and current of that payment, out of
Ireland into England,—it had come to pass that the chiefs were
exchanged for landlords, and the clansman had sunk into able-
bodied paupers.

The details of this frightful famine, as it ravaged those Western
districts, I need not narrate;—they are sufficiently known. It is
enough to say that in this year, 1846, not less than 300,000 perished,

---

2. I have defended poor devils on charges of trespass by gathering sea-weed below high-
water mark, and remember one case in which a large number of farmers near the sea
were indicted *for robbery*, on the charge of taking limestone from a rock uncovered at
low water only—to burn it for spreading on their fields [*Author*].

either of mere hunger, or of typhus-fever caused by hunger. But as it has ever since been a main object of the British Government to conceal the amount of the carnage (which, indeed, they ought to do if they can) I find that the Census Commissioners, in their Report for 1851, admit only 2,041 "registered" deaths by famine alone.

* * *

Letter XXIV

* * *

The Conquest, as I said, was now consummated—England, great, populous, and wealthy, with all the resources and vast patronage of an existing government in her hands—with a magnificent army and navy—with the established course and current of commerce steadily flowing in the precise direction that suited her interests—with a powerful party on her side in Ireland itself, bound to her by lineage and by interest—and, above all, with her vast brute mass lying between us and the rest of Europe, enabling her to intercept the natural sympathies of other struggling nations, to interpret between us and the rest of mankind, and represent the troublesome sister island, exactly in the light that she wished us to be regarded— England prosperous, potent, and at peace with all the earth besides—had succeeded (to her immortal honour and glory) in anticipating and crushing out of sight the last agonies of resistance in a small, poor and divided island, which she had herself made poor and divided, carefully disarmed, almost totally disfranchised, and almost totally deprived of the benefits of that very British "law" against which we revolted with such loathing and horror. England had done this; and whatsoever credit and prestige, whatsoever profit and power could be gained by such a feat, she has them all. "Now, for the first time these six hundred years," said the London *Times*, "England has Ireland at her mercy, and can deal with her as she pleases."

It was an opportunity not to be lost, for the interests of British civilization. Parliament met late in January, 1849. The Queen, in her "speech," lamented that "*another* failure of the potato crop had caused severe distress in Ireland: and thereupon asked Parliament to continue, "for a limited period," the extraordinary power; that is the power of proclaiming any district under martial law, and of throwing suspected persons into prison, without any charge against them. The act was passed, of course.

* * *

* * * Whenever Irishmen grow numerous again, as they surely will, and whenever "that ancient swelling and desire of liberty," as Lord Mountjoy expressed it, shall once more stir their souls—as once more it certainly will—why, the British Government can crush them again, with greater ease than ever; for the small farmers are destroyed; the middle-classes are extensively corrupted; and neither stipendiary officials nor able-bodied paupers ever make revolutions.

This very dismal and humiliating narrative draws to a close. It is the story of an ancient Nation stricken down by a war more ruthless and sanguinary than any seven years' war, or thirty years' war, that Europe ever saw. No sack of Magdeburg, or ravage of the Palatinate, ever approached in horror and desolation to the slaughters done in Ireland by mere official red-tape and stationery, and the principles of Political Economy. A few statistics may fitly conclude this dreary subject.

The Census of Ireland in 1841, gave a population of 8,175,125. At the usual rate of increase, there must have been, in 1846, when the Famine commenced, at least eight and a half millions; at the same rate of increase, there ought to have been, in 1851, (according to the estimate of the Census Commissioners) 9,018,799. But in that year, after five seasons of artificial famine, there were found alive only 6,552,385—a deficit of about two millions and a half. Now, what became of those two millions and a half?

The "government" Census Commissioners, and compilers of returns of all sorts, whose principal duty it has been, since that fatal time, to conceal the amount of the havoc, attempt to account for nearly the whole deficiency by emigration. In Thom's Official Almanac,[3] I find set down on one side, the actual decrease from 1841 to 1851, (that is without taking into account the increase by births in that period) 1,623,154. Against this, they place their own estimate of the emigration during those same ten years, which they put down at 1,589,133. But in the first place the decrease did not *begin* till 1846—there had been till then a rapid increase in the population: the government returns, then, not only ignore the increase, but set the emigration of *ten* years against the depopulation of *five*. This will not do: we must reduce their emigrants by one-half, say to six hundred thousand—and add to the depopulation the estimated increase *up* to 1846, say half a million. This will give upwards of two millions whose disappearance is to be accounted for—and six hundred thousand emigrants in the other column. Balance unaccounted for, *a million and a half.*

3. See note 1, p. 267.

This is without computing those who were born in the five famine years; whom we may leave to be balanced by the deaths from
natural causes in the same period.

Now, that million and a half of men, women, and children,
were carefully, prudently, and peacefully *slain* by the English
Government. They died of hunger in the midst of abundance,
which their own hands created; and it is quite immaterial to distinguish those who perished in the agonies of famine itself from
those who died of typhus fever, which in Ireland is always caused
by famine.

Further, I have called it an artificial famine: that is to say, it was
a famine which desolated a rich and fertile island, that produced
every year abundance and superabundance to sustain all her
people and many more. The English, indeed, call that famine a
dispensation of Providence; and ascribe it entirely to the blight of
the potatoes. But potatoes failed in like manner all over Europe,
yet there was no famine save in Ireland. The British account of
the matter, then, is first, a fraud—second, a blasphemy. The
Almighty, indeed, sent the potato blight, but the English created
the famine.

*   *   *

MICHAEL DAVITT

The Phoenix Park Murders[†]

Michael Davitt (1846–1906), Irish nationalist political leader, worked
in sometimes uneasy alliance with Charles Stewart Parnell (1846–
1891), the leader of the Irish Parliamentary Party in the 1880s during
campaigns for land tenants' rights and Home Rule (limited autonomy)
for Ireland. Davitt opposed Parnell's attempt to retain his political
leadership after Parnell was involved in an adultery scandal. A copy of
Davitt's book is listed in the inventory of Joyce's library in Trieste,
where he lived while he was writing *A Portrait of the Artist as a Young
Man.*

*   *   *

* * * The manifesto was written by a few of us in the hotel * * *
as a declaration absolutely necessary to imparting a sentiment of
unequivocal sincerity to the terms in which the crime was looked

---

[†] From chapter XIX, "The Phoenix Park Murders," *The Fall of Feudalism in Ireland or
The Story of the Land League Revolution* (London and New York: Harper & Brothers,
1904), pp. 359–64.

upon and condemned by the Irish people and their leaders. It was sent at once to the press agencies in Great Britain, cabled to John Boyle O'Reilly, of Boston, for the widest publication in America, and wired to Mr. Alfred Webb, of Dublin, to be printed as a placard, and despatched by Sunday night's last train to every city and town in Ireland, so as to be posted on the walls of the country on Monday morning.

The facts relating to the murders were few, but they created a world-wide sensation. Earl Spencer, the new Lord Lieutenant, made his entry into Dublin on Saturday, May 6th. He was accompanied by Lord Frederick Cavendish, the successor to Mr. Forster in the chief-secretaryship. After the official ceremonies in Dublin Castle were concluded, Lord Frederick Cavendish set out to walk to his official residence in Phoenix Park, about a mile distant. On entering the park gate he was joined by Mr. Burke, the permanent undersecretary for Ireland and recognized head of "The Castle." Both men continued walking in the direction of the chief secretary's lodge. On nearing a spot on the wide roadway, almost exactly opposite the viceregal residence, and distant in a direct line about four hundred yards therefrom, four or five men sprang upon Burke and attacked him with knives. Lord Cavendish attempted to defend the assailed under-secretary, and was himself stabbed and also killed. The time was between half-past six and seven o'clock in the evening. It was still daylight, and the park had its ordinary number of visitors in the usual places of resort. The assailants made off in the direction of Chapelizod, mounting a car which apparently awaited them in that direction, and got clear away before any effort could be made to capture or to track them in their flight. Their subsequent arrest, six months later, their trial and execution for the crime, are now matters of common history.

The motive of the attack on Mr. Burke, who alone was singled out for vengeance, was entirely political. He personified the Castle system of rule, being an Irishman and Catholic who became, on both these grounds, in the view of those who conspired to kill him, the worst type of anti-national official and the strongest prop of alien power. He was credited with being the arch-coercionist of the administration, the employer of informers, and active antagonist of all revolutionary movements. Those who had resolved to kill him were not animated by any purpose friendly to the Land League in their deadly design. It transpired that the chief instigators of the deed of vengeance were inimical to the league movement. But Mr. Burke typified to them the embodiment of English dominance and oppression. He had, they believed, been Mr. Forster's evil adviser, and he had imprisoned men and women of his own race and creed in a despotic manner, his coercionist policy and measures being applied against many men suspected of being Fenians as well as against Land-Leaguers and others. He alone was the object of attack on that fatal Saturday evening. Lord Cavendish's murder was accidental to his presence with and attempted defence of his companion.

* * *

The motive and the making of the Kilmainham treaty appealed to diverging views for support and disapproval. To conservative nationalists and to the large element of Mr. Parnell's personal following the treaty was an adroit political manoeuvre and a notable triumph of party leadership. It appeared to turn the flank of his enemy's position, while it procured at the same time the fall from power of his chief adversary. There was also the release of all the suspects secured, together with the promise of a concession which would relieve a large number of small tenants from the risk of immediate eviction. In addition, there was the prestige of a victorious compromise obtained out of what was felt to be a most dangerous situation, and it was reasoned that the leader who had accomplished all this, while he was still a prisoner in the hands of his enemy, had gained a tactical and decided victory for himself along with very good terms for the people whom he represented.

[Davitt's Differences with Parnell]

On the other hand, these concessions were obtained on the condition that the forces which compelled Mr. Gladstone to change his policy were to be disbanded, while the movement that had given Mr. Parnell his position and power was to disappear. This was virtually the other side of the bargain. The price was too great, and the terms were so obnoxious to the league sentiment in Ireland and America that had not the Phoenix Park catastrophe intervened as a stroke of Ireland's unfriendly destiny, Mr. Parnell's leadership would have trembled in the balance, even should it survive the shock of such a surrender. English rule in Ireland had never been so shaken and demoralized since 1798 as it was in 1881–82, nor had Castle rule ever been so fiercely and effectively assaulted in the century. The country was absolutely ungovernable, while an organization having nearly a million members throughout the world stood behind Mr. Parnell's lead, with abundant friends and ample power to keep the struggle going until the whole system of antinational administration would fall to pieces and necessitate a radical and fundamental change.

* * *

* * * Looked at, therefore, from the point of view of the policy and purpose of the Land League, to destroy landlordism and to demoralize Dublin-Castle rule so as to force a settlement of the agrarian and national problems on radical but rational lines, the Kilmainham treaty was a victory for these menaced institutions and a political defeat of the forces led by Mr. Parnell.

ENGLISH POLITICAL CARTOON AFTER THE PHOENIX PARK MURDERS

PUNCH, OR THE LONDON CHARIVARI.—MAY 20, 1882.

THE IRISH FRANKENSTEIN.

"The baneful and blood-stained Monster * * * yet was it not my Master to the very extent that it was my Creature? * * * Had I not breathed into it my own spirit?'" * * * (*Extract from the Works* of C. S. P-RN-LL, M.P.

From *Punch*, 82 (20 May 1882), 235. Reprinted with permission of the British Library. In small print under the title in the cartoon is the following extract from Mary Shelley's narrative *Frankenstein*, misleadingly attributed to Charles Stewart Parnell: "'The baneful and blood-stained Monster * * * yet was it not my Master to the very extent that it was my Creature? * * * Had I not breathed into it my own spirit?' * * * (*Extract from the Works of* C. S. P-RN-LL, M.P." The document at the monster's feet has a death's head and is signed "Capt Moonlight," the alias of Andrew Scott (1842 or 1845–1880), an Irishman who became a notorious criminal in Australia, where he was involved in daring and violent crimes. His execution in Australia in 1880 for the shooting death of a senior constable had been widely publicized not long before the Phoenix Park murders.

ENGLISH POLITICAL CARTOON AFTER
THE DIVORCE SCANDAL

THE TWO PARNELLS; OR, THE MAN BESIDE HIMSELF.
PARNELL THE PATRIOT AND PARNELL THE TRAITOR.

From *Fun* (December 10, 1890). Reprinted with permission of the Bodleian Library. In the pocket of the Parnell with Satanic wings is a document entitled "Manifesto." At the end of November 1890, Parnell had issued his final political manifesto, a self-serving document that was damaging to Gladstone, his English political ally concerning Home Rule. He apparently thought, erroneously, that the manifesto would distract attention from the divorce scandal.

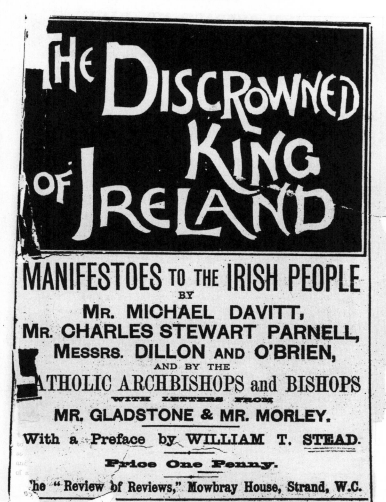

THE DISCROWNED KING OF IRELAND

MANIFESTOES TO THE IRISH PEOPLE
BY
MR. MICHAEL DAVITT,
MR. CHARLES STEWART PARNELL,
MESSRS. DILLON AND O'BRIEN,
AND BY THE
CATHOLIC ARCHBISHOPS and BISHOPS
WITH LETTERS FROM
MR. GLADSTONE & MR. MORLEY.
With a Preface by WILLIAM T. STEAD.

Price One Penny.

The "Review of Reviews," Mowbray House, Strand, W.C.

Pages 277–85 are from *The Discrowned King of Ireland*, ed. William J. Stead (Dublin: Review of Reviews, 1890): front cover (above), back cover (278), inside front cover ("Address"), pp. 16–17 ("An Appeal"), and inside back cover ("Protest"). Reprinted with permission of the National Library of Ireland. The pamphlet's title plays on the popular view before the divorce scandal that Charles Stewart Parnell was the "uncrowned King of Ireland."

IF YOU SUPPORT MR. PARNELL,

REMEMBER!

WILLIAM O'BRIEN says:

"Mr. Parnell's continued Leadership means destruction."

JOHN DILLON adds:

"All the success of the last few years will result in final failure."

MICHAEL DAVITT says:

"The Cause of Home Rule is not only dead but damned for years."

PATRICK FORD says:

"It is his imperative duty to retire."

And the IRISH BISHOPS:

"Surely Catholic Ireland will not accept as its leader a man thus dishonoured, and wholly unworthy of Christian confidence?"

Printed by WILLIAM DUNCAN, at the CARLYLE PRESS, 4, 5, and 7, Bush Harding Street, and 36 — ... Charterhouse Square.

ADDRESS
BY THE
BISHOPS OF IRELAND

At Dublin, on December 3rd

A Meeting of the Standing Committee of the Archbishops and Bishops of Ireland was held at the Archbishop's House, Dublin.

THE COMMITTEE CONSISTS OF FOUR ARCHBISHOPS AND SIX BISHOPS ELECTED TO REPRESENT FOUR ECCLESIASTICAL PROVINCES OF IRELAND.

The following Address was unanimously adopted:—

The Standing Committee communicated by telegraph with their absent brethren of the Episcopacy, and have received the adhesion of the Bishops, whose names, with their own, are signed to the address:—

Address of the Standing Committee of the Archbishops and Bishops of Ireland to the clergy and laity of their flock.

Very Rev. and Rev. Fathers and Fellow-countrymen:—The Bishops of Ireland can no longer keep silent in the presence of the all-engrossing question which agitates, not Ireland and England alone, but every spot where Irishmen have found a home. That question is—Who is to be in future the leader of the Irish people, or, rather, who is not to be their leader?

Without hesitation or doubt, and in the plainest possible terms, we give it as our unanimous judgment that, whoever else is fit to fill that highly-responsible post, *Mr. Parnell* decidedly is not.

As pastors of this Catholic nation we do not base this our judgment and solemn declaration on political grounds, but simply and solely on the facts and circumstances revealed in the London Divorce Court. After the verdict given in that Court we cannot regard Mr. Parnell in any other light than as a man convicted of one of the greatest offences known to religion and society, aggravated as it is in his case by almost every circumstance that could possibly attach to it so as to give to it a scandalous pre-eminence in guilt and shame.

Surely Catholic Ireland, so eminently conspicuous for its virtue and the purity of its social life, will not accept as its leader a man who is dishonoured and wholly unworthy of Christian confidence.

Furthermore, as Irishmen devoted to our country, eager for its elevation, and earnestly intent on securing for it the benefits of domestic legislation, we cannot but be influenced by the conviction that the continuance of Mr. Parnell as leader of even a section of the Irish party must have the effect of disorganizing our ranks, and ranging as in hostile camps the hitherto united forces of our country. Confronted with the prospect of contingencies disastrous, we see nothing but inevitable defeat at the approaching general election, and, as a result, Home Rule indefinitely postponed, coercion perpetuated, the hands of the evictor strengthened, and the tenants already evicted left without the shadow of a hope of ever being restored to their homes.

"Your devoted servants in Christ,

"X MICHAEL LOGUE, Archbishop of Armagh and Primate of All Ireland.

"X WM. J. WALSH, Archbishop of Dublin and Primate of Ireland.

"X T. W. CROKE, Archbishop of Cashel.

"X JNO. MACEVILLY, Archbishop of Tuam.

"X JAS. DONNELLY, Bishop of Clogher.

"X JAMES LYNCH, Bishop of Kildare and Leighlin.

"X FRANCIS J. MACCORMACK, Bishop of Galway and Kilmaeduagh.

"X JOHN MACCARTHY, Bishop of Cloyne.

"X WM. FITZGERALD, Bishop of Ross.

"X BARTHOLOMEW WOODLOCK, Bishop of Ardagh and Clonmaenoise.

"X THOMAS ALPHONSUS O'CALLAGHAN, Bishop of Cork.

"X JAMES BROWNE, Bishop of Ferns.

"X ABRAHAM BROWNRIGG, Bishop of Ossory.

"X PATRICK M'ALLISTER, Bishop of Down and Connor.

"X PATRICK O'DONNELL, Bishop of Raphoe.

"X JOHN LYSTER, Bishop of Achonry.

"X EDWARD MAGENNIS, Bishop of Kilmore.

"X THOMAS MACGIVERN, Bishop of Dromore.

"X JOHN K. O'DOHERTY, Bishop of Derry.

"X MICHAEL COMERFORD, Coadjutor Bishop of Kildare and Leighlin.

"X THOMAS M'REDMOND, Coadjutor Bishop of Killaloe.

"X NICHOLAS DONNELLY, Bishop of Canea.

"Dublin, Dec. 3, 1890"

AN APPEAL TO THE IRISH PEOPLE
BY MR. MICHAEL DAVITT

In the Labour World *of November 27th, Mr. Davitt published the following editorial, entitled "An appeal to the Irish people":—*

The issue which has to be decided by the Irish Parliamentary party on Monday next is plain and unmistakable. That party has to consider one thing, and one thing only—What is best for Home Rule? In our judgment there is no room now for a moment's hesitation, whatever may have been the case a few days ago.

Mr. Parnell has, it is true, claims upon the allegiance and friendship of his colleagues which appeal most strongly to their sense of loyalty and comradeship. They would not be Irishmen, warmhearted, impulsive, and generous, if they did not exhibit these distinguishing qualities of their race when compelled to sit in judgment upon the man under whose banner they have marched and fought for their country during the last ten years; and it cannot be denied that in unanimously re-electing him as their leader, under circumstances which demanded from him the tendering of his resignation, they have given abundant proof of their gratitude for his past services to Ireland and of personal attachment to himself. They are now called upon to weigh the consequences of retaining him in the position which he appears resolved to maintain, at whatever cost to the interests of the cause of which he has been the chief exponent. They cannot be blind to the result which must follow the carrying out of Mr. Gladstone's expressed resolution to retire from politics if Mr. Parnell retains the Irish leadership. Every sane politician in the country knows that without the co-operation of the party led by Mr. Gladstone Home Rule is impossible for years to come.

Will Mr. Parnell allow the hopes which the Irish people have centred in the Liberal alliance to be shattered rather than relinquish even for a time the headship of the Irish party? At the moment it seems as if this were so, and from the report of the proceedings of the meeting of his party it appears he carries with him a majority of Ireland's national representatives. This, then, is the situation which confronts us at the present moment. It is in all conscience grave enough.

Mr. Gladstone's letter puts before the Irish Parliamentary party and the Irish people the clearest and most momentous issue ever submitted to political allies. There can be no possible mistake as to its meaning, or doubt as to the consequences that must ensue if the proposition of the Liberal leader be not accepted. Will Irish members and Mr. Parnell be deaf to the touching appeal which Mr. Sheehy is reported to have addressed to them in behalf of the evicted tenants of Ireland? Do they forget the thousands of homes that have been torn from the peasantry of Ireland during the last ten years—the thousands of evicted tenants who have patiently lived in the hope that Mr. Gladstone and his followers in Great Britain would carry the next general election and be able to give to Ireland a system of domestic government under which the victims of Irish landlordism would be restored to their hearthstones, and Ireland relieved of agrarian and other agitation? Will Mr. W. O'Brien's words, which we print elsewhere, help them to arrive at a salutary decision on Monday?

We are loth to recriminate at this terrible moment, but there is no blinking the fact that the speeches delivered in Dublin, and the action of the Irish party in unanimously re-electing Mr. Parnell, have lost the Irish cause thousands of friends, who it is to be feared will not return, while they have tended to place Ireland in a humiliating position before the nations. In this last respect there are more than the Irish party to blame for a silence that can be construed into tacit condonation of conduct which ought to be more repellent to a nation of Ireland's acknowledged high moral standard than to the English people. Yet the bishops and priests of Ireland have left it to the sturdy Dissenters of Great Britain to make the protest which was called for in the interests of public morality as well as of Home Rule.

However, regrettable as this temporary loss of moral prestige is to the Irish cause, the situation, desperate though it be, may yet be retrieved. If the Irish party, reinforced by an outspoken expression of Irish popular opinion, decide on Monday next to prefer Home Rule to Mr. Parnell, victory may yet be ours. There is no other choice. Last week we made an appeal to Mr. Parnell to save Home Rule and give one more proof of his patriotism and statesmanship. Our appeal has passed unheeded. In some quarters it was for a time even misunderstood. That is so no longer. What we urged a week ago has since been repeated by friends of Ireland everywhere.

Irish members and Irish newspapers have, in the face of the present terrible crisis, besought Mr. Parnell to place country before pride and love of power. They have been treated with a silence bordering on contempt. The friends of Home Rule in Great Britain, beginning with the venerable leader of the Liberal party, have been unanimous in their views. Mr. Parnell declines to yield to prayers or requests. The promptings of duty, of patriotism, of honour, are stifled, and in their place we see the workings of hidden influences which, if permitted free rein, will ruin for a generation the chances of Home Rule for Ireland. * * *

* * *

We need say little more. We implore the Irish race at home and abroad to rise and show themselves equal to this emergency. There may be those who believe that Mr. Parnell can be retained and yet Ireland's cause be saved. We have no such hope. We believe that in the Irish party there is more than one man who can lead it to victory. We believe that there is sufficient patriotism in that party to follow a leader chosen from its own ranks by a majority of its members. Let the Irish race consider these points. We urge them in all earnestness to do this, and with hope and confidence we await a decision. Whatever that decision may be, the Irish cause remains imperishable. It may be thwarted for a time, but not for ever. Of its victory in the end we have no doubt. Monday's decision will postpone it for a generation or retrieve all that is now endangered. May wisdom and courage guide those in whom Ireland's hopes are centred.

PROTEST FROM A CATHOLIC PRIEST

Canon Doyle on the Parnell Scandal

The Rev. Canon Doyle, of Ramsgrange, Arthurstown, has addressed a vigorous letter to the Editor of the *Freeman's Journal* on the subject of Mr. Parnell's position. I take the following extracts from this manly appeal by an Irish priest to be the conscience of the Irish people:—

One of the most shocking scandals I remember to have occurred in my time is the futile attempt made by you and others to whitewash unfortunate Charles Stewart Parnell. Now that all the resolutions on this nasty subject have been passed, and that the country has been swamped under a deluge of feeble fustian, what do they all come to? Why, this, and only this, that Parnell, yet "essential" to Ireland, "can not be done without." I feel it my duty to enter my feeble but solemn protest against this degradation of our just and imperishable cause and of our dear old country. I had to perform many painful duties in the course of my ministry and in my conflicts for our suffering people, but that which devolves on me, now in the advanced evening of a long life, is the most painful of all. Until this divorce case turned up, I entertained for Mr. Parnell the most sincere esteem and profound respect. In the infancy of his political career I went to his assistance with decisive effect, as he was good enough to publicly acknowledge.

How deep must be the guilt of this crime committed in the midday light of the Gospel, and how black the criminal who sacrilegiously tramples under foot the holy bonds of matrimony—the very foundation of civilized society! Yet without one word of repentance, he crawls, reeking from ten years' adulterous concubinage, to claim the leadership of holy Ireland, whose banner, though rent and torn in many a hard-fought battle, is till now as stainless as the driven snow. Until this dark, disgraceful hour no one ever dared to trail it in the mire.

We have now strong reason to suspect why the Vatican is so prompt to visit us with its displeasure. It seems this horrid scandal was well known in what is called "Society" in England, though we heard nothing of it. Our numerous enemies there had abundance of material to send to Rome. * * *

You boast that you and your jerrymandered meetings represent the feeling of Ireland regarding Parnell's leadership. I say you do not. I assert the honest opinion of the country is dead against this infamous man. I venture, further, to prophesy that no Irish constituency will, at the next General Election, accept a candidate at the declaration of the self-convicted, audacious adulterer of One Ash Lodge.[1]

* * * Should any evil befall the Irish cause at this supreme crisis, the blame will rest solely and entirely on those gentlemen of the party who dishonourably and dishonestly have attempted to whitewash Parnell by a snatch vote of jerrymandered meetings in Dublin, falsely declared to represent the feelings of the country. I deliberately assert they do not represent the feelings or the wishes of either priests or people. Did the Parnell *claquers*[2] even condescend to consult the people? Whom did they consult on this most important and vital subject? Did they consult the Catholic clergy? No. Did they consult the people and the leaders of the people throughout Ireland? No, emphatically no. And if ever there were a subject on which the honest, calm, and deliberate opinion of the country was necessary, it is whether they can accept and follow Parnell as a leader after his ten years' adulterous profligacy.

Have you, as a Catholic journalist or a Christian gentleman, and your platform friends, reflected for a moment on the step you have taken? Have you resolved to banish clergymen of every denomination from your movement? It would seem that you have, and to banish with them tens of thousands of honest upright laymen who have been horrified at the *dénouement* of the O'Shea Divorce suit. * * * You have not expelled us by a direct vote, but just as effectually by a side wind. I would respectfully ask you, or any gentleman who attended your late meetings, how could a clergyman of any denomination stand on a platform from which Parnell is cheered, and then stand in his pulpit on the following Sunday, except in a white sheet? How could such a clergyman denounce vice of a similar kind in one of his humble parishioners? Would not the poor man naturally and justly say—"It is because I am poor I am treated after this fashion. If I had an esquire after my name, or an M.P.,[3] I might do what I

---

1. A mistake for, or else an intentional play on, Wonersh Lodge near Eltham in Kent, where Katherine O'Shea, who became Parnell's mistress and eventually his wife, lived when they met and during their affair.
2. "Those who clap" (French); fawning admirers.
3. Member of Parliament. "Esquire": title added to the name of a gentleman because of birth, status, or education.

liked. His reverence denounced me to-day till the dogs would not eat my flesh; yet only last week he was at a great meeting for Parnell, and there he was on the platform cheering him and saying no other man should be our leader, though he is one of the most awful sinners the world ever produced. God help the poor. The rich can do as they like, and we never hear a world about it." That is the position in which you place us, and which no clergyman can on a moment's reflection retain. The masses don't understand your metaphysical distinctions condemning him as an adulterer and admiring him as a politician. If you retain the politician you must retain the adulterer. If you expel the adulterer the politician must go. You say the party will break up. Well, if they are only kept together by so rotten a bond the sooner the better. The lust of M'Murrogh brought us the English invasion and all its evil consequences.[4] It would seem by the infatuation of a few headlong enthusiasts and the cunning of a few scheming barristers the lust of Parnell is about to rivet our chains anew. Where now is the holy zeal that only a few years back cleaned out the Augean Stable[5] of Dublin Castle? * * *

I call upon the faithful fathers and husbands of Ireland, upon the virtuous and loving wives and mothers, upon our modest and chaste young girls, and upon our chivalrous young men, to put an immediate end to this infamy—to call with one voice for the retirement of this unfortunate man from the position he has disgraced, and to insist in the most unequivocal manner on the appointment of a new leader. Thus, and thus only, can peace be restored, and the cause now ripe for settlement be brought to a happy consummation. * * *

4. After taking Dervorgilla, the wife of the rival chieftain Tiernan O'Rourke, Dermot MacMurrough (1110–1171), king of Leinster, asked for help from King Henry II of England, who subsequently became lord of Ireland and initiated eight centuries of English dominance.
5. In Greek mythology, as one of the labors imposed on him as penance for murdering his family, Hercules cleaned the immense, filthy stables of King Augeas of Elis in a single day.

MICHAEL DAVITT

Death of Parnell—Appreciation[†]

Mr. Parnell continued the combat against great odds, with characteristic tenacity, during the summer and autumn of 1891. He
addressed demonstrations in various parts of the country each Sunday for months, travelling from Brighton, in the south of England,
to Ireland on a Saturday, and returning again direct to his home
from the place of meeting. He lost ground steadily in his desperate
campaign, but never lost courage. Doggedly, if hopelessly, he persisted in the struggle until his strength gave way. The end came
with startling suddenness. There had been no tidings of serious
illness, though it was known that his health was breaking down
from the physical strain of weekly journeys from England to meetings in Ireland. He died at Brighton on October 6, 1891. He was
only in his forty-sixth year, and but ten short months had rolled by
since he broke with the majority of his following in refusing to
adopt the course which his wisest friends pressed in vain upon
him. * * *

Parnell's claim to greatness no Irish nationalist, and few Irishmen, will ever deny. To do so would be like ignoring the existence
of a mountain or some other objective fact in nature. His work was
great, and would of itself make the political fame of any man with a
similar record. Like all the world's historic characters, there were
marked limitations to his greatness, not counting the final weakness which precipitated his fall.

His immense popularity with the Irish people was not due to any
Celtic qualities. Of these he had not even a trace. There was no
racial affinity between him and them. He was far less like O'Connell
than even Mr. Gladstone. The great Englishman inherited a Scottish kinship with the Irish nation through his maternal ancestors,
and had some traits of character more Celtic than Saxon. Mr. Parnell was born in Ireland. Beyond this and his descent from English
ancestors of the Pale,[1] there was nothing in habits, temperament, or
individuality that would establish relationship between him and
those whose boundless confidence he had won, except in the common purpose of the national movement which he led.

† From chapter LIII, "Death of Parnell—Appreciation," *The Fall of Feudalism in Ireland
or The Story of the Land League Revolution* (London and New York: Harper & Brothers,
1904), pp. 651–57. Davitt's footnote has been omitted. On Davitt, see p. 271.
1. The English Pale was an area of twenty miles in radius around Dublin fortified with a
ditch and rampart by the English to protect them from attack by the native Irish until
the island could be conquered.

He was a Protestant, leading a nation chiefly Catholic; a landlord, commanding tenants in a war against his own class; a cold, reserved man, at the head of one of the most warmhearted and impulsive of races; a sober, unemotional speaker, who never quoted an Irish poet but once, and did it wrong, in a country remarkable for passion and ornate oratory; a public man and leader who treated his party with icy aloofness for years, who lived away from Ireland most of his time; and who appeared in his conduct towards the Irish people to be absolutely unconcerned as to what they thought of him until the personal issue involved in the unhappy event of 1890 roused him into a fierce contest with those who questioned his right to lead only when the leadership headed directly for disaster.

He was unlike all the leaders who had preceded him in his accomplishments, traits of character, and personal idiosyncrasies. He had neither wit nor humor, eloquence or the passion of conviction, academical distinction of any kind, scholarship or profession, Irish accent, appearance, or mannerism. In fact, he was a paradox in Irish leadership, and will stand unique in his niche in Irish history as bearing no resemblance of any kind to those who handed down to his time the fight for Irish nationhood.

What, then, was the secret of his immense influence and popularity? He was above and before everything else a splendid fighter. He had attacked and beaten the enemies of Ireland in the citadel of their power—the British Parliament. It was here where he loomed great and powerful in Irish imagination. As Wendell Phillips put it on one occasion, Parnell was the Irishman who had compelled John Bull to listen to what he in behalf of Ireland had to say in the House of Commons; and the personal force which had done this, and had flung the Irish question and representatives across the plans and purposes of English parties, in a battle for the Irish people, appealed instinctively to the admiration of those in whose name this work was accomplished.

He was fortunate, too, in being heir to the ripening fruits of his predecessors' labors—the Daniel O'Connells, Fintan Lalors, Gavan Duffys, James Stephenses, and Isaac Butts, who had sown the seed in less propitious days and under darker skies. * * *

* * *

* * * Parnell's prestige and triumphs sprang from a unique kind of blended character, endowed with a magnetic power which made him more formidable than mental culture or oratorical abilities could do. He derived nothing from the profession of political opinions, but everything from an insurrection of social forces led by him in revolt against a system which was the very basis of English government in Ireland, and of aristocratic and class privilege in England—land monopoly. The English classes looked at him as a

desperate revolutionist—which, unfortunately, he was not—because he had the courage and capacity to strike at what was the weakest point in the foreign rule of his country, and also at the very foundations of England's own supremacy—the House of Commons and the land-owning power of those who filled and owned the House of Lords. Political opinions had little or nothing to do with Parnell's work in the days when he won his fame. He was armed with a reformer's crow-bar and not with a politician's note-book. His work was to undermine and pull down what had been chiefly responsible for Ireland's oppression * * *.

* * *

Mr. Gladstone diagnosed Mr. Parnell's political character and purpose clearly during and after the events of 1885–86. He recognized in him a man of great practical capacity, with conservative tendencies scarcely hidden behind the controlling head of a semi-revolutionary agitation. He knew that a successful reformer would be the likeliest personal influence to accept the responsibility of guiding and directing the forces he had led in the revolt against Dublin Castle and landlordism, when once a rational concession of alternatives to these systems would appeal to his sense of patriotic statesmanship. No one more sincerely regretted Mr. Parnell's fall than Mr. Gladstone. "An invaluable man," was his summary of the power and potential qualities of his one-time ally. Not so Lord Salisbury.[2] He took *The Times* estimate of the great Irishman, and persuaded himself that he was a revolutionist, a radical, and an incarnate enemy of the English connection. This was the judgment of prejudice, and not the true estimate of either a penetrating or generous mind.

---

2. Robert Gascoyne-Cecil (1830–1903), 3rd Marquess of Salisbury, Conservative member of the House of Lords who was prime minister at the time of Parnell's death.

PROCLAMATION

POBLACHT NA H EIREANN.

THE PROVISIONAL GOVERNMENT

OF THE

IRISH REPUBLIC

TO THE PEOPLE OF IRELAND.

IRISHMEN AND IRISHWOMEN : In the name of God and of the dead generations from which she receives her old tradition of nationhood, Ireland, through us, summons her children to her flag and strikes for her freedom.

Having organised and trained her manhood through her secret revolutionary organisation, the Irish Republican Brotherhood, and through her open military organisations, the Irish Volunteers and the Irish Citizen Army, having patiently perfected her discipline, having resolutely waited for the right moment to reveal itself, she now seizes that moment, and, supported by her exiled children in America and by gallant allies in Europe, but relying in the first on her own strength, she strikes in full confidence of victory.

We declare the right of the people of Ireland to the ownership of Ireland, and to the unfettered control of Irish destinies, to be sovereign and indefeasible. The long usurpation of that right by a foreign people and government has not extinguished the right, nor can it ever be extinguished except by the destruction of the Irish people. In every generation the Irish people have asserted their right to national freedom and sovereignty ; six times during the past three hundred years they have asserted it in arms. Standing on that fundamental right and again asserting it in arms in the face of the world, we hereby proclaim the Irish Republic as a Sovereign Independent State, and we pledge our lives and the lives of our comrades-in-arms to the cause of its freedom, of its welfare, and of its exaltation among the nations.

The Irish Republic is entitled to, and hereby claims, the allegiance of every Irishman and Irishwoman. The Republic guarantees religious and civil liberty, equal rights and equal opportunities to all its citizens, and declares its resolve to pursue the happiness and prosperity of the whole nation and of all its parts, cherishing all the children of the nation equally, and oblivious of the differences carefully fostered by an alien government, which have divided a minority from the majority in the past.

Until our arms have brought the opportune moment for the establishment of a permanent National Government, representative of the whole people of Ireland and elected by the suffrages of all her men and women, the Provisional Government, hereby constituted, will administer the civil and military affairs of the Republic in trust for the people.

We place the cause of the Irish Republic under the protection of the Most High God, Whose blessing we invoke upon our arms, and we pray that no one who serves that cause will dishonour it by cowardice, inhumanity, or rapine. In this supreme hour the Irish nation must, by its valour and discipline and by the readiness of its children to sacrifice themselves for the common good, prove itself worthy of the august destiny to which it is called.

Signed on Behalf of the Provisional Government,

THOMAS J. CLARKE,

SEAN Mac DIARMADA, THOMAS MacDONAGH,
P. H. PEARSE, EAMONN CEANNT,
JAMES CONNOLLY. JOSEPH PLUNKETT.

On Easter Sunday, April 23, 1916, the day before the Rising began, a thousand copies of the Proclamation of the Irish Republic were printed in Liberty Hall (destroyed by English artillery during the fighting), the headquarters of the Irish Citizen Army, where the newspaper *The Irish Worker* was published. Constance Markiewicz, a commandant in the Irish Citizen Army, read it to a group on the Hall's steps; P. H. Pearse read it formally in front of the General Post Office the next day, when the rebels seized that building. The English executed all seven who signed the document, among others, by firing squad. The image of the Proclamation is reprinted with permission of the National Library of Ireland.

The Irish Literary and Cultural Revival

DOUGLAS HYDE

The Necessity for De-Anglicising Ireland[†]

Douglas Hyde (1860–1949), Irish scholar and outspoken advocate of Irish cultural revival, delivered the address from which these selections are taken at his inauguration as president of the National Literary Society (1892). He was the first president of the Gaelic League (1893) and later became professor of Irish at University College, Dublin (1909–32), an Irish senator (1925 and 1938), and the first president of Ireland (1938–45).

When we speak of "The Necessity for De-Anglicising the Irish Nation," we mean it, not as a protest against imitating what is *best* in the English people, for that would be absurd, but rather to show the folly of neglecting what is Irish, and hastening to adopt, pell-mell, and indiscriminately, everything that is English, simply because it *is* English.

This is a question which most Irishmen will naturally look at from a National point of view, but it is one which ought also to claim the sympathies of every intelligent Unionist,[1] and which, as I know, does claim the sympathy of many.

If we take a bird's-eye view of our island to-day, and compare it with what it used to be, we must be struck by the extraordinary fact that the nation which was once, as every one admits, one of the most classically learned and cultured nations in Europe, is now one of the least so; how one of the most reading and literary peoples has

---

[†] From Charles Gavan Duffy, George Sigerson, and Douglas Hyde, *The Revival of Irish Literature* (London: T. F. Unwin, 1994), pp. 115–61. The author's notes have been omitted.

1. Supporter of the Union between Ireland and England as the United Kingdom of Great Britain and Ireland, which was created by the Act of Union (1800) passed by the British and Irish parliaments. The Home Rule movement, important after 1870, was an effort to modify the Union by giving Ireland limited autonomy. See the 1801 entry in "Key Dates, Events, and Figures," p. 263.

become one of the *least* studious and most *un*-literary, and how the present art products of one of the quickest, most sensitive, and most artistic races on earth are now only distinguished for their hideousness.

I shall endeavour to show that this failure of the Irish people in recent times has been largely brought about by the race diverging during this century from the right path, and ceasing to be Irish without becoming English. I shall attempt to show that with the bulk of the people this change took place quite recently, much more recently than most people imagine, and is, in fact, still going on. I should also like to call attention to the illogical position of men who drop their own language to speak English, of men who translate their euphonious Irish names into English monosyllables, of men who read English books, and know nothing about Gaelic literature, nevertheless protesting as a matter of sentiment that they hate the country which at every hand's turn they rush to imitate.

＊ ＊ ＊

＊ ＊ ＊ Such movements as Young Irelandism, Fenianism, Land Leagueism, and Parliamentary obstruction seem always to gain their sympathy and support.[2] It is just because there appears no earthly chance of their becoming good members of the Empire that I urge that they should not remain in the anomalous position they are in, but since they absolutely refuse to become the one thing, that they become the other; cultivate what they have rejected, and build up an Irish nation on Irish lines.

＊ ＊ ＊

And yet this awful idea of complete Anglicisation, which I have here put before you in all its crudity, is, and has been, making silent inroads upon us for nearly a century.

＊ ＊ ＊

What we must endeavour to never forget is this, that the Ireland of to-day is the descendant of the Ireland of the seventh century, then the school of Europe and the torch of learning. It is true that Northmen made some minor settlements in it in the ninth and tenth centuries, it is true that the Normans made extensive settlements during the succeeding centuries, but none of those broke the

2. Young Ireland, a prominent nationalist group in the 1840s, encouraged national literature, the revival of Gaelic, and repeal of the Union; the Fenian Brotherhood was a
   revolutionary movement advocating the use of force that began in the 1850s among
   Irish in both Ireland and the U.S.; the Irish National Land League, founded by Michael
   Davitt in 1879, demanded peasant proprietorship of the land; Parliamentary obstruction was a technique used by Charles Stuart Parnell and other Irish Members of Parliament to press for action on issues affecting the Irish people.

continuity of the social life of the island. Dane and Norman drawn to the kindly Irish breast issued forth in a generation or two fully Irishised, and more Hibernian than the Hibernians themselves, and even after the Cromwellian plantation the children of numbers of the English soldiers who settled in the south and midlands, were, after forty years' residence, and after marrying Irish wives, turned into good Irishmen, and unable to speak a word of English, while several Gaelic poets of the last century have, like Father English, the most unmistakably English names. In two points only was the continuity of the Irishism of Ireland damaged. First, in the north-east of Ulster, where the Gaelic race was expelled and the land planted with aliens, whom our dear mother Erin, assimilative as she is, has hitherto found it difficult to absorb, and in the owner-ship of the land, eight-ninths of which belongs to people many of whom always lived, or live, abroad, and not half of whom Ireland can be said to have assimilated.

*   *   *

The bulk of the Irish race really lived in the closest contact with the traditions of the past and the national life of nearly eighteen hundred years, until the beginning of this century. Not only so, but during the whole of the dark Penal times[3] they produced amongst themselves a most vigorous literary development. Their schoolmas-ters and wealthy farmers, unwearied scribes, produced innumera-ble manuscripts in beautiful writing, each letter separated from another as in Greek, transcripts both of the ancient literature of their sires and of the more modern literature produced by them-selves. Until the beginning of the present century there was no county, no barony, and, I may almost say, no townland which did not boast of an Irish poet, the people's representative of those ancient bards who died out with the extirpation of the great Mile-sian families.[4] * * * This training, however, nearly every one of fair education during the Penal times possessed, nor did they begin to lose their Irish training and knowledge until after the establish-ment of Maynooth and the rise of O'Connell.[5] * * *

Thomas Davis and his brilliant band of Young Irelanders came just at the dividing of the line, and tried to give to Ireland a new

---

3. A period of nearly a century, which began in the 1690s with the introduction of anti-Catholic penal laws that limited or took away rights, including voting and property ownership.
4. The Milesians were the Gaels, that is, the ancestors of the Irish, who were held to be the descendants of the legendary warrior Mil.
5. St. Patrick's College, Maynooth, authorized in 1795, was the main seminary producing Irish Catholic priests, many of whom had earlier been trained on the Continent. Dan-iel O'Connell (1775–1847) was a moderate nationalist political leader who opposed the Act of Union (1800) and urged its repeal.

literature in English to replace the literature which was just being discarded. It succeeded and it did not succeed. It was a most brilliant effort, but the old bark had been too recently stripped off the Irish tree, and the trunk could not take as it might have done to a fresh one. It was a new departure, and at first produced a violent effect. Yet in the long run it failed to properly leaven our peasantry who might, perhaps, have been reached upon other lines. I say they *might* have been reached upon other lines because it is quite certain that even well on into the beginning of this century, Irish poor scholars and schoolmasters used to gain the greatest favour and applause by reading out manuscripts in the people's houses at night, some of which manuscripts had an antiquity of a couple of hundred years or more behind them, and which, when they got illegible from age, were always recopied. The Irish peasantry at that time were all to some extent cultured men, and many of the better off ones were scholars and poets. What have we now left of all that? Scarcely a trace. Many of them read newspapers indeed, but who reads, much less recites, an epic poem, or chants an elegiac or even a hymn?

Wherever Irish throughout Ireland continued to be spoken, there the ancient MSS. continued to be read, there the epics of Cuchullain, Conor MacNessa, Déirdre, Finn, Oscar, and Ossian continued to be told, and there poetry and music held sway. * * * In fact, I may venture to say that, up to the beginning of the present century, neither man, woman, nor child of the Gaelic race, either of high blood or low blood, existed in Ireland who did not either speak Irish or understand it. But within the last ninety years we have, with an unparalleled frivolity, deliberately thrown away our birthright and Anglicised ourselves. None of the children of those people of whom I have spoken know Irish, and the race will from henceforth be changed; for as Monsieur Jubainville[6] says of the influence of Rome upon Gaul, England "has definitely conquered us, she has even imposed upon us her language, that is to say, the form of our thoughts during every instant of our existence." It is curious that those who most fear West Britainism[7] have so eagerly consented to imposing upon the Irish race what, according to Jubainville, who in common with all the great scholars of the continent, seems to regret it very much, is "the form of our thoughts during every instant of our existence."

* * *

I have no hesitation at all in saying that every Irish-feeling Irishman, who hates the reproach of West-Britonism, should set himself

6. Marie Henri d'Arbois de Jubainville (1827–1910), French historian and philologist, who held the chair of Celtic at the Collège de France.
7. Also West-Britonism; the turning of Ireland into the westernmost province of England.

to encourage the efforts which are being made to keep alive our once great national tongue. The losing of it is our greatest blow, and the sorest stroke that the rapid Anglicisation of Ireland has inflicted upon us. In order to de-Anglicise ourselves we must at once arrest the decay of the language. * * *

We can, however, insist, and we *shall* insist if Home Rule be carried, that the Irish language, which so many foreign scholars of the first calibre find so worthy of study, shall be placed on a par with— or even above—Greek, Latin, and modern languages, in all examinations held under the Irish Government. We can also insist, and we *shall* insist, that in those baronies where the children speak Irish, Irish shall be taught, and that Irish-speaking schoolmasters, petty sessions clerks, and even magistrates be appointed in Irish-speaking districts. If all this were done, it should not be very difficult, with the aid of the foremost foreign scholars, to bring about a tone of thought which would make it disgraceful for an educated Irishman—especially of the old Celtic race, MacDermotts, O'Conors, O'Sullivans, MacCarthys, O'Neills—to be ignorant of his own language—would make it at least as disgraceful as for an educated Jew to be quite ignorant of Hebrew.

We find the decay of our language faithfully reflected in the decay of our surnames. In Celtic times a great proof of the powers of assimilation which the Irish nation possessed, was the fact that so many of the great Norman and English nobles lived like the native chiefs and took Irish names. In this way the De Bourgos of Connacht became MacWilliams, of which clan again some minor branches became MacPhilpins, MacGibbons, and MacRaymonds. * * * Roughly speaking, it may be said that most of the English and Norman families outside of the Pale[8] were Irish in name and manners from the beginning of the fourteenth to the middle of the seventeenth century.

In 1465 an Act was passed by the Parliament of the English Pale that all Irishmen inside the Pale should take an English name "of one towne as Sutton, Chester, Trym, Skryne, Corke, Kinsale; or colour, as white, black, brown; or art or science, as smith or carpenter; or office, as cooke, butler; and that he and his issue shall use this name" or forfeit all his goods. A great number of the lesser families complied with this typically English ordinance; but the greater ones—the MacMurroghs, O'Tooles, O'Byrnes, O'Nolans, O'Mores, O'Ryans, O'Conor Falys, O'Kellys, &c.—refused, and never did change their names. A hundred and thirty years later we

---

8. The area of Dublin within the fortified perimeter that designated English rule.

find Spenser, the poet, advocating the renewal of this statute.[9] By doing this, says Spenser, "they shall in time learne quite to forget the Irish nation. And here-withal," he says, "would I also wish the O's and Macs which the heads of septs have taken to their names to be utterly forbidden and extinguished, for that the same being an ordinance (as some say) first made by O'Brien * * * for the strengthening of the Irish, the abrogation thereof will as much enfeeble them." It was, however, only after Aughrim and the Boyne[1] that Irish names began to be changed in great numbers, and O'Conors to become "Conyers," O'Reillys "Ridleys," O'Donnells "Daniels," O'Sullivans "Silvans," MacCarthys "Carters," and so on.

                              *   *   *

Numbers of people, again, like Mr. Davitt or Mr. Hennessy, drop the O and Mac which properly belong to their names; others, without actually changing them, metamorphose their names, as we have seen, into every possible form. * * *

With our Irish Christian names the case is nearly as bad. Where are now all the fine old Irish Christian names of both men and women which were in vogue even a hundred years ago? They have been discarded as unclean things, not because they were ugly in themselves or inharmonious, but simply because they were not English. No man is now christened by a Gaelic name, "nor no woman neither." Such common Irish Christian names as Conn, Cairbre, Farfeasa, Teig, Diarmuid, Kian, Cuan, Ae, Art, Mahon, Eochaidh, Fearflatha, Cathan, Rory, Coll, Lochlainn, Cathal, Lughaidh, Turlough, Eamon, Randal, Niall, Sorley, and Conor, are now extinct or nearly so. * * * In fact, of the great wealth of Gaelic Christian names in use a century or two ago, only Owen, Brian, Cormac, and Patrick seem to have survived in general use.

Nor have our female names fared one bit better; we have discarded them even more ruthlessly than those of our men. Surely Sadhbh (Sive) is a prettier name than Sabina or Sibby, and Nóra than Onny, Honny, or Honour (so translated simply because Nóra sounds like onóir, the Irish for "honour"); surely Una is prettier than Winny, which it becomes when West-Britonised. Mève, the great name of the Queen of Connacht who led the famous cattle spoiling of Cuailgne, celebrated in the greatest Irish epic, is at least as pretty as Maud, which it becomes when Anglicised, and Eibhlin (Eileen) is prettier than Ellen or Elinor. * * *

9. Edmund Spenser (1552–1599), English poet and colonist in Ireland, argued for the destruction of the Irish language and customs by any means, including violence.
1. The Battles of Aughrim (1691) and the Boyne (1690), both lost by the supporters of James II to the forces of William III. James's defeat confirmed Protestant dominance of Ireland.

Our topographical nomenclature too—as we may now be prepared to expect—has been also shamefully corrupted to suit English ears * * * . Suffice it to say, that many of the best-known names in our history and annals have become almost wholly unrecognisable, through the ignorant West-Britonising of them. The unfortunate natives of the eighteenth century allowed all kinds of havoc to be played with even their best-known names. For example the river Feóir they allowed to be turned permanently into the Nore, which happened this way. Some Englishman, asking the name of the river, was told that it was *An Fheóir,* pronounced In n'yore, because the F when preceded by the definite article *an* is not sounded, so that in his ignorance he mistook the word Feóir for Neóir, and the name has been thus perpetuated. In the same way the great Connacht lake, Loch Corrib, is really Loch Orrib, or rather Loch Orbsen, some Englishman having mistaken the C at the end of loch for the beginning of the next word. Sometimes the Ordnance Survey people make a rough guess at the Irish name and jot down certain English letters almost on chance. Sometimes again they make an Irish word resemble an English one, as in the celebrated Tailtin in Meath, where the great gathering of the nation was held, and, which, to make sure that no national memories should stick to it, has been West-Britonised Telltown. On the whole, our place names have been treated with about the same respect as if they were the names of a savage tribe which had never before been reduced to writing, and with about the same intelligence and contempt as vulgar English squatters treat the topographical nomenclature of the Red Indians. These things are now to a certain extent stereotyped, and are difficult at this hour to change, especially where Irish names have been translated into English, like Swinford and Strokestown, or ignored as in Charleville or Midleton. But though it would take the strength and goodwill of an united nation to put our topographical nomenclature on a rational basis like that of Wales and the Scotch Highlands, there is one thing which our Society can do, and that is to insist upon pronouncing our Irish names properly. Why will a certain class of people insist upon getting as far away from the pronunciation of the natives as possible? * * *

* * * I hope and trust that where it may be done without any great inconvenience a native Irish Government will be induced to provide for the restoration of our place-names on something like a rational basis.

Our music, too, has become Anglicised to an alarming extent. Not only has the national instrument, the harp—which efforts are now being made to revive in the Highlands—become extinct, but even the Irish pipes are threatened with the same fate. In place of the pipers and fiddlers who, even twenty years ago, were comparatively common, we are now in many places menaced by the German band and the barrel organ. * * * A few years ago all our travelling fiddlers and pipers could play the old airs which were then constantly called for, the *Cúis d'á pléidh, Drinaun Dunn, Roseen Dubh, Gamhan Geal Bán, Eileen-a-roon, Shawn O'Dwyer in Glanna,* and the rest, whether gay or plaintive, which have for so many centuries entranced the Gael. But now English music-hall ballads and Scotch songs have gained an enormous place in the repertoire of the wandering minstrel, and the minstrels themselves are becoming fewer and fewer, and I fear worse and worse. * * *

Our games, too, were in a most grievous condition until the brave and patriotic men who started the Gaelic Athletic Association took in hand their revival. I confess that the instantaneous and extraordinary success which attended their efforts when working upon national lines has filled me with more hope for the future of Ireland than everything else put together. I consider the work of the association in reviving our ancient national game of caman, or hurling, and Gaelic football, has done more for Ireland than all the speeches of politicians for the last five years. And it is not alone that that splendid association revived for a time with vigour our national sports, but it revived also our national recollections, and the names of the various clubs through the country have perpetuated the memory of the great and good men and martyrs of Ireland. The physique of our youth has been improved in many of our counties; they have been taught self-restraint, and how to obey their captains; they have been, in many places, weaned from standing idle in their own roads or street corners; and not least, they have been introduced to the use of a thoroughly good and Irish garb. Wherever the warm striped green jersey of the Gaelic Athletic Association was seen, there Irish manhood and Irish memories were rapidly reviving. There torn collars and ugly neckties hanging awry and far better not there at all, and dirty shirts of bad linen were banished, and our young hurlers were clad like men and Irishmen, and not in the shoddy second-hand suits of Manchester and London shop-boys. * * *

I have now mentioned a few of the principal points on which it would be desirable for us to move, with a view to de-Anglicising ourselves; but perhaps the principal point of all I have taken for granted. That is the necessity for encouraging the use of Anglo-Irish literature instead of English books, especially instead of English periodicals. We must set our face sternly against penny dreadfuls, shilling shockers, and still more, the garbage of vulgar English weeklies like *Bow Bells* and the *Police Intelligence.* Every house should have a copy of Moore and Davis.[2] * * * I knew fifteen Irish workmen who were working in a haggard[3] in England give up talking Irish amongst themselves because the English farmer laughed at them. And yet O'Connell used to call us the "finest peasantry in Europe." Unfortunately, he took little care that we should remain so. We must teach ourselves to be less sensitive, we must teach ourselves not to be ashamed of ourselves, because the Gaelic people can never produce its best before the world as long as it remains tied to the apron-strings of another race and another island, waiting for *it* to move before it will venture to take any step itself.

In conclusion, I would earnestly appeal to every one, whether Unionist or Nationalist, who wishes to see the Irish nation produce its best—and surely whatever our politics are we all wish that—to set his face against this constant running to England for our books, literature, music, games, fashions, and ideas. I appeal to every one whatever his politics—for this is no political matter—to do his best to help the Irish race to develop in future upon Irish lines, even at the risk of encouraging national aspirations, because upon Irish lines alone can the Irish race once more become what it was of yore—one of the most original, artistic, literary, and charming peoples of Europe.

WILLIAM BUTLER YEATS

Early Poetry and Prose

Among the Irish writers who were active in Dublin during Joyce's school and university years, William Butler Yeats (1865–1939) was the rising star as poet, playwright, and to a lesser extent fiction writer.

The two poems reprinted here are the early versions that Joyce is most likely to have encountered while he was a student, before Yeats's later revisions.

"Who Goes with Fergus?", quoted in part in episodes 1 and 15 of *Ulysses*, is a lyric from act II of Yeats's 1892 play, *The Countess Cathleen* (originally spelled *Kathleen*), where it occurs in italics without a title. Yeats later reprinted the poem with the title and without italics, independently of the play. The lines of the poem, printed here with the later title, are from *The Countess Kathleen*.

"Michael Robartes Remembers Forgotten Beauty" (1896) appeared with that title in Yeats's *The Wind Among the Reeds* (London, 1899). Yeats

2. Thomas Moore (1779–1852), poet, whose *Irish Melodies* (1808–34) became immensely popular as songs. Thomas Davis (1814–1845), nationalist and poet, famous for leading the Young Ireland movement and for ballads such as "A Nation Once Again."
3. In Irish usage, an area on a farm, set aside for stacking agricultural products such as corn and hay.

later changed the title to "He Remembers Forgotten Beauty." In the 6 April entry of his journal, Stephen repeats the words of the original title.

In chapter XXIII of *Stephen Hero*, the autobiographical fictional narrative that Joyce wrote (and never published) before *A Portrait of the Artist as a Young Man*, the central character, Stephen Daedalus (not Dedalus), discovers and becomes fascinated by the two stories of the occult concerning the characters Owen Aherne and Michael Robartes that Yeats first published privately in 1897 as *The Tables of the Law. The Adoration of the Magi*, with the titles of the two tales separated by a period in the book's title. Stephen can hardly restrain himself from reciting from memory "The Tables of the Law" to a priest, who would have been shocked by the characters' blasphemous attitudes, but he satisfies his impulse by reciting the story to his friend Lynch. When Yeats reprinted the small book with some revisions in 1904, he stated in a prefatory note standing in the place of a dedication that he had been motivated to reprint them because a "young man in Ireland" admired them but none of his other writing. Without being named, Joyce is implied. Yeats dedicated *The Secret Rose* (1897), the collection of stories for which these two separately published tales had originally been intended, to A.E. [George Russell], who appears prominently in episode 9 of *Ulysses* (see note 2, p. 250 above).

Who Goes with Fergus?[†]

Who will go drive with Fergus now,
And pierce the deep wood's woven shade,
And dance upon the level shore?
Young man, lift up your russet brow,
And lift your tender eyelids, maid,
And brood on hopes and fear no more.

And no more turn aside and brood
Upon love's bitter mystery;
For Fergus rules the brazen cars,
And rules the shadows of the wood,
And the white breast of the dim sea
And all dishevelled wandering stars.

Michael Robartes Remembers Forgotten Beauty[‡]

When my arms wrap you round I press
My heart upon the loveliness
That has long faded from the world;

[†] From act II of *The Countess Kathleen* in *The Countess Kathleen and Various Legends and Lyrics* (London: T. Fisher Unwin, 1892), pp. 36.
[‡] From *The Wind Among the Reeds* (New York and London: John Lane, The Bodley Head, 1899), pp. 27–28.

The jewelled crowns that kings have hurled
In shadowy pools, when armies fled;
The love-tales wove with silken thread
By dreaming ladies upon cloth
That has made fat the murderous moth;
The roses that of old time were
Woven by ladies in their hair,
The dew-cold lilies ladies bore
Through many a sacred corridor
Where a so sleepy incense rose
That only the god's eyes did not close:
For that pale breast and lingering hand
Come from a more dream-heavy land,
A more dream-heavy hour than this;
And when you sigh from kiss to kiss
I hear white Beauty sighing, too,
For hours when all must fade like dew
But flame on flame, deep under deep,
Throne over throne where in half sleep,
A sword upon his iron knees,
Brood her high lonely mysteries.

From *The Tables of the Law*†

II

I was walking along one of the Dublin quays, on the side nearest
the river, about ten years after our conversation, stopping from time
to time to turn over the works upon an old bookstall, and thinking,
curiously enough, of the terrible destiny of Michael Robartes, and
his brotherhood,[1] when I saw a tall and bent man walking slowly
along the other side of the quay. I recognized, with a start, in a lifeless mask with dim eyes, the once resolute and delicate face of
Owen Aherne. I crossed the quay quickly, but had not gone many
yards before he turned away, as though he had seen me, and hurried down a side street; I followed, but only to lose him among the
intricate streets on the north side of the river. During the next few
weeks I inquired of everybody who had once known him, but he
had made himself known to nobody; and I knocked, without result,
at the door of his old house; and had nearly persuaded myself that I

---

† Originally intended along with "The Adoration of the Magi" for the collection *The
Secret Rose* (London: Lawrence & Bullen, 1897) but dropped at the publisher's request
and then privately published in *The Tables of the Law. The Adoration of the Magi*
(1897).
1. Members of a secret society that held heretical beliefs and indulged in occult rituals.

was mistaken, when I saw him again in a narrow street behind the Four Courts,[2] and followed him to the door of his house.

I laid my hand on his arm; he turned quite without surprise; and indeed it is possible that to him, whose inner life had soaked up the outer life, a parting of years was a parting from forenoon to afternoon. He stood holding the door half open, as though he would keep me from entering; and would perhaps have parted from me without further words had I not said: 'Owen Aherne, you trusted me once, will you not trust me again, and tell me what has come of the ideas we discussed in this house ten years ago?—but perhaps you have already forgotten them.'

'You have a right to hear,' he said, 'for since I have told you the ideas I should tell you the extreme danger they contain, or rather the boundless wickedness they contain; but when you have heard this we must part, and part for ever, because I am lost, and must be hidden!'

I followed him through the paved passage, and saw that its corners were choked with dust and cobwebs; and that the pictures were grey with dust and shrouded with cobwebs; and that the dust and cobwebs which covered the ruby and sapphire of the saints on the window, had made it very dim. He pointed to where the ivory tablets[3] glimmered faintly in the dimness, and I saw that they were covered with small writing, and went up to them and began to read the writing. It was in Latin, and was an elaborate casuistry, illustrated with many examples, but whether from his own life or from the lives of others I do not know. I had read but a few sentences when I imagined that a faint perfume had begun to fill the room, and turning round asked Owen Aherne if he were lighting the incense.

'No,' he replied, and pointed where the thurible lay rusty and empty on one of the benches; as he spoke the faint perfume seemed to vanish, and I was persuaded I had imagined it.

'Has the philosophy of the *Liber Inducens in Evangelium Æternum*[4] made you very unhappy?' I said.

---

2. Ireland's most famous judicial building, built at the end of the eighteenth century along the banks of the River Liffey in central Dublin.
3. In part I of the story, these tablets are blank and hang in the place normally occupied by the Ten Commandments, which God inscribed on stone tablets, according to the narrative in Exodus of the Old Testament. The narrator learns in that part of the story that the book Aherne has acquired includes a lengthy section focusing on breaking all the commandments.
4. Yeats ascribes this title to the book that has influenced Aherne and Robartes, apparently attributing it to the theologian Joachim of Flora (c. 1135–1202), some of whose prophetic writings were condemned by the Church after his death, though he was never declared a heretic. The title can be translated as *The Book Presenting the Eternal Gospel*. No such work by Joachim is known, but Gerard of Borgo San Donnino (d. 1276), who was influenced by Joachim, produced a work with a similar title. In *Ulysses*, Joachim comes up in Stephen's thoughts in episode 3 (see p. 242).

'At first I was full of happiness,' he replied, 'for I felt a divine ecstasy, an immortal fire in every passion, in every hope, in every desire, in every dream; and I saw, in the shadows under leaves, in the hollow waters, in the eyes of men and women, its image, as in a mirror; and it was as though I was about to touch the Heart of God. Then all changed and I was full of misery, and I said to myself that I was caught in the glittering folds of an enormous serpent, and was falling with him through a fathomless abyss, and that henceforth the glittering folds were my world; and in my misery it was revealed to me that man can only come to that Heart through the sense of separation from it which we call sin, and I understood that I could not sin, because I had discovered the law of my being, and could only express or fail to express my being, and I understood that God has made a simple and an arbitrary law that we may sin and repent!'

He had sat down on one of the wooden benches and now became silent, his bowed head and hanging arms and listless body having more of dejection than any image I have met with in life or in any art. I went and stood leaning against the altar, and watched him, not knowing what I should say; and I noticed his black closely-buttoned coat, his short hair, and shaven head, which preserved a memory of his priestly ambition, and understood how Catholicism had seized him in the midst of the vertigo he called philosophy; and I noticed his lightless eyes and his earth-coloured complexion, and understood how she had failed to do more than hold him on the margin: and I was full of an anguish of pity.

'It may be,' he went on, 'that the angels whose hearts are shadows of the Divine Heart, and whose bodies are made of the Divine Intellect, may come to where their longing is always by a thirst for the divine ecstasy, the immortal fire, that is in passion, in hope, in desire, in dreams; but we whose hearts perish every moment, and whose bodies melt away like a sigh, must bow and obey!'

I went nearer to him and said: 'Prayer and repentance will make you like other men.'

'No, no,' he said, 'I am not among those for whom Christ died, and this is why I must be hidden. I have a leprosy that even eternity cannot cure. I have seen the whole, and how can I come again to believe that a part is the whole? I have lost my soul because I have looked out of the eyes of the angels.'

Suddenly I saw, or imagined that I saw, the room darken, and faint figures robed in purple, and lifting faint torches with arms that gleamed like silver, bending, above Owen Aherne; and I saw, or imagined that I saw, drops, as of burning gum, fall from the torches, and a heavy purple smoke, as of incense, come pouring from the flames and sweeping about us. Owen Aherne, more happy than I who have been half initiated into the Order of the Alchemical Rose, and protected perhaps by his great piety, had sunk again into dejection and listlessness, and saw none of these things; but my knees shook under me, for the purple-robed figures were less faint every moment, and now I could hear the hissing of the gum in the torches. They did not appear to see me, for their eyes were upon Owen Aherne; and now and again I could hear them sigh as though with sorrow for his sorrow, and presently I heard words which I could not understand except that they were words of sorrow, and sweet as though immortal was talking to immortal. Then one of them waved her torch, and all the torches waved, and for a moment it was as though some great bird made of flames had fluttered its plumage, and a voice cried as from far up in the air: 'He has charged even his angels with folly, and they also bow and obey; but let your heart mingle with our hearts, which are wrought of Divine Ecstasy, and your body with our bodies which are wrought of Divine Intellect.' And at that cry I understood that the Order of the Alchemical Rose was not of this earth, and that it was still seeking over this earth for whatever souls it could gather within its glittering net; and when all the faces turned towards me, and I saw the mild eyes and the unshaken eyelids I was full of terror, and thought they were about to fling their torches upon me, so that all I held dear, all that bound me to spiritual and social order would be burnt up and my soul left naked and shivering among the winds that blow from beyond this world and from beyond the stars; and then a faint voice cried, 'Why do you fly from our torches that were made out of the trees under which Christ wept in the Garden of Gethsemane?[5] Why do you fly from our torches that were made out of sweet wood, after it had perished from the world and come to us who made it of old time with our breath?'

It was not until the door of the house had closed behind my flight, and the noise of the street was breaking on my ears, that I came back to myself and to a little of my courage; and I have never dared to pass the house of Owen Aherne from that day, even though I believe him to have been driven into some distant country by the spirits whose name is legion, and whose throne is in the indefinite abyss, and whom he obeys and cannot see.

---

5. The garden in Jerusalem where, according to the New Testament, Jesus experienced anguish just before his arrest the night before his crucifixion.

JOHN MILLINGTON SYNGE

From *The Aran Islands*†

J. M. Synge (1871–1909) was a central figure in the Irish Literary
Revival, which was in progress when Joyce was a university student
and while he was writing *A Portrait of the Artist as a Young Man*. Synge
cofounded the Abbey Theatre with Lady Augusta Gregory (1852–1932)
and W. B. Yeats (see p. 299), and his one-act play *The Shadow of the
Glen* formed part of the Abbey's opening bill in 1904. When Synge's
masterpiece, *The Playboy of the Western World*, premiered there in 1907,
it triggered riots by nationalists who claimed that the play demeaned the
Irish. Even living in Italy beginning in 1904, Joyce would have known
Synge's writings and been aware of these events, which were central to
the developing literary life of Ireland. Among the books in Joyce's
library in Trieste is a first edition of Synge's book *The Aran Islands*,
published in 1907 with illustrations by Jack B. Yeats (1871–1957),
W. B. Yeats's brother. Joyce also would have known Synge's earlier,
brief account of traditional life on the isolated, rugged islands off the
west coast of Ireland, published in 1898 in the *New Ireland Review*.

The following excerpts from *The Aran Islands*, which is based on
Synge's experiences living among the people of the islands, bear direct,
frequently contrasting relation to aspects of Joyce's narrative, especially Stephen's encounter with the birdlike girl on the shore, Davin's
story about meeting in the countryside a wife who wanted to be
unfaithful, Stephen's journal entry of 14 April about an encounter with
an Irish peasant, and his conversation with the dean of studies, who
gives him advice about lighting a fire. At the end of the narrative Stephen is on the verge of leaving Ireland, heading east, presumably for
Europe. *The Aran Islands*, by contrast, presents a powerful attraction
to the west, to a world that is native rather than cosmopolitan.

[*The Birdgirl on the Shore*]

* * *

The drought is also causing a scarcity of water. * * * The water
for washing is also coming short, and as I walk round the edges of
the sea I often come on a girl[1] with her petticoats tucked up round
her, standing in a pool left by the tide and washing her flannels
among the sea-anemones and crabs. Their red bodices and white
tapering legs make them as beautiful as tropical sea-birds, as they
stand in a frame of seaweeds against the brink of the Atlantic.

---

† From *The Aran Islands* (Dublin: Maunsel & Co., Ltd., 1907), pp. 54–55, 112–13, 42–46,
  120–22, 177–78. The text drawn on here is the 1910 reprinting by Maunsel as vol. 3 of
  The Works of John M. Synge.
1. In the idiom of the time, "coming short" means running low, and to "come on a girl" is
  to happen upon her.

Michael, however, is a little uneasy when they are in sight, and I cannot pause to watch them. * * *

* * *

[Girls Wreathed with Seaweed; Trembling and Exultation]

* * *

At the south-west corner of the island I came upon a number of people gathering the seaweed that is now thick on the rocks. It was raked from the surf by the men, and then carried up to the brow of the cliff by a party of young girls.

In addition to their ordinary clothing these girls wore a raw sheepskin on their shoulders, to catch the oozing sea-water, and they looked strangely wild and seal-like with the salt caked upon their lips and wreaths of seaweed in their hair.

For the rest of my walk I saw no living thing but one flock of curlews, and a few pipits hiding among the stones.

About the sunset the clouds broke and the storm turned to a hurricane. Bars of purple cloud stretched across the sound where immense waves were rolling from the west, wreathed with snowy phantasies of spray. * * *

The suggestion from this world of inarticulate power was immense, and now at midnight, when the wind is abating, I am still trembling and flushed with exultation.

[The Tale of the Unfaithful Wife]

Pat told me a story of an unfaithful wife * * * .
Here is his story:—

One day I was travelling on foot from Galway to Dublin, and the darkness came on me and I ten miles from the town I was wanting to pass the night in. Then a hard rain began to fall and I was tired walking, so when I saw a sort of a house with no roof on it up against the road, I got in the way the walls would give me shelter.

As I was looking round I saw a light in some trees two perches off, and thinking any sort of a house would be better than where I was, I got over a wall and went up to the house to look in at the window.

I saw a dead man laid on a table, and candles lighted, and a woman watching him. I was frightened when I saw him, but it was raining hard, and I said to myself, if he was dead he couldn't hurt me. Then I knocked on the door and the woman came and opened it.

'Good evening, ma'am,' says I.

'Good evening kindly, stranger,' says she. 'Come in out of the rain.'

Then she took me in and told me her husband was after dying on her, and she was watching him that night.

'But it's thirsty you'll be, stranger,' says she. 'Come into the parlour.'

Then she took me into the parlour—and it was a fine clean house—and she put a cup, with a saucer under it, on the table before me, with fine sugar and bread.

When I'd had a cup of tea I went back into the kitchen where the dead man was lying, and she gave me a fine new pipe off the table with a drop of spirits.

'Stranger,' says she, 'would you be afeard to be alone with himself?'

'Not a bit in the world, ma'am,' says I; 'he that's dead can do no hurt.'

Then she said she wanted to go over and tell the neighbours the way her husband was after dying on her, and she went out and locked the door behind her.

I smoked one pipe, and I leaned out and took another off the table. I was smoking it with my hand on the back of my chair—the way you are yourself this minute, God bless you—and I looking on the dead man, when he opened his eyes as wide as myself and looked at me.

'Don't be afeard, stranger,' said the dead man; 'I'm not dead at all in the world. Come here and help me up, and I'll tell you all about it.'

Well, I went up and took the sheet off of him, and I saw that he had a fine clean shirt on his body, and fine flannel drawers.

He sat up then, and says he—

'I've got a bad wife, stranger, and I let on to be dead the way I'd catch her goings on.'

Then he got two fine sticks he had to keep down his wife, and he put them at each side of his body, and he laid himself out again as if he was dead.

In half an hour his wife came back, and a young man along with her. Well, she gave him his tea, and she told him he was tired, and he would do right to go and lie down in the bedroom.

The young man went in, and the woman sat down to watch by the dead man. A while after she got up, and 'Stranger,' says she, 'I'm going in to get the candle out of the room; I'm thinking the young man will be asleep by this time.' She went into the bedroom, but the divil a bit of her came back.[2]

_____

2. But she never came back.

Then the dead man got up, and he took one stick, and he gave the other to myself. We went in and we saw them lying together with her head on his arm.

The dead man hit him a blow with the stick so that the blood out of him leapt up and hit the gallery.

That is my story.

[*Queer Places and People; Lighting a Fire*]

* * *

In the evenings I sometimes meet with a girl who is not yet half through her 'teens, yet seems in some ways more consciously developed[3] than any one else that I have met here. She has passed part of her life on the mainland, and the disillusion she found in Galway has coloured her imagination.

As we sit on stools on either side of the fire I hear her voice going backwards and forwards in the same sentence from the gaiety of a child to the plaintive intonation of an old race that is worn with sorrow. At one moment she is a simple peasant, at another she seems to be looking out at the world with a sense of prehistoric disillusion and to sum up in the expression of her grey-blue eyes the whole external despondency of the clouds and sea.

Our conversation is usually disjointed. One evening we talked of a town on the mainland.

'Ah, it's a queer place,' she said; 'I wouldn't choose to live in it. It's a queer place, and indeed I don't know the place that isn't.'

Another evening we talked of the people who live on the island or come to visit it.

'Father——is gone,' she said; 'he was a kind man but a queer man. Priests is queer people, and I don't know who isn't.'

* * *

One evening I found her trying to light a fire in the little side room of her cottage, where there is an ordinary fireplace. I went in to help her and showed her how to hold up a paper before the mouth of the chimney to make a draught, a method she had never seen. Then I told her of men who live alone in Paris and make their own fires that they may have no one to bother them. She was sitting in a heap on the floor staring into the turf, and as I finished she looked up with surprise.

'They're like me so,' she said; 'would any one have thought that!'

Below the sympathy we feel there is still a chasm between us.

3. Developed in her mental abilities.

'Musha,' she muttered as I was leaving her this evening, 'I think it's to hell you'll be going by and by.'

*   *   *

[Rejecting Paris; Choosing Ancient Simplicity]

*   *   *

Even after the people of the south island, these men of the Inish-maan[4] seemed to be moved by strange archaic sympathies with the world. Their mood accorded itself with wonderful fineness to the suggestions of the day, and their ancient Gaelic seemed so full of divine simplicity that I would have liked to turn the prow to the west and row with them for ever.

I told them I was going back to Paris in a few days to sell my books and my bed, and that then I was coming back to grow as strong and simple as they were among the islands of the west.

---

4. The middle island of the three Aran Islands, only slightly larger than Inishere to the south.

Religion

ST. IGNATIUS OF LOYOLA
From *The Spiritual Exercises*†

Saint Ignatius of Loyola (1491–1556) founded the Society of Jesus, also known as the Jesuits, the order within the Roman Catholic Church that established and ran Clongowes Wood College and Belvedere College. Although he probably first drafted *The Spiritual Exercises* in the 1520s, the earliest copy known is from 1541. This immensely influential book consists largely of highly structured meditations to be pursued intently by people in search of spiritual direction. The exercises are meant to strengthen faith and to enhance the experience of faith. Frequently they are undertaken during religious retreats, such as the one Stephen experiences in Part III, and as a result of such retreats. Pinamonti's *Hell Opened to Christians* provides a supplement to the fifth exercise (meditation on hell) during the first week of *The Spiritual Exercises*. A portion from the fourth week has also been included because, rather than emphasizing discipline and abstinence, as do most of the exercises, it projects a positive recognition related to Stephen's experience at the close of Part III.

Annotations

TO GIVE SOME UNDERSTANDING OF THE SPIRITUAL
EXERCISES WHICH FOLLOW, AND TO ENABLE HIM
WHO IS TO GIVE AND HIM WHO IS TO RECEIVE
THEM TO HELP THEMSELVES

First Annotation. The first Annotation is that by this name of Spiritual Exercises is meant every way of examining one's conscience, of meditating, of contemplating, of praying vocally and mentally, and of performing other spiritual actions, as will be said later. For as strolling, walking and running are bodily exercises, so

---

† Trans. Father Elder Mullan, S. J. (New York: P. J. Kenedy & Sons, 1914). For this reprinting, the translator's notes have been omitted. The entire text is available online as a .pdf document: https://selfdefinition.org/christian/Spiritual-Exercises-St-Ignatius -of-Loyola.pdf. The selections are taken from .pdf pages 12, 29–33, 64–69.

every way of preparing and disposing the soul to rid itself of all the disordered tendencies, and, after it is rid, to seek and find the Divine Will as to the management of one's life for the salvation of the soul, is called a Spiritual Exercise.

*   *   *

Fourth Annotation. The fourth: The following Exercises are divided into four parts:
First, the consideration and contemplation on the sins;
Second, the life of Christ our Lord up to Palm Sunday inclusively;
Third, the Passion of Christ our Lord;
Fourth, the Resurrection and Ascension, with the three Methods of Prayer.

*   *   *

[*From* "First Week"]
Fifth Exercise

IT IS A MEDITATION ON HELL

It contains in it, after the Preparatory Prayer and two Preludes, five Points and one Colloquy:

Prayer. Let the Preparatory Prayer be the usual one.[1]
First Prelude. The first Prelude is the composition, which is here to see with the sight of the imagination the length, breadth and depth of Hell.
Second Prelude. The second, to ask for what I want: it will be here to ask for interior sense of the pain which the damned suffer, in order that, if, through my faults, I should forget the love of the Eternal Lord, at least the fear of the pains may help me not to come into sin.
First Point. The first Point will be to see with the sight of the imagination the great fires, and the souls as in bodies of fire.
Second Point. The second, to hear with the ears wailings, howlings, cries, blasphemies against Christ our Lord and against all His Saints.
Third Point. The third, to smell with the smell smoke, sulphur, dregs and putrid things.
Fourth Point. The fourth, to taste with the taste bitter things, like tears, sadness and the worm of conscience.

1. As stated in the First Exercise, "The Preparatory Prayer is to ask grace of God our Lord that all my intentions, actions and operations may be directed purely to the service and praise of His Divine Majesty" (.pdf p. 26).

Fifth Point. The fifth, to touch with the touch; that is to say, how the fires touch and burn the souls.

Colloquy. Making a Colloquy to Christ our Lord, I will bring to memory the souls that are in Hell, some because they did not believe the Coming, others because, believing, they did not act according to His Commandments; making three divisions:

First, Second, and Third Divisions. The first, before the Coming; the second, during His life; the third, after His life in this world; and with this I will give Him thanks that He has not let me fall into any of these divisions, ending my life.

Likewise, I will consider how up to now He has always had so great pity and mercy on me.

I will end with an OUR FATHER.

Note. The first Exercise will be made at midnight; the second immediately on rising in the morning; the third, before or after Mass; in any case, before dinner; the fourth at the hour of Vespers; the fifth, an hour before supper.

This arrangement of hours, more or less, I always mean in all the four Weeks, according as his age, disposition and physical condition help the person who is exercising himself to make five Exercises or fewer.

Additions

TO MAKE THE EXERCISES BETTER AND TO FIND BETTER WHAT ONE DESIRES

First Addition. The first Addition is, after going to bed, just when I want to go asleep, to think, for the space of a HAIL MARY, of the hour that I have to rise and for what, making a resume of the Exercise which I have to make.

* * *

Fourth Addition. The fourth: To enter on the contemplation now on my knees, now prostrate on the earth, now lying face upwards, now seated, now standing, always intent on seeking what I want.

We will attend to two things. The first is, that if I find what I want kneeling, I will not pass on; and if prostrate, likewise, etc. The second; in the Point in which I find what I want, there I will rest, without being anxious to pass on, until I content myself.

* * *

Sixth Addition. The sixth: Not to want to think on things of pleasure or joy, such as heavenly glory, the Resurrection, etc. Because whatever consideration of joy and gladness hinders our feeling pain and grief and shedding tears for our sins: but to keep before me that I want to grieve and feel pain, bringing to memory rather Death and Judgment.

Seventh Addition. The seventh: For the same end, to deprive myself of all light, closing the blinds and doors while I am in the room, if it be not to recite prayers, to read and eat.

Eighth Addition. The eighth: Not to laugh nor say a thing provocative of laughter.

Ninth Addition. The ninth: To restrain my sight, except in receiving or dismissing the person with whom I have spoken.

Tenth Addition. The tenth Addition is penance.

This is divided into interior and exterior. The interior is to grieve for one's sins, with a firm purpose of not committing them nor any others. The exterior, or fruit of the first, is chastisement for the sins committed, and is chiefly taken in three ways.

First Way. The first is as to eating. That is to say, when we leave off the superfluous, it is not penance, but temperance. It is penance when we leave off from the suitable; and the more and more, the greater and better—provided that the person does not injure himself, and that no notable illness follows.

Second Way. The second, as to the manner of sleeping. Here too it is not penance to leave off the superfluous of delicate or soft things, but it is penance when one leaves off from the suitable in the manner: and the more and more, the better—provided that the person does not injure himself and no notable illness follows. Besides, let not anything of the suitable sleep be left off, unless in order to come to the mean, if one has a bad habit of sleeping too much.

Third Way. The third, to chastise the flesh, that is, giving it sensible pain, which is given by wearing haircloth or cords or iron chains next to the flesh, by scourging or wounding oneself, and by other kinds of austerity.

Note. What appears most suitable and most secure with regard to penance is that the pain should be sensible in the flesh and not enter within the bones, so that it give pain and not illness. For this it appears to be more suitable to scourge oneself with thin cords, which give pain exteriorly, rather than in another way which would cause notable illness within.

First Note. The first Note is that the exterior penances are done chiefly for three ends: First, as satisfaction for the sins committed; Second, to conquer oneself—that is, to make sensuality obey reason and all inferior parts be more subject to the superior;

Third, to seek and find some grace or gift which the person wants and desires; as, for instance, if he desires to have interior contrition for his sins, or to weep much over them, or over the pains and sufferings which Christ our Lord suffered in His Passion, or to settle some doubt in which the person finds himself.

\ * * *

[From "Fourth Week"]
Contemplation to Gain Love

Prayer. The usual Prayer.

First Prelude. The first Prelude is a composition, which is here to see how I am standing before God our Lord, and of the Angels and of the Saints interceding for me.

Second Prelude. The second, to ask for what I want. It will be here to ask for interior knowledge of so great good received, in order that being entirely grateful, I may be able in all to love and serve His Divine Majesty.

First Point. The First Point is, to bring to memory the benefits received, of Creation, Redemption and particular gifts, pondering with much feeling how much God our Lord has done for me, and how much He has given me of what He has, and then the same Lord desires to give me Himself as much as He can, according to His Divine ordination.

And with this to reflect on myself, considering with much reason and justice, what I ought on my side to offer and give to His Divine Majesty, that is to say, everything that is mine, and myself with it, as one who makes an offering with much feeling:

Take, Lord, and receive all my liberty, my memory, my intellect, and all my will—all that I have and possess. Thou gavest it to me: to Thee, Lord, I return it! All is Thine, dispose of it according to all Thy will. Give me Thy love and grace, for this is enough for me.

Second Point. The second, to look how God dwells in creatures, in the elements, giving them being, in the plants vegetating, in the animals feeling in them, in men giving them to understand: and so in me, giving me being, animating me, giving me sensation and making me to understand; likewise making a temple of me, being created to the likeness and image of His Divine Majesty; reflecting as much on myself in the way which is said in the first Point, or in another which I feel to be better. In the same manner will be done on each Point which follows.

Third Point. The third, to consider how God works and labors for me in all things created on the face of the earth—that is, behaves like one who labors—as in the heavens, elements, plants, fruits, cattle, etc., giving them being, preserving them, giving them vegetation and sensation, etc.

Then to reflect on myself.

Fourth Point. The fourth, to look how all the good things and gifts descend from above, as my poor power from the supreme and infinite power from above; and so justice, goodness, pity, mercy, etc.; as from the sun descend the rays, from the fountain the waters, etc.

Then to finish reflecting on myself, as has been said.

I will end with a Colloquy and an OUR FATHER.

From the Rev. Father Giovanni Pietro Pinamonti, S.J., *Hell Opened to Christians, To Caution Them from Entering into It*. The frontispiece is from the copy in the National Library of Ireland (Dublin: G. P. Warren, n.d.). The two other images are from the copy in the Boston Public Library (Dublin: Richard Grace, 1840). James R. Thrane established that Joyce drew on an English translation of Pinamonti's text (published originally in Italian in 1688) in Part III in "Joyce's Sermon on Hell: Its Source and Its Backgrounds," *Modern Philology* 57 (February 1960): 172–98. The pamphlet would have been used as a supplement to St. Ignatius's *Spiritual Exercises*, specifically to the meditation on hell from the fifth exercise of the first week, reprinted above. The full pamphlet contains an image of a soul being tortured for each day of the week. Such a pamphlet would likely have played a role at religious retreats, such as the one Stephen participates in during Part III.

THE STING OF CONSCIENCE.

The Sting of Conscience. The Fifth Consideration, For Thursday.
Reprinted with permission of the Boston Public Library.

DESPAIR.

Despair. The Sixth Consideration, For Friday. Reprinted with permission of the Boston Public Library.

Aesthetic Backgrounds

THE VILLANELLE TRADITION IN ENGLISH

In the late decades of the nineteenth century, many English-language poets influenced by French models produced poems in various stylized forms, including the villanelle. A villanelle consists of nineteen lines: five tercets and a closing quatrain, with two refrains and two repeated rhymes. The first and last lines of the opening tercet are repeated in alternation at the end of subsequent tercets, with both appearing in the quatrain. Joyce could have encountered this example by Andrew Lang (1844–1912), whose 1879 prose translation of Homer's *Odyssey*, produced in collaboration with J. H. Butcher (1850–1910), Joyce definitely knew. Joyce uses the word "plenilune," which occurs in Lang's villanelle, in poem XII of *Chamber Music* (see p. 225 above).

ANDREW LANG

To the Nightingale in September[†]

Child of the muses and the moon,
   O nightingale, return and sing,
Thy song is over all too soon.

Let not night's quire[1] yield place to noon,
   To this red breast thy tawny wing,
Child of the muses and the moon.

Sing us once more the same sad tune
   Pandion heard when he was king,[2]
Thy song is over all too soon.

[†] From *Ballades and Rondeaux, Chants Royal, Sestinas, Villanelles, &c.*, ed. Gleeson White (New York: D. Appleton and Company, 1888), p. 255.
1. Choir.
2. In Greek mythology, Pandion, king of Athens, was the father of Procne and Philomel. The nightingale's song is sad because Philomel was raped by her sister's husband, Tereus, and was turned into a nightingale to escape Tereus's wrath after the sisters took revenge on him.

Night after night thro' leafy June
 The stars were hush'd and listening,
Child of the muses and the moon.

Now new moons grow to plenilune[3]
 And wane, but no new music bring;
Thy song is over all too soon.

Ah, thou art weary! Well, sleep on,
 Sleep till the sun brings back the spring.
Thy song is over all too soon,
Child of the muses and the moon.

3. A full moon.

This image of the *Laocoön* sculpture group is reproduced from plate I of Percy Gardner's entry on Greek art, *Encyclopaedia Britannica,* 11th Ed. (London and New York: Encyclopaedia Britannica, 1910), 12.472bis. This edition represents the state of knowledge in the English-speaking world at the time Joyce wrote *A Portrait.* Gardner comments that this work, "signed by Rhodian sculptors of the 1st century B.C., . . . has been perhaps more discussed than any work of the Greek chisel, and served as a peg for the aesthetic theories of

Lessing and Goethe" (491–92; on Lessing and Goethe, see notes 8–9, p. 186). Stephen Dedalus's comments about aesthetics in Part V respond to Lessing's meditations on the character of art, in which the sculpture group plays a central role. The photograph shows the group as Joyce and his contemporaries would have known it but not as we know it today. The statue was found in Michelangelo's day in Rome, broken, without the complete right arm of the central figure. It was mistakenly restored to the form shown in the photograph. Around 1960, it was restored again with significant changes to the handling of the broken arms and the missing one. The image of figures held involuntarily and tormented by a serpent is matched by the woodcuts in Pinamonti's *Hell Opened to Christians*, which Stephen, like his author, would have encountered during his education.

WALTER PATER

The Renaissance[†]

Walter Pater (1839–1894), whose ideas inspired the British Aesthetic movement of the last quarter of the nineteenth century, is most famous for his writings on literature and art. Emphasizing the importance of experiencing beauty in art intensely, those writings were well known to Joyce and to Joyce's older contemporaries Oscar Wilde (see p. 335) and W. B. Yeats (see p. 299). *Studies in the History of the Renaissance,* whose title was eventually shortened to *The Renaissance,* appeared in four editions during Pater's lifetime. The first edition (1873) drew criticism from religious authorities on the grounds that the attitudes expressed in the conclusion placed art above religion. Pater removed the conclusion from the second edition (1877), then restored it in revised form in the third edition (1888). The following excerpts come from a reprinting of the fourth edition (1893), the current edition when Joyce was a student. The inventory of Joyce's library in Trieste lists a slightly later reprinting (1912) by the same publisher. The revised conclusion and the description of the *Mona Lisa* from the essay on Leonardo were famous passages of prose among English-speaking artists and intellectuals during Joyce's youth. In episode 3 of *Ulysses* (see p. 243), Stephen Dedalus's thinking about the philosopher Pico della Mirandola makes clear that Joyce knew the essay on Pico, in which Pater emphasizes the attempt to reconcile ancient Greek culture with European culture of a later time.

Pico della Mirandola

No account of the Renaissance can be complete without some notice of the attempt made by certain Italian scholars of the fifteenth century to reconcile Christianity with the religion of ancient Greece. To reconcile forms of sentiment which at first sight seem incompatible, to adjust the various products of the human mind to each other in one many-sided type of intellectual culture, to give humanity, for heart and imagination to feed upon, as much as it could possibly receive, belonged to the generous instincts of that age. * * *

* * *

It was after many wanderings, wanderings of the intellect as well as physical journeys, that Pico came to rest at Florence. He was then about twenty years old, having been born in 1463. He was called Giovanni at baptism; Pico, like all his ancestors, from Picus, nephew of the Emperor Constantine, from whom they claimed to

---

[†] From *The Renaissance* (London: Macmillan, 1906), pp. 30, 38–49, 122–26, 233–39. One of Pater's footnotes has been omitted.

be descended; and Mirandola, from the place of his birth, a little town afterwards part of the duchy of Modena, of which small territory his family had long been the feudal lords. Pico was the youngest of the family, and his mother, delighting in his wonderful memory, sent him at the age of fourteen to the famous school of law at Bologna. From the first, indeed, she seems to have had some presentiment of his future fame, for, with a faith in omens characteristic of her time, she believed that a strange circumstance had happened at the time of Pico's birth—the appearance of a circular flame which suddenly vanished away, on the wall of the chamber where she lay. He remained two years at Bologna; and then, with an inexhaustible, unrivalled thirst for knowledge, the strange, confused, uncritical learning of that age, passed through the principal schools of Italy and France, penetrating, as he thought, into the secrets of all ancient philosophies, and many eastern languages. And with this flood of erudition came the generous hope, so often disabused, of reconciling the philosophers with each other, and all alike with the Church. At last he came to Rome. There, like some knight-errant of philosophy, he offered to defend nine hundred bold paradoxes, drawn from the most opposite sources, against all comers. But the pontifical court was led to suspect the orthodoxy of some of these propositions, and even the reading of the book which contained them was forbidden by the Pope. It was not until 1493 that Pico was finally absolved, by a brief of Alexander the Sixth. Ten years before that date he had arrived at Florence; an early instance of those who, after following the vain hope of an impossible reconciliation from system to system, have at last fallen back unsatisfied on the simplicities of their childhood's belief.

The oration which Pico composed for the opening of this philosophical tournament still remains; its subject is the dignity of human nature, the greatness of man. * * * For this high dignity of man, thus bringing the dust under his feet into sensible communion with the thoughts and affections of the angels, was supposed to belong to him, not as renewed by a religious system, but by his own natural right. The proclamation of it was a counterpoise to the increasing tendency of medieval religion to depreciate man's nature, to sacrifice this or that element in it, to make it ashamed of itself, to keep the degrading or painful accidents of it always in view. It helped man onward to that reassertion of himself, that rehabilitation of human nature, the body, the senses, the heart, the intelligence, which the Renaissance fulfils. And yet to read a page of one of Pico's forgotten books is like a glance into one of those ancient sepulchres, upon which the wanderer in classical lands has sometimes stumbled, with the old disused ornaments and furniture of a world wholly unlike ours still fresh in them. * * *

He was already almost wearied out when he came to Florence. He had loved much and been beloved by women, "wandering over the crooked hills of delicious pleasure"; but their reign over him was over, and long before Savonarola's famous "bonfire of vanities,"[1] he had destroyed those love-songs in the vulgar tongue, which would have been such a relief to us, after the scholastic prolixity of his Latin writings. It was in another spirit that he composed a Platonic commentary, the only work of his in Italian which has come down to us, on the "Song of Divine Love"—*secondo la mente ed opinione dei Platonici*—"according to the mind and opinion of the Platonists," by his friend Hieronymo Beniveni, in which, with an ambitious array of every sort of learning, and a profusion of imagery borrowed indifferently from the astrologers, the Cabala, and Homer, and Scripture, and Dionysius the Areopagite, he attempts to define the stages by which the soul passes from the earthly to the unseen beauty.[2] * * *

Yet he who had this fine touch for spiritual things did not—and in this is the enduring interest of his story—even after his conversion, forget the old gods. He is one of the last who seriously and sincerely entertained the claims on men's faith of the pagan religions; he is anxious to ascertain the true significance of the obscurest legend, the lightest tradition concerning them. * * *

It is because the life of Pico, thus lying down to rest in the Dominican habit, yet amid thoughts of the older gods, himself like one of those comely divinities, reconciled indeed to the new religion, but still with a tenderness for the earlier life, and desirous literally to "bind the ages each to each by natural piety"—it is because this life is so perfect a parallel to the attempt made in his writings to reconcile Christianity with the ideas of paganism, that Pico, in spite of the scholastic character of those writings, is really interesting. * * * In explaining the harmony between Plato and Moses, Pico lays hold on every sort of figure and analogy, on the double meanings of words, the symbols of the Jewish ritual, the secondary meanings of obscure stories in the later Greek mythologists. Everywhere there is an unbroken system of correspondences. Every object in the terrestrial world is an analogue, a symbol or counterpart, of some higher reality in the starry heavens, and this

1. The burning in Florence, Italy, in 1497 of books, artworks, mirrors, and other items considered immoral by the Italian priest and Florentine ruler Girolamo Savonarola (1452–1498) and his followers.
2. Platonic would mean not narrowly in the mode of the ancient Greek philosopher Plato (c. 427–c. 347 BCE) but Neoplatonic, that is, with a Platonic emphasis on the dominant reality of a nonmaterial realm supplemented by mystical thought, including astrology (based on the belief that celestial bodies influence human affairs), the Cabala (rabbinical mysticism derived from esoteric readings of Hebrew Scripture), and fifth-century mystical writings attributed to Dionysius the Areopagite, who is mentioned in the New Testament as a convert to Christianity (Acts 17:34).

again of some law of the angelic life in the world beyond the stars. There is the element of fire in the material world; the sun is the fire of heaven; and in the super-celestial world there is the fire of the seraphic intelligence. "But behold how they differ! The elementary fire burns, the heavenly fire vivifies, the super-celestial fire loves." In this way, every natural object, every combination of natural forces, every accident in the lives of men, is filled with higher meanings. Omens, prophecies, supernatural coincidences, accompany Pico himself all through life. There are oracles in every tree and mountain-top, and a significance in every accidental combination of the events of life.

This constant tendency to symbolism and imagery gives Pico's work a figured style, by which it has some real resemblance to Plato's, and he differs from other mystical writers of his time by a real desire to know his authorities at first hand. He reads Plato in Greek, Moses in Hebrew, and by this his work really belongs to the higher culture. Above all, we have a constant sense in reading him, that his thoughts, however little their positive value may be, are connected with springs beneath them of deep and passionate emotion; and when he explains the grades or steps by which the soul passes from the love of a physical object to the love of unseen beauty, and unfolds the analogies between this process and other movements upward of human thought, there is a glow and vehemence in his words which remind one of the manner in which his own brief existence flamed itself away.

I said that the Renaissance of the fifteenth century was in many things great, rather by what it designed or aspired to do, than by what it actually achieved. * * * When the ship-load of sacred earth from the soil of Jerusalem was mingled with the common clay in the *Campo Santo* at Pisa,[3] a new flower grew up from it, unlike any flower men had seen before, the anemone with its concentric rings of strangely blended colour, still to be found by those who search long enough for it, in the long grass of the Maremma.[4] Just such a strange flower was that mythology of the Italian Renaissance, which grew up from the mixture of two traditions, two sentiments, the sacred and the profane. * * *

It is because this picturesque union of contrasts, belonging properly to the art of the close of the fifteenth century, pervades, in Pico della Mirandola, an actual person, that the figure of Pico is so

---

3. Literally (in Italian and Spanish), the sacred field, or cemetery, in Pisa, Italy, traditionally thought to be on the site of an earlier burial ground, for which earth was brought from the place of Christ's crucifixion. The strange flower of mixed traditions also suggests the architectural character of the cemetery, which contained many pieces of classical sculpture.
4. Area in Italy that includes part of southern Tuscany and a portion of northern Latium.

attractive. He will not let one go; he wins one on, in spite of one-self, to turn again to the pages of his forgotten books, although we know already that the actual solution proposed in them will satisfy us as little as perhaps it satisfied him. It is said that in his eagerness for mysterious learning he once paid a great sum for a collection of cabalistic manuscripts, which turned out to be forgeries; and the story might well stand as a parable of all he ever seemed to gain in the way of actual knowledge. He had sought knowledge, and passed from system to system, and hazarded much; but less for the sake of positive knowledge than because he believed there was a spirit of order and beauty in knowledge, which would come down and unite what men's ignorance had divided, and renew what time had made dim. * * *

From *Leonardo da Vinci*

[ON THE *MONA LISA* (*LA GIOCONDA*)]

* * *

The remaining years of Leonardo's life are more or less years of wandering. From his brilliant life at court he had saved nothing, and he returned to Florence a poor man. Perhaps necessity kept his spirit excited: the next four years are one prolonged rapture or ecstasy of invention. He painted the pictures of the Louvre, his most authentic works, which came there straight from the cabinet of Francis the First, at Fontainebleau. * * * But his work was less with the saints than with the living women of Florence; for he lived still in the polished society that he loved, and in the houses of Florence, left perhaps a little subject to light thoughts by the death of Savonarola[5]—the latest gossip (1869) is of an undraped Monna Lisa, found in some out-of-the-way corner of the late *Orleans* collection—he saw Ginevra di Benci, and Lisa, the young third wife of Francesco del Giocondo. As we have seen him using incidents of sacred story, not for their own sake, or as mere subjects for pictorial realisation, but as a symbolical language for fancies all his own, so now he found a vent for his thoughts in taking one of these languid women, and raising her, as Leda or Pomona, Modesty or Vanity, to the seventh heaven of symbolical expression.[6]

La Gioconda is, in the truest sense, Leonardo's masterpiece, the revealing instance of his mode of thought and work. In suggestiveness,

5. See note 1, p. 327.
6. Leonardo has elevated the young woman to the level of these mythological and allegorical figures, which were appropriate subjects for Renaissance painting. In Greek mythology, Leda was ravished by Zeus, who took the form of a swan. In Roman mythology, Pomona, goddess of fruit, was associated with amorous adventures. The mention of modesty and vanity together suggests the contradictory implications of her image.

only the *Melancholia* of Dürer is comparable to it; and no crude symbolism disturbs the effect of its subdued and graceful mystery. We all know the face and hands of the figure, set in its marble chair, in that cirque of fantastic rocks, as in some faint light under sea. Perhaps of all ancient pictures time has chilled it least. As often happens with works in which invention seems to reach its limits, there is an element in it given to, not invented by, the master. In that inestimable folio of drawings, once in the possession of Vasari, were certain designs by Verrocchio,[7] faces of such impressive beauty that Leonardo in his boyhood copied them many times. It is hard not to connect with these designs of the elder, by-past master, as with its germinal principle, the unfathomable smile, always with a touch of something sinister in it, which plays over all Leonardo's work. Besides, the picture is a portrait. From childhood we see this image defining itself on the fabric of his dreams; and but for express historical testimony, we might fancy that this was but his ideal lady, embodied and beheld at last. What was the relationship of a living Florentine to this creature of his thought? By means of what strange affinities had the person and the dream grown up thus apart, and yet so closely together? Present from the first incorporeally in Leonardo's thought, dimly traced in the designs of Verrocchio, she is found present at last in *Il Giocondo*'s house. That there is much of mere portraiture in the picture is attested by the legend that by artificial means, the presence of mimes and flute-players, that subtle expression was protracted on the face. Again, was it in four years and by renewed labour never really completed, or in four months and as by stroke of magic, that the image was projected?

The presence that thus rose so strangely beside the waters, is expressive of what in the ways of a thousand years men had come to desire. Hers is the head upon which all "the ends of the world are come," and the eyelids are a little weary. It is a beauty wrought out from within upon the flesh, the deposit, little cell by cell, of strange thoughts and fantastic reveries and exquisite passions. Set it for a moment beside one of those white Greek goddesses or beautiful women of antiquity, and how would they be troubled by this beauty, into which the soul with all its maladies has passed! All the thoughts and experience of the world have etched and moulded there, in that which they have of power to refine and make expressive the outward form, the animalism of Greece, the lust of Rome, the reverie of the middle age with its spiritual ambition and imaginative loves, the

---

7. Andrea del Verrocchio (1435–1488), Florentine sculptor and painter with whom Leonardo studied. Giorgio Vasari (1511–1574), Italian painter and architect best known for his biographies of Italian artists.

return of the Pagan world, the sins of the Borgias.[8] She is older than the rocks among which she sits; like the vampire, she has been dead many times, and learned the secrets of the grave; and has been a diver in deep seas, and keeps their fallen day about her; and trafficked for strange webs with Eastern merchants: and, as Leda, was the mother of Helen of Troy, and, as Saint Anne, the mother of Mary; and all this has been to her but as the sound of lyres and flutes, and lives only in the delicacy with which it has moulded the changing lineaments, and tinged the eyelids and the hands. The fancy of a perpetual life, sweeping together ten thousand experiences, is an old one; and modern thought has conceived the idea of humanity as wrought upon by, and summing up in itself, all modes of thought and life. Certainly Lady Lisa might stand as the embodiment of the old fancy, the symbol of the modern idea.

* * *

Conclusion[9]

[ART AS BURNING WITH A HARD, GEMLIKE FLAME]
Δέγει που Ἡράκλειτος ὅτι πάντα χωρεῖ καὶ οὐδὲν μένει[1]

To regard all things and principles of things as inconstant modes or fashions has more and more become the tendency of modern thought. Let us begin with that which is without—our physical life. Fix upon it in one of its more exquisite intervals, the moment, for instance, of delicious recoil from the flood of water in summer heat. What is the whole physical life in that moment but a combination of natural elements to which science gives their names? But these elements, phosphorus and lime and delicate fibres, are present not in the human body alone: we detect them in places most remote from it. Our physical life is a perpetual motion of them— the passage of the blood, the wasting and repairing of the lenses of the eye, the modification of the tissues of the brain by every ray of light and sound—processes which science reduces to simpler and more elementary forces. Like the elements of which we are composed, the action of these forces extends beyond us; it rusts iron and ripens corn. Far out on every side of us those elements are broadcast, driven by many forces; and birth and gesture and death

8. Italian Renaissance family known primarily for corruption and for the use of violence in the pursuit of power.
9. This brief "Conclusion" was omitted in the second edition of this book, as I conceived it might possibly mislead some of those young men into whose hands it might fall. On the whole, I have thought it best to reprint it here, with some slight changes which bring it closer to my original meaning. I have dealt more fully in *Marius the Epicurean* with the thoughts suggested by it [*Author*].
1. "Heraclitus says, 'All things are in movement and nothing still'" (Greek).

and the springing of violets from the grave are but a few out of ten thousand resultant combinations. That clear, perpetual outline of face and limb is but an image of ours, under which we group them—a design in a web, the actual threads of which pass out beyond it. This at least of flamelike our life has, that it is but the concurrence, renewed from moment to moment, of forces parting sooner or later on their ways.

Or if we begin with the inward world of thought and feeling, the whirlpool is still more rapid, the flame more eager and devouring. There it is no longer the gradual darkening of the eye and fading of colour from the wall,—the movement of the shore-side, where the water flows down indeed, though in apparent rest,—but the race of the mid-stream, a drift of momentary acts of sight and passion and thought. At first sight experience seems to bury us under a flood of external objects, pressing upon us with a sharp and importunate reality, calling us out of ourselves in a thousand forms of action. But when reflexion begins to act upon those objects they are dissipated under its influence; the cohesive force seems suspended like a trick of magic; each object is loosed into a group of impressions—colour, odour, texture—in the mind of the observer. And if we continue to dwell in thought on this world, not of objects in the solidity with which language invests them, but of impressions unstable, flickering, inconsistent, which burn and are extinguished with our consciousness of them, it contracts still further; the whole scope of observation is dwarfed to the narrow chamber of the individual mind. Experience, already reduced to a swarm of impressions, is ringed round for each one of us by that thick wall of personality through which no real voice has ever pierced on its way to us, or from us to that which we can only conjecture to be without. Every one of those impressions is the impression of the individual in his isolation, each mind keeping as a solitary prisoner its own dream of a world. Analysis goes a step farther still, and assures us that those impressions of the individual mind to which, for each one of us, experience dwindles down, are in perpetual flight; that each of them is limited by time, and that as time is infinitely divisible, each of them is infinitely divisible also; all that is actual in it being a single moment, gone while we try to apprehend it, of which it may ever be more truly said that it has ceased to be than that it is. To such a tremulous wisp constantly reforming itself on the stream, to a single sharp impression, with a sense in it, a relic more or less fleeting, of such moments gone by, what is real in our life fines itself down. It is with this movement, with the passage and dissolution of impressions, images, sensations, that analysis leaves off—that continual vanishing away, that strange, perpetual weaving and unweaving of ourselves.

Philosophiren, says Novalis, *ist dephlegmatisiren vivificiren*.[2] The service of philosophy, of speculative culture, towards the human spirit is to rouse, to startle it into sharp and eager observation. Every moment some form grows perfect in hand or face; some tone on the hills or the sea is choicer than the rest; some mood of passion or insight or intellectual excitement is irresistibly real and attractive for us,—for that moment only. Not the fruit of experience, but experience itself, is the end. A counted number of pulses only is given to us of a variegated, dramatic life. How may we see in them all that is to be seen in them by the finest senses? How shall we pass most swiftly from point to point, and be present always at the focus where the greatest number of vital forces unite in their purest energy?

To burn always with this hard, gemlike flame, to maintain this ecstasy, is success in life. In a sense it might even be said that our failure is to form habits: for, after all, habit is relative to a stereotyped world, and meantime it is only the roughness of the eye that makes any two persons, things, situations, seem alike. While all melts under our feet, we may well catch at any exquisite passion, or any contribution to knowledge that seems by a lifted horizon to set the spirit free for a moment, or any stirring of the senses, strange dyes, strange colours, and curious odours, or work of the artist's hands, or the face of one's friend. Not to discriminate every moment some passionate attitude in those about us, and in the brilliancy of their gifts some tragic dividing of forces on their ways, is, on this short day of frost and sun, to sleep before evening. With this sense of the splendour of our experience and of its awful brevity, gathering all we are into one desperate effort to see and touch, we shall hardly have time to make theories about the things we see and touch. What we have to do is to be for ever curiously testing new opinions and courting new impressions, never acquiescing in a facile orthodoxy of Comte, or of Hegel,[3] or of our own. Philosophical theories or ideas, as points of view, instruments of criticism, may help us to gather up what might otherwise pass unregarded by us. "Philosophy is the microscope of thought." The theory or idea or system which requires of us the sacrifice of any part of this experience, in consideration of some interest into which we cannot enter, or some abstract theory we have not identified with ourselves, or what is only conventional, has no real claim upon us.

2. "To philosophize is to dephlegmatize, to bring to life" (German).
3. Georg Wilhelm Friedrich Hegel (1770–1831), German philosopher who claimed that absolute knowledge involves deriving a higher unity from apparent contradictions. Auguste Comte (1798–1857), French thinker who developed the philosophy of positivism, which claims that only the scientific method, with its emphasis on observation, not on speculative thinking, yields authentic knowledge.

One of the most beautiful passages in the writings of Rousseau is that in the sixth book of the *Confessions*,[4] where he describes the awakening in him of the literary sense. An undefinable taint of death had always clung about him, and now in early manhood he believed himself smitten by mortal disease. He asked himself how he might make as much as possible of the interval that remained; and he was not biassed by anything in his previous life when he decided that it must be by intellectual excitement, which he found just then in the clear, fresh writings of Voltaire. Well! we are all *condamnés*, as Victor Hugo says:[5] we are all under sentence of death but with a sort of indefinite reprieve—*les hommes sont tous condamnés à mort avec des sursis indéfinis*: we have an interval, and then our place knows us no more. Some spend this interval in listlessness, some in high passions, the wisest, at least among "the children of this world," in art and song. For our one chance lies in expanding that interval, in getting as many pulsations as possible into the given time. Great passions may give us this quickened sense of life, ecstasy and sorrow of love, the various forms of enthusiastic activity, disinterested or otherwise, which come naturally to many of us. Only be sure it is passion—that it does yield you this fruit of a quickened, multiplied consciousness. Of this wisdom, the poetic passion, the desire of beauty, the love of art for art's sake, has most; for art comes to you professing frankly to give nothing but the highest quality to your moments as they pass, and simply for those moments' sake.

4. In his posthumously published *Confessions* (1782), the Swiss-born French philosopher Jean-Jacques Rousseau (1712–1778) focuses on the first fifty-three years of his life. In the sixth of the twelve main sections of this autobiography, Rousseau presents the illness that he suffered in 1736, which resulted in his undertaking extensive reading and study.
5. Pater is citing *Le Dernier Jour d'un Condamné* (*Last Days of a Condemned Man*; 1829), by the French writer Victor-Marie Hugo (1802–1885). Voltaire: the pen name of the iconoclastic French writer and philosopher François-Marie Arouet (1694–1778), who wrote the satirical narrative *Candide, ou l'Optimisme* (*Candide, or Optimism*; 1759).

OSCAR WILDE

The Picture of Dorian Gray†

Oscar Wilde (1854–1900) was the most successful Irish writer of the generation before Joyce's, until his career and fortunes were ruined when he was imprisoned in England after being convicted in 1895 for homosexual acts. Joyce, W. B. Yeats (see p. 299), and others who were Wilde's younger contemporaries were profoundly influenced by Wilde's life and his writings, which often meditate on art and the artist. The phrase "a portrait of the artist" occurs in the excerpt from the opening chapter of *The Picture of Dorian Gray* (1891) that is reprinted below. Among the volumes that Joyce owned in Trieste is a continental edition of Wilde's book in English published by Tauchnitz (1908). In an essay reprinted on p. 345 below, Hugh Kenner suggests that a pseudonym Wilde used late in life inspired the name Stephen Dedalus.

[*Wilde and His Characters on Realism, Romanticism, and the Artist*]

FROM THE PREFACE

> *The artist is the creator of beautiful things.*
> *To reveal art and conceal the artist is art's aim.*

* * *

> *The nineteenth century dislike of Realism is the rage of Caliban*
> *seeing his own face in a glass.*
> *The nineteenth century dislike of Romanticism is the rage of*
> *Caliban not seeing his own face in a glass.*[1]

FROM CHAPTER I

* * *

In the centre of the room, clamped to an upright easel, stood the full-length portrait of a young man of extraordinary personal beauty, and in front of it, some little distance away, was sitting the artist himself, Basil Hallward, whose sudden disappearance some years ago caused, at the time, such public excitement, and gave rise to so many strange conjectures.

As the painter looked at the gracious and comely form he had so skilfully mirrored in his art, a smile of pleasure passed across his face, and seemed about to linger there. But he suddenly started up,

---

† From *The Collected Edition of the Works of Oscar Wilde*, ed. Robert Ross. Vol. 12. *The Picture of Dorian Gray* (1891) (Paris: Charles Carrington Publisher and Bookseller, 1908), pp. ix, 2–7.
1. See note 1, p. 236.

and, closing his eyes, placed his fingers upon the lids, as though he sought to imprison within his brain some curious dream from which he feared he might awake.

'It is your best work, Basil, the best thing you have ever done,' said Lord Henry languidly. 'You must certainly send it next year to the Grosvenor. The Academy is too large and too vulgar. Whenever I have gone there, there have been either so many people that I have not been able to see the pictures, which was dreadful, or so many pictures that I have not been able to see the people, which was worse. The Grosvenor is really the only place.'

'I don't think I shall send it anywhere,' he answered, tossing his head back in that odd way that used to make his friends laugh at him at Oxford. 'No: I won't send it anywhere.'

Lord Henry elevated his eyebrows, and looked at him in amazement through the thin blue wreaths of smoke that curled up in such fanciful whorls from his heavy opium-tainted cigarette. 'Not send it anywhere? My dear fellow, why? Have you any reason? What odd chaps you painters are! You do anything in the world to gain a reputation. As soon as you have one, you seem to want to throw it away. It is silly of you, for there is only one thing in the world worse than being talked about, and that is not being talked about. A portrait like this would set you far above all the young men in England, and make the old men quite jealous, if old men are ever capable of any emotion.'

'I know you will laugh at me,' he replied, 'but I really can't exhibit it. I have put too much of myself into it.'

Lord Henry stretched himself out on the divan and laughed.

'Yes, I knew you would; but it is quite true, all the same.'

'Too much of yourself in it! Upon my word, Basil, I didn't know you were so vain; and I really can't see any resemblance between you, with your rugged strong face and your coal-black hair, and this young Adonis, who looks as if he was made out of ivory and rose-leaves. Why, my dear Basil, he is a Narcissus, and you—well, of course you have an intellectual expression, and all that. But beauty, real beauty, ends where an intellectual expression begins. Intellect is in itself a mode of exaggeration, and destroys the harmony of any face. The moment one sits down to think, one becomes all nose, or all forehead, or something horrid. Look at the successful men in any of the learned professions. How perfectly hideous they are! Except, of course, in the Church. But then in the Church they don't think. A bishop keeps on saying at the age of eighty what he was told to say when he was a boy of eighteen, and as a natural consequence he always looks absolutely delightful. Your mysterious young friend, whose name you have never told me, but whose picture really fascinates me, never thinks. I feel quite sure of that. He is some brainless, beautiful creature, who should be always here in winter when we have no flowers to look at, and always here in summer when we want something to chill our intelligence. Don't flatter yourself, Basil: you are not in the least like him.'

'You don't understand me, Harry,' answered the artist. 'Of course I am not like him. I know that perfectly well. Indeed, I should be sorry to look like him. You shrug your shoulders? I am telling you the truth. There is a fatality about all physical and intellectual distinction, the sort of fatality that seems to dog through history the faltering steps of kings. It is better not to be different from one's fellows. * * * Your rank and wealth, Harry; my brains, such as they are—my art, whatever it may be worth; Dorian Gray's good looks—we shall all suffer for what the gods have given us, suffer terribly.'

'Dorian Gray? Is that his name?' asked Lord Henry, walking across the studio towards Basil Hallward.

'Yes, that is his name. I didn't intend to tell it to you.'

* * *

After a pause, Lord Henry pulled out his watch. 'I am afraid I must be going, Basil,' he murmured, 'and before I go, I insist on your answering a question I put to you some time ago.'

'What is that?' said the painter, keeping his eyes fixed on the ground.

'You know quite well.'

'I do not, Harry.'

'Well, I will tell you what it is. I want you to explain to me why you won't exhibit Dorian Gray's picture. I want the real reason.'

'I told you the real reason.'

'No, you did not. You said it was because there was too much of yourself in it. Now, that is childish.'

'Harry,' said Basil Hallward, looking him straight in the face, 'every portrait that is painted with feeling is a portrait of the artist, not of the sitter. The sitter is merely the accident, the occasion. It is not he who is revealed by the painter; it is rather the painter who, on the coloured canvas, reveals himself. The reason I will not exhibit this picture is that I am afraid that I have shown in it the secret of my own soul.'

* * *

CRITICISM

Structural Overview of the Narrative

JOHN PAUL RIQUELME
The Parts and the Structural Rhythm of *A Portrait*†

The Parts

Like *Ulysses* and *Finnegans Wake*, *A Portrait* consists of untitled, unnumbered segments grouped into several parts designated by roman numerals. While the conventions of referring to the episodes of *Ulysses* by Homeric titles and to the chapters of the *Wake* by part and chapter numbers were adopted long ago, no similar convention has developed for *A Portrait*. To facilitate reference to specific sections and to indicate their particular placement within the sectional arrangement of the part, I provide the following scheme. Adopting a convention like that for citing chapters of the *Wake*, in my discussion of *A Portrait* I refer to sections by part and section numbers.

Part and Section	Designation	Lines
Part I		
I.1	Prelude	1–41
I.2	Clongowes (playing field; classroom; infirmary)	42–715
I.3	Christmas Dinner	716–1151
I.4	Broken Glasses (smugging; writing lesson, pandybat; rector)	1152–1848

† Revised and elaborated from *Teller and Tale in Joyce's Fiction: Oscillating Perspectives* (Baltimore and London: Johns Hopkins UP, 1983), pp. 232–34. © 1983 Johns Hopkins University Press. Reprinted with permission of Johns Hopkins University Press.

The Structural Rhythm

Besides giving brief numerical designations to the sections of *A Portrait*, this schema provides some evidence for a conjecture about the structural rhythm of Joyce's arrangement. A peculiar sort of unity of effect arises from the juxtaposing of fragmented narrative segments. Part of that unity can be traced to expansions and contractions of narrative focus that become a defining configuration for our experience of the text. My conjecture can be translated into structural terms simply by examining the lengths of the various parts and sections. From such an examination we can describe the narrative structure as made up of three units. The first consists of the first three parts, each of about the same length. The second unit is the climactic fourth part, by far the shortest one, about half the length of any of the three preceding parts. The final unit is the fifth part, by far the longest one, nearly twice as long as Part II, the briefest of the first three.

I emphasize these proportions because they are also the proportions of the narrative configuration of Part V. The unusually long V.1 (longer even than Part II), with its heterogeneous mix of scenes, memories, and dialogues, is the equivalent for the first unit of the larger narrative. The writing of the villanelle, V.2, corresponds to the climactic second unit, Part IV. The talk with Cranly and the journal, V.3 and V.4, provide a denouement, as does all of Part V in the larger scheme. The narrative structure of V, then, duplicates the structure of the entire book. * * *

Joyce stresses this duplicated configuration, one structure nesting within the conclusion of the other, by the way he frames the climaxes of the book and of Part V. In both cases, the sections preceding and following the climactic segments are clearly linked. III.3 presents Stephen in the kitchen of his home idealizing and contemplating with anticipation the food that will be his breakfast after Communion the next morning. In V.1 he is again presented in the kitchen eating a greasy breakfast before leaving belatedly for his classes at the university. * * * V.1 ends and V.3 begins with Stephen on the steps in front of the library. In between the two similar scenes of V, he has decided to break with his past and to leave Ireland. Both climaxes act as intervening segments explaining the transformation that has occurred. * * *

Both the large arrangement of sections and the details framing the climactic portions of the narrative contribute to the structural rhythm and duplication. * * *

My division of the narrative into titled sections responds to Kenneth Burke's suggestion, in "Fact, Inference, and Proof in the Analysis of Literary Symbolism"[1] that the parts be treated as titled "substages." He asks what titles would be appropriate for the five numbered parts, suggesting as possibilities "Childhood Sensibility," "The Fall," "The Sermon," "The New Vocation" (or "Epiphany"), and "The New Doctrine." Burke also comments on the book's structural centers, its quantitative midpoint in the sermon, and its center of narrative reversal, which I call its climax, in Part IV.

1. In *Terms for Order*, ed. Stanley Edgar Hyman (Bloomington: Indiana UP, 1964), 145–72.

Essays in Criticism

HUGH KENNER

Joyce's *Portrait*—A Reconsideration[†]

What you are about to read is a summary of conclusions, without a great deal of evidence. I assume that by now the evidence is pretty familiar. The Joyce canon is not very large, and certainly *A Portrait of the Artist as a Young Man* has been read by everyone not hopelessly given over to the supposition that the novel ceased with Bulwer-Lytton.[1]

I am coming back to it, as I do from time to time, because, fifteen years after I first wrote an essay about it, I still think it is the key to the entire Joyce operation, though I hope I know more about it by now than I did when I wrote my essay. I am not going to deal in local explanations; what I have done along that line is in print, and whoever is interested can find it, while those who are not need not be disturbed.[2] I am simply going to try to describe, as fully and carefully as I can, what the *Portrait* seems to be.

It has been supposed from the beginning that about this at least there is no mystery; for does not the title tell us that it is the portrait of the artist as a young man? To which I think it relevant to answer, that if we are to take this title at its face value, then it is unique among Joyce titles; and since it is too long a title to be printed conveniently upon the spine of a shortish novel—the sort of detail to which Joyce could always be relied on to pay attention—he must have wanted all those words for a purpose, and we had better look at them pretty carefully.

The first thing to be noticed, I think, is that the title imposes a pictorial and spatial analogy, an expectation of static repose, on a book in which nothing except the spiritual life of Dublin stands still: a book of fluid transitions in which the central figure is

---

† From *The University of Windsor Review* 1:1 (Spring 1965): 1–15. Reprinted by permission of *Windsor Review* and the Estate of Hugh Kenner. Notes are by the editor of this Norton Critical Edition.
1. Edward Bulwer-Lytton (1803–1873), English novelist and playwright.
2. The earlier essay, which has been widely reprinted, is "The *Portrait* in Perspective," in Kenner's *Dublin's Joyce* (Bloomington: Indiana UP, 1956), 109–33.

growing older by the page. The book is a becoming, which the title tells us to apprehend as a being. I shall have more to say about this in a moment; let me first draw attention to two more things we may notice in the title. One of them is this, that it has the same grammatical form as "A Portrait of the Merchant as a Young Man" or "A Portrait of the Blacksmith as a Young Man." It succeeds in not wholly avowing that the Artist in question is the same being who painted the portrait; it permits us to suppose that he may be the generic artist, the artistic type, the sort of person who sets up as an artist, or acts the artist, or is even described by irreverent friends as The Artist. I do not press this theme, though I shall later extract a consequence or two from it. The third thing the title says is that we have before us a Portrait of the Artist *as a Young Man*. Now there is a clear analogy here, and the analogy is with Rembrandt, who painted self-portraits nearly every year of his life beginning in his early twenties. Like most Joycean analogies, however, it is an analogy with a difference, because the painter of self-portraits looks in a mirror, but the writer of such a novel as we have before us must look in the mirror of memory. A Rembrandt portrait of the artist at twenty-two shows the flesh of twenty-two and the features of twenty-two as portrayed by the hand of twenty-two and interpreted by the wisdom of twenty-two. Outlook and insight, subject and perception, feed one another in a little oscillating node of objectified introspection, all locked into an eternalized present moment. What that face knows, that painter knows, and no more. The canvas holds the mirror up to a mirror, and it is not surprising that this situation should have caught the attention of an Irish genius, since the mirror facing a mirror, the book that contains a book, the book (like *A Tale of a Tub*) which is about a book which is itself, or the book (like *Malone Dies*) which is a history of the writing both of itself and of another book like itself, or the poem (like "The Phases of the Moon")[3] which is about people who are debating whether to tell the poet things he put into their heads when he created them, and are debating this, moreover, while he is in the very act of writing the poem about their debate: this theme, "mirror on mirror mirroring all the show," has been since at least Swift's time the inescapable mode of the Irish literary imagination, which is happiest when it can subsume ethical notions into an epistemological comedy. So far so good; but Joyce, as usual, has brooded on the theme a great deal longer than is customary, and has not been arrested, like Swift or Samuel

3. Dialogue poem published in *The Wild Swans at Coole* (1919), by the Irish writer W. B. Yeats (see p. 299). *A Tale of a Tub:* prose satire (published 1704) by the Irish writer Jonathan Swift (1667–1745). *Malone Dies:* the middle work in a trilogy of novels by the Irish writer Samuel Beckett (1906–1989); originally published in French as *Malone Muert* (1951), then in the author's English translation in 1956.

Beckett or even Yeats, by the surface neatness of a logical antinomy.
For it inheres in his highly individual application of Rembrandt's
theme, that the Portrait of the Artist as a Young Man can only be
painted by an older man, if older only by the time it takes to write the
book. Joyce was careful to inform us at the bottom of the last page
of this book that it took ten years. We have a Portrait, then, the subject of which ages from birth to twenty years within the picture space,
while the artist has lived through ten more years in the course of
painting it.

There follows a conclusion of capital importance: that we shall
look in vain for analogies to the two principal conventions of a normal portrait, the static subject and the static viewpoint, those data
from which all Renaissance theories of painting derive. The one
substantial revision I would want to make in the essay on this book
I wrote in 1947 is its title; I entitled it "The *Portrait* in Perspective,"
and the more I think about the matter now the more I see that the
analogies of perspective are simply inapplicable. The laws of perspective place painter and subject in an exact geometrical relation
to one another, in space and by analogy in time; but here they are
both of them moving, one twice as fast as the other. The *Portrait*
may well be the first piece of cubism in the history of art.

I have already hinted that a few of the topics on which we have
come already will require further development; so I am not really
through with the title yet. But let us open the book and see what we
discover. We discover, behind and around the central figure, what
Wyndham Lewis[4] described as a swept and tidied naturalism, and
nowhere more completely than in the places, the accessory figures,
the sights and sounds, the speeches and the names. Joyce is famous
for his meticulous care with fact; "he is a bold man," he once wrote,
"who will venture to alter what he has seen and heard." He used, in
Dubliners and *Ulysses*, the names of real people, so often that their
concerted determination to sue him the minute he should step off
the boat became, I think, an implacable efficient cause for his long
exile from Ireland, which commenced virtually on the eve of the
publication of *Dubliners*. The BBC had an unfortunate experience
a few years ago, when they broadcast in all innocence a radio tran-
scription of the funeral episode in *Ulysses*, with its story about the
pawnbroker Reuben J. Dodd, whose son was fished out of the Liffey
by a boatman. Father rewarded the boatman with two shillings, and
someone comments, "One and eightpence too much." A few days
later there arrived at Broadcasting House a letter signed "Reuben
J. Dodd, Jr." Since one does not receive letters from fictional

---

4. Percy Wyndam Lewis (1882–1957), Canadian-born writer and painter who spent his
   career mainly in England.

characters, the BBC dismissed it as a joke, until they were persuaded, to their heavy cost, that it was no joke. It is clear that for
Joyce authenticity of detail was of overriding moment. If actual
names were artistically correct, he used them at whatever risk. If
they were not, he supplied better ones, but always plausible ones.
So far so good. And what stares us in the face wherever we open the
first sustained narrative of this ferocious and uncompromising realist? Why, a name like a huge smudged fingerprint: the most implau-
sible name that could conceivably be devised for an inhabitant of
lower-class Catholic Dublin: a name that no accident of immigra-
tion, no freak of etymology, no canon of naturalism however
stretched, can justify: the name of Stephen Dedalus.

It seems to me very odd that we accept this name without protest; it is given to no eccentric accessory figure, but to the central
character himself, the subject of the *Portrait*. But I cannot see that
it has ever had the sort of effect Joyce must have intended: he must
have meant it to arrest speculation at the outset, detaching the central figure at once from the conventions of quiet naturalism. What
has happened instead is instructive: for Joyce is the best case available of the principle that the history of the reception of a writer's
works is one of the basic data of criticism. Joyce himself, as the
Satanic antinomian,[5] attracted attention as soon as the book did,
and far more strongly; it was at once assumed that the book was
nothing more than a thinly veiled autobiography. It was a natural
assumption from this premise, that the author treated his early self
with considerable indulgence, especially since the Stephen of the
Portrait seemed clearly destined to turn into the man Joyce was
supposed to be. So it seemed clear that the name of Stephen Dedalus should be scrutinized for a piece of indulgent symbolism: and
indeed it yields this symbolism quite readily, the strange name a figure of prophecy, prophecy of light and escape, and fabulous artifice.

Now it is true that Joyce exploits the symbolism of the name, in
the latter part of the book; but if we could somehow get Joyce himself
out of our minds for a moment, and consider the early part of the
book on the terms it seems to impose, we should see a central figure
with a name so odd it seems a pseudonym. And indeed it seems to
have been modelled on a pseudonym. It combines a Christian martyr with a fabulous artificer. I think it very likely that it was based
on another name constructed in the same way, a name adopted by
a famous Irishman which also combines a Christian martyr with
a fabulous wanderer. The model, I think, is the name Sebastian

---

5. Adhering to the doctrine of antinomianism, which maintains that salvation comes
   through faith and divine grace, not through obedience to laws.

Melmoth, which was adopted during the brief time of his continental exile by the most lurid Dubliner of them all, Oscar Wilde.

Wilde built his pseudonym of exile deliberately. Sebastian—Saint Sebastian—may be described as the fashionable martyr of 19th-century aestheticism. Melmoth—*Melmoth the Wanderer*—was the hero of a novel written 80 years before by yet another Irish romancer, Charles Maturin. The two names joined the Christian and the pagan, the sufferer and the exile; in combination they vibrate with a heavy mysterious exoticism, linking Wilde with the creed of beleaguered beauty and with the land of his ancestors, affirming at the same time something richer and stranger about this shuffling Irish scapegoat than would seem possible, in Wilde's view, to a countryman of people with names like Casey, Sullivan, and Moonan. It is a haunting homeless name, crying for exegesis, deliberately assumed by a haunted, homeless man. He was a man, furthermore, in whom Joyce did not fail to see enacted one of his own preoccupations, the artist as scapegoat for middle-class rectitude. And in modelling, as I believe he did, the name of the hero of his novel on the pseudonym of the fallen Wilde, Joyce was, I believe, deliberately invoking the Wildean parallel.

To give this remark a context, let me now say as plainly as possible what I think the *Portrait* is. The *Portrait* is a sort of Euclidean demonstration,[6] in five parts, of how a provincial capital—for instance Dublin, though Toronto or Melbourne would do—goes about converting unusual talent into formlessly clever bohemianism. This demonstration is completed in *Ulysses*, when the bourgeois misfit *par excellence* turns out to be the bohemian's spiritual father. (The principle, by the way, that underlies the spiritual paternity of Bloom and Stephen is the simple and excellent scholastic maxim that opposites belong to the same species.) Now Dublin, by the time Joyce came to look back on the process to which he had barely escaped falling victim, had already extruded the arch-bohemian of a generation, Oscar Wilde, and Wilde had completed the Icarian myth by falling forever. If we are going to be consistent about the symbolism of names, it should be clear that Stephen is the son of Dedalus, and what the son of Dedalus did was fall. It seems clear that Joyce sees Stephen as a figure who is going to fall, not as a figure who is going to turn into the author himself. It is in *Ulysses*, of course, that we last see Stephen, aged twenty-two; and I think it significant that Joyce remarked one day to Frank Budgen,[7] while he was engaged on the figure of Leopold Bloom in *Ulysses*, that Stephen no longer interested

6. A logical proof involving deductive principles and clearly defined axioms, as in the geometric proofs by the Greek mathematician Euclid (c. 325–265 BCE).
7. English painter (1882–1971), who wrote *James Joyce and the Making of "Ulysses"* (1934), based on conversations with Joyce.

him as Bloom did; for Stephen, he said, "has a shape that can't be changed." This seems decisive; but let us go back to Wilde a moment. It is, to put it plainly, possible if not sufficient to regard the *Portrait* as a lower-class Catholic parallel to Wilde's upper-class Protestant career.

This idea, for all the attention that has been devoted to Joyce's work, remains absurdly unfamiliar. Let me expand it. I am not arguing that Joyce hated Stephen, or could not bear Stephen, or was satirizing Stephen. I am merely pointing out that Joyce, though he used everything usable from his own experience, was creating all the time a character not himself, so little resembling himself that he may well have been suggested by the notoriety of a famous compatriot who had died only a few years before the first version of the book was begun. One of the incidents for which even the careful researches of Mr. Kevin Sullivan[8] have turned up no prototype whatever, the caning of Stephen by schoolfellows because he refuses to "admit that Byron was no good," may even have been contrived as an Irish parallel to the famous indignities Wilde suffered at Oxford.

I have said that Joyce used everything usable from his own experience to create a character not himself. Now the evidence multiplies, as biographical trivia come to light, that Joyce did this with all his characters; but the party line of Joyce exegesis is wonderfully accommodating. When we learn, as I learned recently from an eyewitness of the Paris years, that he liked grilled kidneys for breakfast, we at once remember the familiar opening lines of the second section of *Ulysses*: "Mr. Leopold Bloom ate with relish the inner organs of beasts and fowls. . . . Most of all he liked grilled mutton kidneys, which gave to his palate a fine tang of faintly scented urine." This would seem to be a clear example of Joyce's way of using any detail that was handy, including, or especially, the most intimate trivia of his own existence, in the process of building from the inside a fictional creation. But this is not what we are normally told. When such details come to light the analogy of Stephen is trotted out. Stephen shares many experiences and attitudes with his author, because Stephen is Joyce. Now here is Bloom sharing characteristics with his author, therefore Bloom is Joyce. Mr. Ellmann actually commits himself (p. 369) to the judgment that Bloom is Joyce's mature persona, and avers (p. 309) that the movement of *Ulysses* "is to bring Stephen, the young Joyce, into *rapport* with Bloom, the mature Joyce."[9]

It is surely wiser to work the analogy of Stephen the other way. If Bloom shares characteristics with Joyce and is plainly not Joyce,

8. Kevin P. Sullivan, *Joyce among the Jesuits* (New York: Columbia UP, 1958).
9. Richard Ellmann, *James Joyce* (New York: Oxford UP, 1959).

then Stephen, merely because he shares characteristics with Joyce, is not necessarily Joyce either.

I sketch this argument because it seems to be called for, not because I think it especially enlightening. If we want to know what Joyce is doing with the character called Stephen, we shall arrive at nothing conclusive by checking our impressions against the evidence of what he does with Leopold Bloom, simply because Leopold Bloom is—like Stephen himself, for that matter—a special case. He is a special case because he is so greatly elaborated; one would expect a good number of the author's own characteristics to find their way into the portrait of Bloom simply because so many small characteristics are needed for the presentation of a character on such a scale. The people who turn up in the short stories provide a much better control group. Can we find in *Dubliners* any useful prototypes of Stephen Dedalus, useful because formed in a similar way, but so controlled by the smaller scale and the unchanging viewpoint that we may have less trouble deciding what they are meant to signify? The answer is that we can find a great many.

There is Mr. James Duffy, for instance, in "A Painful Case." Mr. Duffy has been endowed with the author's Christian name, and a surname with just as many letters in it as there are in Joyce. (This is a tiny point, to be sure, but Joyce was a great counter of letters.) He has moved out of Dublin, though it is true that he has not moved far, only as far as suburban Chapelizod. He elected Chapelizod because he found all the other suburbs of Dublin "mean, modern and pretentious." He is a man obsessed with ideas of order, with pattern, symmetry, classification: he expresses these impulses by, among other things, the care with which he arranges his books. Like his creator, who kept a notebook headed "Epiphanies," he keeps on his desk a sheaf of papers headed "Bile Beans," held together by a brass pin, and in these papers he inscribes from time to time a sorrowful or sardonic epigram. The woman with whom he attempts to strike up a relationship is named Mrs. Sinico, which was the name of a singing teacher Joyce frequented in Trieste. He has even translated *Michael Kramer*, as Joyce had done in the summer of 1901. The manuscript of his translation is exceptionally tidy: the stage directions are written in purple ink. And he listens, as did the author of *Exiles* and of the final pages of *Finnegans Wake*, to "the strange impersonal voice which he recognized as his own, insisting on the soul's incurable loneliness. We cannot give ourselves, it said: we are our own." "Ourselves, oursouls, alone," echoes Anna Livia across thirty years. Mr. Duffy, in short, is A Portrait of the Artist as Dublin Bank-clerk.

Or consider Jimmy Doyle, in "After the Race," whose name is Jimmy Joyce's with only two letters altered. Jimmy Doyle, who

352 HUGH KENNER

becomes infatuated with continental swish and hangs around racing drivers, owes detail after detail of his taste for the anti-Dublin to the life of Jimmy Joyce, who even made a few shillings during his first bleak winter in Paris by interviewing a French motor-racing driver for the *Irish Times*. Or consider Little Chandler in "A Little Cloud," with his taste for Byron, his yearning after a literary career, his poverty, his fascination with escape from Dublin, his wife and baby. Almost every detail of his story has its source in the author's life. Or consider finally Gabriel Conroy, in "The Dead."

Gabriel Conroy, who is sick of his own country and has "visited not a few places abroad," who writes book reviews, as did Joyce, for the *Daily Express*, teaches language, as did Joyce, parts his hair in the middle, as did Joyce, wears rimmed glasses, as did Joyce, clings to petty respectabilities, as did Joyce, has taken a wife from the savage bogs of the west counties, as did Joyce, snubs people unexpectedly, as did Joyce, and is eternally preoccupied, as was Joyce, with the notion that his wife has had earlier lovers: Gabriel Conroy, attending a festivity in a house that belonged to Joyce's great-aunts, and restive in his patent-leather cosmopolitanism among the provincials of the capital by the Liffey, is pretty clearly modelled on his author by rather the same sort of process that was later to produce Stephen Dedalus.

There is nothing original in these observations, and we have not by any means exhausted the list of Joycean shadow-selves who turn up in these strangely intimate stories. But when we find them in the stories, instead of in an equivocally autobiographical novel, we can see more clearly what they are. They are not the author, they are potentialities contained within the author. They are what he has not become.

The sharpest exegetical instrument to bring to the work of Joyce is Aristotle's great conception of potency and act. Joyce's awareness of it, his concern with it, is what distinguishes him from every other writer who has used the conventions of naturalism. Naturalist fiction as it was developed in France was based on scientific positivism, its conviction that realities are bounded by phenomena, persons by behaviour, that what seems is, and that what *is* must be. But Joyce is always concerned with multiple possibilities. For a Zola, a Maupassant, a Flaubert,[1] it is simply meaningless to consider what might have been; for since it was not, it is meaningless to *say* that it might have been. In the mind of Joyce, however, there hung a radiant field of potentialities: ways in which a man may go,

1. The French novelists Émile Zola (1840–1902), Guy de Maupassant (1850–1893), and Gustave Flaubert (1821–1880). All were naturalists, in the sense that they presented everyday realities in believable ways.

and correspondingly selves he may become, bounding himself in one form or another while remaining the same person in the eyes of God. The events of history, Stephen considers in *Ulysses,* are branded by time and hung fettered "in the room of the infinite possibilities they have ousted." Pathos, the dominant or subdominant Joycean emotion, inheres in the inspection of such limits: men longing to become what they can never be, though it lies in them to be it, simply because they have become something else.

All potentiality is bounded by alien and circumstantial limits. The people in *Dubliners* are thwarted, all of them, by the limitation of potentiality the city imposes. They sense this, all of them, and yearn to remove themselves, but in their yearning they are subjected to another scholastic axiom, that we cannot desire what we do not know. If they have notions of what it would be like to live another way, in another place, they confect these notions out of what Dublin makes available. The story called "A Little Cloud" presents the counter-Dublin in what is unmistakeably Dublin's image, a roisterer and journalist named Ignatius Gallagher, who incarnates for Little Chandler the possibility of liberation. But Ignatius Gallagher himself is simply fulfilling Dublin appetites, and enacting Dublin tavern images of rebelliousness. The story called "Eveline" posits this theme still more sharply. Eveline's token of escape is a sailor called Frank, which is just the right name for him. Frank is "kindly, manly, open-hearted," like a stage sailor, and when Eveline's father says "I know these sailor chaps" he is probably right. There is nothing discernible in Frank that is not part of the stock-in-trade of the Dublin common dream, as enacted in the music-halls every night. Having said this, we should go on to say (1) that all our knowledge of Frank comes through Eveline, and (2) that we cannot really say that Eveline sees Frank at all; she sees a kind of approximation to Frank, assembled out of a list of characteristics—kindness, manliness, openheartedness, etc.—with which Dublin has supplied her. So the Frank she considers fleeing with is a chimera of her own mind, and in refusing to decide to flee, in fearing Frank, she is refusing herself, fearing herself. "Eveline" is another of those Irish mirror-stories of which we were speaking. If Frank, or the image of Frank, is the counter-Dublin, he is the counter-Dublin made in her imagination out of pieces of Dublin, which is all her imagination has to work with. And opposites belong to the same species. That is why Stephen says, in *Ulysses,* that if Socrates step forth from his house today, it is to Socrates that his steps will tend.

I hope no one thinks that I am forgetting Stephen Dedalus all this time. I am supplying a context for all those people in *Dubliners* who resemble the author, so as to supply in turn a context for the

ways in which Stephen Dedalus resembles the author. At every
moment of his life, the author, like anyone else in Dublin or anywhere else, was confronted with decisions and choices, courses of
conduct elected or not elected; and each of these in turn, branches,
if he elects it, into a whole branching family of further courses, or
if he does not elect it, branches into a whole different family of
branching courses. If the nose on Cleopatra's face had been shorter,
the destiny of the world would have altered; if the swan had not
come to Leda, Troy would not have fallen, nor Homer educated
Greece, nor Greece Rome, and we should none of us perhaps exist.
So there lies before a man an indefinitely large potentiality of
events he may set in motion, ways he may go, and selves he may
become. But each way, each self, each branching upon a branch, is
supplied by Dublin; so the field, however large, is closed. In Dublin
one can only become a Dubliner; a Dubliner in exile, since the exile
was elected from within Dublin and is situated along one of the
many paths leading out of Dublin and so connected to Dublin, is a
Dubliner still. Even refusing Dublin is a Dublin stratagem.

He contains, then, within him, multitudes. All the people in
Dubliners are people he might have been, all imprisoned in devious
ways by the city, all come to terms of some sort with it, all meeting
or refusing shadow-selves who taunt them with the spectre of yet
another course once possible but possible now no longer. *Dubliners*
is a portrait of the artist as many men. And it foreruns the more
famous *Portrait* in one other aspect also, that while it has one subject the subject does not stay still in time. The boy in the first story,
"The Sisters," does not become Gabriel Conroy, but he might. Eveline does not become Maria in "Clay," but she might. Bob Doran in
"The Boarding-House" does not become Little Chandler in "A
Little Cloud," but he might. And none of the men becomes James
Joyce, nor none of the women Nora Joyce, but they might: they contain those potentialities. It is only by a fantastic series of accidents
that anyone becomes what he does become, and though he can be
only what he is, he can look back along the way he has come, testing it for branching-points now obsolete.

So the subject of *Dubliners* is a single subject, metamorphosing
along many lines of potentiality as the circle of light directed by the
story-teller moves through time, picking out, successively, a small
boy of the time when he was himself a small boy, or adolescents of
the time when he was an adolescent. Each story obeys, or seems to
obey, the pictorial convention of a fixed perspective, subject and
viewer set in place until the work of portrayal is finished. The book,
however, is a succession of such pictures; or better, it is the trace of
a moving subject, seen from a moving viewpoint which is always
very close to him.

And if we apply this account to *A Portrait of the Artist as a Young Man* we shall find that it applies exactly: the moving point of view, product not only of a book ten years in the writing but of a standpoint which remains close to the subject as he moves; the moving subject, passing from infancy forward for twenty years; and the subject himself a potentiality drawn from within the author, the most fully developed of the alternative selves he projected over a long life with such careful labor. If the differences between Stephen and Joyce seem small, all differences are small, and it is always small differences that are decisive. One has only to accept or refuse a causal opportunity, and the curve of one's life commences a long slow bending away from what it otherwise would have been. This line of argument is not only Aristotelian[2] but wholly familiar to a man brought up, like Joyce, in a climate of clerical exhortation. From the time he could first remember hearing human words, he must have listened to hundreds of homilies, ruminations, admonitions, developing the principle that it is the little sins that prepare the habit great sins will later gratify, or that the destiny of the soul is prepared in early youth, so that there is nothing that does not matter.

So Stephen is a perfectly normal Joyce character, not the intimate image of what Joyce in fact was, but a figure generated according to a way of working that came naturally to him in a hundred ways. Stephen, unlike a character in *Dubliners*, is followed with unflagging attention for twenty years instead of being exhibited as he was during the course of a few hours. But like the characters in *Dubliners*, who also do many things Joyce did, he also leaves undone many other things Joyce did, and does many things Joyce did not. And these, if you accept my account of Joyce's way of thinking on human destiny, are not trivial divergences, but precisely the many small points of decision that make him Stephen and not Joyce.

And, to recapitulate further, Joyce was fascinated by the way Dublin contrives to maintain its life-long hold on its denizens. He himself made no pretence of having escaped the city, except in body; he remained so thoroughly a Dubliner that he kept in repair to the last his knowledge of the shops and streets, pressing visitors from the distant town for news of civic alterations, or carefully making note of the fact that such-and-such a place of business had changed hands. Stephen's talk of flying by nets of language, nationality, religion, remains—Stephen's talk. One does not fly by Dublin's

---

2. In accordance with the thinking of the Greek philosopher Aristotle (384–322 BCE), with regard to potential and act, mentioned earlier in the essay, and the logical relation of cause to effect.

nets, though the illusion that one may fly by them may be one of Dublin's sorts of birdlime.

Once we are in possession of the formula for Stephen, his many little points of divergence from his creator cease to point toward mysterious formal requirements. Stephen is a young man rather like Joyce, who imagines that he is going to put the city behind him; he is going to fly, like Shelley's skylark; and he is going to fall into cold water, like Icarus, or like Oscar Wilde. Given this formula, Joyce used everything he could find or remember that was relevant, all the time fabricating liberally in order to simplify and heighten a being whose entire emotional life is in fact an act of ruthless simplification. Consider the famous retreat, and the hell-fire sermon which scares Stephen into the only act of capitulation he is ever to make to a priesthood which rules by fear. Mr. Kevin Sullivan, in a very careful investigation of Joyce's time at Belvedere, has showed that if we try to fit the events of the book into the author's life the chronology is impossible. The retreat, for instance, is represented as occurring in 1898 (when December 3 fell on a Saturday), and in 1898 James Joyce was not a secondary schoolboy but a college freshman. Mr. Sullivan also notes that for James Joyce "a Jesuit retreat was neither a terrifying nor a unique experience," since during his Belvedere school years he made at least five of them. And the familiar notion of phrases from a scarifying sermon burning themselves on the appalled young Joyce's mind, to be reproduced years later by Joyce the artist in a paroxysm of stupefied recall, rather dies away when we are shown, with a table of parallel passages, Joyce the artist constructing the sermon in cold blood from the Sodality Manual, a book which would have been his *vade mecum*[3] during the two years when, on account of his intellectual and spiritual eminence, he served as prefect of the Sodality. And these are the years to which, if we insist on believing the *Portrait* (or for that matter the recollections of people who recalled the *Portrait* more vividly than they did their own half-century-old impressions) we must assign him a time of wallowing in brothels. Another writer has since shown that while the passages Mr. Sullivan cites from the Sodality Manual are very close, a certain hell-fire pamphlet[4] that was circulating in Dublin at the turn of the century is even closer; the more reason, of course, to doubt that a set of rhetorical commonplaces would have affected Joyce as they are supposed to have affected Stephen.

---

3. Guidebook that would be constantly available; literally "go with me" (Latin). "Sodality Manual": the manual of the devotional fellowship, or sodality, used at Belvedere College.
4. Pinamonti's *Hell Opened to Christians* (see p. 317).

I have a last observation to make, which concerns Joyce's tone. I am always a little surprised to find myself cited, from time to time, as the bellwether of the Stephen-hating school of critics. It is clear that Stephen is not hateful, though he is irritating when he is being put forth by the massed proprietors of the Joyce Legend as an authentic genius. Considered as a genius, he is a tedious cliché, weary, disdainful, sterile; he writes an exceedingly conventional poem in the idiom of the empurpled nineties, indeed a poem Wilde might well have admired, one which seems unlikely to pass beyond the nineties. He has, as Joyce said, a shape that can't be changed.

Or has by the end of the book. But when we were first considering the title of the book, we noticed that the title imposes a look of pictorial repose on a subject constantly changing. We noticed, too, the author's announcement, on the last line of the last page, that he had spent fully ten years revolving the subject and revising and re-revising the writing. As we observed that we had a Portrait with a difference, neither subject nor artist united in a normal geometrical relationship. This is the last thing I want to stress. What we normally call "tone" is the product of a fixed relationship between writer and material. It is the exact analogy of perspective in painting. Its two familiar modes are utter sympathy and sustained irony. Irony says, "I see very well what is going on here, and I know how to value it." But Joyce's view of Stephen is not ironic; it is not determined by a standpoint of immovable superiority. Sympathy says, "Withhold your judgment; if you undervalue this man you will offend *me*." Joyce's view of Stephen is not sympathetic either, by which I mean that it is not defensive, or self-defensive. Like a Chinese painter, or a mediaeval painter, Joyce expects our viewpoint to move as the subject moves. We are detached from Stephen, we comprehend his motions and emotions, we are not to reject him nor defend him, nor feel a kind of embarrassment on the writer's behalf. We have not "irony," we have simply the truth. This is so until the end. At the end, when Stephen's development ceases, when he passes into, or has very nearly passed into, the shape that can't be changed, then he is troubling; and we sense, I think, a little, Joyce deliberately withholding judgment.

It is a terrible, a shaking story; and it brings Stephen where so many other potential Joyces have been brought, into a fixed rôle, into nothing; into paralysis, frustration, or a sorry, endlessly painful, coming to terms: for the best of them, a meditating on restful symbols, as Gabriel Conroy, stretched out in living death beside his wife, turns to the snow, or as Leopold Bloom, in the room of his cuckolding, thinks on the intellectual pleasures of water. For all the potential selves we can imagine stop short of what we are, and this is true however little we may be satisfied with what we are.

Dubliner after Dubliner suffers panic, thinks to escape, and accepts paralysis. It is the premise of the most sensitive of them, as it is for Stephen Dedalus, that the indispensable thing is to escape. It was Joyce's fortune that having carried through Stephen's resolve and having escaped, he saw the exile he accepted as the means of being more thoroughly a Dubliner, a citizen of the city that cannot be escaped but need not be obliterated from the mind. He celebrated it all his life, and projected the moods through which he had passed, and for which he retained an active sympathy, into fictional characters for each of whom the drab city by the Liffey, whatever else it is, is nothing at all to celebrate.

JOHN PAUL RIQUELME

[Dedalus and Joyce Writing the Book of Themselves]†

> The genius in the act of artistic generation . . . is miraculously like the uncanny fairy tale figure that can roll its eyes inward to observe itself, becoming simultaneously subject and object, at once author, actor, and spectator.
> —Nietzsche, *The Birth of Tragedy*

Oscillating Perspective

In my commentary on *Finnegans Wake*, I explain how Joyce provides the reader in various ways with the means for achieving an oscillating perspective. That perspective is a viewpoint for reading that vacillates between mutually defining poles, just as our perception of the relation between figure and ground in some optical illusions may shift. The vacillating viewpoint is available in Joyce's writing much earlier than the *Wake*, as early, in fact, as *A Portrait of the Artist as a Young Man*. Joyce creates it through style in the continuing refinement of his techniques for rendering consciousness that he develops during the writing of *Dubliners* and *Stephen Hero*. The subtle intermingling of third- and first-person perspectives that Joyce effects in *A Portrait* is the most significant change in the style of his autobiographical work, one that differentiates it clearly from *Stephen Hero*. The mixing of narrator's and character's

---

† Abridged and slightly revised from *Teller and Tale in Joyce's Fiction: Oscillating Perspectives* (Baltimore and London: Johns Hopkins UP, 1983), pp. 48–64, 250–52. © 1983 Johns Hopkins University Press. Reprinted with permission of Johns Hopkins University Press. Page references have been replaced with part and line numbers of this Norton Critical Edition. Some cited passages might differ slightly from the equivalent passages in this volume. Epigraph translated by the editor of this Norton Critical Edition from Friedrich Nietzsche, *Nietzsche's Werke, Erste Abteilung. Band I. Die Geburt der Tragoedie*. Fritz Kroegel, ed. Leipzig: C. G. Naumann, 1895.

views and voices in *A Portrait*, which is prepared for by aspects of *Dubliners*, will become the given of *Ulysses*, the stylistic element the later work starts with, deviates from, then returns to in "Penelope." It is also an early step toward the radical superimposing of voices in *Finnegans Wake*.

In addition, Joyce encourages the oscillating perspective in *A Portrait* by constructing his narrative to avoid the pretense that his narration is a transparent vehicle for plot. He eschews that pretense through subverting the conventions of realism. Generally speaking, in fiction those conventions, including a single telling voice or style and a coherent chronological presentation, are undercut when the narration includes apparently heterogeneous material: diagrams, documents, or stories-within-the-text. Joyce achieves some of his most arresting and puzzling effects in *A Portrait* by injecting heterogeneous elements into the narrative. By disrupting the semblance of a continuous flow of narrative, these elements draw attention to the book's artifice, to its status as art, and to themselves as relatively independent of the text containing them. * * * They set up countermovements in the reading process that may engender an oscillating perspective on the totality of the work's details.

In this regard, Joyce's autobiographical fiction resembles another eccentric work, a fictional autobiography, Laurence Sterne's *Tristram Shandy* (1759–67). Sterne's book is one of the most famous heterogeneous instances in the history of fiction, in part because the narrator's divagations distract the reader repeatedly from any passive response to the text based on unquestioned assumptions about what a novel should be and what its implications may legitimately include. Sterne's book contains blank, black, and marbled pages, as well as ellipses, diagrams, and a musical score. * * *

* * *

Although Joyce's *A Portrait of the Artist as a Young Man* is neither as obviously idiosyncratic as *Tristram Shandy* nor as unusual as Joyce's later fictions, like them, it is only marginally a *novel*, if by that term we mean a prose narration that abides by the canons of realism. These works include elements of form revealing disequilibria in the conventions of the telling that are startling and, at times, disquieting. In *A Portrait* the disturbing elements that raise the question of the book's marginal status are most prominent at the beginning and the ending. These are the locations of the text's margins, its borders with a world not delimited by the language of the story. Title, epigraph, and journal are the gates into and out of Joyce's work. They provide for the reader portals of discovery, margins to be negotiated and filled during the reading process.

* * *

Many critics who have written on *A Portrait* interpret that work autobiographically, claiming that it is based on details of Joyce's youth. Generally, they adduce the title as evidence for the link between the life and the work of art: the portrait is of the artist who writes the book. Unquestionably, strong evidence supports this kind of autobiographical reading. But an autobiographical interpretation of a different sort is also possible, one that sees Stephen Dedalus as the teller of his own story. * * * Implicit in the story of Stephen Dedalus's growth to maturity is the process by which his book emerges from previously existing texts that Stephen knows, some of which he has written himself. *A Portrait* is both the author's autobiographical fiction and the autobiography of the fictional character. It provides the portrait of both artists.

Any interpretation that suggests Stephen may be the narrator will take exception to most readings that dwell on the problem of irony, or aesthetic distance, and on the impersonality of the narration.[1] By emphasizing the narrator's invisibility and the would-be dramatic or objective presentation of Stephen, those readings cannot account adequately for either the narrator's recurring presentation of Stephen's consciousness or the various paradoxes of the narration that make describing the details of the story and its form so difficult. Although there can still be disagreements concerning the precise mix of the narrator's attitudes toward the central character at any given moment in the story, if Stephen narrates, the large problem of his future as an artist can no longer be at issue. If he writes his own tale, the story itself as text provides the strongest possible indication that his choice of vocation will yield more valuable work than the writing he produces within the narrative. And the narration indicates exactly what kind of artist Stephen has become. The teller in *A Portrait*, like the purloined letter of Poe's story,[2] is well-hidden out in the open, where anyone who cares to look can find him.

Dislocations in Style and Story

A Portrait of the Artist contains displacements in both narrative and narration, story and telling. The literal displacements include the moves of the Dedalus family from one residence to the next

---

1. For a review of discussions of aesthetic distance in *A Portrait*, see James J. Sosnowski's "Reading Acts and Reading Warrants: Some Implications for Readers Responding to Joyce's Portrait of Stephen," *James Joyce Quarterly* 16 (Fall 1978/Winter 1979): 43–63. Thomas F. Staley provides a helpful overview of trends in the criticism of *A Portrait* in "Strings in the Labyrinth: Sixty Years with Joyce's *Portrait*," in *Approaches to Joyce's "Portrait": Ten Essays*, ed. Thomas F. Staley and Bernard Benstock (Pittsburgh: University of Pittsburgh Press, 1976), pp. 3–24. * * *
2. "The Purloined Letter" (1845), by the American writer Edgar Allan Poe (1809–1849).

always less attractive abode, compounded with Stephen's displacements from school to school, from Clongowes to Belvedere to University College. "Still another removal" (IV.577), Stephen exclaims to himself during the scene in the kitchen with his siblings at the end of IV.2. In Stephen's boyhood and adolescence, sex and religion replace one another in mutually modifying and mutually defining alternation, until their ultimate displacement through coalescence in Stephen's choice of art as vocation. In the future projected by the book's ending, this last development will be last in the sense of previous. That future may bring a series of further developments, each transforming the last from final to merely previous. Stephen's choice of vocation is accompanied by suggestions of the next physical displacement, his planned departure from Ireland, which will take him eventually not just to Paris, but to Trieste.

Displacements in *A Portrait* are temporal as well as spatial and stylistic as well as literal. The ending indicates that Stephen may be entering a period of more mature adulthood, which will replace his young adulthood, the most recent in a series of states stretching back through adolescence to childhood and infancy. The displacements of style are both those of Stephen as developing artist and of the narrator as mature artist. As William M. Schutte has pointed out, "*Portrait*, like *Ulysses* and *Finnegans Wake*, has no one style."[3] By entwining strands of language into a narrative, the teller of the story reaches back through the past to the origins of Stephen's development as an artist. * * *

* * * In *A Portrait*, by shifting styles Joyce meets a special challenge: to present a wide variety of stylistic exercises that would simultaneously mark the development of a young character's aesthetic sensibilities and form the basis for the writer's exhibition of his own technical mastery. In the various styles of portraiture we have proof of both the character's aesthetic sensitivity and the narrator's virtuosity. The same language serves two purposes. From time to time Joyce directs his adventure in styles toward culminating passages of discovery and self-revelation in which the heightened language vividly calls attention to the relationship of narrator's skill to character's state of mind. The writing of the villanelle in Part V will be especially important in this regard for our consideration of the teller's merging with character in *A Portrait*.

During the displacing of earlier parts of the narrative by later parts, the teller modulates among his different styles of narration,

3. William M. Schutte, editor's introduction, in *Twentieth-Century Interpretations of "A Portrait of the Artist as a Young Man"* (Englewood Cliffs, NJ.: Prentice-Hall, 1968), p. 14. In the fourth section of his introduction to this volume of essays (pp. 10–14), Schutte provides what he calls a "summary account" of the styles that is quite helpful, though brief.

including a "vague, nineteenth-century romanticism," "exalted, almost hysterical lyricism," "workaday prose," and the language of Pater and the decadents.[4] In general, the narration consists of anonymous representations of scene, action, and dialogue in the third person together with the report of Stephen's thoughts, also in the third person. The thoughts of other characters are not reported. This sort of presentation allows Joyce a great deal of flexibility. Modulation from one style to another can be smoothly executed as a shift in the character's thinking within the often relatively unobtrusive framework of third-person narration. Some of the more violent, jarring shifts of style occur at the breaks between typographically demarcated segments of the narrative, between the five parts, and between the nineteen smaller sections making up those parts.[5]

There are so many modulations of style in A Portrait that any endeavor to characterize generally the details of narration will prove inadequate in some respects. Part of the work's richness and appeal is a verbal texture so variable that it defeats all attempts at reduction to a simple pattern. But the fluctuations do develop in a general direction as the narrative proceeds. In broad terms, the style shifts from psycho-narration narrowly conceived toward narrated monologue; that is, it moves from the narrator's discourse concerning the character's mind to a presentation that also includes the character's mental discourse rendered as the narrator's language. Occasionally, the narrator employs the technique of quoted monologue, language that we understand as the character's supposedly unmediated mental discourse because it employs first person and present tense. The general distinctions between psycho-narration, quoted monologue, and narrated monologue will emerge as we examine specific passages in A Portrait.[6] Each technique affects our stance toward character and teller and our sense of the teller's relationship to the tale. All three occur in the context of third-person narration. While we may want to distinguish between them for the purposes of analysis, they hardly ever occur in complete isolation from one another.

Of the three, the most problematic is the narrated monologue, also known as erlebte Rede and as le style indirect libre, a technique

---

4. All pointed out by Schutte in his introduction to Twentieth-Century Interpretations of "A Portrait," pp. 13–14.
5. See "The Parts and the Structural Rhythm of A Portrait," on p. 341.
6. I have adopted the terms psycho-narration, quoted monologue, and narrated monologue from the typology Dorrit Cohn presents in Transparent Minds: Narrative Modes for Presenting Consciousness in Fiction (Princeton: Princeton University Press, 1978). She draws extensively on Joyce for examples illustrating her categories. * * *

Joyce would have found in Flaubert.[7] This device involves the rendering of the character's consciousness in the third person and the past tense. Although there may be no explicit announcement of mental process in the narrator's language, we understand the passages as thoughts occurring to the character in the first person and in the present tense. The present time of the action, as opposed to the past time indicated by the narration, is often emphasized by deictic adjectives and adverbs (ones that point to specific contexts of time or place, such as *here* and *now*) and by demonstrative pronouns, which create a sense of immediacy. Here arises the crucial complication that Joyce develops with such subtlety in both *A Portrait* and *Ulysses*. The reader translates the third person into "I" during the reading process. We speak the character's subjectivity, as do narrator and character in their different ways. The use of third person and past tense indicates a tendency toward a fusion of character's voice with teller's voice. The ambiguous merger of voices makes it difficult, even impossible, for the reader to distinguish between the cunningly combined voices of character and narrator. Because the technique requires the reader to translate third person into first and to attempt discriminations, however difficult, between the merged voices, it necessitates the reader's active recreative rendering of the narration. The reader *performs* the text of narrated monologue with a special kind of involvement because of the device's unusual nature.

Quite frequently, the narrator in *A Portrait* summarizes Stephen's thoughts as psycho-narration employing verbs of consciousness prominently either in the past tense or as infinitives. There are numerous examples from the book's early pages: "felt" (I.48), "wondered" (I.105), "to remember" (I.159), "knew" (I.376, I.733, I.796). Occasionally several verbs indicating thought are clustered together. In one paragraph early in I.2 (I.181–98), there are six instances of such verbs. In general, in this portion of the narrative, there is little emphasis on the complex combination of voices that appears later.[8] The reader can easily distinguish the narrator's discourse about Stephen's thoughts from the presentation of scene and dialogue; for instance, in the alternation between these two complementary aspects of the narration in I.3, the Christmas dinner. As Stephen grows older, the narrator's techniques for presenting his thoughts change. Verbs denoting mental process still occur but less frequently, and other words connoting thought supplement them. Predicates less directly evocative of consciousness, often together with a

7. Gustave Flaubert (1821–1880), French novelist. *Erlebte Rede:* "experienced (in the sense of felt) speech" (German). *Le style indirect libre:* "free indirect style" (French).
8. Some exceptions to this general description are I.1 and such passages as the paragraph in I.3 beginning "Why did Mr Barrett . . ." (I.801).

prepositional phrase, become the reminders that we have access to Stephen's mind.

In II.2, when Stephen begins wandering the streets of Dublin alone, the passages describing his adventures contain just as many indicators of thought as do some earlier passages, but the indications are of a different order. Stephen makes a map of the city "in his mind." As he follows physically the routes of this internal map, the verb "to wonder," used before in the past tense, now occurs as a present participle, "wondering." While an explicit reference to mental process is still provided, the transformation of the verb denoting thought from a predicate to a modifier makes the reference less obtrusive. Instead of telling us that Stephen thought, felt, or remembered, the narrator presents Stephen's impressions as they "suggested to him," "wakened again in him," or "grew up within him" (II.232, II.234, II.239). As before, the references to thought are clustered together, though they are more muted now. These last three predicates and the two preceding quotations are all from a single paragraph. And the predications of thought, even these muted ones, begin to be supplemented or replaced by a new affective vocabulary presenting mood, as in the phrases "mood of embittered silence" and "angry with himself" (II.245, II.247). Or nouns and verbs not necessarily denoting mental activity, such as "vision" and "chronicled" (II.249, II.251), take on connotations that suggest consciousness because of their use in context.

There are two distinctions implicit in the alternation between scene and psyche that occurs in the work's first sections: the distinction between an external world and the character's mind and between narrator and character. Starting in Part II both begin to be blurred in various ways. The alternation becomes overlap when the narrator quotes Stephen's thoughts in II.2 using the same typographical indicator, the dash, that previously identified only direct discourse: "—She too wants me to catch hold of her, he thought. That's why she came with me to the tram. I could easily catch hold of her when she comes up to my step: nobody is looking. I could hold her and kiss her" (II.350–53). The character's interior speech is utilized here as the equivalent of a stage monologue or aside in drama. It has the form of direct discourse but a different effect. In II.3 the narrator carries his modifications further during Stephen's encounter with his schoolmate Heron just before the play. We are given the narrative of Stephen's heretical essay and the drubbing it leads to as scene, dialogue, and action (II.638–791). But this narrative occurs in Stephen's mind. His memory now is rendered in nearly the same way as the narrator's presentation of the external world. The growing resemblance between the two modes of narration prepares for the more radical alignment of teller and character that occurs later.

The more striking fusion of inner and outer and of character and teller begins emerging in the next part, when the teller adopts the narrated monologue while presenting the retreat in III.2. As in the narration of the Christmas dinner, the telling alternates between an external scene (the sermons) and Stephen's reaction to the outer world. Although the narrator continues to employ techniques introduced in previous sections, there are some crucial modifications. These changes suggest, among other things, the intensity of Stephen's reaction to events. Section III.2 consists of an introductory talk and three sermons that take place on consecutive days. The initial, prominent use of narrated monologue occurs in the passage presenting Stephen's walk home the first evening after the introductory talk: "So he had sunk to the state of a beast that licks his chaps after meat. This was the end; . . . And that was life" (III.338–43). The device is especially manifest because Joyce uses demonstrative pronouns in a paragraph otherwise relatively free of them. The statements can be easily transformed into the character's speech to himself in first person and present tense. In the paragraph that follows, the narrator presents the initial sermon, on death and judgment (III.351–465), in a curious way. He renders it not as direct discourse, the technique he uses to report the two subsequent sermons on hell, but as speech mediated by Stephen's consciousness. The brief passage of narrated monologue acts as the preparation for this odd filtering of Father Arnall's words through Stephen's mind. The narration of the sermon begins in the past tense with a series of verbs and phrases indicating Stephen's consciousness is being rendered: "stirring his soul," "fear," "terror," "into his soul," "he suffered," "he felt" (III.351–54). In the middle of the sermon, although the dashes of direct discourse are absent, the past tense is replaced with a mixture of tenses, including present and future, much closer to the quotation of the later sermons as speech.

After this lengthy report of Stephen's consciousness during the first sermon, the alternation of passages focusing on psyche with those focusing on scene is again established, but now the narrated monologue has become a recurring feature of the narration. The narrator employs it briefly but regularly throughout the remainder of III (instances occur in lines 466–77, 529–36, 812–21, 871–79, 1284–93, 1447–71, 1546–53).[9] In III.3 Stephen's thoughts are quoted directly, once with a dash indicating direct discourse when

9. This and the following lists provided parenthetically are meant to be indicative only, not exhaustive.

he hears voices (III.1213–17), but at other times without the dash as apparently unmediated interior exclamations: "Confess! Confess!" (III.1321). While this last exclamation can be read as a direct presentation of Stephen's thought, the similar one, "For him! For him!" (III.1287), that occurs only a page earlier is an instance of narrated monologue. We read "For him" as "For *me*," understanding the third person as applying to the character.

With a device as problematic as narrated monologue, there will almost certainly be some disagreement among readers concerning the application of the term to specific passages. Whatever the differing judgments about the particular passages I have identified as narrated monologue, the general point concerning the sudden, recurring appearance of the technique in the narration is irrefragable: these numerous possible instances of narrated monologue grouped together in Part III mark a significant shift in the style. The shift is increasingly toward renderings of Stephen's intensely felt thoughts that create an ambiguity concerning the relationship of the style to the character's language. In the two remaining parts the narrator freely employs in combination the various techniques he has used to present Stephen's mind. Once the reader has grown accustomed to the different modes for representing consciousness that have been introduced seriatim over the course of nearly 150 pages, the teller can rely on the reader's newly created capacity for responding to the salmagundi of techniques that will now be employed in the narration.

The narrator has been making a persona for the reader as well as for himself in his portrayal of Stephen. The reader has learned the conventions of the literary techniques that the author uses to compose his own self-representation as teller and to present Stephen's gradually developing sensibilities. Only after all the techniques have become thoroughly established as conventions of the fiction can the narrator begin to shift rapidly from one to another. The swift alternation of devices evoking the hard, gemlike flame of Stephen's mind occurs in the book's two climactic segments: at the end of IV.3 when Stephen is on the strand, and during Stephen's composing of his villanelle in V.2. At the end of IV.3, the narrator gives us Stephen's interior exclamations, "Yes! Yes! Yes!" (IV.810), combined with possible instances of narrated monologue, (IV.810–21, IV.883–90, IV.900–02) and with Stephen's thoughts quoted as if they were direct discourse: "—Heavenly God! cried Stephen's soul, in an outburst of profane joy" (IV.876–77). Near the end of my discussion of *A Portrait,* I shall deal with the implications of the similar combination in V.2.

In V.1 and V.3 there are numerous instances of narrated monologue (V.129–61, V.175–211, V.1918–40, V.2047–82, V.2111–32,

V.2507–17). The narrator also employs at great length the technique he used in II.3 by presenting Stephen's memories while he is walking to the university as scene, action, and dialogue (as in the long recollection of Davin's story about his walk in the country and his encounter with the peasant woman [V.265–334]). The ambiguity about the source of the narration's language is particularly pronounced throughout V. Repeatedly the narrator introduces long passages of Stephen's thoughts by asserting first that Stephen "watched" (V.394), "saw" (V.435), "looked at" (V.1124), or "had heard" (V.623) something, then that someone or something "seemed" (V.396, V.440, V.445, V.488, V.527, V.549, V.625) a certain way. These passages omit the phrase "to him" or "to Stephen," which would identify explicitly the language to follow as Stephen's rather than the narrator's. The narrator will introduce a long paragraph of revery with only a brief reference to "Stephen's mind" (V.643–44), which the reader may tend to forget, or he will conclude rather than introduce such a long paragraph with a phrase indicating the passage was Stephen's "thought" (V.1935). As in so many other late passages, the effect is to align the teller's voice and the character's, if only temporarily. The residual and cumulative sense of merger created by such alignments molds the reader's stance toward the narration with particular force. While *some* distinctions can be made between teller and character (this discussion would not have been possible without them), the passages ask us again and again to consider the relationship of the two voices that are so complexly mixed.

The subtly mingled but counterpointed language of teller and character emerges vividly in the book's second half, primarily because the narrated monologues together with the related techniques appear frequently beginning in III.2. Along with the seemingly intimate presentation of Stephen's thoughts, in Part V the reader encounters longer and more elaborate statements to his companions than Stephen has made earlier. His voices, both internal and public, are thrust to the foreground. At the book's ending, it is primarily these voices that determine the reader's overall judgment of Stephen's potential.

Journal and Epigraph:
Beginning and Homeward Glance

The representations of Stephen's consciousness that occur in Part V are particularly relevant for understanding the relationship of narrative to narration in *A Portrait*. The following paragraph, in which Stephen comments silently on Cranly's remark about a fellow student, is typical of the last section:

It was his [Cranly's] epitaph for all dead friendships and Stephen wondered whether it would ever be spoken in the same
tone over his memory. The heavy lumpish phrase sank slowly
out of hearing like a stone through a quagmire. Stephen saw it
sink as he had seen many another, feeling its heaviness depress
his heart. Cranly's speech, unlike that of Davin, had neither
rare phrases of Elizabethan English nor quaintly turned versions of Irish idioms. Its drawl was an echo of the quays of
Dublin given back by a bleak decaying seaport, its energy an
echo of the sacred eloquence of Dublin given back flatly by a
Wicklow pulpit. (V.762–72)

Such insertions, made by the narrator during his report of conversations, amount to brief digressions. As part of a commentary on
time in fiction, Jean Ricardou remarks on the effect passages like
this one can have in a narrative. Because of their length, they dis-
rupt any illusion of a continuous flow of time in the plot by calling
attention to the time of the narration. As Ricardou says, they
emphasize "the writing (habitually concealed by the story)."[1] When
their prominence begins to define the mode of narration, as it does
in A Portrait, in Ricardou's formulation the work "ceases to be the
writing of a story to become the story of a writing."[2] The passage
emphasizes writing in two senses, as process of narration and as
style of language. The teller's activity of narrating is emphasized in
ways it cannot be through the quotation of dialogue. And attention
is drawn to the specific kind of language employed, particularly in
this passage, in which Stephen explicitly makes contrasts between
various styles.

As narration, A Portrait includes all the styles mentioned in the
paragraph and many more. They are the literary styles the character has heard or read (and sometimes spoken) and that the narrator
has adopted in his written mimicry of the character's mind and the
character's world. At times we understand them primarily as styles
within the narrative; at other times, as styles of the narration.
When the styles characterize Stephen's thoughts intimately presented, distinguishing narrative from narration is often no longer
possible. * * * The language of the narration is opaque. We see *it* as
well as the story communicated, just as Stephen sees the phrase
Cranly speaks. Stephen understands the semantic meaning of
Cranly's words and the implication of Cranly's style. And the reader
understands the implications of the narration, including the recurring reports of Stephen's thoughts.

1. Jean Ricardou, "Time of the Narration, Time of the Fiction," trans. Joseph Kestner,
James Joyce Quarterly 16 (Fall 1978/Winter 1979): 13.
2. Ricardou, p. 11.

Through an energetic echo that gives back Stephen's eloquence, the narrator fuses inextricably with character. There is no means for disentangling Stephen's attitudes from the voice of the narrator who speaks them. The two voices are linked by the author's act of writing, a mediating process we become aware of through the style of narration but can never experience directly. We know the product and its implications but not the process itself. Instead, we experience the analogous mediating process of the act of reading, which aligns *our* activities of mind with those of character and teller. As Wayne Booth has said, "any sustained inside view, of whatever depth, temporarily turns the character whose mind is shown into a narrator."[3] The narrator's reiterated shifts between internal and external views make *A Portrait* a work about the transforming of a character into an artist in which style regularly turns the character into a teller. When the style includes narrated monologue, the reader shares the role of teller with the character by speaking the character's mind.

The final style adopted by the narrator, one especially pertinent to the present inquiry, is that of the journal, from which the entries of 20 March through 27 April are apparently only an excerpt. In the narrative's fictive chronology, as distinct from the chronology of narration, the journal is the last example of Stephen's styles as well. The potential ambiguity of the word "last" is the crux of the difference between the narrative and the narration. The style of the journal displaces the villanelle, the aesthetic theory, and the other examples of Stephen's expression—written, spoken, and internal—that are either directly presented or alluded to earlier. In its turn, the styles of the entire book displace that of the journal. The dual, interlocking process of feedback points to the problem of the ending and the end toward which the narrative tends. Two styles, the teller's and the character's, not just one, are brought to conclusion, or at least partial closure, in the one document that can be read as two documents. The journal kept by a character is also a portion of a narrative reported by the teller.

There is an acute disequilibrium between process and product, between Stephen's activity of keeping a journal and the portion reproduced by the narrator through an act of quotation that resembles the reporting of dialogue. * * * The shifting focus becomes particularly evident for the reader of *A Portrait* who attempts to reconcile the journal in its fictional and textual contexts (of story and of narration) with the title and the epigraph of the title page and with the dates and places noted on the final page. All these

3. Wayne C. Booth, *The Rhetoric of Fiction* (Chicago: University of Chicago Press, 1961), p. 164.

parts of the book are relatively independent of what falls between them. Their implications do not appear at first to be wholly integrated with the remainder of the book as coherent aspects of style and story. This apparent failure of integration provides grounds for interpreting *A Portrait* as preposterous in that word's etymological sense.

Before and after, pre- and post-, are made to exchange places and to interact reciprocally. The exchange and interaction are manifest in the ending, from the perspective of which the reader revises the provisional interpretations generated up to that state of the reading. At the end of any narrative the reader engaged in an interpretive process experiences the preposterous aspect of reading. The reader's new perspective for scrutinizing the text's details allows a look backward that sees the text in retrospective arrangement. That arrangement modifies and displaces provisional readings, which are now seen anew in revision. The reading process flows temporally from the present to the past as the reader experiences portions of the text becoming parts of new contexts that are the bases for reinterpretations. Prospective and retrospective, provisional and revisionary judgments merge as the reader encounters and assimilates the conceptual implications of the narrative's form. The reader's experience of retrospective rearrangements shifting places through time duplicates the character's experience when he becomes the teller of his own tale in retrospect.

The closing of both book and journal with the notation of dates and places, "Dublin 1904/Trieste 1914," presents in small the problematic, preposterous quality of the entire work. The reader must decide whether the references are part of the story or part of the writing, whether they are appropriate to the product or to the process of creation. Like the title, they refer at once to both product and process, to both character and author as artists. The autobiographical bases of the dates and places are well known. They point to the time and locations at which the author initiates and completes the writing of the book. Joyce finished *A Portrait* in Trieste just over ten years after leaving Dublin. Serial publication began in 1914.[4] The authorial, autobiographical significance in no way diminishes the relevance the references possess for Stephen Dedalus's story. There is a complicated, uncanny doubling lurking within and behind the apparently innocent closing that is a *post scriptum*. This doubling that occurs through the telling of the story is more radical than most interpretations have allowed. * * *

---

4. For a discussion of the dates of composition see Schutte's introduction to *Twentieth-Century Interpretations of "A Portrait,"* pp. 5–7.

The strange duplication becomes apparent once dates and times are both understood as referring to Joyce's process of writing *and* to the story of Stephen Dedalus as it appears to develop beyond the time of the excerpt printed from the journal. Although no exact dates are ever provided for Stephen's activities earlier in the narrative, Dublin is obviously the place appropriate to the journal and to much of the action, and 1904 is within the limits of probability suggested in the fiction. Nineteen fourteen would be the year and Trieste the place in which Stephen completes the transforming of the journal into a book that is the simulacrum of Joyce's. The last portion of *A Portrait* presents what comes first with respect to the remainder of the text. In Stephen Dedalus's fictional life, which includes his life as a writer of fiction, the keeping of the journal precedes the completing of the book. The last—that is, the most recent—stage of Stephen's development as an artist is presented through the narration, not in the narrative. The dates and places that stand both inside and outside the story are the signatures of author and character as writers, their superimposed self-portraits painted in the corner of the finished canvas. They are the equivalent of the closing that Stanislaus Joyce reports his brother intended to append to *Stephen Hero,* "the signature, *Stephanus Daedalus Pinxit.*"[5]

In Ovid's *Metamorphoses* the line quoted as epigraph to *A Portrait* refers to the mythic artist Daedalus, the "old father, old artificer" (V.2791) mentioned at the end of Stephen's journal. Ovid presents Daedalus setting his mind to work upon unknown arts. As with the notations at the book's end, the question of the epigraph's meaning concerns its referent. Like the journal, the epigraph is presented as a fragment quoted out of its original context. For the epigraph, but not for the journal, the original context is available to be examined. There is no evidence that the fragmentary journal actually has an origin in the same way as the epigraph does. In the *Metamorphoses* the epigraph's context indicates Daedalus's longing for home:

> Homesick for homeland, Daedalus hated Crete
> And his long exile there, but the sea held him.
> . . . He turned his thinking
> Toward unknown arts, changing the laws of nature.[6]

In the case of Ovid's Daedalus, the act of turning the mind to work on obscure arts has an explicit cause and an explicit effect. Daedalus fashions wings for himself and for Icarus in order to escape from a

5. Stanislaus Joyce, *My Brother's Keeper: James Joyce's Early Years,* ed. Richard Ellmann (New York: Viking Press, 1958), p. 244.
6. Ovid, *Metamorphoses,* trans. Rolfe Humphries (Bloomington: Indiana University Press, 1955), Book VIII, ll.182–88, p. 187.

prison and return home. Daedalus's work violates the laws of nature through the accomplishment of a feat seemingly beyond human possibility. The result also includes the death of Icarus, an apparently unavoidable concomitant of the mature artist's act of making in order to escape.

At the beginning of A *Portrait* as well as at its end, Joyce challenges the laws of conventional narrative by turning his own mind to intricate arts that result in a death and a doubling through the creation of a ghostly presence for the artist in a voice that repeats itself. Like the designations of place and time, the epigraph refers to the Dedalian character as well as to the Daedalian author. When the character's role as son is over after the final page, his fatherly role as teller is born phoenixlike to return home on the first page. Character transforms himself into artist as the son becomes his own father. Essential to the transformation is the importance of home in both Ovid's work and Joyce's. The act of producing the portrait combines the longing for home with the homecoming itself. * * *

* * *

In A *Portrait,* because Stephen exhibits the antithetical traits of Daedalus and Icarus in his two manifestations, the Daedalian narrator can present the young protagonist in the guise of an Icarus transforming himself into a Daedalus. Both Odysseus and Daedalus are homesick and homeward bound in their myths. At the end of A *Portrait* Stephen is outward bound, having determined to serve no longer. Stephen's decision to leave is necessarily connected for the reader to his act of keeping a journal, for the presentation of the journal signals Stephen's departure. But the keeping of the journal, which indicates the decision to write as well as to leave, is glossed by the epigraph. In order to write Stephen turns his mind to obscure arts, arts that lead him far from home, as Daedalus is led far from home, but these arts inevitably bring him back to a home, not literally but literarily. The subject of the journal that ostensibly announces departure from home, like the subject of the book containing the journal, is home, as well as the displacements of wandering. For Joyce, to turn the mind toward intricate arts is to look homeward. In the act of refusing to serve the home, the artist makes it possible for the home to serve him as the primary material for his art. Daedalus and Icarus, Sicily and Crete, Trieste and Dublin, 1914 and 1904, Stephen as teller and Stephen as character all merge in the book's oscillating focus. In A *Portrait* and later, the homeward look, no matter how intricately expressed in and as wanderings of style, involves a merging that occurs in the encounters of reader and teller and of reader and character. In Joyce's fiction the two encounters are not necessarily distinct.

The language of the one book casts two shadows, projects two images related by superimposition as in a palimpsest. The character who tells his own tale never writes on a tabula rasa. He always and inevitably displaces the past by erasing it and writing over the erasure, even when the writing constitutes a recapturing of the past as well as a displacing of it. Like Tristram Shandy and every other teller, Stephen Dedalus as writer can never capture himself or his own process of writing. He can only suggest the nature of the activity of writing as self-portrayal, as self-representation. The pretext for the narration given in the title, to portray a young, developing artist, precedes the reader's experience of the story. But the prior text for the character, the writing that precedes the text temporally in the character's experience, is the journal that is part of the book as well as prior to it. That journal allows the reader to redefine the narrative in a new frame of reference. By experiencing the earlier text as both behind the later one and within it, the reader can see through, as well as by means of, the story's pretense.

BONNIE KIME SCOTT

[The Artist and Gendered Discourse][†]

[*Joyce and Muted Female Culture*]

* * * Joyce's present availability owes much to the industry and support of women in publishing. Joyce's nurturing by females was not just a fortunate fall into female altruism. He was selected from other modernists because the women involved found revolutionary affinities in Joyce. Joyce began under male patronage—his father's. John Joyce had his son's poem on Charles Stuart Parnell published privately. Presumably, it echoed the father's sense of history. Next, the prestigious British periodical *The Fortnightly Review* published his review on Ibsen (1900). With the exception of the relatively conventional poems in *Chamber Music* (1907), Joyce's increasingly experimental and iconoclastic works met with rejections. *St Stephen's,* his college newspaper, censored his attack on the Irish literary revival, "The Day of the Rabblement," and Joyce published it privately with an equally marginal essay on women's education by Irish feminist and friend Francis Skeffington. The bourgeois

† From *James Joyce* (Atlantic Highlands, NJ: Humanities P International, 1987), pp. 16–17, 20–22, 31–33, 47–53, 86–88, 112–16, 120, 128–29. Reprinted by permission of the author. Some of the author's footnotes have been omitted. Information from her bibliography has been incorporated into her footnotes. Page references for *A Portrait* have been replaced with part and line numbers of this Norton Critical Edition. Some cited passages might differ slightly from the equivalent passages in this volume.

readers of *The Irish Homestead* objected to the stories that became *Dubliners*, so publication ceased after three. With *Dubliners* still unpublished, Joyce's prospects for *A Portrait* seemed gloomy until Ezra Pound put him in touch with the daring women editors of *The Egoist*. Dora Marsden and Harriet Shaw Weaver were willing to deal with printers' fears of litigation, to defy the norms of established literature and the economics of the marketplace, as were other female editors of small, individualist magazines.

The gynocritical concept of a muted female culture applies well to the operations of women editors and publishers of Joyce. *The Egoist* was descended from suffragist periodicals (*The Freewoman*, later renamed *The New Freewoman*), and staffed by feminists, including Rebecca West, H.D., and Bryher (Winnifred Ellermann). As writers, these women were neglected during the years when Joyce studies grew into an industry, but their muted modernist tradition has drawn the attention of feminist critics and publishers * * *. Joyce was living in Trieste when his work began appearing in *The Egoist*, and the only woman connected with the enterprise that he came to know personally was Weaver. If so disposed, he could have read the work of Weaver, West and H.D. in *The Egoist*.

Weaver re-made the quaint role of literary patronage in a style of her own, learned partially from her participation in Victorian women's roles. She avoided poses of authority and airs of social superiority, offering instead common sense, practical nurture, and the psychological support that came from utter dependability and loyalty. Weaver's support of Joyce began with handling the details of periodical publication of *A Portrait*, including the same sort of haggling with printers that so delayed *Dubliners*. She eventually changed from periodical publishing to book publishing. The Egoist Press was established "on non-commercial lines" with the aim of making "operative an influence capable of transforming our entire world of form-thought and action."[1] Its Joyce list included several editions of *A Portrait*, as well as English editions of *Ulysses*, *Exiles*, *Dubliners*, and *Chamber Music*. Weaver also published T.S. Eliot, Wyndham Lewis, Ezra Pound, Marianne Moore, H.D. and Dora Marsden, a list with a generous presence of women writers.

* * *

[*Stephen, History, and Literature*]

In *A Portrait of the Artist as a Young Man*, Stephen Dedalus begins early to absorb the lessons on the Romans, the Greeks and Napoleon.

---

1. *The Egoist*, December 1919, 71.

He thinks that there are right answers about history, and examples of greatness to be followed, even in family life. There should be simple monological solutions to problems involving gender, like the question posed by the bully, Wells, "Do you kiss your mother before you go to bed?" (I.246–47). Personal application of male historical paradigms is evident in the aftermath of the pandybat incident. A priest has beaten Stephen's hand as punishment for Stephen's having broken his glasses. The dynamics of phallic power over excised or castrated vision invite gender-based interpretations, but the boys cannot articulate them. Stephen's peers state his grievance in classical historical terms: "The senate and the Roman people declared that Dedalus had been wrongly punished" (I.1625–26). Stephen responds:

> He would go up and tell the rector that he had been wrongly punished. A thing like that had been done before by somebody in history, by some great person whose head was in the books of history. . . . Those were the great men whose names were in Richmal Magnall's Questions. History was all about those men and what they did and that was what Peter Parley's Tales about Greece and Rome were all about. (I.1635–45)

On his way to secure justice from the highest school authority, Stephen displays internalized male-biased values that allow him to feel superior to his punisher. His name, Dedalus, connects him to the great men of the classics he has studied: "The great men in the history had names like that and nobody made fun of them. . . . Dolan: it was like the name of a woman that washed clothes" (I.1701–04). Stephen has learned that women in domestic service deserve low regard; great men in history are respectable. * * *

Stephen develops a reputation as a prize-winning student over the years. His memory is excellent; his knowledge of the catechism can be used later to divert a priestly instructor from unprepared lessons (III.131–33). The Jesuits of Belvedere are convinced that they have a potential recruit (IV.362–66). But long before he must use a "habit of quiet obedience" (IV.326) to disguise other interests from the priests, the young Stephen searches out different angles, de-centering Jesuit-style learning. Stephen tries, but only half-heartedly, to compete on one of two teams named (with significant indifference to Irish nationalism) for the historical English factions of York and Lancaster in the Wars of the Roses. Due to illness, Stephen's mind works feverishly, eluding a more customary discipline. On a more normal day, Stephen had listed his name at the head of a hierarchy, ranging from self to universe (I.300–08). But on this day, Stephen's mind wanders from manly competition to colour, rearranging and inventing. Stephen displays little respect for the

hierarchy of colours accorded to high and low places. He thinks of
the flower (usually a female emblem) originally attached to the
colour symbolism. He introduces off-shades and plays with a chias-
mic structure (parallelism in reverse order that achieves symmetry
rather than hierarchy): "White roses and red roses: those were
beautiful colours to think of. And the cards for first place and second place and third place were beautiful colours too: pink and
cream and lavender. Lavender and cream and pink roses were beautiful to think of" (I.191–95). At his second school, Belvedere, Stephen cannot attend to a typical history lesson; he is troubled by the
concentration on names which veil and mute what interests him:
"royal persons, favourites, intriguers, bishops passed like mute
phantoms behind their veil of names" (III.845–46). His mind is
diverted at this time by his own mysteries—a sense of sin with a
prostitute, and concern for his soul * * * (III.479–501). Stephen
grows more openly critical of the educational process at University
College. He cuts his English lecture, but imagines his peers at their
Jesuit rituals, their heads "meekly bent as they wrote in their notebooks the points they were bidden to note, nominal definitions,
essential definitions and examples or dates of birth or death, chief
works" and so on (V.134–37). Stephen turns the available instruction toward a different form of history. He seeks social rather than
political, militant history, often finding his cues in language, however ill-chosen by his instructors:

> The crises and victories and secessions in Roman history were
> handed on to him in the trite words *in tanto discrimine* and he
> had tried to peer into the social life of the city of cities through
> the words *implere ollam denariorum* which the rector had
> rendered sonorously as the filling of a pot with denaries.
> (V.194–98)

His new history of pots rather than battles has affinity with feminist history, as defined by feminist historians like Gerda Lerner.
Ulysses offers many discussions of military engagements, but Stephen figures in them peripherally, if at all. He is less involved in the
historical debates of the "Eumaeus" episode than is Leopold Bloom,
though they agree momentarily on the values of pacifism. As if to
emphasize his distaste for the subject, he requests, rather affect-
edly, "O, oblige me by taking away that knife. I can't look at the
point of it. It reminds me of Roman history" (*U* 16.814–6).[2]

* * *

2. *Ulysses,* ed. Hans Walter Gabler (New York: Vintage, 1986) [*Editor*].

Though Stephen is indebted to classicism and scholasticism, and though he makes the canonized British master Shakespeare the subject of his central literary discourse in *Ulysses*, these authorities receive significant challenges from Stephen, his audience, and Joyce, as the arranger of *Ulysses*. Stephen is not even prepared to say he believes in the theories he expresses on Shakespeare. In *A Portrait*, Stephen acknowledges weariness after searching the "spectral words of Aristotle and Aquinas," and is relieved by "the dainty songs of the Elizabethans," and gladdened by his passage through "the squalor and noise and sloth of the city" (V.88, V.89, V.110). Stephen is "disheartened" by "the firm dry tone" of the dean of studies, outlining a Jesuitical method of exploring beauty through a set of distinctions (V.565–93). He is not eager to become an "unlit lamp" or a "faithful servingman of the knightly Loyola" (V.488, V.586).

Clearly without Jesuit endorsement, Stephen had sought out romantic texts like Dumas' *The Count of Monte Cristo*. One appeal of these texts was their romantic visions of women like Mercedes. Stephen has prized other romantic writers who offer comparable distanced female inspirational figures for questing. Foremost is Byron, who provides the form for Stephen's poem to E.C. (II.361–64), and for whom Stephen sustains a beating by virile schoolfellows. Byron had been denounced by Stephen's schoolmate Heron as immoral and heretical.

In Blake, Stephen encountered a profoundly radical critique of cultural hegemony, one which contributed to his re-vision of history * * *. "The most enlightened of Western poets" referred to in an essay Joyce wrote in 1902 was Blake, according to Joyce's brother, Stanislaus (*CW* 74–5).[3] Interestingly, Blake was ensconced alongside Joyce in Sylvia Beach's bookshop. The romantic temper, with its heritage of the French Revolution, its denial of hierarchies, and its greater interest in subjective and unconscious human experience, added new dimensions to Joyce and to his persona, which brought him closer to the sensibilities of revolutionary women writers like Mary Wollstonecraft, Mary Shelley and Charlotte Brontë.

Even in his pursuit of classical male writers, Stephen adopted his own course. The final chapter of *A Portrait* shows Stephen decentring classical teaching to suit his interests. He reads Ovid and Horace with the Jesuits, but is distracted by the whimsical words used to translate Ovid and by the human imprint of the "timeworn pages" of his copy of Horace (V.199–203). In John Henry Newman,

3. *The Critical Writings of James Joyce*, ed. Ellsworth Mason and Richard Ellmann (New York: Viking, 1959) [*Editor*].

Stephen admires a writer approved for the modern Jesuit canon, but values, not the theology, but the "silver-veined prose." Stephen also seeks out the heretics of ecclesiastical history. He defends Bruno of Nola to the dean of students, just as he had defended Byron with his contemporaries. Stephen is not physically punished for this allegiance, but he reminds the dean that Bruno was brutally burned. In a book review on Bruno (1903), Joyce agrees with the author's view of Bruno as a revisionist of scholasticism. Joyce appreciates Bruno's pluralist attitude * * *. Bruno's system has various poles, "by turns rationalist and mystic, theistic and pantheistic." Joyce reiterates Coleridge's identification of Bruno as a "dualist" (CW 133–4). Thus Bruno offers a greater sensitivity to alternative paradigms than the more monological scholastic thinking, but we should recall that dualistic thinking is also suspect as a male-generated paradigm by Marxist and post-structuralist feminists. Where Brunonian binaries operate in Joyce, their function must be deconstructed; where they are synthetic or question the usual hierarchy, they may offer a positive paradigm. Bruno's supposed abhorrence of the multitude is endorsed by Joyce in "The Day of the Rabblement." This supports the pose of aloof, romantic artist, and is more difficult to accommodate to a feminist position. The multitude scorned by Bruno and Joyce, however, may be most objectionable for its mindless support of hegemonic culture.

Stephen's thoughts are also crossed by the modern continental playwrights Gerhart Hauptmann and Henrik Ibsen, who are serious alternatives to the classical curriculum of the Jesuit university. Interestingly, Joyce specialized, not in the classics but in modern literature, the subject usually chosen by female students. Ibsen has surprisingly little place in A Portrait, considering Joyce's substantial effort to claim his place in the dramatic canon in such essays as "Drama and Life," "Ibsen's New Drama," "Catalina," and "The Day of the Rabblement." Joyce's major performance at the university was not on the well-canonized Shakespeare, Stephen's choice for the library discourse [in Ulysses], but on Ibsen. In "Drama and Life," Joyce notes that the "Shakespearean clique" had toppled an already failing classical dramatic tradition. Yet he sets about dismissing Shakespeare in turn, finding him a writer of "literature in dialogue." Ibsen is preferable as a writer of a higher and more collective "dramatic" art (CW 39, 45ff.). Stephen's few thoughts on Hauptmann and Ibsen suggest that they provide him with images and attitudes not available in the canon. Thoughts of Hauptmann come to Stephen from the sensuous "rainladen trees," evocative of the girls and women in his plays. Ibsen is a revolutionary "spirit" that "would blow through him like a keen wind, a spirit of wayward boyish beauty" (V.71–73, V.81–83). * * *

[*The Discourse of the Father*]

* * * While examining issues of canonical history and literature, we charted Stephen Dedalus' acquisition of academic male discourse from the classical and theological education provided by the Jesuits. [Stephen absorbs] a second male discourse [from] his father, Simon. * * *

Simon Dedalus offers his son's first rhetorical model in the story-telling at the opening of *A Portrait of the Artist as a Young Man*. Lacanian theory[4] associates the paternal phallus with the *logos* or word, as well as the laws by which society operates, hence the importance of this narration in supplying Stephen with the rules of discourse. By making "Baby Tuckoo" or Stephen the subject or centre of his narrative, Simon encourages the self-centered, egotistical, solipsistic narrative so obvious throughout Stephen's artistic development. The early story-telling is one in a series of vignettes where Stephen witnesses a performance, a personal or political discourse by his father, and is moved to sort out his own personal history and eventually his artistic course. Mrs Dedalus, on the other hand, has had most of her performances edited out of *A Portrait*. Dialogues are recalled, not recorded at length. She complies generally with the stereotypically feminine roles of accompanist and observer, displaying a muted and inhibited discourse, or providing a mouthpiece for the words of the father or the patriarchal church.[5] We see her teamed with Stephen's Aunt "Dante," but never in exclusively female company.

Simon's major performances include the Christmas dinner scene, where he is patriarchal host—wielder of the knife, dispenser of the sauce, and instigator of the political discussion that divides the family along gender lines and sunders Stephen's sense of a moral world order. Simon is again on stage in Cork (II.946–1275), where he sentimentally recalls his personal past, including his prowess with women and his attachment to his father. In another scene, Simon makes a political speech outside the former Irish House of Commons, regretting the diminishment of public men (II.1276–1301). Scattered through *A Portrait* are his pearls of paternal wisdom. To facilitate Stephen's male-bonding at school, Simon advises "never to peach on a fellow" (I.86). Simon's discourses have their antecedents in *Dubliners* in the speech of Joe Hynes in "Ivy Day in the Committee Room" and the banquet address of Gabriel Conroy in "The Dead." Simon says less in *Ulysses*, but he moves about the

---

4. In the work of the French psychiatrist Jacques Lacan (1901–1981) [*Editor*].
5. Colin MacCabe suggests that the father's authority as narrator is juxtaposed by the sound of the mother in this opening scene. See *James Joyce and the Revolution of the Word* (London: Macmillan, 1979), 55–6.

male preserves of the city, and everywhere he is or has been, we find recollections and repetitions of his discourse. Significantly, so does Stephen. The rhetorical tropes of the headlines printed in "Aeolus" are related to his discourse. Simon's sort of talk culminates in the "Cyclops" chapter of *Ulysses*[6] but echoes still in the *Finnegans Wake* speeches of the four chroniclers and Shaun as "Jaun the Boast" (*FW* 469.29)[7] with his "barrel of leaking rhetoric" (*FW* 429.8), "stone of law" (430.6), and ["preaching to himself" (467.9)]. Hugh Kenner describes the spectacle of a man speaking in public as "a paradigmatic communal act, offering to make sense of what he and his listeners confront together." He suggests that Dublin men simply lack the sense of history needed to carry off more than "pieces of inappropriate virtuosity" or "Pyrrhonism in the pub."[8] I suggest that their failures lead us on to deconstruct the male speech act itself, and to recover alternate acts and conceptions of community more inclusive of women, and less characterized by forced unities.

Even though his economic prowess steadily declines in *A Portrait*, Simon clings to a rhetoric of masterful command. When he can no longer afford to send Stephen to prestigious Clongowes Wood College, Simon takes pride in having arranged with Father Conmee for Stephen's place in the local Jesuit school, Belvedere. His self-satisfaction comes from a sense of knowing and manipulating a system and implies complicity in social and intellectual hierarchies and male networks. He performs for the family, with Mrs Dedalus as his assistant. The narrator implies criticism, with references to his busy tongue and calculations of Simon's repetitions:

> One evening his father came home full of news which kept his tongue busy all through dinner. . . .
> —I walked bang into him, said Mr Dedalus for the fourth time, just at the corner of the square.
> —Then I suppose, said Mrs Dedalus, he will be able to arrange it. I mean about Belvedere.
> —Of course he will, said Mr Dedalus. Don't I tell you he's provincial of the order now?
> —I never liked the idea of sending him to the christian brothers myself, said Mrs Dedalus.
> —Christian brothers be damned! said Mr Dedalus. Is it with Paddy Stink and Mickey Mud? No, let him stick to the jesuits in God's name since he began with them. They'll be of service to him in after years. Those are the fellows that can get you a position. (II.392–410)

---

6. The twelfth episode of that novel; "Aeolus" is the seventh [*Editor*].
7. New York: Viking, 1939 [*Editor*].
8. *Joyce's Voices* (Berkeley: U of Calif. P, 1978).

The most extensive, varied, virtuoso performance by Simon is the earlier Christmas dinner scene, which also marks an epoch in Stephen's cultural passage into manhood. Stephen has survived the anxieties of the young male world at Clongowes and is fulfilling a dreamed-of return home. Triumphal return to the family from the larger, public world of Clongowes was a male pattern and freedom in that era. * * * Stephen also takes on the privileges of an adult occasion and an Eton suit, a uniform of social prestige, notably of British public school design. Simon's tears at seeing the suit betray a male identification, Simon thinking back to his father (I.812–16). Stephen recalls the suit years later, and Leopold Bloom has a vision of his long-dead son in similar garb in *Ulysses*.

The argument which develops at Christmas dinner is strongly marked by gender. Simon has been out walking with his radical nationalist friend Mr Casey. The Sunday or holiday walk is another male institution. Politics is a usual topic, and a suburban pub is a probable destination, since drinking laws limited serving to bonafide travellers. Stephen joins his father and Uncle Charles on their constitutionals. He listens and thinks that he is finding a future for himself.

> Trudging along the road or standing in some grimy wayside publichouse his elders spoke constantly of the subjects nearer their hearts, of Irish politics, of Munster and of the legends of their own family, to all of which Stephen lent an avid ear. . . . The hour when he too would take part in the life of that world seemed drawing near and in secret he began to make ready for the great part which he felt awaited him. . . .
> (II.79–88)

Simon Dedalus comes to Christmas dinner prepared by discussion with a like-minded Parnellite to vindicate his fallen political hero. In this territory of mixed gender, Simon meets opposition in Mrs Riordan (Dante), whom Stephen takes as a figure of some intellectual and moral authority, but already sees as subordinate to males and a disappointment in life. He assumes she knows less than priests and recalls his father's assessment of her as a "spoiled nun" (I.996). Stephen is clearly more interested in Mr Casey, an exotic from a sphere of male action and violence, while Dante is a regular domestic feature. Stephen imagines Casey's bold adventures and dangerous connections through the half-told recollections cherished by his father. He likes to sit by Casey and looks "with affection" at his face, which has the same "fierce" appeal that attracted the boy of "An Encounter"[9] to the exotic female figures of detective

9. Second story in *Dubliners* [*Editor*].

fiction (I.990–92). Thus Stephen enters the dinner scene with a
male bias. At the end, when Dante storms out consoled and accompanied by Mrs Dedalus, Stephen is fixed with the men.

Simon Dedalus has an array of rhetorical devices. Cryptic allusions to tales shared with Mr Casey give them mysterious attrac-
tiveness and exclude Dante. Simon's first remark to her accentuates
their different worlds:

> —You didn't stir out at all, Mrs Riordan?
> Dante frowned and said shortly:
> —No. (I.748–50)

Dante's curtness suggests pre-existing difficulties; perhaps she
anticipates the baiting techniques that regularly appear in Simon's
apparently jovial discourse. Simon does arouse her finally with an
anticlerical recollection to the appreciative Mr Casey. Simon admires
a "good answer" made to a canon who had spoken of politics from
the pulpit. Dante is alone in her defence of the role of the church,
though Mrs Dedalus seems a sympathizer, silenced by her husband's
domination. Dante comes across as a defender of strict moral priori-
ties. Her thinking and even her rhetoric derive from church fathers,
not from any female culture. The defence, once summoned, is relentless and ends in the apocalyptic, vengeful discourse of a hell-fire
sermon: "Devil out of hell! We won! We crushed him to death!" It is
impossible to idealize this discourse or identify it as a feminist alternative to Simon's. Its product is sex war.

Simon's speech is far more amusing than Dante's and his tearful
breakdown at the end of the scene tends to evoke the reader's sympathy. His discourse is just as sinister as Dante's, however. We have
seen two examples of baiting. There are others, calling the turkey's
tail "the pope's nose," and a reference to "strangers" in the neighbourhood (foreign intruders, to an Irish audience) (I.903, I.912–
13). Simon moves on to *ad hominem* invective against priests:
"Respect! he said. Is it for Billy with the lip or for the tub of guts up
in Armagh? Respect!" Simon adds the dimension of physical mimicry, "a grimace of heavy bestiality and . . . a lapping noise with his
lips" (I.923–24, I.932–33). In the late parts of his performance,
Simon receives his friend's support, Mr Casey providing useful
nods and reinforcing echoes of Simon's opinions. To Dante's charge
of "renegade" Catholicism, Casey embraces a significantly male-
identified Catholicism: "I am a catholic as my father was and his
father before him . . ." (I.970–71). Indeed, Catholicism does have
different male and female versions in Ireland, Joyce suggests
repeatedly.

Casey's own narrative performance is the story of "the famous
spit." Casey creates himself as the hero at the centre of his

narrative. As in the larger Christmas dinner scene, there is female opposition, an old woman, who like Dante lacks the wit so apparent in the men. Casey prepares his response, holding off through several of her verbal assaults, the delay in the narrative arousing the curiosity of his audience and Simon's appreciative prompting. The woman plays right into his hands, presenting her face for his *"Phth!,"* which Casey delivers twice, for effect, in his narrative. Like Simon, he also has skills of mimicry, which he turns toward the representation of her screams and exclamations (I.1047–52). Casey's spit offers paradigms of male physical and sexual assault upon a woman grown despicable by age as well as speech. Male production denies female speech. The old woman's message, a condemnation of Parnell's extramarital love, Kitty O'Shea, shows complicity in the moral norms of male hegemony, a familiar aspect of woman's consciousness in the shared culture, to which Joyce was sensitive.

Simon's final subject at Christmas dinner, the fall of the great man of Irish history, Charles Stuart Parnell, [reveals his] version of Irish history[. It] is peopled by great and infamous men, and treats of a series of wars and political struggles, much like the Roman history studied by young Stephen * * *. In Ireland, as Kenner notes, defeat and betrayal are recurrent outcomes, and the discourse takes on tones of regret and nostalgia for bygone greatness. Simon's lists of former heroes and gross betrayers are long and embellished, the heroes including his male ancestors. He began his Christmas remarks with a gesture toward the portrait of his grandfather, "condemned to death as a whiteboy" (I.1086). In Cork, Simon reminisces tearfully about his father. In the street by the old House of Commons, he recalls Flood, Grattan and other parliamentarians predating the Act of Union (a parliamentary unification of Ireland with England which occurred in 1800). Simon follows his citation of the heroic grandfather with a well-prepared list of traitor priests:

> —Didn't the bishops of Ireland betray us in the time of the union when bishop Lanigan presented an address of loyalty to the Marquess Cornwallis? Didn't the bishops and priests sell the aspirations of their country in 1829 in return for catholic emancipation? Didn't they denounce the fenian movement from the pulpit and the confessionbox? And didn't they dishonour the ashes of Terence Bellew MacManus? (I.1101–07)

Simon's final tearful utterances on Parnell are familiar to readers of "Ivy Day in the Committee Room," where Joe Hynes shares both the subject and the discourse, as he will again on the all-male occasion of the funeral in the "Hades" chapter of *Ulysses*. Stephen's memories of Paris in the "Proteus" episode of *Ulysses* are haunted by a fallen Fenian father, Kevin Egan.

* * *

[Stephen and Women]

Joyce's mythical explorations of the construction of the psychological subject greatly favour the male subject, beginning with ones resembling himself—the male persona of *Chamber Music,* the boys in *Dubliners,* and of course Stephen Dedalus. Hélène Cixous suggests that the becoming of the subject is a perpetual theme in Joyce, starting her analysis with "The Sisters,"[1] but extending it to include Stephen.[2] This is a concept which helps us around Stephen Dedalus' classic Aristotelian value of "stasis," and his apparent identification with the father, and one that moves him toward the mythic principle of "transitionality" that Lauter has found in women poets.[3] We have considered the male cultural influences on Stephen's development * * *, and can leave his development in terms of identification with the father to Joyce's Freudian critics.[4] What seems more controversial in feminist terms is his mode of rejecting his mother and other women. Feminists, led by Florence Howe, have been particularly troubled by Stephen's viewing of female subjects like the bird-girl as "other," as defined by Simone de Beauvoir in *The Second Sex.*[5]

Stephen makes some rather artificial, literary constructions of woman as "other" or distant muse that are less constructive than deeper, psychological contacts that spring from his mother. The artificial literary constructions show the immature artist's handling of male-devised literary and liturgical conventions, and are what was found deficient in early feminist critiques. In *Stephen Hero,* when Stephen has his first significant contact with a lively, desirable young woman, Emma Clery, he finds her "image" incongruous to his aesthetics and the verses he has composed: "He knew that it was not for such an image that he constructed a theory of art and life and a garland of verses and yet if he could have been sure of her he would have held his art and verses lightly enough" (*SH* 158).[6]

1. First story in *Dubliners* [*Editor*].
2. Hélène Cixous, "Joyce: the (r)use of writing", in *Post-structuralist Joyce,* ed. Derek Attridge and Daniel Ferrer (Cambridge, Eng.: Cambridge UP, 1984), 15–30.
3. Estella Lauter, *Women as Mythmakers* (Bloomington: Indiana UP, 1984) [*Editor*].
4. I recommend Edmund Epstein, *The Ordeal of Stephen Dedalus* (Carbondale: Southern Illinois UP, 1971) and Sheldon Brivic, *Joyce between Freud and Jung* (Port Washington, NY: Kennikat, 1980).
5. Florence Howe, "Feminism and Literature," in *Images of Women in Fiction: Feminist Perspectives,* ed. Susan Koppelman Cornillon (Bowling Green, OH: Bowling Green U Popular P, 1972), 260.
6. Ed. John J. Slocum and Herbert Cahoon (New York: New Directions, 1963) [*Editor*].

Joyce had a comparable feeling of incongruity between Nora Barnacle[7] and the image he had cultivated for *Chamber Music*.

Joyce's early verses idealize the parts of woman he has seen emphasized by the decadents (her golden hair [*CP* 13],[8] her bosom, which is good for male reclining [14]), or in icons of the Virgin Mary (the sombre eyes, the snood, the colour blue [19]), or in Elizabethan songs (the "merry green wood" and her "pretty air" [16–18]). Joyce's maiden has a "little garden" (21) but, unlike the stronger Eve, she doesn't cultivate it. She must be summoned or sung to as she sits at a window. "Love" is a solitary male persona, who at one point in the cycle upbraids the beloved for destroying male friendship or perhaps access to a male god: "He is a stranger to me now/ Who was my friend" (25). Throughout, the adored but distrusted maiden is more absent than present, a distant object of conventional, not physical, desire.

Stephen's musing on the unencountered, literary Mercedes is comparable. He finds passive brooding is preferable to interactions with real, noisy children:

> He did not want to play. He wanted to meet in the real world the unsubstantial image which his soul so constantly beheld. * * * They would be alone, surrounded by darkness and silence: and in that moment of supreme tenderness he would be transfigured . . . Weakness and timidity and inexperience would fall from him in that magic moment. (II.173–85)

The bird-girl Stephen views at the close of chapter 4 of *A Portrait* is gazed at (to use Irigaray's[9] concept of basic Greek aesthetics) and rendered poetic, but she is not psychologically encountered. Compared to the *Chamber Music* girl, there is a slightly fuller catalogue of her body, slender legs and full thighs. But the dove she is transformed to was in *Chamber Music* and is a suspiciously religious icon; her likeness to the Virgin Mary is even more strikingly rendered. Though Stephen claims that "her image had passed into his soul forever" and he experiences an ecstasy that is at least partly sexual ("His cheeks were aflame; his body was aglow; his limbs were trembling"), Stephen still represents a woman in conventional terms of the religious call to a vocation. His much-analysed "Villanelle of the Temptress," with its reliance on eucharistic trappings, is a comparable failure. The eucharistic metaphor is troubling, not just because of its religious conventionality, but because of its

7. James Joyce's companion (1884–1951), muse, and then wife, who was from the west of Ireland [*Editor*].
8. *Collected Poems*. New York: Viking, 1957 [*Editor*].
9. Luce Irigaray (b. 1930), Belgian psychoanalyst and feminist cultural theorist [*Editor*].

mixture of spiritual selfishness with the implicit intention to consume the host.

A more significant journey into the unconscious comes after Stephen's bird-girl construction has vanished. He reclines on a nurturing mother earth, then falls into a sleep that is also a fall into a flushed womb through rose-like labia:

> * * * the earth beneath him, the earth that had borne him, had taken him to her breast.
>
> He closed his eyes in the languor of sleep. * * * A world, a glimmer, or a flower? Glimmering and trembling, trembling and unfolding, a breaking light, an opening flower, it spread in endless succession to itself, breaking in full crimson and unfolding and fading to palest rose, leaf by leaf and wave of light by wave of light, flooding all the heavens with its soft flushes every flush deeper than the other. (IV.901–13)

* * *

From the very first scene of *A Portrait*, Stephen takes note of his father's stories. But using a variety of his senses, he also carefully notices his mother's emissions. She has a nice smell; she plays music and encourages his dance, an art form usually associated with women in Joyce. At Clongowes Wood College, he remembers "her feet on the fender and her jewelly slippers were so hot and they had such a lovely warm smell" (I.15–16, I.129–31). She has an erotic relation to language. Her image serves his definition of the word kiss: "His mother put her lips on his cheek; her lips were soft and they wetted his cheek; and they made a tiny little noise: kiss" (I.278–80). This begins Stephen's focus upon maternal lips.[1] Described as soft and wet, the lips suggest not just her mouth, but her vulva, and both are "they" or two. Irigaray focuses upon the diffuseness of sexuality women experience in their bodies. The two lips of the vulva are only one aspect of the multiple sites and surges of female libidinal energy, as opposed to the singular identity and orgasm of the male's penis and corresponding phallocentric language.[2] The lips produce minimal sound, and no word. This is fitting as an aspect of female silence. Yet the sound which is not a word is onomatopoetic and becomes the partial source of the word for Stephen.

---

1. Maud Ellmann works with language and lips, Stephen's as well as his mother's, in "Disremembering Dedalus: *A Portrait of the Artist as a Young Man*," in *Untying the Text: A Post-Structuralist Reader*, ed. Robert Young (Boston and London: Routledge & Kegan Paul, 1981), 189–206.
2. Luce Irigaray, from "This sex which is not one," in *New French Feminisms*, ed. Elaine Marks and Isabelle de Courtivron (Amherst: U of Massachusetts P, 1980), 100–1, 103.

Mrs Dedalus elicits written words in the form of a letter from young Stephen at Clongowes; he is ill and wants to return to his primary source of nurture. Stephen asks, "Please come and take me home" (I.586–87). This is classically Oedipal, but also offers an intriguing relationship between language and the maternal body. Stephen closes *A Portrait* with another female writing form, the diary, which contains a number of entries on his mother as well as Emma, but, at this stage, expresses a determined leave-taking.

Nancy Chodorow's revisions of the theory of the Oedipus complex suggest that young men are helped in resolving their desire for the mother by replacing her with the women they encounter as prospective and actual mates.[3] Stephen continues to read the semiotics of the maternal body in the girls and women he meets, and to note occurrences of silence and suggestions of alternative languages. His own imagery re-creates female pulsions and genital forms. Stephen notices water "falling softly in a brimming bowl" at the culmination of chapter 1 of *A Portrait* (I.1848). He reads, almost as language, the look in the eyes of a girl and the pressure of her hand; her nonverbal expressions have a fluid, soothing effect that reaches to his brain and body even in memory, setting a pattern for future reception of female semiotics.

> He could remember only that she had worn a shawl about her head like a cowl and that her dark eyes had invited and unnerved him. . . . Then in the dark and unseen by the other two he rested the tips of the fingers of one hand upon the palm of the other hand, scarcely touching it and yet pressing upon it lightly. But the pressure of her fingers had been lighter and steadier: and suddenly the memory of their touch traversed his brain and body like an invisible warm wave. (II.807–16)

Stephen's first encounter with a prostitute involves more communication by gesture and pressure than actual language on her part, or significantly, on his:

*   *   *

* * * Her round arms held him firmly to her and he, seeing her face lifted to him in serious calm and feeling the warm calm rise and fall of her breast, all but burst into hysterical weeping. Tears of joy and relief shone in his delighted eyes and his lips parted though they would not speak.

*   *   *

3. Nancy Chodorow, *The Reproduction of Mothering* (Berkeley: U of Calif. P, 1978), 167.

With a sudden movement she bowed his head and joined her
lips to his and he read the meaning of her movements in her
frank uplifted eyes. It was too much for him. He closed his
eyes, surrendering himself to her, body and mind, conscious of
nothing in the world but the dark pressure of her softly parting
lips. They pressed upon his brain as upon his lips as though
they were the vehicle of a vague speech; and between them he
felt an unknown and timid pressure, darker than the swoon of
sin, softer than sound or odour. (II.1437–42, 1450–58)

Stephen begins with an effort to control the situation by speech but
the prostitute's own "vehicle of a vague speech" moves him to
uncharacteristic silence, submission and almost to hysterical weeping. "Hysterical," derived from "hyster," the Greek word for womb,
is a negative symptom attributed particularly to women by Freud; it
has been rehabilitated in some feminist theory as an expressive and
useful form for organizing language.[4] Stephen ceases his gaze and
opens his brain and body to an alternative experience, which is
articulated in terms of the female body's warmth, the rise and fall
of her breast, the pressure of her soft parted lips, experiences
darker and softer than the intellectual, moral or sensuous experiences he has known in the world, but reminiscent of his mother's
early kiss.

Even during his reactionary period of self-imposed asceticism,
Stephen is receptive of muted voices merged with female form, the
ubera or breasts. He takes as his text the other-worldly "Song of
Songs":[5]

A faded world of fervent love and virginal responses seemed to
be evoked for his soul by the reading of its pages . . . An inaudible voice seemed to caress the soul, telling her names and
glories, bidding her arise as for espousal and come away, bidding her look forth, a spouse, from Amana and from the mountains of the leopards; and the soul seemed to answer with the
same inaudible voice, surrendering herself: *Inter ubera mea
commorabitur.* (IV.180–88)

Stephen's soul is feminine in pronoun and behaviour. The final surrender unites feminine soul with maternal bosom, an expression of
primal feminine affinity, even lesbianism. Stephen's production of
language or art is frequently inspired by the maternal, female body,
the muse as semiotician. In his discourse with Lynch, Stephen

4. Robin Tolmach Lakoff, "Women's language," in *Women's Language and Style*, ed.
[Douglas] Butturff and [Edmund L.] Epstein (Akron: L&S Books, 1978), 152.
5. See note 7, p. 132 [*Editor*].

admits that scholasticism is not enough to go beyond asthetics to actual creation:

> So far as this side of esthetic [sic] philosophy extends Aquinas will carry me all along the line. When we come to the phenomena of artistic conception, artistic gestation and artistic reproduction I require a new terminology and a new personal experience. (V.1268–72)

Lynch enjoys the sexual metaphors, but postpones the discussion— forever, as far as A Portrait goes. In the scene where Stephen composes his villanelle, the word emerges from the womb: "O! In the virgin womb of the imagination the word was made flesh. Gabriel the seraph had come to the virgin's chamber" (V.1543–45).

Stephen's openness to female semiotics as a marginal form of communication is in keeping with his feelings of marginality as an Irish speaker of English:

> * * * His language, so familiar and so foreign, will always be for me an acquired speech. I have not made or accepted its words. My voice holds them at bay. My soul frets in the shadow of his language. (V.556–59)

Notably, it is the soul, the female aspect of himself, that frets. Stephen also recognizes that he has special and different things to do with words. He meditates upon a phrase he has made, "A day of dappled seaborne clouds":

> * * * was it that, being as weak of sight as he was shy of mind, he drew less pleasure from the reflection of the glowing sensible world through the prism of a language manycoloured and richly storied than from the contemplation of an inner world of individual emotions mirrored perfectly in a lucid supple periodic prose? (IV.698–703)

Stephen's interests here, though not comprehensive of Joyce, bear elements of what has been identified as male as well as female literary form. His direction toward an "inner world" diverts him from the masculine realm. His multiple interests, his fascination with rhythm, his willingness to watch colours in the process of changing, and his "supple periodic prose" suggest multiplicity, fluidity and recycling, aspects attached to the female body and female writing. But the "periodic" also suggests what Virginia Woolf called the masculine sentence;[6] at this point Stephen aspires to the exact and culminating phrase, a control of language and desire for

---

6. Virginia Woolf, A Room of One's Own (1928; New York: Harcourt Brace and World, 1963, 79).

representation (though different in its inward direction) that has
been identified with male language. Stephen's habit of imposing
Latin on an encounter with a young girl, *mulier cantat* (V.2479),
and mother love, *amor matris* (U 2.165), is also questionable as a
form of linguistic distancing, learned through the church.

* * *

[*Joyce and Women's Language*]

The language of flowers is one way that the female body is "written"
(as Cixous and practitioners of *écriture féminine*[7] put it) in Joyce,
though it is not exclusively identified with female writers. In [one]
passage in *A Portrait* * * * a rosy glow seems to open into a metaphorical journey into labia for Stephen. Molly Bloom takes up her
husband's identification of her body with flowers, "Yes he said I was
a Flower of the mountain yes so we are flowers all a womans body
yes that was one true thing he said in his life" (U 18.1576–7). Bloom's
gift of eight poppies was effective in wooing Molly. As "Henry
Flower," Bloom gives Martha Clifford a subject to write about, and
he thinks again of the affinity of women to flowers in terms of silence:
"language of flowers. They like it because no-one can hear" (5.261).
ALP, in encouraging HCE near the end of the *Wake*, describes her
hands "in the linguo of flows" (621.22). Issy's accompanying girls
are written as flowers and flowers typically triumph over ruins in the
Wake landscape.

In *Finnegans Wake*, female identities write themselves in several
ways. This is somewhat surprising in the case of the mother, whom
we have seen written but not writing in early Joyce. According to
Susan Rubin Suleiman, female as well as male writers offer a written, but not a writing mother.[8] The "Mamafesta"[9] or hen's letter is
probably the most obvious woman's writing, though there is constantly the issue of forgery by Shem or Issy,[1] or even T.S. Eliot,
where the language of "The Waste Land" seems evident. The text is
written, written over and analysed, becoming a collective expression of both genders, a palimpsest, an anastomotic text.[2]

---

7. "Female writing" (French) [*Editor*].
8. "Writing and Motherhood," in *The (M)other Tongue: Essays in Feminist Psychoanalytic
   Interpretation*, ed. Shirley Nelson Gardner, Claire Kahane, and Madelon Sprengnether
   (Ithaca, NY: Cornell UP, 1985), 356–60.
9. Word from *Finnegans Wake* that suggests both the mother and a manifesto [*Editor*].
1. In the Earwicker family of *Finnegans Wake*, Shem is one of the male children, and Issy,
   or Iseult, is the only female child [*Editor*].
2. Characterized by anastomosis, the connection among individual parts of a branching
   system into a network, as in the capillary connections in the vessel network of the
   human circulatory system [*Editor*].

* * *

Woman's language has some variants in Joyce. It may be as ancient as the cuneiform wedge or as common as Molly's *lingua franca*. It makes do with available surfaces, an egg or a rock. It is an essential variant for the male writer, and allows him a measure of self-criticism. Female modernism, as constructed by Joyce, does not show off with densities and portmanteau words: "But how many of her readers realise that she is not out to dizzledazzle with a graith uncouthrement of postmantuam glasseries from the lapins and the grigs" (*FW* 112.36–113.2). Though he may raise a "meandering male fist" of control, the action is sure to be mocked by his own female writer. Female language may flow in and from the body, or be woven or played as music. The aesthetic of women's language is sufficiently broad to embrace both the goddess and Stephen Dedalus in the artistic life-sustaining process: "As we, or mother Dana, weave and unweave our bodies, Stephen said, from day to day, their molecules shuttled to and fro, so does the artist weave and unweave his image" (*U* 9.376–8). We find ALP a musician-weaver. "Windaug," she weaves like Penelope, making music as did Mrs Dedalus in Stephen's first perceptions of her. She also unweaves, flowing away into impersonality and recombination of gender, as she rejoins her sky mother and sea father. ALP is allowed lush sound, but no personal ambition. There is no culminating, final sentence. Her language is as interrupted, interruptable as the final half-sentence of *Finnegans Wake*. Yet her feminine language is what provides the umbilicus, the "vicus" of recirculation,[3] and offers a new politics of relationship and authorship. As she flows to the sea, Anna thinks of the writer of "work in progress" (the working title Joyce used for *Finnegans Wake*) and says with confidence, "But it's by this route he'll come some morrow" (625.13–14).

Anna's route cannot fully satisfy the woman writer or gynocritic who has a shaping vision, a self-defining ambition and tradition, along with her physical female form, to equate with language. Still, the French feminist paradigms of writing the feminine enrich our reading of Joyce, taking us beyond Freud and beyond structuralism. A troubling possibility is that Joyce's writing of woman still serves a male author's ego, proving he can move into "other" forms. On the other hand, if the move is made, not in the spirit of epic conquest, but as wanderer-gatherer and re-viewer of writing, we should wish for more male writers who will follow in Anna's wake.

---

3. "Vicus of recirculation" (*FW* 3.2). "Vicus" suggests, among other meanings, a road [*Editor*].

CHRISTINE FROULA

[Male Initiation, Recovering Buried Femininity, and the Villanelle in *A Portrait of the Artist as a Young* WoMan][†]

* * *

In exploring the reciprocal yet mutually interfering psychodynamics of individual and collective desire, Joyce * * * brings to light some profound psychohistorical and cultural consequences of the son's early identification with the maternal body under the psychosocial law that forbids that identification and dictates its repression. His writings thus contribute to the modernist project of investigating the unconscious dynamics of subjectivity and culture in fundamental and startling ways, even as they make good Stephen Dedalus's vow to forge in the "smithy" of his soul or psyche a critical conscience for his race. If, as Freud wrote, conscience is the repository of the "cultural past," Joyce's ambition to forge an as yet uncreated collective conscience puts the rethinking of the cultural past at the heart of modernity's critical enterprise. Departing from earlier feminist views of Joyce as a misogynist, a patriarch, an inventor of *écriture féminine*,[1] a masochist, I ally Joyce's vow to bring his culture's collective unconscious to consciousness and conscience with the revolutionary energies of feminism and psychoanalysis. * * *

* * *

In framing Joyce's self-portraiture as cultural critique, I locate the autobiographical dimension of his work not in any naive, necessary, or simple correspondences between his artist-figures and himself, the represented events of their lives and the actual events of his own, but in their status as fictional self-projections—virtual selves created and performed through writing—whose adventures belong first to the life of Joyce-the-artist and only secondarily (when at all) to Joyce's life as actually lived. As we shall see, the texts at moments explicitly assert this continuity between Joyce-the-artist and his characters, with a self-irony that silently hoists on its

---

† From *Modernism's Body: Sex, Culture, and Joyce* (New York: Columbia UP, 1996), pp. xi–xii, 2, 34, 37–38, 41, 43–50, 53–55, 58–66, 68–72, 259–60, 266–67, 269–71, 273–74. Copyright © 1996 Columbia University Press. Reprinted with permission of Columbia University Press. Some of the author's notes have been omitted. Page references for *A Portrait* have been replaced with part and line numbers of this Norton Critical Edition. Some cited passages might differ slightly from the equivalent passages in this volume.
1. See note 7, p. 390 [*Editor*].

petard[2] the unwary reader who would patronize his characters at the expense of his cultural analysis. With Cindy Shermanlike masquerade,[3] parody, and play, Joyce projects autobiographical artist-figures whose unruly desires are ostentatiously mediated yet not entirely subdued by his culture. * * * Much is at stake in the jocoserious[4] self-irony of these performative self-representations, for, far from comfortably distancing the artist (and by extension his readers) from his characters, as pure irony would do, it unsettlingly implicates him—and with him, his readers—in his culturally derived personae and the critique they set in motion.[5]

* * *

Although Joyce composed his villanelle long before he began writing *A Portrait of the Artist as a Young Man*, Hans Walter Gabler concludes from manuscript evidence that Joyce incorporated the villanelle episode into *Portrait* in final form only in 1914, after he had written out the rest of the work in fair copy, and "appreciably later at that."[6] If Gabler is right, the villanelle scene culminates *Portrait*'s compositional history if not its narrative, consolidating a stage of artistic development not only for Stephen (whose villanelle is the only one of his poems *Portrait* transcribes) but for Joyce, who, in completing it, completed *Portrait* itself.

The cry that announces the villanelle's conception—"O! In the virgin womb of the imagination the word is made flesh"—famously figures Stephen's labor to forge his literary authority as a transsexual Annunciation in which the Virgin/artist transmutes words into the

2. The proverbial expression "hoist with his own petard," meaning blown up by their bomb, that is, injured by a device meant to harm others (*OED*), originates with Shakespeare (*Hamlet* 3.4.214) [Editor].

3. The American artist Cindy Sherman (b. 1954) is known for her photographic self-portraiture as various imagined personas, often in extravagant costumes and makeup [Editor].

4. Partly jocular, partly serious (*OED*); used by Joyce in episode 17 of *Ulysses* [Editor].

5. My readings [of *Ulysses* and *Finnegans Wake* later in *Modernism's Body*] in subsequent chapters flesh out the position on Joyce's self-portraiture I sketch here, particularly the crucial distinction between the comfort of ironic distance and Joyce's unsettling self-irony. For a useful discussion of the decades-long debate on the question of irony in Joyce's characterization, see James. J. Sosnoski, "Reading Acts and Reading Warrants: Some Implications for Readers Responding to Joyce's Portrait of Stephen," *JJQ* [*James Joyce Quarterly*] 16 (1979): 43–63. On Joyce, gender, and the genre of autobiographical fiction, see my "Gender and the Law of Genre: Joyce, Woolf, and the Autobiographical Artist-Novel," in *New Alliances in Joyce Studies*, ed. Bonnie Kime Scott (Cranbury, N.J.: Associated University Presses, 1988), pp. 155–64.

6. The villanelle remained unpublished until *Portrait* appeared in 1916, but Stanislaus Joyce reports that Joyce actually wrote it around 1900 when he was about Stephen's age (*My Brother's Keeper*, ed. Richard Ellmann [New York: Faber and Faber, 1958], pp. 100, 158; JJ [Richard Ellmann, *James Joyce: New and Revised Edition* (New York: Oxford UP, 1982), 76 n]). Hans Walter Gabler, "The Seven Lost Years of *A Portrait of the Artist as a Young Man*," in *Approaches to Joyce's Portrait: Ten Essays*, ed. Thomas F. Staley and Bernard Benstock (Pittsburgh: University of Pittsburgh Press, 1976), p. 44.

symbolic "flesh" of his poem.[7] But how does this aspiring modern artist come to cast himself as the Virgin in his psychodrama of creativity * * *? And what is his accomplished but indisputably premodernist verse, with its eucharistic iconography, doing in a self-portrait of an avowedly "modern" artist at work? Rather than attribute this seeming incongruity to Joyce's ironic distance on the residual idle blasphemy of his younger artist-self, I shall situate Stephen's bold masquerade as Virgin/artist of the villanelle within *Portrait's* exploration of the psychohistorical and psychosocial processes of his male initiation, by which his culture imposes—and he both embodies and dissects—its law of gender. * * *

                                        *   *   *

Drawing on anthropological and psychoanalytic descriptions of male initiation to frame *Portrait* as a narrative of Stephen's initiation into a culture inseparable from gender, [I] trace Stephen's progress toward his Virgin/artist identity through his subjection and resistance to such initiatory agencies as family, school, church, state, and literary and folk cultures.[8] I shall first outline certain paradigms of male initiation that alert us to the narrative and imagistic structures of *Portrait's* initiation story and then chart Stephen's progress from his initiatory "death" through a prolonged liminal (or threshold) state to his forging of a new identity within his fathers' culture. This identity is consolidated in the villanelle scene—the first fully realized scene of writing in Joyce's canon and one that self-ironically displays his amalgamated Daedalian Virgin/artist powers, refracting the social contradictions of gender through the young artist's culturally constructed "body."[9] * * *

7. As Suzette Henke puts it in "Stephen Dedalus and Women: A Portrait of the Artist as a Young Misogynist," in *Women in Joyce,* eds. Henke and Elaine Unkeless (Bloomington: Indiana University Press, 1982), Stephen attempts to "usurp [female] procreative powers" through an "aesthetic endeavor [that is] a kind of 'couvade'—a rite of psychological compensation for the male's inability to give birth" (97).

8. For a comparison of initiatory paradigms in the *Odyssey* and *Ulysses,* see Erwin R. Steinberg, "Telemachus, Stephen, and the Paradigm of the Initiation Rite," *JJQ* 19 (1982): 289–301, who locates Stephen at the end of *Ulysses* within the liminal and marginal state that Victor Turner [in *The Ritual Process: Structure and Anti-Structure* (Chicago: Aldine, 1969), 128] associates with artists and prophets. Steinberg does not view Stephen's search for artistic identity as continuous with Joyce's realization of it nor consider the gender dynamics of Stephen's initiation.

9. Readings of the villanelle scene have tended to reinstate certain repressions it dismantles, including the psychodynamics of cross-gender desire. [In "The Villanelle Perplex: Reading Joyce" (*JJQ* 25 [Fall 1987]), Robert Adams Day notes that the villanelle is a "crux" about which either we "happily feel we can keep on arguing . . . forever, or we feel a deep if vague conviction that the crux can be solved (also forever) if someone will only use the right method" (69); Day, who includes a useful bibliography of criticism and debate, reads the villanelle scene as Joyce's demonstration that the young Stephen fails to meet his own artistic criterion of impersonality: "Talent is there, but Cupid gets in the way" (83). Robert Scholes, "Stephen Dedalus, Poet or Esthete?," in *A Portrait of the Artist as a Young Man: Text, Criticism, and Notes,* ed. Chester G. Anderson (New York: Viking, 1968), pp. 468–80, also interprets the scene in terms of oedipal

Paradigms of Male Initiation

* * *

Portrait's narrative of Stephen Dedalus's initiation roughly follows the three stages analyzed by van Gennep and Turner,[1] whereby the boy undergoes separation from his mother's world and symbolic death as his mother's child; proceeds through a disorienting, identityless liminal stage in which temporary, fleeting, virtual selves are tried on and cast off like masks; and, through "rites of incorporation," is at last "reborn" or consolidated as a masculine subject, his fathers' child. Stephen's initiation into his culture's law of gender begins with a crisis of identity, represented as illness and symbolic "death," as that law forces him to split off and repress his early maternal identification (stage 1). He then passes through a long liminal stage of virtual and temporary identifications, during which he is a kind of empty mirror in which myriad cultural identities are fleetingly and insubstantially reflected (stage 2). When at last he "reincorporates" his identity in his fathers' culture, it is by forging an artistic authority that enables him to reintegrate his lost mother/ self (outwardly complying with the law of gender while escaping through a loophole in his art)—an authority he learns from such cultural fathers as Yahweh/Adam, Zeus, and Daedalus, whose symbolic wombs become the matrix for his own (stage 3).[2] Outfoxing the forces of cultural repression, Stephen/Joyce's art traces the buried life of his early mother/self as it furtively seeks expression, at first through unconscious identifications with actual and imaginary women and later in an art that self-ironically exposes the mechanisms of repression in the very act of fulfilling forbidden desire. Even as Joyce's art reproduces his culture's law of gender, I shall be arguing, it also puts it radically in question. By exposing its workings, Joyce not only makes art out of his symptom but makes his symptom that of his culture, and his self-vivisection, a cultural anatomy. To that extent, he moves beyond the fathers in whose

---

rather than identificatory desire; the villanelle is addressed to "a muse who is a traditionally feminine and mythic figure. . . . For the virgin who lured the seraphim from heaven a flowing chalice is raised in celebration" (478).

1. Arnold van Gennep, *The Rites of Passage* (Chicago: U of Chicago P, 1960); Turner, *The Ritual Process* [Editor].
2. See Eva Fetter Kittay, "Womb Envy: An Explanatory Concept," in *Mothering: Essays in Feminist Theory*, ed. Joyce Trebilcot (Totowa, NJ: Rowman and Allanheld, 1984), pp. 94–128, esp. 109–115 * * *. On Zeus's swallowing of the pregnant Metis to give birth to Athena, see Robert Fagles and W. B. Stanford, "The Serpent and the Eagle," in *Aeschylus: The Oresteia,* trans. Fagles (New York: Viking/Bantam, 1982) [Author]. In Judaism, Yahweh is the creator of the universe, the one god. Adam is the original patriarch in Christian history. Zeus, god of thunder, is the king of the ancient Greek gods. Daedalus, the great inventor and craftsman in Greek mythology, is, as a wise father, the dominant figure by contrast with his foolish son, Icarus [Editor].

image he fashions himself into the critical modernity Stephen claims in his manifesto to Cranly.

Stage 1. Initiatory Death: "Farewell, my mother!"

Portrait's first section, which begins with the moocow story Simon tells his son and concludes with Stephen's triumph in the pandybat episode at Clongowes, narrates both Stephen's physical separation from his mother and his enforced renunciation of that part of himself identified with her. * * *

*   *   *

The allusive fragments of language with which Joyce surrounds the infant Stephen intimate the loss he must sustain in order to gain the fathers' world: not only home and mother but the part of himself identified with the maternal world. These early rehearsals of male initiation introduce Stephen's experience at Clongowes, the scene of his initiatory death. Stephen arrives still closely tied to his mother, who admonishes him tearfully as she kisses him good-bye not to "speak with the rough boys in the college. Nice mother!" (I.78). At first he experiences this new world in her terms: "It was nice and warm to see the lights in the castle. . . . And there were nice sentences in Doctor Cornwell's Spelling Book. . . . It would be nice to lie on the hearthrug before the fire" (I.110–20). But soon the older, bigger Wells—the sadistic self-appointed priest of Stephen's initiation * * *—intervenes, driving a wedge of self-consciousness between his mother-identified self and the masculine self his initiation installs in its stead. * * *

*   *   *

Obscurely recognizing Wells's authority—"Wells must know the right answer for he was in the third of grammar"—Stephen responds accurately if unconsciously to the performative grammar of male initiation by internalizing the damned-if-you-do/damned-if-you-don't embarrassment in which Wells traps him as a new anxiety about kissing. Once a spontaneous expression of affection associated with his "nice" mother, kissing now becomes an alienated object of analysis: "Was it right to kiss his mother or wrong to kiss his mother? What did that mean, to kiss? . . . His mother put her lips on his cheek; her lips were soft and they wetted his cheek; and they made a tiny little noise: kiss. Why did people do that with their two faces?" (I.275–80). Recurring throughout *Portrait*, the kissing phobia Wells's teasing engenders in Stephen symptomatically registers the barrier of repression his initiation sets up not only between himself and his mother but between himself and the earlier self continuous with her, figured in all the women he finds himself unable to kiss.[3]

Wells brutally enforces Stephen's initiation into masculine culture by shouldering him into the rat-infested square ditch. Like the ritual tortures of some initiation ceremonies, this baptism-by-slime—the ostensible cause of the delirious fever that frames much of the Clongowes narrative—dramatizes a violent break with his mother. Having found it impossible to avoid "the rough boys" as his mother has warned him to do, Stephen now has occasion to heed his father's instruction "whatever he did, never to peach on a fellow" (I.85–86). His immersion allegorizes a death-by-drowning of his early mother/self and the origin of an unconscious haunted by this repressed ghost; and his illness refracts his inner crisis through the expressionist lens of his delirium. "Sick in your breadbasket," says Fleming sympathetically, but Stephen "was not sick there. He thought that he was sick in his heart if you could be sick in that place" (I.221–22). He mourns his mother's world and his former state: he counts the days until Christmas vacation and longs to return to his infancy, remembering how he saw from the train to Clongowes "a woman standing at the halfdoor of a cottage with a child in her arms. . . . It would be lovely to sleep for one night in that cottage before the fire of smoking turf, in the dark lit by the fire, in the warm dark" (I.387–91). But already, this regressive yearning evokes fear of losing the separate, masculine self Stephen's initiation is causing him to forge: "But, O, the road there between the trees was dark! You would be lost in the dark. It made him afraid to think of how it was" (I.392–94).

The narrative stages the violent and traumatic sacrifice of Stephen's mother-identified self to Clongowes's culture of "rough boys" as a symbolic, initiatory death, from which, bedridden in the infirmary, he appeals to his mother to save him in an imaginary letter: "Dear Mother / I am sick. I want to go home. Please come and take me home. I am in the infirmary. / Your fond son, / Stephen" (I.585–89). Dreaming of death, he inwardly performs his own elegy with a song his nurse once sang:

> *Dingdong! The castle bell!*
> *Farewell, my mother!*
> *Bury me in the old churchyard*
> *Beside my eldest brother.*
> *My coffin shall be black,*
> *Six angels at my back,*

3. Joyce took Aloysius for his confirmation name after Aloysius Gonzaga, patron saint of Clongowes, said to be so holy that he refused to look at, let alone kiss, his mother (*JJ* 230–31).

Two to sing and two to pray
And two to carry my soul away. (I.606–13)

As Stephen is ill not in his "breadbasket" but in his "heart," his lament commemorates not his body's death but the symbolic death of the early "soul" or psyche that his Clongowes experience teaches him to murder and bury, as his elder "brothers"—Wells and the rest—have done before him.

Stage 2. Threshold Dramas: Memory and Mummery

Although the Clongowes narrative ends in momentary heroic triumph as Stephen's schoolmates celebrate his protest against his unjust pandying, his experience at the school does not complete his initiation but leaves him lingering in melancholy between his lost early self and a future identity as a son of the fathers that he has yet to forge. Throughout much of *Portrait* he remains, in Victor Turner's words, a liminal or "threshold" person, "neither here nor there; . . . betwixt and between the positions assigned and arrayed by law, custom, convention, and ceremonial."[4] In the infirmary, Stephen associates his initiatory death with Parnell's actual death, which, through the bitter exchange at the Dedalus Christmas dinner, comes to stand for the mysterious, evidently dangerous masculine estate that he knows he must enter: "It pained him that he did not know well what politics meant. . . . When would he be like the fellows in poetry and rhetoric?" (I.345–48). Years later, he still has not wholeheartedly acceded to the fate of being his father's son. When, traveling with his father in Cork, he finds the word *Foetus* cut in a school desk while searching for Simon's initials, the sight shocks him into remembering his repressed early self and its symbolic death:

> . . . he had . . . dreamed of being dead, . . . of being buried then in the little graveyard . . . But he had not died then. Parnell had died. . . . He had not died but he had faded out like a film in the sun. He had been lost or had wandered out of existence for he no longer existed. How strange to think of him

---

4. Turner, *The Ritual Process*, p. 95. Turner describes the three phases as follows: "The first phase (of separation) comprises symbolic behavior signifying the detachment of the individual or group either from an earlier fixed point in the social structure, from a set of cultural conditions (a 'state'), or from both. During the intervening 'liminal' period, the characteristics of the ritual subject (the 'passenger') are ambiguous; he passes through a cultural realm that has few or none of the attributes of the past or coming state. In the third phase (reaggregation or reincorporation), the passage is consummated. The ritual subject, individual or corporate, is in a relatively stable state once more and, by virtue of this, has rights and obligations vis-à-vis others of a clearly defined and 'structural' type; he is expected to behave in accordance with certain customary norms and ethical standards binding on incumbents of social position in a system of such positions" (94–95).

passing out of existence in such a way, not by death but by fading out in the sun or by being lost and forgotten somewhere in the universe! It was strange to see his small body appear again for a moment: a little boy in a grey belted suit. (II.1161–75)

Seeking his father's initials, which are also his own, Stephen finds instead a word that evokes his early self merged with the mother, a self now "buried" or "lost," "faded out" or "wandered out of existence," "forgotten somewhere in the universe" upon his initiation into masculine culture. The word *Foetus* shatters the (in Stephen's case, fragile) repression that keeps this early self buried in his unconscious and estranges him from the still-tentative masculine identity that binds him into his fathers' world. Stranded on the threshold between his lost childhood and his paternal identity, he repeats like empty tokens the signs that constitute him as "his father's son" [II.1208]: "I am Stephen Dedalus. I am walking beside my father whose name is Simon Dedalus. We are in Cork, in Ireland. Cork is a city. Our room is in the Victoria Hotel. Victoria and Stephen and Simon. Simon and Stephen and Victoria. Names" (II.1152–55).

This sudden apparition of Stephen's forbidden self through the barrier of repression that founds his masculine identity opens an abyss between him and the world of his fathers:

His mind seemed older than theirs: it shone coldly on their strifes and happiness and regrets like a moon upon a younger earth. No life or youth stirred in him as it had stirred in them. He had known neither the pleasure of companionship with others nor the vigour of rude male health nor filial piety. Nothing stirred within his soul but a cold and cruel and loveless lust. His childhood was dead or lost and with it his soul capable of simple joys, and he was drifting amid life like the barren shell of the moon. (II.1260–68)

Stuck in melancholy liminality, Stephen mirrors his lost "soul" or psyche in the weary, wandering, uncompanioned moon of Shelley's fragment "To the Moon": *"Art thou pale for weariness / Of climbing heaven and gazing on the earth / Wandering companionless . . ."* (II.1269–71). Apostrophized by Shelley as "chosen sister of the spirit," the moon would seem to be female here as elsewhere in Joyce. But here, the moon's "barren shell" figures that femininity as lost or dead, and Stephen himself as a vessel emptied of early maternal plenitude, a bitter remnant of that lost female self that he opposes to his fathers' alien world. Contrasting his barren moon with their young and lively earth, his empty lust with their "rude male health," he memorializes and grieves for a "dead or lost" child-hood that he remembers only dimly and cannot revive, with a sense of loss that the pleasures and privileges of the masculine estate—male companionship, manly vigor, "filial piety"—do not assuage. Momentarily exposing his masculinity as masquerade, Stephen evokes a vestigial female self so deeply buried that it can emerge from repression only as loss, death, the emptied-out shell of a bar-ren moon.

The Cork scene confirms the long liminal state that Stephen passes through after leaving Clongowes. He walks the fathers' world like a ghost of his earlier self, "fade[d] like a film in the sun," while covertly reanimating his lost female self by projecting it upon actual and imaginary women even as he pursues his masculine education. Outwardly, he tries to learn by heart the words of his father and uncle Charles, preparing for the "great part" he feels awaits him in the world (II.88). Inwardly, he dramatizes his exile from his lost mother/self by playing the Count of Monte Cristo, who, proudly and tragically distanced from Mercedes in her rose garden, acts out a variant of Stephen's refusal to kiss with the line, "Madame, I never eat muscatel grapes" (II.111). Stephen makes Mercedes—whose rose garden recalls the "green rose" of art that will resurrect his buried self—his ideal not of a desired object but of a desired self, an animated mirror in whom he seeks himself "transfigured" [II.184].

* * *

* * * [A] failed real-life kiss inspires Stephen's first poem, "To E—C—," wherein "when the moment of farewell had come the kiss, which had been withheld by one, was given by both" (II.386–87). Stephen sits apart at a children's party as "E—C—" flirts with him, "flattering, taunting, searching, exciting his heart" (II.316). As they ride home on the tram, Emma's eyes[5] "beneath their cowl" remind him that in "some dim past, whether in life or in revery, he had heard their tale before" (II.336–87). With this glimpse of his lost self (and possibly, too, of his childhood friend Eileen) in Emma's eyes, erotic desire fails ("I could easily catch hold of her . . . nobody is looking. I could hold her and kiss her. But he did nei-ther") while identificatory desire obscurely quickens, to be fulfilled in his writing of the poem (II.351–54).

Stephen's one previous attempt to write a poem, on Parnell, has degenerated into names and addresses of Clongowes classmates as "his brain had then refused to grapple with" his theme (II.370–71). But if male heroics leave him cold, the vicissitudes of kissing kindle in Stephen's imagination an art that, like the words "green rose,"

5. E—C— is later identified by her first name, Emma (III.483, 506, 518) [*Editor*].

symbolically creates what "you could not have" in real life. The poem's symbolic kiss, that is, acts out less erotic desire (in this scene E—C—'s body is almost as attenuated as her name) than the restoration of the maternal identification that Wells's kissing riddle has long before broken. As he practices, for the first time, the poetics foreshadowed in his green rose, the artist-son's symbolic power to transform the failed kiss into one "given by both" bodies forth his secret hope that the female self he "could not have" in the real world might exist "somewhere" (I.198). So, at least, suggests the episode's closing scenario: after finishing the poem, Stephen enters "his mother's bedroom and gaze[s] for a long time in the mirror of her dressingtable," as though his act of symbolic creation may have resuscitated the early self once mirrored in his mother; as though seeking visible proof that he has discovered in his art the means to his long-fantasized transfiguration (II.389–90). In *Portrait*'s first vignette of the artist at work, then, Stephen abandons the historical-heroic poetics his Clongowes initiation encouraged to rewrite history in the image of his secret desire. His poem's symbolic kiss makes good losses sustained in the actual world by reviving in the symbolic realm the desire his male initiation has forced him to bury. The ghost of the buried child who sang farewell to his mother in the Clongowes infirmary returns in his mother's mirror.

But Stephen's first poem only temporarily rejoins the masculine and repressed feminine selves split apart by his male initiation. Two years later, on the day of the school play in which he plays a "farcical pedagogue" [II.480], he is still lingering on the threshold of identity. Emma is expected to attend, and all day Stephen remembers their tramride and his poem; but now he hopes for "some further adventure," a consummation in life rather than in the self-transfiguring art that his self-conscious masculinity now impedes: "The old restless moodiness had again filled his breast as it had done on the night of the party but had not found an outlet in verse. The growth and knowledge of two years of boyhood stood between then and now, forbidding such an outlet" (II.617–21). The conflict between Stephen's poetics and his "boyhood" is temporarily submerged as he dons what he usually experiences as the "mummery" of masculinity and seems "For one rare moment . . . to be clothed in the real apparel of boyhood" [II.892–94]—while little Bertie Tallon, cross-dressed in a pink dress, golden wig, sunbonnet, and face paint, parodies the younger poet-self who sought his transfigured image in his mother's mirror (II.505–16). But his hope comes to nothing; Emma does not meet him afterward. Life fails to provide the transfiguration he has earlier sought through art. * * *

* * *

Stage 3. Rebirth: Daedalian Wings, or What Birds Were They?

Stephen awakens to his artistic vocation, and incorporates his new identity in his fathers' culture, through his Daedalian epiphany,[6] a cultural inheritance of symbolic wings that reintegrates his male body with his "female" soul or psyche, enabling him to fly. Walking impatiently while his father arranges his entrance to the university, he meets schoolboy acquaintances swimming in the sea below the Bull bridge and sees in their "pitiable nakedness" his own: "Perhaps they had taken refuge in number and noise from the secret dread in their souls. But he, apart from them and in silence, remembered in what dread he stood of the mystery of his own body" (IV.760–63). As they playfully mock his name, Stephen suddenly hears its prophetic meaning in the "noise of dim waves" and sees "a winged form flying above the waves":

> What did it mean? . . . a hawklike man flying sunward above the sea, a prophecy of the end he had been born to serve and had been following through the mists of childhood and boyhood, a symbol of the artist forging anew in his workshop out of the sluggish matter of the earth a new soaring impalpable imperishable being? (IV.775–81) * * *

This epiphany transposes the language of swooning, tremulous passion evolved through his Marian devotions and mystical ecstasies to Stephen's new, secular identity. No longer is his female soul alien to his male body: following in his cultural father's wingflaps, Stephen joins his radiant, wild, windswept limbs with his soaring soul in the image of the Daedalian father whose art exempts him from the laws of nature. His soul awakens from the death-in-life of his boyhood as his long-sought transfiguration takes place. * * *

> Where was his boyhood now? Where was the soul that had hung back from her destiny, to brood alone upon the shame of her wounds and in her house of squalor and subterfuge to queen it in faded cerements and in wreaths that withered at the touch? Or where was he? (IV.843–47)

This Daedalian transfiguration shows up as shams all Stephen's previous forms of furtive self-expression. The verb "to queen" casts a cold eye on his erstwhile mumming in the livery of the Church, as though his soul has been only masquerading in *jupes*,[7] feigning resurrection while still buried alive. Repossessing his she-soul in and

---

6. An event involving the appearance of a divine or supernatural being (*OED*). For details concerning Joyce's own use of the word, see note 1, p. 460 [*Editor*].
7. "The skirts" (French). Mentioned with reference to the garb of Capuchin priests in Belgium when Stephen is offered the chance to become a priest (IV.279–83) [*Editor*].

as himself, Stephen finds himself translated to a new place ("Or where was he?")—the third stage of his initiation, wherein he consolidates his masculine identity in his fathers' culture.

But how exactly does paternal Daedalian identity liberate Stephen from his liminal suspension in the undertow of his own repressed femininity? * * *

* * *

Stephen quickly learns from his "old father" how to use the law of gender to change the laws of nature, for scarcely has he heard the "prophecy" in his "strange name" than he finds he too can fly. Not coincidentally, on his maiden voyage on his new symbolic wings, he * * * transforms a human being into a bird: "A girl stood before him in midstream. . . . She seemed like one whom magic had changed into the likeness of a strange and beautiful seabird" (IV.854–56). The "magic" * * * here is nothing other than writing—the Daedalian artist's transfiguring words:

> * * * Her slateblue skirts were kilted boldly about her waist and *dovetailed* behind her. Her bosom was *as a bird's* . . . slight and soft *as the breast of some darkplumaged dove*. . . .
>   . . .
> —Heavenly God! cried Stephen's soul, in an outburst of profane joy. (IV.861–77, my emphases)

* * * Stephen's affirmation of his own creativity—"Yes! Yes! Yes! He would create . . . a living thing" (IV.810–12)—as he walks from the Bull bridge toward Howth * * * is immediately (in Stephen's mind) and retrospectively (in Joyce's text) realized in his transformation of a girl into a bird. * * * Inscribing his signs upon her flesh, the male inventor changes the laws of nature. Praising her creator ("Heavenly God!"), he praises himself, the inventor who changes her flesh into his words.

The girl's metamorphosis is proof of Stephen's own—of the transfiguration he has awaited since childhood. Like the poem "To E—C—," his newfound *artes ignotae*[8] reawaken and reintegrate his buried "female" self as he learns how to use the symbolic law of gender to change the law of nature, to turn his lack of an actual womb into a Daedalian symbolic womb/wings. His art not only transfigures the girl into a bird but transfers her body's attributes to his—"a faint flame trembled on her cheek. . . . His cheeks were aflame; his body was aglow; his limbs were trembling" (IV.875–80)—until,

---

8. "Unknown arts" (Latin); the strange skills that the mythological craftsman Daedalus uses as an inventor [*Editor*].

in yet another revisionist Annunciation, she becomes a Gabriel-like
"wild angel" hailing Stephen's Mary:[9]

> * * * A wild angel had appeared to him . . . to throw open
> before him in an instant of ecstasy the gates of all the ways of
> error and glory. (IV.886–89)

Receiving her image in his soul or psyche as Mary receives the
Word, Stephen once more depicts himself called "to recreate life
out of life." Through his newly discovered art, the Virgin/artist res-
urrects the early mother-identified self his male initiation has
forced him to bury: "the earth that had borne him, had taken him
to her breast." * * * [H]e luxuriates in the feminine ecstasy he has
now symbolically incorporated:

> His soul was swooning into some new world. . . . A world, a
> glimmer, or a flower? Glimmering and trembling, trembling
> and unfolding, a breaking light, an opening flower, it spread in
> endless succession to itself, breaking in full crimson and
> unfolding and fading to palest rose, leaf by leaf and wave of
> light by wave of light, flooding all the heavens with its soft
> flushes, every flush deeper than other. (IV.906–13)[1]

Over the empty grave of his resurrected female self now blooms the
rose of Stephen's art.

Daedalus's example, then, teaches Stephen's born-again psyche/
soul to soar not only over the "drownded" boys and his own "dread"
body, "the grave of boyhood," but over female bodies too. His Daedalian transfiguration assuages his melancholy over his buried
female self by endowing him with a symbolic creativity both modeled on and exalted over female procreativity. Reborn as Daedalian
artist, Stephen reincorporates within his now indisputably masculine identity the "female" self that he has repressed, mourned, and
surreptitiously kept alive through his long liminal stage. * * *
Changing nature's laws, Stephen fashions a symbolic womb out of
his "secret dread" of his male body and his "worship" of the girl's
and soars on winged words above both girl and "drownded" boys
(IV.761, 868, 792).

---

9. A transformed version of the announcement recorded in the Bible in which the archangel Gabriel tells the Virgin Mary that she will give birth to Jesus [Editor].
1. Cf. Henke, "Stephen Dedalus and Women," in *Women in Joyce*, Henke and Unkeless,
eds., who, arguing that "Stephen's fear of woman and contempt for sensuous life are
among the many inhibitions that stifle his creativity," views this image of female
orgasm as a voyeuristic exercise in "romantic self-indulgence" (pp. 96, 102).

The Villanelle: Flesh Made Bird Made Word Made Flesh

Portrait's villanelle scene consolidates the third stage of Stephen's initiation, his incorporation of his new identity as Daedalian/Virgin artist. The finale of *Portrait's* compositional process, the villanelle scene traces the psychohistorical genesis of a poem Joyce had composed fourteen years earlier * * *. In keeping with Stephen's emphasis on artistic process, *Portrait's* narrative of the villanelle's composition upstages the poem itself. * * *

This self-portrait of the artist "forging anew in his workshop out of the sluggish matter of the earth a new soaring impalpable imperishable being" (IV.780–81) shows him symbolically incorporating feminine attributes as he gives birth from his "virgin womb" (V.1543) to "a living thing" (IV.812)—not just the villanelle, which hardly merits this description, but his narrative self-portrait, which is to say, himself as "modern" artist. * * * [Joyce] capitalized on Stephen's Daedalian epiphany and his newfound art of turning girls into birds by reframing his account of the villanelle/"Eucharist" that had "come to" Joyce in 1900 as yet another Annunciation scene. * * * But now Stephen works his Daedalian magic on Emma (as I call her for convenience, although her name does not occur in this scene), changing her too into a bird who plays the Holy Ghost— the dove that mediates the impregnating Word—in this latest Annunciation.

Stephen deftly accomplishes Emma's metamorphosis in the prelude to the villanelle scene. Watching her leave the library with her friends, he feels his anger at her for flirting with the priest wane: "And if he had judged her harshly? If her life were a simple rosary of hours, her life simple and strange as a bird's life, gay in the morning, restless all day, tired at sundown? Her heart simple and willful as a bird's heart?" (V.1519–22). When he awakens the next morning as the Virgin/artist, * * * this Emma-bird is the "spirit," announced by "Gabriel the seraph," that infuses him with the "rose and ardent light" of "her strange willful heart," thereby engendering his poem/ Word:

> * * * O! In the virgin womb of the imagination the word was made flesh. Gabriel the seraph had come to the virgin's chamber. An afterglow deepened within his spirit, whence the white flame had passed, deepening to a rose and ardent light. That rose and ardent light was her strange willful heart, strange that no man had known or would know; willful from before the beginning of the world: and lured by that ardent roselike glow the choirs of the seraphim were falling from heaven. (V.1543–51)

The Daedalus myth and the Annunciation converge in Emma's metamorphosis into a "simple" bird/sacred dove, not just iconographically but in the primal-word psychodynamics in play throughout Stephen's initiatory progress, whereby a single word or identity encompasses apparent opposites: high/deep, sacred/profane, masculine/feminine * * *.

Emma's uses as a model for Stephen's artist-identity arise, in fact, not from her particular qualities but from the generic femaleness that the self-fashioning artist first envies and exalts and finally appropriates in his symbolic art so satisfactorily that his anger is quelled. The villanelle scene dramatizes a symbolic miming of female sexuality similar to that analyzed by Bettelheim[2] in initiation rites and adolescent fantasies and play. As Virgin/artist, Stephen not only changes Emma's female flesh into the bird/Word that he incarnates in the symbolic "flesh" of his poem, thereby conceiving, gestating, and giving birth to his work of art. More subtly, he imitates the essential, that is bodily or natural, sign of biological femaleness—menstrual blood—in the scene's images of blood and roses and in the villanelle's cycling form. As certain male initiation rites imitate this natural law of female sexuality, so Stephen explicitly parallels his sexual initiation (or "sin") to Emma's menarche, which he imagines as the moment when "the strange humiliation of her nature had first came upon her," "the dark shame of womanhood" humbling and saddening her (V.1730–35). * * * As the "rose and ardent light" that "was her strange willful heart" [V.1546–48] becomes "the roselight in his heart" [V.1581–82], Emma's incorporated bird-heart inspires the beating rhythms, periodic rhymes, cycling refrains, and blood-flowing chalice of the villanelle that now issues from his body and brain. Culminating Stephen's initiatory progress, the villanelle scene mimes women's natural, cyclical "enchanted days" [V.1554], changing nature's law into his own creative Annunciation.

The villanelle's eucharistic imagery mediates Stephen's symbolic incorporation of the divinity he projects upon Emma. As her willful rose-heart shines its "rays of rhyme" [V.1557] down on him, Stephen imagines the world as an altar from which he sends "smoke of her praise" [V.1571] up to the deified Emma. In the sacrifice of the Mass, the communicant partakes of divinity by eating the god's body and blood, symbolized in the Eucharist and communion wine. So the artist-priest Stephen first symbolically dismembers Emma in an imaginary *sparagmos*[3] ("[r]ude brutal anger . . . broke up violently

2. Bruno Bettelheim, *Symbolic Wounds: Puberty Rites and the Envious Male* (Glencoe, IL: Free P, 1954) [*Editor*].
3. An ancient Greek word meaning the act of tearing to pieces, used to refer to the dismemberment of a living sacrifice in the rites of the god Dionysus [*Editor*].

her fair image and flung the fragments on all sides" [V.1645–47])
and then incorporates her fragmented attributes. Lying in bed,
he makes "a cowl of the blanket" and, "seeing himself" with "his
closely cowled head," remembers how "she had worn her shawl
cowlwise about her head" [V.1696–1707] in the tram after the
children's party. Cowled like Emma and the Virgin, he imagines his
own ascension to the idealized and fetishized femininity he projects
on them, seeing in "the great overblown scarlet flowers of the tattered wallpaper . . . a roseway from where he lay upwards to heaven
all strewn with scarlet flowers" and even feeling the same emotions
his poem projects on Emma: "Weary! Weary! He too was weary of
ardent ways" (V.1697–1701).

With these words, the question that cycles through the villanelle
("*Are you not weary of ardent ways?*") circles back to its origin, Stephen. His symbolic merging with Emma through this eucharistic
communication of qualities continues in the "languor" that he
attributes first to himself and then to her ("his soul had passed
from ecstasy to languor. . . . Her eyes, dark and with a look of languor, were opening to his eyes") and the ambiguous grammar that
entangles her "lavish" limbs with his: "Her nakedness yielded to
him, radiant, warm, odorous and lavishlimbed. . . ." (V.1736–45).
Imagining her soul conscious of his "homage" and her body enfold-
ing him "like a shining cloud," he consummates their union by
transmuting her fantasized flesh into the poem that "flow[s] forth
over his brain," now complete in the fertile, flowing chalice/womb
of his imagination (V.1739–48). In this light, the villanelle scene
deconstructs the eucharistic rite as a symbolic transubstantiation
of male body and blood in parallel with the biological menarche
that Eliade projects as "the mystery of blood," sign of a naturally
sacralized femininity.[4]

The villanelle, then, articulates the "vague speech" earlier impressed
on Stephen's brain by the prostitute's kiss as a Word that both
mystifies and mimes the "element" of generic female sexuality.
The Eucharist "come[s] to" him as Emma's imagined body, which
the artist's words make "flesh" as both the body of his poem and his
narrative self-portrait. As the narrative shows him symbolically
incorporating one after another of Emma's attributes, his anger and
envy are soothed into an "unbroken . . . hymn of thanksgiving" and
then into "quiet indulgence," just as the celebrants' "broken cries
and mournful lays" resolve into "one eucharistic hymn" in the villanelle (V.1681–90).

---

4. Mircea Eliade, *Rites and Symbols of Initiation: The Mysteries of Birth and Rebirth*,
trans. Willard R. Trask (New York: Harper, 1958), 42 [*Editor*].

Critics have debated whether Stephen awakens from a wet dream to write his poem, masturbates on completing it, or entirely sublimates his Virginal sexuality.[5] For our purposes, what is most interesting is that the scene's end adumbrates (not for the first time, since Emma's absence is the condition of the symbolic kiss "given by both" in "To E—C—") the onanistic writing economy whereby Joycean artists create symbolically in self-conscious parallel to female procreativity. * * * Stephen's newfound art of turning girls into birds while taking flight on symbolic wings enables him to resolve anger and envy into an ironic "homage"—less to Emma, ultimately, than to himself, the only bird remaining at the scene's close. Clutching not Emma but his own *petit oiseau*,[6] Stephen inaugurates a narcissistic writing economy that compensates him for missing bodies, body parts, and bodily powers * * *.

Portrait's analysis of Stephen's writing economy marks a crucial difference between *Stephen Hero*'s and *Portrait*'s narrative modes. As Joyce moves from narrating external events to dissecting the artist's inner life, he abandons traditional realist narrative for the scalpel of modernist realism, and the realist character Emma for an imago of the artist-son's buried femininity * * *. *Portrait*, in short, is not a love story but a psychohistory of male initiation, driven by the vicissitudes of forbidden identificatory desire; and its depiction of frustrated and sublimated sexual desire should not obscure the villanelle scene's real drama (or the cultural critique it implies): its self-ironic dissection of the sexual dialectics underlying masculine creativity. *Portrait* is a story of writing in which artist and self-portrait create each other, and the artist's obscure object of desire is ultimately not Emma but the writing by which he symbolically recovers his buried femininity. Incorporating Emma-as-bird within the soaring Daedalian artist, the villanelle scene substitutes its textual body for Emma's absent one and the poem's "liquid letters," flowing rhythms, and cycling rhymes for her mystified female sexuality.

If, in *Stephen Hero*, Stephen vents contemptuous anger at Emma and her priest, *Portrait*'s villanelle and narrative enact his rivalry with and triumph over them both. Appropriating eucharistic ritual to an art that splits it open to expose its psychogenesis, Stephen inverts the hierarchy of priest over artist, sacred over profane: "she

5. See especially Charles Rossman, "Stephen Dedalus' Villanelle," *JJQ* 12 (Spring 1975): 281–93; Bernard Benstock, "The Temptation of St. Stephen: A View of the Villanelle," *JJQ* 14 (Fall 1976): 31–38; Day, "Villanelle Perplex," p. 79 and passim; and Mary Reynolds, *Joyce and Dante* (Princeton: Princeton University Press, 1981), 178–83, 194–99, 262, who compares Stephen's spiritualized eroticism to Dante's.
6. "Little bird" (French), a term of endearment between lovers that can be addressed to a man or a woman [*Editor*].

would unveil her soul's shy nakedness . . . to one who was but schooled in the discharging of a formal rite rather than to him, a priest of eternal imagination, transmuting the daily bread of experience into the radiant body of everliving life" (V.1675–79). His eucharistic "sacrifice" of Emma dispels his rage as his Daedalian artist outsoars her Emma-bird: even as he incorporates her sublime bird-heart within his Virgin/Daedalian identity, he reassures himself as to her actual lowness: "the strange humiliation of her nature," "the dark shame of womanhood," the merely natural blood/"roses" that his *artes ignotae* imitate and surpass (V.1730–35). The strategic inversions of highness and lowness in the male artists' metamorphos[i]s of * * * the girl on the strand [is] repeated in the villanelle scene's exchanges between male and female; sacred and profane; theology and art; Emma with her priest and the Virgin artist-priest.

On Weariness of Ardent Ways: Psychopolitical Symptoms

* * *

* * * Emma is in Stephen's eyes not just a woman who rejects him for cowardly reasons but an emblem of a colonized Ireland's subjection to the presumptive authority of the Roman Catholic Church and British state. Both of these authorities imposed sexual repression through a sex/gender system that Joyce represents as a powerful determinant of Ireland's political oppression. *Portrait* unforgettably links the subjection of desire to Church and state in Irish Catholic culture to Ireland's colonial fate in the devastatingly sad and terrifying fight at the Dedalus family's Christmas dinner over the priests' castigation of Charles Parnell for his adulterous liaison with Kitty O'Shea. The priests' fatal influence in Parnell's downfall—their sacrifice of "the man that was born to lead us" [I.1094], and with him Ireland's political freedom, to the Church's authority over sexuality—writes huge the uncritical subjection Stephen sees and condemns * * *. The villanelle scene's critique of "ardent ways" cracks open the interlocking psychodynamics of sexual and political subjection as exemplified by, though hardly exclusive to, what the heartbroken Mr. Dedalus and Mr. Casey call Ireland's "unfortunate priestridden . . . Godforsaken race" (I.1075–81).

* * * By *Portrait*'s end, this figural Irish woman as a type of her race and his own, an image of colonized desire emerging from a repression profoundly complicit in Ireland's political oppression, has become yet another prototype for Stephen's dialectical self-fashioning. Her

awakening consciousness metamorphoses into his vow "to forge in the smithy of my soul the uncreated conscience of my race" [V.2789–90] her mind's conditions of darkness, loneliness, and secrecy into his of silence, exile, and cunning.

Parlaying Irish women's imagined awakenings to desire into his vow to forge a modernist conscience, Joyce fashions his artist-identity itself as a primal word encompassing both deep and high: unconscious and consciousness, peasant and artist-priest, mute secrecy and narrative art, batlike woman and hawklike man, her dark, lonely, unmet desire and his heroic sunward flight, and, not least, slow, furtive, awakening consciousness and conscience as knowing-with (con + science) instead of knowing alone. * * *

Stephen, then, makes his image of Irish women's sexual subjuga-tion and the split consciousness it entails a model for Ireland's political oppression and the colonial subject's divided conscious-ness; and he makes their imagined awakenings the motive of an art that strives to transform unconscious subjection into conscious desire, lonely consciousness into collective conscience, and collec-tive conscience into political freedom. * * *

* * *

Stephen's final interview with Emma, recorded in *Portrait*'s con-cluding diary, suggests that his self-vivisection has (at least tempo-rarily) advanced him beyond the symptom of projecting on her his own lost femininity—that is, beyond the masculinity his initiation story has dissected. "Talked rapidly of myself and my plans," he reports. "In the midst of it unluckily I made a sudden gesture of a revolutionary nature. I must have looked like a fellow throwing a handful of peas into the air. People began to look at us. She shook hands a moment after and, in going away, said she hoped I would do what I said" [V.2765–70]. Stephen briefly confronts the contra-diction between his feelings for the "temptress" of the villanelle and his "new" liking for the real Emma: "Now I call that friendly. . . . Yes, I liked her today . . . and it seems a new feeling to me. Then, in that case, all the rest, all that I thought I thought and all that I felt I felt, all the rest before now, in fact. . . . . . O, give it up, old chap! Sleep it off!" (V.2771–76). * * * In *Portrait*, Stephen declines to pur-sue the implications of their friendly "end," perhaps because such a resolution would prematurely foreclose the delicate balance between the belief he needs to embody his culture's fictions of gen-der and the unbelief he needs to dissect them. If Stephen seems to have moved beyond the psychodynamics that the villanelle scene painstakingly dissects, the fact that he conceives his art as demysti-fying a cultural unconscious that essentializes gender commits him to keeping this tension in play.

By the end of *Portrait*, in other words, Stephen/Joyce has established both his autobiographical hero and the modernist-realist method by which he lays open his culturally constructed psyche. * * *

* * *

JOSEPH VALENTE

Thrilled by His Touch: Homosexual Panic and the Will to Artistry in *A Portrait of the Artist as a Young Man*†

* * *

The modern educational system in general and the elite boarding school in particular, where boys learned the ways of male entitlement under the pressure of powerful and labile erotic pulsions, have afforded a prototypical arena for the experience of homosexual panic.[1]

Joyce not only betrays just this sort of sexual unease in his private correspondence, but, I will be arguing, he communicates these attitudes to his fictive alter ego, Stephen Dedalus, in a more explicitly "panicky" mode, which affects the most crucial decisions Stephen enacts: his appeal to Conmee, his refusal of the priesthood, his assumption of an aesthetic vocation, his self-exile. A number of critics have, over the years, pointed to the emergence of homoerotic energies in *A Portrait*, for example, in the smugging episode or in Stephen's final interview with Cranly, and several have even asserted the importance of these same energies as a component of Stephen's psychology.[2] What I would like to demonstrate is that

---

† From *James Joyce Quarterly* 31:3 (Spring 1994): 167–88. Reprinted with permission of the publisher and the author. Rev., exp. in *Quare Joyce*. Ed. Joseph Valente. Ann Arbor: U of Michigan P, 1998. Some of the author's notes have been omitted. Page references for *A Portrait* have been replaced with part and line numbers of this Norton Critical Edition. Some cited passages might differ slightly from the equivalent passages in this volume.

1. [On homosexual panic, see] Eve Kosofsky Sedgwick, *The Epistemology of the Closet* (Berkeley: Univ. of California Press, 1990), pp. 182–212, and *Between Men* (New York: Columbia Univ. Press, 1985), pp. 83–96. On page 195 of *Epistemology*, Sedgwick doubts whether the "arguably homosexual" objects of her own analysis properly bear out or embody the experience of homosexual panic, which "is proportioned to the non-homosexual identified elements of . . . men's character." Accordingly, she continues, "if Barrie and James are obvious authors with whom to begin an analysis of male homosexual panic, the analysis I am offering here must be inadequate to the degree that it does not eventually work just as well—even better—for Joyce, Faulkner, Lawrence, Yeats etc." In this respect, my essay can be seen as a continuation of Sedgwick's project, an attempt not only to explore Joyce's writing by way of her conception but also to demonstrate the adequacy of her conception by way of Joyce's writing. Further references to these works will be cited parenthetically in the text as *Closet* and *Men*.

2. These critics include James F. Carens, "A Portrait of the Artist as a Young Man" in *A Companion to Joyce Studies*, ed. Zack Bowen and James F. Carens (Westport:

Joyce's phobic denial or denegation[3] of his own homoerotic energies makes its way into the novel as a *fundamental determinant* of its basic narrative structure and hence of Stephen's destiny. By taking this approach, I do not mean to imply any simple autobiographical identification of the figure of Dedalus with that of Joyce. I do mean to propose, however, that the combination of projection, disavowal, and self-awareness connecting author and alter ego comprises a certain homoerotic ambivalence whose operation in the text helps to demystify Stephen's strongest claim to being Joyce's surrogate, his will to artistry.

The very title of the novel invokes the homoerotic scenario and does so in a characteristically Joycean fashion, by establishing, at the outset, the text as intertext. As Vicki Mahaffey suggested to me, the phrase "a portrait of the artist" is a quite peculiar locution, which makes its derivation from one work in particular, Oscar Wilde's *The Picture of Dorian Gray,* that much more assured, especially since Dorian's portrait *keeps* him at the age of a young man. During the opening scene of Wilde's famous novel, Basil tells Henry:

> [E]very portrait that is painted with feeling is a portrait of the artist, not of the sitter. The sitter is merely the accident, the occasion. It is not he who is revealed by the painter; it is rather the painter who . . . reveals himself.[4]

In this light, Stephen can be taken either as a self-portrait in the ordinary sense or as a self-portrait strictly by virtue of being "a portrait painted with feeling," a condition likely to disfigure the ordinary self-portrait with a certain self-indulgence. Stephen must, therefore, not only be seen as both Joyce and not Joyce, but he must also be seen as revealing Joyce precisely to the extent that he is *not* a self-depiction (being instead merely a portrait painted with feeling) and disfiguring Joyce to the extent that he *is* a self-depiction, altered by that feeling.

But Joyce's interest in the intercourse between revelation and representation in Wilde exceeded questions of the pragmatics of self-portraiture. It had a nakedly ethico-political edge as well. Joyce's primary response to *The Picture of Dorian Gray* was disappointment that Wilde had dissembled in presenting the homosexual charge

---

Greenwood Press, 1984), pp. 255–359; Jean Kimball, "Freud, Leonardo and Joyce" in *The Seventh of Joyce,* ed. Bernard Benstock (Bloomington: Indiana Univ. Press, 1982), pp. 57–73; Chester Anderson, "Baby Tuckoo: Joyce's Features of Infancy," in *Approaches to Joyce's "Portrait": Ten Essays,* ed. Thomas F. Staley (Pittsburgh: Univ. of Pittsburgh Press, 1970), pp. 136–42. Further references to these works will be cited parenthetically in the text.
3. Freud's term for admitting to consciousness by denying [*Editor*].
4. Oscar Wilde, *The Picture of Dorian Gray* [see p. 335—*Editor*].

binding Dorian, Basil, and Henry, that Wilde's own complex self-representation had not been more of a (sexual) revelation.

> I can imagine the capital which Wilde's prosecuting counsel made out of certain parts of it. It is not very difficult to read between the lines. Wilde seems to have had some good intentions in writing it—some wish to put himself before the world—but the book is rather crowded with lies and epigrams. If he had had the courage to develop the allusions in the book it might have been better. I suspect he has done this in some privately-printed books.[5]

Like this letter, however, which conspicuously declines to develop "the allusions in the book" any more than Wilde does, leaving the homosexuality therein an "open secret," Joyce's title repeats the gesture of circumspection, leaving the *homotextual* relations between his novel and Wilde's at the level of "epigram." Or perhaps it would be truer to say, Joyce's title answers Wilde's conscious circumspection with an unconscious disavowal; it simultaneously reveals and conceals the intense homotextual relation between his *Bildungsroman* and his precursor, revealing the "textual" affinity, in its most Derridean sense,[6] while concealing or eliding the "homo." Whereas the "feeling" that makes Dorian's portrait a "portrait of the artist" involves Basil's homoerotic attraction to his "sitter," as Joyce recognizes, Joyce's "feeling" for his "sitter" could only be construed as narcissistic, a modality of desire properly understood as the precondition for any object relation, homo- or hetero-. That is to say, by remaining at the level of epigram, *A Portrait of the Artist* translates the "open secret" of *Dorian Gray*'s sexual economy into an open option or open possibility.

A similarly displaced homotextual relation reveals itself in the symbol of Stephen's Irish art * * *, the impossible green rose. Stephen's aesthetic career begins on a significant pun, significantly repeated.

> *O, the wild rose blossoms*
> *On the little green place.*

He sang that song. That was his song. (I.9–11)

And again,

---

5. *Selected Letters of James Joyce,* ed. Richard Ellmann (New York: Viking, 1975), 96 [*Editor*].
6. Jacques Derrida (1830–2004), Algerian-born French philosopher and founder of deconstruction, which explores how meaning comes into being [*Editor*].

Perhaps a *wild* rose might be like those colors. And he remembered the song about the *wild* rose blossoms on the little green
place. (I.195–97, my emphasis)

Joyce underlines and clarifies the pun in *Finnegans Wake*, where it
serves to stake the process of history on the wages of illicit
sexuality:

has not levy of black mail from the times the fairies were in it,
and fain for *wilde* erthe blothoms followed an impressive private reputation for whispered sins? (*FW* 69.02–04, my
emphasis)[7]

With this in mind, Stephen's subsequent musing—"But you could
not have a green rose. But perhaps somewhere in the world you
could" (I.197–98)—unmistakably recalls Wilde's famous "green
carnation," which was the symbol both of the artifice of the imagination, the conventional reading of Stephen's rose, and a badge of
the homosexual subculture of *fin de siècle* England,[8] a sense that
Stephen's flower intimates *sotto voce*. At a certain level, Joyce is
grounding Stephen's aesthetic vocation in an inarticulate homoeroticism or rather, as we shall see, in an inability or unwillingness
to articulate his homoerotic cathexes directly, a simultaneous experience, denial, and diversion of them, rooted in his Clongowes
education.

  Stephen's thoughts on the green rose immediately follow his
ruminations on Simon Moonan, the homoerotic implications of
which are, of course, patent * * *:[9]

  —We all know why you speak. You are McGlade's suck.
  Suck was a queer word. The fellow called Simon Moonan
that name because Simon Moonan used to tie the prefect's
false sleeves behind his back and the prefect used to let on to
be angry. But the sound was ugly. Once he had washed his
hands in the lavatory of the Wicklow Hotel and his father
pulled the stopper up by the chain after and the dirty water
went down through the hole in the basin. And when it had all
gone down slowly . . . [it] made a sound like that: suck. Only
louder. . . . There were two cocks that you turned and water
came out: cold and hot. . . . and he could see the names printed
on the cocks. That was a very queer thing. (I.149–63)

7. New York: Viking, 1939 [*Editor*].
8. In his own words, Wilde "invented that magnificent flower," the green carnation, as a
"work of art"—Richard Ellmann, *Oscar Wilde* (New York: Vintage, 1987), pp. 424–25.
The green carnation became a symbol of aestheticism, memorialized in Robert
Hichens, *The Green Carnation* (New York: Dover Publications, 1970) [published anon-
ymously in 1894—*Editor*].
9. See [Kimball (66) and] Leonard Albert, "Gnomonology: Joyce's 'The Sisters,'" *JJQ* 27
(Winter 1990), 360–61.

I have quoted this passage at length because:

1. through the repeated use of terms like suck, queer, cocks, and so forth,[1] it establishes a psychosymbolic association among Stephen's developing fever, his long-standing fascination with and aversion to standing water and waste, and an embryonic homosexual possibility and panic;

2. it sets an erotic context for understanding the sort of homosocial roughhousing that lands Stephen in the square ditch and causes his fever. Stephen, remember, a designated mama's boy, will not trade his dandyish "little snuffbox" for Wells's macho "hacking chestnut, the conqueror of forty" (I.124–25); the box and the nut function as genital symbols for the respectively feminized and masculinized positions of Stephen and Wells. Since the incident exemplifies the sexualized aggression that Joyce attributed to English boarding school activities, and since Joyce was likewise shouldered into the ditch, with similarly febrile consequences (*JJII* 28),[2] it is worth noting that the square ditch runs along the perimeter of Clongowes and forms its boundary with the old English pale.[3] It is, in other words, a border zone where the masculinized Anglo-Saxon "conqueror" and the feminized Irish conquered meet and, partly as an effect of the conquest itself, where their ethno-racial differences are both marked, even exaggerated, and overridden, even erased. With respect to Joyce's cherished distinction between the rampant homoeroticism of English public school life and the comparative innocence of its Irish counterpart, the square ditch constitutes an objectified instance of "the proximate"[4] itself, in effect, a thin margin of dissociation into which the subject might always land or be pushed and his kinship with the other be uncomfortably reaffirmed;[5]

3. it establishes a basis on which to overcome an inveterate critical assumption—an Enlightenment prejudice really—that because Stephen does not fully grasp the implications of the

---

1. Elaine Showalter correctly contends that the term "queer" had homosexual connotations before the yellow nineties, let alone the twentieth century, began. All subsequent references to and uses of the term will assume a distinct homosexual valence—*Sexual Anarchy* (New York: Viking, 1990), p. 112.
2. Richard Ellmann, *James Joyce* (New York: Oxford UP, 1982) [*Editor*].
3. For this information, I am grateful to Vicki Mahaffey, who gathered it on a visit to Clongowes in 1992.
4. On "the proximate," see Jonathan Dollimore, *Sexual Dissidence* (New York: Oxford Univ. Press, 1991), pp. 14–17 [expansion and relocation of author's note—*Editor*].
5. This dynamic of proximate-ness played itself out quite humorously in Joyce's indirect dialogue with H. G. Wells. Wells objected to the "'cloacal obsession'" of *A Portrait*. Joyce's reply to Frank Budgen reveals the kind of ethno-racial dichotomy that we have been adducing: "'Why, it's Wells's countrymen who build water-closets wherever they go.'" But in a private comment to another friend, Joyce acknowledged, "'How right Wells was!'" (*JJII* 414).

"smugging" scandal until later on, he is not really party to the homosexual energies circulating among the Clongowes students as they remember or recount the "crime" and anticipate the similarly titillating punishment.

As it turns out, these three narrative functions are strictly correlative. For it is not the appropriately named Athy's prosaic specification of Moonan and Boyle's offense ("smugging") nor even his poetic acting out of their chastisement ("It can't be helped;/It must be done./So down with your breeches/And out with your bum"—I.1325–28) that most powerfully eroticizes the scene. It is instead the way that Stephen elaborates upon these accounts and the way that his elaborations interact with other environmental cues like the sound of the cricket bats.

Regarding the crime, it is Stephen who seeks to exculpate Simon Moonan and, in the process, reveals the direct libidinal impact that young man has had upon him:

> What did that mean about the smugging in the square? . . . It was a joke, he thought. Simon Moonan had nice clothes and one night he had *shown him a ball of creamy* sweets that the fellows of the football fifteen had rolled down to him along the carpet. . . . It was the night of the *match against the Bective Rangers* and the ball was made just like a red and green apple only it opened and it was *full of the creamy sweets.* (I.1244–52, my emphases)

Stephen's earlier fantasy about leaving on vacation already incorporated his experience with Moonan in a plainly, if unconsciously, homoerotic fashion: "The train was full of fellows: a *long, long chocolate train* with *cream facings*" (I.465–66, my emphases). This is a classic instance in which commonplace homosocial reinforcement, highlighted by the affiliation with team sports, merges almost seamlessly with the "most reprobated" sexual imagery and investments. Once again, Stephen undergoes the panic that this double bind arouses as * * * a dread associated with waste and sitting urine:

> But why in the square? You went there when you wanted to do something. It was all thick slabs of slate and water trickled all day out of tiny pinholes and there was a queer smell of stale water there. (I.1270–73)

Being the site of a certain mutual genital exposure, the male lavatory space always carries some homoerotic potential; as a result, the introduction of an *explicitly* sexual element, tapping as it does Stephen's existent fear and confusion, renders the excremental function itself "queer" and therefore unspeakable for him. You went to the lavatory to "do something" that apparently dares not be named.

Regarding the punishment, Stephen's dread and Stephen's desire are simultaneously on display.[6] He imagines the prospect of being caned less in terms of pain than in terms of "chill": "It made him shivery to think of it and cold. . . . It made him shivery" (I.1337–39). That this chill bespeaks a sexualized *frisson* becomes immediately evident in Stephen's focus on the ceremonial unveiling of the "vital spot" (I.1321): "He wondered who had to let them [the trousers] down, the master or the boy himself" (I.1342–43). Stephen's speculation on the protocol involved suggests a mutuality of participation in the act of undressing that bares the sexual energy animating the exemplary discipline. His subsequent vision of the caning itself implies a literalized dialectic or reciprocity between beater and beaten that issues in a sense of positive and implicitly homoerotic pleasure:

> [Athy] had rolled up his sleeves to show how Mr Gleeson would roll up his sleeves. But Mr Gleeson had round shiny cuffs and clean white wrists and fattish white hands and the nails of them were long and pointed. Perhaps he pared them too like Lady Boyle. . . . And though he trembled with . . . fright to think of the cruel long nails . . . and of the chill you felt at the end of your shirt when you undressed yourself yet he felt a feeling of queer quiet pleasure inside him to think of the white fattish hands, clean and strong and gentle. (I.1346–57)

As the passage mushrooms into a full-blown, if displaced, sexual fantasy, Stephen takes center stage as the subject of warring sensations, an outer chill and an inner glow, an anticipated pain and an experienced pleasure, an involuntary engagement but a voluntary imagining, a sexual affect at once savored and denied. Indeed, Joyce exploits the equivocality of the word "queer" in this passage in order not only to mark the homoerotic nature of Stephen's ambivalence but also to mark the ambivalent, uncanny impact of the homoerotic upon Stephen, his mixture of fear and fascination, attraction and repulsion, which is the recipe for a "panic" borne of "proximate-ness."

This proximate-ness, in turn, with its ambivalent affect, gives a sharply ironic twist to Stephen's subsequent pandying. It is not just that Stephen receives punishment for something he never did, scheme to break his glasses, nor even that he is made the scapegoat for a sexual scandal he imperfectly comprehends, which is how he comes to interpret the matter (I.1659–68); no, what is ironic is that, in the unconscious, where the thought or the wish can stand for the

6. Carens speaks of the Clongowes episode as denoting an element of sexual ambivalence in Stephen (p. 319).

deed and carry the same transgressive force,[7] there is indeed a certain symmetry, if not equity, to Stephen's chastisement. If, as Stephen and the other boys suspect, the pandyings actually respond to the homoerotic indulgences of the smuggling "ring," then Stephen can be seen as an accomplice after the fact, participating vicariously in these indulgences through his fantasy-construction of Mr. Gleeson's discipline. In fact, the imagined caning and the real pandying communicate with one another precisely through Stephen's erotic preoccupation with his masters' hands. Having taken a "queer quiet pleasure" from the contemplation of Mr. Gleeson's "white fattish hands, clean strong and gentle," Stephen seems to expect something of the same gratification from the prefect's fingers, in which he initially discerns a like quality, and Stephen finds Father Dolan's betrayal of this sensual promise to be, in some respects, the most galling aspect of the whole episode. His mind returns to it obsessively in the aftermath.

> [H]e thought of the hands which he had held out in the air with the palms up and of the firm touch of the prefect of studies when he had steadied the shaking fingers. (I.1559–62)

> He felt the touch of the prefect's fingers as they had steadied his hand and at first he had thought he was going to shake hands with him because the fingers were soft and firm: but then in an instant he had heard the swish of the soutane sleeve and the crash. (I.1586–90)

> And his whitegrey face and the nocoloured eyes behind the steelrimmed spectacles were cruel looking *because* he had steadied the hand first with his firm soft fingers and that was to hit it better and louder. (I.1597–1600, my emphasis)

Since we are dealing with Stephen's *perception* of the scene, the insistent, fetishistic repetition of "soft," "firm," "fingers," "touch," and "steadied," along with the bizarre causal priority accorded Dolan's duplicitous touch, must be seen as registering some sort of baffled desire as well as trauma or rather an overlapping of the two psychic movements. Stephen's trauma at the pandying fixates upon the master's touch because that is where Stephen's unconscious wishes insert themselves into both the smuggling scandal and the larger homosocial-sexual economy of Clongowes. It is the point at which he has eroticized, and so from a certain point of view merited, the priests' brutal sanctions on such eroticism.

---

7. This is what Freud means by the omnipotence of the unconscious wish, a crucial motif everywhere in his work. See, in particular, chapter 3 of *Totem and Taboo* [*The Standard Edition of the Psychological Works of Sigmund Freud*, ed. James Strachey (London: Hogarth P, 1961)], vol. 13, pp. 94–124.

Stephen's subsequent protest at the injustice of his thrashing likewise belies his fascination with the male body, which is, of course, the vice being penalized.

> [A]nd the fifth was big Corrigan who was going to be flogged by Mr Gleeson. That was why the prefect of studies had called him a schemer and pandied him for nothing. . . . But he [Corrigan] had done something and besides Mr Gleeson would not flog him hard: and he [Stephen] remembered how big Corrigan looked in the bath. He had skin the same colour as the turf-coloured bogwater in the shallow end of the bath and when he walked along the side his feet slapped loudly on the wet tiles and at every step his thighs shook a little because he was fat. (I.1662–73)

Stephen wants to assert a distinction between guilty, robust Corrigan and poor little innocent Dedalus. But in doing so, he discloses a familiarity with Corrigan's physique apparently gleaned from watching his "every step" "in the bath," and the desire such familiarity would suggest seems further corroborated by the way Corrigan's bodily image simply takes over Stephen's juridical meditation. At the same time, his comparison of Corrigan's pigmentation to the dirty water in the bath recalls his own immersion in the square ditch and so indicates how profoundly this desire interfuses with dread.

Far from resolving this double bind, Conmee's vindication of Stephen and his schoolmates' ensuing homage only cements it. After his interview with the rector, Stephen is "hoisted" and "carried . . . along" (I.1824–25) in a homosocial bonding ritual that obviously makes him quite uncomfortable, for he immediately struggles to extricate his body from their grasp. And it is only once "[h]e was alone" that "[h]e was happy and free" (I.1833–34). He then proceeds to dissociate himself in a categorical fashion from any sense of triumph over the prefect and so, by extension, from the celebratory fellowship of his peers. The reason is not far to seek. The very image in which his sense of gratification crystallizes, a sound "like drops of water in a fountain falling softly in a brimming bowl" (I.1847–48), is but the inverse of his image of the dreaded "smugging" square, "all thick slabs of slate and water trickled all day out of tiny pinholes." The aestheticized emblem of personal fulfillment thus encodes and carries forward the cloacal image of taboo sexual longing. Just as the prospect of painful social humiliation—being singled out for a caning—triggers in Stephen a "queer quiet pleasure" amid anxiety, owing to its homoerotic undercurrents, so the fruits of Stephen's social victory trigger an unconscious anxiety amid validation, an anxiety registered along the associative chains of Stephen's mental imagery.

In this regard, the fact that this ambivalent water rhapsody actually emanates from a game of cricket, a sport exported from the elite playing fields of England to those of Ireland, implicates the author's unconscious as well in the structure of homoerotic disavowal. As Trevor L. Williams has argued, Joyce frames Stephen's success with a motif of colonial-cultural hegemony as a way of qualifying or undercutting its ultimate meaningfulness, in keeping with the alternating elevation/deflation mechanism of the narrative as a whole.[8] But in the process, Joyce necessarily undermines his own cherished distinction between the athletic customs of English and Irish boarding schools at precisely the moment when the sexual anxiety that distinction was intended to forestall infiltrates the crowning symbol of Stephen's young life—the brimming bowl.

Stephen's failure to resolve his "homosexual panic," in spite of his social victory, presages Joyce's treatment of the issue through the remainder of the novel, beginning with Stephen's entry into nominally heterosexual activity, from courtship rituals to whoring practices. Joyce consistently surrounds Stephen's participation in these things with forms of gender inversion, which, by the end of the century, was the dominant model of homosexuality in both the popular imagination and in the work of prominent sexologists like Havelock Ellis, Richard Krafft-Ebing, Edward Carpenter, and Freud (all of whom Joyce read).[9] As an effect of this pattern, the homoerotic surfaces in the text neither as a simple alternative to nor an anomalous deviation from some naturalized heteroerotic incitement, but as an element uncannily symbiotic with that incitement and menacing to its normalization.

First, just *before* the Harold's Cross children's party—Stephen's "coming out" as a heterosexual male—an old woman, possibly a relative of Stephen's, with a "whining voice" mistakes him for a female, repeating the phrase "I thought you were Josephine" several times (II.290, II.300). Often treated as an isolated epiphany,[1] this interlude has little if any pertinence to the rest of the narrative, other than being the first of several instances in which gender inversion attaches specifically to Stephen. As such, it can be read as one of those incompletely processed "lumps" in which the subterranean concerns of a text concentrate themselves in a nearly

8. Trevor L. Williams, "Dominant Ideologies: The Production of Stephen Dedalus," in *The Augmented Ninth,* ed. Bernard Benstock (Syracuse: Syracuse Univ. Press, 1988), p. 316.
9. Havelock Ellis and J. A. Symonds, *Studies in the Psychology of Sex,* vol. 1, *Sexual Inversion* (London: Wilson & MacMillan, 1897); Edward Carpenter, *The Intermediate Sex* (Manchester: Labour Press, 1896); Baron Richard Von Krafft-Ebing, *Psychopathia Sexualis* (London: F. G. Rebman, 1892); Freud, *Three Essays on Sexuality, Standard Edition,* vol. 7, pp. 136–48; see Richard Brown, *James Joyce and Sexuality* (Cambridge: Cambridge Univ. Press, 1985), pp. 78–107.
1. See note 1, p. 460 [*Editor*].

illegible form. In support of this thesis, I would note that just *after* the party, Stephen actually bears out this gender (mis)identification in terms of the standard Victorian sexual typology.[2] On the tram ride home with E__ C__, he assumes what was thought to be the essentially, even *definitively* feminine role of sexual passivity and withdrawal, receiving without responding to her sexual advances.

Once again, just before E__ C__'s attendance at Stephen's Whitsuntide performance, their first encounter since the party, a significant instance of gender misidentification supervenes. There appears backstage "a pinkdressed figure, wearing a curly golden wig and an oldfashioned straw sunbonnet, with black pencilled eyebrows and cheeks delicately rouged and powdered" (II.501–03). The presiding prefect asks facetiously, "Is this a beautiful young lady or a doll that you have here, Mrs Tallon?" (II.508–09). It turns out, of course, to be the "girlish figure" of a boy, "little Bertie Tallon," a circumstance that provokes "a murmur of curiosity" and then "a murmur of admiration" from the other boys (II.505, II.512, II.504, II.514–15). In Stephen, however, this transvestite spectacle precipitates a telling "movement of impatience. . . . He let the edge of the blind fall and . . . walked out of the chapel" (II.517–19). Why would Stephen react or overreact in this fashion? Perhaps because the superimposition of the signifiers of feminine desirability upon a schoolboy's already "girlish figure," the accompanying expression of the other schoolboys' admiration, and the disingenuous participation of the prefect combine to tap the ambivalence at the heart of Stephen's sexual desire (Carens 304–05), by recalling the roots of that ambivalence in his own school experience as the "little" boy, the mama's boy, the feminized boy. A subsequent passage, however, indicates that still more is at stake.

> All day he had thought of nothing but their leavetaking on the steps of the tram at Harold's Cross. . . . All day he had imagined a new meeting with her for he knew that she was to come to the play. The old restless moodiness had again filled his breast as it had done on the night of the party but had not found an outlet in verse. The growth and knowledge of two years of boyhood stood between then and now, forbidding such an outlet: and all day the stream of gloomy tenderness within him had started forth and returned upon itself in dark courses and eddies, wearying him in the end until the pleasantry of the prefect and the painted little boy had drawn from him a movement of impatience. (II.612–25)

---

2. Freud actually declares, "He understood now that active was the same as masculine, while passive was the same as feminine"—*An Infantile Neurosis, Standard Edition*, vol. 17, p. 47.

And why does the moodiness attached to Stephen's sexual "growth and knowledge," not to mention the restlessness accumulated over his day of brooding on Harold's Cross, vent itself *specifically* in response to a schoolboy's drag performance? Perhaps because Stephen's sexual ambivalence, tapped by this transvestic scenario, persists in such a way as to disturb the ease of his enlistment in the rolls of compulsory heterosexuality, his dalliance with E__ C__ being a critical step in this process. Notice, in this respect, that Stephen figures his feelings for E__ C__ as a "stream of gloomy tenderness" moving "in dark courses and eddies," a metaphor that unmistakably keys into and recirculates the homoerotic valences and associations of Stephen's past experience with dark or eddying courses of water: the square ditch, the sink at the Wicklow Hotel, the shallow end of the bath at Clongowes. Given this commingling of the "streams" of heterosexual affect with the "courses" of (water) closeted homosexual desire, Stephen's prescription for calming his heart after he misses E__ C__, the "odour" of "horse piss and rotted straw" (II.943–44), seems a recognizable enough displacement.

Finally, Stephen's venture into the brothel area is characterized by a literal and symbolic inversion of the phallic mode of heterosexual activity. He serves as the object or locus rather than the agent of penetration. First, "subtle streams" of sound "penetrated his being." Then, "[h]is hands clenched convulsively and his teeth set together as he suffered the agony of . . . penetration" (II.1404–06). Upon entering the prostitute's room, it is Stephen who becomes "hysterical," Stephen who is "surrendering himself," and Stephen who is penetrated by "the dark pressure of her softly parting lips" (II.1453–55). Moreover, Joyce frames Stephen's long anticipated (hetero) sexual transfiguration with lavatory motifs familiar from Clongowes. He depicts Stephen prowling "dark slimy streets" (II.1396), being penetrated by the "subtle streams" of sound, and issuing "a cry which was but the echo of an obscene scrawl which he had read on the oozing wall of a urinal" (II.1411–13). In this way, Joyce unsettles the popular *Bildungsmythos* of a young man's self-conscious graduation from homosexual play to heterosexual maturity and (re)productivity, and he replaces it with an ambivalent complication, a progressive overlapping and interfolding of sexual preferences that is registered at one level of self-narration only to be denied or externalized at another. Such interfolding even extends to Stephen's repentance for these sexual excesses at the religious retreat. For his nominally *heterosexual* sins, he imagines an eternal punishment expressive of his profound dread at his unacknowledged *homosexual* desires: a weedy field of "solid excrement" populated by bestial creatures with long phallic tails and faces whose similarity to and contact with the field give them an anal cast (III.1263, III.1267–82).

Keeping this sexual ambivalence at bay (what we might call the normative working through of homosexual panic) exerts a subtle yet potent pressure on the subsequent course of Stephen's development. On the one hand, his unconscious anxiety about the homoerotic component of his sexual drives can be seen as fueling his repentance and the renunciation of their illicit enactment. On the other hand, and more importantly, a gradual accretion of images and associations of sexual inversion and memories of the homosocial interplay at Clongowes work to hold Stephen back from the logical terminus of his recovered piety, turning his consideration of the religious life toward a relieved demurral.

The latter point becomes evident over the course of his vocational interview with the director of Belvedere. The director opens the interview with a comment on "the friendship between saint Thomas and saint Bonaventure" and goes on to criticize the feminine design of "[t]he capuchin dress" (IV.264) known as "[l]es jupes" (IV.279–80). Stephen's silent embarrassed response is a meditation upon the "soft and delicate stuffs" (IV.292) of women's clothing followed by a meditation on the Jesuit body, in both senses of the term:

> His masters, even when they had not attracted him, had seemed to him always intelligent and serious priests, athletic and high-spirited prefects. He thought of them as men who washed their bodies briskly with cold water and wore clean cold linen. (IV.308–12)

In a context thus informed by questions of homosocial affection and institutionalized cross-dressing, the director's ensuing gesture of releasing the blindcord suddenly cannot but trigger, in both Stephen and the reader, the unconscious memory of Bertie Tallon in drag and Stephen's own impatient responses: letting the edge of the blind fall.

As Stephen leaves the director, he begins to envisage his daily life as a priest in more concrete detail, and the (homo)eroticized traces of the past gather more thickly and affect him more intensely:

> The troubling odour of the long corridors of Clongowes came back to him. . . . At once from every part of his being unrest began to irradiate. A feverish quickening of his pulses followed. (IV.483–87)

An olfactory cue, always the strongest for Stephen, puts him in the grip of an excitement that cannot be explained on a purely nonsexual basis or in terms of simple attraction or repulsion, but only by way of the annihilating proximate-ness of a taboo desire, its alien and alienating intimacy. The memory of the bathhouse atmosphere at Clongowes returns to Stephen with precisely this quality, being *in* and yet not *of* him:

> His lungs dilated and sank as if he were inhaling a warm moist unsustaining air . . . which hung in the bath in Clongowes above the sluggish turfcoloured water. (IV.489–92)

The last phrase, it should be noted, substantially repeats Stephen's mesmerized description of big Corrigan's naked body. So when Stephen goes on to ground his refusal of the clerical life on "the pride of his spirit which had always made him conceive himself as a being apart in every order" (IV.503–05), he represses one of his libidinal aims in the service of the larger economy of desire that feeds his "panic." Stephen does not, as he later thinks, refuse the priesthood by obedience to a "wayward instinct" (IV.654) but rather by the fear of yet another "wayward instinct" implicated in his possible acceptance. This misprision resonates specifically in the odd, ambiguous phrase "apart in [not from] every order" (IV.504–05). To be "apart in" an order, after all, is also to be "a part in" that order; it is to find oneself in a situation of belonging and estrangement simultaneously, the condition of the proximate.

   That Stephen's professedly homosocial discomfort cannot be dissociated from homosexual anxiety grows even clearer during the climactic scene on the strand, where he receives his "true" calling. His fetishistic (which is to say implicitly misogynistic) overvaluation of the bird girl's physical presence follows a correspondingly aversive overreaction to the physical presence of his unclothed schoolmates.

> It was a pain to see them and a swordlike pain to see the signs of adolescence that made repellent their pitiable nakedness. Perhaps they had taken refuge in number and noise from the secret dread in their souls. But he, apart from them and in silence, remembered in what dread he stood of the mystery of his own body. (IV.758–63)

The phallic ("swordlike") nature of Stephen's pain, his confounding of his dread of others with a dread of self, and finally the now familiar solace that he takes in a fantasy of dignified solitude, all indicate a recurrence of Stephen's homosexual panic. The representation of his state of being upon removing himself from the spectacle of his naked classmates even recalls the description of his state of being upon extricating himself from his classmates' celebratory embrace at Clongowes.

He was alone. He was unheeded, happy and near to the wild heart of life. (IV.848–49)

He was alone. He was happy and free. (I.1833–34)

The crucial development on this occasion is that Stephen is able to legitimate his resource of splendid isolation through the romantic myth of the artist.

* * *

Here we have then the erotic hinge on which the *Künstlerroman* aspect of the narrative can be said to turn. Whereas the religious life figures for Stephen the perilous slide of homosocial relations toward homosexual exposure, prompting his flight, the aesthetic vocation figures the sublimation of homosocial ties through the elaboration of a heteroerotic ideal. It thus serves as a kind of supplement to the heterosexual imperative, a subsidiary distancing or mediating agency of homosocial bonds. That the heterosexual imperative should need the supplement of aesthetic transformation, however, is a sign of its ultimate vulnerability.

Such vulnerability is borne out in Stephen's friendship with Cranly, which features the closest thing *A Portrait* has to a French triangle: Stephen projects upon Cranly a mutual competitive interest in E__ C__. This triangle is modeled in turn onto an oedipal triangle, in which the paternalistic Cranly remonstrates with Stephen over the proper devotion to be paid his mother. We seem, in other words, to be moving toward what Sedgwick would see as a normative heterosexual/homophobic resolution. But it does not work. For if Stephen requires a heteroerotic ideal to sublimate his stubborn homoerotic ambivalence, his rarefaction of E__ C__ paradoxically renders her too shadowy and insubstantial a figure to mediate his powerful homosocial relationship with Cranly. Stephen's fleeting sense of romantic rivalry notwithstanding, Cranly increasingly comes to *take over* the place of E__ C__ as Stephen's object of affection. True to the terms of the novel outlined thus far, this transfer of erotic intensity and intimacy to a male figure passes through the register of religious intercourse.

Shortly before Stephen's initial thoughts of Cranly, there occurs a moment of gender misidentification of the sort that occurs prior to Stephen's first date with E__ C__. Stephen's father adverts to him as a "lazy bitch" (V.41). Joyce hereby intimates a structural parallel between Stephen's relations with E__ C__ and Cranly, a sort of dueling courtship. Stephen's thoughts themselves are fairly bursting with a barely repressed homoeroticism. He begins by wondering:

> Why was it that when he thought of Cranly he could never raise before his mind the entire image of his body but only the image of his head and face? (V.146–48)

The habit of mind Stephen observes would seem to locate Cranly, like the aestheticized image of Venus, exclusively "in a mental world" (V.1136), in this case by substantially blotting out his bodily existence. But the "mental world" in which Stephen would cloister his friend is sacerdotal rather than aesthetic; as the following passage indicates, Stephen's identification of the clerical orders with marked homosocial-sexual bonding has survived his rejection of them:

> The forms of the community emerged from the gustblown vestments. . . . They came ambling and stumbling, tumbling and capering, kilting their gowns for leap frog, holding one another back . . . smacking one another behind . . . calling to one another by familiar nicknames . . . whispering two and two behind their hands. (V.646–61)

The largely confessional nature of Stephen's mental intercourse with Cranly, in which he recounts "all the tumults and unrest and longings in his soul" (V.156–57), plugs directly into this homoerotic fantasy of church life, too directly, in fact, to escape Stephen's notice altogether. Even as he contemplates Cranly's "priestlike face," Stephen is brought up short remembering "the gaze of its dark womanish eyes," and "[t]hrough this image" of gender inversion, "he had a glimpse of a strange dark cavern of speculation" (V.152–63)—the very cavern, I would submit, that the present essay has traversed.

Stephen does not really explore this "cavern" until his last interview with Cranly, when he announces his imminent departure from Ireland. Most readers of this scene have followed Richard Ellmann in taking the "homosexual implications" to emanate largely, if not entirely, from Cranly—"Stephen's friend is as interested in Stephen as in Stephen's girl" * * *.[3] But Stephen is the one taken with Cranly's "large dark eyes" (V.2509), which he earlier finds "womanish"; Stephen is the one who inquires, with significant double entendre, "[A]re you trying to make a convert of me or a pervert of yourself?" (V.2429–30); and Stephen is the one whose sexual interests are left most ambiguous:

> Yes. His face was handsome: and his body was strong and hard. . . . He felt then the sufferings of women, the weaknesses of their bodies and souls: and would shield them with a strong and resolute arm and bow his mind to them.

---

3. [Ellmann, *James Joyce*, 117.] An exception is Carens, who takes specific issue with Ellmann, arguing that Stephen is "drawn" to Cranly and partakes of "the current of latent homosexuality in the scene" (pp. 304, 323).

> Away then: it is time to go. A voice spoke softly . . . bidding him go and telling him that his friendship was coming to an end. (V.2509–16)

Stephen here follows the cultural script of placing the figure of woman between himself and his homosocial counterpart, just as he did with the swimmers and with Lynch, but beside Cranly she disappears into a vapid generality. By the end of the passage, in fact, it is hard not to see Cranly as Stephen's *real* object of sexual rivalry rather than a rival for the favor of another. As if to emphasize this gender inversion, when an actual woman appears further on, mediating the "strife of their minds," Stephen perceives her in masculine terms; he sees her "small and slender as a boy" and hears her voice "frail and high as a boy's" (V.2483–87). That the transferential woman now figures in Stephen's mind as male reflects the preeminence of Cranly in his affections.

Finally, if Cranly initiates the physical contact in this encounter, Stephen is the one who responds positively to it. Moreover, having eroticized the priestly office since his time at Clongowes, Stephen insistently positions Cranly as a cleric manqué, a priest without portfolio or the "power to absolve" (V.160). In this way, Stephen can himself experience sexual *frisson* without institutional subordination. This may, in fact, be the key to Stephen's relationship with Cranly. In order that Stephen may resolve the trauma of the doubtful or duplicitous "touch" of his masters, such as Father Dolan, he enlists Cranly to extend to him the "touch" of a doubtful mastery, a touch that elicits a less immediate sense of dread. But precisely because Stephen can be so "thrilled by his touch" (V.2585–86), Cranly embodies the most profound danger yet to Stephen's heterosexual self-conception. He not only represents the persistence of Stephen's religious sensibility in and despite his apostasy ("your mind," he says, "is supersaturated with the religion in which you say you disbelieve"—V.2335–36), but he also represents the persistence of its homoerotic attractions in and despite Stephen's aggressively heterosexual aesthetics.

As the vessel of this persistence, I would suggest, Cranly plays *the* decisive role in motivating Stephen's self-exile. For at this point Stephen can only reconstruct the aesthetic mission as a safely heterosexual adventure by making its completion somehow contingent upon separating himself from the "one person . . . who would be more than a friend" (V.2599–600), however much Stephen would like to project that sentiment onto Cranly alone. Surely it is no coincidence that this pivotal conversation with Cranly breaks off, assuring Stephen's departure, just when the issue of homosexual attraction and involvement, which has been diverted, displaced, and misrecognized throughout the novel, is finally if inconclusively broached. Stephen's last unanswered question, "Of whom are you speaking?" (V.2607), virtually epitomizes homosexual panic as a neurotic obsession with the identity, status, and location of homo-hetero difference and virtually defines Stephen as its captive.

Can we extend the diagnosis to Joyce and to his leavetaking? This question can only return us to the pragmatic riddles concerning self-revelation and fictional representation introduced at the outset of this essay. The unstable differential equation between Stephen and Joyce, wherein the protagonist conceals the author by standing for him, means that self-portraiture is its own refuge, requiring no deliberate forms of secrecy. All of the disclosures that Joyce might have packed or wanted to pack into his depiction of Stephen, including the display of homoerotic desires and discomforts, ultimately prove indistinguishable from the exercise of poetic license as a mode of denial. That is to say, regarding such things as erotic preferences, the ontology of self-portraiture makes the candor Joyce demanded of authors easy because it makes the credulity of the reader impossible. A portrait of the artist is an open closet.

GREGORY CASTLE

Coming of Age in the Age of Empire: Joyce's Modernist *Bildungsroman*[†]

> We live in an age when men treat art as if it were meant to be a form of autobiography.
>
> Oscar Wilde, *The Picture of Dorian Gray*

* * * Seamus Deane argues that Stephen Dedalus is primarily known to readers at first by quotations; by the end of the novel, he is quoting himself: "the narrated Stephen becomes the narrator Stephen."[1] In terms of development, he is for the most part what he has read or, as Deane puts it, borrowed:

> His idea of the soul and its relation to the body is at first a borrowed one . . . culled from the teaching of his religious superiors and later confirmed by his reading of literature, especially

---

† From *James Joyce Quarterly* 50:1–2 (Fall 2012–Winter 2013): 359–84. Originally appeared in *JJQ* 40:4 (Summer 2003). Copyright © for the *JJQ*, University of Tulsa, 2012. Reprinted with permission of University of Tulsa. Some of the author's notes have been omitted. Page references for *A Portrait* have been replaced with part and line numbers of this Norton Critical Edition. Some cited passages might differ slightly from the equivalent passages in this volume.
1. Seamus Deane, introduction to *A Portrait of the Artist as a Young Man* by James Joyce, ed. Deane (1916; New York: Penguin Publishers, 1993), p. xvi.

Dante. But, worst of all, Stephen feels the threat of his borrowed culture when it seeks to co-opt him, when it tries to recruit him into its system of institutionalized borrowing, either through the vocation of the priesthood or through a commitment to Irish nationalism. (xviii)

Deane might have added the vocation of teaching to his list of possible institutionalized forms of borrowing, for Stephen is frequently depicted in scenes of instruction, both as a student and as a pedagogue. Elsewhere, Deane has noted that Stephen is the novel's first intellectual hero and that thinking—or, more precisely, an "intellectual vocation"—is an important element in his narrative of development.[2] However, the experience of intellectual life that Deane describes is far from the harmonious socialization that Fritz Martini (and a host of other theorists of the genre) considers the *raison d'être* of the *Bildungsroman*:[3] the "idea of cultivation . . . through a harmony of aesthetic, moral, rational, and scientific education [which] had long been common property of Enlightenment thought."[4]

The idea of education through self-cultivation (*Bildung*) belongs to the era of self-assured modernity, the era of the "all-round, self-realizing individual."[5] * * *

Along with Johann Wolfgang von Goethe, Friedrich Ernst Daniel Schleiermacher, Friedrich von Schiller, and others associated with Weimar and Jena from the 1790s through the 1830s, [Wilhelm von] Humboldt developed th[e] notion of an "inner culture" attained through practices of self-cultivation * * *.[6] This was classic Renaissance humanism energized by new fields of knowledge—especially the emerging disciplines of anthropology, biology, political economy, comparative religion, and the phenomenon described by Edward Said as "Orientalism"[7]—as well as new theories and new methods of analysis. This intellectual climate encouraged the development of a narrative form that symbolically harmonized the diverse aspects of social experience, often depicting this process in dialectical terms. The *Bildungsheld* (hero of development) of such

---

2. Deane, *Celtic Revivals: Essays in Modern Irish Literature 1880–1980* (Winston-Salem: Wake Forest Univ. Press, 1987), p. 76.
3. "Novel of development" (German), in the sense of growth to maturity through self-cultivation. The plural is *Bildungsromane* [Editor].
4. Fritz Martini, "Bildungsroman—Term and Theory," *Reflection and Action: Essays on the Bildungsroman,* ed. James Hardin (Columbia: Univ. of South Carolina Press, 1991), p. 5.
5. Jürgen Habermas, *The Philosophical Discourse of Modernity: Twelve Lectures,* trans. Frederick Lawrence (Cambridge: MIT Press, 1987), p. 64.
6. For a good general background text on this era in German thought, see Bruford, *Culture and Society in Classical Weimar, 1775–1806* (London: Cambridge Univ. Press, 1962). See also Todd Kontje, *The German Bildungsroman: History of a National Genre* (Columbia: Camden House, 1993).
7. See Edward Said, *Orientalism* (New York: Vintage Books, 1978).

narratives is delivered into a position of security and authority, symbolized by a unity of desire and social responsibility. This essentially Romantic unity was thought capable of annulling—through dialectics or an ideal of organicism—any resistance to harmonious development the hero might meet from internal or external forces. Rebellion against this destiny, which is determined by the objective destiny of history, is countenanced only if the hero returns, still young, but a little wiser, to the fold—a prodigal son, artistic rebel *and* good bourgeois, returning to close the circle.

In the classical *Bildungsroman*, exemplified by Goethe's *Wilhelm Meisters Lehrjahre (Wilhelm Meister's Apprenticeship)*,[8] the hero makes a detour from the family business in order to travel with a dramatic troupe. But his sojourn in the marginal world of the theater is only one stage towards the *telos*[9] of his self-development, for he is ultimately inducted into an elite society of sensitive and enlightened men and women, a spiritual rendition of the bourgeois life Wilhelm left behind when he began his journey. * * *

* * * Goethe's paradigmatic *Wilhelm Meister's Apprenticeship* reveals the difficulty in attaining the ideal of *Bildung,* in attempting to harmonize desire with history, to resolve reflection in action, action in reflection. This problem persists as the philosophical ideal of *Bildung* is uneasily translated into the dominant ideology of self-formation in the nineteenth century and as the personal goal of self-sufficiency becomes the impersonal state requirement to become socialized.

* * * [A]s I will demonstrate, the modernist *Bildungsroman,* especially in colonial societies, thrives on the kinds of social conflicts * * * traditionalist critics deem unsuitable for the proper Germanic "philosophico-spiritual" *Bildungsroman.*

Outside of the German critical tradition, Franco Moretti has taken a hard line of a different sort.[1] He argues that there was, in fact, a vigorous *Bildungsroman* tradition in nineteenth-century France and, more problematically, in England. It is not national origins, however, but late modernity that hampers the authentic development of the form. Moretti argues, in brief, that beginning in the late nineteenth century we witness the degeneration of a form that had once provided the young bourgeois hero a map of "the way of the world." He sees the demise of the form primarily as a result

8. Johann Wolfgang von Goethe, *Wilhelm Meisters Lehrjahre (Wilhelm Meister's Apprenticeship)* (Berlin: J. F. Unger, 1795–1796), and published in translation as *Wilhelm Meister's Apprenticeship,* ed. and trans. Eric A. Blackall, vol. 9, *Goethe: The Collected Works* (1795–1796; Princeton: Princeton Univ. Press, 1995). * * *

9. "End, purpose, ultimate object or aim" (*OED*) (Greek) [*Editor*].

1. Franco Moretti, *The Way of the World: The Bildungsroman in European Culture,* trans. Albert Sbragia (London: Verso Press, 1987). Further references will be cited parenthetically in the text.

of its development in the English context. The English *Bildungs-roman* develops, he believes, amid the stability and conformity of English social and political life: "Here is a solid world sure of itself and at ease in a continuity that fuses together 'tradition' and 'progress.' It is a world that cannot and does not want to identify with the spirit of adventure of modern youth" (213). For Moretti, "liberal-democratic civilization" meant the end of a "philosophico-spiritual" tradition; the English *Bildungsroman* "has absorbed and propagated one of the most basic expectations of liberal-democratic civilization: the desire that the realm of the law be certain, universalistic, and provided with mechanisms for correction and control" (213). The implication is that social and political developments at the end of the nineteenth century had rendered the *Bildungsroman* inadequate as a model for identity formation, for the harmonious cultivation of the self. Moretti's argument about the exhaustion of the *Bildungsroman* form, because it is predicated on the inadequacy of its conventional modes of narrative development and characterization, resembles that of the Germanists who argue that the form cannot exist outside of the terrain marked out for it by German Enlightenment thinkers nearly two hundred years ago. But far from languishing at the turn of the century, as Moretti argues, the *Bildungsroman* enters a period of revival and transformation and becomes a powerful and relevant form for the negotiation of complex problems concerning identity, nationality, education, the role of the artist, and social as well as personal relationships. This is especially true in the works of Irish modernists like Joyce, who was able to translate disempowerment into narratives of survival, even if survival meant dissent and, ultimately, exile.

For this is what *Bildung* often turns out to be, in a reading that stresses the links between narrative form and social power: a dissent from social order, from the conventions of self-cultivation, a dissent as well from the ideas of pedagogy and parenting that sanction restrictive and punitive models of development. These ideas had developed within a classical *Bildungsroman* tradition in Europe and England, which begins with Goethe and encompasses Honoré de Balzac, Gustave Flaubert, Charles Dickens, Charlotte and Emily Brontë, George Eliot, George Meredith, and a handful of others. The fundamental features of the form, as the modernists inherited it, include: a rebellion against the father and the social values he represents, the desire for self-mastery and the journey away from father and home, apprenticeship and vocation, the instrumental function of women along the way, crises in the process of self-development, and the reconciliation with the father and social values, often represented as a symbolic return. These elements represent the stages of development—stylized and to some degree

idealized—within bourgeois culture. In turn, the representations
serve as models for the reader. Nineteenth-century *Bildungsromane*, in depicting these stages, generally focused on the hero's
more prosaic social relations, primarily those involved in pursuing
a vocation and a spouse.

*   *   *

By and large, the English tradition produced narratives that privileged stable, traditional positions in commerce or the arts and
legal marriages that symbolized the union of spiritual and temporal
desires. * * * The *Bildungsromane* of Balzac and Flaubert, in which
the hero leaves the provinces in order to achieve artistic or social
success in Paris, is of obvious interest to anyone reading Joyce's
Bildungsroman. In this tradition, the goal of harmonious socialization, of induction into the symbolic system of the dominant class
(and thus into the languages of power), is never met: either it is
frustrated or deferred to some future time or totally forestalled in
the face of crushing and irredeemable social failure. In any case,
the failure to socialize, if not accounted for, must be assimilated
dialectically within a transcendent and triumphant unified self. It
is the desire of the prodigal son that underwrites these classical
narratives of development and return. This self-legitimating closed-
circuit is ideally suited to the task of creating models of bourgeois
socialization.[2]
    It is in a general thematics of dissent from this ideological func-
tion and refusal of its legitimating authority that we find the modernist impulse in Joyce's *Bildungsroman*. For this reason, *A Portrait*
is perhaps the most compelling example of the way the modernist
Bildungsroman manages to retain and even emulate the formal
structures of a genre whose conceptual foundations and thematic
concerns are at the same time subjected to critique and revision.
Joyce does this not primarily by altering the structure of the legiti-
mizing narrative in some subversive way but by narrating new
norms of development that are either marginal or heterodox, that
critique the various components of the classical *Bildungsroman*.
Thus, *A Portrait* attempts to establish new ways to represent the
relations between the developing subject and social and familial
institutions. In the opening chapters, these relations are difficult
because of the young Stephen's hypersensitivity to his own social
and pedagogical oppression. Take, for example, the concluding section of the first chapter, in which Stephen rebels against the authority of his teachers and gains the approbation of his peers. He walks

---

2. I have discussed this historical background at length in my "Book of Youth: Reading
Joyce's *Bildungsroman*," *Genre*, 22 (Spring 1989), 21–28.

the gamut of "great men" [I.1701] of history, presents his case to the Rector, then returns to his fellows, who "made a cradle of their locked hands and hoisted him up among them and carried him along till he struggled to get free" (I.1824–26). The figures of Father Dolan and the Rector are the masculine embodiments of Church authority; by the end of chapter 1, Stephen successfully asserts himself against these authorities only to find himself still under their sway. In a characteristic reverie, Stephen curtails his own rebellion: "he would not be anyway proud with Father Dolan. He would be very quiet and obedient" (I.1834–35). In this microcosm of the *Bildung* narrative, we see that the only way out for a Catholic Irish colonial subject is to capitulate to the Church and rise up in the hierarchy.

A few years later, Stephen's participation in a Whitsuntide play, * * * coincides with a crisis of being in which the son refuses the lessons of his father. After the play, he collapses in nearly incoherent disappointment: "That is horse piss and rotted straw, he thought. It is a good odour to breathe. It will calm my heart. My heart is quite calm now. I will go back" (II.943–45). The full import of the lessons he learned that night come home to him while on a visit to Cork with his father, who is seeing to the dissolution of some of the family's property at auction. What Stephen learns is that his own path is not the one of mild, gentlemanly heroism that Simon Dedalus gasses on about in the Cork pubs with his old cronies. * * *

Chapter 2 narrates Stephen's burgeoning desire to be far from such a cultural authority, far from "the constant voices of his father and of his masters, urging him to be a gentleman" (II.841–42). His response at first is a kind of passive refusal of what is expected of him. Only later, in chapter 5, does he actively dissent from normative models of development—on patently anticolonial grounds— and normative conceptions of the self, particularly the *artistic* self. In chapter 2, while presumably learning manhood from his father, he travels mentally to a time during which "he was happy," far from "hollowsounding voices": "beyond their call, alone or in the company of phantasmal comrades" (II.854–58). The trope of return ("I will go back" [II.945]) links this episode with the general pattern of return inscribed in and by the narrative hegemony of the *Bildungsroman* form, while, at the same time, his "[p]ride and hope and desire like crushed herbs in his heart" [II.930–31] sustain him as he gathers his forces to leave his father's world behind. The "growth and knowledge of two years of boyhood" (II.620) have left him moody and gloomy, susceptible to the trauma of discovering that his "education of the senses" was the antithesis of the socialization proffered by his father: the making of a "bloody good

434 GREGORY CASTLE

honest Irishmen," who associates with "fellows of the right kidney" (II.1118). But this vision of the gentleman is really retrospective wish fulfillment on Simon's part, and Stephen later indicates how well he knows it when he "enumerate[s] glibly his father's attributes": "A medical student, an oarsman, a tenor, an amateur actor, a shouting politician, a small landlord, a small investor, a drinker, a good fellow, a storyteller, somebody's secretary, something in a distillery, a taxgatherer, a bankrupt and at present a praiser of his own past" (V.2372–76). The displacement of paternal authority from an abstract principle to multiple or serial subject positions signals the disintegration of the authority of the father, both as parent and as Law. It also dramatizes the inadequacy of the father (and of father figures) to perform reliably as a mentor for young Stephen. *A Portrait* opens with the establishment of the Father's authority, by emphasizing the relations of domination that exist between father and son. Simon's bearing in the Christmas dinner scene is at first authoritative, but by the conclusion of the vignette, as Stephen notes, "terrorstricken," his "eyes were full of tears" (I.1151). Moreover, Simon Dedalus's scheme to have Stephen train under Mike Flynn, who "had put some of the best runners of modern times through his hands" (II.52–53), underscores the total lack of understanding on the father's part of his son's talents and ambitions.[3] The famous schoolroom scene in Cork, where Stephen reads an inscription that shocks him by naming his own "monstrous reveries," illustrates the bankrupt potential of the Father's Law (II.1067). The inscription of the body as "*Foetus*" [II.1050] on a desk, like the "horse piss and straw," asserts the priority and power of the maternal-as-Real over the exhausted Father. It confirms the degradation of all his idealizations and with them the *Bildung*-plot in which they were instrumental. It throws him back to a point prior to (or beyond) the Symbolic, the Law of the Father: "By his monstrous way of life he seemed to have put himself beyond the limits of reality" (II.1143–45). He soon attempts to use the money he wins in essay contests "to build a breakwater of order and elegance against the sordid tide of life without him and to dam up, by rules of conduct and active interests and new filial relations, the powerful recurrence of the tides within him" (II.1347–51). He is, in effect, attempting to make up for the inadequacy of the Father's Law (the "sordid tide of life without him"), but he also realizes that his own desires (the "tides within him") are every bit as destructive as the conventional authority represented by his father and the socialization of Irish gentlemen.

3. Stephen is certainly not interested in conventional schoolboy heroics, as his dismissal of Heron as a "sorry anticipation of manhood" indicates (II.837).

Critique of and capitulation to the imperatives of *Bildung* can easily become confused with one another, especially when a critique of normative modes of development is conducted within the strict formal limits of the *Bildungsroman*. Questions concerning the difficulty of critiquing conceptions of the self, subjectivity, social or national identity—the array of *topoi*[4] associated with the question of Irish modernism—arise within a form whose conventions are tied in myriad ways to an Enlightenment conception of *Bildung* that had begun, in the mid-nineteenth century, to resolve the adversarial relationship between the individual and the State through dialectics. Is it possible, in short, to remain within the main coordinates of the *Bildungsroman* tradition and at the same time create a hero who *dissents* from that tradition? I think it is possible, and it is this very act of dissent that begins to propel the genre toward new modes of expression and new modes of inharmonious but *achieved* development.

A Portrait, principally in its treatment of the ideological effects of theology and pedagogy, takes a critical view of the conventions of socialization, especially insofar as they are marked by the Enlightenment idea of self-cultivation. * * * Rather, it narrates scenes of instruction and ideological interpellation, in which the subject resists a social system that seeks to produce rational individuals. * * *

* * * But we might speculate that the instrumental view of education serves imperial and ecclesiastic but not necessarily personal interests. This is especially the case in metrocolonial situations with regard to identity formation and the viability of the educated colonial subject. It is in an attempt to explain the paradox of the educated colonial subject that Joyce's texts pay so much attention to schoolroom scenes—and I mean formal classroom experience in both national and sectarian schools as well as alternative forms of public instruction.[5] If * * * education eventually becomes consolidated within the institutional structure of society, then there is little room for the kind of self-formation that *Bildung* requires. The modernist *Bildungsroman* represents the failure of classical *Bildung* in this institutional climate; but it also maps new points of resistance in the processes of formation and encourages the emergence of new conceptions of self-formation that are more often concerned with evading and resisting socialization, with disharmonious social spheres or with hybrid, ambivalent, sometimes traumatic processes of identity formation. By challenging the pedagogical assumptions of the genre—that is, by narrating a failed or problematic

---

4. Plural of topos, meaning "motif or theme" (*OED*) [*Editor*].
5. This is, of course, true of *Stephen Hero* and *A Portrait* but also of significant portions of *Ulysses* and *Finnegans Wake*.

educational odyssey followed by the beginning of an artistic apprenticeship in exile—Joyce effectively challenges the historical and
ideological values the classical *Bildungsroman* more or less overtly
legitimizes and celebrates.

In its classical form, the *Bildungsroman* narrates a harmonious
social dialectic; such a narrative form cannot convey the traumatic
social development of colonial subjects.[6] In the National schools,
colonial students had to choose dissent or alienated assent to foreign values imposed upon them; a similar choice arose in Catholic
schools, though they did make some appeal to national values.[7] Stephen's desire to dissent from the choice by taking the option of
exile at the end of *A Portrait* grows out of a prior enthusiastic assent
to an ideal of *Bildung* that had become alienated and then finally
bitterly resented. His desire for freedom from this transformed,
rationalized *Bildung* with its coercive master-narrative of bourgeois
self-development is no less desperate or desperately felt for being
the desire of a metrocolonial subject. In fact, proximity, cultural
and geographic, to the metropolitan center might increase the psychological, if not physical, damage that failed socialization can
cause in a colonial situation. By the same token, a shared language
and, to some degree, a shared aesthetic culture mean that an intel-
lectually gifted young man like Stephen can find ways to resist the
impossible norm of imperial sociality and thus to open up possibilities of subjectivity and historical agency denied by classical *Bildung*. We might, in short, ask if a colonial *Bildungsroman* is even
possible.

•

As I have argued above, alongside the development of the modernist *Bildungsroman* from the 1890s through the 1930s, we see a
general breakdown in the authority of the essential, autonomous
self, a general challenge to traditional models of identity formation,
and a broad crisis * * * of normative socialization. This breakdown
in socialization in colonial society creates the conditions for what
Albert Memmi calls "an internal catastrophe," a form of arrested

---

6. As many postcolonial theorists argue, colonial power cannot conceive of subjectivity as
a property of subaltern individuals. Subjectivity is not really an option for the colonized, who are materially present though socially and politically nonexistent. What we
tend to find instead is the subjective trauma of revolt against conditions that bear upon
the felt experience and (one can only propose) the consciousness of colonized individuals. See my "Confessing Oneself: Colonial *Bildung* and Homoeros in Joyce's *A Portrait
of the Artist as a Young Man*," *Quare Joyce*, ed. Joseph Valente (Ann Arbor: Univ. of
Michigan Press, 1998), pp. 160–62. * * *

7. On the idea of "alienated assent" as a pedagogical strategy, see Gayatri Chakravorty
Spivak, "The Burden of English," *Postcolonial Discourses: An Anthology*, ed. Gregory
Castle (Oxford: Blackwell Publishers, 2000), pp. 53–72.

development unique to the colonial situation.[8] * * * Education in colonial societies—in effect, national state education systems imposed by colonial administrators—far from furthering development, typically distorts or arrests it at crucial points of adolescence and young adulthood. In Joyce's *Bildungsroman*, formal education plays a more complicated role, for Stephen Dedalus is educated in denominational schools (first Clongowes, then Belvedere College) that had found their niche within colonial society and that offered limited access * * * to the classical *Bildungsroman* tradition. And while such schools offered a superior grade of education, they also exposed students to forms of eroticized pedagogical violence unique to the Catholic educational system. The situation is complicated by a lack of vocational options that compounds the limitations experienced in the school system. As in many other colonial contexts, the two spheres of development, public and private, are radically incommensurate, not least because the dominant cultural ideals of British imperialism are foreign and imposed more or less coercively and totally, reaching into the very interior of the colonial subject. The economic models of development that governed the prosperity of England at home were precisely those that devastated Ireland.[9] In the absence of viable means of social reform, this unevenness often led to arrested or catastrophic development in society and in the individual. At the limits of what is normative (generically and socially), the desire for the self becomes interiorized, illicit and phantasmal. The cultural ideals (transcendence, white male dominance, secularism, positive science, and so forth) that accompany colonial domination do not represent the sociality into which Stephen would desire to be harmoniously integrated. Neither does self-sufficiency seem a viable option. What is offered instead is a contest. But rather than pit the subject's interiority against a set of normative and regulative ideals, colonial *Bildung* splits the subject and pits it against itself in a form of psychological dehiscence. Put another way, the colonial subject must orient the process of self-development against a norm that, in a "proper" context (especially a metropolitan one), produces a sovereign, autonomous (not to say self-sufficient) subject. The desire for the self, for self-cultivation, becomes a desire directed not only against a given norm (in this case, of socialization) but against norms themselves, normativity as

---

8. Albert Memmi, *The Colonizer and the Colonized* (New York: Orion Press, 1965), p. 99. Frantz Fanon's work is relevant on this point as well—see the case studies in *The Wretched of the Earth*, trans. Constance Farrington (New York: Grove Weidenfeld, 1963). Further references to both the Memmi and Fanon works will be cited parenthetically in the text.

9. Terry Eagleton, in *Heathcliff and the Great Hunger: Studies in Irish Culture* (London: Verso Press, 1995), pp. 1–27, illustrates the economic disparities between Ireland and Britain. * * *

such. One positive result for Stephen (as for other colonial and postcolonial *Bildungshelden*)[1] is a consciousness of contradiction: the desire for self-formation, which in the classical *Bildungsroman* is tied to normative socialization, appears to the colonial or subaltern subject as a transgression, something illegitimate and disharmonious—an impossible dream. The colonial *Bildungsroman*, like the female form that began to flourish alongside the Goethean prototype, articulates this failure, this failed dream.[2]

The fact that, for Stephen, this formal schooling is offered under the auspices of the Roman Catholic Church (rather than the colonial rulers) does not lessen the possibility of "internal catastrophe." For the likes of Stephen, a university education in Ireland at the turn of the century was a guarantee of little more than the requisite degree for rising up in the Church. Indeed, the normative pathways of socialization offered by the Church are among the first that Stephen refuses. In the "cold lucid indifference" (III.47) that pervades the opening of chapter 3, we have a prelude not to liberation from a colonial condition but rather to a more sweeping engulfment in a characteristically Irish narrative of salvation. The language of sin in which Stephen couches his rebellion against the Church is telling, as is the pride he takes in "his own sin," the "loveless awe of God" that precludes "false homage" (III.68–70). The consciousness of sin, like the consciousness of an interdiction, holds Stephen in a providential narrative of development. A discourse of sin makes him a subject because he sins. We see him gradually succumb to the sinfulness of the very sensualism that appeared to set him free: "a faint glimmer of fear began to pierce the fog of his mind" (III.340–41). The authority of the Father shifts from the totally ineffectual Simon Dedalus to the hypereffective Father Arnall. The theological fervor of the latter's discourse at the retreat, intensified by the Loyolan intricacies of "composition,"[3] signals the hegemony of a providential discourse that cannot be easily rejected, that seeks to contain and defuse colonial *Bildung* by creating a transcendent space of reconciliation of the individual with the Church and God, thus compensating for social injustice. As part of this containment, the retreat discourse cancels the coming into consciousness of sexuality. In the middle of the retreat, Stephen imagines he is married

1. Plural of *Bildungsheld* (German), the protagonist, or hero (*Held*), of a *Bildungsroman* (novel of development) [*Editor*].
2. On the "female *Bildungsroman*," see Elizabeth Abel, Marianne Hirsch and Elizabeth Langland, eds., *The Voyage In: Fictions of Female Development* (Hanover, NH: Univ. Press of New England, 1983), and [Susan] Fraiman's *Unbecoming Women* [(New York: Columbia Univ. Press, 1993)].
3. In his *Spiritual Exercises* (see pp. 311–16), St. Ignatius of Loyola presents composition of place as part of disciplined contemplation. It involves the contemplative person's imagining the details of a scene from scripture or experience, taking up a place in the scene, and then experiencing the effects [*Editor*].

to Emma (III.518–22), thus enacting in fantasy the marriage of personal desire and social expectations so often narrated in the classical *Bildungsroman*. The power and presence of the Blessed Virgin Mary, here as elsewhere in Joyce, fulfills the function of the absent but powerful Father who stands behind and guarantees the machinations and symbolizations of the classical *Bildungsroman*. Ecclesiastical constraints and cancellations serve to negate any potential for political education by rigidly prescribing the nature of mental activity. St. Ignatius of Loyola's *Spiritual Exercises,* which govern Father Arnall's sermon and Stephen's reaction to it, seem in and of themselves to be unambiguous testimony to the subversive and profane power of an idle mind.[4]

Stephen's entrapment in the discourse of salvation clarifies and rigidifies his subjection, leaving him farther than ever from the promised land of classical *Bildung*. There is no journey abroad, no ameliorating rebellion from the Father and his social values that can lead to a return before it is too late. There is only stasis and damnation, which hobble the trajectory of *Bildung*. The "mild proud sovereignty" (IV.767) that Stephen asserts after finally refusing the call to the priesthood does not represent a successful practice of *Bildung*. * * * Stephen's sovereignty of self is far too tenuous, far too much like a defense mechanism. This is why he is tempted at first by the prospect of a spiritual vocation. He is singled out and asked about his "desire to join the [Jesuit] order" (IV.366), an offer of vocation that comes closest to fulfilling the principal requirement of the classical *Bildungsroman*. Indeed, here we are faced with an anomalous situation, for it is rare in colonial contexts for the disavowed subject to be taken into the fold. The Church in Irish colonial society thus mediates between the imperial domain of proper *Bildung* and the colonial terrain of catastrophic development. Stephen is invited to take a position of social power, which he does not underestimate as his mock-serious performance of priestly duties suggests (IV.392–516).[5] But these duties mainly support the stasis that assimilates and stymies all development; it is an abstract, ceremonial power calculated to guarantee all the more fully the political powerlessness of the colonial subject. * * *

The narrative of salvation, the totalizing narrative of development that thwarts self-formation and imposes the *telos* of spiritual

---

4. St. Ignatius of Loyola, *The Spiritual Exercises of S. Ignatius of Loyola* (Saint Omers, France: Nicolas Joseph Le Febre, 1736) [see the excerpts on pp. 311–16—*Editor*]. On the "Ignatian spiritual model," and its significance for Stephen's sacramental identity, see Jonathan Mulrooney, "Stephen Dedalus and the Politics of Confession," *Studies in the Novel,* 33 (Summer 2001), 170–71. Further references to the Mulrooney article will be cited parenthetically in the text.

5. I discuss Stephen's parodic performance in terms of his reworking of confessional discourse and confessional acts in "Confessing Oneself" (pp. 170–73).

redemption and absolution in its place, begins to unravel as the spiritual energies that usually drive the processes of development along familiar pathways are recathected in order to serve an awakening artistic style. Precisely at the moment of initiation into the Church, * * * Stephen demurs and rejects a destiny laid out in advance by the Jesuit order. The vocation refused in the director's office is instead accepted in a profane and erotic mimicry conducted in the open air on a walk from Byron's pub to the strand along Dublin Bay. He encounters larking, naked boys and a girl bathing at the shore. The call of art comes amid a confusion of mind as Stephen moves from disharmonious rebellion to ecstatic self-affirmation. He is less self-sufficient than he is self-contained, "elusive of social and religious orders" [IV.531], a Nietzschean solitary.[6] He realizes that "the oils of ordination would never anoint his body. He had refused. Why?" (IV.655–66). The answer to this question is the university, precisely the space where we might suppose a traditional *Bildung*-plot would unfold: "The university! So he had passed beyond the challenge of the sentries who had stood as guardians of his boyhood and had sought to keep him among them that he might be subject to them and serve their ends" (IV.630–33). Stephen's desire to attend the university is in obedience to "a wayward instinct" (IV.654), one that we can connect to his early fascination with the very processes of his own understanding: "By thinking of things you could understand them" (I.1269). He was eight or nine when he solemnly thought these words, but they are now as apt a description of his self-wonder as they were then. His fascination with his own consciousness as an "inner world of individual emotions mirrored perfectly in a lucid supple periodic prose" (IV.701–03) confirms his sense of autonomy from social authorities. He is quite willing to give himself up to an aesthetic experience that would afford him a new path of development. Those moments on the shore, before he sees the birdgirl, are powerful ones in which he asserts his independence from normative modes of socialization. The cacophony of boys' voices and the iteration of his name in a pseudo-Greek form lend the scene a certain archaic eroticism:

6. But see Dominic Manganiello, in "Reading the Book of Himself: The Confessional Imagination of St. Augustine and Joyce," *Biography & Autobiography: Essays on Irish and Canadian History and Literature,* ed. James Noonan (Ottawa: Carleton Univ. Press, 1993), p. 159, who argues that *A Portrait* offers Stephen "as the prime specimen of the self-sufficient individual whose ambition is to beget a new race in his own image and likeness" [*Author*]. In his 1883 book, *Also sprach Zarathustra* (*Thus Spoke Zarathustra*), the German philosopher Friedrich Nietzsche (1844–1900) presented the *Übermensch,* or superior human being, as an ideal. This superior being would reject widely held attitudes in Judeo-Christian society that focus on fulfillment in some other world and would instead concentrate on earthly life. To become such a being, the individual refuses conventional perspectives and proceeds in a solitary way [*Editor*].

—Stephaneforos!
His throat ached with a desire to cry aloud, the cry of a hawk
or eagle on high, to cry piercingly of his deliverance to the
winds. This was the call of life to his soul not the dull gross
voice of the world of duties and despair, not the inhuman voice
that had called him to the pale service of the altar. An instant
of wild flight had delivered him and the cry of triumph which
his lips withheld cleft his brain.
—Stephaneforos! (IV.796–804)

The misrecognition of his name frames a Nietzschean refusal to be
held down by abstractions and "dull gross voices." It is, to be sure,
infused with a homoerotic desire, but this desire is itself articulated within a "call of life to his soul" symbolized by the birdgirl.
The homoerotic atmosphere of the preamble to the scene featuring
the birdgirl underscores, as does his objectification of her, the distance Stephen has traveled from the compulsory heterosexuality
subtly insisted upon in most classical *Bildungsromane*.

   With respect to his relations with girls and women, Stephen lives
in a fantasy world. When he is not the romanticized hero out of *The
Count of Monte Cristo*, he is championing the apostate Lord Byron
and getting thrashed for his trouble (II.732–91). His adolescence is
represented in a series of transformations in which Eileen Vance,
E. C., Mercedes, the unnamed prostitute, the birdgirl—all come
under the sway of a budding *Bildung*-process, a period of self-
discovery and awakened desire on the part of an artist who imaginatively transforms real and fictive women into instruments of his
own struggle for artistic freedom.[7] Early on, the emotions evoked in
Stephen are romanticized longings, vaguely erotic "premonition[s]"
[II.176] of an "unsubstantial image" [II.175]. In short order, his
desires, though still inchoate, become more insistent, and he can
connect them to real girls in an immediate way, as when he with-
draws "into a snug corner of the room" [II.309–10] at a children's
party and feels E. C.'s glance "travel . . . to his corner, flattering,
taunting, searching, exciting his heart" (II.315–16). * * * E. C.
excites in Stephen the power of youth, that supreme emblem of late

7. On Stephen's adolescent attitude toward girls and women, specifically the way in
   which E. C. serves "primarily as a means to fulfill Stephen's own needs," see Margaret
   Church, "The Adolescent Point of View toward Women in Joyce's *A Portrait of the Artist
   as a Young Man*," *Irish Renaissance Annual*, 2, ed. Zack Bowen (Newark: Univ. of Delaware Press, 1981), 158–65. Of special importance for understanding Stephen's relationship with E. C. is Christine Froula's *Modernism's Body: Sex, Culture, and Joyce*
   (New York: Columbia Univ. Press, 1996), pp. 47–69 [see p. 392—*Editor*]. See also
   Suzette Henke, "Stephen Dedalus and Women: A Portrait of the Artist as a Young
   Misogynist," in *James Joyce and the Politics of Desire* (New York: Routledge Publishers,
   1990), pp. 50–84.

Victorian modernity that Moretti sees as one of the ideological motifs of the nineteenth-century *Bildungsroman*.[8]

Stephen's experiences with women constitute a series of duplications in which women are more or less interchangeable icons of his mental attitudes or of significant points along the way of his self-formation. In both cases, he conforms to the conventions of the *Bildungsroman* tradition, in which women are primarily important for their secondary status, their instrumentality in forwarding the desires of the male *Bildungsheld*. But he also undermines the conventions when he confounds his own sexual identity with that of women around him, as in the concluding scene of chapter 2, where he feels "some dark presence moving irresistibly upon him from the darkness," a murmuring female presence, and "he suffered the agony of its penetration" (II.1405–06). Whether we read this scene as confounding sexual and gender identities or screening for homoerotic desire, it is clearly not the normative experience of the young *Bildungsheld*, for whom women are supposed to be helpmates and selfless partners, not monstrous, vampiric presences or "batlike souls" that can only derail the *Bildung*-process. Given the catastrophic nature of colonial *Bildung*, it should come as no surprise that women, real and iconic, should succeed less in facilitating than in distancing Stephen irrecoverably from harmonious socialization. His mother, after all, packs him off for exile.

In Joyce's modernist *Bildungsroman*, then, women do not cease to be instrumental to the young hero; rather, their instrumentality takes on a new function and value, one that includes the rejection of prior bourgeois and colonialist values. There is, additionally, a kind of criticism lodged in this instrumentality, one that goes to the heart of the gender politics of the classical *Bildungsroman*. At the end of chapter 2, when Stephen finds himself with the unnamed prostitute, he suffers the "agony of penetration." * * * This perhaps predictable collapse of gender certainty is followed and compounded by a feverish and panicky journey to a confessional that contrasts with the stasis of the retreat and simultaneously recalls and links itself with the wanderings that close chapters 2 and 4 in a haze of vague, vampiric sexuality. Stephen's confession at the end of chapter 3 structurally aligns itself with his fall into sin, with the suggestion that confession must therefore share in the subversive quality

8. Moretti writes:

> Virtually without notice, in the dreams and nightmares of the so called "double revolution" [in effect, the simultaneous rise of mobility and interiority. Author], Europe plunges into modernity, but without possessing a culture of modernity. If youth, therefore, achieves its symbolic centrality, and the "great narrative" of the Bildungsroman comes into being, this is because Europe has to attach a meaning, not so much to youth, as to modernity. (p. 5)

of sin. At the end of chapter 4, the appearance of the birdgirl—the "envoy from the fair courts of life" (IV.887–88)—mocks and aestheticizes sin, repositioning the instrumental figure of woman as profane icon of a secular aesthetic priesthood.

•

In the modernist era, the *Bildung* concept cannot contain or explain a colonial condition or experience, cannot make sense of the dehiscent interiority of the colonial subject, cannot recognize it, much less legitimize it. For the utter dissolution of paternal and pedagogical authority is, in large measure, the effect of colonial violence, specifically, the imperialist ideology that turned Catholic Irish men and women into objects of sexual and racial discrimination. No longer the subjects of traditional narratives of self-formation and social integration, these colonial subjects were officially disavowed—materially present though politically nonexistent and thus reduced to caricatures of themselves. As I have suggested above, Joyce succeeds in his critique of *Bildung* not so much by challenging these narratives of self-formation but by subtly undermining the mainspring of the ideological traditions they express. This mainspring is education and its accompanying "structures of feeling."[9]

In restagings of the *mise en scène* of acculturation and public instruction—in the classroom, the library and the street—we find the destabilizing and critical potential of Joyce's modernist *Bildungsroman*. Stephen's education takes place in the recently founded Catholic University College, but the curriculum was typical of European universities, and so, to this extent, he was unable to escape fully the influence of conventional discourses of formation.[1] In *A Portrait*, we see an array of strategies for resisting pedagogical hegemony. One such strategy, perhaps inevitable in an Irish Catholic context, is a profane confessional discourse that provides opportunities for dialogue and debate, for freedom of expression that the lecture hall and classroom (not to mention the orthodox confessional) do not offer. The "appropriation of Catholic confessional language," according to Jonathan Mulrooney, enables Stephen to see "how language creates reality" (169). It also enables the free expression of disparate and conflicting modes of knowledge, power and desire; this is especially

9. See Raymond Williams, *Culture and Society: 1780–1950* (1958; New York: Columbia Univ. Press, 1983). Also relevant is Williams's *The Country and the City* (New York: Oxford Univ. Press, 1983). A "structure of feeling" refers to an idea of culture as an organic, communal belonging that invests individual subjects with a solidity and sense of position within society that is sometimes lost and certainly hard to sustain in an alienating modern culture. It includes complex formations of affective and material relations, networks of "felt experiences" requiring obligations to individuals, to class groupings, or to the nation.

1. See Jill Muller, "John Henry Newman and the Education of Stephen Dedalus," *JJQ*, 33 (Summer 1996), 593–603.

evident in the confessions that Stephen makes to Davin, Lynch, and Cranly.[2] What I would like to emphasize here is that the characteristic intention of confession, understood as a sacramental speech act, is the disburdening of the self. The orthodox sacrament of confession upon which these secular confessions are modeled is highly scripted, leaving spaces for certain kinds of categorical or generic responses. The confessor, acting in the capacity of a transhuman conduit, accepts the penitent's burden of sin and grants the specified absolution and penance. The liturgical details are, of course, abandoned by Stephen, but the idea of disburdening thus takes on a compensatory increase in intensity and purpose. Once he has reached University College, he begins to shape confessional discourse into a dialogic space in which he can perform his ongoing experience of his own psychological and artistic development. Joyce exploits the subtle paradox of a confessional mode of enunciation that is highly ritualized and impersonal but that elicits information of a very personal nature. As it was in the early Christian Church, so confession in *A Portrait* becomes a public forum for the modern artist-priest, despite the confessional intimacy Stephen forms with his friends. Unfortunately, those to whom he confesses, like the "peasant student" Davin (V.222), are very often terrorized by what they hear.

Chapter 5 is a chapter of refusals and mockery, of confessions and usurpations. In the first vignette (V.1–1522), Stephen repudiates home, Church, nationalism, and internationalism; he also articulates an aesthetics that mimics theology by resignifying its essentialism and transcendental triumph over material social conditions. Significantly, Ireland is itself rejected in the form of the woman who seduces Davin, the "batlike" woman (V.1667), the inevitable vampire lover who has haunted Stephen since Eileen Vance and will continue to haunt him in the form of his mother's ghost in *Ulysses*. Stephen seems to take on some of the power of Davin's rejection of the woman and repeats it when this figure is conflated with E. C. during the reverie surrounding his composition of the villanelle. Both figures are refined out of existence in a blaze of sacramental eroticism:

> *Above the flame the smoke of praise*
> *Goes up from ocean rim to rim.*
> *Tell no more of enchanted days.*

2. I have discussed these profane confessions at length in "Confessing Oneself" (pp. 164–65, 174–78). See also Vicky Mahaffey, "Père-version and Im-mère-sion: Idealized Corruption in *A Portrait of the Artist as a Young Man* and *The Picture of Dorian Gray*," and Joseph Valente, "Thrilled by His Touch: The Aestheticizing of Homosexual Panic in *A Portrait of the Artist as a Young Man*," in *Quare Joyce* (pp. 121–36, 47–75) [see p. 411 for Valente's essay—*Editor*].

> *Our broken cries and mournful lays*
> *Rise in one eucharistic hymn.*
> *Are you not weary of ardent ways?* (V.1755–60)

This resignification of sacramental images, like so many of Stephen's other highly stylized, self-conscious performances, is meant to signal an attitude of refusal that is intertwined with a moment of affirmation and acceptance. The mock-serious mime of priestly duties in chapter 4 becomes here a more fully invested performance of self-ordination, in which Stephen becomes "a priest of the eternal imagination" (V.1677). In the villanelle, the language of a sacramental mystery that Stephen ostensibly rejects affirms and articulates the spiritualized desire that colors his own "ardent ways."

Ironically, this desire, which lies behind Stephen's restagings, allows for a certain recovery of the sacred even within a secular, eroticized confession. Confession—as an effect or outcome of sacramental desire expressed in a disburdening speech act—always involves a sacred attitude toward the past. Virtue and sin become the dominant ways about which to talk about the past, particularly the biographical past that makes up the narrative of development. History, understood in these terms, becomes a confession of sin, of recent sin, of possible sin.[3] It also becomes an index of the Catholic colonial subject's catastrophic development: growing up is a continuous confrontation with one's own sinfulness, with one's inadequacies. Of course, this conception of sin is bound up, early on at least, with the child's sense of awe in regard to God the Father who sees and knows all. It is no surprise that Stephen dreams of heroic action as he meditates on stealing altar wine, reminding himself of Napoleon [I.1391–1410], nor is it a surprise when, later, he refuses to take a sacrilegious communion, fearing the "chemical action which would be set up" in his soul "by a false homage to a symbol behind which are massed twenty centuries of authority and veneration" (V.2458–60).

Confessional discourse inevitably will find a prominent place in a modernist narrative of Irish Catholic childhood and adolescence such as *A Portrait*. In Joyce's *Bildungsroman*, confession takes on a subjective resonance and valence; it becomes an erotic and dialogical performance only partly structured by sacramental desire. The secular confessions in Joyce's texts are deeply politicized, which means that a sense of history and of historical injustice has led to a feeling of indignation that can no longer be contained within the

---

3. See Michel Foucault, *The History of Sexuality*, vol. 1, trans. Robert Hurley (New York: Vintage Books, 1988), especially parts two and three, on the ubiquity of priestly curiosity: the not-yet-done, even the not-yet-thought, which are potentially sinful. See also Mary Lowe-Evans, "Sex and Confession in the Joyce Canon: Some Historical Parallels," *Journal of Modern Literature*, 16 (Spring 1990), 563–76.

protective tower of the traumatized colonial artist's "mild proud sovereignty." In such a social world, a secular confessional discourse—one in which feelings of alienation, inadequacy, and general dissociation are confronted and interrogated—can become a political discourse. If used within a cultural project of political education, such a discourse becomes a revolutionary one, something akin to Frantz Fanon's "fighting literature, a revolutionary literature, and a national literature" (222)—a literature that would "call . . . on the whole people to fight for their existence as a nation" (240).

As a species of fighting literature, *A Portrait* targets the social ideologies and institutions that posit as their goal the smooth socialization * * * of the viable subject into the dominant class. Like many "transculturated" postcolonial *Bildungsromane*, it narrates developmental trauma, the catastrophic adolescence of a young man denied certain kinds of normative educational goals and vocations held out as most prized by the colonizers.[4] Joyce ends *A Portrait* with Stephen poised on the verge of leaving Dublin for Paris,[5] already psychologically alienated from the social world in which he grew up, the network of material and emotional relations seeming less like a structure of feeling and more and more like a trap set especially for him. The dialectical energies of development become internalized, and Stephen appears to thrive only in an inner world that lacks the harmony Humboldt thought essential to self-sufficiency and wholeness. His return to Dublin after his sojourn in Paris, revealed to the reader in several oblique flashbacks in *Ulysses*, is a parody or deconstruction of the return inscribed in the classical *Bildungsroman*. * * * Continuing the process begun in *A Portrait*, *Ulysses* redefines the historical agency and destiny at the heart of bourgeois self-formation. The young pedagogue who sees nothing amiss in swerving from history to poetry to riddles to silence in the "Nestor" episode instinctively (if half-consciously) undermines the ideological aims of the history lesson he is supposed to be teaching. The material reality underpinning his elegiac sense of the past is that of a disavowed, internally split colonial subject.

4. As Memmi has pointed out, the colonizer is himself "a tempting model very close at hand"; the "turncoat" native desires to "become equal to that splendid model and to resemble him to the point of disappearing in him" (p. 120). For "transculturation," see Maria Helena Lima, "Decolonizing Genre: Jamaica Kincaid and the *Bildungsroman*," *Genre*, 26 (Winter 1993), 431–59. Lima writes, "Regions which have undergone European colonization constitute particularly interesting sites to observe what I call generic transculturation since different cultures will transform the 'originary' genre to serve their particular needs. . . . Post-colonial writers have had to invent stories and allegories of 'self' and 'other,' mythologies of their own that begin to translate their complex heritage" (p. 433).
5. Readers learn only in the early episodes of *Ulysses* that Stephen relocates temporarily to Paris after the last events reported in *A Portrait* [Editor].

The [opening] episodes constitute a supplement to *A Portrait,* a revision of history from the teacher's point of view. At the same time, they introduce new strands of Joyce's increasingly parodic critique of nationalist modes of historical mythmaking, particularly the role of such myths in projects of political education. Stephen's failed *Bildung* serves in these ways to point up the inadequacy of normative models of self-cultivation and education, for they do not represent the catastrophic processes of growing up in the colonies. Thus, Joyce's structural excesses undermine the coherence of the *Bildung*-plot—even the French and English versions of failed harmony—for it takes multiple narratives to relate it. The narrative of formation is rewritten and critiqued, with increasing rigor, in a textual series beginning with the sketch "A Portrait of the Artist" and ending (more or less) in *Ulysses.*[6]

Coming of age in Dublin has led Stephen to feel, as he realizes so pronouncedly on his return from exile, a sense of alienation from himself, from the young man who not so long ago possessed a "mild proud sovereignty." Insofar as it serves as a "dangerous supplement" to Joyce's *Bildungsroman,*[7] *Ulysses* narrates this sense of belatedness, this elegiac mood of recollecting a catastrophic youth. However, Stephen's problematic colonial *Bildung* functions critically within Joyce's modernist *Bildungsroman* because it points up the inadequacy of normative models of self-development and education that neither alleviate nor represent the "internal catastrophe" of coming of age in the age of empire. His struggle with the processes of socialization, together with Joyce's struggle to represent those processes, indicates some of the problems the modernist *Bildungsroman* faces—and not just in the colonial territories but in the entire field of late modernity.

6. Susan Stanford Friedman, in "(Self)Censorship and the Making of Joyce's Modernism," *Joyce: The Return of the Repressed,* ed. Friedman (Ithaca: Cornell Univ. Press, 1993), pp. 21–57, argues that this textual series constitutes a "composite" text that can be read in terms of unconscious desire and repression. See also Maud Ellmann, "Disremembering Dedalus: 'A Portrait of an Artist as a Young Man,'" *Untying the Text: A Post-Structuralist Reader,* ed. Robert Young (Boston: Routledge and Kegan Paul, 1981), p. 191. Ian Crump charts the changes in Stephen's aesthetic theory through the same series in "Refining Himself out of Existence: The Evolution of Joyce's Aesthetic Theory and the Drafts of *A Portrait,*" *Joyce in Context,* ed. Vincent Cheng and Timothy Martin (Cambridge: Cambridge Univ. Press, 1992), pp. 223–40 [*Author*]. In 1904 Joyce produced a narrative essay, "A Portrait of the Artist," available in *The Workshop of Dedalus,* 60–68 [*Editor*].
7. On the idea of the supplement as a "dangerous" excess of signification, see Jacques Derrida, *Of Grammatology,* trans. Gayatri Chakravorty Spivak (Baltimore: Johns Hopkins Univ. Press, 1976), pp. 144–45, 167.

DEREK ATTRIDGE

A Portrait of the Artist as a Young Man[†]

The Child

It pained him that he did not know well what politics meant and that he did not know where the universe ended. He felt small and weak. When would he be like the fellows in poetry and rhetoric? They had big voices and big boots and they studied trigonometry. That was very far away. First came the vacation and then the next term and then vacation again and then again another term and then again the vacation. It was like a train going in and out of tunnels and that was like the noise of the boys eating in the refectory when you opened and closed the flaps of the ears. * * * Only prayers in the chapel and then bed. He shivered and yawned. It would be lovely in bed after the sheets got a bit hot. First they were so cold to get into. He shivered to think how cold they were first. But then they got hot and then he could sleep. It was lovely to be tired. He yawned again. Night prayers and then bed: he shivered and wanted to yawn. It would be lovely in a few minutes. He felt a warm glow creeping up from the cold shivering sheets, warmer and warmer till he felt warm all over, ever so warm and yet he shivered a little and still wanted to yawn.

The bell rang for night prayers and he filed out of the studyhall after the others and down the staircase and along the corridors to the chapel. The corridors were darkly lit and the chapel was darkly lit. Soon all would be dark and sleeping. There was cold night air in the chapel and the marbles were the colour the sea was at night. The sea was cold day and night: but it was colder at night. It was cold and dark under the seawall beside his father's house. But the kettle would be on the hob to make punch.

[I.345–74]

Before his first fictional foray into print with 'The Sisters' in 1904, Joyce had begun an ambitious and fairly traditional autobiographical novel whose protagonist he called Stephen Daedalus, the name—combining a Christian saint and a mythical Greek craftsman—he was also to use as a pseudonym for the publication of his short story. He called the huge novel *Stephen Hero*, on the model of 'Turpin Hero', an anonymous ballad about the famous highwayman he is said to have sung at parties. In 1905, having completed twenty-four of the planned sixty-three chapters, he set it aside to concentrate

[†] From *How to Read Joyce* (London: Granta Books, 2007), pp. 23–39. Reprinted with permission of Granta Books. Page references for *A Portrait* have been replaced with part and line numbers of this Norton Critical Edition. Some cited passages might differ slightly from the equivalent passages in this volume.

on *Dubliners*, and by the time he returned to it his entire conception of the work had changed. First serialized in 1914–15 and then
published in the United States as a book in 1916, the revised novel
covered the same territory—the life of an aspiring Dublin writer
from childhood to college—but its new title, *A Portrait of the Artist
as a Young Man*, signals, ironically, the distance from his earlier self
which Joyce had achieved. Whether 'the artist' refers to the actual
creator of the work (as in paintings with similar titles), thus high-
lighting the autobiographical dimension, or whether it indicates a
more generic notion of artisthood, the final phrase cannot but suggest a contrast between youth and maturity. But unlike 'The Sisters',
A Portrait avoids intimations in the writing itself of the older author's
presence; the style matches each stage of development of the subject,
and the reader is left to judge the degree of irony with which his attitudes and actions are to be viewed.

Joyce never finished, or published, *Stephen Hero*, though after
his death an edition of the surviving fragments—some eleven
chapters—was brought out. *A Portrait* marks a radical shift from
the earlier project, and constituted a breakthrough (not just for its
author but for European literature) in its evocation of a growing
boy's developing sense of language and its potential in the world,
from the innocent responsiveness of the child to the would-be
sophistication of the young adult. In five long chapters Joyce charts
his hero's growth not by a continuous narrative but by a series of
episodes separated sometimes by extensive temporal gaps. Part of
the interest of each one is registering the new phase of Stephen's
growth and what it implies about the intervening period; and it is
often the details of the language that provide the most subtle clues.
And there is much to engage the reader in each phase: we follow
Stephen's intense responses to the conflicts of Irish politics, the
demands of sexual desire, the temptations of the religious life, the
orthodoxies and restrictions of a moralistic society, the passions of
friendship and the fascinations of art, all taking place against the
background of a family slipping inexorably down the economic lad-
der, just as Joyce's own family did.

Reactions to the work were mixed: many reviewers admired the
vividness of Joyce's representation of a boy's and a young man's psychology, the variety and power of the writing, the honesty of the
treatment of sex and religion. Many others found it disgusting in its
use of 'privy-language' and its interest in 'the sex-torments of adolescence' (to quote one reviewer); others thought it long-winded and
inattentive to the reader's needs. Pound,[1] through whose efforts the

1. Ezra Pound (1885–1972), American poet and critic [*Editor*].

novel was first published as a serial in the English little magazine *The Egoist*, promoted it as a truly European work in the tradition of Flaubert. Wells,[2] who admired the novel immensely in spite of his commitment to a very different kind of fiction, was more aware of its Irish, and anti-English, dimension, a dimension that has only fairly recently been fully explored. The variety of responses matched the complexity of the book, which provides a series of images of turn-of-the-century Dublin through eyes growing in acuity and a mind increasing in disenchantment, until complete rejection seems the only solution—yet one that the book's ironies keep the reader from entirely accepting. This Ireland is emphatically not the Ireland of the Irish Revivalists,[3] whose star, in any case, was beginning to fade. In the year the book was first published, the Easter Rising in Dublin marked a turning point in Ireland's history,[4] and the traumatic years that followed had less room for dreams of a mythical past.

Young Stephen Dedalus (Joyce changed the surname from Daedalus, making it slightly less Greek) is a boarder at Clongowes Wood College, the Jesuit-run school in county Kildare that Joyce himself had been sent to at the age of six. It is the year 1891, when Joyce would have been nine; unlike Joyce, however, Stephen—who is also about nine—appears to be in his initial term at school, counting the days to the Christmas vacation when he will return home. The first of the two episodes set at Clongowes follows Stephen from the evening of a day in October to the following evening; within this short span of time, Joyce conveys vividly a young child's experience of strangeness and alienation as he adapts to a new and often harsh environment. The vividness of this particular twenty-four hours is augmented by Stephen's having contracted a fever, although we are not told explicitly of this since he is not aware of the cause of his unnaturally sharp perceptions.

His new surroundings keep exposing his ignorance: at the moment captured in the passage above, he is supposed to be studying his geography lesson but the textbook has instead set off a train of associations leading him to think about political arguments at home and about the extent of the universe. Joyce has created a style that,

2. H. G. Wells (1866–1946), English writer who identified the anti-English dimension of *A Portrait* in his review of the book, "James Joyce" (*Nation* XX [24 February 1917]: 710, 712. Gustave Flaubert (1821–1880), French novelist noted for his realism and his commitment to a precise style [*Editor*].
3. The Irish Literary Revival, or Irish Literary Renaissance, in the late nineteenth century and early twentieth, involved Irish writers committed to the goals of cultural nationalism, including Ireland's Gaelic and mythological heritage. W. B. Yeats (see p. 299) was a central figure [*Editor*].
4. See the Proclamation of the Irish Republic, Easter Rising, on pp. 289–90 [*Editor*].

while not imitating the writing of a boy of Stephen's age (it does not have mistakes, for instance), conveys his unsophisticated thought patterns and elementary grasp of concepts. Much of it is in what is known as 'free indirect discourse': the grammatical form of the sentences is that of ordinary narration (not 'then I can sleep' but 'then he could sleep'), but the vocabulary and style are those of the character. The sentences are simple and short, and Joyce does not avoid the repetitions that would be objectionable in a mature style: 'did not know'—'did not know'; 'big voices'—'big boots'.

The repetitions that make up the alternation of term time and vacation are expressed in repetitions in the language, as Stephen counts out to himself the new organizing rhythm of his life. He is no longer trying to solve the riddles of politics or astronomy, nor processing his new life: his feverishness has concentrated his attention on his own body and on his immediate need for sleep and warmth. The ideas of coldness and heat dominate his thoughts as he imagines being in bed. If we pick out the words that signal these ideas we find a chain of terms in which neither state feels permanent, since each gives way eventually to its opposite: 'shivered'—'hot'—'cold'—'shivered'—'cold'—'hot'—'shivered'—'warm'—'cold'—'shivering'—'warmer'—'warmer'—'warm'—'warm'—'shivered'. What comes across are not just ideas, of course, but that physical experience of sensitivity to both warmth and cold that we associate with a heightened body temperature; particularly telling is the displacement of the boy's own state to the 'cold shivering sheets' he imagines touching his skin. Stephen does not know it, but his shivering and yawning (and, in an example of Joyce's accuracy as a recorder of physical experience, *wanting* to yawn without being able to do so) are symptoms of an incipient fever that will cause him to be sent to the sickroom the following morning, symptoms which the reader has noticed from much earlier in this episode.

Repetition, therefore, serves Joyce's purposes as a realistic evocation of a child's way of thinking and, at the same time, as a particularly effective way of conveying powerful experiences, physical and psychological, to the reader. Writers who look back at childhood experience in adult language can often diminish its intensity by framing it in a mature outlook. There is a degree of such framing in 'The Sisters', though the adult language in that case serves as a substitute for the boy's intensity of feeling. Here, however, Joyce conveys Stephen's experience, and Stephen's language, to us without modification.

Not only the syntax but the vocabulary, too, is appropriate for a child. Most of the words are simple, and the adjectives in particular lack the detail of an older speaker: 'small', 'weak', 'big', 'hot', 'cold', 'lovely', 'warm', and so on. However, one occasionally senses that Stephen's use of a word is in part an attempt to explore its meaning for himself. He has been doing this with 'politics' and 'universe' and now he is getting to grips with the words, and concepts, 'vacation' and 'term', further extending an analogy that had come to him earlier in the evening when, in a spasm of misery in the refectory, he had 'leaned his elbows on the table and shut and opened the flaps of his ears' (I.223–24). But there is one word Stephen clearly does not know the meaning of—and it is his ignorance that is significant. The older boys—always a source of particular fascination and fear for the younger boys—not only have big voices and big boots but they study something called 'trigonometry'. Stephen has no doubt heard this impressive-sounding word, and for him it stands for that world of learning from which he is excluded and to which, at this stage of his life, he cannot imagine gaining access.

The bell rings and the pupils leave the studyhall, Stephen apparently bringing up the rear. (Notice how Joyce omits the hyphen when he writes 'studyhall'; this will become a trademark of his style, often producing a more concentrated compound word than the normal hyphenated version.) Again we are given only Stephen's perceptions, and only in language appropriate to his age and his physical condition. Repetition is once more a feature of the prose, and once more the words are simple ones: 'darkly lit', 'darkly lit', 'dark', 'dark'; 'cold', 'cold', 'colder', 'cold'; 'night', 'night', 'night', 'night'. As he sits in the chapel for prayers, he is aware of little other than the coldness and the darkness, both of which seem concentrated in the marble chapel furnishings, which are 'the colour the sea was at night'. It is at once a childish association in childishly laborious language (not 'the colour of the sea at night') and a striking one. The experience producing the association is less one of colour—the sea at night is black or very close to it, as no doubt are the marbles—than one of being enclosed by a cold substance: Stephen moves from the 'cold night air' to the marbles to the night sea, and then in the following sentence to the coldness of the sea. Here is a similar process of puzzling something out for himself that he had been through with regard to politics, the universe, and the rhythm of term and vacation. It is a process that characterizes much of Stephen's intellectual growth from the first page of the book, where we encounter the beginnings of his observations about the changing temperatures in bed: 'When you wet the bed first it is warm then it gets cold.'

The reason why Stephen's thoughts swerve to the sea when there is no apparent cause becomes clearer in the penultimate sentence: the sea is associated with his home, just as the train which provides him with an analogy for the term–vacation rhythm is in his mind because it is what will take him back to his family for Christmas. And the warmth and security of home is felt all the more strongly when it is imagined in contrast to the cold and dark outside—and, more specifically, to the seawall holding back the accumulation of cold and darkness in those black waters. The vocabulary suddenly changes as a comforting image comes to Stephen's mind: the cheerful kettle next to the fire in readiness for a warming drink.

The brilliance of Joyce's writing is such that the subtlety of his method is scarcely noticed by most readers, who respond directly to its evocation of childhood intensities of emotion and physical experience. Although in his later works there is often a more showy aspect to his stylistic achievements, the sure touch he exhibits in choosing the right word for the purpose seldom abandoned him.

The Artist

He drew forth a phrase from his treasure and spoke it softly to himself:

—A day of dappled seaborne clouds.

The phrase and the day and the scene harmonised in a chord. Words. Was it their colours? He allowed them to glow and fade, hue after hue: sunrise gold, the russet and green of apple orchards, azure of waves, the greyfringed fleece of clouds. No, it was not their colours: it was the poise and balance of the period itself. Did he then love the rhythmic rise and fall of words better than their associations of legend and colour? Or was it that, being as weak of sight as he was shy of mind, he drew less pleasure from the reflection of the glowing sensible world through the prism of a language manycoloured and richly storied than from the contemplation of an inner world of individual emotions mirrored perfectly in a lucid supple periodic prose?

He passed from the trembling bridge on to firm land again. At that instant, as it seemed to him, the air was chilled; and looking askance towards the water he saw a flying squall darkening and crisping suddenly the tide. A faint click at his heart, a faint throb in his throat told him once more of how his flesh dreaded the cold infrahuman odour of the sea: yet he did not strike across the downs on his left but held straight on along the spine of rocks that pointed against the river's mouth.

* * * In the distance along the course of the slowflowing Liffey slender masts flecked the sky and, more distant still, the dim fabric of the city lay prone in haze. Like a scene on some vague arras, old as man's weariness, the image of the seventh city of Christendom was visible to him across the timeless air, no older nor more weary nor less patient of subjection than in the days of the thingmote.

Disheartened, he raised his eyes towards the slowdrifting clouds, dappled and seaborne. They were voyaging across the

deserts of the sky, a host of nomads on the march, voyaging high
over Ireland, westward bound. The Europe they had come from
lay out there beyond the Irish Sea, Europe of strange tongues
and valleyed and woodbegirt and citadelled and of entrenched
and marshalled races. He heard a confused music within him as
of memories and names which he was almost conscious of but
could not capture even for an instant; then the music seemed to
recede, to recede, to recede: and from each receding trail of
nebulous music there fell always one longdrawn calling note,
piercing like a star the dusk of silence. Again! Again! Again!
Again! A voice from beyond the world was calling.
    —Hello, Stephanos!
    —Here comes The Dedalus!
    —Ao! . . . Eh, give it over, Dwyer, I'm telling you or I'll give
you a stuff in the kisser for yourself . . . Ao!

                                                    [IV.688–737]

Young Stephen is obliged to leave Clongowes, as his real-life model
had to do, when the family fortunes decline, and after a spell at
home (or rather homes, since the financial difficulties entail several
decampings) he is enrolled at Belvedere College, another Jesuit
school, this time in the centre of Dublin. (Again, he is following in
Joyce's own footsteps.) While he is there, a three-day religious
retreat for the pupils has a profound effect on him: in an act of
confession he admits that he has been seeking sex with prostitutes
and, feeling cleansed, he embraces a new devotional regimen. His
evident religious commitment leads to an interview with the director of the school, who proposes that he train for the priesthood. It
is a decision on which the entire course of his life will depend. As
he imagines his first night in the dormitory as a novice, memories
of the cold corridors of Clongowes flood back; there is an echo of
the earlier passage as he feels 'a feverish quickening of the pulses'
[IV.487]; and he realizes that he cannot go down this road.

    Casting off his adolescent piety, he experiences a new attach-
ment to his family, in all their neediness, and a new possibility presents itself thanks to his academic achievements: the university.
(Not Trinity College, a Protestant stronghold at the time, but University College, Dublin, then under Jesuit auspices.) While his
father is discussing this possibility with the Belvedere tutor, Stephen, impatient at the long wait, heads towards the nearby Bull,
the seawall that forms one of the arms containing Dublin Bay. It is
a moment at which an alternative pathway is opening up for him,
central to which will be the art of the writer.

Jumping to the passage above—it comes towards the end of the
fourth chapter—from the one discussed previously makes the shift
in style obvious. Once again Joyce uses free indirect discourse, so

that what appears to be a narrator's description is coloured by the kind of vocabulary and syntax Stephen himself might use at this stage of his life. He is now perhaps sixteen years old,[5] and has absorbed the language and some of the attitudes of his favourite poets. The nineteenth century is almost at its end, and many of the highly regarded writers of the day value fine expression over strict realism. We can see their influence on Stephen not only in the phrase he utters in response to the scene before him—'A day of dappled seaborne clouds'—but in the language by means of which the action is described. 'He drew forth a phrase from his treasure' is just a little too precious to be taken entirely seriously: Stephen's image of his mind as a trove of poetic expressions suggests that he has some way to go before he will achieve maturity as an artist.

At the same time, Stephen's fascination with language, which has been a continuous thread from the beginning of the book, holds some promise for the budding writer. He doesn't simply take for granted the poetic quality of the phrase he has spoken to himself; he interrogates its power to charm and move him. In so doing, he explores two possible sources of this power: the play of images conjured up by the words, and their shapeliness of sound and rhythm—what he calls 'the poise and balance of the period itself'. Before rejecting the former, he gives it its full due by dwelling on the colours suggested by each significant word, *day, dappled, seaborne, clouds*. However, this elaboration can itself only be carried out in further words, which both strengthens and weakens Stephen's argument against the power of images—strengthens it, because it shows that we never escape the words into a realm of pure colour, weakens it, because these further phrases do succeed in evoking a rich sense of the different colours. (Note again two of Joyce's fused compounds, 'seaborne' and 'greyfringed'; there are many other examples in the passage.)

The preference that he exhibits for the sound and movement of the words over their semantic associations could lead to writing of superficial beauty but little strength—a failing to which Joyce was not immune, particularly in his poetry, though he succumbed to a lesser extent than many of his contemporaries. The phrase he is investigating is not without semantic interest, but Stephen ignores this aspect: in particular, we might ask, how can clouds be said to be 'seaborne'? It requires an annotated edition to discover that the phrase is not original to Stephen, but in the book he has taken it from the adjective is the more logical 'breeze-borne'.[6] Yet 'seaborne'

5. He may be slightly older. During the confession in Part III, he tells the priest that he is "sixteen" (III.1511). We do not know how much time has passed [*Editor*].
6. See Don Gifford, *Joyce Annotated: Notes for 'Dubliners' and 'A Portrait of the Artist as a Young Man'*, 2nd edn, Berkeley: University of California Press, 1982, p. 219. The

has a resonant suggestiveness that the more obvious alternative lacks, inviting us to puzzle over it a moment: are the clouds being borne across the sea? or are they borne by (and born from) the sea's moisture?

It is also to Stephen's credit that he is willing to entertain a somewhat reductive explanation for his predilection: his shortsightedness, which may be what leads him to prefer language's evocation of the inner realm of feeling over its representation of shapes and colours. Yet the passage demonstrates that these are not separable: Stephen's feelings are conveyed as much by the words detailing what he sees as those dealing directly with his inner experience. Take the second sentence of the following paragraph: he senses a sudden coldness in the air, and looking towards the water sees 'a flying squall darkening and crisping suddenly the tide'. It is a wonderfully economic description, each word contributing fully to the mobile image, the slightly unusual placing of the adverb adding urgency to the motion, the verb 'crisping' retaining its older meaning of 'curling' with an added suggestion of 'making chilly' (as in a 'crisp morning'). But at the same time, the sudden change in the sea's appearance (occurring, so it seems to Stephen, at the moment he steps onto firm land) implies a change in his outlook, as the word 'askance' also suggests. This is confirmed by the surprising 'faint click at his heart' and 'faint throb in his throat' that accompany his registering of the alteration in the weather; now it becomes difficult to separate the inner and outer worlds, as Stephen seems to hear and feel his own bodily organs. These bare monosyllables convey admirably the tug of fear that is as much physical as emotional, and we note too that it is his 'flesh' that dreads the sea's odour, as if his entire body were possessed of the sense of smell. We recall young Stephen at Clongowes connecting the coldness of the marbles in the dark chapel with the cold, dark sea (and when we meet him again in *Ulysses* his dread of the sea has not abated).

Can we take this compelling writing to be a reflection of Stephen's own skill with words? Is it, that is to say, a form of free indirect discourse, as the previous paragraph clearly is? The question is not easy to answer, and it is one of the fascinating features of the book that we're often not quite sure when we are reading the words of an accomplished storyteller, the narrator created by Joyce, and when we are getting a hint of Stephen's own verbal talents at a particular stage of his life. Here, though, the contrast between the

---

phrase comes from Hugh Miller, *The Testimony of the Rocks* (1857). That Stephen is not making up beautiful phrases but culling them from unlikely places in his reading hints at a creative process more like Joyce's in his later work and less like the contemporaries he seems to be imitating, though Joyce could not have expected his readers to pick this up.

lavish poetic style of the previous paragraph and the vivid economy of this one may suggest that we are now observing Stephen from the outside.

In spite of his feeling of apprehension, Stephen chooses to walk along the wall jutting into the sea (which is made to seem more risky than it really is by the words 'spine', 'rocks' and 'pointing'), rather than the safe ground of North Bull Island to his left. (It is typical of Joyce that this scene of inner drama takes place in a concretely located environment, still traceable in Dublin today; his very distance from Ireland seems to have provoked an obsession with accuracy of geographical detail.) Again the outward action is inseparable from the mental and emotional decision which Stephen is facing: although walking one way rather than another is a trivial choice, and although it is a difficult one only because of an irrational phobia, it signals a will to face danger rather than take the easy option.

The light changes again, as if the threat has been overcome, though not to sunlit brilliance. Instead, all is dim, hazy and vague as Stephen looks across the bay to the city. We are back with the heightened poetic language with which the passage began: words seem chosen for their suggestiveness and emotional effect rather than their visual accuracy. Stephen thinks of the River Liffey as 'slowmoving', though he cannot see its motion from where he is standing; Dublin is lying 'prone' because it seems to him like a lifeless face-down body, though it is hard to give this any literal meaning. Just as the hazy light evens out the visual field, so Stephen's mood banishes any sense that the passage of history brings about change, and consequently any hope of making a difference to the city he has grown up in. His knowledge of history and early literature—evident in his association of the cityscape with the tapestry image on an arras, his allusion to the 'thingmote' or Viking ruling council, and his naming Dublin 'the seventh city of christendom'[7]— produces only a feeling that the centuries have achieved nothing. No wonder he is 'disheartened'.

If Ireland seems to offer no future for the aspirant artist, is there an alternative? Suddenly the narrator's—and presumably Stephen's—language changes gear, as the clouds referred to earlier are transformed into desert travellers and their imagined origin is described in high poetic terms. Europe, strange and romantic, now beckons the would-be artist (for Stephen, 'Europe' clearly means 'continental Europe'); all he has read and heard about crystallizes

7. No satisfactory source for this splendid phrase, which Joyce was fond of, has, to my knowledge, been found. Although it has been used in debates in the Irish parliament as if it were an established epithet, it is not certain that it pre-dates Joyce.

into a longing to experience the magical centres of the culture that
has formed part of his education from childhood. From now to the
end of the book these voices call out to Stephen.

But a question haunts the attentive reader. How seriously are we
to take Stephen's weary view of his home city and the marvellous
European alternative he imagines? Don't those poetic phrases border at times on cliché? 'Old as man's weariness'; 'a host of nomads
on the march'; 'woodbegirt and citadelled'—there is a linguistic
self-indulgence about such phrases, very different from the sharp
economy of 'darkening and crisping suddenly the tide'. And what
about the repetition of words? In the earlier episode young Stephen's thoughts are marked by the repetition of key terms, suggesting the stage of linguistic development he has reached; now,
however, repetition is a deliberate poetic device which can be
powerful but can easily tip into archness or banality. (Where the
younger Stephen looks forward to feeling straightforwardly 'tired',
it is typical of the older Stephen that the word that comes to mind
is the poetic 'weary'.) It is not always easy to say where the border-
line lies. For most of this passage, the repetitions seem purposeful
and restrained; for instance, 'old'—'older' and 'weariness'—'weary'
are part of a controlled rhetorical structure, even though the sentiments may not stand up to much scrutiny. But 'music'—'music'—
'recede'—'recede'—'recede'—'receding'—'music'? This sequence is
harder to justify. Is Stephen allowing himself to fall under the spell
of words and their attendant myths? Is there something just a little
too poetic about the 'one longdrawn calling note, piercing like a
star the dusk of silence', attractive though that last complex metaphor is?

One kind of answer is given by Joyce's next novel, *Ulysses*, in
which we meet Stephen after his European dream has proved fruitless. But another kind of answer is immediately forthcoming: just
as Stephen hears, or imagines he hears, a voice from beyond the
world calling to him, another voice breaks in, a voice very much
from this world. His school friends are bathing nearby, and their
shouts puncture the mood of high poetry. Nothing could be further
removed from the language of Stephen's reverie than the coarse
repartee of the bantering adolescents. If Stephen wants to succeed
as an artist, he has to find a way—as Joyce did—of incorporating
these voices as well.

Stephen, however, has yet to see this, and he refuses to join in
the horseplay, finding instead his ideal of beauty, and his promise
of a new life, in a wading girl. Joyce brings to bear on the scene the
full force of his poetic rhetoric, and unless we remember the caus-
tic voices of his schoolmates we are in danger of succumbing to
Stephen's vision of himself and his future as an artist. At the same

time, it would be wrong to regard such moments as purely ironic: this is indeed a turning point in Stephen's education as an artist, and although he has much more to learn than he realizes, it marks his permanent rejection of the religious life, the other possible vocation that had beckoned.

The final chapter finds Stephen at university, interacting vigorously with fellow students, writing poetry overloaded with vague imagery, pursuing his studies in a less than studious manner, articulating an aesthetic theory, pursuing a frustrating and unsatisfactory involvement with a girl, and feeling more and more the need to escape the confining bounds of home, nation and church. The last few pages, in the form of a diary, give us Stephen's own words as he prepares to leave Ireland, and contain notable signs of a growing maturity in the writing. Not only are some of the entries powerfully evocative without the striving for effect characteristic of his earlier moments of rapture or gloom, but he is now capable of mocking his own excesses. After a highly wrought passage recalling the view of Dublin from the Bull wall—'Faintly, under the heavy night, through the silence of the city which has turned from dreams to dreamless sleep as a weary lover whom no caresses move . . .' [V.2728–30]— we find the entry: '11 April: Read what I wrote last night. Vague words for a vague emotion' [V.2737–38]. When we meet Stephen again, such self-criticism has become habitual, though the poetic impulse has not been extinguished.

TOBIAS BOES

A Portrait of the Artist as a Young Man and the "Individuating Rhythm" of Modernity[†]

A Portrait of the Artist as a Young Man concludes with a brief postscript: "Dublin 1904 Trieste 1914" [V.2793–94]. In contrast to the similar phrase that James Joyce would later append to Ulysses, the two terms of this addendum aren't connected by hyphens indicating a spatiotemporal continuity, but instead remain discrete entities, as though to indicate that the work had been carried out twice. A more suitable ending to a novel that similarly frustrates the conventions of the well-made plot by its constant vacillation between disjunctive and conjunctive tendencies could hardly be imagined. A

† ELH 75 (Winter 2008): 767–85. © 2008 Johns Hopkins University Press. Reprinted with permission of Johns Hopkins University Press. Some of the author's notes have been omitted. Page references for A Portrait have been replaced with part and line numbers of this Norton Critical Edition. Some cited passages might differ slightly from the equivalent passages in this volume.

Portrait refuses to develop smoothly: at times it moves forward by leaps and bounds, skipping from one phase in Stephen's life to another; at others it seems to merely spin around in circles, as each new episode takes on a disturbing resemblance to those that preceded it.

The tension between these narrative vectors can also be felt on the level of style. The epiphany and the leitmotif, the two devices that more than any others define Joyce's prose, are essentially opposites of one another.[1] The epiphany is fundamentally disjunctive: by "transmuting the daily bread of experience into the radiant body of everliving life" (V.1677–79), it necessarily destroys the flow of mundane reality and therefore also the continuity of sensation. As *A Portrait* demonstrates time and time again, the only way to follow up on an epiphany is with a chapter or section break. The leitmotif, on the other hand, is entirely conjunctive: it points out the prosaic underpinnings of lofty emotions and ties each stage in the development of both plot and protagonist back to the ones that preceded it. The endearingly frustrating nature of Joyce's text stems from the fact that epiphany and leitmotif can hardly be separated from one another. Stephen's famous encounter with the bird-girl on Sandymount Beach is at once radically disjunctive, pushing him "on and on and on and on" (IV.880), and symbolically overdetermined, invoking a network of well-established motifs that includes birds, Mariolatry, eyesight, falling water, and several others. Stephen's paradoxical resolution at the end of the novel says it all: "I go to encounter for the millionth time the reality of experience and to forge in the smithy of my soul the uncreated conscience of my race" (V.2788–90). His aspiration is for a conscience that is as yet "uncreated," but in order to achieve it he has to tread down a path that has been walked a million times before.

The ambiguous status that the concept of "development" thus occupies in Joyce's novel is perhaps best demonstrated by the inevitable contradictions one encounters in the canonical attempts to

---

1. The scholarly literature on either of these devices is far too vast to comprehensively summarize here. Richard Ellmann's *James Joyce* (Oxford: Oxford Univ. Press, 1959) and Hugh Kenner's *Joyce's Voices* (Berkeley: Univ. of California Press, 1978) remain valuable starting points. For an overview of recent research on the literary epiphany, see the essays collected in Wim Tigges, ed., *Moments of Moment: Aspects of the Literary Epiphany* (Amsterdam: Rodopi, 1999). Franco Moretti's *Modern Epic: The World System from Goethe to García Márquez* (London: Verso, 1996) presents a highly influential comparison of epiphany and leitmotif in Joyce's fiction and ultimately argues for the primacy of the latter [Author]. Epiphany is a Christian feast day celebrating the revelation of Jesus Christ as God incarnate, but Joyce used the term to mean an unexpected manifestation, whether elevated or grittily embodied, that causes an insight or recognition. Joyce called some prose vignettes that he wrote early in his career epiphanies, and he incorporated some of them and other moments of revelation in his longer works. Critics writing about Joyce use the term, sometimes loosely. A leitmotif (German: *Leitmotiv*) is a repeated musical phrase, but literary critics use it by extension to refer to recurring elements in the language or narrative of a text [Editor].

classify *A Portrait* as a *Bildungsroman,* or "novel of development."[2] In order to reconcile Joyce's work to the tradition, Jerome Hamilton Buckley, for example, is forced to dismiss great chunks of it as "unnecessarily long-winded" and to assert, somewhat counterintuitively, that "indecision and inconclusiveness" have always characterized the endings of classical *Bildungsromane.*[3] Breon Mitchell has to similarly downplay the paradox of the novel's title, which in Hugh Kenner's words "impose[s] a pictorial and spatial analogy, an expectation of static repose, on a book in which nothing except the spiritual life of Dublin stands still."[4] On the other hand, Franco Moretti, who sees the *Bildungsroman* merely as an obstacle delaying the rise of the modernist novel, celebrates precisely the indecision of the final chapter as Joyce's ultimate vindication. By asserting prosaic reality over poetic meaning, leitmotif over epiphany, and (in Moretti's own terms) Gustave Flaubert over Arthur Rimbaud, Joyce has earned for himself the status of a modernist writer: "the merit of *Portrait* lies in its being an unmistakable failure" as a novel of development.[5]

In short, any approach to Joyce's work that conceives of *Bildung* as a teleological process, a smooth and gradual journey towards individual and collective destiny, is bound to be frustrated by the contradictory dynamics of his novel. A very different methodology, however, is provided by Mikhail Bakhtin's fragmentary study of the spatiotemporal form (or of what he in other contexts called the "chronotope") of the classical *Bildungsroman.* Bakhtin's essay can

2. I intentionally translate the German word *Bildungsroman* as "novel of development" rather than as "novel of formation," because the English use of this term much more closely resembles that of the German word *Entwicklungsroman,* which quite literally means "novel of development." The characteristic features of *Bildung*—a pedagogical ideology associated with German classicism and romanticism, and with such figures as J. G. Herder, Johann Wolfgang von Goethe, Friedrich Schiller, and Alexander von Humboldt, to name just some examples—are almost entirely absent in the Anglophone context. This slippage in usage is regrettable and has caused many a headache in comparative literary studies, but it is by now unavoidable. For a standard treatment of the concept and history of *Bildung,* see W. H. Bruford, *The German Tradition of Self-Cultivation: "Bildung" from Humboldt to Thomas Mann* (Cambridge: Cambridge Univ. Press, 1975). Its relationship to British culture is discussed in the introductory chapter of Gregory Castle's *Reading the Modernist Bildungsroman* (Gainesville: Univ. Press of Florida, 2006), 1–29. [Reprinted in this edition (pp. 428–47), from an article that preceded publication of Castle's book, is a version of part of the commentary on Joyce from his book—*Editor.*]
3. Jerome Hamilton Buckley, *Season of Youth: The Bildungsroman from Dickens to Golding* (Cambridge: Harvard Univ. Press, 1974), 238, 246 [*Author*]. *Bildungsromane* is the plural form [*Editor*].
4. Kenner, "The Cubist *Portrait,*" in *Approaches to Joyce's Portrait: Ten Essays,* ed. Thomas F. Baley and Bernard Benstock (Pittsburgh: Univ. of Pittsburgh Press, 1976), 171. See Breon Mitchell, "*A Portrait* and the *Bildungsroman* Tradition" in *Approaches to Joyce's Portrait,* 61–76.
5. Moretti, *The Way of the World: The Bildungsroman in European Culture,* 2nd ed. (London: Verso, 2000), 243 [*Author*]. Flaubert (1821–1880), French novelist noted for his realism and his commitment to a precise style. Rimbaud (1854–1891), French poet whose writing has at times a hallucinatory aspect [*Editor*].

for present purposes be reduced to two main propositions. First, that "man's individual emergence" in the novel of development "is inseparably linked to historical emergence," and second, that this emergence takes the form of a dialogue between linear and cyclical temporalities.[6] In his analysis of *Wilhelm Meister's Apprentice Years*, the novel with which Johann Wolfgang von Goethe inaugurated the *Bildungsroman* tradition in 1796, Bakhtin notes of Goethe's writing that in it the "background of the world's buttresses *begins to pulsate* . . . and this pulsation determines the more superficial movement and alteration of human destinies and human outlook."[7] For Bakhtin, Goethe's genius lies in his ability to mediate between the cyclical experience of time characteristic of the pre-modern agrarian society into which he was born and the essentially linear, progressive "historical time" that comes to dominate during the last thirty years of the eighteenth century.[8]

The advantage of such a Bakhtinian approach to the *Bildungsroman* is that it allows one to understand the tension between conjunctive and disjunctive, cyclical and emergent elements of Joyce's novel not as deviations from a norm but as the forceful assertion of a dynamic that has defined the genre from the very beginning. And indeed, the spatiotemporal form of *A Portrait*, like that of *Wilhelm Meister*, originates in and directly responds to a specific historical constellation. Like Stephen Dedalus, Ireland during the early years of the twentieth century was tossed back and forth between two different ways of representing temporal experience, and two different conceptions of historical development: on the one hand, that of the Irish Renaissance,[9] for which real improvements in Ireland could be achieved only through the revival of the cultural values of a bygone era; and, on the other hand, that of progressivism, according to which the hope of the nation lay in a break with the past and a corresponding leap into modernity.[1] The problem of the Irish diaspora, which also becomes the central problem of *A Portrait*,

6. Mikhail Bakhtin, "The *Bildungsroman* and its Significance in the History of Realism," in *Speech Genres and Other Late Essays*, trans. Vern W. McGee (Austin: Univ. of Texas Press, 1986), 23.
7. Bakhtin, 30; my emphasis.
8. Bakhtin, 26.
9. See note 3, p. 450 [*Editor*].
1. Unionism belongs to this second category, because it sees British colonial rule as essentially setting the pace and direction for Ireland's march into modernity. Jed Esty has recently written with great erudition on the relationship between the *Bildungsroman* and what Esty, following the postcolonial theorist Dipesh Chakrabarty, calls the "not yet" of imperial modernity ("Virginia Woolf's Colony and the Adolescence of Modernist Fiction," in *Modernism and Colonialism: British and Irish Literature, 1899–1939*, ed. Richard Begam and Michael Valdez Moses [Durham: Duke Univ. Press, 2007], 77). [Reprinted in this edition (pp. 482–502), from a chapter in Esty's book *Unseasonable Youth*, is Esty's later commentary on *A Portrait*, which draws on the essay mentioned here—*Editor*.]

provides merely one manifestation of this conflict.[2] As the famous debate between the citizen and Leopold Bloom in the "Cyclops" chapter of *Ulysses* illustrates, the cultural reactionaries of 1904 saw the post-famine exodus[3] as a means by which Ireland would ulti-mately replenish itself—a systolic expansion of the nation's life-blood that would ultimately lead to a diastolic contraction: "But those that came to the land of the free remember the land of bond-age. And they will come again and with a vengeance, no cravens, the sons of Granuaile, the champions of Kathleen ni Houlihan."[4] For the progressivist Bloom, on the other hand, the diaspora simply helps fulfill the definition of a modern nation as the same people living in different places. The final lines of *A Portrait*, in which Ste-phen expresses his desire to renew the Irish nation precisely by leaving it behind him, congeal these warring conceptions of histori-cal development into a dialectical image.

The historical situation that generates the tension between cycli-cal and emergent temporalities in *A Portrait* is as much a product of the early twentieth century as Goethe's *Wilhelm Meister* was a product of the outgoing age of Enlightenment. Joyce's novel resists Moretti's hypothesis of the destruction of the *Bildungsroman* genre at the hands of modernist style, but this does not imply that *A Por-trait* represents merely an updated version of Goethe's accomplish-ment, a relay station by which a literary form is exported from the European metropole towards the underdeveloped imperial periph-ery. Instead, it responds to the challenges of its own culture and its own time with stylistic grace and subtlety.

Joyce's 1904 essay "A Portrait of the Artist,"[5] which contains the first seeds of the novel he would complete a decade later, serves as a useful guidepost to the young artist's attempts to adapt the novel of development to his concrete historical situation. At the begin-ning of this essay, Joyce declares his dissatisfaction with all repre-sentations of personal growth premised upon the "characters of beards and inches," and thus implicitly also with traditional con-ceptions of the *Bildungsroman*, which valorize growth that occurs organically and in gradual increments.[6] He casts his lot instead with

---

2. For a recent theory of the peculiar nature of Irish modernity, see Joe Cleary, "Toward a Materialist-Formalist History of Twentieth-Century Irish Literature," *boundary* 2 31.1 (2004): 207–41.
3. See The Great Famine in "Key Dates, Events, and Figures" (p. 263) and John Mitchel, "On the Great Famine" (pp. 266–71). "Famous debate": In episode 12 of *Ulysses*, a mili-tant Irish nationalist referred to as the citizen presses Bloom, who is of Jewish ances-try, on the question of Bloom's nation. During the discussion, Bloom expresses an inclusive understanding of the concept of nation that transcends geographical location [*Editor*].
4. Joyce, *Ulysses*, ed. Hans Gabler (New York: Vintage, 1986), book 12, lines 1372–75.
5. See note 7, p. 464 [*Editor*].
6. Joyce would, of course, have approached the *Bildungsroman* tradition (which at any rate lacked a name until Wilhelm Dilthey introduced this term to modern criticism in

those who "seek through some art, by some process of the mind as yet untabulated, to liberate from the personalized lumps of matter that which is their individuating rhythm, the first or formal relation of their parts."[7] This metaphor of an "individuating rhythm" once again points to a structural compromise between cyclical and progressive elements, between a temporal sequence that moves relentlessly forward and one in which individual stresses are repeated and thereby create compositional units (musical bars, or, in Joyce's case, sections and chapters).

The study of "individuating rhythms" as they manifest themselves in concrete historical situations and in the everyday experiences of ordinary people was also the focus of the late work of the French sociologist Henri Lefebvre.[8] His conclusions not only prove extraordinarily fruitful for the study of *A Portrait* but also provide an interesting complement to Bakhtin's narratological approach, with its altogether different intellectual foundation. Like his Russian contemporary, Lefebvre regarded time and space as inextricable from one another; he was well aware, for example, that the temporal rhythms pulsing through the boulevards of a colonial city can be very different from those that hover in its back alleys. In his most extensive project of "rhythmanalysis," a study of the patterns of everyday life in Mediterranean cities, Lefebvre concluded that, "the large Mediterranean towns appear to have always lived and still to live in a regime of compromise between all the political powers. Such a 'metastable' state is the fact of the polyrhythmic."[9] "Polyrhythmicality" in this context should be understood as the simultaneous existence in close spatial proximity of life-worlds that place differing emphases on the linear and cyclical elements that constitute historical experience. The forum, for example, in which each successive ruler reconfigures public life through a series of legal and even architectural adjustments coexists with older parts of town in which traditions pass on unchanged from one generation to the next.

1906) primarily through the impact it left on nineteenth century French and English novels of literary realism. It does not appear that he had read Goethe by 1904, though Mitchell has suggested that Stanislaus Joyce came up with the name *Stephen Hero* by analogy to *Wilhelm Meister* ("William Master"). See Mitchell, 63–65, esp. 65 n.5. Ellmann reports that as late as 1915, Joyce dismissed Goethe as *"un noioso funzionario"* (a boring civil servant) (406).

7. Joyce, "A Portrait of the Artist," in *The Workshop of Daedalus. James Joyce and the Raw Materials for A Portrait of the Artist as a Young Man*, ed. Robert Scholes and Richard M. Kain (Evanston, IL: Northwestern Univ. Press, 1965), 60.

8. I am sincerely indebted to a seminar presentation given by Tom Sheehan of Florida Atlantic University at the Modernist Studies Association Conference (2005) for an introduction to Henri Lefebvre's theories and some preliminary theses regarding their applicability to the analysis of colonial societies.

9. Lefebvre, *Rhythmanalysis: Space, Time and Everyday Life*, trans. Stuart Elden and Gerald Moore (London: Continuum, 2004), 92.

Joyce, of course, always conceived of Dublin—to which in *Ulysses* he famously refers as the "Hibernian Metropolis"—as an essentially Mediterranean city.[1] *A Portrait* was largely executed in Pola and Trieste, and as in *Ulysses*, the imaginary reconstruction of Joyce's hometown owes as much to the wine-dark as it does to the snot-green seas.[2] Stephen's call to spread his wings and arise from the Daedalian labyrinth—"Bous Stephanoumenos! Bous Stephaneforos!" (IV. 739–40)—is voiced in Greek and comes to him through a group of young boys who look as though they had just stepped onto Cythera out of the foamy breakers of the Aegean.

This analogy suggests that *A Portrait* might offer more than merely a *rhythmic* approach to the development of its protagonist. The novel in fact moves beyond Joyce's initial resolution and towards a radical *polyrhythmicality* that achieves for narrative a similar breakthrough as Igor Stravinsky's contemporaneous *Le sacre du printemps* did for music.[3] *A Portrait*, divided as it is into numerous discontinuous sections, constantly displaces its protagonist from one environment (and thus also one rhythm) into another: Clongowes, Belvedere, and University College, but also the Dedalus' living room, the brothels of Night Town,[4] and the downtown thoroughfares. Stephen oscillates back and forth between those influences that urge him to move forward in life and those which encourage him to linger and thus to see his identity as essentially predetermined by the past. Jesuit priests, university instructors, and Unionist schoolfellows studying for the entrance exams to colonial careers form one extreme of a range of possible responses to the Irish historical situation; his father's drinking companions and the whores of Night Town form another. The network of allusions between these influences is complex and reciprocal. The peasant woman who invites Davin to spend the night in her arms, for example, provides an inverted double of Stephen's muse on the seashore: a kind of nocturnal bat-woman to his diurnal bird-girl. As a consequence, Stephen is constantly struggling to synchronize his internal beat with an ever-changing environment. Traces of the rhythms he has experienced continue to resonate in his unconscious, in much the same way in which the earliest lessons in theology that he received as a school boy find their way into his "mature"

1. Joyce, *Ulysses*, 7.1–2.
2. Wine-dark translates into English Homer's description of the sea in *The Odyssey*, which, in episode 1 of *Ulysses*, Buck Mulligan jokingly replaces with snotgreen (see p. 234 above) [*Editor*].
3. *Le sacre du printemps* (*The Rite of Spring*), an experimental 1913 orchestral work by the Russian–born composer Igor Stravinsky (1882–1971), caused a sensation when first performed, in Paris, with avant-garde choreography by the Russian-trained dancer Vaslav Nijinsky (1890–1950). It eventually influenced many composers [*Editor*].
4. The red-light district in central Dublin during Joyce's youth [*Editor*].

statement of aesthetic rebellion. He vacillates between being a priggish assimilationist and a "lazy idle loafer" (I.1461).

Martin Swales has brilliantly summarized the operative logic of the classical *Bildungsroman* as that of a transformation of contiguity into continuity—of a synchronic "beside-one-another" (*Nebeneinander*) of potential selves into the diachronic "after-one-another" (*Nacheinander*) of realized actuality.[5] *A Portrait* breaks with this operative logic by refusing to cast its lot with a single "after-one-another," a single rhythm. Multiple versions of the self and multiple interpretations of success and personal growth compete for attention, in much the same way that differing historical rhythms pulse and flow through the back alleys, institutions, and public places of Dublin. Stephen himself intensely experiences the tensions that condition his personal development. On the night of one of his greatest successes, for instance, right after his triumphant performance in the Whitsuntide play at Belvedere, the young man abandons his admiring family in a state of nervous tension and finds reprieve only once he has inundated himself in the intense physicality of the poorer areas of town near Marlborough Street: "That is horse piss and rotted straw, he thought. It is a good odour to breathe. It will calm my heart. My heart is quite calm now. I will go back" (II.943–45).

Unlike in the traditional *Bildungsroman*, in which the progress of the hero eventually takes on a harmonious rhythmic structure that illustrates the shape of a larger underlying historical current, Stephen's development in *A Portrait* remains internally contradictory. A product of the polyrhythmic texture of his colonial surroundings, Joyce's hero might thus be described as having a "syncopated" identity. Jumping back and forth between the individual strands that constitute Irish historical experience, he is often internally at odds with his immediate surroundings. But as anyone who has ever spent time contemplating Stephen's monologues on Irish identity will recognize, this tension is as productive as it can be painful. Kenner once observed that:

> in the mind of Joyce there hung a radiant field of multiple possibilities, ways in which a man may go, and corresponding selves he may become, bounding him by one outward form or another while he remains the same person in the eye of God. The events of history, Stephen considers in *Ulysses*, are branded by time and hung fettered "in the room of infinite possibilities

---

5. Martin Swales, *The German Bildungsroman from Wieland to Hesse* (Princeton: Princeton Univ. Press, 1978), 28–36. The terms *Nebeneinander* and *Nacheinander* are, of course, borrowed from G. E. Lessing's famous distinction between pictorial and verbal art in the *Laocoön* [*Author*]. See pp. 323–24 and notes 8–9, p. 186 [*Editor*].

they have ousted." Pathos, the subdominant Joycean emotion, inheres in the inspection of such limits: men longing to become what they can never be, though it lies in them to be it, simply because they have become something else.[6]

Kenner's basic approach is correct, but his conclusions are altogether too pessimistic. *A Portrait* does not eulogize a lost possibility, nor does it quietly resign itself to the triumphal march of history. Instead, it offers a celebration of life in a colonial society caught between tradition and modernity in all its confusing, contradictory, and sometimes also disheartening complexity, filtered through the mind of an individual desperately trying to compose his "individuating rhythm" amidst a polyrhythmic tapestry. Only in the mind of *Ulysses'* obsequious Mr. Deasy could history be conceived of as a singular train of events moving "towards one great goal, the manifestation of God."[7] Stephen believes, on the other hand, that God manifests himself locally, as a mere "shout in the street"—a creed that binds historical revelation to spatiotemporal contingencies. The traditional *Bildungsroman*, of course, is structured as a poetic correlate of Deasy's historical hypothesis, leading up to that cathartic moment when error is transformed into insight and development brought to a convenient closure. *A Portrait,* on the other hand, refuses such a teleological structure on a variety of levels.

Fredric Jameson, whose work continues to be inspired by Lefebvre's, summarizes some of the central insights also reached by the rhythmanalytical project when he explains that "the subjects or citizens of the high-modern period are mostly people who have lived in multiple worlds and multiple times—a medieval *pays*[8] to which they return on family vacations and an urban agglomeration whose elites are, at least in most advanced countries, trying to 'live with their century' and be as 'absolutely modern' as they know how."[9] *A Portrait,* of course, contains its own highly unpleasant version of such a "return to a medieval *pays* on family vacation," in the form of the trip to Cork in the third chapter of the novel. This episode aptly illustrates how *A Portrait* manages to transmute the deep historical rifts that run through Irish society at the *fin de siècle* into a "rhythmic" experience. The excursion begins with a detailed description of Stephen's impressions during the journey on the Dublin-Cork night train. As the train leaves the station, the boy is

6. Kenner, "The Cubist Portrait," 179. Kenner's reference is to Joyce, *Ulysses*, 2.50.
7. These phrases and the one in the next sentence appear in the excerpts from *Ulysses* in this volume. See the end of the episode 2 excerpt, p. 241 [*Editor*].
8. "An area in the countryside whose inhabitants feel a communal cohesion, as they would if they lived in a territory held by a medieval count" (French) [*Editor*].
9. Fredric Jameson, *Postmodernism, or, The Cultural Logic of Late Capitalism* (Durham: Duke Univ. Press, 1991), 366.

overcome by a curious feeling of detachment that enforces a definite rupture between his present self and his personal recollections:

> As the train steamed out of the station he recalled his childish wonder of years before and every event of his first day at Clongowes. But he felt no wonder now. He saw the darkening lands slipping past him, the silent telegraphpoles passing his window swiftly every four seconds, the little glimmering stations, manned by a few silent sentries, flung by the mail behind her and twinkling for a moment in the darkness like fiery grains flung backwards by a runner. (II.948–55)

A consummate modernist subject, Stephen is no longer capable of feeling any wonder, for wonder presupposes rootedness in familiar circumstances.[1] Yet as he continues on towards an uncertain destination, Stephen leaves all prior allegiances behind him. He appears as a monadic subject, an entity cutting a solitary path through historical time and into the promise of modernity. As the landscape that he has known for all his life fades into darkness, his primary markers of experience become the passing "telegraphpoles," which no longer frame recognizable vistas, but instead measure out the relentless advance of empty time at the rate of one bar every four seconds.

In a move that is typical of A Portrait, however, a psychosexual component is immediately added to Stephen's exhilarating experience of modernist vertigo. His self-assured demeanor on the train corresponds to a simultaneous debasement of his father, who now appears to him stuck in the past, futilely clinging to experiences that history has long since condemned to irrelevancy: "Stephen heard but could feel no pity. The images of the dead were all strange to him save that of uncle Charles, an image which had lately been fading out of memory" (II.960–63). Stephen tosses his personal recollections into the darkness behind him in roughly the same way in which the night train flings backwards the "fiery grains" of the provincial postal stations. His father, who still held a position of supreme respect in his life during the Christmas dinner scene, now seems to him ludicrous—a weak old man who nurses the fires of past passions with occasional sips from his pocket flask. In Sigmund Freud's terms, Stephen might be said to have successfully resolved an Oedipus complex,[2] and the endless succession of telegraph poles

---

1. As Sigmund Freud famously pointed out, the step-sibling of wonder, the uncanny (das Unheimliche), similarly results from a violation of the underpinnings of familiar reality (das Heimliche).
2. In Greek mythology, Oedipus becomes king of Thebes, but in doing so commits patricide without knowing that he has killed his father and then commits incest by marrying his mother unknowingly. Freud's notion of the Oedipus complex focuses on a child's conflicting feelings toward the same-sex parent and the opposite-sex parent,

flanks not only a trail into historical modernity, but also one that leads towards an unencumbered personal development.

But as night yields to day, Stephen's initial exhilaration also has to make room for a very different, and much more depressing, experience:

> The cold light of the dawn lay over the country, over the unpeopled fields and the closed cottages. The terror of sleep fascinated his mind as he watched the silent country or heard from time to time his father's deep breath or sudden sleepy movement. The neighborhood of unseen sleepers filled him with strange dread as though they could harm him: and he prayed that the day might come quickly. (II.969–75)

For the first time since his evening departure, the Irish landscape becomes visible as something more than a mere abstraction, something more than a dark mass of shades broken up every four seconds by a pole. And what Stephen views through his window isn't just any landscape—and certainly not the urban agglomeration of Dublin in which he has lived for most of his life—but rather a *paysage*[3] of cottages and "unpeopled fields," an almost mystical vision of rural Eire. Suddenly, the previous feeling of detachment and disjunction gives way to a definite sense of place: the experience of a locality that is steeped in custom, organic social experience, and intransigent historical continuity.

Stephen's sense of his own position in the world changes in accordance with the landscape that he glimpses outside of his window. Suddenly, his father's presence—so easily dismissed just a few hours ago—takes on an almost claustrophobic heaviness, and the dim outlines of the fellow passengers in his compartment inspire in him a strange dread. His experience of time changes as well. His attention is no longer held by the passing telegraph poles, which measure out the advance of historical time in a relentlessly repetitive mechanical continuity, but by his father's heavy breathing and occasional sleepy movement. The mechanical thus yields to the biological, and mere repetition is replaced by the organic cycle of pulmonary activity. Time no longer progresses, but appears almost at a standstill.

Psychologically, this change corresponds to a relapse into a pre-Oedipal state for Stephen, in which the physical proximity of his father becomes a source of almost unmanageable anxiety. To contain

---

about desiring one or the other erotically or hating one or the other. The resolution asserted for Stephen here concerns his newfound disdain for his father, which is then displaced by a sense of confusion [*Editor*].

3. "Landscape or countryside" (French), here with the sense of a locale from an earlier era [*Editor*].

his fears, he has recourse to what Freud in *Totem and Taboo* calls the "power of magical thinking" and defines as the belief that wishes, thoughts and prayers can effect direct changes in the world.[4] Stephen's prayer, "addressed neither to God nor saint, began with a shiver, as the chilly morning breeze crept through the chink of the carriage door to his feet, and ended in a trail of foolish words which he made to fit the insistent rhythm of the train; and silently, at intervals of four seconds, the telegraphpoles held the galloping notes of the music between punctual bars" (II.976–81).

An important change occurs over the course of these four lines. The telegraph poles that fly by outside of the window are no longer merely described as markers of a spatiotemporal contiguity, but as the "punctual bars" that create an underlying "rhythm" for the "galloping notes" of Stephen's prayer. Stephen's prayer is the direct result of his Oedipal anxiety and his apprehension of a spatiotemporal situatedness that negates his earlier feelings of modernist vertigo. Clock time and circadian time, the linear and unbroken expanse of the railroad tracks and the cyclical movement of pulmonary activity have blended into the apprehension of a rhythmical structure.

This episode not only illustrates how Stephen creates an "individuating rhythm" out of the overlap between progressive and regressive influences, but also demonstrates the essential parallelism to which Joyce subjects the themes of historical and psychosexual development in his novel. The nativist, cyclical elements of *A Portrait* are consistently gendered as female and associated with maternal and gestational imagery: Stephen's mother, whose death sometime in the interstice between *A Portrait* and *Ulysses* will force the young poet to return to Ireland; Emma * * *, whom Stephen sexually desires yet at the same time loathes for her obsequious attempts to learn Gaelic; the peasant woman who attempts to lure Davin into her bed; and most forcefully, perhaps, the "old sow that eats her farrow" (V.1055) to which Stephen impatiently compares his native country. Throughout the book, the young poet will struggle to liberate himself from the heavy burden of a nationalist movement that self-consciously aims not for revolutionary rupture but for a renaissance—a "rebirth" of lost cultural values and thus the continuation of a matriarchal lineage.

The progressivist influences of *A Portrait*, on the other hand, are largely associated with imperial institutions that assume a superegoic function in the nascent mind of Stephen Dedalus. The Jesuit school system, for instance, exerts a castrating power over the

4. Sigmund Freud, *Totem and Taboo: Some Points of Agreement Between the Mental Lives of Savages and Neurotics*, trans. James Strachey (New York: Routledge, 1950), 94–124.

young man, forcing him either to throw his lot with the colonizer or else to risk symbolic impotence alongside the rest of an underdeveloped Irish nation. Father Arnall's sermon, which forms both the literal and the symbolic centerpiece of Joyce's novel, illustrates this dynamic especially well. The priest begins his descriptions of hell with a proem reminding his students of the future that awaits them in colonial service—a future imagined as the very negation of present circumstances: "Many of the boys who sat in these front benches a few years ago are perhaps now in distant lands, in the burning tropics or immersed in professional duties or in seminaries or voyaging over the vast expanse of the deep or, it may be, already called by the great God to another life and to the rendering up of their stewardship" (III.257–62). From this proem, the sermon gathers force over the span of almost forty pages before it culminates in an elaborate metaphor intended to dramatize the quite literally inconceivable duration of an eternity of suffering:

> You have often seen the sand on the seashore. How fine are its tiny grains! And how many of those tiny little grains go to make up the small handful which a child grasps in its play. Now imagine a mountain of that sand, a million miles high, * * * and imagine that at the end of every million years a little bird came to that mountain and carried away in its beak a tiny grain of that sand. How many millions upon millions of centuries would pass before that bird had carried away even a square foot of that mountain, how many eons upon eons of ages before it had carried away all. Yet at the end of that immense stretch of time not even one instant of eternity could be said to have ended. (III.1058–75)

The image of sand that needs to be cleared away from a beach has become a familiar symbol of the progressive urge ever since Goethe finished the second part of his *Faust* in 1832.[5] But in Father Arnall's hellscape, this struggle for improvement has been converted into a futile and repetitive activity: hell quite literally is development at a standstill, a denial of the teleological promise modernity holds out to its faithful disciples.

Another instance of rhythmic composition occurs early in the fifth chapter of *A Portrait*, as Stephen, afflicted with a guilty conscience because he is late for a lecture, makes his way through downtown Dublin. * * * Stephen, if anything, is far too much "in tune" with the surrounding city. For him, there exists a psychic

---

5. Goethe's drama and its central motif find a powerful explication in Marshall Berman, *All That Is Solid Melts Into Air: The Experience of Modernity* (New York: Simon and Schuster, 1982), 37–86.

continuity between the world of exterior sensations and the world of interior rumination:

> Through [the memory of his friend Cranly] he had a glimpse of a strange cavern of speculation but at once turned away from it, feeling that it was not yet the hour to enter it. But the night-shade of his friend's listlessness seemed to be diffusing in the air around him in a tenuous and deadly exhalation and he found himself glancing from one casual word to another on his right or left in stolid wonder that they had been so silently emptied of instantaneous sense until every mean shop legend bound his mind like the words of a spell and his soul shriveled up, sighing with age as he walked on in a lane among heaps of dead language. His own consciousness of language was ebbing from his brain and trickling into the very words themselves which set to band and disband themselves in wayward rhythms. (V.162–74)

In this passage, Stephen's memories of Cranly diffuse into the atmosphere around him, where they seem to poison the signs and shop legends, leaving only "heaps of dead language." In response to this figurative murder, Stephen's own "consciousness of language" (a purely subjective mental operation, just like his earlier recollection) appears to drain out of him in an attempt to restore life to the goings-about in the street. Exterior observation and interior psychic process mingle in the production of a "wayward rhythm."

* * * In *A Portrait* * * * meaning is still immanent to the subject, rather than a product of outside circumstance. Stephen succeeds in synthesizing his confused surroundings in an act of linguistic creation, a "band of wayward rhythms" that can be wrapped around them to artificially enforce stability. All of which is to say that the rhythmic shape of history in this novel emerges from and through the protagonist, rather than independently of him, as it will in the later and more radical *Ulysses*.[6]

This conversion of a historical experience into poetic language also explains the peculiar texture of Joyce's novel: its oscillation between disjunctive and conjunctive elements and its reliance on the antagonistic techniques of epiphany and leitmotif. For after all, both style and structure of *A Portrait* reflect the growing consciousness of its hero, from the infantile babblings on the opening page to

---

6. As Robert Spoo puts it, "[i]n *Ulysses* an expansive format and epic scope eagerly accommodate history as a theme, going so far as to make it the organizing principle of the second episode. In *A Portrait*, however, history is important because it belongs to Stephen's emerging sense of self, and this personal imperative causes historical issues to be registered in psychological and poetic terms, in sudden flashes of image and metaphor, allusion and luminous detail, as Stephen's mind and story dictate" (*James Joyce and the Language of History* [Oxford: Oxford Univ. Press, 1994], 39).

the transition into the diary form in the closing chapter. And if the form of this novel is explicitly shaped by the polyrhythmic historical experience that serves as its content, then it only makes sense that it would attempt to move in multiple directions at once. Michael Levenson recognized as much twenty years ago, when he attempted an intervention to save Joyce critics from their paralyzing obsession with "irony," defined long ago by Wayne Booth as a refusal to take sides.[7] According to Levenson, "Joyce is less concerned to submit sentiment to the astringencies of irony than to conjoin all pertinent implications and to disclose the copresence of incongruous designs. Stronger than the attraction of irony is the allure of the pun, which depends not upon a collision but upon a union of meanings and which functions at every level of Joyce's work."[8]

Epiphany and leitmotif are, in other words, nothing less than a stylistic precipitate of the conflicting vectors that defined Irish intellectual life in the early years of the twentieth century. The epiphany, for example, is unmistakably aligned with the modernist aesthetics of rupture, and with the Nietzschean blink of an eye (*Augenblick*).[9] In the *Stephen Hero* manuscript, Stephen himself defines it as "a sudden spiritual manifestation, whether in the vulgarity of speech or of gesture or in a memorable phase of the mind itself."[1] This emphasis on the epiphany's sudden and unexpected appearance stresses its family resemblance to the shock, that other quintessential symptom of modernist experience. Like the shock, the epiphany renders the everyday strange by disrupting the comfortable distance that ordinarily exists between the objective world and an apprehending subject. But while the shock reduces the objective world to a jumble of meaningless signifiers that encroach upon and threaten to overwhelm the subject, the epiphany increases the distance between the two until the objective world is quite literally consumed in a moment of radiant and pure signification.[2] Here, again, is Stephen Dedalus on his morning walk to University College:

7. In his highly influential study, *The Rhetoric of Fiction* (Chicago: U of Chicago P, 1961), the American critic Wayne C. Booth suggests trenchantly that Joyce's narrator does not give us sufficient guidance to judge Stephen positively or negatively; as a consequence, the narration makes it impossible to settle the critical debate concerning whether the presentation is ironic or sympathetic. See in particular Booth's pp. 323–26 [*Editor*].

8. Michael Levenson, "Stephen's Diary in Joyce's *Portrait*: The Shape of Life," *ELH* 52 (1985): 1033–34.

9. Literally in the glance (or, we would say more idiomatically in English, the blink) of an eye, by which is meant "a moment or instant" (German). By the word, the German philosopher Friedrich Nietzsche (1844–1900) means a transforming moment [*Editor*].

1. Joyce, *Stephen Hero* (Norfolk: New Directions, 1963), 211.

2. Walter Benjamin, the most important theorist of the shock, cites as one of its consequences the "demolition of the aura" (*Charles Baudelaire: A Lyric Poet in the Age of High Capitalism*, trans. Harry Zohn [London: Verso, 1983], 154; translation modified). The epiphany, by contrast, might be defined as an attempt to mend this aura and to return a sensation of organic wholeness to a fragmented age [*Author*]. By aura,

His thinking was a dusk of doubt and selfmistrust lit up at moments by the lightnings of intuition, but lightnings of so clear a splendor that in those moments the world perished about his feet *as if it had been fireconsumed*: and thereafter his tongue grew heavy and he met the eyes of others with unanswering eyes for he felt that the spirit of beauty had folded round him like a mantle and that in revery at least he had been acquainted with nobility. But when this brief pride of silence upheld him no longer, he was glad to find himself still in the midst of common lives, passing on his way amid the squalor and noise and sloth of the city fearlessly and with a light heart. (V.100–111; my emphasis)

For Friedrich Nietzsche, the "blink of an eye" was the fragile contact zone between the unrealities of the past and the future in which the new enters into our world. He dreamt of a reformed humanity that might break the shackles of historicism and live entirely for the present. Joyce, who went through a brief Nietzschean phase in early life, but essentially left the philosopher-prophet behind him once he moved out of the Martello Tower,[3] is considerably less grandiose in his fictions. Nevertheless, a similar confidence in the restorative powers of the new informs the structure of the epiphanies in *A Portrait*.[4] In the very best of them, Stephen Dedalus finds himself yanked out of his habitual surroundings and born aloft on a current of pure historical time that drives him forwards with relentless momentum. This is the case, for example, with the famous "bird-girl" epiphany:

He turned away from her suddenly and set off across the strand. His cheeks were aflame; his body was aglow; his limbs were trembling. On and on and on and on he strode, far out over the sands, singing wildly to the sea, crying to greet the advent of the life that had cried to him.

Her image had passed into his soul for ever and no word had broken the holy silence of his ecstasy. Her eyes had called him, and his soul had leaped at the call. To live, to err, to fall, to triumph, to recreate life out of life! A wild angel had appeared to him, the angel of mortal youth and beauty, an envoy from the fair courts of life, to throw open before him in an instant of ecstasy the gates of all the ways of error and glory. On and on and on and on! (IV. 878–90)

Benjamin means the specificity and authenticity of the work of art as experienced by the person who encounters it [*Editor*].

3. The former coastal fortification in which Stephen and Buck are living in episode 1 of *Ulysses*, part of which is reprinted in this edition (see pp. 232–38 and note 6, p. 55) [*Editor*].

4. For more on Joyce's flirtation with Friedrich Nietzsche, see Ellmann, 142, 162, 172.

The key phrase in this passage clearly is the twice-repeated "on and on and on and on," an expression of the vertiginous experience of modernity. It is true that not all epiphanies are quite as optimistic as this one.

Leitmotifs, on the other hand, function in a manner that is diametrically opposed to that of epiphanies in *A Portrait*. Instead of emphasizing historical ruptures, they reiterate continuities, and instead of focusing on the contingency of the subject, they restrict personal options and underscore necessity. In the closing paragraphs of the first chapter of the novel, for example, Joyce offers a detailed and psychologically realistic description of Stephen's exuberant feelings after he elicits an apology of sorts from the rector of Clongowes Wood College over the unjust beating administered by Father Dolan: "The cheers died away in the soft grey air. He was alone. He was happy and free: but he would not be anyway proud with Father Dolan. He would be very quiet and obedient: and he wished that he could do something kind for him to show him that he was not proud" (I.1833–37). The text then continues with a paragraph that enumerates Stephen's surroundings in sensual detail—the color of the air, the smell of the fields. But when the description shifts into an auditory register, it takes on symbolical overtones: "The fellows were practicing long shies and bowling lobs and slow twisters. In the soft grey silence he could hear the bump of the balls: and from here and from there through the quiet air the sound of the cricket bats: pick, pack, pock, puck: like drops of water in a fountain falling softly in the brimming bowl" (I.1844–48).

The onomatopoetic sequence "pick, pack, pock, puck" is introduced in an attempt to realistically render the noise that a cricket ball makes when it strikes a wooden bat, but the concluding simile draws attention to an additional symbolic meaning generated by the textual interplay of Joyce's novel. For the sound of water striking a bowl recalls Stephen's earlier memories of the time that his father took him to the lavatory of the Wicklow Hotel ([I.153–58]) and of the time when his classmate Wells shouldered him into the same sewage ditch into which "a fellow had once seen a big rat jump plop into the scum" (I.126–27). Stephen's moment of victory is thus implicitly connected with two previous episodes in which he showed weakness, and his triumphant rupture with past experience is ironically diminished. If the epiphany results in a consumption of everyday reality in a flame of pure signification, then the leitmotif asserts the continued material presence of just this ordinary reality. The Joycean leitmotif never consists of exact repetitions of previous symbolic material, however, and therefore points not towards stasis, but towards a cyclical emergence in time. The dozens of different motifs that circulate in *A Portrait* gain in complexity with each and every occurrence. In a word, they develop. Their structuring logic isn't that of the closed circle, but rather that of William Butler Yeats's "widening gyre."[5]

Previous attempts to relate *A Portrait* to the *Bildungsroman* tradition * * * were unable to fully account for these two aberrant kinds of development using the terms laid out by canonical theories of *Bildung*. Neither the transformative, disjunctive pull of the epiphany, nor the conservative, conjunctive recurrence of the leitmotif submit to what Joyce attacked in 1904 as the "character of beards and inches." They do, however, combine to form an "individuating rhythm" not just of Stephen's tortured mind, but also of the Irish historical situation at the beginning of the twentieth century. Caught in what Lefebvre would designate as a "metastable" state at the fringes of the British imperial world, Ireland vacillates between a full immersion in the cultural and economic exchanges of modernity and the revival of more ancient identity formations. *A Portrait* illustrates this contradictory dynamic by narrating Stephen's gradual move towards a diasporic vocation that is imagined both as a radical break with the homeland and as its symbolic renewal. Epiphany and leitmotif represent the antagonistic—yet closely intertwined—extremes of this development. By switching back and forth between them, Joyce not only creates a "polyrhythmic" texture previously unknown to Anglophone fiction, but also moves the time-honored novel of development firmly into the age of empire and towards an engagement with many of the historical traumata that would come to define the twentieth century.

KATHERINE MULLIN

Joyce's Bodies[†]

Joyce's preoccupation with the body is notorious. *Ulysses'* fame stems almost as much from its reputation as a 'dirty book', banned for much of the twentieth century in many English-speaking countries, as for its prominence as a foundational text of experimental modernism. * * *

---

5. Among Yeats's many articulations of the historical gyre, the most famous is, of course, the one given in the poem "The Second Coming," in *The Collected Poems of W. B. Yeats*, ed. Richard J. Finneran, rev. 2nd ed. (New York: Scribner, 1996), 187 [*Author*]. On Yeats, see p. 299 [*Editor*].

† From *James Joyce*, ed. Sean Latham (Dublin and Portland, OR: Irish Academic P, 2010), pp. 170–72, 177–81, 187–88. Reprinted with permission of Irish Academic Press. Some of the author's notes have been omitted. Page references for *A Portrait* have been replaced with part and line numbers of this Norton Critical Edition. Some cited passages might differ slightly from the equivalent passages in this volume.

Joyce's troubling interest in the body and its dark places * * * was heralded as early as 1906, when the struggling young author, unknown and adrift in Trieste, fulminated against a climate of prudishness dominating his home-town. The immediate cause of his wrath was an article in the Irish nationalist journal *Sinn Féin* deploring the 'venereal excess' of those British soldiers barracked in Dublin who spent their evenings in the city's red light district. Joyce was particularly incensed to learn that the journalist was the poet and critic Oliver St John Gogarty, his former companion in his own brothel adventures, later fictionalized as Buck Mulligan in *Ulysses*. Writing to his brother Stanislaus, Joyce castigated Gogarty's 'lying drivel about pure men and pure women and spiritual love and love for ever' as 'blatant lying in the face of truth'.[1] In retaliation, he promised to 'put down a bucket in my own soul's well, sexual department' and 'in my novel inter alia . . . plank the bucket down' before his appalled literary associates back in Dublin. What interests me here is not so much Joyce's declaration of intent to write his sexual autobiography in *Stephen Hero*, later revised into *A Portrait of the Artist as a Young Man*, as the way in which the body and its unpalatable preoccupations are presented as the proof, even the guarantor, of a new literary authenticity. On the threshold of his career, Joyce flaunts his writing as a form of bracing, liberating indecent exposure. The body, even its 'sexual department', is to be hauled up and displayed as an antidote to the prudish disingenuousness of his contemporaries. Through representing the body and its concerns openly and without obfuscation, Joyce vows that his writing will transcend and rebuke the intellectual and aesthetic dishonesty of his literary rivals.

*   *   *

* * * [T]he somatic constriction Joyce so relentlessly describes as peculiar to Dublin is potentially fatal to the artist. That problem forms one of the chief themes of *A Portrait of the Artist as a Young Man*, the book eventually issuing from Joyce's 1906 threat to flaunt his 'sexual department' before a prudish Dublin literati. Whereas *Dubliners* delineates the stifling symbiosis between the body and all kinds of narratives—from old men's stories through newspaper reports to popular songs—*A Portrait* is ostensibly concerned not so much with the processes of narrative consumption as with the alchemy of artistic production. Yet, as in *Dubliners*, Joyce begins by showing how a child is taught to associate the inhibition of the body with the regulation of the text. Indeed, the first page of the

1. *Letters of James Joyce*, Vol. II, ed. Richard Ellmann (New York: Viking, 1966), 191–92 [*Editor*].

novel associates Stephen Dedalus's first lesson in bodily restraint with the bowdlerization of a song he has learnt to call his own. '*O, the wild rose blossoms / On the little green place*' (I.9) is a sanitized version of the popular ballad 'Lilly Dale' (1852), in which the word 'place' has been substituted for 'grave' in order to transform a song about desire, loss and death into a palatable nursery rhyme. Stephen himself, however, has modified the song further, lisping '*O the geen wothe botheth*' (I.12), inviting much speculation about what a 'green rose' might signify. Is the flower appropriately Irish, as might befit this first act of creation? Might it, more darkly, hint at the green carnation worn by Oscar Wilde, an Irish artist whose martyrdom for his sexual transgressions animated one of Joyce's Triestine essays?[2] These questions hang in the air as the coloured narrative moves on to 'When you wet the bed first it is warm then it gets cold' (I.13). Stephen's first attempt to find his own voice is thus repeatedly entwined with his attempt to regulate his wayward body. As in *Dubliners*, the opening episode of *A Portrait* immediately problematizes the relationship between body and text.

This early intimation that Stephen's artistic progress will be closely bound up with his body is sustained throughout the novel. At Clongowes School still more compelling somatic secrets interrupt his attempts to comprehend the mysteries of language. When two lines from the Litany of the Blessed Virgin Mary, '*Tower of Ivory. House of Gold*', baffle Stephen, he interprets the words through his friend Eileen's 'long thin cool white hands' and her 'fair hair' which 'streamed out behind her like gold in the sun' (I.1267– 69). Accessing language by mapping it on to the body comes naturally to Stephen, but the strategy fails him when he is called upon to decipher the still more mysterious word 'smugging'. Learning that some of his school-fellows are to be flogged for this obscurely named crime, Stephen muses, 'What did that mean about the smugging in the square' (I.1244–45), wondering if the transgression has something to do with the graffiti of the walls of the 'square', or school latrines: 'Perhaps that's why they were there because it was a place where some fellows wrote things for cod?' (I.1283–84). What 'smugging' actually means is still a subject of some dispute, and I have argued elsewhere that it most plausibly signifies some form of collective masturbation, the focus of an abiding anxiety throughout boys' public schools in Britain and Ireland at the time.[3] Crucially, however, the word's suggestive indeterminacy invites a telling frisson between bodily and textual transgression. A forbidden

---

2. James Joyce, "Oscar Wilde: The Poet of 'Salome'," *Critical Writings of James Joyce*, ed. Ellsworth Mason and Richard Ellmann (New York: Viking, 1959), 201–05 [*Editor*].
3. See K. Mullin, *James Joyce, Sexuality and Social Purity* (Cambridge: Cambridge University Press, 2003), pp. 83–115.

text, for Stephen here as much as for the boy in 'An Encounter',[4] is loosely associated with corporal punishment, and, at some dimly understood level, with sexual desire.

These associations between writing and the abject sexual body are inevitably sharpened in adolescence. In the second chapter Stephen travels with his father to Cork and visits the university where the older man once studied. There, father and son tour the anatomy theatre, where Mr Dedalus seeks out the initials he once carved on a desk. Anatomy and inscription are, however, bound together in a second sense when Stephen finds another carving which devastatingly speaks to his own sexual anxieties: 'On the desk before him he read the word *Foetus* cut several times into the dark stained wood' (II.1049–50). This 'sudden legend', suggestive of an abortive or sterile sexuality, seems to publish his own 'mad and filthy orgies' (II.1101–2) to the world, and his mortification increases as he reads into '[t]he letters cut in the stained wood of the desk' the stigmata of his own 'bodily weakness and futile enthusiasms' (II.1100). Stephen's tendency to map the body on to writing, already established at Clongowes, here takes on the weight of epiphany[5] as the connection between word and body becomes intensely personal. What is at stake here is not simply adolescent sexual panic, but Stephen's half-grasped understanding of the inextricable relationship between his physical and his creative life. Indeed, the word 'Foetus' itself takes on a quasi-corporeal form in this episode, as it 'capered before his eyes as he walked back across the quadrangle' (II.1063–64). It follows, therefore, that Stephen should choose to spend some of the money gained from his schoolboy literary successes, 'the moneys of his exhibition and essay prize' (II.1282–83), on losing his virginity with one of Dublin's many prostitutes. The second chapter closes with his dramatic turn from finding solace in literature, particularly 'the soft speeches of Claude Melnotte' (II.1386), to seek out 'sin with another of his kind' (II.1398–99). As '[t]he verses passed from his lips', displaced by 'the inarticulate cries and the unspoken brutal words' (II.1393–94) of desire, Stephen is nonetheless unable to leave behind the world of language as he compares his 'cry for an iniquitous abandonment' to 'the echo of an obscene scrawl which he had read on the oozing walls of a urinal' (II.1411–13). This is the third of the novel's pointed conflations of sexuality with graffiti, recalling both Stephen's childhood misunderstanding that 'smugging' is forbidden writing on the lavatory walls, and his encounter with the word 'Foetus' in the Cork lecture theatre.

As the third chapter of the novel unfolds, Stephen's future as an artist is shown to be dependent upon his ability to resist and,

---

4. The second story in *Dubliners* [Editor].
5. See note 1, p. 460 [Editor].

ultimately, reject cultural incitement to regulate his body's wayward appetites. Father Arnall's infamous hell-fire sermon ironizes
the Christian doctrine of the Word made flesh through its relish for
the physical. His command of the language of bodily disgust
inspires a somatic response in Stephen, who leaves the sermon
beset by 'Bodily unrest and chill and weariness' (III.1228–29), and
subsequently disciplines himself into a regime of strict denial. This
system of physical constraint, however, connects to a familiar form
of narrative circularity. Like the old man in 'An Encounter', Stephen too slips into a pattern of monologic repetition as his life 'circled about its own centre of spiritual energy' (IV.30–31). His
religious practices—most notably reciting the rosary or attending
confession—ensnare Stephen in a stifling cycle of 'confess and
repent and be absolved, confess and repent again and be absolved
again, fruitlessly' (IV.227–28) as he repeats the same words time
and again. This sense that the body's suppression crushes and sti-
fles creativity—and is thereby fatal to the development of the artist—is underlined at the close of the fourth chapter when Stephen,
having rejected a religious life, perceives his alternative vocation
embodied in the form of the bird-girl. The bathing young woman is
both artist's muse and erotic spectacle, and Stephen's response to
her hovers ambiguously between aesthetic reverence and ardent
desire: 'His cheeks were aflame; his body was aglow; his limbs were
trembling' (IV.879–80). This epiphany, closing the fourth chapter
and apparently betokening Stephen's future artistic destiny, points
the way to the reconciliation of body and text in the young artist's
future career. Yet, as the fifth and final chapter reveals, Stephen
cannot so easily put aside a mistrust of the body that compromises
his aesthetic ambitions.

Stephen's predisposition to view the body and art as irreconcil-
able is evident in his 'applied Aquinas' (V.1268) theory of aesthetics.
During his ambulatory lecture to Lynch, he insists that the 'kinetic'
arts are 'pornographical or didactic' in exciting 'desire or loathing',
and are therefore 'improper arts' (V.1109–11). To illustrate his thesis,
Stephen invokes a sequence of examples which repeatedly exclude
the body from his own personal theory of art. He begins by casting
out the pierced heart of the girl fatally wounded in the hansom cab
from his definition of the tragic [V.1099–1102]. Next, he refutes
Lynch's suggestion that his desire for the Venus of Praxiteles is a
bona fide artistic response, dismissing his reaction as 'simply a reflex
action of the nerves' (V.1146–47). With 'Let us take woman' (V.1225),
Stephen moves on to a convoluted attempt to divorce sexual attraction from artistic appreciation in an effort to articulate a clear distinction between 'eugenics' and 'esthetic' (V.1235). The final flourish
of Stephen's tendency to isolate art from the body is evident in the

example he chooses to explain the three aesthetic elements of *integritas, consonantia* and *claritas*:

> —Stephen pointed to a basket which a butcher's boy had slung inverted on his head.
> —Look at that basket, he said.
> —I see it, said Lynch.
> —In order to see that basket, said Stephen, your mind first of all separates the basket from the rest of the visible universe which is not the basket. The first phase of apprehension is a bounding line drawn about the object to be apprehended. (V.1353–60)

Stephen's theory of art here accomplishes the decapitation of the butcher's boy: his explication depends upon the erasure of the boy's unruly body from the picture. In this erasure, I would suggest, is rooted much of the narrative's notorious ironic distance from its protagonist. The much-debated artistic merits of his villanelle depend in part upon the tension between Stephen's aesthetic theories and the blatantly erotic processes of its composition. 'O! In the virgin womb of the imagination the word was made flesh' [V.1543–44], thinks Stephen, but 'the temptress of his villanelle', awakening from her 'odorous sleep' with a 'look of languor' (V.1742–43), states the radical extent of the narrative's interrogation of this biblical trope.[6] This moment of creation is suggestive not so much of divine inspiration as of autoerotic fantasy, and even the form of the villanelle, through its layers of rhythmic repetitions, implies masturbation. The villanelle episode thus refutes Stephen's own aesthetic theorizing by locating the body at the heart of artistic practice. The theme is further elaborated in *Ulysses*, where Joyce's ironic meditation upon 'the word made flesh' is confirmed and deepened within both the form and the content of the novel.

* * *

* * * Pound[7] was not alone in his unease over Joyce's somatic preoccupations. Virginia Woolf also dismissed *Ulysses* in a 1922 diary entry as the work of 'a queasy undergraduate scratching his pimples', damning it as 'an illiterate, underbred book, the book of a self-taught working man, and we all know how distressing they are, how egotistic, insistent, raw, striking and ultimately nauseating'.[8] Woolf's recourse to tropes of acne and nausea to describe the

---

6. The passage echoes New Testament passages concerning the future birth of Jesus. At the moment "the Word was made flesh" (John 1:14), Gabriel, an archangel, not a seraph, announces to Mary the character of her pregnancy (Luke 1:26–38) [*Editor*].
7. See note 1, p. 449 [*Editor*].
8. V. Woolf, entry for 16 August 1922, in A. Bell and A. McNeillie (eds), *The Diary of Virginia Woolf, Volume* 2: 1920–1924 (London: Hogarth Press, 1978), pp. 188–9

pungency of Joyce's writing could easily belong in the seventh chapter of *Finnegans Wake*. There Joyce gleefully pastiches reactions like Woolf's and Pound's, insisting instead on the centrality of the body, in all its unpalatable vulgarity, to his art. It is a position sustained, in multiple ways, throughout Joyce's literary career, from *Dubliners* and *A Portrait of the Artist as a Young Man*, where the suppression of the physical is repeatedly linked to the stifling of the creative imagination, through to *Ulysses* and *Finnegans Wake*, where bodies and texts become increasingly enmeshed. * * *

JED ESTY

"Elfin Preludes": Joyce's Adolescent Colony[†]

Among the many urban settings Joyce uses to capture the dilatory mind and shifting moods of Stephen Dedalus in *A Portrait,* some of the most resonant are the Liffeyside quays and docks where our hero, the itinerant aesthete of Dublin, walks the margins of national space and courts the barely definable needs of his growing soul:

> A vague dissatisfaction grew up within him as he looked on the quays and on the river and on the lowering skies and yet he continued to wander up and down day after day as if he really sought someone that eluded him. (II.238–42)

Stephen's dockside wanderings fill the middle spaces in a long narrative of becoming; they point to a durable symbolic connection between an inchoate adolescent selfhood, an uncertain and unsanctioned form of desire, and the quays and rivers that connote Stephen's own marginal or provincial place in a vast system of economic modernization. Such scenes, with their overtones of juvenile wanderlust, verge at times on banal romanticism. But they also recall a specific frame of literary reference: Beginning with [George] Eliot's Maggie Tulliver and her fateful downstream journey on the Floss, we [readers of Esty's book] have encountered a series of protagonists whose coming-of-age plots have been disrupted by

---

[*Author*]. Woolf (1882–1941) was an English novelist and essayist; her Hogarth Press declined to publish *Ulysses* [*Editor*].

† "From *Unreasonable Youth: Modernism, Colonialism, and the Fiction of Development* (Oxford and New York: Oxford UP, 2012), pp. 144–59, 247–49. Reprinted with permission of Oxford University Press through PLSclear. Some of the author's notes have been omitted. Bibliographic information has been supplied in editorial brackets and footnotes. Page references for *A Portrait* have been replaced with part and line numbers of this Norton Critical Edition. Some cited passages might differ slightly from the equivalent passages in this volume.

As Esty mentions in his commentary on Joyce, Esty's book focuses on "the novel of subject formation in the age of empire" (see p. 485 below).

commerce and traffic running outside the symbolic boundaries of local or national territory. From Conrad's maritime empire and its dispersal of the soul-nation allegory to Wells's "unassimilable enormity of traffic" and its diffusion of the condition-of-England novel to Woolf's impenetrable London economy and its framing of [Rachel Vinrace's] voyage out,[1] we have been charting a close correspondence between antidevelopmental novels and a vast, disruptive global-colonial system of social and economic reorganization. We have been charting, in other words, symbolic tensions between the waterways of late Victorian or new Imperial capitalism and the territorialized spaces of national identity, tensions that seem to have altered the basic contours of the modern(ist) bildungsroman.

In *Portrait*, Joyce figures experience, especially traumatic experience, in a hydraulic system of images: pools and puddles, rivers and reservoirs, tides and currents, sweat and spittle, holy and profane liquids that wash over and run through Stephen.[2] Joyce sets the flow of sin and squalor against the elaborate bulwarks and levees of Stephen's own making: the patterning and ordering devices of arcane scholarship, churchly abstraction, aesthetic theory, and self-mythologization. Consider, for example, this typical passage, from chapter 2:

> He had tried to build a breakwater of order and elegance against the sordid tide of life without him and to dam up, by rules of conduct and active interests and new filial relations, the powerful recurrence of the tides within him. Useless. (II.1347–51)

The tides of sexual awakening within and urban degradation without converge in Stephen's encounter with a Dublin prostitute. But the conflict is more than just sexual; it goes to Stephen's attempt to assert moral and temporal control over the process of his own formation; at a formal level, tides and breakwaters mark Joyce's attempt to manage the flow of time and story line. Water and waterways signify time in a generalized existential or purely narrative

---

1. Earlier sections of Esty's book provide commentaries on the works and authors mentioned here. Maggie Tulliver is the central figure in *The Mill on the Floss* (1860), by the English novelist George Eliot (Mary Ann Evans) (1819–1880). The Polish-born English novelist Joseph Conrad (1857–1924) published narratives that often dealt with characters who experienced life at sea. "Unassimilable enormity of traffic" is a phrase referring to London streets, by contrast with the open sea, from *Tono-Bungay* (1909), by the English novelist H. G. Wells (1866–1946). Rachel Vinrace is the central figure in *The Voyage Out* (1915), by Virginia Woolf (see note 8, p. 481) [*Editor*].

2. Maud Ellmann provides a sensitive close reading of the novel's "economy of flow" ["The Name and the Scar: Identity in *The Odyssey* and *A Portrait of the Artist as a Young Man*," in *James Joyce's* A Portrait of the Artist as a Young Man: *A Casebook*, ed. Mark A. Wollaeger (New York: Oxford UP, 2003), 158–65].

sense (the stream of consciousness, one might say), but here they also signify time in a more textured, perhaps even geopolitical, sense, since they open at both the literal and symbolic levels to the boundless world of modernization unchecked and unbalanced by the soul-nation allegory.

Like Rachel Vinrace, albeit in a more self-consciously dramatic way, Stephen oscillates between self-consolidation and self-dissolution; both resist the socialization process and value the fluidity of adolescence. * * * In *Portrait*, the water imagery—right down to the "swirling bogwater" [V.2712] of Stephen's closing diary—flows across chapters, breaking up the plot with sensual repetitions that attune Stephen to alternative temporalities of drift, stasis, and regression.

If *Portrait* can be read as typical of a larger modernist problematic—in which subjective narratives of arrested development seem to cluster around themes of colonial backwardness and globally uneven development—it also stands apart from our earlier examples for at least two immediate and related reasons. First, it gives us a more thorough objectification of the bildungsroman: This protagonist not only embodies the displacement of action by thought, but he also theorizes an entire aesthetic program around the principle of stasis or arrested development. Joyce sets Stephen's ideas about aesthetic stasis into the historical context of emergent Irish nationhood, giving us a full demonstration of the ways in which modernist experimentation can denaturalize the soul-nation allegory of the Goethean novel.[3]

Second, as we take up the case of Joyce, we move from ambiguously positioned exiles and dissidents within the British metropolitan or colonial sphere to a writer generally taken to represent the "colonized" population. Even so, we should recall the methodological caveats introduced by the editors of and contributors to *Semicolonial Joyce*,[4] a book that refines our understanding of the postcolonial Joyce: Ireland represents a special case of what Joseph Valente has called "metrocolonial"[5] status, and Joyce (or his alter ego Stephen) a special case of the highly educated and cosmopolitan Irish intellectual. If Stephen understands himself as partial heir

3. In *Wilhelm Meister's Apprenticeship* (1795–96), by the German writer Johann Wolfgang von Goethe (1749–1832), the protagonist's progress to maturity is a movement toward alignment with the conception and expectations of his nation that inform the narrative's social context. By asserting that modernist writing denaturalizes the link between character and nation, Esty means that it challenges the alignment as ideal and determining [*Editor*].

4. Ed. Derek Attridge and Marjorie Howes (Cambridge, Eng.: Cambridge UP, 2000) [*Editor*].

5. A term referring to a colonial situation that is in close proximity to the empire's metropolitan center. Valente uses the term in his essay "Neither Fish Nor Flesh: Joyce and the Conundrum of Irish Manhood" (*Semicolonial Joyce*, 96–127) [*Editor*].

to a baleful legacy of colonial impositions (witness the "tundish" scene), he also takes the iconic figure of the credulous Irish "peasant" to constitute the true subject of both British and "Roman" conquest. With this in view, we can say that Joyce's work appears here as a new variation on this study's governing theme, that is, the novel of subject formation in the age of empire. Reading Joyce and Woolf in semitandem, we can see important differences that can be ascribed to the divergent historical experiences of imperial and colonial cultures, but we can also appreciate the striking fact that, on both sides of the colonial divide, modernist fiction seems to challenge and scramble the Bakhtinian formula of "national-historical time."[6]

Irish national emergence is obviously a problem of identity formation for Stephen and of aesthetic practice for Joyce. *Portrait* narrates a continuous tension between experiential flux and the time-shaping force of national identity. In the opening chapter, Stephen famously gives order to the (traumatic) disorder of experience by locating himself within a nested geography of classroom, school, town, county, nation, continent, planet, and universe (I.300–308). This signal moment of Ptolemaic[7] self-assertion both reinterprets and, in a sense, travesties the soulmaking apparatus of the Goethean hero who builds a nascent intellect out of a kind of cultural global-positioning system always set to the cardinal point of the cosmopolitan self. Such devices—the most hoary conventions of the modern novel as a technology of self-fashioning—are deployed by Joyce but also torqued until they lay bare their own status as conventions. This one in particular, the location of the self within a concentric model of political geography, gets tested and exposed as Stephen doggedly exits the circles of family, church, school, and nation.

Joyce inventories the stock conventions of the bildungsroman in every episode of the novel, but some episodes in particular give us a deeper sense of how he interrupts the forward motion of the soul-nation allegory. Chapter 1, for example, takes up the motif of illness as an antidevelopmental tool * * *. Stephen's early illness at Clongowes Wood College * * * seems placed in such a way as to suggest that it is a psychosomatic reaction to narrow ideologies of

6. M. M. Bakhtin, "The *Bildungsroman* and its Significance in the History of Realism: Toward a Historical Typology of the Novel," in *Speech Genres and Other Late Essays*, trans. Vern W. McGee (Austin: U of Texas P, 1986), 25. Bakhtin, (1895–1975), a Russian literary theorist, uses the term to project an enabling social condition for the *Bildungsroman*, or "novel of development" (German), that avoids the disruption of experiencing time as unbounded under capitalism because nations create apparent temporal boundaries that stabilize the experience of time [*Editor*].

7. Referring to the theory promulgated by the Greek astronomer Ptolemy (c. 100–c. 170 CE) that the Earth is the fixed center of the universe [*Editor*].

gender and class. First of all, his fever follows an early incident of sexual panic * * *. And his bout of unfitness ends, significantly, with the death of the national hero Parnell; it seems therefore to manifest a disorder not just of body but of spirit, a malady rooted in the problem of national destiny.

From this early point on, Stephen seeks to disburden himself of Irish icons while Joyce establishes a persistent tension between national spaces or traditions and the flow of subjective or private time. Whereas in the traditional bildungsroman, national territory and national history are often the narrative and epistemological containers that orient the hero in space and time, here the hero insists that he must break out of the cage of national identity in order to access some fresh, unfiltered knowledge of his place in the sensual and social universe. Read back against the history of the bildungsroman as the genre of European modernization, *Portrait* seeks to update and to objectify long-standing generic formulae, dislodging the soulmaking project from the moralizing time of national history by revealing the Irish national project as a belated, flawed, and often debilitating basis for Stephen's aesthetic education.

* * * Joyce in *his* apprenticeship-as-arrested-development fiction wages a campaign of revisionary reading and writing, always regis- tering the particular problems of the Irish artist or what Seamus Deane has called the "provincial intellectual."[8] Traumatic repetition and ritualized behavior shape Stephen and give Joyce the occasion to expand the logic of serialized experience in several directions. * * * [C]utting against the "tyranny of plot" * * *, he assembles his *Portrait* as a series of recurring motifs that make each of the five chapters seem like retellings of the same story as much as phases in a single story. The contest between plot development and symbolic repetition—always on display in the novel to some extent, as J. Hillis Miller has demonstrated so elegantly[9]—becomes more overt than usual here in Joyce's schematic plot. Joyce uses serialized motifs to undercut linear emplotment * * *. Even now it is surpris- ing how thoroughly Joyce uses repetition and recursion to make a novel whose end circles back to its beginning. If Hugh Kenner's celebrated reading of *Portrait* reveals that the first few pages of the text anticipate all that will follow, Michael Levenson's reveals that the final few pages recapitulate all that has come before. Taken

---

8. Deane has in mind a distinctive kind of provincializing process, though, in which Joyce's major fictions, especially *Ulysses*, turn tables to underscore the provincialism of the English domestic novel tradition [*Celtic Revivals* (Winston Salem, NC: Wake For- est UP, 1987), 75–91].

9. Esty is referring to the central thread of Miller's *Fiction and Repetition* (Cambridge, MA: Harvard UP, 1985) [*Editor*].

together, they remind us that Joyce's novel works by superimposing linear and circular form.[1]

Levenson notes that the diary form that takes over in the final chapter implies, by its very nature, that Stephen's life story is, page by daily page, a never-ending one (1019). Pericles Lewis offers a similar account of the novel's potentially infinite plot: "Joyce converts the disillusionment plot structure from a single, momentous event in the life of the protagonist into an indefinite process, coextensive with life itself"[2] As Joyce prepares his hero to exit the nation, he shifts from a closed to an open genre (novel to diary). This gesture * * * cinches the modernist novel's revision of national closure in the bildungsroman, throwing open the gates to the potential narrative infinities associated * * * with colonial modernity.

The notions that Stephen's life is not a (linear) narrative and that Stephen's life is *only* narrative, that is, an infinite narrative with no closure, are, of course, mirror images of each other. *Portrait* thus stands as the clearest example of a metabildungsroman in which the central, most indispensable device—developmental time—is subjected to a remarkably thorough articulation into two broken halves. All development, all the time, is the same, finally, as the absence of development. This is no mere narrative ruse or modernist gimmick, but also a deep, if deeply oblique, commentary on the postcolonial nation whose self-fulfillment is itself perpetually deferred because it is perpetually under development. The fissile logic of Stephen's coming of age, always happening and thus never happening, corresponds quite exactly to Joyce's vision of Ireland as a radically unfinished project. In "Ireland, Island of Saints and Sages," Joyce ventures the following conditional portrait of a true Irish cultural renaissance:

> It would be interesting, but beyond the aims I have set myself this evening, to see what the probable consequences would be of a resurgence of this people; to see the economic consequences of the appearance of a rival, bilingual, republican, self-centered and enterprising island next to England, with its own commercial fleet and its ambassadors in every port throughout the world; to see the moral consequences of the appearance in old Europe of Irish artists and thinkers, those

1. In his essay on the "cubist *Portrait*" [in *Approaches to Joyce's Portrait: Ten Essays*, ed. Thomas F. Staley and Bernard Benstock (Pittsburgh: U of Pittsburgh P, 1976, 171–84)], Kenner lays out the patterns that recur within each chapter. Levenson, for example, observes that "a leading pattern in the novel is the *series*, which depends not on movement toward an end but on the recurrence of identities and similarities" ["Stephen's Diary in Joyce's *Portrait*: The Shape of Life," *ELH* 52.4 (Winter 1985): 1026, 1020].

2. *Modernism, Nationalism, and the Novel* (Cambridge, Eng.: Cambridge UP, 2000), 30 [Editor].

strange souls, cold enthusiasts, artistically and sexually unin-
structed, full of idealism and incapable of sticking to it, childish spirits, unfaithful, ingenuous and satirical, "the loveless
Irishmen" as they are called.[3]

Since the frame of reference for Stephen in *Portrait* is not the actual
emergent postcolonial nation, but an idealized Ireland of an indefinite future, it follows that the temporality of the national allegory is
the time of pure potentiality, an adolescent counternarrative of
national destiny made to fit those "childish spirits," Irish artists and
thinkers.[4] This picture of Ireland as a nation of great potential but
unworthy political self-formation in the present mirrors, and perhaps structures, the novel's portrait of Stephen. The fundamental
split in Joyce between a sardonic rejection of Irish nationalism in
practice and a playful utopian interest in a renascent Ireland takes
aesthetic form in *Portrait* as the plot of incomplete formation for
both hero and nation.

At the pragmatic level of composition, though, the novel has to
blend the uninflected temporality of mere becoming and the shaped
temporality of discrete experience; the result is Joyce's epicyclical
scheme of five chapters split between repetition and progress.[5] Facing such a temporal scheme, many readers have seen *Portrait* as a
fairly conventional bildungsroman at bottom, propelled by the careful work Joyce does to "age" the style and diction of each chapter in
apparent correspondence to Stephen's growth. Yet * * * it makes
equal interpretive sense to say that the novel's changing style marks
a limit in Stephen's maturity, perhaps even that stylistic advances
throw into relief the recursive elements of the plot and the persistently adolescent features of Stephen's thinking.[6] Taking the force

3. James Joyce, *Occasional, Critical and Political Writing*, ed. Kevin Barry (Oxford, Eng.:
   Oxford UP, 2000), 125 [*Editor*].
4. For a useful outline of the novel's structure and symmetry, see [John Paul Riquelme,
   Teller and Tale in Joyce's Fiction: Oscillating Perspectives (Baltimore: Johns Hopkins
   UP, 1983), 58–64, 232–34]. On pure potentiality, see Kenner: "In the mind of Joyce
   there hung a radiant field of multiple possibilities" (179). Seamus Deane likewise
   observes that Joyce operates in a field of open possibility: "The unfinished and the
   uncreated culture provided the opportunity for the most comprehensive, the most finished, the most boundlessly possible art. The colonial culture produced imperial art"
   (97).
5. Tobias Boes has recently explored the novel's use of repetition to cut progress, citing Joyce's
   own concept of the "individuating rhythm" to describe what Boes calls a "structural
   compromise between cyclical and progressive elements" [see p. 464 above—*Editor*].
6. Traditional criticism of *Portrait* has been, in my view, likely to err, at least in emphasis,
   in the direction of seeing the novel as a continuation rather than a dramatic revision of
   the bildungsroman template. Breon Mitchell, for example, allows that the novel "contains an implicit critique of the *Bildungsroman*," but focuses on the way that Joyce's
   narrative conforms to the generic expectations set by Goethe ["A Portrait and the *Bildungsroman* Tradition," in Staley and Benstock, 72]. And Jerome Buckley notes that
   "Joyce sums up, even as he transforms, the traditions of the nineteenth-century *Bildungsroman*" [*Season of Youth: The Bildungsroman from Dickens to Golding* (Cambridge, MA: Harvard UP, 1974), 226]. The summing up may be a more critical act than

of style, plotting, and characterization together, we might say that the novel warps and defamiliarizes the conventions of the novel of progress, but does not destroy them. * * * Joyce follows Stephen's mental voice into a minute rendering of sensory and cognitive experience and, underneath that, a prismatic account of language itself. Stephen does not just recall, but reenacts, revises, and revisits events and the words used to store and distort them in the mind. Once stationed outside the lines of Goethean destiny, Stephen exhibits signs not just of arrested, but also of accelerated, development: He is by turns premature and immature, juvenile and fusty. He leapfrogs ahead of his time, then treads the temporal waters. In essence, the figure of Stephen is recalcitrant to the standard narrative sequence of youth-into-age.[7] Mixed temporal effects in Joyce— the co-presence of over- and underdevelopmental logic—disorganize the socialization plot in several ways at once.

Few things happen once in *Portrait*. Repeated and remembered episodes (the square ditch at Clongowes, for example) offer a psychologically realist depiction of a layered mind developing its recursive path through life and give the plot its strongly patterned symmetries. Within the diegetic frame,[8] Stephen conducts a proud and holy campaign to separate himself from the crowd, to force his socialization narrative onto a separate and privileged track. Stephen's hyperindividuation parodies self-formation as an aesthetic and social value; he exposes the epigenetic logic[9] of the bildungsroman ideal by dwelling on the mythic act of self-creation. Stephen's ludic fascination with self-authoring continues, of course, into *Ulysses*; here it takes the form of a callow, even arrogant, mission to

---

Buckley allows in his discussion. A more recent interpretation that accords more with my own sense of the novel's relationship to genre conventions is Jessica Berman's: "The end of *Portrait* signifies neither the hero's triumph, maturation, nor his reincorporation into society; but rather the explosion of the conventional *Bildungsroman* along with its enforcement of liberal subjectivity, its insistence on a unified perspective, and its insistence on language as a transparent expression of that perspective" ["Comparative Colonialisms: Joyce, Anand, and the Question of Engagement," *Modernism/modernity* 13.3 (2006): 477].

7. Vicki Mahaffey observes that a combination of psychoanalytic effects—Lacanian "père-version" and what she counter-punningly terms "im-mère-sion"—works in *Portrait* both to hasten and to retard the aging process; Mahaffey rightly traces this set of effects from Joyce back through to Wilde, reading both as participants in a joint study of "unnatural youthfulness" linked not just to tender aestheticism, but to a half-articulated sense of Irish underdevelopment [Vicki Mahaffey, *States of Desire: Wilde, Yeats, Joyce, and the Irish Experiment* (New York: Oxford UP, 1998), 81, 53] [*Author*]. *Père* and *mère* mean father and mother (French). According to the French psychoanalyst Jacques Lacan (1901–1981), perversion involves a turning toward the father. Mahaffey characterizes corrupt desire informed by the father as homophobic and misogynistic, while corrupt desire informed by a dominating mother is hidden, that is, immersed and closeted [*Editor*].

8. The diegetic frame is the plot, as opposed to nondiegetic elements, which are not within the narrative, such as style of narration [*Editor*].

9. A logic that is of the surface, that is, not something that has developed from an originating internal process [*Editor*].

shrug off the burdens of identity politics and group formation. In chapter 2, a precocious Stephen has already turned rebellious moods into personal policy by rejecting the standards of middle-class Irish Catholic male identity. Asked to play the role of gifted redeemer to a series of corrupt, fallen, or dishonored institutions, he tries instead to deny the "din of all these hollowsounding voices," the voices telling him to be a gentleman, a good Catholic, a devout son to a bankrupt father, a decent mate to his fellows, and a hale, manly patriot to champion poor Ireland's "fallen language and tradition" (II.849). To save himself—to become himself—Stephen vows to join "the company of phantasmal comrades" (II.858).

Stephen's preference for phantasmal comrades over against any functional male subgroup not only marks out a key point of departure from the Goethean prototype of the *bildungsheld,*[1] Wilhelm Meister, but it also serves to emphasize to readers a particular crisis of Irish masculinity in which both rebellion and authority can, it seems, be articulated only in terms pre-scripted by the stereotype factory of the Anglo-Irish colonial encounter. Stephen's double bind in the face of patriarchal and national/imperial authority comes into sharp focus during the trip to Cork with his father in chapter 2. Stephen proudly recoils from his father's coarse bonhomie, leaky libido, profligate drinking, and masculine bravado—all of which are accentuated as father and son rejoin the father's old mates in Cork. The acid commentary of Stephen's interior monologue conveys familiar adolescent disgust at the foibles of the older generation, but this cliché of youth takes on greater force when Stephen refuses to be identified not just with his father but with his grandfather. Joyce embeds the drama of disfiliation[2] within a legible array of national types and stereotypes, so that it expands into a wider story of Irish national and colonial disaffiliation (II.1074–1275). Simon's friends hector shy Stephen throughout the scene until one unnamed Corkman asks him which of two Latin slogans is correct: "*Tempora mutantur nos et mutamur in illis* or *Tempora mutantur et nos mutamur in illis*" (II.1200–1201). Seamus Deane renders the line as "Circumstances change and we change with them" and suggests that the comparison of the two phrases—both grammatically correct—is merely academic (*Portrait* 295). But the slight variation, when viewed through the central lens of the soul-nation allegory, takes on an interesting inflection: "Times change and we change with them" or "Times change and we are changed by them." The shift from a parallelism implied by "with" to the causality implied by

---

1. The protagonist (German), or hero (*Held*), of a *Bildungsroman* (novel of development) [*Editor*].
2. Filiation is "the fact of being the child of a specific parent" (*OED*). Disfiliation is the refusal of filiation [*Editor*].

"by" contains in a grammatical nutshell an entire open question around which *Portrait* as a late or metabildungsroman might be said to revolve: Is the self a product of its historical circumstances or a self-producing, self-authoring entity restricted—but not wholly formed—by its circumstances?

In particular, Stephen wonders whether he can break from the traditions and values embodied by his bluff and rivalrous jackass of a father. Is rebellion—already cataloged by Arnoldian ethnology[3] as a cliché of the Irish soul, already jocosely dismissed by his father as a toothless adolescent pose—even possible for Stephen under these conditions? How to rebel within an Irish nationalist culture of failed rebellion? Watching his father and friends drink a self-satisfied toast, Stephen imagines a crisp break between the generations:

> An abyss of fortune or of temperament sundered him from them. His mind seemed older than theirs: it shone coldly on their strifes and happiness and regrets like a moon upon a younger earth. No life or youth stirred in him as it had stirred in them. He had known neither the pleasure of companionship with others nor the vigour of rude male health nor filial piety. (II.1259–65)

Where the youth of his father and his ilk is of the conventional, phased kind—discrete and free and pleasurable—Stephen's is an unpredictable, idiopathic style of youth, riddled with inhibitions, devoted to abstract rewards of aestheticized intellection, and elastic in its temporality. Failure to be youthful here means failure to observe a proper youth-age sequence; failed youth also provides the aegis for Stephen's sweeping rejection of male companionship and homosocial bonds. Stephen's alienation from the spectacle of youth as pre-manhood constitutes a serious falling away from the homosocial Goethean subsociety, understood as the key agent of social reconciliation for the bourgeois-bohemian apprentice. If the Goethean hero (recycled, for example, in the Dickens novel)[4] seeks paternity everywhere, Joyce's hero seeks to *reject* paternity everywhere, claiming proud exclusion from the homosocial clique as well as the national patrimony. For Stephen, naturally, this obsessive and disfiliative plot cycle has the effect, as the passage makes perfectly clear, of scrambling both the social repertoire and the organicized timetable of youth-maturity.

3. For the English critic and poet Matthew Arnold (1822–1888), ethnology was the science of origins with respect to peoples, that is, races understood as nations. He characterized the Irish people as inherently rebellious in *On the Study of Celtic Literature* (1867) [*Editor*].
4. The prolific English novelist Charles Dickens (1812–1870) wrote such widely admired novels as *Great Expectations* (1861), a *Bildungsroman* whose central character, Pip, is an orphan who longs to find a father figure [*Editor*].

Stephen, operating only semiautonomously from the indirect discourse of the narrator, casts this social fracture as a temporal break between himself and his own past:

> His childhood was dead or lost and with it his soul capable of simple joys, and he was drifting amid life like the barren shell of the moon.
>
> > Art thou pale for weariness
> > Of climbing heaven and gazing on the earth,
> > Wandering companionless . . . ?
>
> He repeated to himself the lines of Shelley's fragment. Its alternation of sad human ineffectualness with vast inhuman cycles of activity chilled him, and he forgot his own human and ineffectual grieving. (II.1266–75)

Stephen's lunar self-image implicitly refutes the *Tempora mutantur* of the crony from Cork: Where that motto speaks to the integrated and reciprocal relation between the subject and his times, Stephen becomes the companionless moon, quite out of joint with his times.

Stephen's interest in the Shelley fragment centers on the *alternation*, not integration or synthesis, between human and inhuman activity, between inner experience and outer signs, a problem chilled and condensed into an impersonal verse form. Stephen articulates via Shelley a problem—am I overdetermined or self-determining?—that cannot be resolved.[5] Joyce thus positions Stephen not simply as the typical protagonist of a disillusionment plot, a rebel in the face of bourgeois compromise, but also as a belated subject who marks the breakdown of the core soul-nation allegory. In particular, Stephen's capacity for masochism allows Joyce to describe subject formation in terms of an overidentification with authority, and thereby to balance out the rebellious Luciferian streak of Stephen's "non serviam."[6] Reading *Portrait* this way, we can understand afresh some of Stephen's self-glorification and self-mortification; they make sense not just as adolescent emotionalism but as signs of Joyce's attempt to modernize literary character. With recent colonial, semicolonial, and postcolonial Joyce criticism in mind, we might say that *Portrait* casts the struggle of Irish national emergence as a historical condition for Joyce's novelistic critique of the European novel of progress.

If Stephen's rebellious individualism and Joyce's modernist will to innovation take the form of an adolescent indifference to

---

5. On the "extreme form of the tension" that Stephen experiences between self-determination and social determination, see Pericles Lewis[, *Modernism, Nationalism, and the Novel* (Cambridge, Eng.: Cambridge UP, 2000),] 30–31.

6. "I will not serve" (Latin). The statement is often attributed to Satan when he rejects God's dominance. See *A Portrait*, III.556 and V.2297 [*Editor*].

the narrative conventions of moralized, nationalized progress, they must then confront the temporal registers that fall outside the model of shapely progress: static and infinite time. And these are not just theoretical markers of time in *Portrait,* but take their place inside the rhetoric and ideology of the very authorities against which Stephen attempts to rebel, that is, the colonial and imperial centers of patriarchal power. Stephen's volatile self-understanding in relation to those sources of patriarchal authority accounts in part for the length and detail of Father Arnall's hell sermon—an episode during which Stephen's propensities for self-mortification and self-glorification blur into one. What makes that long passage even more germane to Stephen's place at the center of a colonial novel of arrested development is that, as Tobias Boes has aptly noted, the priest's vision of hell is "development at a standstill" [p. 471 above]. Indeed, Joyce lingers on the infernal rhetoric so as to give Stephen—and readers—a foretaste of eternity itself: "ever, never; ever, never" (III.1105–06). Eternal damnation, in other words, feels like pure narrativity with no closure.

But the rhetorical reach of Father Arnall's sermon extends beyond hell to an alternative language of destiny too:

> Time has gone on and brought with it its changes. Even in the last few years what changes can most of you not remember? Many of the boys who sat in those front benches a few years ago are perhaps now in distant lands, in the burning tropics or immersed in professional duties or in seminaries or voyaging over the vast expanse of the deep or, it may be, already called by the great God to another life. (III.255–261)

This official and clichéd account of the boys' pathways to adulthood emphasizes service in two alien hierarchies, the Catholic church and the British empire. More to the immediate point, it describes futures—professions, priesthood, death, and imperial adventure—that are grand callings, tilted toward the romanticized extremes of adventure and of destiny. Life, it seems, is a mission and a project, and the diction ("distant . . . vast . . . expanse . . . deep . . . great") directly echoes the endless, boundless qualities the sermon associates with eternal hellfire. The future stretches to far horizons rather than attaching to fixed and stable places. The extranational authorities that dominate *Portrait* have their own versions of infinity: the empire's endless Great Game[7] of imperial expansion and the church's boundless rhetoric of hell. Nowhere in

---

7. The political and diplomatic clashes, focused on Afghanistan and surrounding areas, between the British Empire and the Russian Empire in the nineteenth century, largely initiated by the British to preclude the possibility that the Russian Empire would invade India [*Editor*].

Portrait is the language more clearly anatomized for the way in which it connects destiny and adventure itself to the twin imperialisms of Rome and London and to the bad infinities (spiritual, spatial, existential) that they seem to represent. The sermon is a lurid, sensually rich version of a never-ending story: precisely what a novel of arrested development threatens to become if it generates no inner checks. To get outside the soul-nation allegory of nineteenth-century convention is thus to risk confrontation with or suspension in a demoralized, nonprogressive temporality—the empty chronos that is the dark other of the bildungsroman itself.

* * * Joyce must find a way in *Portrait* for Stephen, as a figure, to remain poised between the Scylla of pat and linear national *Bildung* on the one hand and the Charybdis of shapeless or empty time on the other.[8] At the thematic level, this means giving fictional form to an alternative ideal of Irish nationality outside the prescriptive and restrictive canons of official nationalism.[9] The complexity of *Portrait* and its reception by postcolonial critics especially has always been that Stephen seems to be a nationally representative type who also rejects nationalism (if not nationality); that is, he can be read as representatively or typically Irish only in his paradoxical disavowal of the burden of Irishness. The novel thus preserves and cancels the apparatus of the soul-nation allegory, splitting the national hero between residual and emergent times, between recursive patterns and sequential narration. In making Stephen a specialized talent and a highly self-conscious historical thinker, Joyce breaks with the Lukács-Scott model of the "typical" realist or historical protagonist since, as Lukács suggests, "a biographical portrayal of a genius . . . conflicts with the means of expression peculiar to epic art".[1] The modern epic genres of historical and realist fiction, that is, require the average or middling hero, but Stephen cannot operate like a Scott hero because he is not a historiographical innocent. He knows too much and, what is more,

---

8. Two dangers in the path of Odysseus' homeward journey in *The Odyssey*, only one of which he can avoid because they occupy opposite sides of a strait through which he must sail: Scylla is a rapaciously cannibalistic monster; Charybdis, a monster who generates a giant whirlpool that destroys ships. *Bildung:* "development" (German) [*Editor*].

9. Seamus Deane makes the point clearly: "It was at such moments in his fiction that Joyce rewrote the idea of national character and replaced it by the idea of a character in search of a nation to which he (Joyce-Stephen) could belong" [*Strange Country: Modernity and Nationhood in Irish Writing since 1790* (Oxford, Eng.: Oxford UP, 1997), 96].

1. Georg Lukács, *The Historical Novel*, trans. Hannah Mitchell and Stanley Mitchell (Boston: Beacon P, 1962), 303. Lukács (1885–1971) was a Hungarian Marxist theorist and critic who opposed the modernist turn away from realism because he saw it as undermining political engagement for social change. Sir Walter Scott (1771–1832) was a prolific Scottish historical novelist whose historical realism Lukács praised for fostering a consciousness of history that could lead to revolutionary social change [*Editor*].

he takes history too personally. He cannot function as the unwitting embodiment of historical forces but must be a kind of delectator of historical possibility, positioned at the far side of a century chock-full of historical fiction canonized in the wake of Scott for its ability to narrate collective destiny under the sign (however naturalized) of the nation.[2]

Even more particularly, we can think of Stephen's aesthetic individualism as a mark and symptom of a colonial intellectual's suspicion of the logic of the representative type. * * * *Portrait* modernizes the historical novel for a new century of devolutionary and decentering social and political movements, that is, for historical forces and events that cannot be fit to Lukács's unilinear metanarrative of national emergence. One might say then that Joyce uses Stephen to update the symbolic function of the Scott hero for a heterochronic world of alternative modernities. * * * Joyce operates in the novel under the aegis of national allegory, but not of developmental historicism, with the result that all the buried correspondences between soul and nation are brought to the surface and exposed as semifunctional, sometimes ironized to the point of near breakdown. It is important to emphasize that, however much the would-be iconoclast Stephen imagines himself escaping or opposing nationalism as a creed, he cannot escape the force of nationality as an epistemological precondition for historical being.

If Joyce updates and dialectically transcodes the mode of Scottian historicism, the procedure unfolds at several levels, with the Irish urban novel self-consciously breaking from the gentrified codes of Victorian English fiction; the plot of sexual irresolution opposing both standardized marriage and gendered socialization; the plot of national irresolution opposing the mythic emergence of the nation as the political expression of the people; the narrative of the egoistic cosmopolitan artist breaking from the convention of the representative (national) protagonist; and the *Kunstlerroman*[3] centered on a passive, even decadent, artist-antihero shifting away from the tale of the Political Action Hero à la Scott. The national coding of these shifts is significant: Joyce sees in Scott a Celtic precursor working inside the greater British or Anglophone sphere,

---

2. Along these lines, David Lloyd describes the Irish subject's peculiar relation to history: "Where the colonizer in his modernity appears able to dismiss the past with the easy forgetting of a historicist consciousness, the colonized is always in the position of having too much history, a history that detains and divides him" [*Irish Times: Temporalities of Modernity* (Dublin: Field Day, 2008), 90]. The detaining and dividing interrupt the allegorical subsumption of historicist logic into the body of the *bildungsheld* so that Joyce's adolescent subject cannot square a linear sequence of youth/adulthood with a teleological model of national self-fulfillment.

3. A *Bildungsroman* concerning an artist's growth to maturity (German) [*Editor*].

but he even more openly identifies with a Flaubertian (or Wildean) lineage as against the classic English brand of realism.[4]

Such a reading certainly resonates with Joyce's stated understanding of the difference between Irish and English literature, particularly in the case of the novel. For Joyce, the signal instance of English realism is *Robinson Crusoe*,[5] the novel of self-formation and of British colonial modernity par excellence. *Crusoe* is prophetic, Joyce states, of the centuries of British expansion and colonization that followed it. As Joyce notes in his 1912 lecture "Realism and Idealism in English Literature," *Crusoe* inaugurates the great tradition of English stories centered on an emergent self working in tandem with colonial and economic modernization:

> The true symbol of British conquest is Robinson Crusoe who, shipwrecked on a lonely island, with a knife and a pipe in his pocket, becomes an architect, carpenter, knife-grinder, astronomer, baker, shipwright, potter, saddler, farmer, tailor, umbrella-maker, and cleric. He is the true prototype of the British colonist. (*Occasional* 174)

Crusoe, the hero of modern British imperialism, is also the hero of English realism. He is the maker of his own destiny, literally and physically, and the activist archetype of what Hannah Arendt calls *homo faber* (man the maker),[6] to which Stephen is the ironic colonial antitype. Indeed Stephen seeks both to invert and to usurp the role of *homo faber* in the antidevelopmental story of *Portrait*, first by establishing the passive antihero, then by converting that antihero into a symbolic smith, a forger of national myth, a Daedalian hero for an unheralded race.

If Joyce transvalues the concept of *homo faber* in *Portrait*, it is not just to play on the colonial dynamics of active/passive heroes but to explore the problem of the enunciated and narrated self from the point of view of minor literature or of a colonized relationship to language.[7] The inversions of *Portrait* violate developmental time;

---

4. Although Gustave Flaubert (see note 2, p. 450) was a realist, his writing, like Oscar Wilde's (see p. 335), was highly refined by comparison with English realism. As a French writer, Flaubert was literally outside the British sphere. Although literally inside it, Wilde openly challenged English attitudes and its tradition of realism [*Editor*].

5. Novel (1719) by the English writer Daniel Defoe (c. 1660–1731) [*Editor*].

6. Arendt (1906–1975), a German political philosopher, used this Latin phrase to identify humans as manipulating the environment by means of tools [*Editor*].

7. In *James Joyce and Nationalism* [London: Routledge, 1995], Emer Nolan offers an excellent account of "the uncertain, divided consciousness of the colonial subject, which [Joyce] is unable to articulate in its full complexity outside his fiction" (130). Colonial self-alienation was something Joyce understood as central to Irish culture at large; he wrote that Ireland "entered the British dominion without forming an integral part of it. It almost entirely abandoned its language and accepted the language of the conqueror without being able to assimilate its culture or adapt itself to the mentality of which this language is the vehicle" (*Occasional* 159).

they also—as the masochistic and self-negating elements of Stephen's subject formation suggest—address a type of self-alienation endemic to the colonized position. Faced with this predicament, Stephen self-consciously assumes the mantle of the Irish artist but allocates the burden of Irish iconicity to the people around him (particularly women).[8] Both crones and cronies figure in this game, as Stephen measures his adolescent national ideals against the failings of harridanish Cathleens, secondhand *aislings*,[9] clay-footed men, and vainglorious or politically correct fools that populate his Dublin. Stephen's oedipal/anti-oedipal anxiety about maternal and sexual plots involving women, most of which cast him as the passive or childlike object of a devouring other, are as bound up with his disaffected patriotism as are all the episodes of disavowed male homosociality.

Inspired by his mate Davin's story of a lonely Irish peasant woman on the roadside, Stephen elaborates Davin's adventure into a fantasy for his own private sense of national mission, seeing in his mind's eye the woman "as a type of her race and his own, a batlike soul waking to consciousness of itself in darkness and secrecy and loneliness" [V.330–32]. But in the next moment, Stephen quickly dispels this vision by concentrating on a real Irish girl, a flower seller of "ragged dress and damp coarse hair and hoydenish face" (V.341–42). Even so, he remains taken with the motif of the batlike soul—his and the woman's—folding into his personal mythology the idea of himself as the savior of a shrouded people. He effects a Cartesian separation of the body and mind of Ireland, assigning the former to the predictable female icon and reserving the latter as the basis for his own Parnassian intervention.[1] In other words, Stephen projects himself beyond the logic of the hero who embodies national destiny by imagining himself as the artist who conceives it. This requires not only a kind of self-removal and spiritual exile, but a thwarting of the narrative conventions of the historical novel and the bildungsroman alike. Stephen's mode of fashioning a destiny is to imagine the awakening of an other; he routes his concepts of the future through passive fantasies of self-negation. Joyce thus

8. Christine Froula offers a succinct and critical account of the ways in which Stephen arrogates to himself the feminist critique of patriarchal institutions in Ireland [*Modernism's Body: Sex, Culture, and Joyce* (New York: Columbia UP, 1996), 66–72; reprinted in part on pp. 392–411].

9. Traditional Irish poems that present Ireland in a vision as a woman. "Secondhand" suggests imitated rather than authentic. "Harridanish Cathleens": Irish women who, like Cathleen ni Houlihan, mythical emblem of Ireland, are old. A harridan is a gaunt old woman (*OED*) [*Editor*].

1. "Parnassian": referring to Parnassianism, a French literary movement of the third quarter of the nineteenth century that emphasized strict literary form. "Cartesian": referring to the French philosopher René Descartes (1596–1650), who claimed that body and mind were distinct [*Editor*].

estranges the Goethean project of self-formation, introducing in its place a colonial dialectic of self-possession vexed and vitiated by self-dispossession.

* * * [F]or Joyce we must imagine that a more direct sense of colonial history [by comparison with Virginia Woolf] conditions the critique of male destiny as the symbolic proxy for national emergence. Joyce isolates and reorganizes that symbolic tie between soul and nation, particularly with regard to its traditional narrative destination of self-fulfillment or self-possession. It makes strict formal sense that *Portrait* must hang fire on Stephen's coming of age rather than produce a straightforward or traditional postcolonial novel of emergence (which is what a strictly nationalist cause might see as the desideratum for the Irish novel in 1916). As a result, *Portrait,* with all its idiosyncratic elements marking it off as a creative response to particular aspects of Irish experience, also takes part in a larger modernist project, the critical dismantling of the temporal and allegorical givens of the historical bildungsroman centered in the European nation-states.

The modernizing frame of the industrial nation-state allows the ideal or classic bildungsroman to project a certain synchronization between economic and emergent modernity as the joint horizon of closure. Joyce's *Portrait,* by contrast, is an object lesson in the disjunction between Ireland's political modernity—as ratified by the march toward independent republic status—and its economic conditions—a breach mediated by the cultural and aesthetic projects of the Irish Renaissance.[2] But as a putative "novel of development" *Portrait* has a special status within the Revival or Renaissance era; in its rewiring of the bildungsroman into a novel of pure adolescence it continually signifies the problem of Ireland's own partial or *alternative* modernity.

From *Dubliners* on, Joyce is a keen and cold observer of economic underdevelopment, and of the contradictions between debased and debasing economic conditions on the one hand and the highflying rhetoric of Irish cultural modernity on the other. As he notes in "Ireland, Island of Saints and Sages," "The economic and intellectual conditions of his homeland do not permit the individual to develop" (*Occasional* 123). Irish literary and historical studies of the last many years have centered on the various kinds of anachrony produced by the specific colonial, semicolonial, or metrocolonial conditions of Irish modernity, with special attention to the variations between Irish modernization processes and the norms or standards set by Euro-American narratives of reformation, liberalization, industrialization, secularization, and urbanization. In Attridge

2. See note 3, p. 450 [*Editor*].

and Howes's *Semicolonial Joyce,* one of the best recent treatments of these questions within Joyce studies, Marjorie Howes, Luke Gibbons, and Enda Duffy all address uneven development in Ireland—what Howes defines as the "geographical expression of the contradictions of capital" (Attridge and Howes, 61).[3] In *Dubliners,* Joyce frames that contradiction spatially using the famous structuring motif of paralysis. In *Portrait,* he uses scenes of transit through Dublin to underscore his parodic inversion of the Goethean soulmaking narrative and its cosmopolitan-elite modes of travel. And toward the end, he emphasizes a shift in scale from the hero who leaves behind the provinces for a national capital to the hero who wishes to leave behind a provincialized nation for the metropolitan center.

But flight never quite wins out over nets in *Portrait.* From the perspective of his own expatriated status, Joyce can see that the art of the Irish genius is an art made not from what Cranly jeeringly exposes as a bogus ideal of "unfettered freedom," but from the tension between self-determination and social conditions (V.2544). Joyce does not condescend to Stephen's ideal of a radical individuation that would save him from the burdens of the young Irish artist, but neither does he accept the idea that a workable aesthetic can emerge for Stephen from his dreams of companionless exile. Moreover, Stephen himself offers an oblique aesthetic rationalization of paralysis as stasis, valuing the Aristotelian principle of "arrest" as against the kinesis of plot (desire/loathing).

Of course, Stephen's theory of aesthesis is a tragic-dramatic one, not a narrative one: It is therefore outflanked by or subsumed within the narrative frame. This is not just a theoretical or generic fact about novels, but the topic of what appears to be some of Stephen's most scholasticist contemplation. Drawing from Aquinas,[4] he hypothesizes that even when two people or two cultures apprehend different objects according to different scales of beauty, both are proceeding through certain universal or fixed "stages . . . of all esthetic apprehension" (V.1257–58). His analysis, in other words, depends on breaking the instant of apprehension into a process of stages, so that he recaptures a narrative sequence out of what would seem to be a moment in time. Not surprisingly, Stephen's reflections on aesthetic process conjure for his friend Donovan the thought of Goethe and of Lessing's *Laocoön* (V.1323–25). Donovan's allusion may be shallow, but Joyce's is not: Stephen is working at questions about the relation of temporal to nontemporal art in

3. For a further account of uneven development and cultural anachronism in modern Irish literature, see Terry Eagleton's description of the "archaic avant-garde" [*Heathcliff and the Great Hunger* (London: Verso, 1995), 273–319].
4. See note 7, p. 111 [*Editor*].

the line of Lessing and Goethe just as Joyce is attempting to inter-
polate antinarrative elements into a conventional narrative genre.[5]
If Lessing stands for the attempt to separate art into plastic and
poetic (spatial and temporal) media, Goethe stands in a sense for
the synthesis of the spatial and the temporal in narrative form. The
ghost of Goethe presides quietly over Joyce's attempt to square
developmental and antidevelopmental time. * * * Goethean allusions signal a formal problem and a historical predicament to which
the novel of unseasonable youth seeks to respond.

Even among * * * stalled-adolescent protagonists * * *, Joyce's
Stephen stands for the diagrammatic clarity with which he reorganizes the humanist motif of Goethean destiny. His story is almost
entirely built from minutely subjective responses to the call of the
future: His action is its contemplation. After the spiritual retreat of
chapter 3, a cross and stupefied Stephen consumes a greasy meal
and feels himself a mere "beast that licks its chaps after meat."
"This was the end," he thinks, and gazes out at dull Dublin:

> Forms passed this way and that through the dull light. And
> that was life. The letters of the name of Dublin lay heavily
> upon his mind, pushing one another surlily hither and thither
> with slow boorish insistence. His soul was fattening and con-
> gealing into a gross grease, plunging ever deeper in its dull fear
> into a sombre threatening dusk, while the body that was his
> stood, listless and dishonoured, gazing out of darkened eyes,
> helpless, perturbed and human for a bovine god to stare upon.
> (III.342–50)

Listless and dishonored, Stephen Dedalus stands as an anti-hero
devoid of enterprise and motivation and hope—all the qualities
that define the protagonist in a novel of progress.[6] His soul resonates to the world outside his window. The dullness and dusk of
the city are assimilated to him as features of his own self, reflecting the shared inanition and squalor of ego and city. Disaggre-
gated, the letters D U B L I and N go hither and thither without
purpose or direction—a perfect symbol of the vectorless anachrony of Dublin, signifying moreover the lost animation of Stephen's soul and the slippage from a novel of development to a novel
of antidevelopment.

5. See notes 8–9, p. 186 and note 3, p. 484. Stephen mentions Lessing's treatment of
   visual arts as spatial and literature as temporal without explicitly aligning himself with
   the contrasting synthesis of space and time that Esty ascribes to Goethe. Esty's view of
   Goethe appears to be influenced by Bakhtin's comments on Goethe in relation to the
   Bildungsroman (see note 6, p. 462).
6. As Rebecca Walkowitz points out, the "syntax of 'while' captures the wandering of
   Stephen's mind" and keeps the temporality of the novel at a pitch of irresolution [*Cosmopolitan Style: Modernism Beyond the Nation* (New York: Columbia UP, 2006), 68].

Joyce's techniques for rewiring the bildungsroman are, as we have seen, inflected by a distinctive Irish experience of colonial modernity, but he also inherits many of the same historical and literary-historical conditions that shaped the work of Woolf, Wells, Wilde, Conrad, Schreiner, and Kipling.[7] In all these cases, prolonged or lingering youth embodies an antidevelopmental logic that registers not only the moralized or eschatological time of the nation and its imperial extension (development to a fixed point of political actualization), but the open-ended and boundless time of capitalism in the age of empire. Seeking to assimilate the open yet uneven form of postnational development, Joyce must confront the same kind of closural problem that bedeviled most of these earlier writers: What kind of terminal plot makes sense in the face of a never-ending narrative of modernization, especially once the chronotope[8] of national *Bildung* has been demystified or disqualified? More precisely, what kind of narrative maneuvers can represent both the infinity of world-historical development and the residual time-shaping power of the organicized nation (and its symbolic familiar, the biographical novel)?

In one of his visionary moments, Stephen seems to recognize the root problem in the narrative of endless becoming or pure potential; listening to the music of his soul, he seems almost to make a sly address to the formal problematic of the novel itself:

> It was an elfin prelude, endless and formless; and, as it grew wilder and faster, the flames leaping out of time, he seemed to hear from under the boughs and grasses wild creatures racing. (IV.641–44).

On the surface, this music reflects Stephen's wayward instincts, but the flames and hoofbeats of an amorphous and boundless energy also describe the Joycean narrative itself, straining to manage the infinite with some token of the finite. The language of Stephen's grandiosity is the same language that records for the reader the danger of formlessness: if Stephen's horizons are ever-enlarging and ever-receding, no lines can finally be crossed, no act fully realized. His own experience stands and remains as an "elfin prelude" to some larger achievement. By this light, the novel itself comes to seem an elfin prelude not just by extratextual reference to *Ulysses*, but by its own operations, in which moments—however epiphanic— keep melting into their own failed immanence, paling before the vast

---

7. Joseph Rudyard Kipling (1865–1936) English writer, the author of *Kim* (1901). Olive Schreiner (1855–1920), South African writer, the author of *Story of an African Farm* (1883) [*Editor*].
8. The interrelationship of time and space forming the language of a particular literary genre. A term used by M. M. Bakhtin (see note 6, p. 462).

potentialities that extend out of them, and beyond them. * * * *Portrait* devolves, from this perspective, into a long ironic prelude * * *.

Since a novel that never ends (and never begins) is an impossible artifact, an antidevelopmental fiction must in some sense adapt the metabildungsroman strategy of writing not beyond, but about, the contradictions of the national coming-of-age tale.[9] The antidevelopmental logic so thoroughly tested in *Portrait* situates Stephen at a modernist switchpoint where a double temporal register is needed, one that incorporates without synthesizing the moralized time of progress (soul and nation) and the empty time of pure chronos,[1] manifested in the endless revolutions of global modernity. But if this is a logic immanent to the text, it is not a "resolution" or synthesis available to Stephen Dedalus himself. Arrested forever at the threshold of flight, Stephen is interred in his diary, not self-actualized by it or in it.[2] In this sense, even with his Promethean intellect afire, Stephen is * * * closer in his frozen youth to death than to life.

9. Pericles Lewis assesses the function of Stephen as a national redeemer, arguing that "in embracing his moral unity with the Irish race, he will reconcile his ethical self with his socially constructed identity"; however, Lewis goes on to note that "Joyce's own attitude towards this ideal [of the individual who redeems the nation] seems to have been more complex and ambivalent than Stephen's" (48). I would emphasize the second portion of that interpretive stance, and suggest that Joyce's ironization of Stephen reveals the hubris of Stephen's epigenetic conception of himself as the self-made redeemer of a new nation.
1. Chronos (Greek) means time. Pure chronos would presumably be time unstructured by social attitudes, such as those supporting the notion of progress [*Editor*].
2. Patricia [Meyer] Spacks offers a forceful account of the novel as a failed bildungsroman in which Stephen progresses very little: "Stephen yields nothing of his youthful romanticism, he grows out of nothing. Instead, he grows more fully into a self of boyish ardency, boyish self-absorption, boyish conviction of infinite possibility. He refuses to grow up. Should we deplore or applaud?" [*The Adolescent Idea: Mythos of Youth and the Adult Imagination* (New York: Basic Books, 1981), 254–55].

DANIEL AURELIANO NEWMAN

A *Portrait of the Artist* as a 'Biologist in Words': Language, Epiphany and Atavistic *Bildung*†

> A developing organism is . . . a system struggling with the help of its ancestral tendencies to survive and to convert itself into successive viable shapes.
> —Gavin de Beer, 'Embryology and Evolution'[1]

'In the history of words there is much that indicates the history of men', writes James Joyce as a student at University College. This history, he continues, is forged by a vanguard of literary master-pieces, 'landmarks in the transition of a language, keeping it inviolate, directing its course straight on like an advancing way, widening and improving as it advances but staying always on the high road'.[2] Joyce's enthusiastic rhetoric of national destiny, perfectibility and imperialism may seem surprising in light of his later writings, which would so playfully yet forcefully attack notions of historical progressivism. But these are the words of a youth seventeen or eighteen years old, written for the approval of a schoolmaster. Anyhow, Joyce would soon disavow them, submitting the parallels between development, evolution, history and philology to increasingly byzantine travesties and parodies.

'Oxen of the Sun'[3] offers a stark case, with its overdetermined parallelism of fertilisation, embryological development, parturition, biological and linguistic evolutions, and progressive inebriation. Its seemingly linear structure conceals numerous reversions, which produce a humorous yet urgent critique of recapitulation theory.[4] * * *

---

† From *Modernist Life Histories: Biological Theory and the Experimental Bildungsroman.* (Edinburgh: Edinburgh UP, 2019), pp. 54–70, 72–73, 75–79. Reprinted with permission of Edinburgh University Press through PLSclear. Some of the author's notes have been omitted. Bibliographic information has been supplied in editorial brackets and footnotes. Page references for *A Portrait* have been replaced with part and line numbers of this Norton Critical Edition. Some cited passages might differ slightly from the equivalent passages in this volume.

1. In Gavin de Beer, ed., *Evolution: Essays on Aspects of Evolutionary Biology* (Oxford, Eng.: Clarendon, 1938), 63. Reprinted with permission of Oxford UP [*Editor*].
2. "The Study of Languages," *Critical Writings of James Joyce,* ed. Ellsworth Mason and Richard Ellmann (New York: Viking, 1959), 28–29 [*Editor*].
3. Episode 14 of *Ulysses,* in which Joyce imitates in a chronological sequence well-known styles of English literature [*Editor*].
4. The theory of recapitulation, sometimes called the biogenetic law, involves centrally the claim that ontogeny recapitulates phylogeny, that is, that individual creatures develop in size and structure through stages that mimic the evolutionary history of their species. "Ontology recapitulates phylogeny" originated with the German zoologist and philosopher Ernst Haeckel (1834–1919) [*Editor*].

Superimposing the history of English prose and the growth of 'Stephen the embryo' (as Joyce put it to Frank Budgen),[5] 'Oxen of the Sun' is a condensed rewriting of Joyce's earlier *Bildungsroman*.[6] Like 'Oxen', if less outrageously, *A Portrait of the Artist* uses gestation as an ordering principle and likewise uses a stylistic progression to formalise its thematic focus on development. * * *

* * * *A Portrait* engages covertly with the embryological and evolutionary biology more visibly exploited in 'Oxen'. * * * [For earlier critics of *A Portrait*] recapitulation serves as a metaphorical rather than literal connection between the novel and biological theories of development. * * * The critical readiness to overlook biology's potential interpretive contributions has obscured some of Joyce's crucial manoeuvres in his modernist reformulation of *Bildung*.

Though most recent critics read *A Portrait* as a critique or reformulation of the genre, it is sometimes read as a straightforward *Bildungsroman*. In structure and theme, indeed, the novel rather closely follows the generic outline of the classical *Bildung* plot. * * * [However, Stephen's] epiphanies puncture rather than propel the linear *Bildung* plot, allowing the past (personal, historical, evolutionary) to check the momentum of Stephen's progressive development. The implications of these checks are neither simply psychoanalytical nor merely antiquarian: they put Joyce's formal strategies into inextricable relation to his thematic treatment of literary history, colonialism and racial origins.

There are, in this sense, more affinities between *A Portrait* and the later novels than critics of earlier generations might have believed. * * * *Portrait* already torqued the classical *Bildung* plot. Despite its apparent linearity, the narrative is riddled with reversions, many of them triggered by Stephen's epiphanies. The seemingly chronological plot is crossed-stitched with what Kevin Ohi calls 'queer atavism—by unrealizable worlds, reticulated and non-subordinated developments, and non-communicating cells'[7]— though I might generalise it here as modernist atavism. If Joyce's novel endorses the ideal of *Bildung*, the form it generates in order to narrate Stephen's development nevertheless abjures the chronology, gradualism and recapitulatory structure of the classical *Bildung* plot.

In progressivist models of history, the past serves as anchor and spur for the individual's forward development, but this past must be past. The retention or return of past forms is thus a pathological

5. *Letters of James Joyce,* Vol. I, ed. Stuart Gilbert (New York: Viking, 1957, rev. 1966), 140 [*Editor*].
6. See note 3, p. 429 [*Editor*].
7. *Dead Letters Sent: Queer Literary Transmission* (Minneapolis: U of Minnesota P, 2015), 91 [*Editor*].

reversal, an atavism. And such reversals are exactly what happen, time and again, to Stephen's development. Throughout *A Portrait*, Stephen experiences what he interprets as setbacks in the fulfilment of the artistic 'end he had been born to serve' (IV.634). These checks less often come from the external world than most theories of the *Bildungsroman* would predict; though not unaffected by familial and social realities, Stephen rolls rather well with the world's punches. What really frustrates his aspirations are internal events, almost all of them involving a private encounter with sexuality and reproduction, at the locus of convergence between the artistic mind and 'the bestial part of the body able to understand bestially and desire bestially' (III.1340–41).

This convergence occurs in and through language. For Stephen, verbal mastery in speech and in art amounts to a transcendence of the 'sensible world', to an ascension to a pure and spiritual 'inner world of individual emotions' (IV.700–702). In classical theories of *Bildung*, language plays a central role in channelling development from the body upwards to the successively higher levels of mind and spirit; the child's growing linguistic competence therefore evidences a growing capacity for disembodied abstract thought and aesthetic and spiritual experience. Max Müller famously argued that 'language is the Rubicon which divides man from beast' as part of his anti-evolutionary belief that 'the science of language will yet enable us to withstand the extreme theories of the Darwinians, and to draw a hard and fast line between man and brute'.[8] As Tecumseh Fitch puts it, 'Müller effectively substituted "language" for the soul that played the key distinguishing role in earlier religion and philosophy'.[9] Other post-Darwinian linguists incorporated language acquisition into the great system of recapitulation * * *. For [Ernst] Haeckel, language acquisition was in fact more than just another proof of his biogenetic law: the apparent fact that language acquisition recapitulates glossogeny (language evolution) supplied a keystone for his monistic philosophy, bridging animal morphology with human culture.

There is thus a specific logic behind Stephen Dedalus's ambition to use a *verbal* art to 'forg[e] . . . out of the sluggish matter of the earth a new soaring impalpable imperishable being' (IV.780–81). Language, as he sees it, will propel him to maturity and purity, away from childhood, animality, the body and sexuality. * * *

---

8. Quoted in Tecumseh Fitch, *The Evolution of Language* (Cambridge, Eng.: Cambridge UP, 2010), 395. Müller's disagreement with Darwin specifically concerned the possibility that language usage as a human practice could have developed from animal language. Müller was motivated to blunt the force of nineteenth-century intellectual developments that resulted in skepticism about religious faith [*Editor*].
9. Fitch, 395 [*Editor*].

[H]owever, Joyce had his doubts about recapitulation and wished 'to attack with drawn sword'.[1] His *Bildungsroman* consequently ensures that language never sheds the materiality which Stephen so fervently denies. Try as he might to isolate language from the body, words persist in mediating between the realm of art and the sexual, reproductive body.[2] Given the Manichean linkage of body with gross animality and language with mind and spirit, the intercalation of bodily and linguistic stages of Stephen's development effectively confuses the parallel lines of progressive change demanded by recapitulation.

Throughout *A Portrait* and his oeuvre, Joyce exults in transgressing boundaries between the primitive and the civilised, merging human and animal, sacred and secular, high and low, Symbolist and Naturalist,[3] beautiful and ugly. Joyce deploys language against Stephen's idealistic notions of development, staging his experience with words not as stepping-stones to the future but as reversions 'back into the perambulator' (V.2221)—and back into ancestry. The medium of Stephen's chosen art puts paid to the comforting belief that 'the past was past', as he tells himself after his climactic confession (III.1581–82). The past survives actively in the present, either in literal remainders or in displaced form. While the text of *A Portrait*, tightly focalised through Stephen, is good at concealing the marks of the body and its foetal, historical and animal residues, these are ironically preserved in their linguistic analogue.

Rather than moving inexorably and irreversibly from body to mind to spirit, Joyce's *Bildung* plot is grounded in a language encrusted with reversions. Ironically, the modern form of expression sought by Stephen is atavistic.[4] Within the framework of recapitulation

---

1. James Joyce, *Joyce in Padua*, ed. and trans. Louis Berrone (New York: Random House, 1977), 19 [*Editor*].
2. In 'Language, Sex, and the Remainder in *A Portrait*', Derek Attridge stresses 'the relation between implicit sexuality and overt attention to language, especially to single words' [in Derek Attridge, *Joyce Effects: On Language, Theory, and History* (Cambridge, Eng.: Cambridge UP, 2000), 64]. Brook Miller [*Self-Consciousness in Modern British Fiction* (New York: Palgrave Macmillan, 2013)] devotes a chapter to Stephen's inability to grasp the hylomorphism of body and soul [the union of body and soul. *Hylomorphism* is a nineteenth-century term for the ancient Greek philosopher Aristotle's notion that being is compounded of matter and form—*Editor*]. These readings, and mine, are consistent with Jessica Berman's view that *A Portrait*'s 'intensely heteroglossic' narrative consistently exceeds and ironises the limitations of Stephen's individual perspective [*Modernist Commitments: Ethics, Politics, and Transnational Modernism* (New York: Columbia UP, 2011), 122] [*Author*]. *Heteroglossia* is the term that the Russian literary theorist M. M. Bakhtin (1895–1975) used for the layered convergence of varied worldviews in novelistic discourse [*Editor*].
3. The late nineteenth-century European movement in literature and the arts known as Symbolism strove to present immutable truths through images and language not limited to everyday realities. By contrast, the Naturalist movement of the same period focused on material and social realities [*Editor*].
4. In *Stephen Hero* Stephen calls himself 'modern', prompting Cranly to dismiss the difference between 'ancient' and 'modern' [James Joyce, *Stephen Hero* (London: Jonathan Cape, 1969), 190 and 190–91]. When Stephen counters that 'the modern spirit is

theory, atavism is the result of an incomplete ontogeny, one which has failed to work through its full phylogenetic itinerary. Atavism is thus inimical to the classical *Bildungsroman* as a chronicle of modern subject formation. * * * Dana Seitler clearly identifies the threats atavism poses to the modes of identity formation which structure the genre. As a 'mixed temporal entity', the atavistic body 'produces modern subjectivity as less certain, less determinedly structured by the idea of continual progress'; as a remainder of the 'unenlightened, uncivilized, stateless time of human prehistory',[5] atavism confounds the individual's movement towards 'enlightenment', defined by Kant, in the language of *Bildung*, as 'man's emergence from his self-immaturity'.[6] Though Stephen Dedalus writes in his diary that 'the past is consumed in the present' and thus 'brings forth the future' (V.2718–20), Joyce's novel models a radically different relationship between past and present.

A *Portrait* resists the recapitulatory structure of the classical *Bildungsroman*, as well as Stephen's desire to transcend the bodily, by forcing the archaic and animal to coexist, albeit tensely, with the modern and artistic. Rather than rejecting the ideal of *Bildung*, however, the novel's unsettling marriage of sexuality, language and artistic self-cultivation represents one of modernism's most pointed reminders that the body participates in and throughout the process of self-formation. Its participation manifests as a reversion in *A Portrait* nonetheless because it must contend throughout the narrative, but especially in the later chapters, with a philosophical tradition and generic expectations which view the body as a primitive precursor to the emergence of civilised, spiritual maturity. From this perspective, the body's active part in Stephen's development continues long after it should have been abandoned in favour of more grown-up concerns.

These reversions manifest primarily in two closely related forms. The first is in Stephen's response to language, which far from striking him as pure, abstract or spiritual, affects him erotically and carnally. The second is the epiphany,[7] an aesthetic response whose effect on the narrative is to put the plot on hold. Various critics have variously named the resulting pauses. Tobias Boes, like me,

---

vivisective' whereas 'the ancient spirit' accepted ideas on faith, Cranly significantly asks, 'I suppose you do know that Aristotle founded the science of biology' [*Stephen Hero* 190–91]. Atavism is the "resemblance to grand-parents or more remote ancestors rather than to parents; tendency to reproduce the ancestral type in animals or plants" (*OED*) [*Editor*].

5. Dana Seitler, *Atavistic Tendencies: The Culture of Science in American Modernity* (Minneapolis: U of Minnesota P, 2008), 66 [*Editor*].
6. Immanuel Kant, *Political Writings*, 2nd Ed., ed. H. S. Reiss, trans. H. B. Nisbet (Cambridge, Eng.: Cambridge UP, 2003), 54 [*Editor*].
7. See note 6, p. 402 [*Editor*].

calls them epiphanies.[8] * * * Whatever they are called, these epiphanies are consistently triggered by language (thus the two forms of
reversion mentioned above are in fact one). This fact seems to have
escaped critical attention. Nor have critics noted that Stephen's
epiphanies involve various forms of temporal regression, awakening
his cultural and animal memories from 'the slumber of centuries'
(II.1425). For despite what Stephen implies in his aesthetic theory,
epiphanies may arrest movement but they are not timeless. As the
narrator describes them, epiphanies drag Stephen's thoughts or
emotions back in time, either into personal flashbacks or into
visions of the historical or pre-historical past. Thus Stephen sees
through the 'strange eyes' [I.436] of his younger self and of his fore-
bears, both human and 'infrahuman' (IV.709). A fascinating corol-
lary emerges from this interpretation: Stephen's epiphanies have a
material origin (in the senses and the body) but an apparently transcendental effect—a seamless merger of Symbolist and Naturalist
ideas producing a distinctly modernist aesthetic.

My interpretation of words as a reversionary force suggests a
partial solution to the problem of ironic distance which has long
troubled readers of A Portrait. It is only from Stephen's perspective
that the flesh represents entrapment and the frustration of Bildung;
Joyce's text, by contrast, celebrates the sexual body which connects
'the history of words' to 'the history of men'.[9] While Stephen envi-
sions his artistic development as a forward and upward line from
flesh to spirit, the narrative stages his encounters with words as a
series of atavistic returns to the animal body. * * * [W]ords subvert
Stephen's desired developmental trajectory in A Portrait. Figured as
a large embodied archive, language refuses to be mastered in the
service of Stephen's artistic destiny or reduced to a 'progress' from
'lyrical' through 'epical' to 'dramatic' modes [V.1444–58]. Language
pulls his growth as an artist off the rails of any predetermined historical template.

Language Acquisition and A Portrait's Ontogenetic Structure

A Portrait's structure mirrors Stephen's developing consciousness,[1]
and because his sense of reality is primarily linguistic, the clearest

---

8. For Boes's essay, see p. 459 [Editor].
9. Joyce, "The Study of Language," 28 [Editor].
1. The correlation between style, psychic development and gestation was first noted
   by Stanislaus Joyce [My Brother's Keeper, ed. Richard Ellmann (Cambridge, MA: Da
   Capo, 2003), 17] then developed into a critical framework by Sidney Feshbach ["A Slow
   and Dark Birth: A Study of the Organization of A Portrait of the Artist as a Young Man,"
   James Joyce Quarterly 4:4 (1967): 289–300] and by Richard Ellmann [James Joyce
   (Oxford, Eng.: Oxford UP, 1965), 307]. Critics of all theoretical stripes have followed
   suit * * *.

marker of his development is language. Stephen's consciousness emerges from the stream of language with which he interacts, privately in his mind, in dialogue with others and in literature. As in most *Bildungsromane*, Stephen's ontogeny unfolds over the course of the story's duration spanning infancy to young adulthood. But Joyce, who offers few objective markers of passing time, allows this progression to be expressed—and, by readers, experienced—mainly through stylistic changes in the discourse. * * *

Because the narrator's syntax and style grow ever more complex, Stephen may seem to be maturing progressively, irreversibly, as expected given the narrative grammar of *Bildung* and, as we have seen, of recapitulation. Yet the maturing style also provides the best record of the ongoing embodied nature of Stephen's development. Language implicates the body from the very beginning of the novel and, despite Stephen's pretensions, does so to the end. In the opening vignette, the toddler Stephen tries to sing '*O, the wild rose blossoms*' only to produce '*O, the geen wothe botheth*' (I.12); his lack of verbal control marks the written text as a production of still clumsy oral organs. * * * Seeking direct access to 'the features of infancy' * * *, Joyce *shows* the fumbling productions of Stephen's infant tongue, presenting the passage of time not teleologically but as 'a fluid succession of presents'.[2]

Painting a series of experiential portraits, Joyce couples development and thus narrative structure with Stephen's sensory and perceptual world (that muddy zone between mind and body) and with his anatomy (his immature vocal apparatus). The opening passage's sensuousness reflects a mind almost wholly constituted by perception. Stephen soon masters speech enough to hide its patent link with his mouth and throat, but whenever he tries to express himself, to forge an identity and destiny for himself, the language he has inherited dampens his forward momentum with a contrary impulse, as if to 'revert at once to its physiological and its cultural roots'.[3] His fascination with language remains ineluctably embodied, either directly through its vocal production or indirectly through its impact on the emotions and physical desire. Stephen cannot help but connect language with excremental and sexual functions, through which it consistently marks the presence of the flesh. Joyce was a 'biologist in words' long before Beckett coined the epithet in 1929.[4]

---

2. James Joyce, "A Portrait of the Artist" [narrative essay], *The Workshop of Daedalus: James Joyce and the Raw Materials for* A Portrait of the Artist as a Young Man, ed. Robert Scholes and Richard M. Kain (Evanston, IL: Northwestern UP, 1965), 60 [*Editor*].
3. Derek Attridge, *Joyce Effects: On Language, Theory, and History* (Cambridge, Eng.: Cambridge UP, 2000), 66 [*Editor*].
4. Samuel Beckett, "Dante . . . Bruno . . . Vico . . . Joyce," in *Our Exagmination Round his Factification for Incamination of Work in Progress* (1929; London Faber & Faber, 1961), 19 [*Editor*].

Decisive moments in Stephen's development are consistently marked by the turbulent convergence of language and biology. Just before accepting his artistic destiny, Stephen sees some school-fellows bathing in the sea. He is pained to see 'the signs of adolescence' revealed by 'their pitiable nakedness' because they mirror his own physical transformation, reminding him 'in what dread he stood of the mystery of his own body' (IV.762–63). Such reminders are inconvenient for a budding artist who cannot fathom art in the bodily realm. To neutralise the physical affinity with his peers, then, Stephen appeals to his linguistic superiority. Yoking the bathers' bodies to their 'banter', he uses his own 'formal[ity] in speech' (V.229) as a fulcrum for distinguishing himself. His speech is so different that the bodily likeness can only be deceptive! Having established this difference, he can smugly reflect on 'how characterless they looked' (IV.755) compared with his own self-conscious individuality. Thus de-individuated, viewed 'collectively', the boys and their 'banter' confirm 'his mild proud sovereignty' (IV.766–67). Stephen can then reconceive his physical puberty as a spiritual metamorphosis from puerile body to mature spirit: 'His soul had arisen from the grave of boyhood, spurning her graveclothes' (IV.809–10). As Joyce presents it, however, this developmental vision is unmistakably one of Stephen's protective delusions.

Immediately after the swimming boys, he sees a girl and imaginatively transforms her 'into the likeness of a strange and beautiful seabird' (IV.855–56). She resists his spiritual vision, however, with an overdetermined reminder of her bodily reality: 'her long slender bare legs were delicate as a crane's and pure save where an emerald trail of seaweed had fashioned itself as a sign upon the flesh' (IV.856–59). Stephen tries to refine the girl's 'boldly' [IV.862] exposed thighs out of existence, anticipating his thoughts 'on the correspondence of birds to things of the intellect' [V.1798–99] and, in the figure of ibis-headed 'Thoth, the god of writers' (V.1810), on the rarefied realm of literature. But the seaweed mars the illusion of sexual purity and pure language, demonstrating that language may conceal the body like clothing but, like clothing, cannot erase it and may even emphasise its sexual allure.

Throughout the novel, the carnality of language fuses the novel's form and content. The changing prose styles literally incorporate its developmental plot. The novel's structural mechanics are therefore visible in the behaviour of individual words and motifs—some words and motifs more than others. Though Stephen finds all words 'mysteriously alive,'[5] the liveliest are those relating to sex and

5. Frank Budgen, *James Joyce and the Making of* Ulysses (Bloomington: Indiana UP, 1960), 57 [*Editor*].

reproduction. In this context, the encounter with 'foetus' is catalytic; more than any other moment in the novel, it reveals the interpenetration of developmental and reproductive dynamics, a permeability which unsettles his aspiration to follow the classical route to *Bildung*. From the moment of the encounter onwards, Stephen will consistently translate language into sexual thoughts and reactions. This translation is unbidden and disturbing, laying bare the sensuality and materiality of the medium he strives to spiritualise. Stephen's reaction to 'foetus' is visceral, betraying the body's oneness with the mind: thus the word 'startled his blood', and Stephen is 'shocked'

> to find in the outer world a trace of what he had deemed till then a brutish and individual malady of his own mind. His monstrous reveries came thronging into his memory. They too had sprung up before him, suddenly and furiously, out of mere words. (II.1065–69)

'*Foetus*' is the objective correlative of his adolescent fantasies: it expresses what his animal body sensed only dumbly, and it answers his 'wondering' about where—'from what den of monstrous images' (II.1071–72)—his lust originates. Though he will later admit that true art can excite sexual emotions, acknowledging that 'I also am an animal', he nevertheless persists in quarantining his animal nature in favour of 'a mental world' (V.1136) where language is purified and disembodied. Being 'monstrous', however, the images elicited by 'foetus' refuse to cooperate with Stephen's dualism. * * * His sexual 'thoughts', 'reveries', and 'dreams' may be in the mind, but they bear the mark of the flesh and the beast. Stephen founds his mythic identity on the invention of human flight, but Daedalus was also responsible for the monstrous hybrid Minotaur.[6]
 * * * *Portrait* ties dirty words to the sexual body and, in spite of Stephen, to art. Readings of a novel, *The Count of Monte Cristo*, frame his visits to Nighttown[7] and his tendency to connect lust with utterance: 'a cry for an iniquitous abandonment, a cry which was but the echo of an obscene scrawl which he had read on the oozing wall of a urinal' (II.1411–13). He seeks an outlet for 'the wasting fires of lust' which figure as 'soft speeches', 'verses pass[ing] from his lips', 'inarticulate cries', 'unspoken brutal words' and a 'murmur' (II.1392–94; 1403). Though these vocal and verbal manifestations of lust might suggest Freudian displacement, they do not protect him from unconscious desires or from his 'humiliating sense of transgression' (II.1373). Rather than transcending the sexual body,

---

6. See note 1, p. 3 [*Editor*].
7. See note 4, p. 465. *The Count of Monte Cristo*: See note 5, p. 54 [*Editor*].

his language is mired in it. This reversionary dynamic recalls Joseph Valente's reading of the Nighttown passage, which links Stephen's conflicted feelings about dirty water to the novel's resistance to the 'Bildungsmythos of a young man's self-conscious graduation from homosexual play to heterosexual maturity and (re)productivity.' In its place Joyce stages 'a progressive overlapping and interfolding of sexual preferences' [that affect Stephen's development; for Valente's essay, see p. 411]. My focus on embodied language suggests that the complicating effects of same-sex desire on the Bildung plot, so persuasively diagnosed by Valente, are only one manifestation of the novel's reversionary dynamics; according to recapitulation theory, homosexuality is one of many forms of developmental arrest at a pre-mature, atavistic stage.

* * * Stephen's encounter with 'Foetus' is formative. It fuses word and lust, cementing the bonds between reproductive flesh and creative mind which inform the rest of the narrative. From now on, his mind will insistently excavate traces of the sexual body from words and literature. * * *

Yet Stephen persists in imagining 'his spiritual progress' (IV.59) as the progressive mastery of words and the transcendence of the flesh. In his religious phase, he finds solace in 'the simple fact that God had loved his soul from all eternity, for ages before he had been born into the world, for ages before the world itself had existed' (IV.76–78)—that is, when he was bodiless, all soul. After baring his body to the pleasures of Nighttown, the devotional Stephen pictures his 'spiritual progress' as a different kind of undressing. Rather than expose his flesh, he imagines casting it off

> as if his very body were being divested with ease of some outer skin or peel. He had felt a subtle, dark, and murmurous presence penetrate his being and fire him with a brief iniquitous lust: it, too, had slipped beyond his grasp leaving his mind lucid and indifferent. (IV.85–89)

Likening spiritual awakening to the metamorphosis of a butterfly, which emerges from the chrysalis having completely reabsorbed and reorganised its larval body, Stephen deludes himself that he is unconnected to his own childhood self. Later in the novel, when he notes his mother 'remembers the time of her childhood', he admits only doubtfully that she also remembers 'mine if I was ever a child' (V.2717–18). For all his desire to cordon off the past in the past, Stephen faces opposition from a text whose distinctive use of motif supplies not only the forward momentum generated from the accumulation of repetitions,[8] but also a reciprocal backward impulse.

8. See Boes, 459–60.

After his confession, Stephen's 'lucid and indifferent' state may flatter his sense of having progressed beyond the temptations of the flesh, but a textual déjà vu suggests otherwise. When he was a habitual visitor of Nighttown, a strikingly similar 'cold lucid indifference reigned in his soul' (III.47). Together, the two instances of lucid indifference, the debauched and the devotion, generate a rather hybrid aesthetics in which the artist is simultaneously disembodied and embodied, 'within or behind or beyond or above his handiwork, invisible, refined out of existence, indifferent, paring his fingernails' (V.1467–69). In theory Stephen refines all sensuousness from aesthetics, but his *experience* of artistic creation as 'the word . . . made flesh' 'in the virgin womb of the imagination' (V.1543) is hilariously sexual. Writing his villanelle may have 'kindled again his soul', but its generation in the afterglow of a wet dream also 'fulfill[s] all his body' (V.1740–41).

* * * It is one of Joyce's abiding ironies that Stephen persists in his distrust and disgust of the flesh: the more the budding poet engages with words, the more insistently they lead back to the body.

Epiphany as Atavism

Stephen builds his future on words, but those words force him back into the past. When he hears 'kiss' and 'suck', he relives his mother's bedtime kiss and the hotel lavatory. * * * Such flashbacks, being personal, require no appeal to evolutionary theory; they resemble Proust's[9] or other kindred models of unconscious memory. Other words bring Stephen deeper in time, back before his birth, his historical era or even his species. In these cases memory is an insufficient explanation. 'Foetus' reveals a past Stephen never saw: in the empty anatomy theatre 'he seemed to feel the absent students about him . . . A vision of their life, which his father's words had been powerless to evoke, sprang up before him out of the word cut in the desk' (II.1051–55). In the pub afterwards, Stephen feels older than his father's peers (II.1260), as if his epiphany had tapped him into 'the conscience of [his] race' (V.2790).

* * *

To investigate the reversionary power of language and its effects on Stephen's *Bildung*, let us turn to a long passage in the fifth chapter. Having just observed how his friend Cranly reacts to a 'gross name' ('ballocks') [V.2048, 2035], then watched his love interest Emma pass by, Stephen recites to himself a line of sixteenth-century

9. In his novel *À la recherche du temps perdu* (*In Search of Lost Time*) (1913–1927), the French writer Marcel Proust (1871–1922) presented intense instances of involuntary memory [*Editor*].

verse, misremembering Thomas Nashe's 'Brightness falls from the air' as 'Darkness falls from the air' (V.2125, 2078). The misquotation initiates a narrative pause, and in the long description which follows Stephen experiences a vivid and multi-staged immersion into Elizabethan times. At first the words evoke a 'trembling joy, lambent as a faint light', but they inevitably grow monstrous with 'the darkness of desire': 'What was their languid grace but the softness of chambering?' he wonders (V.2089–90). Earlier in the same chapter, the thought of 'chambering' had 'stung his monkish pride' and spoiled the 'pleasure' he seeks in lyrics such as Ben Jonson's 'I was not wearier where I lay'. A seemingly innocent distraction from the 'spectral words of Aristotle and Aquinas' the pleasure Stephen finds in 'the dainty songs of the Elizabethans' is a slippery slope, leading inexorably to the 'shadow under the windows of that age' to 'a phrase, tarnished by time, of chambering and false honour' (V.86–95). From Nashe's lyric the immersion into Elizabethan times is more intensely sensorial:

> he tasted in the language of memory ambered wines, dying fallings of sweet airs, the proud pavan, and saw with the eyes of memory kind gentlewomen in Covent Garden wooing from their balconies with sucking mouths and the pox-fouled wenches of the taverns and young wives that, gaily yielding to their ravishers, clipped and clipped again. (V.2092–97)

Though 'dainty' (V.89), the Elizabethan lyrics are infected by (and infectious with) the sordidness and sexual obsessions of their age. * * * Stephen's lovely 'ambered wines' are perverted by the 'pox-fouled wenches' whose sexuality and allure are fossilised along with the beauty in the lyrics he admires.

The passage takes a remarkable turn when Stephen's increasingly sexual vision of Elizabethan times combines with the lingering smell of Emma: 'Vaguely first and then more sharply he smelt her body. A conscious unrest seethed in his blood. Yes, it was her body he smelt, a wild and languid smell, the tepid limbs over which his music had flowed desirously' (V.2105–09). Nashe's song has ineluctably led Stephen's mind to sex. His sensitivity to Emma's odour, harkening back to his mother's 'nicer smell' (I.15), is also a reversion to a deeper, pre-human past. Olfactory arousal was in Joyce's time frequently listed as an atavism, and as Havelock Ellis argues in *Sexual Selection in Man*, 'the grosser manifestations of sexual allurement by smell belong, so far as man is concerned, to a remote animal past which we have outgrown.' Nevertheless, Ellis adds, 'the latent possibilities of sexual allurement by olfaction . . . still remain ready to be called into play', especially in 'exceptional and abnormal persons' who include, as he notes earlier, 'poets and novelists.'[1]

Perversion begets perversion: the associations triggered by Nashe snowball and grow ever more bestial. As Emma's smell fades, leaving the image of 'the secret soft linen upon which her flesh distilled odour and a dew' (V.2109–10), a louse appears on Stephen's neck. As though generated by his arousal, or by the allusion to 'dew' (a Joycean euphemism for semen), the insect reminds Stephen that lice were once thought to be 'born of human sweat' (V.2117), products of the body which

> were not created by God with the other animals on the sixth day. But the tickling of the skin of his neck made his mind raw and red. The life of his body, ill clad, ill fed, louse-eaten, made him close his eyelids in a sudden spasm of despair and in the darkness he saw the brittle bright bodies of lice falling from the air and turning often as they fell . . . He had not even remembered rightly Nash's line. All the images it had awakened were false. His mind bred vermin. (V.2117–27)

So close on the heels of Emma's odorous passage, mere hours after the composition of the Symbolist villanelle, the louse and its association with Nashe's poem is the novel's ironic riposte to Stephen's opposition of sex and art. The louse further bestialises Stephen's initially idyllic vision of Elizabethans, lending a vampiric and entomological allure to the 'kind gentlewomen . . . with sucking mouths' (V.2094–95), and reminding us that Nashe's song, 'In Time of Pestilence', is a report from a time of plague (a disease transmitted by fleas, another insect with sucking mouthparts, one with a long history in erotic poetry). Steven Connor, in his wonderful essay on flies in Beckett, calls the louse an 'anomaly-animal' along with other 'imperfect creatures' which confound philosophical systems, taxonomies and moral hierarchies because they 'do not belong to created nature'.[2] Joyce's louse enables reality to counteract Stephen's bias towards the idealist aspect of *Bildung* with its dialogic counterpart in bodily existence—what Michael Minden calls 'the body's insistent refusal to coincide with the products of the mind, of social, historical or philosophical consciousness'.[3] 'Lice', notes Jean-Michel Rabaté, 'embody the stubborn resistance of nature or the

1. Havelock Ellis, *Studies in the Psychology of Sex: Sexual Selection in Man* (Philadelphia: Davis, 1905), 110–11, 73 [*Editor*].
2. Steven Connor, *Beckett, Modernism and the Material Imagination* (Cambridge, Eng.: Cambridge UP, 2014), 60, 48 [*Editor*].
3. Michael Minden, *The German Bildungsroman: Incest and Inheritance* (Cambridge, Eng.: Cambridge UP, 1997), 21 [*Editor*].

body to ideas'.[4] It is indeed thanks to the louse on Stephen's neck that we catch a glimpse of his suffering, malnourished body. * * *

Stephen's 'mind bred vermin': uncreated by God, born of the body, the louse travesties his ideal conception of language and art. It therefore worries him that the insects are self-begotten * * *. As an ironic rejoinder to Stephen's perspective, the louse joins Lynch in exposing the 'scholastic stink' of Stephen's aesthetic theorising, which includes such questions as *'Can excrement or a child or a louse be a work of art?'* (V.1432–33). Louse and Lynch both counter Stephen's Manicheism by accepting the body's excretions—dung, offspring or vermin alike—into the larger Joycean realm of art. Because Stephen sees art as refined or transmuted nature, as 'life purified in and reprojected from the human imagination' (V.1465), he has good reason to worry about language's bodily origin.

Also ironic is the fact that Stephen's most intense aesthetic experiences coincide with a state of sexual exhaustion. After his wet dream, Stephen completes his villanelle overcome with 'languorous weariness' and the certainty that 'soon he would sleep' (V.1702–05). 'The languor of sleep' he felt after his birdgirl epiphany (IV.903) is retrospectively revealed as similarly if less literally post-orgasmic. Nowhere is the reversionary power of the epiphany clearer than in the moments following his vision of the birdgirl. The drowsiness following the intensely personal 'profane' or 'quiet' joy (IV.876–77, V.75) is an awakening onto a strangely expansive vista which is geological, evolutionary, even astronomical in scope: 'his eyelids trembled as if they felt the vast cyclic movement of the earth' (IV.903–04). * * *

* * *

Two moments in particular demonstrate how Joyce deploys deep-time reversions against Stephen's own overly idealistic conception of progressive *Bildung*. In both moments, Stephen's ontogeny and phylogeny visibly interact, but they do not run parallel in accordance with recapitulation theory. When his bathing friends call him 'Dedalos' and 'Bous', Stephen suddenly sees history before his eyes: 'all ages were as one to him' (IV.770). Linked to Daedalus,

> he seemed to hear the noise of dim waves and to see a winged form flying above the waves and slowly climbing the air. What did it mean? Was it a quaint device opening a page of some medieval book of prophecies and symbols, a hawk-like man flying sunward above the sea, a prophecy of the end he had been

4. Jean-Michel Rabaté, *James Joyce and the Politics of Egoism* (Cambridge, Eng.: Cambridge UP, 2001), 86 [*Editor*].

born to serve and had been following through the mists of
childhood and boyhood . . . ? (IV.773–79)

Stephen's journey from 'the mists of childhood and boyhood'
towards 'the end he had been born to serve'—the vocational *telos*[5] of
the *Bildungsroman*—is also a return to the mythic past of Daedalus.
Where recapitulation demands parallelism (embryo → adult : ancestor → descendent), Joyce supplies a chiasmus (childhood → maturity :
ancient Crete ← modern Dublin). Chiasmus, as Elliott Gose has
shown, is one of *A Portrait*'s ruling figures, characterising everything from phrases and sentences to chapters and, indeed, the
novel as a whole.[6] Through its mirroring structure, chiasmus
exposes Stephen's delusion that 'the past [is] past' (III.1581–82);
the past is the very substance to his prophetic visions.

*   *   *

Stephen feels words most strongly when their history, etymological, literary or personal, is sexual, but he is disposed to ignore this
fact by his sense of 'destiny' and his Catholic education. Only rarely
does Stephen appear receptive to their embodied nature. When
Davin tells him about the woman of the Ballyhoura Hills, Stephen's
haunted response is produced or at least intensified by the fact she
is shirtless, pregnant and offering milk. As usual, Stephen tries dis-
tilling his response to sexualised or reproductive language into a
spur for *spiritual* self-development: the 'soul waking to the consciousness of itself' (V.331–32). But the body is intransigent.
Thoughts remain stuck on 'the figure of the woman . . . calling the
stranger to her bed', and the 'soul' he extricates from Davin's tale is
not angelic but animal, 'batlike' (V.331). Every movement forward
and upward is thus marbled with reversion. Even in the cathartic
moments following his confession, when Stephen thinks 'life lay all
before him' (III.1562), his sense of destiny is undercut by a pun
which situates his future in the past: 'before him'.

This dual temporality, which structures the plot of *A Portrait*,
recurs finally in Stephen's famous and famously perplexing vow to
'go to encounter for the millionth time the reality of experience'
(V.2788–89). There is a paradox in the notion of experiencing
something for the millionth time, and while the expression may
reflect the muddle of Stephen's youthful romanticism, it also cuts
to the heart of the novel's reversionary *Bildung* plot. Pericles Lewis
has argued that when Stephen vows to 'forge in the smithy of [his]
soul the uncreated conscience of [his] race' (V.2789–90), Joyce

---

5. "End, purpose, ultimate object or aim" (*OED*) (Greek) [*Editor*].
6. Elliott B. Gose, "Destruction and Creation in *A Portrait of the Artist as a Young Man*,"
   James Joyce Quarterly 22:3 (1985): 259–70 [*Editor*].

articulates a modernist nationalism that 'places an emphasis on the role of the race in shaping the individual's experience'.[7] * * * Lewis's explanation * * * is markedly at odds with Stephen's character, with his vow not to 'serve that in which [he] no longer believe[s] whether it call itself [his] home, [his] fatherland or [his] church' (V.2575–77) and with Joyce's stated scepticism concerning nationalism and myths of national identity. More problematic is Lewis's implication that the artist must submit to national history by replaying it,[8] just as the organism in Haeckel's biogenetic law is a mere effect of phylogenetic causes. The notion of experiencing reality 'for the millionth time' suggests a more complex historical engagement than the recapitulatory dynamic * * *. [Instead] the past, including the non-Irish past of English language and literature, detains Stephen in his attempts to 'forge ahead' and 'go forth to encounter reality' (I.180, IV.424).

The relation between past, present and future which emerges from Stephen's encounters with verbal and corporeal reality are too kaleidoscopic and indeterminate to fit Lewis's effectively palingenetic model of national conscience. The narrative dynamic of *Bildung* in *A Portrait* is not recapitulatory; it is simultaneously forward and backward or, to quote one of the novel's recurrent phrases, 'hither and thither' (III.1269, 1272, 1278; IV.348, 488–89, 872, 874–75; V.1797). Stephen's vow to 'forge in the smithy of my soul the uncreated conscience of my race' may suggest finality—but not closure. It has the same unnerving indeterminism of an earlier cry, 'on and on and on and on!' (IV.889–90) * * *. Indefinite movement forward is progress without teleology, and progress without an end is anathema to the classical *Bildung* plot.[9]

7. Pericles Lewis, *Modernism, Nationalism, and the Novel* (Cambridge, Eng.: Cambridge UP, 2000), 1 [*Editor*].
8. Lewis, 2 [*Editor*].
9. Franco Moretti, *The Way of the World: The Bildungsroman in European Culture*, 2nd Ed, trans. Albert Sbragia (New York: Verso, 2000), 90 [*Editor*].

James Joyce: A Chronology

1882	February 2	James Augustine Joyce born to John Stanislaus Joyce and Mary Jane ("May") Joyce, in Dublin
1884	December	Joyce's closest brother, Stanislaus, born
1888		Joyce enrolls at the Jesuit-run Clongowes Wood College, in Sallins, County Kildare, the most highly regarded Catholic preparatory school in Ireland
1891		Family finances result in Joyce's withdrawal from Clongowes
1892		Attends the Christian Brothers School in central Dublin
1893		Enrolls in the Jesuit-run Belvedere College in Dublin as a day student
1894		Travels to Cork with his father, who is liquidating the last of the family holdings there
1896		Selected to be prefect of the Sodality of the Blessed Virgin Mary; attends a retreat; becomes sexually active
1898		Begins studies at Royal University, now University College, Dublin
1899		Attends the opening of W. B. Yeats's controversial play *The Countess Cathleen* and refuses to support protests about the play
1900		Publishes a review of the iconoclastic Scandinavian playwright Henrik Ibsen's *When We Dead Awaken* in the respected *Fortnightly Review*
1902		Graduates from University College; departs for Paris, supposedly to study medicine
1903	April	Returns to Dublin because of illness of his mother, who dies in August
1904		Teaches at a school in Dalkey; lives briefly in a Martello tower at Sandycove. Writes

poems and stories and begins work on the autobiographical novel *Stephen Hero*. Meets Nora Barnacle, with whom he departs for Europe to teach English in a Berlitz School in Pola, Italy, then part of the Austro-Hungarian Empire

1905   Moves to a job at the Berlitz foreign-language school in Trieste. Son, Giorgio, born. Submits *Chamber Music* and a version of *Dubliners* to publishers, but encounters rejections and reversals. Stanislaus joins the family in Trieste

1906   Works briefly in Rome for a bank. Begins expanding *Dubliners*

1907   Returns to Trieste. *Chamber Music* published in London. Daughter, Lucia, born. Finishes "The Dead," the closing story of *Dubliners*. Begins reworking the material of *Stephen Hero* into *A Portrait*

1908   Finishes the first three numbered parts of *A Portrait*

1909   Visits Ireland twice, first with Giorgio, when he signs a contract for the publication of *Dubliners*, and then to arrange for the opening of the first cinema in Dublin, the Volta, on behalf of Triestine investors

1912   Members of the family travel to Galway and Dublin. *Dubliners* is not published because of demands for changes and libel concerns

1914   Encouraged by Ezra Pound, Joyce completes *A Portrait*, which is published serially in *The Egoist*. *Dubliners* is published. World War I starts, causing the possibility of internment in Trieste because of Joyce's British passport. Begins writing *Ulysses*

1915   Completes the play *Exiles*. Family is allowed to move to neutral Switzerland, where they settle in Zürich

1916   *A Portrait* is published in the United States

1917   Completes the first three episodes of *Ulysses*. Joyce's difficulties with his eyes require the first of numerous operations. Harriet Shaw Weaver begins providing financial support, which continues beyond Joyce's death (with her payment of funeral expenses)

1918		*Exiles* published in England. *Ulysses* begins to appear serially in *The Little Review* in the U.S.
1919		Family able to return to Trieste because the war has ended
1920		Family moves to Paris after Pound's encouragement. *Little Review* publication is stopped by the authorities because of supposed obscenity
1922	February 2	*Ulysses*, set by French printers, is published in Paris for Joyce's fortieth birthday by Sylvia Beach through her bookshop, Shakespeare and Company
1923		Begins writing *Finnegans Wake* under the working title *Work in Progress*
1927		Shakespeare and Company publishes *Pomes Pennyeach*. Portions of *Work in Progress* begin to appear in *transition*
1929		Samuel Beckett and others publish *Our Exagmination Round His Factification for Incamination of* Work in Progress
1931		James Joyce and Nora Barnacle marry in London. Joyce's father dies
1932		Birth of first grandchild, Stephen Joyce, to Giorgio and Helen Joyce
1933		A court in the U.S. declares that *Ulysses* is not obscene, enabling publication there. Hospitalization of Lucia for mental illness (the first of many virtually continuous institutional stays for schizophrenia until her death, in 1982)
1934		Random House publishes *Ulysses* in New York
1939		*Finnegans Wake* published in New York and London. The Joyces leave Paris for the south of France because of World War II
1940		After the Germans take control of France, the Joyces move to Zürich
1941	January 13	Joyce dies of a perforated ulcer and is buried in Fluntern cemetery, Zürich
1951		Nora Barnacle dies, in Zürich

Selected Bibliography

Joyce's Writings

Long Narratives

Stephen Hero (incomplete; published posthumously, 1944)
Stephen Hero: New Edition (with additions; ed. John J. Slocum and Herbert Cahoon; 1963)
A Portrait of the Artist as a Young Man (1916)
Ulysses episodes serialized in *The Little Review* (1918–20)
Ulysses (1922)
Finnegans Wake (1939)

Short Stories

Dubliners (1914)

Essays and Other Prose and Poetry

Chamber Music (1907)
Collected Poems (1936; consists of *Chamber Music* [1907], *Pomes Penyeach* [1927], and "Ecce Puer" [1932]).
Exiles, A Play in Three Acts (1918).
The Critical Writings of James Joyce. Ed. Ellsworth Mason and Richard Ellmann. New York: Viking, 1959.
Occasional, Critical, and Political Writing. Ed. Kevin Barry. Oxford, Eng.: Oxford UP, 2000.
Poems and Shorter Writings: Including Epiphanies, Giacomo Joyce, *and* "A Portrait of the Artist." Ed. Richard Ellmann, A. Walton Litz, and John Whittier-Ferguson. London: Faber and Faber, 1991.
The Workshop of Dedalus: James Joyce and the Raw Materials for A Portrait of the Artist as a Young Man. Ed. Robert Scholes and Richard M. Kain. Evanston, IL: Northwestern UP, 1965.

Other Materials

The James Joyce Archive. 63 Volumes. Ed. Michael Groden et al. New York and London: Garland Publishing, 1977–79. [Reproduces prepublication material in photographic facsimile.]
Letters of James Joyce. Vol. I. Ed. Stuart Gilbert. New York: Viking, 1957, rev. 1966. Vols. II–III. Ed. Richard Ellmann. New York: Viking, 1966.
Selected Letters of James Joyce. Ed. Richard Ellmann. New York: Viking, 1975. [Contains some letters not previously collected.]

Bibliographies

Slocum, John J. and Herbert Cahoon. *A Bibliography of James Joyce, 1882–1941.* New Haven: Yale UP, 1953.

Biographies

Bowker, Gordon. *James Joyce: A New Biography.* New York: Farrar, Straus and Giroux, 2012.

Ellmann, Richard. *James Joyce.* New and rev. ed. New York: Oxford UP, 1982.

Jackson, John Wyse and Peter Costello. *John Stanislaus Joyce: The Voluminous Life and Genius of James Joyce's Father.* New York: St. Martin's P, 1998.

Joyce, Stanislaus. *My Brother's Keeper: James Joyce's Early Years.* Ed. Richard Ellmann. New York: Viking, 1958.

Maddox, Brenda. *Nora.* Boston: Houghton Mifflin, 1988. [Biography of Joyce's wife.]

McCourt, John. *The Years of Bloom: James Joyce in Trieste, 1904–1920.* Dublin: Lilliput P, 2000.

Criticism

• indicates works included or excerpted in this Norton Critical Edition.

• Attridge, Derek. *How to Read Joyce.* London: Granta Books, 2007.
——. "'Suck was a queer word': Language, Sex, and the Remainder in *A Portrait of the Artist as a Young Man.*" *Joyce Effects: On Language, Theory, and History.* Cambridge, Eng.: Cambridge UP, 2000. 59–77.

Benstock, Shari. "The Dynamics of Narrative Performance: Stephen Dedalus as Storyteller." *English Literary History* 49:3 (1982): 707–38.

Bloom, Harold, ed. *James Joyce's* A Portrait of the Artist as a Young Man. Modern Critical Interpretations. New York: Chelsea House, 1988.

• Boes, Tobias. "*A Portrait of the Artist as a Young Man* and the 'Individuating Rhythm' of Modernity." *ELH* 75 (Winter 2008): 767–85.

Booth, Wayne C. "The Problem of Distance in *A Portrait of the Artist.*" *The Rhetoric of Fiction.* 2nd ed. Chicago: U of Chicago P, 1983. 323–36.

Brady, Philip and James F. Carens, eds. *Critical Essays on James Joyce's* A Portrait of the Artist as a Young Man. New York: G. K. Hall, 1998.

Brivic, Sheldon. "Gender Dissonance, Hysteria, and History in James Joyce's *A Portrait of the Artist as a Young Man.*" *James Joyce Quarterly* 39 (2002): 457–76.

Brockman, William S. "*A Portrait of the Artist as a Young Man* in the Public Domain." *The Papers of the Bibliographical Society of America* 98:2 (2004): 191–207.

Brown, Richard. *James Joyce.* New York: St. Martin's P, 1992.

Burke, Kenneth. "Fact, Inference, and Proof in the Analysis of Literary Symbolism." *Terms for Order.* Ed. Stanley Edgar Hyman. Bloomington: Indiana UP, 1964. 145–72.

• Castle, Gregory. "Coming of Age in the Age of Empire: Joyce's Modernist *Bildungsroman.*" *James Joyce Quarterly* 50:1–2 (Fall 2012–Winter 2013): 359–84. Originally in *James Joyce Quarterly* 40:4 (Summer 2003).

Cheng, Vincent J. "Coda [to 'Catching the Conscience of a Race']: The Case of Stephen D(a)edalus." *Joyce, Race, and Empire.* Cambridge, Eng.: Cambridge UP, 1995. 57–74.

Church, Margaret. "The Adolescent Point of View toward Women in Joyce's *A Portrait of the Artist as a Young Man*." *Irish Renaissance Annual* 1. Ed. Zack Bowen. Newark: U of Delaware P, 1981. 158–65.

Cixous, Hélène. "Reaching the Point of Wheat, or A Portrait of the Artist as a Maturing Woman." *New Literary History* 19:1 (Autumn 1987): 1–21.

Connolly, Thomas E., ed. *Joyce's Portrait, Criticisms and Critiques.* New York: Appleton-Century-Crofts, 1962.

Deane, Seamus. "Joyce and Stephen: The Provincial Intellectual." *Celtic Revivals: Essays in Modern Irish Literature, 1880–1980.* London: Faber and Faber, 1985. 75–91.

Deming, Robert H., ed. *James Joyce: The Critical Heritage, Volume One, 1902–1927* and *Volume Two, 1928–1941.* New York: Barnes and Noble, 1970.

Eco, Umberto. *The Aesthetics of Chaosmos: The Middle Ages of James Joyce.* Transl. Ellen Esrock. Cambridge, Mass.: Harvard UP, 1989.

Eide, Marian. "The Woman of the Ballyhoura Hills: James Joyce and the Politics of Creativity." *Twentieth Century Literature* 44:4 (Winter 1998): 377–93.

Ellmann, Maud. "Disremembering Dedalus: *A Portrait of the Artist as a Young Man*." *Untying the Text: A Post-Structuralist Reader.* Ed. Robert Young. Boston and London: Routledge & Kegan Paul, 1981. 189–206.

• Esty, Jed. *Unseasonable Youth: Modernism, Colonialism, and the Fiction of Development.* Oxford, Eng.: Oxford UP, 2012.

Feshbach, Sidney. "A Slow Dark Birth: A Study of the Organization of *A Portrait of the Artist as a Young Man*." *James Joyce Quarterly* 4:4 (1967): 289–300.

• Froula, Christine. *Modernism's Body: Sex, Culture, and Joyce.* New York: Columbia UP, 1996.

Gabler, Hans Walter. "The Genesis of *A Portrait of the Artist as a Young Man*." *Critical Essays on James Joyce's A Portrait of the Artist as a Young Man.*" Ed. Philip Brady and James F. Carens. New York: G. K. Hall, 1998. 83–112.

Gifford, Don. *Joyce Annotated: Notes for Dubliners and A Portrait of the Artist as a Young Man.* 2nd Ed. Berkeley. U of Calif. P, 1982.

Gose, Elliott B., Jr. "Destruction and Creation in *A Portrait of the Artist as a Young Man*." *James Joyce Quarterly* 22 (1985): 259–70.

Harkness, Marguerite. *A Portrait of the Artist as a Young Man: Voices of the Text.* Boston: Twayne, 1990.

Henke, Suzette. "Stephen Dedalus and Women: A Portrait of the Artist as a Young Narcissist." *James Joyce and the Politics of Desire.* New York and London: Routledge, 1990. 50–84.

Howes, Marjorie. "'Goodbye Ireland I'm going to Gort': geography, scale, and narrating the nation." *Semicolonial Joyce.* Cambridge, Eng.: Cambridge UP, 2000. 58–77.

Jacobs, Joshua. "Joyce's Epiphanic Mode: Material Language and the Representation of Sexuality in *Stephen Hero* and *Portrait*." *Twentieth-Century Literature* 46:1 (2000): 20–33.

Kenner, Hugh. "The Cubist *Portrait*." *Approaches to Joyce's "Portrait": Ten Essays.* Ed. Thomas F. Staley and Bernard Benstock. Pittsburgh: U of Pittsburgh P, 1976. 171–84.

• ———. "Joyce's *Portrait*—A Reconsideration." *The University of Windsor Review* 1:1 (Spring 1965): 1–15.

———. "The *Portrait* in Perspective." *Dublin's Joyce.* Bloomington: Indiana UP, 1956. 109–33.

Kershner, R. B. "The Artist as Text: Dialogism and Incremental Repetition in *Portrait*." *English Literary History* 53:4 (1986): 881–94.

Klein, Scott. "National Histories, National Fictions: Joyce's *A Portrait of the Artist as a Young Man* and Scott's *The Bride of Lammermoor*." *English Literary History* 65:4 (1998): 1017–38.

Lawrence, Karen. "Gender and Narrative Voice in *Jacob's Room* and *A Portrait of the Artist as a Young Man*." *James Joyce: The Centennial Symposium.* Ed. Morris Beja, et al. Urbana: U of Illinois P, 1986. 31–38.

Leonard, Garry. "When a Fly Gets in Your I: The City, Modernism, and Aesthetic Theory in *A Portrait of the Artist as a Young Man*." *Advertising and Commodity Culture in Joyce*. Gainesville: UP of Florida, 1998. 175–207.

Levenson, Michael. "Stephen's Diary in Joyce's *Portrait*—The Shape of Life." *English Literary History* 52:4 (1985): 1017–35.

Lewis, Pericles. "The Conscience of the Race: The Nation as Church of the Modern Age." *Joyce through the Ages: A Nonlinear View*. Ed. Michael Patrick Gillespie. Gainesville: UP of Florida, 1999. 85–106.

Lowe-Evans, Mary. "Sex and Confession in the Joyce Canon: Some Historical Parallels." *Journal of Modern Literature* 16:4 (1990): 563–76.

Mahaffey, Vicki. "Père-version and Im-mère-sion: Idealized Corruption in *A Portrait of the Artist as a Young Man* and *The Picture of Dorian Gray*." *Quare Joyce*. Ed. Joseph Valente. Ann Arbor: U of Michigan P, 1998. 121–38.

———. *Reauthorizing Joyce*. Cambridge, MA: Cambridge UP, 1988.

Manganiello, Dominic. *Joyce's Politics*. Boston and London: Routledge & Kegan Paul, 1980.

———. "Reading the Book of Himself: the Confessional Imagination of St. Augustine and Joyce." *Biography & Autobiography: Essays on Irish and Canadian History and Literature*. Ed. James Noonan. Ottawa: Carleton UP, 1993. 149–62.

McCourt, John, ed. *James Joyce in Context*. Cambridge, Eng.: Cambridge UP, 2009.

Muller, Jim. "John Henry Newman and the Education of Stephen Dedalus." *James Joyce Quarterly* 33:4 (1996): 593–603.

• Mullin, Katherine. "Joyce's Bodies." *James Joyce*. Ed. Sean Latham. Dublin and Portland, OR: Irish Academic P, 2010. 170–88.

———. "'True Manliness': Policing Masculinity in *A Portrait of the Artist as a Young Man*." *James Joyce, Sexuality and Social Purity*. Cambridge, MA: Cambridge UP, 2003. 83–115.

Mulrooney, Jonathan. "Stephen Dedalus and the Politics of Confession." *Studies in the Novel* 33:2 (Summer 2001): 160–79.

• Newman, Daniel Aureliano. *Modernist Life Histories: Biological Theory and the Experimental Bildungsroman*. Edinburgh: Edinburgh UP, 2019.

Nolan, Emer. *James Joyce and Nationalism*. London and New York: Routledge, 1995.

Noon, William T. *Joyce and Aquinas*. New Haven: Yale UP, 1957.

Norris, Margot. "Stephen Dedalus, Oscar Wilde, and the Art of Lying." *Joyce's Web: The Social Unraveling of Modernism*. Austin: U of Texas P, 1992. 52–67.

Parrinder, Patrick. *James Joyce*. Cambridge, Eng.: Cambridge UP, 1984.

Peake, C. H. *James Joyce: The Citizen and the Artist*. Stanford, CA: Stanford UP, 1977.

Rabaté, Jean-Michel. *James Joyce: Authorized Reader*. Baltimore: Johns Hopkins UP, 1991.

———. *Palgrave Advances in James Joyce Studies*. Houndsmills, Eng.: Palgrave Macmillan, 2004.

Radford, F. L. "Dedalus and the Bird Girl: Classical Text and Celtic Subtext in *A Portrait*." *James Joyce Quarterly* 24:3 (1987): 253–74.

Riquelme, John Paul. "Desire, Freedom, and Confessional Culture in *A Portrait of the Artist as a Young Man*." *A Companion to James Joyce*. Ed. Richard Brown. Oxford, Eng.: Blackwell, 2007.

———. "*Stephen Hero* and *A Portrait of the Artist as a Young Man*: Transforming the Nightmare of History." *Cambridge Companion to James Joyce*. Second Ed. Ed. Derek Attridge. Cambridge, Eng.: Cambridge UP, 2004. 103–21.

• ———. *Teller and Tale in Joyce's Fiction: Oscillating Perspectives*. Baltimore and London: Johns Hopkins UP, 1983.

Roche, Anthony. "'The strange light of some new world': Stephen's Vision in *A Portrait*." *James Joyce Quarterly* 25:3 (1988): 323–32.

Rossman, Charles. "Stephen Dedalus and the Spiritual-Heroic Refrigerating Apparatus: Art and Life in Joyce's *Portrait.*" *Forms of Modern British Fiction.* Ed. Alan Warren Friedman. Austin: U of Texas P, 1975. 101–31.

Scholes, Robert. "Stephen Dedalus, Poet or Esthete?" *PMLA* 89 (1964): 484–89.

Schwarze, Tracey-Teets. "Silencing Stephen: Colonial Pathologies in Victorian Dublin." *Twentieth-Century Literature* 43:3 (1997): 243–63.

Schutte, William, ed. *Twentieth-Century Interpretations of 'A Portrait of the Artist as a Young Man.'* Englewood Cliffs, NJ: Prentice-Hall, 1968.

• Scott, Bonnie Kime. *James Joyce.* Atlantic Highlands, NJ: Humanities P International, 1987.

Seed, David. *James Joyce's* A Portrait of the Artist as a Young Man. New York: St. Martin's P, 1992.

Seidel, Michael. *Exile and the Narrative Imagination.* New Haven: Yale UP, 1986.

Senn, Fritz. "The Challenge: *ignotas animum* (An Old-fashioned Close Guessing at a Borrowed Structure)." *James Joyce Quarterly* 16:1–2 (1978–79): 123–34. Repr. in *Joyce's Dislocutions: Essays on Reading as Translation.* Ed. John Paul Riquelme. Baltimore and London: Johns Hopkins UP, 1983. 73–84.

Sosnoski, James J. "Reading Acts, Reading Warrants, and Reading Responses." *James Joyce Quarterly* 16:1–2 (1978–79): 43–63.

Spoo, Robert. *James Joyce and the Language of History.* New York: Oxford UP, 1994.

Spurr, David. "Colonial Spaces in Joyce's Dublin." *James Joyce Quarterly* 37:1–2 (1999–2000): 23–42.

Staley, Thomas F. and Bernard Benstock, eds. *Approaches to Joyce's "Portrait": Ten Essays.* Pittsburgh: U of Pittsburgh P, 1976.

Tropp, Sandra. "'The Esthetic Instinct in Action': Charles Darwin and Mental Science in *A Portrait of the Artist as a Young Man.*" *James Joyce Quarterly* 45:2 (Winter 2008): 221–44.

Valente, Joseph. "The Politics of Joyce's Polyphony." *New Alliances in Joyce Studies.* Ed. Bonnie Kime Scott. Newark: U of Delaware P, 1988. 56–69.

• ———. "Thrilled by His Touch: Homosexual Panic and the Will to Artistry in *A Portrait of the Artist as a Young Man.*" *James Joyce Quarterly* 31:3 (Spring 1994): 167–88. Rev., exp. in *Quare Joyce.* Ed. Joseph Valente. Ann Arbor: U of Michigan P, 1998. 47–75.

Wollaeger, Mark A, ed. *James Joyce's* A Portrait of the Artist as a Young Man: *A Casebook.* Oxford, Eng.: Oxford UP, 2003.